HENRY WILLIAMSON

THE GOLDEN VIRGIN

'Objects of hate are but our own chimaerae.
They arise from wounds within us.'
Father Aloysius.

ALAN SUTTON PUBLISHING LIMITED

To
RICHARD ALDINGTON

First published in 1957 by Macdonald & Co (Publishers) Ltd

First published in this edition in the United Kingdom in 1996
Alan Sutton Publishing Limited
Phoenix Mill · Far Thrupp · Stroud · Gloucestershire

British Library Cataloguing-in-Publication Data.

A catalogue record for this book is available from the British Library.

ISBN 0–7509–1215–4

Cover picture: detail from The Battle of the Somme *by Richard Caton Woodville (1856–1927) (after). (Private Collection/Bridgeman Art Library, London)*

ACKNOWLEDGEMENT

The author is indebted to the Hon. Lady Salmond for permission to quote, in the story, verses from *Into Battle*, by Captain the Hon. Julian Grenfell, D.S.O., who died of wounds in May, 1915.

The version used in the following pages, which differs slightly from that printed in *The Oxford Book of English Verse* (New Edition 1939) and also from another version in *Bright Armour, Memories of Four Years of War*, by Monica Salmond (Faber & Faber Ltd.), is taken from 'the rough copy scribbled and hardly altered in Julian's small pocket diary'.

Printed in Great Britain by
The Guernsey Press Company Limited,
Guernsey, Channel Islands.

INTRODUCTION

HENRY WILLIAMSON was a writer of tremendous energy and tenacity. He wrote over fifty books, innumerable short stories and articles in newspapers and magazines, and literally thousands of lengthy letters. Most of his books were long and there were several typescript versions for each one. His compulsion and need to write ruled the whole of his life.

His first book *The Beautiful Years* was published in 1921. In 1951, thirty years and thirty-five books later, there appeared the first volume of his long novel in fifteen volumes, *A Chronicle of Ancient Sunlight*, whose hero, Phillip Maddison, is based on Henry Williamson himself. Apart from being an absorbing story of the life of an extraordinary man, the entire *Chronicle* is a fictionalized social history of the first half of the twentieth century.

The first volume, *The Dark Lantern,* opens with a scene where a man called Richard Maddison is out collecting moths on a summer night when he is set upon by two ruffians. Richard Maddison is based on Henry Williamson's own father, William Leopold Williamson, and this scene and most of the characters and incidents throughout the entire series are based on real scenes, characters and incidents from Henry Williamson's own life, and that of his family and friends. The element of fiction and transposing of real events with imagined ones does, however, mean that nothing can be taken for granted.

William Leopold Williamson was a bank clerk by profession who, in May 1893, married Gertrude Eliza Leaver in a secret ceremony. This dramatic tale is to be found in *The Dark Lantern*. Their first child, Kathleen Mary, was born in 1894, while Henry William Williamson was born on 1 December 1895 at 66 Braxfield Road in Brockley, south-east London. A third child, Doris Mary, was born in 1898. Soon after, William Leopold bought one of the new houses being built next to 'Hilly Fields' in Lewisham, and so the family moved to 11 [now 21] Eastern Road, where the main part of Henry Williamson's childhood and adolescence was spent. A blue commemorative plaque was placed here in 1984 under the aegis of The Henry Williamson Society and Lewisham Council.

Henry Williamson's mother came from a family who had been farmers in Bedfordshire and the young Henry was very friendly with his Bedfordshire cousins in whose home he felt more relaxed; we find all the relations woven into the tapestry of the *Chronicle*. An earlier branch of the family had originated from Devon, which Henry Williamson always claimed as his spiritual home and where he was to live for the greater part of his life.

In 1907 he obtained a scholarship to Colfe's Grammar School in Lewisham. He was not psychologically suited to the strict discipline of school life, preferring to roam the countryside collecting birds' eggs, but he was not a disgrace either: he became Captain of Harriers [cross-country running] and was in the school rifle team. His feelings, friendships and adventures gave him plenty of writing material and are marvellously captured in an early book, *Dandelion Days,* and later in *Young Phillip Maddison*, the third volume of the *Chronicle*.

On leaving school in the summer of 1913 Henry Williamson became a clerk in the Sun Fire Insurance Company, which becomes the 'Moon' Fire Office in the *Chronicle*. In the early summer of 1914 he went on holiday to stay with his Aunt Mary Leopoldina [Theodora in the novels], who rented a cottage in the tiny village of Georgeham in North Devon. This holiday made a great and lasting impression on the young Henry Williamson. He loved the wild coastal scenery of the nearby Braunton Burrows and the cliff promontory known as Baggy Point. This idyllic impression was further reinforced because shortly afterwards the First World War broke out and soon Henry Williamson was a soldier in the battlefields of Flanders.

He had enlisted into the ranks of the London Rifle Brigade the previous January, and was mobilized on 5 August 1914, embarking for the battlefields at the beginning of November. This period is related in the fourth volume of the *Chronicle*, *How Dear is Life*, where Phillip actually joins The London Highlanders, who also leave for the horror of the trenches. The ensuing volumes, *A Fox Under My Cloak*, *The Golden Virgin*, *Love and the Loveless* and *A Test To Destruction*, are all devoted to coverage of the war, interspersed with scenes of amorous and hilarious adventures of home leave, and service in this country training to be an officer, many of them episodes which were personally experienced by Henry Williamson himself. These books are considered by many critics to be some of the best that have ever been written about the First World War.

The war affected him greatly, particularly the extraordinary Christmas Truce of 1914, when he discovered that the German soldiers – the enemy – were fighting for the same ideals as the British: God and their country. He realized the futility and destruction of war and this determined his life's work: to show the world, through writing, that truth and peace lay in beauty and the open air. This was reinforced when, in 1919, stationed in Folkestone with the Dispersal Unit, he discovered a copy of Richard Jefferies' book, *The Story of my Heart,* and read in rapt attention what was to him 'a revelation of total truth'. He began to write seriously from then onwards.

After demobilization in September 1919, Henry Williamson returned to live at his parents' house, where he behaved rather wildly for a few months. At the beginning of 1920 he obtained a job as motoring correspondent for the *Weekly Dispatch* and was soon having short nature sketches published in various newspapers and periodicals while he worked on his first novel. But he found life in the family home too narrow and frustrating because his father disapproved of everything he did. Finally they quarrelled irrevocably, and in March 1921 Henry left home for the cottage in Georgeham whose lease he took over for £5 a year. This period of his life is related in *The Innocent Moon,* the ninth volume of the *Chronicle,* although Phillip's courtship and marriage with 'Barley' and her subsequent death in childbirth soon after is a fictionalized version of what in real life was a frustrated love affair.

The Beautiful Years, the first volume of his tetralogy *The Flax of Dream,* was published that autumn. From then on Henry Williamson wrote and published a book (sometimes two books) more or less every year, almost to the very end of his long life.

In 1924 he embarked on an ambitious project: a novel depicting the life story of an otter. To procure material he joined the Cheriton Otter Hounds and at one of their meets he saw a beautiful young woman, Ida Loetitia Hibbert, whom he soon decided was his ideal partner. They were married in May 1925. She is Lucy Copplestone in the *Chronicle* and we first read about their courtship and subsequent marriage (and Henry's quarrels with her brothers) in the tenth volume, *It was the Nightingale.*

Tarka the Otter was published in October 1927 to much acclaim, especially after it was awarded the Hawthornden Prize for Literature the following year. A letter arrived from T.E. Lawrence, Lawrence of Arabia, who wrote to say he had 'sizzled with joy' on reading it, thus starting a correspondence and friendship between the two men.

With the £100 prize money Henry Williamson bought a field on the hill above Georgeham and built himself a Writing Hut which was to be his refuge throughout his life.

In *The Power of the Dead* Phillip goes off to learn farming from his uncle, Sir Hilary Maddison, who owns twelve hundred acres of downland with its own trout stream. In real life Henry and his wife and two sons moved to Shallowford in the village of Filleigh near South Molton in Devon, where there are, of course, several hundred acres of farmland and a trout stream. Henry set to work to improve the trout fishing and to write a book about another water creature, to be called *Salar the Salmon*. He published several more books and made two long visits to America, where his books had always been well received, at this time. His family increased and was complicated by the fact that his secretary, known in the novels as Felicity, also bore him a child.

In early May 1935 he wrote a letter to T.E. Lawrence asking if he might visit him to discuss a writing project for a friend, Victor Yeates, who had just died; Lawrence rushed out on his motorbike to send him a telegram in reply and as he returned had an accident from which he subsequently died. Later that year Henry was invited to visit his great friend Sir John Heygate, who was working in a film studio in Germany, and to attend the huge Nüremburg Rally being addressed by Adolf Hitler. Henry also saw and was greatly impressed by the German Youth Movement and the agricultural and industrial reforms Hitler was instigating. We must remember here that Henry had a German grandmother, and that his own ideas that 'truth and peace lay in beauty and the open air' coincided with what he saw happening in Germany. Later he was to call Hitler 'Lucifer', the fallen angel. This era is covered in *The Phoenix Generation*, the twelfth volume of the *Chronicle*.

Once *Salar* was published Henry Williamson felt he needed to move on to find fresh material. Two books, the charming *The Children of Shallowford* and the factual *Goodbye West Country*, relate the family's life at Shallowford in an interesting saga. Having seen the portents of war looming, he decided now to become a farmer and in 1937 bought a very run-down farm on the north Norfolk coast to which, amid much turmoil, the family moved. *A Solitary War* relates Phillip's [and Henry's] struggles to turn the 'bad lands' into a viable farming unit. Once in Norfolk Henry Williamson was persuaded to attend a meeting of the British Union of Fascists where he met its leader Sir Oswald Mosley. As a new farmer Henry felt the BUF's agricultural policy held the answer to the country's troubles, and Mosley became his new hero. Mosley is Sir Hereward Birkin in the *Chronicle* novels. *Lucifer Before Sunrise* continues the story of the farming struggle in wartime England. He also covers the farming era in *The Story of a Norfolk Farm* and *The Phasian Bird*.

It was a harrowing time for the family. Henry was exhausted and irritable, trying both to run the farm as a perfect system and to write to earn enough money to keep everything going. At the end of the war it was obvious that things could not continue as they were. The farm was sold but the tensions were so great that the family broke up. Henry returned to his field in Devon alone, although he always maintained close touch with his ex-wife and his children.

The last volume of *A Chronicle of Ancient Sunlight* also has Phillip returned to Devon, living alone on Exmoor. This tremendous novel, *The Gale of the World*, culminates in an epic description of the storm that led to the flooding and devastation of Lynmouth in 1953. Afterwards, Phillip, finding himself still alive, decides that he can at last start to write his Chronicle – opening with a shy young man out with his dark lantern mothing on 'the Hill' and including all his friends in ancient sunlight . . .

In real life, on his return to Devon Henry Williamson met and soon married his second wife, Christine Duffield, and their son was born in 1950. He built a larger studio in the Field, and bought a large, comfortable and convenient caravan, but eventually also bought a cottage in nearby Ilfracombe. And he began in earnest to write *A Chronicle of Ancient Sunlight*, publishing one volume almost every year between 1951 and 1969. His second marriage could not withstand the pressure of his difficult personality and this tremendous workload, and he and Christine were divorced in 1964.

Despite the attentions of friends and family Henry was then permanently lonely. His last book *The Scandaroon*, the story of a racing pigeon, was published in 1972. Many years previously he had drawn up plans to build a large house in the Field and he now achieved that ambition although he never lived in it. He finally gave permission for a film to be made of *Tarka the Otter*. With his life's purpose over he was now tired and ill and eventually was taken into a nursing home on the outskirts of London run by Alexian monks. The filming of *Tarka* went ahead unknown to him. He died aged nearly eighty-two years old on 13 August 1977 on the very same day that the death scene of Tarka was being filmed in the exact spot that he had placed it over fifty years previously, and a few days later he was buried in a simple grave in the church-yard at Georgeham, in a plot he had bought many years before.

ANNE WILLIAMSON
Summer 1994

Readers who are interested in the life and work of Henry Williamson might like to know that there is a Henry Williamson Society. Meetings are held twice a year and the Society's *Journal*, with a wide range of articles on his life and work, is published in the spring and autumn of each year. For further information please contact the Membership Secretary:

Mrs Margaret Murphy, 16 Doran Drive, Redhill, Surrey, RH1 6AX.

Further Reading: *Henry Williamson: Dreamer of Devon*, an illustrated biography, written by Anne Williamson, was published by Alan Sutton Publishing Limited in August 1995.

A Chronicle of Ancient Sunlight

Part One

THE WILD BOY

"It might have been thought that War, with its weeping nights and solitary mornings, would have silenced rumour; that the fearing and faint at home would have been infected by the radiant and courageous abroad, and that such unknown human sufferings as the world went through in 1914 would have made men kind; but it was not so.

From the first day the cry went up that we were to 'hunt out the Germans in our midst', and you had only to suggest that the person you disliked for reasons either social or political had German blood or German sympathies and a witch-hunt was started as cruel and persistent as any in the fourteenth century.

Our treatment of aliens was worse than that of any of the Allies. We crushed their business, ruined their homes, boycotted their families and drove their wives into asylums. Not a voice was raised from Christian pulpits; but Prelates were photographed on gun-carriages chatting to soldiers on the glories of battle."

The Autobiography of Margot Asquith.

"Some craven scruple
  Of thinking too precisely on the event,
  A thought which quartered, hath but one part wisdom
  And ever three parts coward. . . ."

Shakespeare's *Hamlet.*

Chapter 1

NIGHT THOUGHTS

In 1910 a company was formed in London with the style and title
of Temperance Billiard Halls Ltd. Its object was to build the
sort of places where youth of the poorer classes might enjoy
companionship other than that found in street and public house,
of the kind synonymous with all that was dreaded by parents
who hoped that their boys would not go wrong. Several of these
halls were built in the suburbs during the most optimistic period
of Liberalism in power, if not in flower, in the first decade of the
twentieth century.

The word *billiards* was, among the aspiring classes which dwelt
in the new suburbs of red and yellow brick, in uneasy association
with Victorian liquor, bar lights, and unmentionable worse
things connected with women. To help overcome existing preju-
dice, and lest any doubts arise as to the spirit and capability of
the impulse towards the setting up of healthy, innocent recreation
for the young, Temperance Billiard Halls Ltd. had caused to be
let into the outside wall of each building a panel of glazed green
tiles with letters and figures announcing the reassuring fact that
the company had a capital of £100,000.

One such hall had been built in south-east London, beside a
high road leading into Kent, where cabbage and potato fields
were still under cultivation only a mile or so away, despite the
extension of new roads of creosoted blocks of jarra wood and rails
for the brown and yellow electric trams of the L.C.C. The hall
stood on what had been grazing land below the South Eastern
and Chatham Railway embankment. The site had been chosen,
among other reasons, for its nearness to the Conservative Club
across the road, a high-toned place where even the most successful in trade had not yet succeeded in rubbing shoulders with
the old and established professions of the borough. True, the
entrance to the garden surrounding the Club was almost hidden
by a most unfortunate jerry-building which had sprung up almost
overnight owing to a lapse of the steward of the ground landlord,

the Earl of Dartford: an oversight the more strange since the solicitor concerned was a member of the Club, and presumably had put a restrictive covenant upon the use to which the ninety-nine-year leasehold of the parcel of land beside the Club entrance would be put by the emptor. It was a case of the old tag in reverse, *caveat vendor*; for now, where once lilacs and laburnums had grown, stood a pawn shop, its three large gilt balls hanging beside the Club entrance for all to see, and many, including Dr. Dashwood, to make jokes about. "So convenient for the Members, don't you know."

The entrance into the billiard hall was well back from the kerb of the wide pavement which had taken the place of the original sidewalk. Once over the threshold, no parent was likely to continue in doubt as to the hall's respectability, for the walls of the porch were decorated with two panels in plaster, Law on the left, and Commerce on the right; groups of female figures made familiar by Burne-Jones and others of the fashion in art. Law stood with bandaged eyes and sword, holding scales, Commerce with ball and sceptre among some of the subject races of Empire. With artistic daring, Queen Victoria had become a young woman with blonde hair hanging down her back, swathed all in white.

Over the porch was fixed the legend:

THE GILD HALL
Billiards
Refreshments

the letters of which gleamed but dully on a raw Saturday night in the late autumn of 1915. Owing to Zeppelin raids the glass lanterns of street lamps had been covered with deep blue paint except for a small margin around their bases, and the only other lights in the street came from passing tramcars, and negligible wavering yellow spots from bicycles and horse-drawn carts.

Outside the porch two girls were standing in hesitation. One of them was peering into the well of light coming through glass doors, beyond which could be seen a floor possibly of marble, set with tables at which young people were sitting, looking about them, or playing some game among cups of coffee.

"Why, it's only dominoes, it's just an ordinary place after all, Nina!"

"I told you it was, Mavis! Only you wouldn't believe me."

"Well, what does he come here for, then?"

"Phil has to go somewhere, I suppose."

"Why? Why can't he stay at home sometimes, with Mother? I'll tell you what! It's like one of the Mecca coffee rooms in the City, where men go to spoon with the waitresses!"

"Anyway, let's go in and see, shall we?"

They entered into warmth and light, amidst a murmur of young voices, of girls in large black straw hats and pigtails—flappers, in fact—and youths, some of them in uniform, sitting at tables amidst laughter and the sliding rattle of dominoes. In the centre of the floor was a sunken circular pool in which goldfish moved languidly. Beyond other glass doors could be seen a multiplication of hanging dark green cones casting pyramids of light upon arms, heads, and faces intent around little emerald lawns, whereon rolled white and multi-coloured balls.

The taller of the two girls led the way to a table in a far corner, and sat down with her companion. "Well," she said, with a trace of disappointment, "I don't see him anywhere, do you, Nina?"

"Are you sure he hasn't gone to the Hippodrome?"

"Oh, he never goes there on Saturday nights! Too rough. No, I bet he's in Freddy's bar, with Desmond, who sponges on him!"

The waitress came, and the fair girl, who was short and sturdily built, ordered coffee. When the two cups came she passed the sugar bowl to her friend, who helped herself and then appeared to fall into a state of dream, as slowly she stirred her coffee and stared before her. Nina waited, wondering what was upsetting her now. She had learned never to ask questions, which almost invariably brought forth a startled, "Why do you ask?"

Mavis of the brown eyes reflective with inward thoughts that often held a fixed stare of mournful vagueness usually told her perplexities and troubles to her great friend Nina; Nina so considerate of the feelings of the imperious Mavis, always ready to give, to put herself out to help the often-unhappy and (to Nina) the beautiful Mavis. No young man had looked twice at Nina, an Anglo-Saxon young woman who might have been any age between eighteen and twenty-eight. So the fair ruddy-faced Nina lived much in the feelings of the brunette, cream-complexion'd Mavis, who at times had a radiant expression, her large eyes filling with light and animation, which caused men covertly to observe her, and some to pay direct attention to her. But Mavis, to Nina's relief, wanted none of them: she said she

did not like men, because of their crude ways, and lack of the
things of the soul.

Mavis had a blank in her; in part, life for her was a dark
tunnel in which her soul dreamed of celestial, ideal things. The
tunnel was akin to fear, and death: the dead image of the father
she had adored, until without warning he had kissed her, when
she was thirteen, in a strange way; a distressing way, for immediately afterwards he had become blank and cold with guilt;
and having no self-consciousness, no self-knowledge, had transferred his self-dislike upon the object of its cause, the figure in
bud of Mavis. For a long time afterwards the words of his angry
voice had the power to darken her to hopelessness. *I do not love
you*, he had cried; and never resurrected himself from the tomb
of his guilt, under which love lay buried. The child's hazel eyes
had become blackthorn-dark with brooding, the spines grown
dully inwards.

"I think it's *terribly* unfair, Nina!"

"Life often is unfair," replied Nina, who had got that thought
from one of John Galsworthy's novels.

"I mean," said Mavis, "that my only brother should behave
as he does."

"I don't quite know what it is you have against him, Mavis.
After all, soldiers drink rum in the trenches, and Phillip's been
out to France twice, you know."

"Yes, but look how *much* he drinks!" Mavis sipped her coffee.
"Not bad, is it? Still, for tuppence—— Why aren't you having
yours?"

"I was waiting for the sugar, Mavis."

"Well, you are silly! Why didn't you ask me to pass it?"

"I didn't like to interrupt your thoughts."

"Oh, don't be so fussy!"

Nina put on a mild and pleasant expression. She was used to
soothing her friend, whom she secretly loved: Mavis of the delicate ears and profile, the wistful lips, the limpid brown eyes which
made Nina think of shadowed forest pools.

"Do you swear to keep a secret, Nina?"

"I never breathe word of what you tell me, you must know
that, Mavie."

"It is Mother. She is worrying herself to death over Phillip.
He's her favourite, you know. Oh yes! Neither I nor Doris get a
look in where Phillip is concerned. Well, she is so upset now by
what is happening, that she told me she was thinking of going to

see the landlord of the public house he haunts, for he is killing himself, the way he is going on! He's getting all this sick leave, and all he's doing is making himself worse."

"But perhaps he is ill, Mavie. He was gassed at Loos, didn't you tell me?"

"That's what *he* said, but I don't believe it! There's nothing wrong with him, except that he drinks! I hear him being sick in his room when he comes back, night after night! He has his own key, and opens the front door and shuts it very slowly, hardly a sound. I can hear distinctly at the end of the passage, with my door open, you know. It's like a sounding board. I hear him coming up the stairs on hands and knees, then creeping over the oilcloth down the passage, and into his room. No, you ought not to laugh! It isn't really funny. Now you've made me laugh!" But she checked herself, "No, it's really tragic!" Her eyes held tears. "You see, it's Mother! I always know when he's going to be sick, for I hear the pot slide from under the bed, then he gets off the bed and draws up his elbows and knees, I think, and so tries to minimise the noise of retching! It's horrid, I tell you, to have a brother people talk about, Nina! You aren't his sister, so you can't possibly understand what the feeling is!"

"I've never heard anyone say anything about him, Mavie."

"Ah, but you live more than a mile away, you would if you lived near Randiswell! There everyone knows he ran away from the Germans at Messines, while Peter Wallace and his brothers stayed, and were bayonetted, defending the doctor, who was kneeling by the wounded! No, don't stop me, I know what you are going to say about gossip, but I know it's true! One of the men who was with Phillip then, called Martin, has a father who is one of our messengers at Head Office, and Martin told his father that Phillip deserted him, when the two of them were bringing up ammunition, to save his own skin!"

"Oh, Mavie, I don't believe it! People say things about everyone, if you listen to them!"

"But Phillip himself told Mother that it *was* true! He said he left Martin because he lay down, and wouldn't get up. Then again, he says that he pretended to be a chemist before he joined the army, to avoid being sent over the top at Loos. So they made him a gas officer, and he says, quite openly, that he gassed all his own men! And everybody knows our father is half-German, though he hates the Germans, for what they have done. Phillip doesn't mind telling Mr. Jenkins in that public house that the

German soldiers are as good as ours! That's the awful thing about it—he has no shame at all. It will break Mother's heart! And on top of it all, there's this horrible drinking!"

On returning from the battle of Loos some weeks before, having transferred to a home unit, Second-lieutenant Phillip Maddison had obtained a week's leave, ostensibly to replace kit lost in battle; and after that week, he had got a further week's sick-leave. This luck, as he called it, had come about through Dr. Dashwood, a recent acquaintance, who in the Conservative Club, over double whiskeys, had said, "I don't like the sound of your pipes, Middleton, come along and let me sound your bellows." Leading Phillip into the billiard-room, Dr. Dashwood, with professional fixity upon his purple face, listened through the worn and grubby pink rubber tubes of a stethoscope pressed upon selected places of a thin chest and ribs. A murmur, a distinct murmur, the doctor announced, stuffing his apparatus back into his overcoat pocket.

"Can't let you go back like that, Middleton. You've had two spells at the Front, so let someone else have a turn. I'll give you a note to Toogood at the Workhouse. D'you know 'im?"

"I've heard of Dr. Toogood, that's all," replied Phillip, not liking to ask why he should be sent to a Workhouse doctor. Was Dashwood blotto? One could never quite tell.

"Toogood's now a colonel in the R.A.M.C.," remarked Dr. Dashwood, as though he had read his thoughts. "The Infirmary has been turned into a hospital for Tommies, Middleton." Dr. Dashwood staggered sideways, recovered, hooked his umbrella over his elbow, and putting on his bowler hat, led the way back to the bar. There he ordered two more double whiskeys.

"If you don't mind, I won't have any more, Doctor. But will you have one with me?"

"Thank you, my dear Middleton," said Dr. Dashwood, bowing. "But the rules of the Club forbid. You are my guest. Help yourself to seltzer." Courteously he placed the syphon by Phillip's glass. Not wanting to hurt the old boy's feelings, Phillip sipped the whiskey, suppressing a shudder, while hoping that it would not make him shoot his bundle. Making his expression amiable, he refrained from watching while Dr. Dashwood scrawled something with his big fat fountain pen on Club writing paper, and signed it with a flourish. Then waving the paper to and fro, to dry the ink before putting it in an envelope, he gave it to Phillip, with another bow.

Would the Club address give the game away? For Dr. Dashwood, according to Mrs. Neville, was well-known for his tippling.

Furthermore, had Dr. Dashwood written *Middleton*, when his name was Maddison? He had not liked to correct the doctor, lest it spoil the genial spirit of himself being Middleton.

Half an hour and two whiskeys later, Phillip left the smoke room of the Conservative Club and walked with glassy determination across the croquet lawn beyond the billiard room, and so to the banks of the Randiswell. There, with one hand on the weeping willow trailing some of its branches into the dirty water, he was sick. Afterwards a desire to hide his shame led him, with faltering steps, across the lawn and to the billiard room where, as he told his great friend Desmond and Mrs. Neville his mother at their flat later that evening, he got into a dugout under the table, and passed out.

"When I had got rid of the fumes and the nausea it was tea-time. Dr. Dashwood gave me some bromide. And before I went to see Toogood at the Workhouse I bought some violet cachous, and took care to turn my face away when the old boy sounded me. Anyway, it's awful to breathe in anyone's face. I think he appreciated this, for he gave me a week's extension. So here I am!"

"*Did* Dr. Dashwood write *Middleton*, Phillip?" asked Mrs. Neville.

"I couldn't read any of his writing, Mrs. Neville."

"Just as well!" cried the fat woman, with sudden laughter. "Still," she added, solemn again, "if he is a bit of a rogue, he is a charming rogue, I'll say that for him."

The extra leave took Phillip to Friday night. He was due to report to his new unit in Essex on the Saturday morning. But on his last night Desmond was not on duty with the searchlights, and on the Saturday morning Phillip put off his start for a cup of coffee in the flat, then another cup, then a quick game of snakes-and-ladders while eating bread and cheese; after which he took Desmond on the back of his motor cycle to Freddy's bar in the High Street for a glass of beer, and as they were coming out in walked Dr. Dashwood. After a round of drinks they went for one for the road, as the doctor called it, in the Conservative Club, where, said the doctor, "Auld Scottie" whiskey, unlike Teacher's he had had before, was as mild as milk, and the very thing to kill any bug which might be exploiting the dull patch in Phillip's lung.

"The trouble with me, Doctor, is that I have never been able

to stop my thoughts racing about in all directions," said Phillip.
"When I was a child, I called this to myself the battle of the brain.
I find it awfully hard to control thoughts of disaster, even of
torture, however much I try to reason things out. I suppose it is
bad form not to conceal one's thoughts, but then I'm not a
gentleman. Also, I'm a frightful coward, and always have been.
And, as you can see, I have no reserve, as mother is always telling
me. I just can't help saying what I think."

It was a handicap to have too much imagination, Dr. Dashwood
said, kindly, after Phillip had returned to the Club to thank him
for a further week's leave. "Sometimes I think I am all imagination, and by a freak was born with the spirit of a hare," went on
Phillip, and thereupon told the doctor why he had transferred to
a home-service unit.

"I get absolutely stiff and trembling with fear, when I think
of facing machine guns again. That's why I applied to be a gas
officer at Loos, because I couldn't face the idea of going over the
top. I was given several days light duty afterwards, for a slight
gassing, but I didn't really get gassed at all. I saw men who did.
Their faces and bodies turned the colour of plums, with saliva all
over their chins and tunics. Slugs seemed to like it, when they
were dead. You don't see those things in the papers."

"My dear Middleton, as I told you, you have too much imagination! Why should such details be put in newspapers? Surely
the right thing is to keep them out? You don't see what goes on
in any hospital, 'in the papers'. Now to change from the general
to the particular, I don't like that bronchial rasp you have. Come
into the billiard room, and let me sound your bellows. Yes, definitely you have a dull patch. I'll give you a note to Toogood."

"But you've just given me one, Doctor!"

"Oh, did I? Well, that calls for a celebration!"

It was Dashwood who had done the wheezing, Phillip thought,
not himself; but the main thing was that he had another week's
leave, and would be with his great friend Desmond again.

The Gild Hall was filling up with its Saturday evening crowd,
now that the shops closed early at half past seven, owing to the
war. Large straw hats of black, set well back on the head, worn
with white blouses and dark skirts above the ankle, with black
cotton gloves to the elbow, appeared to be the fashion among
those flappers who wore their hair in plaits either over a shoulder
or down the back. Many of the youths, the more envied ones,

were in uniform, although obviously under military age. Others had dressed themselves in brown shoes with slacks, sharply creased, some with turn-ups; or brown boots with lace-up breeches; both styles unauthorised and worn only on leave, to suggest a gentility above that of the ordinary private soldier. Their jackets, too, had been altered, to take away the issue roughness, to show the shape of the torso—all from aspiration to glory and freedom.

The manager of the Gild Hall was now, as he put it to himself, in evidence, as he stood beside the pay-box leading to the billiard hall proper. He was an upright figure with thin white hair, wearing an ancient pattern of frock coat with celluloid collar, dickey, ready-made flat black tie held in place by elastic, and stringy waxed moustaches that looked as though they had been thick and bushy. A scrawny neck and prominent Adam's apple stood out of the oversize celluloid collar. This great-grandfatherly teetotal figure gave forth contentment with life, as he surveyed the youthful throng before him.

Mavis was playing dominoes, with Nina. The smooth, slurring slide of the ivory and ebony pieces, the feel of them to the finger-tips was of summer childhood, when she had loved all the world and was loved by everyone, all the faces round the big mahogany table in the sitting room, which had a new leaf in it, brought up from under the floor, through the trapdoor, because Aunt Liz and cousins Polly and Percy had come to stay, and Dads was ever so jolly as he played games of halma and ludo with them, and promised prizes of Callard and Bowser's cherry toffee bars in silver paper. It was summer, and a wet day, but the rain did not matter, for everything was so jolly and shining inside the sitting room. Then it was dark and sad again, and it was Phil's fault, for Dads opening his roll-top desk had found out that some of the toffee was gone, and Phil had told a lie, saying that he had not opened the desk with one of the keys on Mother's key-ring, when he had; and Mummie had scolded her for saying that he had told a lie, and Dads had sent Phil upstairs to take down his trousers for a caning, and he had cried like a baby as he left the room and Mummie had cried, too, and it had spoiled the lovely feeling of summer and the rain on the window.

"Don't you feel it awfully hot in here, Nina? Let's go, shall we? There's no point in our stopping."

"But I've just ordered some more coffee, Mavis."

"We can tell the girl we don't want it."

Nina was used to the sudden peremptory moods of her friend;
and as her care was to save her from being upset, she got up to
speak to the waitress, being sensitive about cancelling an order
only when the tray should arrive. She was half way to the girl,
who was standing by the pay-box at the entrance to the billiard
hall proper, when she heard loud voices, then a prolonged cry
between a cheer and a yell, as the glass doors leading in from the
porch were pushed open and three figures staggered into the
room, arm in arm, barging into one another with laughter. She
recognised Phillip, his friend Desmond, and a smaller, dark man
in a blue suit and bowler hat, carrying an ebony cane with large
silver top, and wearing an eyeglass, who, she thought, must be
Eugene, the Brazilian friend of Desmond.

They stood by the sunken pool, and appeared to be arguing
about something, hands on one another's shoulders. Their voices
were loud, everyone was looking at them, the domino games
suspended. Nina saw that Phillip's jacket was dripping with
water, as though a jug had been tipped over him, as indeed it
had, by Mrs. Freddy in the bar over the road. Anxious for her
friend, Nina went back to Mavis, whose eyes were dark and
anxious.

"Are they tipsy?" she whispered.

"I don't think so."

"Why didn't you let me go when I first said I wanted to? I
knew something like this would happen, you know! I have second-
sight, like Mother! Listen, what are they saying?"

The argument was apparently about whether they should play
three-handed snooker, or Eugene and Desmond play a hundred
up at billiards. Mavis winced at the loudness of the voices. Phillip
was drunk, she decided; his cap was pulled down on the side of
his head, and he had the weak, foolish grin on his face that made
him look so undignified. Thank goodness he was not in uniform!

Very soon her worst fears, or previsions, were realised.

"All right, you two birds go and play," she heard her brother
drawl. "I'll come and watch." He followed them to the door.
The manager stood there. She saw him put a hand on Phillip's
chest, before saying something inaudible to him.

The two others went through the door, leaving Phillip standing
there. Then he tried to go through the door into the billiard
room, after the others. The manager stopped him. In the silence
she heard him say, "I've asked you to leave, now go quietly,
sir."

While he continued to stand there, a fourth figure entered the Gild Hall, wearing raincoat and bowler hat, carrying an umbrella. Seeing Phillip, he went towards him. Mavis recognised Tom Ching, and her spirit darkened. So that was it; he and Phillip had been drinking together!

"Look, that awful creature! He's the cause of it, I bet. Oh look what's happening."

Throwing off Ching's offered arm, Phillip said something to the manager; then holding out his arms he began to walk, or totter, backwards, as though he had lost all sense of balance. Back he went, a dozen paces, and fell into the goldfish pool.

Mavis went out, followed by Nina. Outside in the murky air she said, "Oh, I would have died if anyone had recognised me as his sister!"

Opposite the fire station, at the turning to Randiswell, the friends said goodbye, for Nina's way lay to the south.

"See you tomorrow, usual time? Don't be late, will you? And swear on your honour that you will never tell anyone what happened tonight?" Mavis allowed herself to be kissed, then she hurried across the road, unaware that she was being followed by Tom Ching, who had as powerful an impulse towards his image of Mavis as she had towards the image of her lost father.

Tom Ching was Phillip's age. He was not in uniform because he was a second-grade clerk employed in the Admiralty. His excuse for not having joined up was his indispensability. He was reserved; but there was talk of a Military Service Bill coming before the Commons, and "Cuthberts in Whitehall being combed out", and sent into the services. This was one of Ching's dreads, for he had nothing in himself with which to resist the terrors of death should he have to face what Phillip had gone through at Messines with the London Highlanders, and again at the first battle of Ypres. If Phillip's heritage of courage had been dissipated in childhood by the cold ignorance of a righteous father at odds with his wife, Ching's had been liquidated by an early horror of knowing what his father did to his mother; of himself doing the same thing, in fascination and horror (at first) with his sister; and being found out, by a father who did not punish him, but in his heavy, fleshy way told him that he had committed one of the great sins which can eat into the soul of a family. This had not shocked the youth, who had been at school at the time, so much as being told by his sister, later on, that father had since done the same thing to her.

Now the father was paralysed, a mass of soft pink and white flesh above a formless heavy face, looked after by the daughter. The mother, a mental invalid, was in Peckham House, an asylum.

These complications had emphasised Ching's feeling for the ideal, which for some years now had been centred on Mavis; but he practised his love alone, in the thoughts of unattainable deeds. And to help escape his guilt, he had taken to drinking rum, a drink acceptable to his stomach, apparently, for unlike Phillip after three or four quarterns of whiskey, he was never sick.

He hurried after Mavis, in order to confirm his worst fears.

In the sitting room of the Maddison house the curtains were drawn against Zeppelins and the cold November night. A coke fire glowed brightly in the hearth. It was an extravagance on his part, in war-time too, to have built up a fire so late, thought Richard, as he lay back in his armchair, legs and feet stretched to the polished steel fender. But he was not to be on special constabulary duty again until the Monday, and all Sunday's ease lay before him. He lay back with a sigh of contentment, his cup of hot water on the plush table-cloth beside him, and took up a blue-covered booklet which he had purchased for one penny that afternoon from the London book-stall where, regularly every month, he called for his favourite *Nash's and Pall Mall Magazine*.

Always meticulous when he was not emotionally disturbed, Richard read the title-page carefully.

Report of the Committee on Alleged German Outrages appointed by His Majesty's Government and Presided over by The Right Hon. Viscount Bryce, O.M., etc., etc., formerly British Ambassador at Washington.

He read the first two pages of the preamble, and then his eye wandered. He turned to Part 1, *The Conduct of the German Troops in Belgium*, read a little, and turned over again to read a passage about Liége. Villages around the fortress burned . . . systematic execution of civilians, by being summarily shot . . . survivors of volleys bayonetted, including a young girl of thirteen. He breathed deeply, and took a few sips of hot water.

There followed page upon page of the same thing, shooting, bayonetting, burning. Where were the rapings? He turned over more pages, until he came to Part 2 (b) *The Treatment of Women and Children*. He was reading with horror entwined in fascination when his wife came into the room. His privacy thus being broken into, he put down the booklet.

"I am ready, Dickie, if you would like to play a game of chess," said Hetty, almost gaily.

"You're back early, aren't you?"

"Yes, dear, Papa wants to write a letter, so I shall go back later for the game of piquet."

It did not take much to make Richard feel unwanted. She could put herself out for her father, but would she ever do the same for him? He picked up the blue book and went on reading; but soon the disharmony of his thoughts broke into indignation.

"Listen to this incident, Hetty! It took place not far from the district where your convent stands, or did stand, at Wespelaer, a little more than a year ago. I can only thank heaven that Mavis came home last year in the nick of time."

"'On the afternoon of the 14th or 15th August, three German cavalry officers entered the house and demanded champagne. Having drunk ten bottles, and invited five or six officers and three or four private soldiers to join them, they continued their carouse, and then called for the master and the mistress of the house: 'Immediately my mistress came in', says the valet de chambre, 'one of the officers who was sitting on the floor got up, and, putting a revolver to my mistress' temple, shot her dead. The officer was obviously drunk. The other officers continued to drink and sing, and they did not pay great attention to the killing of my mistress. My master and the officer went into the garden, the officer threatening my master with a pistol. My master was then forced to dig the grave, and bury the body of my mistress in it. I cannot say for what reason they killed my mistress. The officer who did so was singing all the time'."

"Terrible, terrible," murmured Hetty, making a clicking noise between tongue and palate.

"But that is not the worst, Hetty!

'One witness reports that a young girl who was being pursued by a drunken soldier at Louvain appealed to a German officer, and that the offender was then and there shot: another describes how an officer of the 32nd Regiment of the Line was led out to execution for the violation of two young girls, but reprieved at the request or with the consent of the girls' mothers. These instances are sufficient to show that the maltreatment of women was no part of the military scheme of the invaders . . .'"

Richard's voice ceased. He put down the Report, with a further feeling of being cheated. However, there was the clean, unopened copy of *Nash's* at his elbow. He turned to his wife and said rhetorically,

"What is the point of publishing an indictment of German military brutality, which we know exists, if in the same breath the Report exonerates the guilty? In my opinion such two-facedness is typical of that old woman Asquith, whose wife, the blatant 'Margot', openly visited German officer prisoners at Donnington Hall in Lincolnshire, taking with her hampers of the best comestibles from Curling and Hammer, and playing tennis with them, while her country is at war, and her husband Prime Minister!"

"Yes, Dickie, it is all very wrong. Shall I get the chess board? Or do you feel too tired to play tonight?"

"Oh," he said airily. "Do not let me keep you from your duties in the house next door." Richard's relationship with his father-in-law was one of dislike reduced to nullity. As his wife went out of the room he said, "Now, if you please! Do not be late. I want to be in bed by eleven, and cannot get to sleep until every member of this house is in bed, you know that."

Hetty knew that he was worried about Phillip, about whom she had gone next door, to speak to Papa. "I shan't be long, Dickie," as she left the room, her heart feeling lighter.

"Let the cat in, as you go out, will you? I don't want Zippy to catch cold, waiting in that draughty porch."

"Very well, Dickie."

Soon the cat was in the room, purring, purring, purring, to see its master again—and the warm fire.

During the years a cat had been almost the only medium by which tenderness was released in the Maddison household. There had been three cats, all called Zippy. Zippy never upset anyone, by interfering. Having security from want, fear, and entanglement by sex, Zippy was always in the same mood. In the short days of the duller half of the year Zippy followed the sun around the house, from one resting place behind glass, to another; cushion, chair, window sill, top of wicker dirty-clothes-basket, table beside balcony window. In the season of light, Zippy lived a country gentleman's life. His landed property was the garden and part of the Backfield, where sparrows, mice, frogs, moths, and daddy-long-legs existed for the chase. A surgical operation long forgotten and preceded by a howl of finality had spared Zippy the pangs and aspirations of love; and being nimble, Zippy was generally able to avoid the periodical clashes with female cats, which smacked the neuter's face if Zippy did not immediately flee from their insults and oaths. So Zippy took it out of small birds and mammals, which it left bedraggled and maimed when it had had what Richard, often expressing impatience with what he called his wife's sentimentality, described as its sport.

Had Hetty shown less obvious distress, less melting pity when smaller, weaker things were hurt and despairing, it is possible that her husband would have been less critical of her so-called sentimentality. He had been brought up in the country, and knew the balancings of nature, of life and death. A bird taking a butterfly, a cat the bird in its turn, should be outside a man's feelings. Privately, he preferred that the cat should run after what he called his drag—a rabbit's foot tied to string.

Now, taking the lure from his desk, Richard and the cat played together. The chase went on for several minutes around the bulbous mahogany legs of the table, under the mahogany bookcase, the gramophone stand, over the chairs. Finally the string was fastened to the handle of the door, so that the furry foot hung clear of the carpet. Thus the game was rounded off, until the cat had had enough, and went back to its place, to tuck paws under before the fire; then Richard untied the lure, and locked it away until the next time.

Mavis looked back as she crossed the humped bridge over river and railway, and saw that Ching was following her. She felt disgust. He had written letters to her; she suspected that he waited in the grass behind the garden fence, to watch her when she went to bed in the end room. Where poor, gentle Alfred Hawkins had once crept, to leave little poems for her in a crack of one of the posts. Until——

She put away the terrible childhood scene that Phillip had been responsible for.

Mavis hurried on, to escape Ching's attentions. He kept pace with her. Then, turning into Charlotte Road, with its leafless polled chestnuts, she decided to walk slower. Why should she have to run away from anyone? Perhaps he had something to tell her about Phillip. Perhaps he had not been drunk, after all, but only ill. Impossible. There was nothing the matter with him —except that he was going the way of Uncle Hugh. Poor Mother! Father bullying her on one hand, Phillip destroying her peace of mind on the other. Mother was a saint. Her whole life had been given to her husband and her son, and both treated her shabbily. Men were utterly selfish. Grandpa had knocked her down when he had found out about her secret marriage to Father, when she was carrying Phillip; and she had been unconscious for hours, in a kind of fit. And now Phillip was showing himself just as bad as Father, and in his time, Grandpa.

What did Ching want to say to her this time? The usual grovelling?

She allowed him to overtake her just before the turn up Hillside Road. It would be better there, than outside the house.

He took off his bowler hat, and stood before her. At first he could not speak. She heard him swallowing, and felt calm. But if he tried to kiss her suddenly, she would poke him with her umbrella—one of the new three-quarter size models, called The Gay Paree, price four and eleven three in Beeveman's Store near the Obelisk. Mavis had borrowed the money from her mother to buy it, and Hetty, after protest, had made her promise to pay the money back next salary day, for the money was out of the housekeeping, and food was now very expensive, she said. Mavis had paid it back, reluctantly, then borrowed it again the next day to pay for her lunches.

"Mavis, I humbly beg your pardon for accosting you like this. Will you forgive me?"

"What, are you tipsy too?"

"I swear it was none of my doing! I was only being a good Samaritan. Phillip was overcome by gas."

"By whiskey, you mean!"

"Well, only a very little. Please, Mavis, do not judge him!"

"You mean you don't want me to judge you, I suppose?"

"Oh, I do not matter at all. It is for Phillip that I hasten to plead. He is not well. He has a lesion on one lung."

"Who told you, I should like to know?"

"I heard it on high authority."

"Don't tell me it was that Dr. Dashwood!" she cried derisively. "We all know what he is!"

Ching said humbly. "It may be a matter of grave concern. Even of life and death."

"I bet! What is it, then?"

Encouraged by her matter-of-fact manner, Ching felt easier in himself, and correspondingly flummoxed about what he could say. He pretended.

"Well, the high authority is Phillip himself. After all, it is a matter of life and death to him."

Mavis laughed. "Pooh, I don't believe you know what you're talking about, Ching!"

"As a matter of fact, I do. It concerns the love of his life."

"Oh, that old thing! That is only his pretence! Besides, Helena Rolls cares nothing for him. Why should she? His talk about eternal love is entirely one-sided! So one-sided, in fact, that it doesn't stop him from going after at least one other girl."

"I never have, I swear," said Ching hoarsely. He clasped his hands. "Mavis—Mavis——"

"I know that you're only pretending, you know! Why do you?"

"Please don't be unkind," he groaned. "I can't help feeling— as I do. Can't we be just friends? Oh please—that's all I ask— I know I'm no good—please don't be angry——" Ching, to his remote satisfaction, managed to break into tears.

For a moment Mavis was shocked in a way that surprised her. Her mood of brittle scorn fell away, and she felt that Ching was part of the sadness of the world. There was only one way by which one's personal sorrows could be harmonised with those of the world.

"Do you mind if I say something to you, Ching?"

"Yes, Mavis, of course, of course, anything!"

"Go and see Father Aloysius at St. Saviours, in the High Street, and he will tell you what to do."

"Yes, you go there with your friend Nina, I know."

"Well, you go too, Ching. Now I must go. Please do not think anything more about me, I am only a substitute for something else in your eyes. Father Aloysius will explain it all to you."

"You mean there's no hope for me otherwise?" he moaned.

"I can't say any more, Ching. Everyone has their troubles, you know."

Ching passed away in the darkness, and Mavis went on up Hillside Road, dullness overcoming her as she drew near her home.

Richard, lying back in his armchair, was feeling some sort of freedom, as he read about life on the Western Front, obviously an account at first hand, in *Nash's*. BILLET NOTES, *being casual pencillings from a Fighting Man to his Mother*, was obviously the real thing. Why couldn't his own son tell him what he had always wanted to know about the front, instead of replying in monosyllables, if at all? If only he himself were younger, he would join up and get away from the drudgery and restriction that had been his life for two and twenty years now.

Dearest,—I have just emerged from a dug-out that would make you stare. Now, there are dug-outs and dug-outs. They all aim at being a home from home, but this one was fairly It. It hadn't a carpet, but it was furnished with old oak (loot from a German trench whose previous occupants had obviously looted it from someone else). In it we ate our dinner off delicate Sèvres plates and drank out of rare old cut glasses. A dug-out de luxe! But even the common or garden dug-out shows some attempt at cosiness.

I am coming to the conclusion that man is considerably more of a real home-maker than woman. What woman, living as we do, would, without the incentive of male companionship, go into the trouble of trying to make a mud cave into the semblance of a civilised house? A woman living alone, especially in a temporary abode, troubles little or not at all about her personal comfort. She doesn't even take pains about food. She only studies these two amenities of life if she has a man to share them. Now we, on the contrary, always have a desire to make the best of circumstances. We collect (or steal) planks, bricks, doors, and windows to help give a semblance of civilisation to our funk-holes. The men keep the trenches neat and make gardens behind the parados. A sense of humour gives spice to the task. It shows in the names bestowed upon our residences—'The Keep', 'Minenwerfer Villa', 'The Gasworks'. 'Myholme' is also very popular. But there's something beside humour that incites Tommy to put up a board marked 'Trespassers will be Prosecuted' over his kitchen garden. He means it. His impotent rage when a German shell ignores the prohibition is comic to a degree.

After one of these annoyances some of the men of my company in desperation stalked a German sentry, brought him in alive, and made him write in huge German characters the words KARTOFFELN GARTEN—VERBOTEN, which they hoisted on a board facing the enemy's lines. I believe that sentry is secretly being kept as a hostage against further damage!

Your loving
CHOTA

Richard laughed delightedly, the whole scene was most vivid, he could see it all happening. He lay back in his chair before the bright and crackling coke fire, stretching his toes in his old carpet slippers, feeling a sense of continuity with life as he unfrogged the ancient pleated smoking jacket that had belonged to his father. He felt he was cosy in a dug-out, with his soldiers' pet Zippy contentedly lying beside a brazier.

Before settling down again with his magazine, he poured himself another cup of hot water from the kettle simmering in front of the fire, then lifting the cat to his knee, covered it with *The Daily Trident*, so that Zippy could feel safe, as in a cave or hollow tree. All being settled, he lay back to read; but hardly had he turned the page when the bell of the front door rang. He sighed: his evening alone was ended.

"Good evening, Father."

"Hullo, Mavis. Don't forget to wipe your boots on the mat, if you please."

"It's quite dry out, Father."

"Even so, it is a good habit, which you children do not seem yet to have learned."

"Is Mother in?"

"She is where she prefers to be—next door."

"Will it be all right if I have my bath now, Father?"

"Why do you ask? You know very well your Mother said it was available for you tonight. Only don't take too much hot water—the price of coal is very nearly prohibitive as it is."

Without further words, Richard went back to his chair, and Mavis disappeared upstairs. It took him five minutes to feel clear again; and back with Chota.

At twenty past ten Hetty gave her brief little trill to the bell; Richard sighed; his period of peace was over.

"Mavis returned while you were away, Hetty, and is having her tub. Have you seen anything of Master Phillip?"

"No, dear, but I expect him any moment now."

"Oh you do, do you? Have you any special reason for knowing that he will, for once, be home before midnight?"

"I don't suppose Phillip will be long now, Dickie. He likes to walk about at night, he says he can think clearer then."

"So the Wild Boy thinks at night, does he? Are you sure you are not confusing the word *think* with another that rhymes with it?"

"Phillip has had a lot on his mind, Dickie, one way and another. He always was a thoughtful boy."

"A pity he does not think more about others, or his home, if that is the case."

In an exasperated voice Richard went on, "Do you think that you can pull the wool over my eyes with such an explanation?

But there, you have always shielded that best boy of yours! Do not deceive yourself that I am ignorant of what has been going on! Night after night he has been coming home the worse for liquor! Now don't try and defend him, as you always tried to do when he was a boy! You spoiled him, let me tell you! It is high time you realised that Phillip will have to stand on his own feet!"

Despite her anxiety about her son, Hetty saw the funny side of these words. No, no, it was not funny, her sudden mind-picture of Phillip, perhaps at that very moment unable to stand upright. Mary, Mother of God, help my son, she tried to transmit through her brain, as she strove against another picture of Hughie, her dearest brother, thin and shambling, dying of *locomotor ataxia*. She must hope for the best about Phillip; she must pray for guidance to come to him. Should she go to see Dr. Dashwood, and ask him not to encourage Phillip in his loose ways? People were beginning to talk about it. Mrs. Feeney, the charwoman, had mentioned it only that morning.

"I saw Master Phillip the other evening, coming out of the Conservative Club with Dr. Dashwood, m'm. It's not my place to speak about it, but it would be a pity if someone so much older was to lead Master Phillip astray. If you'll excuse me mentioning of it, m'm."

"Yes, of course, Mrs. Feeney. You are a very old friend, and have known Phillip since he was little. Between ourselves, that very self-same thought has been worrying me."

Mrs. Feeney knew all about the fate of poor Mr. Hugh next door; but she knew her place, and would never have mentioned to the mis'ess about Master Phillip, except that Dr. Dashwood was so well known for his liking for the bottle.

Hetty had been to see Mrs. Neville about it; to be momentarily reassured by that tolerant woman with a "There's no harm in our boys, Mrs. Maddison! My boy Desmond and your Phillip are only young, dear! They mean no harm by it! Don't you worry, Phillip is all right. They can take care of themselves, if I know those two boys! What friends they are! I call them David and Jonathan, David being Phillip, of course."

Hetty was not so sure. She knew Phillip's weaknesses; from the first he had been almost fearfully susceptible to everything around him, so that his life had seemed to be one long round of trouble, so mischievous, excitable, curious, and wilful had he been. And what was he but a boy still, so young for his age, despite having been twice to the front. Was it the rum in the trenches that had started him off on his intemperate habits?

Another thing had disturbed Hetty: something his Father must never be allowed to find out. She had seen cousin Polly in her nightdress coming out of Phillip's bedroom, after they had returned home late from seeing *Tonight's the Night* at the Gaiety in the Strand. It was in the Strand that Hughie had contracted that terrible illness which had ruined his hopes for marrying Dora, and led to paralysis and early death of her gifted brother. Was Phillip to go the same tragic way? Better Polly than a stranger; even so, one bad habit led to a worse habit, more often than not. Had not Hughie, while protesting love for Dora, at the same time fallen into temptation with a complete stranger? O, how could men do such things?

As for Phillip, he had confided in her, that very morning, that he would never cease to love Helena Rolls; but that, she knew, was more a feverish obsession with him than something real—what was called calf-love. What a strange boy he was; almost at times he seemed to be two distinct persons.

She poured herself a cup of hot water. Richard had decided to give up his nightly cup of cocoa for the sake of economy, and also for reasons of health. The cost of living was going up; and he felt that he slept the better, with fewer worries arising to upset his mind, on what he called a clean stomach.

The Daily Trident was being flicked slightly at one corner, Zippy's ear was being tickled by the paper. "Poor Zippy, did I cover you up too much, then, poor Zippy?" Tenderly Richard lifted the newspaper, and scratched Zippy's ears. The cat purred gratefully; and thus encouraged, Richard took up *Nash's Magazine* and turned to the serial by Robert W. Chambers, *Athalie, the Romance of a girl with a strange power*, for a few moments; but his wife's presence got between him and the beautiful, luring heroine. Putting down the magazine, he turned to his wife and said, with an explosion of irritability,

"There's another matter on my mind that I think you should know about! I do not at all approve of what Phillip has been saying in that low haunt of his in the High Street! Things get about, let me tell you, among certain of our special constables who shall remain nameless! I do not know what Phillip did during his recent visit to France, or what part, if any, he took in the Loos battle, for he apparently has no desire to tell me any of his doings, but he can hold forth, from what I hear, in no uncertain voice about the conduct of affairs in the Army overseas! And, furthermore, he is saying things in the enemy's favour which will get him into serious trouble one of these days! More than one person has reported to me, at the Station, what they have overheard him to say in that public house he frequents. Hark! Was that a bomb?"

Richard's thoughts were of Mathy, the redoubtable Commander Mathy whose raids on England had been made with such skill that, it was thought, he worked with spies—many German spies—throughout the country.

Only the crackle of coke, and the purring of the cat, was audible in the room. Hetty thought of her elder daughter, Mavis, alone in the end bedroom upstairs. Her footfalls were softly audible. The girl was highly nervous, and terrified of Zeppelins.

Richard sipped his hot water. "No, I do not think it could have been a bomb. Zippy's ears always go up when Zeppelins are about, he hears the engines a long way off, don't you, Zippy dear?" He fondled the cat's neck and head, talking to it in a crooning voice. It was the only personality in the house which he had not, unwittingly, turned from him.

The hearkening mother heard heavier footfalls overhead, from her son's bedroom. Thank goodness that Dickie was a little deaf, she thought, as there came two bumps, as of shoes being torn off. Then the noise of a bed spring extending. She went out of the room; and when she came in again she said almost gaily: "Phillip is in bed after all, Dickie!"

"H'm!" said Richard, as he took up *Nash's*, "I suppose that I, as the mere master of this house, can consider myself to be extremely fortunate if I see the Wild Boy for breakfast tomorrow, or will he then be sleeping off the effects of his 'night thoughts'? When is he going back to duty, do you know? Even a visitor to an hotel has the courtesy to give notice when his room is no longer required, you know."

"He has one more week, I think, Dickie, before going to his new duties."

Why his son had "exchanged", as he put it, from the Gaultshire Regiment in France to a non-combatant unit at home, Richard did not know; but he could guess.

Phillip lay in bed, knees drawn up to chin for warmth and companionship. The "battle of the brain", as he had called it since childhood, was raging in his head. He was near to despair, a not unusual condition of his living.

When the worst of the "battle" was over he turned about and rearranged the sheet which he had drawn tightly about his neck. After settling down, instinctively he nipped between the edges of his lips a fold of the sheet; and feeling some relief in the smoothness of the material against his face, sighed deeply with the hope of sleep.

The habit of nipping and holding the sheet between his lips was a survival from babyhood, when in his cot he had had two objects of consolation for the loss of protecting maternal warmth: a thumb to suck, and a strip of white silk from an old petticoat of his mother's to hold over his face. The strip was given him, at night, when he cried for his mother.

Richard in those days had wanted his wife for himself in bed; he had wanted, also, quietness at night; and though he disapproved of both thumb and silk he had not openly objected to what he had called the baby's soporifics during the first year of the child's life.

Soon after the first birthday anniversary he considered that the time was come for reformation. A bad habit was a bad habit; the sooner it was broken, the sooner it would be forgotten. Sonny must learn not to cry for his mother, too. So at the age of fifteen months the child was put in a room by himself, with Anky, and told that to suck Thumb was very, very naughty. If he cried, too, he would be smacked.

Thus, Richard thought, the boy would, from an early age, learn to face the hardships of life.

Chapter 2

GREY TOWERS

At eight o'clock one morning of the following week, Richard took a letter coming through the box of the front door as he passed on his way to breakfast. It was addressed to his son. The flimsy envelope from France was franked by a signature which he made out to be *H. J. West, Capt.*, and bore the oval red rubber stamp of the Base Censor. It had been redirected from *Brickhill House, Beau Brickhill, Gaultshire.*

Richard had to leave the house at eight twenty-two a.m. to catch his train from Wakenham station over the hill. His daughter Mavis caught the next train, which enabled her to get to the office in time for its opening for business at half-past nine. The younger girl, Doris, was still at school, and left at twenty-five to nine.

Breakfast was usually silent. Richard, looking at *The Daily Trident*, spoke only when he had some fault to point out, such as taps left to drip, bedrooms left untidy "for your mother to attend to"; or the boot-cleaning box in the scullery had not been put back, with its brushes and Japanese blacking pot upright, under the scullery table.

Phillip, urged by his mother to come down for breakfast with the others, "out of courtesy to your Father, dear", appeared just as Richard was putting his table-napkin into its ivory ring.

"Good morning, Father. Good morning, Mother. How do you do, Mavis. Hullo, Doris. Thanks for purring, Zippy."

"There's a letter for you, from France," said Doris.

"Good lord! 'Spectre' West!" He sat down. "May I have permission to open it, sir?"

The unexpected courtesy surprised Richard.

"Good news, I hope," he said, when his son had read the letter.

"Yes, Father. A friend of mine in hospital is getting on well."

"I see it has been re-directed from Brickhill, Phillip," said Hetty.

"Westy is in the Gaultshires, Mother."

Phillip put the letter in his pocket, and added milk to his porridge. He still felt sick, and would have preferred a glass of cold water.

"Pass your brother the sugar, Mavis."

"No thanks—really. I never have sugar——"

As soon as Richard had shut the front door behind him, Mavis cried, "Why do you pretend that you live at Brickhill, can you tell us that?"

When he did not reply, she went on, "I know! It's because it's a swankier address than poor old Wakenham."

Hetty screwed up her eyes, and made a *moue* with her lips to Mavis, meaning be quiet. "Won't you tell us what it says, Phillip?"

"Oh, it's just an ordinary letter, Mother." He went on trying to eat his porridge, while calculating from experience how long it would be before he would have to get rid of it. Not, he hoped, while Mavis was in the house.

Experience did not betray him. Afterwards, alone with his mother, he showed her the letter. "On the condition, Mother, that you do not breathe a word of what it says to anyone."

"Well, perhaps it would be better if I did not see it, if it's like that, dear."

"No, it's not that. Only it isn't true, that's all."

He gave her the letter, and Hetty read with surprise that grew to tearful emotion. The writer declared that the bar to his Military Cross, "which came up with the rations", should have gone to Phillip, and would have gone, too, if he had not left the regiment after the damned fine show he put up during the flank attack on Lone Tree Ridge.

"'Spectre' West wasn't there, you see. He was hit before we started. It was all over when we got to Lone Tree. The Germans had chucked it. No more ammunition. Anyway, the Welch had already got right behind them. It was awful good luck for us."

"He says he is sorry you have left the 'Mediators', Phillip. That surely shows——"

"I told the Colonel afterwards that I was up at Cambridge before the war. I was nervous because I had only been to a grammar school when all the other officers were public school men. So I pretended I was a ''varsity m'n'. I've got no guts, I never had any. Tell that to Father if you like, but not that other rot."

"Why, I wonder, must you always insist on showing yourself in the worst light? Always as a boy you were without reserve of any kind. You should have more pride, Phillip."

"Oh Mother, for God's sake——" He hastened away to the lavatory. Later—"I feel better now. But no bacon, for heaven's sake. Just a cup of weak tea. A large one. Put it in a basin. Here, let me get one. That's the sort, holds a quart. Thank God tea at home doesn't taste of chloride of lime." The thought made him quaver; the quaver took him back to the lavatory.

"You ought never to drink spirits, you know, Phillip. You have a weak stomach. That was always your trouble as a child. Now try and eat a little dry toast, and later on I'll make you some beef tea. It was always good for you, after train sickness, do you remember?"

"Yes, and so was brandy," replied Phillip. "But I'd rather have some plain hot water at the moment. If it's all the same to you, Hetty," he added, almost jauntily.

Saturday morning; his leave was up. "Everything is flat, Des, now I'm leaving you." Just one more drink at Freddy's; but when they came out of Freddy's after only two half-pints of beer, Phillip ready to run and vault into the saddle and dash away to the thuds of his open exhaust, music in his ears, there was the motor bike sunken down on its rear, with a flat tyre.

"She must have heard my very words, and taken them literally," said Phillip. "Good old girl. Let's shove her to Wetherley's, and get him to mend the puncture." The inner tube was perished. Wetherley had no replacement in stock.

A *For Sale* notice on a runabout motor car caught Phillip's eye. Only £60! He bought it at once, not so much for its appearance, as the thought of his own appearance driving his own motor car. Having bought it, he asked what it was, and if it was in good condition. Mr. Wetherley assured him that it was the best 1909 model of a Swift he had driven. It had a two-cylinder water-cooled engine. The grey paint was new, and so was the varnish. Mr. Wetherley folded and put into his pocket-book the cheque for £60, and said he would try and sell the motor cycle for £15 without taking commission. The sudden transaction now had its effect; Phillip wondered if his cheque would be dishonoured by Cox & Co., his bankers.

"However, it will be all right by the first of the month. Then some field allowances are due, Mr. Wetherley, so don't worry."

"I do not worry, sir," said Mr. Wetherley. "I have had the pleasure of serving your father for many years now. Indeed I sold him the first All-Black Sunbeam in the district. There is no question, sir, of doubting the word of the son of such a gentleman as Mr. Maddison."

Phillip felt that he must hope for the best, as the garage owner showed him how to get to Hornchurch, pointing out the route on the map, by way of the Blackwall Tunnel under the Thames. This done, he explained about the oiling of the engine, by the drip feed visible behind glass on the dashboard.

"Don't forget to push down the hand pump as soon as the oil stops dripping into the bowl."

Mr. Wetherley checked the milled screw controlling the drip, and gave it two extra clicks.

"Don't turn it on more unless you want to go fast, say over thirty-five. Otherwise you may oil a plug. You'll find her a useful little runabout."

Phillip's two-mindedness now showed itself. "I suppose," he

said, doubtfully, "you wouldn't let me have a test run before I actually—well, I have, haven't I? Anyway, I think I'll test it, before I really start off."

"I'd be very pleased to take you for a run, sir."

"Well, thanks. Could you take me to my home a minute? It's quite a steep hill." A wild hope that Helena Rolls or her mother would see the car pierced him.

Desmond was left at the garage, since three in front would be a squeeze. Mr. Wetherley drove as far as Randiswell, then Phillip took the wheel. The Swift went easily up Hillside Road, and to his alarmed delight, there was Helena coming out of her gate with her mother.

The motor was praised, then—"Why have you not been to see us, Phillip?" He could not reply; and Mrs. Rolls said, "Well, when you are next on leave, don't forget, will you?" The full look of Helena's eyes was upon him; he felt enveloped and dissolved, and was relieved when they had gone on down the road, for now he could release his feelings of joy, rush in and bang at the door and tell Mother the terrific news, in which the Swift was for the moment forgotten.

His mother and younger sister Doris came out to admire it, though Hetty looked a little anxious. "Are you sure you can drive it, Phillip?"

"Easily! I'll take you all out to Reynard's Common and the Fish Ponds when I come home next. Well, cheerho. I mustn't keep old Wetherley waiting. Give my love to everyone." Mr. Wetherley was on the opposite pavement, apparently interested in the sheep on the slopes of the Hill beyond the railings. Together they went down the road, the tyres crackling on the flinty surface. Waving at Mrs. Neville in her window, Phillip drove safely back to the High Street. There Desmond was awaiting him on the kerb.

Phillip had driven a motor car before, and soon he felt mastery of the Swift. With Desmond beside him he drove up the hill and on to the Heath, and down into Greenwich. At the mouth of the Blackwall Tunnel stood a military policeman on duty. He said that a brigade of field guns had just gone through, and another was expected, the tunnel being temporarily closed to all other traffic. "You have a pass, sir, of course?"

Phillip pointed to the O.H.M.S. plate tied on the side of the bonnet. Standing aside, the redcap saluted. Phillip raised a negligent hand, as a staff officer might, he thought, and praying that he would not grate the gears when starting off, let in the

clutch and drove on with a wild feeling of possible self-destruction
into the circular brick mouth of the tunnel.

"My God, and we've got no lamps!" he said to Desmond,
with a laugh, as they rushed into darkness.

The car drove itself; then gradually seemed to be guided by
two golden threads overhead. These were carbon-filament bulbs
lining the roof, stretching away to a minuteness that dipped in
the centre, the middle of the river. Suddenly he became aware
of an army lorry just in front of him. The tunnel was ammoniacal
with horse-dung; he too, like the solid-tyred 'bus in front, was
slipping about.

With relief he drove into cold fresh air to see masts and funnels
of steamers rising above rows of black and crushed-in little sooty
brick houses, with black sheds and warehouses, cranes, army
lorries, and, as he drove on, sudden rows of field guns, olive-green
and wheel to wheel along a sort of wharf. A notice board by a tall
iron gate set with spikes and barbed wire was headed *East India
Dock*. The surface of the cobbled streets came up through the
shackle bolts of the springs and reproduced myriad contours in
their bones.

There was a market, with stalls and donkey shallows, a litter
of paper and rotten fruit all across the road, lean dogs routing and
fleeing from boys with sticks held as guns, and wearing old badge-
less khaki caps. Other boys with pails were collecting horse dung.

It was a mild November day, with no wind. The river mist
and smoke hung as daze in the low arc of the iodine-brown sun.
Tall chimneys and towers darkened the dull skyline rising upon the
ancient flats of the riverside. Smells, industrial and chemical,
moved in layers upon them: paint, iodoform, picric acid, and a
whiff of pear-drops, from the waterside factories of Silvertown.

"There is the great chemical concern of Brunner, Mond and
Company," said Desmond. "The Zeppelins are always trying to
find it. The whole district is given over almost entirely to war
work."

They drove away from the sprawl of street and factory, coming
to an open level prospect of deep brown ploughlands, of dark and
stunted oak trees in sooted hedgerows, acid pastures, sad-looking
stacks of hay and corn, and untidy fields of cabbages and roots—
the environs of industrial London. Phillip began to feel depressed
with the level colourlessness of the extending country, which
seemed to have upon it the mark of death. Here the bittern and
the duck among the reeds had seen the marching of the Romans,

while the sails moved up the broad Thames, not then held back by wall and bank; the marshman went, and the ploughman came, and now the factories were waiting to kill the land forever with their weight of brick and steel, a countryside sentenced to industrial death.

"I suppose there is still some wildfowling down on the marshes somewhere, Desmond?"

"It's been stopped since the war, all down this coast. My cousins on my father's side live in Essex, and they told me."

It was the first time Desmond had spoken to Phillip about his father's people. Phillip wanted to hear more, and waited for him to speak. When he did not, Phillip glanced at his face. Desmond said, looking straight ahead, "My father's people have lived in Essex for centuries."

"Are your mother's people from Essex, too?"

"My mother hasn't got any relations."

Desmond was holding his head so still, staring ahead, that Phillip wondered what was the matter. Desmond's usually pale face was faintly pink.

Phillip drove on, silence between them. He felt slight distress that Desmond had never wanted to confide in him, his great friend. He had always shared everything with Desmond—secrets of his nests in the old days, his permits in Knollyswood Park and elsewhere, his holy-of-holies the Lake Woods—where Desmond had taken his school-friend Eugene, without first asking if he might do so. He had told Desmond everything about himself; but Desmond had never really shared any of his secrets with him.

"I say, Des, I've had most frightful luck." He told his friend about the invitation from Mrs. Rolls. "I'll call there next time I come on leave!"

Feeling happy, he stopped to examine the engine under the bonnet. Everything looked clean and polished and painted.

"It's worth the money, don't you think, Des?"

"I don't know. I haven't driven her."

"Of course, why didn't I think of it! You take the wheel now. After all, you let me drive your uncle's Singer. You can take her back this afternoon, if you like. That is, if I can't get week-end leave."

Desmond drove on for a mile, then he put on the brake, turned the switch, and sat still. Looking at Phillip intently with his pale blue eyes he said slowly and quietly, "I've wanted to tell you something for a long time."

Surprised by his manner, Phillip asked what it was.

"It concerns Helena Rolls."

"Yes."

"You may not like what I am going to say."

"Go on, say it."

"I consider that you are wasting yourself on something quite vain."

"But how do you know it is quite vain?" said Phillip, feeling weak.

"Because it is obvious to everyone except yourself. She isn't your sort. She laughs at you behind your back."

"How do you know, Des? Who told you?"

"I shan't say. But I do know. Just as I know that you are losing your happiness because of her. She isn't worth it."

Phillip hardly knew what to say. What did Desmond know? Had he been talking to someone who knew the truth? No doubt Mrs. Rolls was only being kind. She was sorry for him, that was it. The Swift, his hopes of the new life with the Navvies' battalion, all seemed grey, like the mist over the fields.

"Why can't we be as we were? Aren't I enough for you?" asked Desmond.

"Well Des, of course you're my great friend, but honestly, what I think about her does not affect you and me."

"I say it does."

Phillip laughed, partly from nervousness. Desmond gripped his arm.

"Does it seem a matter only for laughing, that I am concerned for our friendship?"

"Let go my arm! Aren't you being just a little melodramatic, old chap?"

"Very well, if that's your attitude, I've no more to say."

The Swift was standing under a large oak. A labourer in front was digging in a deep ditch beside the road, on which lay many acorns, some squashed by carts which were unloading dung on the stubble field over the hedge.

"Is this the way to Becontree Heath?" Phillip called out.

"Straight on, sir, and turn left at the village."

"What's the name of the village?"

"Thet be Dagenham."

Desmond drove on unspeaking, and in half an hour they were at Hornchurch. Asking for the headquarters of the battalion, Phillip was told it was at Grey Towers, the turrets of which could be seen among trees.

Fifty yards inside the gate was a wooden hut, set to one side of the gravel drive. He stopped, and knocked at the door, entered, and saw a red-faced youth half-risen from a blanket-covered trestle table and shouting, "What the bloody hell do you want? I told you I haven't got the blasted book of railway warrants, didn't I?"

To Phillip's surprise the young captain was addressing an old major, whose face showed amusement.

"Second Lieutenant Maddison reporting for duty, sir!"

"—— off!" replied the captain amiably. "This isn't the Orderly Room. Anyway you're bloody late."

"Can you direct me to the Orderly Room, sir."

"The Old Man and the Adj. are in town. This is 'A' Company's Office. —— off!"

"Where shall I —— off to, sir?" asked Phillip, observing a look of humour in the eyes of this very young captain. Before the captain could reply, he gave brief details of himself, standing to attention, aware that the large hands before him on the blanket table were red and raw, the lips thick, the band of the new service cap already saturated with hair-oil, the fingers yellow with nicotine.

The old major looked at Phillip quizzically. "Weren't you the young feller that come to see Colonel Broad at Alexandra Palace, on a motor-cycle with O.H.M.S. painted across the forks?"

"Yes, sir."

"You had a nerve, didn't you, to call yourself O.H.M.S.?"

"I was on His Majesty's Service, sir."

"Is that your car outside?" asked the captain suddenly looking up.

"Yes, sir."

"Is that O.H.M.S. likewise?"

"Yes, sir."

"Who's the tommy sitting in it?"

"He's a friend taking the runabout back to London for me."

"You couldn't have timed it better, cock! The major and I've got to hop up to town On His Majesty's Service, so your friend can take us. You've been posted to Captain Kingsman's Company. Go and ask the mess sergeant where that is. I'll show you the mess, I'm just going there myself."

He got up, shook himself into a greatcoat, with red piping on the epaulettes set with very new gilt stars, and said to the major, "We're in Meredith, we're in! I'll bring your old iron back tonight O.H.M.S. You don't mind my borrowing it, do you?"

"It's got no lamps, sir."

Outside the mess house Phillip gave Desmond a pound note, saying, "In case you need some petrol. If not, borrow it. Shove the 'bus in Wetherley's before lighting-up time. I must get some carbide head-lamps. Meanwhile, ask him if he's got any oil lamps, though O.H.M.S. will get past any copper."

With mixed feelings Phillip watched the major getting in beside Desmond, to slam the door with violence. What about my new paint and varnish, he thought, as the captain put a nailed boot on a mudguard to get into the dickey seat, where he lolled sideways, knees up, breeched thighs and leather legs angular as he rested his spurs on the other mudguard. With a grating of gears the runabout drove away round the drive, the captain giving him a wave of his heavy ash-wood riding-crop.

"Of all the blasted cheek," said Phillip, as he walked towards the ivy-covered house, and went through the porch into the hall.

"Good afternoon," said a short, spruced-up officer, coming down the uncarpeted wooden stairs. "My name is Milman. May I be of assistance? I'm going away on four days' leave, and my bed is at your disposal if you need one. Perhaps I may show you your room? The mess president is away, at the moment. What about your valise?"

"I didn't bring it. I hoped to be able to go back for it. Can you tell me where I can find Captain Kingsman?"

"He's just gone on week-end leave."

"Oh hell. Who's in command of the Company, in his absence, d'you know?"

"Captain Bason."

"Where can I find him?"

"He's just left for Town," said a tall dark subaltern coming down the stairs.

"I think I can fix you up with some kit," smiled Milman. Phillip had liked him at once. He was alert, dapper, with brown upturned moustaches, and looked about twenty-five.

"I'd like to introduce to you my great friend, Thompson," he said.

"How do you do?" said Phillip.

"Very well, thank you. And you?"

"Not so dusty."

"Splendid! Let me show you the geography of the place."

"This way," said Milman, giving way for Phillip to follow Thompson.

Upstairs, in a large bare room with camp-beds, Phillip waited while one found him a towel, the other offered use of razor, soap, and folding camp mirror. An ancient batman stood by, a thin broken-pearly forelock pressed with water on his brow. Long horizontal waxed strings of a Matabele moustache wandered around the lobes of his ears. His left breast had all the old ribands.

While this was going on, a third officer at the far end of the room remained standing there with his back turned to the others. He was dipping a toothbrush into a saucer, and rubbing it into his hair. Milman, doing the honours, called to him across the room, "May I introduce——" whereupon a lined face set with sandy eyes under sparse hair lying back in streaks from the forehead was turned in their direction.

"Permit me to finish my toilet before you assault me in my dressing-room with your blasted pretentiousness, will you?" and the owner of the voice returned to work with the toothbrush.

Milman, for a moment, seemed to be quelled. He looked a little helpless, then recovering, said to Phillip, "May I offer you the services of my batman to show you the geography of the place?"

"Don't forget the 'laounge'," called out the man with the toothbrush.

"Very good, sir!" cried the batman. "It's a nice little place, you'll find, and very comfortable, is the laounge. You can enjoy yourself there."

Phillip imagined himself telling Mrs. Neville all about the comic scene: the batman's head on his stringy neck shaking slightly; his cheeks sunken, the spikes of his waxed moustache sticking out wider than his ears, despite the ears being set almost at right angles to the skull. The ears of an earnest, human cabbage, saying, "We'll come to the laounge presently, sir. I'll show you it all in good time. First, here is the geography of the place!" He flung open a door, inviting Phillip to enter. "A moment, sir!" as he pushed past him, apparently to remove a solitary floating match-stick by pulling the plug. "Very comfortable, sir, you see."

"And this is the bath-room," as he flung open another door. As though to demonstrate further the principle of water seeking the lowest level, he turned on first one tap, then the other.

"Nothing like a good 'ot bath once-ta-week, sir!"

"I prefer a cold tub, myself," said Phillip.

"Yes, sir, a pukka sahib's cold tub, quite right, sir! This way, sir, mind the stairs, sir, they're slippery with elbow grease."

At the bottom by the newel post the small officer with the Kaiser moustache was waiting. With a wave of the hand he stepped back from the open door of a room, to allow Phillip to enter before him. The batman hurried in afterwards, saying, "This 'ere's the laounge, sir. Now if you'll excuse me, it's my turn to be the wine-waiter straight away." He disappeared.

"Will you care to have a drink with me?" said Milman, with a couple of twists upon his moustache. "You will? I'll ring for the wine-waiter."

The old batman reappeared, wearing a white jacket, and apologising for not wearing what he called the 'mascot'. He took the order, and while he was away, Milman's friend, Thompson, joined them. Phillip began to enjoy himself. It was better than he had expected. The batman came in with a tray bearing three glasses of whiskey, and a siphon of soda. He now wore, proudly it seemed, a small silver shield on a chain round his neck, engraved PORT. He nodded and smiled at Phillip like an old friend, and said, "Sorry, gents, I forgot me gloves this time. Wood, all wood," as he tapped his head.

Phillip thought that he would show no surprise at this unusual sort of mess. Seeing his eyes on the silver label, Milman said, when the waiter had gone, "The label should be worn for mess dinner, of course, and then only on social nights when the King's health is proposed by the orderly officer."

"I see. Is that an old regimental custom?"

"I rather think it was an idea of Major Fluck, the Mess President."

"Oh yes?"

At this point Thompson said to Milman that they had not too much time if they were to catch their train, and making their excuses for leaving him alone, the two friends went upstairs together; to reappear, as Phillip was ordering himself another whiskey, in identical greatcoats with slung haversacks, calf-skin gloves, and leather-covered short canes. Both looked in the door to say, "Au revoir", before departing. He watched the two walking down the drive in step, Milman taking long strides and Thompson short ones.

He sat down with *The Daily Trident*. Opening it, he read that fireworks had been forbidden in London "under severe penalties", on Guy Fawkes' night. Then the *communiqué* from the Western Front. Nothing of further interest, so throwing down the newspaper, he collected a pile of periodicals on his lap. The first was an old copy of *Land and Water*. An article on Strategy by Hilaire Belloc caught his eye. Uncle Hugh used to quote a poem about the Boer War by Belloc, something about gold and diamond mines, a satire. Belloc's article proving to be unreadable, he turned the pages of *Punch*. They reminded him of unfunny jokes in the dreary dentists' room in the High Road, so *Punch* fell to the floor with *Land and Water*. *Tit Bits* flopped on top of *Punch*. He read the *Things we want to know* column in *London Mail*, then took *The Times*, to seek in the *Roll of Honour* casualties in the Gaultshires; a few names only, none he recognised; obviously the Loos casualties were not yet published. His eye ran down *The London Gazette*, wondering if there had been any promotions in the other regiments with which he had served. Ah, Flynn, the bed-wetter, had resigned his commission in the Cantuvellaunians, on grounds of ill-health. Who else had been hoofed out? He sought other entries of officers coming unstuck, or *stellenbosched*, as Lieut. Brendon, who had served in the Boer War, called it. There were several ways in which an officer could be turfed out of the army, beginning with *resigns on account of ill-health*, otherwise incompetence, for genuine ill-health would merit *invalided out of the service*, which meant a pension. *Resigns his commission* was rather bad, but *Resigns his commission, the King having no further use for his services*, was worse. *Dismissed the service by sentence of a General Court Martial* was a disgrace. *Cashiered* was the end of all things, for you would not then serve again, even as a private.

He pressed the bell, and ordered a large whiskey and soda; then taking out his pocket book, added the sum of £1 to the column of figures which represented previous loans to Desmond, now a total of £19 10s. He had kept account of these items as he kept his own column of receipts each month from pay and allowances, and also half-quarterly payments of salary from the Moon Fire Office. With relief he determined that his account, when Wetherley's cheque had been presented, would still be about £11 in credit. Officers who gave dud cheques, or stumers as they were called, faced court-martial, and at best dismissal from the service; at worst, they were cashiered. He had known that his account was in funds, and knew also that Wetherley had some security for £10 at least in the motor-bike.

There was another column for money borrowed by Eugene, totalling £13. He had no thoughts of money ever being paid back; both were his friends, and money anyway was to be spent, or used, on behalf of friends. He had given his mother £5, to help with the housekeeping—which meant Mavis's constant demands for money, as she spent most of her salary on clothes, which were a sort of fetish with her—some women were mad on clothes, why, he could not think.

He was putting away his pocket diary when he was aware of somebody else in the room, although he had heard no sound. Turning his head, he saw the elderly subaltern, who had been at work with toothbrush and saucer in the bedroom. It seemed polite to stand up, since he was a newcomer.

"No need to get up," said an even voice. "Although one appreciates the courtesy to another senior by age. Has Milman gone? He gets my goat with his damned mincing ways. Bogus little man!"

Phillip thought that the less he said the better; he was wary of this man with the face of a faded desert cat.

The hard yellow eyes in the rutted face seemed to be weighing him up as he leaned sideways and pressed the bell. Almost at once the wine-waiter or butler labelled PORT wobbled through the door. His scanty hair was flatter than before, his moustaches curled upwards in thin strings, and white cotton gloves seemed about to drop off his fingers as he put his tray down.

"Bring me a large pink gin, and see that it is Pickelson's this time, not Hooth's."

"Certainly, sir, very good, sir!"

The old fellow picked his way out, a model of Victorian military earnestness.

"What did you think of our Cabin Boy? He was an apprentice in the Merchant Service last week, and came straight to the battalion on his eighteenth birthday as a captain. What it is, to have a socialist member of Parliament for a father! Was that your motor?"

"Yes."

"Did you lend it, may I ask?"

"Well——"

"Probably you are quite right. The thing here is to be on the right side, as apparently you have already realised. I should advise an upstanding, handsome young man like yourself to pay court to the Colonel's daughter, then you may find yourself with three pips instead of one. But you'll find Milman a keen rival, I warn you."

The speaker walked up and down in front of the fire, and went on, "If you're not doing anything else, would you care to come to

Town with me, and look for a couple of girls? The place is beginning to swarm with enthusiastic amateurs, as you probably know."

Phillip had never been to the West End at night, and from what he had heard from his mother, it was a highly dangerous place; there it was that Uncle Hugh had come a cropper. This man was obviously a bad companion.

"I'm orderly officer, I'm afraid."

A tall motor car stopped outside the window. "I would have appreciated your company. I've got very few friends in London, having lived abroad before the war."

Phillip offered the other a cigarette; which, without a glance, was refused.

"I smoke my own. Turkish. American tobaccos offend my sense of smell."

He selected a fat oval cigarette from a gold case, and fitted it carefully, after tapping, to his dry lips. "I was in tobacco before the war, at Smyrna, and managed to bring back a thousand or so with me. Turkish leaf will soon be unobtainable in this country, there is little left in bond. What will happen after the war, I dare not think. The Gyppies are capturing the market now, since Turkey is blockaded. Well, it was a good life while it lasted. For all its filth, Smyrna is the place to live! Give me a twelve-year-old Circassian girl who has been properly trained, to come into a man's bed, slowly, past his feet, gradually to his knees, and you can have all your English flappers!"

Discomposed and silent, attracted yet repelled, Phillip stood by while the other put on a short fawn-coloured pea-jacket with flapped pockets that ended on the same line as his tunic. Then he fitted on a floppy trench cap, the brim of which was set at an angle to cut the line of the brow: and having put up jacket collar, stuck hands in pockets, hunched shoulders, thrust out chin, he turned his face so that a wolfish profile was visible.

"That's the stance. The bum-freezer gets a girl, where the common or garden greatcoat with its protective swaddling has no attraction at all."

"How do you mean?"

"The hunched shoulders and slightly bowed back tend to emphasise the look of a lonely soldier. It arouses the maternal instinct. Next, the prowling young female notices the bum-freezer, the shortness of which emphasises the desirability of the buttocks and the length of one's legs. One must stand still, of course, the quintessence of a lonely soldier, thus inducing in the girl that baby-in-the-bulrushes feeling."

The driver sitting at the wheel of the Argyll landaulette beyond the window gave two hoarse honks on the horn. The man in the pea-jacket swirled the remains of the pink gin in his glass, tossed the liquid into his mouth, appearing to catch it at the back of his gold teeth without touching either tongue or metal; then holding back his head, he let the liquid run down his throat.

"I can see that your education has been neglected, my young friend. Another time let us pursue further the all-important subject of *l'amour*." With a short cane under one arm he turned at the door to say, "No good with a walking-stick! That's the prop of the English country gentleman, making love as he rushes his fences in the hunting field."

With considerable relief Phillip saw him getting in beside the driver; then with a grind of Glaswegian machinery the Argyll moved off, and out of sight, but not of sound, around the bend of the carriage sweep.

Phillip returned to the fire. What could he do? He saw the mess waiter in the doorway, and called him. The man wobbled forward. The ends of his moustaches, he noticed, were wet.

"Who was that officer?"

"Mr. Wigg, sir. A real gent, sir."

"Oh! Are there any other officers about?"

"Most on'm's already gone on leaf, sir."

"Where's the mess sergeant?"

"Gone 'ome to see 'is missus, sir. On week-end leaf, sir."

"Are you going on week-end leaf?"

"What me, sir? I'm the wine-waiter, sir!"

"Good. Let me have another large whiskey and soda, will you."

When it had been brought, he said, "What do you all do here, when you are here, I mean? Dig trenches?"

"We 'ave done a spot o' diggin' in the past, sir, but not lately. The boys goes for rowt marches, drills like on the square, care of arms in 'uts, and generally prepares themselves for what's to come."

"What is to come, do you know?"

"Well, if you arst my opinion, sir, I say the future will always come with what it brings. More I wouldn't like for to say, sir."

"I see. What else do the boys do, wine-waiter?"

"We provides guards for bridges and factories dahn by the

river, sir. Some goes on detachment, guarding prisoners of war, and providin' escort duties, sir."

"Lines of communication, in fact," said Phillip with satisfaction. With any luck he would see out the war in England from now on.

And then remembering 'Spectre' West and the Gaultshires, he ordered another whiskey, to drink the health of lost faces.

What the hell could he do? Risk going back to Wakenham, in the hope of meeting Desmond and Eugene in Freddy's? Supposing, meanwhile, he was sent for? Or a Zeppelin dropped thermite canisters on the huts while he was absent? If only he had reported earlier, he might have got leave, too. However, he must hang around, in case he were wanted. No more miking with this new lot! He must make a good impression. He rang the bell.

"Bring me another whiskey and soda, will you?"

When he had signed a chit for this, he said, "Is there Church Parade tomorrow?"

"Oh yes, sir! The Ganger allus takes it, sir."

"Ganger?"

"Beg pardon, no offence, sir, that's what we call the Colonel, sir."

"Really? Now can you tell me, is there any geography on the ground floor?"

"Oh yes, sir. Follow me, sir. Choice of two, sir."

"One will be enough for the moment."

On returning to the ante-room, or lounge as it was called, he picked up *La Vie Parisienne*, and returned to his creaking wickerwork armchair. Remembering what Wigg had said about Circassian girls, he refrained from looking at the picture on the cover until he was lying back with his feet up, cigarette smoke straying past eyes, preparatory to using his imagination with the slightly yellow, svelte, and semi-naked body in diaphanous underwear. But somehow the picture did not give the benison hoped for; the more he tried to imagine it real, the flatter surface it remained. Had poor old Father felt like that when he had looked at the same sort of pictures in the *Artist's Sketch Book of Parisian Models* which he kept locked in his desk in the sitting room? He recalled his own feeling of fascination, after he had opened the desk with a key on his mother's ring and gone through the contents of Father's desk, to look for the revolver kept there, and had come upon the book, which he had smuggled into the lavatory, the only private reading room in the house. He must have been about nine or ten at the time. Even now, the thought of Father looking at such pictures flurried him. He flung away *La Vie*, scornfully.

Then he picked it up again, and tried once more to find in it rest, light, and relief from dark depression overcoming him. Damn the bloody rag! He hid it under a large and heavy *Atlas of the World*, before lying back in the chair, wondering how he could possibly get through the rest of the day, the rest of his barren life. What *was* there left in his life? Then through his depression arose the face and hair and eyes, like a dream of everlasting summer, of Helena Rolls.

He sighed, and thrust away the vision. It was no good thinking of her ever again. She had loved cousin Bertie, and now that he was dead, she would keep him in her heart for ever. Even though dead, Bertie was still real to her; while he, Philip, had never been real even to himself. That was the terrifying truth.

Thinking of cousin Bertie, such a splendid man in contrast to his feeble self, Phillip's depression became so acute, his thoughts so devastating, so annihilating, that he uttered an involuntary shout of acceptance of his own shame and damnation.

The mess waiter appeared at the doorway. "Ready for another little drop, sir? Keeps the cold out, sir, in a manner of speakin'." He grinned somewhat unsteadily, as though he had been keeping the bottle warm.

Phillip pretended to be asleep. The mess waiter tottered away. Lying in the chair he felt himself sinking under the helplessness of his thoughts. He would always feel the dark weight within when he thought of Helena. What could he do about it? Desmond had tried to help him; he had rebuffed Desmond. What could he do, *what could he do*, he shrieked within himself. He could no longer force himself on her, as he had, idiotically, in the past. O, the damned silly idiocies of himself! Humiliations, silly lies which everyone saw through—his life was ruined. Why had he not remained in France with the Gaultshires? By now he might have found release from the dark shadow that had, so far back as he could remember, always been near him, sometimes threatening to press his life away. Only in death perhaps would he be free from the shadow of himself.

Was death the end? Mother believed in life after death; Father scoffed at her for it. Yet how could the person, who was his mind, or self, survive when it was made up of myriads of impressions, all from his feelings, all little cell-like photographs of sight, hearing, taste, smell and touch. When a bullet broke the store-house of self, inside the skull, how could those myriads of photographs survive, or the personality that they made up? Why should they survive, what use were they to life? If only he could stop his thoughts.

To remain alive was to continue to endure the nihilism of time rushing by, soundless and vain, atoms whirling in a void, creating life that must be destroyed, leaving blanks to be filled by other speck-like atoms whirling in darkness. Life was sadness, sadness, sadness; ache, ache, ache; until you were dead. His mother's words came into his mind—*Happiness comes only when we can forget ourselves*. And yet she was seldom if ever really happy. How could anyone forget himself or herself?

He pulled from his pocket a letter he had forgotten, given him by his mother that morning, before he left home. Mother had asked him to read it slowly, and to consider very very carefully every word that his grandfather had written to him.

Wespelaer
  Hillside Road
    Wakenham, S.E.

My dear Boy

I spoke to your Mother last night about your incipient but regrettable propensity for *strong* drink—There is nothing stationary in this world—our lives, character, thoughts are always rising or falling and perhaps the most insidious and awful in its result is drink—but not that alone—Indiscretions. Thoughtless folly of all sorts is paid for in months and years to come in the most painful suffering—now, my dear Phillip, have the strength of mind to disregard the habits and minds of any companions. You will learn with experience how rare commonsense thought and conscience are but you can never visualise what remorse, and physical suffering, is accrued by acts lightly and thoughtlessly made in youth. Cut them now and firmly resolve not to drink any spirits except a medicinal dose under exceptional circumstances such as a little rum after severe exposure and trench work.

If you are beyond the influence of reason—think of your Mother and her noble conduct and example and how she has sacrificed herself to start her children on the road to happiness, and think of the result of your folly to her. She is not strong, and the consequences of your folly may be far more awful than you think *now*.

I have a little money for my children and their children, and I have not exercised self denial and much thought and work to have that money fooled away. You have the potentiality of a successful and with

moderation in all things a happy life. Be master of your mind and
don't throw your chance away——

It was obvious what the old man was driving at. *His* eldest
son, Uncle Hugh, had died of syphilis, which he had got after
being sent down from Cambridge. As though he would be such
a fool as to go with one of those awful prostitutes he and Desmond
had heard about in London! Gran'pa was old-fashioned. And
who wanted his money? If he ever left him any in his will, he
would give it away to the nearest hospital.

He thought to throw the letter on the fire, but something
stopped him. Somehow it was like hurting poor old Gran'pa, to
do that. Putting it in his pocket book, he lay back, feeling himself to be drawn once more into the flow of empty Time. The
image of Helena floated before him, her face under her fair
crowning hair shining with the sun, her eyes blue and frank as
the sky. It was all over now, he had deliberately destroyed his
ideal on the night of his return from Loos, after the Zeppelin
raid, when he had gone into the sheepfold on the Hill with
cousin Polly. Henceforward his ideal was dead to him; dead,
dead, dead.

Such was life; everything passed away; the fields and wood-
lands of boyhood became built upon; streets and pavements and
lamp posts arose where warblers and willow wrens had sung;
nothing ever remained the same. All the dead lying at that very
moment upon the battlefield of Loos were slowly becoming part
of the chalky soil—the chalk that was one vast tumulus of shells,
aeons of shells of the salt, salt sea. Each shell had once been a
house of life, born but to die, each in its dying to add to the salt
of the sea, or the soil of the earth. So it was with men. And
nothing could ever be done about it.

He lay still, floating through time; he thought of the sadness
of Mother's face, as he remembered it before he could walk,
before he could speak; he recalled Father's angry voice, the fear
of himself and his sisters, sitting still under Father's pale-blue-
eyed anger, his voice thin as a fret-saw—poor old Father, he had
never had a chance, from what Aunt Belle used to say about his
early life at home, with *his* angry and often tipsy father. What
a grind his life had been from the start: how many thousand times
did Father say he had walked over London Bridge to the office,
that very office which he himself could never return to after the
war, *if* he lived until after the war? Father taking long strides

over London Bridge, on the same worn paving stones, thirty
thousand times was it? Without a friend in the world—Father
who had once spoken so happily, Mother had said, of having a
friend in his son. And what a son: selfish, cowardly, a liar,
deceitful: better if he had been killed.

He lived again the glassy, beyond-fear feeling of the attack on
that Sunday, the second day of the battle, across the Lens—La
Bassée road, when most of the Cantuvellaunian crowd had
copped it. Poor old Strawballs, Jonah the Whale, O'Connor, and
all the old faces that had ragged him after he had set fire to the
Colonel's *Times* during one guest night, for a joke. It had not
been the drink he had taken, for he always knew much clearer
what he was doing when tight than when he was sober. What a
bounder they must have considered him. Now, like cousin
Bertie, they were all dead on the field of honour.

What did it *really* mean, *on the field of honour*? Father spoke of
honour, as though it was part of life, his own life, for instance.
Well, if living like that was honour, he was quite content to
remain as Father had often told him he was, lacking in all sense
of honour. *Field of honour*—that ghastly mess at Loos!

"Bring me another spot of old-man whiskey, will you?" He
would wait until the winter was over, and then apply to go back
to the Gaultshires. He lay back in the armchair, eyes closed, legs
crossed at ankles, hands folded on chest, resting himself in the
terrible beauty of gun-flashes filling the darkness with light.

Chapter 3

NEW WORLD

On the following Saturday morning Phillip's company commander, a quiet elderly captain, asked him if he would care to take
him to Southend-on-Sea in his motor. Captain Kingsman explained that he had to go on duty, to inspect a detachment of
the company, and the cost of the journey would be borne by
an allowance of threepence a mile, recoverable from Eastern
Command *via* the Orderly Room.

"You may as well have it as a hired driver," he said, "and if
you care to spend the night at my place about a dozen miles away
from the salubrious mud-flats, you'd be most welcome."

Phillip hesitated, for he had been imagining himself driving up Hillside Road, in the glory of his motor car, and perhaps daring to ask Helena Rolls to come for a ride with him. Then Wigg across the breakfast table said, "May I propose myself for a lift as far as Southend, Captain Kingsman? I'm on leave since last night. Or would three be a crowd?"

"You must ask Maddison, it's his motor," said Kingsman.

"Yes, certainly," replied Phillip, "there's room in the dickey. And thank you for your offer of hospitality, Captain Kingsman." He felt depressed at the prospect.

It was a fine morning, and when he brought the Swift up the drive, a fourth man was waiting beside the other two. He wore an eyeglass, and was bending and straightening a whangee cane as he stared straight before him. Phillip recognised the red pug-face and pale eyelashes and hair of Cox, with whom he had been on a three-weeks' course at Sevenoaks when first he had been gazetted, in the spring.

The presence of Cox, waiting with the others, made him shy. He remembered the way Cox had scorned him, after an unsuccessful walk (for Cox) up and down the main street of Sevenoaks, Cox rattling his whangee cane at girls, to attract them. Cox's irritability had increased with his non-success, which he had said was due entirely to Phillip's presence 'putting the birds off'.

"I don't suppose you remember me, you one-piecee bad boy?" Cox said, with defensive challenge.

"Oh yes I do," replied Phillip. "You had no success with your wood-pecker rattle, remember?"

"I haven't the least idea what you're talking of."

"That Shanghai custom you told me about. The Rattle!"

"You're still quite mad, I see. This one-piecee bad boy——" said Cox, to the others, "filled the night with groans and yells in the room I shared with him at the Royal Oak, until I could bear it no longer. He hurled boots about in the darkness, thinking they were bombs."

"Seriously, Cox, don't you remember our walk down the hill to the Picture Palace and back?"

"You're making it all up. Besides, when did *you* do any walking? When you weren't attacking the enemy by night, you were chasing him, apparently, in clouds of dust. This one-piecee bad boy——" went on Cox, "had about half a dozen stink-machines, one for every day of the week."

"I was testing various motor cycles, as a matter of fact."

"At any rate you've got a decent vehicle now. Can you find room for me? My wife's staying at Southend-on-Sea, and I want to bring her back here, as I've found lodging in the village. We'll come back by the train, of course."

Phillip saw the reason why Cox had shut him up about Sevenoaks. He did not want to be reminded of his past.

"If you don't mind wedging yourself in the back with Wigg——There aren't any steep hills, I hope——"

"The very thing for hills," said Cox, taking some white balls from his pocket. "They never fail. Drop them into the petrol, and they put life into the oldest crock. Remove all carbon from piston tops and cylinder heads."

"What are they?"

"Speed pills. Also they increase consumption by fifteen per cent."

Phillip sniffed them. "They smell like moth pills to me."

"Speed pills," replied Cox. "My contribution to the petrol supply. Quite frankly, I've got to support a wife on my pay——Speed pills will do the trick. I always used them in my Studebaker in Shanghai."

Phillip had read, in *The Boy's Own Paper*, of camphor propelling small wooden boats, so it might possibly do the same for an engine. But might it be a practical joke of Cox's. After all, sugar dropped into petrol turned black as treacle, and clogged the carburettor jet.

"Are you sure you aren't ragging, Cox?"

"Do I look like the sort of person who hurls boots at hotel room walls at one o'clock in the morning? That's settled. No more talkee-talk, Wigg and I will ride in the dickey."

"Moth balls are harmless," said Captain Kingsman, quietly; and Phillip dropped them into the tank.

"I'm glad this car isn't a moth, Cox! I say, mind the paint, please. The step up is this side, for next time."

Cox had mounted on the mudguard, while Wigg had used the step. Phillip swung the handle, and seated himself at the wheel.

"Camphor has a very low flash-point, and burns with a smoky flame, while tending to decrease the speed of the detonation," said the quiet captain. "So it has a use in preventing knocking, when the spark is well advanced."

"Are you keen on motor cars, sir?"

"Very; but don't call me 'sir'. My name is Kingsman. I'm

a barrister by profession, and an amateur racing-driver by inclin-
ation."

"Have you raced on Brooklands, Captain Kingsman?"

"Occasionally."

Phillip began to enjoy the adventure. The engine, too, responded
to this amazing information by an audible sucking in of breath.
The carburettor began to whisper hoarsely as it fed to the cylinders
the juice of the speed pills. Had Captain Kingsman given them
to Cox? Faster and faster turned the engine, with a pleasing
double thrust of its twin connecting rods.

Phillip was so exhilarated that he was over a cross-roads before
he saw them, causing a boy on a bicycle in panic to wobble and a
pig being driven by the boy to stop a couple of inches off the
front wheel, get into reverse, shudder, and bolt squealing into the
boy, pitching him and bicycle into the ditch.

"A miss is as good as a mile!" Phillip said to Captain Kingsman, who was thoughtfully stroking his moustache.

"That is an epitaph as good as any."

While Phillip was wondering what he meant, Captain Kingsman said, "Is this a particularly favourite route of yours to
Southend?"

"No, I've never been here before. I thought that perhaps you
knew the way."

"Well, one can get on to the road by the next turn to the left,
about two miles ahead."

The road was narrow but straight, with an occasional thatched
cottage along it. To show off the Swift's paces, Phillip kept the
pedal pressed to the floorboard. It might almost have been a
steam-engine under the bonnet, he thought, so smoothly did it
thrust away at the crankshaft with its nine iron horses.

Captain Kingsman spoke again. Phillip said he was sorry, he
could not hear. Captain Kingsman shouted, "I fancy nine
hundred R.P.M. is the safe limit for this type of engine, with
the unmodified flywheel."

"I see, thank you," Phillip shouted back, his foot still hard down.

Captain Kingsman shouted, "Your engine is now doing almost
eleven hundred revvs!"

Phillip looked over his shoulder and shouted, "I think there
must be something in your speed pills, Cox, you old rattler!"

Captain Kingsman tugged at his moustache. He was about to
ask Phillip to stop, when a yellow whangee cane rapped the
driver on the shoulder.

"Not so fast, one-piecee mad boy!" yelled Cox. "It's horribly bloody cold at the back."

"We'll stop at a pub and get some hot Irish whiskey soon, boys!" shouted the driver. "Olley-Olley-Olley!" he yelled, as he pressed down the accelerator.

Captain Kingsman was now crouching up in his seat, hand covering moustache and mouth, as though meditating a problem —or ready to roll himself into a limp ball. His eyes were fixed on the glass cylinder containing the oil-drip. Then he tripped the switch and unscrewed the oil regulator, so that the drip became a stream; then it ceased to fall.

"Don't declutch! Keep her in gear! Close the throttle!" He switched on. "Now declutch and let the engine idle a few moments, to get the oil circulating!"

The car came to a standstill. The water around the engine was boiling.

"Switch off, but don't touch the radiator cap!"

Clouds of steam arose from in front. They waited until the rumbling ceased. Then Captain Kingsman said, "May I look under the bonnet? Ah, as I thought, your oil tank is empty. Another few seconds, and your big ends would have run their white metal. Have you a spare oil can? Do you mind if I look? Ah, here it is." He poured out a little, rubbed it between finger and thumb, sniffed it, decided it was thick enough, and said, "Shall I fill your tank?"

"Thanks. I'd forgotten about the oil. Very careless of me, I'm sure."

"This will do until we get to a garage. There's one of sorts near Horndon-on-the-Hill."

They got back under the scuttle.

"Not so fast this time, one-piecee mad boy," said Cox, rapping with the cane.

The driver kept the needle at thirty-five. "How's that for you, Rattler?"

"Bloody awful cold."

The needle dropped to thirty. "How's that?"

"Damned cold."

"We don't need a speedometer when Cox is aboard," said Phillip to Kingsman. "At forty he's horribly bloody cold, at thirty-five he's bloody awful cold, at thirty, damned cold! Let's see what speedometer says at twenty-five."

"How are you feeling now, Cox?"

"Still cold."

They were approaching a straw stack beside the road. The driver stopped again, and getting down, gathered an armful, which he stuffed between puttee'd legs and the interior of the dickey. Cox's face had a bluish tinge, and the eyeglass seemed to have cut more into his flesh.

"Anyway, it's a damned sight better than being in a flooded trench, Rattler. Here, take my British warm."

"Don't you want it yourself?"

"I'm inured."

Nothing could ever be so bad as the Diehard T-trench.

Cox took the wool-and-camel-hair coat and put it over his knees, ramming it down beside his legs, watched anxiously by Phillip, who was proud of his neat coat, with the gilt stars on the shoulder-straps. He felt the more uneasy when Wigg tugged up one side of the coat to cover his knees. Cox tried to pull it back. Wigg held on. They bickered.

"Steady on, you rookies!" cried Phillip. "I think it's no good, really. Half a mo', I'll get some more straw. That will be much better, like thatch, cool in summer and warm in winter."

"But the wind will blow it away, without your coat."

"All right, do have it, but please leave it in one-piecee."

During this time, Captain Kingsman had sat unspeaking, looking to his front, a slightly amused expression on his face.

The engine took a lot of swinging before it would start. When it did fire, it kicked the handle, and raced backwards, as though on a spring.

"Damn, the timing must have slipped!"

"Too much aphrodisiac," said Wigg.

"What's that?" asked Phillip, preparing to swing the handle again.

"Speed pills," said Cox.

"Do be careful, one can easily break one's wrist," said Captain Kingsman. "It's sometimes advisable to hold the handle with the other hand. May I show you?"

He got out, and having seen that the switch was off, stopped to fill the cylinders with gas by pulling the engine over twice with his right hand; then half turning round to hold the handle with the fingers of his left hand, said "Switch on!" and gave a sudden jerk. The engine fired.

"One doesn't risk breaking one's thumb that way."

"Thanks very much for the tip, Captain Kingsman."

Phillip had been driving for a few more minutes when Captain Kingsman remarked, "There's another tip I learned in racing—to hold the wheel at four o'clock and eight o'clock, elbows well into ribs. In that position, if a driver has a burst front tube he is in a position instantly to control a wobble."

"Like this?"

"That's the position. And in turning, if one passes the wheel from hand to hand, keeping the elbows down, one is in position to control the steering if one has suddenly to turn away."

Phillip thought that Captain Kingsman corrected a fault in a way unlike that of any other man he had known. He did not say things directly, to snub you or to tick you off, but said them without putting himself between you and what you were doing.

The dull day was now being transformed; sunshine broke through the clouds, colour became alive.

"Would you like to take a turn at the wheel, Captain Kingsman?"

"I would!" cried Cox immediately. "I'll change with you." He heaved himself out of the dickey, while straws flew back in the eddy.

Phillip hid his feeling of being put upon as he got in beside Wigg.

"Do you mind stopping at Horndon-on-the-Hill," said Captain Kingsman over his shoulder, to Phillip in the back. "There's a thirteenth century wooden belfry on the church which might be worth your while to visit."

They came to this at the beginning of a village, where stood a church with a squat belfry, in shape like the crown of a Puritan's hat. It was being re-roofed on one side; ladders led up to scaffolding and a plank platform. No-one was about, so while Cox and Wigg went to find a pub, Captain Kingsman and Phillip climbed up.

Standing near the apex, Phillip saw shipping upon the leaden reaches of the Thames extending away to the west where the horizon of smoke and sun in haze upon London enclosed the green prospect. A finger's breadth to the south of west was a glint in the haze, a flicker of hard bright light as of a heliograph uncertain of its message.

"I say, isn't it simply wonderful! I'd no idea the Thames estuary could look like this. I wonder what that flickering comes from."

"I rather think," said Captain Kingsman, "that must be the Crystal Palace."

Phillip felt subdued. Once he had thought that north-west Kent, now south-east London, was quite the best place to live, particularly Wakenham and the Hill, with its view of the Crystal Palace and the wonderful firework displays on Thursday summer nights, the whites of strolling tennis players glimmering in the twilight, and best of all, the real country only a few minutes' bike ride away.

"Why did you sigh?" asked Kingsman.

"Oh, I don't know."

Kingsman observed the nervous look in the face beside him, and wondered what was the cause. He said nothing more. They got down the ladder and went into the church, where, resting on the floor, was a massive dark oak cage supporting the bells above.

Two slate slabs lay on the floor—one of *Jasper Kingsman*, who died in 1688, the other to *Jonah Kingsman*, both barristers of the Middle Temple.

"The older one gets, the more one feels a sense of security through one's forebears, particularly if one happens to be the last of one's line. I have a feeling that I belong here, although I was born in India, and so far as I know no Kingsman has lived here for over a hundred years."

Outside the lych-gate Phillip said, "I think I know what you mean. I was born not far from the Crystal Palace, but I feel that my real home is in Gaultshire, where my mother's people came from. I think I would rather be buried there, than in London, though best of all, since one has to die sometime, is a battlefield grave."

Kingsman was hesitating, as though to speak or not to speak, when Phillip said, "Do you mind if we find the others and have a drink? A short life and a merry one, that's my motto!"

When the Swift stopped at a garage near the esplanade of Southend-on-Sea Cox and Wigg left for their different ways, while Phillip accompanied Captain Kingsman who had to inspect a detachment of troops on the pier. As they went down the long board walk Kingsman said, "So you knew Cox before, did you? Some of the red pepper of the East seems to have got into his system. Too much sun in China, perhaps. He was married while we were stationed here, to a girl in his billet. She lives with her people. I fancy he finds it difficult to make ends meet on a second-lieutenant's pay."

"I wonder what happened to his fiancée, the one he had when he was at Sevenoaks, I mean. It seemed to me rather strange to want to pick up girls, when he was engaged to be married."

"Well, I suppose life is more difficult for some of us than for others," said Captain Kingsman, to discourage any further gossip. He changed the subject. "This mud is all a present from London, I suppose."

The tide was out. Black sludge extended for miles. A fresh breeze was exhilarating. Phillip thought it fun to make regular strides over the boards, and at the same time to try to avoid stepping on a crack. It was more than a mile to the end, and he had to stare intently, with constantly changing pace. At the end of the pier were buildings and huts occupied by the Royal Naval Air Service. When he stopped it was beside three old men who were fishing, and speaking to one, he saw that they were blind. They were employed at night to listen for the note of the Maybach engines, which powered the Zeppelin gondolas. Their sense of hearing was the more acute because of the loss of sight, said Kingsman.

When he had paid the detachment, and they had inspected quarters, Captain Kingsman said to Phillip that they were free, and if they left right away, they would be at his home in time for luncheon. The Swift meanwhile had had its oil drained and the sump refilled, for temporary oil, suitable for Ford engines only, had been put in at Horndon-on-the-Hill.

"Do you mind if we have a quick drink, Captain Kingsman?"

"Well, can it be a quick one?"

Coming out of an hotel, Phillip invited his company commander to drive, but Kingsman declined, saying that he so enjoyed looking at the country, particularly when there was no hurry to get from place to place. Phillip understood what he intended to convey; something as it were apprehended in the retina of the eye, and not by a frontal stare. So he drove at a steady thirty, and was pleased with himself when his company commander said, "It is paradoxical how the steadier one drives, the faster is progress made. Speed is a relative condition of movement; the more one consumes oneself to go faster, the longer seems the journey."

"Do you mind if we stop for a drink, Captain Kingsman?"

"Well, I don't think we shall have time. I telephoned from

the pier that we would arrive about ten minutes to one. Can you wait until then for some beer?"

"Oh yes, of course, Captain Kingsman."

At last they came to a road between thin and tall willow trees growing in parallel straight lines behind trimmed quickthorn hedges bordering the road. Kingsman explained that the heavy clays of the rodings grew the best wood for cricket bats in England. Pheasants flew up, from under oaks in a meadow.

"Are you a shooting man?"

"Only in a small way."

"It's remarkable how the eating qualities of a cock pheasant, a young bird particularly, vary between late October and late November, in this part of the world. In October, the barley they pick up on the stubbles puts on flesh that is inclined to be without much taste, but after a week or two of acorns, the bird has a nutty flavour, equal with a full-bodied burgundy. If they're smoked, they're excellent."

"The only bird I ever smoked was a sparrow, when I tried to roast it on a green stick over a wood fire, while making tea in a billy can. Both tasted of the same smoke!"

Was his remark rather pert? He was relieved when Captain Kingsman laughed. "I tried a water-hen when I was a boy, baking it in clay, but even my puppy refused it."

"Was that here in Essex, sir?"

"Do drop the 'sir', it makes me feel quite old! Call me Jasper. No, this is my wife's country. The next turning to the right is ours. In about half a mile."

Woods succeeded water-meadows and willows. A level area of gravel opened up on the other side of the road, with a view of a lodge with twisted brick chimney stacks of damson colour issuing smoke, tall iron railings with gilded decorations on top, and open gates of iron-work.

"In here?"

"Yes. The house is half a mile on."

It looked as though Kingsman lived in a big country house. There would be servants; he hadn't brought a dressing-gown, never having had one. Still, he could wear his British warm over his pyjamas when he went to the bathroom. Oh, and bedroom slippers! He had never had any of those, either. He had only twelve shillings. How much ought he to tip the butler? Then there was petrol to be bought on the way back.

The house was cream-coloured, with two huge pillars rising

beside the entrance seen across a lake fringed with reeds. The drive curved round the lake, and leaving it behind went on between smooth lawns to the Palladian front of the house. As the Swift stopped, Phillip noticed a heraldic wolf's head ensculped on the key stone of the arch above the porch, its tongue pierced by an arrow. Yes, there was a butler, opening the door.

Smiling, he drew it wide open as he walked backwards in a way that made the smile, the bow, the good-morning and the arc of the opening door all part of one motion. A sovereign tip at the very least; he was probably more used to getting fivers! With the thought of In for a penny, In for a pound, Phillip entered a hall panelled in oak, with an open hearth, on which smouldered a six-foot section of beech-tree. The chimney piece above was coloured with armorial bearings, and around the hall itself stood suits of burnished armour. A dog bounded down the stairway that was open to the light through a large southern window, and again from a glass dome far above in the roof. The dog, a setter, came gently to Phillip with feathering tail and touched his hand with its cold nose, then without pause went on to its master, talking in its throat and appearing to find some diffi-culty in speaking, due to excitement that was controlled. Only its tail waved more furiously; and then, overcome by the reaction of having waited all the morning for this moment, it opened its mouth wide and let out a small noise between yawn and yowl.

Mrs. Kingsman came down the stairs after the dog, smilingly towards them both. She greeted her husband as though he too were a guest, Phillip thought, with a manner that seemed arti-ficially bright. She held out a limp hand to him, while looking into his eyes with a frail sort of lost look. Her eyes seemed to dwell upon him with vague questioning before a light came in them and she said, with sudden animation, "I am so glad you could come with Jasper, was it fun in your little motor? I do hope you had a good journey?" He saw that she carried two tallow candles in her hand.

Captain Kingsman led him down a stone-cold passage to a little room with a wash-hand basin in an iron frame, and a table on which stood a tarnished looking-glass. On a cloth were ivory-backed hair-brushes inlaid with a gold monogram. They looked to be quite new. He was left alone, and when he went back to the hall the butler was waiting for him beside a tray on a side-board, on which were various bottles of beer. He chose Bass, which was quietly poured into a long thin glass on which a hunting scene had been cut, he thought, with a diamond. He waited while the glass was placed on a silver tray and offered to him, where he stood a yard away, wondering where the others had gone. The butler with his slight bow left the room.

How could he get away? And tomorrow was Sunday, a prospect of dull and suspended life, against which his mental struggle was quelled before it began. If only he could get to a pub, if only Kingsman were not so old and staid.

As he sipped the bitter drink he heard voices above. When Mrs. Kingsman was beside him again he thought she looked less distraught, although her eyes were still far away in thought. The same remoteness of manner had come upon Kingsman, as though the easy-going, genial personality Phillip had known in the company office and the mess at Grey Towers had been subdued by the dark oak of the hall, part of the very sameness of time, beams and posts which had stood for centuries, bearing with stone mullioned arch and wall and coign the weights of a house that had stood since the Tudors, for father and son, uncle and nephew, until the present owner, the heiress who had married Jasper Kingsman.

The luncheon was very simple, it might have been one in his own home, except that it was the butler who put the fish pie on the table before Mrs. Kingsman, and not Doris. Mrs. Kingsman filled the plates which the butler took round with the same gentle gravity, following with a tureen of brussels sprouts on one side and peas on the other. He sat quietly, alert and polite to all that was said, feeling that the conversation was forced, and that it was his nervousness that was the cause of it, for he did not know what to say. He thought that he was a dull person, and suffered a little and for comfort withdrew into himself and sat on his hands part of the time, to feel less stiff and more in balance with himself. He got off his hands when Mrs. Kingsman said,

"My husband tells me you have recently come back from France, Mr. Maddison. Did you see anything of the Royal Flying Corps when you were out there?"

"We did not see one scout 'plane during the entire battle of Loos, Mrs. Kingsman. Of course the weather was dud at times, and our machines were outmatched by the Fokkers, which can fire through their propellers, and so our chaps in their Martinsydes, Morane Parasols, and dud old B.E.'s and F.E.'s hadn't a hope. Anyway our staff is hopeless, the whole battle was a

ghastly mess-up in every way. Where the R.F.C. was I don't
know, probably having a binge miles away from it all. They
get even more pay than our old navvies, and have tremendous
champagne parties."

"Not all the time, surely?" said Kingsman, quietly.

"Well, quite often, from what I heard. And I do know that for
the four days I was on the battlefield, not one 'plane was to be
seen. Again and again I heard our chaps asking where the R.F.C.
was, and then the German reserves came up unspotted, and
when we went over to the attack on Sunday, whole battalions
were mown down. Nobody knew where or how or why they were
there, and some of the reserves, who came up late and hungry,
fired at one another, never having seen a German. No observation by the R.F.C., obviously."

Neither Kingsman nor his wife spoke. The butler stood unmoving as Phillip finished his pudding, while Mrs. Kingsman
played with a fork and a few scraps on her plate. It was a relief
when the meal was over and Mrs. Kingsman told the butler they
would have coffee in the smoking-room. There to his surprise,
she smoked a cigarette with them, taking nervous puffs at it
while talking about the birds which came to her bird-table,
including nuthatches and woodpeckers. This mood did not last,
for the distant look came back into her eyes and she left, murmuring about writing some letters.

When she had gone, Kingsman said, "I expect you would like
to see your room," and Phillip wondered if they had both found
him a bore, and to make matters worse, he had begun to stutter.
In silence he walked beside Kingsman up the broad stairs to
where on the first landing a long corridor with leaded windows
all along one side of the house led to what he thought was a wing.
Coats-of-arms in stained glass were let into all the leaded case-
ments of the windows. It was the Long Gallery, said Kingsman,
and faced north to give an even light upon the pictures hanging
along the opposite wall.

Opening a door beyond the gallery, he said as Phillip hesitated, "Do go in, won't you." Inside the room he said, "You
might care to rest for a bit, or write letters; if there is anything
you want, you'll ring, won't you?"

Phillip saw a tester bed, a table with a rack holding very blue
writing paper, envelopes, sealing wax and pens, a bowl of mixed
apples and pears, and a green plate with gilt edging on which lay
a gold dessert knife. The uneven glass of a bookcase reflected the

flames of the wood fire burning in the hearth. His haversack lay on a stool.

"At three o'clock, in about an hour's time, Dolly and I usually go for a walk, you might care to see the gardens, such as they are at this time of the year, but do please yourself. We'll be down in the hall at three. Ring if you want anything, won't you," and Kingsman went out and shut the door.

Phillip thought he would write a letter to Mrs. Neville, telling her of his extraordinary adventure, and the mysterious atmosphere in the house, while examining a piece of blue writing paper embossed in white *Tollemere Park, Chelmsford, Essex*, with a telephone number and station name of the Great Eastern Railway. But first he must explore. Carefully opening a door, after warning coughs, he found himself in a bathroom, with many immense pipes wrapped in some sort of bandages heavily covered with cracked white enamel; and opening a second door, discovered a dressing-room, with a thing like a commode without pan, but with sort of bicycle handles for holding on, and a base covered with leather hiding some sort of springs. It had a wooden handle projecting from the back, by which it could be jigged up and down. What was it, a liver rattler? Perhaps in the old days of two-bottle port men, this was necessary as well as foxhunting six days a week. Or was it for the summer, anyway it was a horrible looking thing.

It appeared that he had the wing to himself. After exploring the landing, and hearing only heavy silence which hung in the shut air with the fog of his breath, he walked on tip-toe to the gallery, and examined the last two pictures, which had seemed to be different from the others as he had walked past them with his host.

One was of a family group, Jasper Kingsman and his wife with a small boy sitting in dappled sunlight under a laburnum tree with its yellow blooms hanging down and the house in the background across lawns with clumps of rhododendrons. Next to this picture, which was signed *Sargent*, was the portrait of a boyish figure wearing a brown leather flying helmet carelessly left unfastened, and showing the dark fur lining. His leather coat was open, too, revealing the wings of a scout pilot, and under the wings the riband of the Military Cross.

Phillip stared up at the face. It was smiling slightly, the eyes were a deep blue, the features delicate and sharp, almost childlike in their innocence. Where had he seen the picture before?

Of course, it had been one of the pictures in the Royal Academy of the past summer, and photographs of it had appeared in the newspapers. Hadn't it been painted by someone called Orpen? He looked, and saw the name in the corner. How strange, that Captain Kingsman had never spoken of having a son.

He went along the gallery, looking at the portraits of men and women, most of them in family groups, with fresh, easy faces as though nothing had ever worried them, all ideally happy in the country that belonged to them. This appearance changed when he came to the Jacobean period; faces became sterner, with little ruffs and beards and eyes looking out beyond ideal country scenes, as though thoughtful with trouble in the time of religious struggles; then, into the Tudor period, the men looking more cocky, in both dress and manner, as though feeling the world was wide and they were masters of it.

He listened on the edge of the main landing. There was no sound. He crossed over behind the heavy oak balustrade, and tip-toed down a passage, drawn by a flickering light. When he reached another passage he saw an image of the Virgin holding the dead Christ, set in an alcove in the wall, before which was a small bunch of flowers in a bowl. The *pieta* was lit by two candles, or tapers Mother called them, which had burned away half their lengths. It was like the street boys' grottos, which they made once a year and exhibited on the pavements for pennies. Had the grotto the same derivation as the *pieta*, or was it earlier—relic of Great Pan being dead?

So the Kingsmans were Roman Catholics.

The walk was dull, he could feel nothing in the countryside, which was bleak and bare and desolate as the small red sun went down like a wound in the flesh of a man lying dead on no man's land. How could he get through the rest of the day; why had he come; he might by now have been with Desmond and Eugene; even Tom Ching's face would be welcome in Freddy's or the Gild Hall; and here he was, his life fret-sawed away into pieces by his mind taking him all over the place, and tomorrow was Sunday, the dead dull day of the week. He would not be able even to go with Mother and Doris to sit in the gallery of St. Simon's church, in the hope of seeing Helena Rolls below in her family pew; vain and hopeless as that would be.

In this mood of feeling lost within himself, as a hoar frost began to settle over the level landscape, and partridges were calling

rustily, he returned with the Kingsmans to tea with muffins in the
hall and sat upon the edge of a deep leather armchair before a fret
of flames beginning to arise in triumph all along the other half of
the six-foot length of split beech trunk, which two men had carried
into the hall as they had set out for their walk. When the electric
light was switched on he saw on the wall beside the corner of the
hearth where Mrs. Kingsman sat with her work-basket, a small
frame covered by glass in which hung a Military Cross.

A visitor arrived during tea. He wore the black-skirted cassock
of a priest. The setter seemed to writhe with suppressed joy to
see the figure, as it took in its mouth the pair of slippers which
Phillip had noticed on the other side of the hearth, of blue velvet
embroidered with what looked like a flowery pattern. The dog
advanced with high steps towards the newcomer, who stopped
to pat it before going to Mrs. Kingsman to take her hand in both
of his. Then to Kingsman; and turning to Phillip, who had stood
up when the visitor arrived, was introduced as Father Aloysius.

The newcomer brought life into the room, as he set about
eating with zest the muffins from a covered dish that had been
kept warm on the hearth.

"You walked, I suppose, Lulu?"

"Rather! It helped to clear the miasmas from my mind. I
was beginning to feel like Shakespeare's 'vagabond flag upon the
tide, that rots itself with motion'. But I was sorry to leave my
many friends, I had no idea they would feel the parting as I did.
I've spent the last two years," he said, turning to Phillip, "in a
London suburb south of the river—a place that George the
Second, travelling by coach from Kent on his way to London
early one morning, called 'long lazy lousy Loos'am,' having
apparently watched door after door opening along the High
Street to see his subjects yawning and scratching their heads as
the Royal Coach passed by. Of course the Hanoverians, as you
know, were not exactly popular then."

"No—I mean yes."

"How did you come, by Liverpool Street, Lulu?"

"I was lucky to get a lift in a motor going over Woolwich
Ferry to Chelmsford, Dolly. My word, it's good to see the rodings
ridge-and-furrow again! There's something about a London
suburb, a nervous tension, an underlying anxiety, a suppression
of true living that is not of the town and certainly not of the
country, which is most hard to combat."

Phillip wondered if this was the same Father Aloysius that his mother had spoken of, as being 'such a good man', the priest-in-charge of St. Saviour's in the High Street.

"What did you think of your chaplains in France?" went on the priest, turning to him.

"I can hardly judge, sir, I saw only one, and he preached a sermon that told us only that Zero day was not far off. The troops call chaplains the Royal Staybacks."

The priest laughed. "What did your man say, can you remember?"

"He said, 'This is the greatest fight ever made for the Christian religion, a fight between the mailed fist and the nailed hand.'"

"That sounds like the Bishop of London."

It was too late to leave now; darkness had come, and there were no lamps on the Swift. His great lonely bedroom! He remembered what Father had always said about Roman Catholic priests: how they tried to control other people's lives, and although supposedly devoted to things spiritual, they were great acquirers of property. But Father disliked Roman Catholics because his mother had come from a German Lutheran family which had suffered from persecution. Anyway, what did it matter? All religions were the same—merely made up from people's fears and desires.

The others began to talk about people they knew, including someone called "Margot". The only Margot Phillip had heard of was the Prime Minister's wife, and to his surprise this was the same person. The Kingsmans must be very high up, if they were intimate friends of the Asquiths. He must be careful not to say anything against the war.

"The newspapers are dreadful," said Mrs. Kingsman. "Poor Margot! That wretched *canard* about her visit to Donnington Hall, to play tennis with the German officer prisoners there, is still going the rounds. Even my head gardener believes it to be true. Margot says she does not even know where Donnington Hall is."

Phillip remembered that Mrs. Asquith's visit was one of the things that made Father furious with the Liberal Prime Minister. He might have known it! *The Daily Trident* had right across its chief page, *A Real British Victory at Last!* on the Monday following the attack at Loos . . . *The Daily Liar*.

"Even if she did go to visit old friends, I don't see anything wrong in it," he could not help saying.

To his surprise the priest exclaimed, "Bravo! Therein lies hope. Tell me, do many think like you do, in France?"

"I don't think so. Or if they do, they don't say so. You see——"
he began tremulously, but could not finish.

"Henry Asquith is so good," he heard Mrs. Kingsman saying.
"He will not defend himself. He will not believe that they are
intriguing against him."

"One of the disadvantages today of being a Balliol man," said
Kingsman.

"Tell me," said the priest softly, leaning across the sofa to
Phillip, "would it have been a help if you had had a padre with
your men in the line, sharing their lives, one to whom they could
confide their unhappiest thoughts?"

This was so strange a question that Phillip did not know what to
reply.

"One to whom a man could tell even his fears of being killed?"

"I think he would be killed just the same, whether he told his
fears or not, if his time had come, sir."

"You know Julian Grenfell's 'Into Battle', of course?"

"No—I don't, I'm afraid."

"Oh, my dear boy! It is one of the great poems of the war, with
Rupert Brooke's 1914 sonnets! It is your meat and drink, as a
soldier! Where can we find you a copy?"

"I have kept *The Times*, Lulu!"

Mrs. Kingsman got up, a strange exalted smile on her face, and
went up the stairs.

"Julian was our friend," said the priest, softly. "At Balliol
nearly ten years ago he was known as Roughers, or the Rough
Man. He was tremendously keen on physical fitness, delighting in
all beauty, fired by great poetry, feeling kinship with animals,
particularly horses, that was our dear, dear Rough Man, with his
stock whip, cracking its lash with a noise like a pistol shot! But
since all human qualities must have their defects, for what is man
but a wayward pilgrim unto God, Julian had the fault of in-
tolerance. Thus, he could not bear the sight of one fellow undergraduate in particular, and would hunt him whenever he saw
him, hurling that great thong of his stock-whip until the lash
exploded about the ears of the fleeing Jew . . . who is now, in the
whirligig of time, an A.D.C. to a general in France, while our
dear Roughers has died of wounds," ended the priest, with a
smile.

Phillip did not know what to say to this. He remembered his
father saying that grandfather Twiney was a Jew. What did it
matter, anyway, what religion a man was?

As Mrs. Kingsman came down the stairs with *The Times*, the priest went on, "You will know your Heraclitus," and he quoted for nearly half a minute, while Mrs. Kingsman waited. "You remember your Greek?"

"I did not learn Greek, sir."

"Oh, do forgive me, I did not intend——" The priest got up and took the newspaper from Mrs. Kingsman. Spreading it open on the table he said softly, "Read it to us, my dear Maddison," and then he began to pace the room, touching his rosary.

> *The naked earth is warm with Spring*
> *And with green grass and bursting trees*
> *Leans to the sun's gaze, glorying,*
> *And quivers in the sunny breeze.*
> *And life is Colour and Warmth and Light*
> *And a striving evermore for these;*
> *And he is dead who will not fight.*
> *And who dies fighting hath increase.*

Phillip read on, transfixed, as scenes of the countryside he had known with such happiness rose before him with so startling a clearness that he lowered his eyes, waiting for the tears which filled them to go.

> *The kestrel, hovering by day,*
> *And the little owls that call by night,*
> *Bid him be swift and keen as they,*
> *As keen of ear, as swift of sight.*

> *The blackbird sings to him: "Brother, brother,*
> *If this be the last song you sing,*
> *Sing well, for you may not sing another,*
> *Brother, sing."*

"Do go on, Phillip!" said Kingsman. "Yes, do," said Mrs. Kingsman. They watched the slim figure hesitating, then the nervous stroking of dark hair with a hand; the indrawn breath, the voice clear, gentle, and firm.

> *And when the burning moment breaks,*
> *And all things else are out of mind,*
> *And only Joy of Battle takes*
> *Him by the throat and makes him blind,*

Through joy and blindness he shall know,
Not caring much to know, that still
Nor lead nor steel shall reach him, so
That it be not the Destined Will.

The thundering line of battle stands,
And in the air Death moans and sings;
But Day shall clasp him with strong hands,
And Night shall fold him in soft wings.

In the silence that followed he could hear the flap of the flames
and the slight clicking of beads; then the low voice of Father
Aloysius began to pray in Latin. Captain Kingsman and his wife
bowed their heads, followed by Phillip. He felt himself to be small
and simple, and blessed.

"And now," said the priest, as he drew up his chair, "tell me
about your Redpoll herd, Dolly, and if the cows are doing their
duty. I am looking forward to that bowl of cream, and that
blackberry and apple pudding that Marty in the kitchen, bless
her, knows so well how to make."

What a marvellous poem, Phillip was thinking, again and again.
And yet——

It was a marvellous dinner, he thought, looking round the table
lit by tapers burning in Elizabethan holders of hand-wrought
silver. Now he knew why he had felt that something was wrong
with the Kingsmans, and the explanation was as sad as it was
simple: he had taken for granted that all homes, or the people in
them, were like his own. These people were kind, and because
they were kind they were polite to one another. And they did
not show their feelings or their spiritual bruises because they were
not bruised. Even the death of their only son had not broken as it
were their skins. Father Aloysius before they had gone into dinner
had whispered to him that their son, their only child, had been shot
down during the battle of Loos by the German airman Boelcke
flying a Fokker; so, said the priest, "Let us not speak harshly of
the mistakes or deficiencies of others. We are all pitiful in our
errors, our lives are composed of joy and of Virgil's *lacrimae rerum*,
'the tears of things'."

The dinner had begun with oxtail soup, and with it the butler
had three-quarter filled a small glass with dark red sweet wine,
which somehow just suited the soup. On the decanter was a silver

label, *Madeira*. Asked by Father Aloysius (dare he call him 'Lulu', wondered Phillip, and thought it better to keep his distance) what it was, Kingsman replied, "Bual Solera, 1826". After the soup came pink fish, which he thought was salmon; but Kingsman said it was sea-trout, which had been in the ice-house since last September. With this fish was a cold pale wine which made Phillip think of a sea-cave, by still water; they were allowed two three-quarter glasses only of this wine, which Kingsman said came from a Jesuit monastery on the banks of the Rhine, the *Forster Jesuitengarten*. By the time his plate was taken away Phillip was no longer metaphorically sitting on his hands; he was soaring happily in this new world of grace and friendship. With the pheasant came two more three-quarter glasses of claret, *Château Haut-Brion* bottled, said Kingsman, before the Franco-Prussian war, in 1862.

Now he knew why people talked about food and wine, which when matched, and balanced, had a wonderful effect on one, of life at its best, without any feeling of being tight.

By the time the blackberry and apple pudding came in, with cream in a bowl dull yellow which he realised was gold, he floated in timeless happiness. What wonderful people he had met, owing to the war! Then, thinking of his own home—of the constriction of spirit there, of his mother's anxiety and fear of upsetting the feelings of his father, of his sister Mavis who was not like other girls, but critical and never satisfied, and ashamed of him as she was of Father—he sighed, thinking that he had no right to be so happy. If only the others at home could know that such happiness *was* possible on earth——

Father Aloysius seemed to know what he was thinking, for after a glass of port to finish the dinner, with cob nuts and Cox's orange pippins, when they returned to the hall for coffee, he seated himself beside Phillip and during talk said that he had met both his mother and his sister, and that both held him in deep affection.

"My sister, Father?"

"You look surprised, Phillip. Your sister loves you dearly. Does that seem strange? I notice that your hands are usually clenched, as though you are holding yourself in. That is a sign of nervous strain. Do forgive me if I am too personal."

"I am very glad, Father. I like to find out the truth of things."

"To know the truth of oneself takes courage. And what is so good about you, if you will allow me to say so, is that you are not bitter about others. But one must not be bitter about oneself, Phillip. That leads to self-hate, which in the end splinters one, and the splinters hurt others. Self-centredness, the Old Adam, has to die, you know, or change rather, before one can find spiritual freedom, which is the love of God."

"When I was a boy," said Phillip, getting up to walk about the room, "I wanted some bullets for my catapult, to shoot wood-pigeons with. I had a bullet-mould, so I melted down some lead soldiers in a frying pan over the gas stove. Suddenly each one shrunk and the colours dropped away with its shape and a little bright blob ran where its feet had stood. I have been thinking! How does 'Into Battle' stand at the melting moment of action, when warmth and light and colour fall from men's lives, when first surprise, then desperate fear, comes upon them, and sometimes screams for help? How does it stand in the glare of action?"

"A man is not only a soldier, a toy soldier if you like," said the priest. "He has a soul. And if he is aware of that soul, and has fortified himself with self-discipline, with the help of God, his soul will uphold him in the terrors of the Abyss suddenly opening upon life as he has known it."

"Yes, Father, you are right. But 'when the burning moment breaks', and he goes forward, I am unable to believe that it will be 'only the Joy of Battle' that takes hold of him."

"Roughers was a cavalryman, you must remember."

"Yes, I see."

"Have you ever tried to write poetry, Phillip?" said Kingsman.

"Oh, I'm no good at it, Jasper. Do you mind my calling you Jasper? I'm afraid it slipped out."

"I've been asking you to call me by my name ever since this morning, you ass!"

"Hurray, I love being called an ass," said Phillip, stretching himself out on the sofa.

"And now," said Jasper, "auction! No more war, Phillip. When Dolly comes back, we'll cut for partners. You don't play? It's like whist, the partners bid for trumps, that's all. The one who gets the bid plays the hand. We play only for small stakes, as in the mess, sixpence a hundred."

As they were going upstairs with lighted candlesticks the priest said to Phillip, "How wonderful, that during the many times I walked up to the Heath, on my nightly walks around Greenwich, with its history of a thousand years and more, that I should have

passed your old school! I believe that you have an uncommon gift
of clarity; bear all things with that gift, Phillip." Seeing that the
youth looked puzzled he said, "Bear *with* all things."

"I'd like to ask you one thing, if I may, Father. Why did
Catholics torture and burn people at the stake? Or, like G. K.
Chesterton, if I remember rightly"—he could hear Uncle Hugh
saying it—"say, as a Catholic, that the writings of Thomas Hardy
reminded him 'of the village atheist brooding over the village
idiot'. Or people worshipping relics like toe-nails and bones?"

"Well, to answer your three questions in order. There are
insensitive men and sensitive men; and sometimes the most
sensitive are at times the most self-tortured, and therefore torturing. Objects of hate are but our own chimaerae. They arise from
wounds within us. So we seek scapegoats, to void our own hurts."

"Yes, I see what you mean, Father."

"Chesterton's criticism of Hardy was made at an off-moment,
I think. Even fine poets do not always see with what Goethe called
paradise-clearness."

"But do Catholics damn people like Hardy?"

"Men are men, of all sorts and conditions, Phillip. It is not for
me to say who are bad men, or good men, whether they are
Catholics or not. I myself love the writings of Hardy. Indeed, I
chose his works as the subject of my doctor's thesis in theology,
arguing that he is naturally a religious man, and a visionary,
whose compassion shines again and again like Shakespeare's
taper—you remember, 'How far that little candle throws its
beams, So shines a good deed in a naughty world.' Hardy's
spirit burns steadily, he is one of the lights of humanity.

"Now about relics, Phillip. The people love shows, and they
love goodness, and we all grieve in our hearts when loved ones are
gathered from us. Being mortal, we cling to relics—a ring, a letter,
a field post-card, or perhaps a cigarette case with initials on it—a
photograph, the first lock of hair clipped from a baby's head. Our
friends die, our children are killed in battle, the bone or fragment
of the saint is cherished accordingly."

"Yes, Father. Thank you very much for explaining it to me."
Phillip went down the Long Gallery, his candle flame fluttering,
while the faces in the portraits seemed to be alive, and sharing a
spirit that lived within the house.

Chapter 4

NEW BROOM

On the next Friday night Phillip's hopes of getting home to see Desmond were dashed when he saw in Orders that he was Orderly Officer for the next day. Well, he would do his duty strictly, like cousin Bertie. The entire camp needed to be smartened up. Grey Towers, a well-to-do tradesman's villa of mid-Victorian days, was in a disgraceful state. Cinders and eggshells strewed the muddy paths through the trees, with potato peelings and empty bully beef cans. Old sodden newspapers lay about. He would put in a report about the extremely slack condition of the camp.

As he walked towards the hutments an old shaky man with watery eyes and forage cap perched precariously on the centre of his skull approached him, obviously preparing with some anxiety to salute. Up went a hand with thick fingers spread between nobbly joints, jerk went the poor old head sideways, knees came up so that he just avoided a stagger, and a hand wavered at him. Philip returned his best salute, and stopped to speak.

"Didn't I see you at Alexandra Palace, last August? I thought so. How are you?" He shook hands.

The old fellow said he mustn't grumble, but his boots hurt something terrible. It was his blue veins, he explained.

"I had frost bite in France, and so I can sympathise. Ask your company quarter-master sergeant to try and get you a more comfortable pair. Take his name and number, sergeant!"

"Very good, sir."

The old fellow looked nearer eighty than seventy as he walked away. The orderly sergeant, cane under arm, waxed moustache, thin like trench bayonets said, "There's several old 'uns 'ere."

He was an old sweat himself if ever there was one, thought Phillip, noting the beery face, the medal ribands of Egyptian campaigns.

"We've grandads, and not a few great-grandads. They sign on for the pay, six bob a day, sir, more'n twice a time-servin' sergeant instructor gets. But queer things goes on everywhere in time o' war, sir."

"Yes, your old Adjutant went to quod for half-inching Government property, didn't he?"

"Yes sir, and he's not the only one. I mean, sir," said the sergeant, stopping and facing him. He hesitated, then began again. "Well, sir, if you understand my meanin', I could say a lot, sir, were I a mind to. The food we get in the sergeant's mess is not fit for pigs. I reckon someone ought to write to John Bull about it."

"Why that bloody rogue Bottomley? Why not me, as orderly officer, sergeant? Isn't he supposed to receive all complaints? Come on, out with it!"

The sergeant gave him a glance in which surprise, fear, and evasive cunning were mixed.

"I don't want to lose me pension, sir."

"What's wrong with the food, anyhow?"

"Mustn't grumble, sir."

"H'm. Well, we'll go and see the guard room."

"Tell you what, sir, there's a prisoner there, and the orderly officer is within 'is dooty to ask if a prisoner 'as any complaints about his food, sir."

"Lead on, sergeant."

The sentry on guard outside carried a black swagger stick with nickel top instead of a rifle. He was a man younger than the run of navvies Phillip had seen so far, and managed a fair salute. The sergeant, however, rated him in a loud voice. "Can't you do better'n that, my lad? Come smartly to attention when you see an orficer approachin'. Let me see the forefinger of your left 'and in line with the seam of the trouser next time!"

Phillip entered the creosoted building in time to see the N.C.O. in charge of the guard sweeping a heap of coppers into one hand, while another man thrust a pack of cards under the brown blanket covering the trestle table at which several soldiers were sitting.

"Guard—SHUN," roared the N.C.O., saluting. "Guard present and correct, sir."

"So I noticed. What is it, pontoon or nap?"

"Nap, sir."

"Solo whist has its points, as a change. Stand easy. I would like to see the man in the cell."

The guard sergeant looked at the orderly sergeant. Then staring at nothing the orderly sergeant cried, "Orfficer to see prisoner!" in a loud but hollow voice.

In silence the key was put in, the door was half opened, the guard sergeant shouted, "Prisoner, SHUN!"

The orderly sergeant said to Phillip that he had better follow him, and gave him a wink. "Troublesome customer in 'ere, sir."

"Then he has a grievance. That's what I'm here for."

The room inside was lined, like the door, with sheet-iron. The brown iron on the door was dented, as from many kickings. It was lit by a single electric bulb high in the wooden ceiling. The prisoner seemed to have absorbed the grimness of iron-encasement as he stood by the only object in the room, a palliasse bed in three sections on the dirty floor. He had a sullen unshaven face, his dark eyes seemed to be darker with suppressed anger, or pain. He stood bootless, beltless, and minus his braces, so that his trousers were about to fall down. He was a huge man, with lips the thicker for being swollen, his nose was likewise swollen and blood-crusted. There was a long cut upon one swelled cheek-bone.

"Any complaints?" asked Phillip, deciding that the man had been brought in fighting drunk.

"No!" replied the prisoner, in a hoarse voice.

"How's the food?"

"Bloody muck, not fit for a bloody pig."

"Steady my lad, before an orfficer!" cried the sergeant.

"Oh, I heard ever so much worse language than that during the first battle of Ypres," said Phillip, amiably. "Now tell me, how did you get hurt like that?"

"I falled down."

"Yes, it happens to us all sometime or other." To the orderly sergeant, "Has iodine been put on those cuts?"

"No sir."

"Then he should be treated at once."

"Medical orderly's hut closed, sir."

"Then it must be opened."

"Next sick parade at nine o'clock tomorrow morning, sir."

"Then we'll have a special one now."

He lifted the left side of his tunic and with a rip of stitches opened his field dressing. He broke the iodine capsule, and saying, "This will smart a bit on your cheek, but I'll let you put it yourself on your lips. I saw a man with lock-jaw in France, and it was not a pleasant sight."

"Don't go near him, sir," said the orderly sergeant, softly past one spike of his moustache. The prisoner heard, and glowered at the sergeant.

"He's all right," cried Phillip, enthusiastically. "So is anyone who wears both the Queen's and King's ribands for South Africa! Ask the sergeant of the guard to let him have a hot cup of fresh tea, with plenty of sugar. What is your name?" to the prisoner.

"Pimm, that's a very good name. Now be a good fellow, and let me treat that cut on your cheek-bone."

He went forward, and in silence dabbed the iodine on the cut. The prisoner looked at him, unmoving. "There, that's done. Like to have my handkerchief to do your lips? It's quite clean. You can have it, if you like."

The prisoner put the iodine on his lips. Phillip smiled at him, saying, "Good man. Sergeant, don't forget that cup of char. Plenty of sugar in it, if Pimm wants it. Right, we'll go and see the cookhouse now."

"Want yer snot rag, sir?" said the prisoner, holding out the khaki handkerchief.

"It's a present for you, Pimm. I've been under arrest in my time, and I know what it feels like. I'll come and see you later on."

They left the iron room. The door was locked again.

"Christ A'mighty, there ain't many like you, if you'll pardon the remark, sir," said the sergeant, on the way to the cookhouse. "You took a risk, sir, you know."

Feeling mellow and pleased with himself, Phillip replied, "Oh, surely not, sergeant? Pimm is a good fellow. The officers I knew when I was a private, in France, all looked after their men. That's what an officer is for. In a good battalion, anyway. It's you fellows, the N.C.O.'s, who have all the dirty work. An officer should be a soldier's friend."

"In the old army, yes sir, I agree, but this ain't the old army."

"But Pimm is an old soldier—in both senses of the term! How did he get those bruises on his face? I saw drops of blood on the floor, and they weren't from deep cuts. Did he scrap in the guardroom?"

"It isn't my business to say, sir."

"Why can't you tell me?"

"You 'eard what 'e said, sir, 'e fell down."

"What's all the mystery about?" said Phillip, stopping.

"I can't say, sir, I'm only the orderly sergeant."

They walked on towards the cookhouse, a place of lime-washed corrugated iron, grease, and coal. Thick smoke poured from a chimney. Beyond was a heap of white bread, hundreds of loaves piled together, thousands of loaves under the trees.

"My God, and a soldier in France is lucky if he can get two small slices of bread in his ration once a week! And what the hell is all that?"

He walked to a pit wherein joints and bones lay piled on top of each other. There was among them the whole side of a bullock.

"Does the Adjutant know about this waste?"

"The farmer takes it away, sir, for to feed his pigs."

"And who gets the money?"

"Ah, now you're asking something, sir!"

"No wonder the war is costing five million pounds a day. There's several cartloads of meat wasted here, all going rotten, and at least a couple of lorry-loads of loaves."

"It's the same everywhere, sir. Everyone makin' money except the tommy, what does the fightin'."

"I don't think I want to see the inside of the cookhouse. The outside is enough."

"Cooks are off duty now, sir, anyway."

"Do they wear smoke-helmets? They should. Right, I'll see you at guard mounting at six o'clock. See to it that the prisoner Pimm gets his cup of tea."

"Very good, sir."

The sergeant changed his manner. "It was the colonel what marked 'm, sir. Only don't fer Gawd's sake let on that I told you. I don't want to be broke, sir."

"Colonel Broad?"

"Yes sir. It was that or a court martial, sir, for insubordination. The colonel goes to see Pimm, and offers him a good 'iding or a court martial, in which case the man will be for the glass 'ouse, sir, and his pay be stopped, and 'is missus and kids suffer. Pimm knows that, and before 'e can say which 'e'll take, the Ganger, as they call the Colonel, batters 'is gums good and proper. 'E'll let 'im out on Monday, sir, and there won't be no more trouble."

"Rough justice, sergeant."

"Yes sir, and the men understand it."

"It's not as bad as it looks, then?"

"It's what they all bin used to, sir."

"Well, I take it that there are no complaints, sergeant?"

"None whatever, sir! I allus says, let sleeping dogs lie. Oh, before I forgets it, sir, the orderly orfficer ain't supposed to go near the men's quarters before lights out, sir."

"Why is that?"

"To avoid trouble, sir. The men gets paid today, and they're only navvies arter all, if you understand my meanin'."

At guard mounting the orderly sergeant said, "Pimm 'ad his cup of char, sir, and we give 'im some sausages and bread. The men liked what you did, if you'll excuse me tellin' you. But you'll remember to keep clear of them huts, won't you, sir? We don't want no trouble."

This made Phillip all the more determined to see what went on. It reminded him of the music hall song

Where did Robinson Crusoe go
With Friday on Saturday night?

for these old navvies were like a lot of ancient Crusoes, who drew each Saturday afternoon the immense pay of forty-two shillings each.

After the pubs and canteen had been closed, the men staggered back to their quarters, singing, rolling and fighting. He watched from behind a tree two buck navvies taking terrific swings at each other, men who a few moments before had been coming along holding one another up, arms round necks. Phillip thought he knew all the swear words in the cockney's vocabulary, but some of the things said were pretty awful, he thought, coming from the lowest level of slum living. He had heard remarks from wretched boys in the fever hospital which had made him wince, boys in whose thoughts nothing was sacred; but these navvies when fighting drunk taunted one another with far worse phrases. Could a father really make his small children do what was said? Incest took place, of course, often among the poor in crowded rooms, but that was nothing to what he heard from the two who had been calling one another "matey" only a few moments before, and then fallen out.

The scenes in the huts, or rather on the hut floors, were mild compared with the language. Taking care to remain hidden, he watched one scene beyond an open door; men lay about in all attitudes, in pools of their own urine. The sergeant had told him that a man might take as many as forty pints in a boozer at night, and it had seemed to be an exaggeration; but now he saw, in hut after hut, figures dispread and inert on wet floors, an occasional shaggy figure sitting up and singing. In one hut, asprawl with figures, four men of about forty years of age, real buck navvies, he thought, were doing what some of the senior boys in the school Cadet Corps at Bisley had done in a tent openly and without shame, to see who could race the others.

He went from hut to hut, all with doors open, and watched. In one a man was staggering about, the only one on his feet, roaring out that he had been home to see his old woman, but when he got there, he found she had on the kicking strap. A flow of obscenity followed, then:

"I give it to 'er, I give it to 'er jus' like this——" and the man lurched at the stove, swinging his fist. He hit the iron pipe so that the chimney collapsed and fell on the floor and smoke came with flames out of the broken upright end of the pipe. The man went down on the floor, groaning.

Phillip went in to have a look and thought that it was unlikely to set fire to the room, as the stove was now a fire-pail and the fire would gradually die out. Six times the pay of the fighting tommy in France, no wonder they behaved like beggars on horseback! Before the war, sixteen shillings a week; now, forty-two.

The only report he would make, thought Phillip, would be to Mrs. Neville when he saw her next; and even to her, he would have to censor at least one of the scenes.

It certainly was a rag-time battalion of Kitchener's Army he had come to, he thought, as he leaned against a wall of the drawing-room of Grey Towers, one of several other junior subalterns taking part in the weekly Social as it was called.

Dinner was over. The ladies were in the drawing-room, knitting and talking among themselves. With the exception of the Colonel's daughter, the ladies were matronly, homely individuals of between forty and fifty years of age: Mrs. Broad, Mrs. Fluck, Mrs. Crump, Mrs. Gleeson, Mrs. Stiff. Their husbands had been time-served N.C.O.'s, retired for many years before the war. Now they were back again, and having the time of their lives—as majors, and prospective lieutenant-colonels; for, it was said, several new battalions were to be formed out of the original Navvies. There they sat: Crump, Fluck, Gleeson and Stiff, all together in one corner, smoking pipes and playing cards—not exactly bridge, but pontoon: a crafty lot taken altogether, he thought, wicked old devils who knew all the tricks, all trying to line nests which before the war had certainly not been feathered. Now some of the feathers were in evidence: round the necks, as boas, of Mesdames Crump, Fluck, Gleeson and Stiff.

Phillip laughed as he thought of what Wigg had told him: that every grocer in Ilford and Romford had been visited at various times by one or another of these gentry, in connection with possible deals for probable Regimental Institute "comforts for the troops" —extra rations such as custard powders, prunes, fresh vegetables, and cocoa for the canteens—to be bought with a secret commission returned to each C.O. when the new battalions were formed. "Jam," it was called.

As the now-idle new broom leaned against the wall there were voices in the passage outside. "Steady!" "Take it easy!" "All right, keep your wool on", etc.; then through the open door came a pushed piano. Miss Broad turned pale. Milman was going to accompany her on the piano; then they were going to sing a duet. After that, she was going to play the piano accompaniment of *The Broken Melody*. At intervals during the afternoon fragments of this ordeal had been audible in and around Grey Towers. Now the dreaded moment was come. Milman smiled at her reassuringly. She smiled back, her eyes still anxious. Phillip sympathised. He liked Milman.

When the violinist was rubbing resin on his bow, Wigg sauntered over to Phillip. "Look at Milman," he said, *sotte voce*, "little gutscraper!"

Phillip gave Wigg an amiable look, and remained silent, thinking that sotty votshy just about summed up Wigg.

"By the way, did the Cabin Boy ever thank you for letting him use your motorcar, when you first arrived?"

"Yes, thanks. What's more, he gave me four gallons of juice. I thought it quite decent of him."

"Yes, at Curling's expense."

"I don't understand."

"He took two cans from the pit-store in the stable, didn't he? Well, those cans were kept there, and had been paid for, by Little Boy Curling. The Cabin Boy took them without as much as a by-your-leave."

"But surely Colonel Broad pays for the petrol Curling uses when he drives him about in his 'Prince Henry' Vauxhall?"

"Not on your life! Little Boy Curling takes the C.O. to the House of Commons, at other times he takes the Colonel's wife shopping in Regent Street, or to a *matinée*, where I bet he pays for the tickets. What it is to have for father the richest grocer in London, who bought himself a baronetcy by paying thirty thousand pounds to the Liberal Party's coffers."

Phillip wondered about those two tins of petrol. After the tremulous singing of *When you Come down the Vale, Lad, There's Music Everywhere*, he crossed the room to Curling and asked him. The duet, *O that We Two were Maying!* was about to begin.

"Tell me, Curling, have you missed four gallons——"

"S-sh!" said Curling, his head seeming to shrink into his

shoulders. He put a finger half-heartedly to his lips, his eyes were those of a subdued little boy. He wore leggings and breeches; other subalterns had changed into slacks, but Curling was apparently on duty all the time, ready to drive Col. Broad, M.P. whenever he or England might require the services of his grey open motor-car with the beaky radiator and arrow-fluted bonnet. Second-lieutenant Curling had one main sorrow; he had been promised a second pip by the Colonel last July, and still he had only one on each sleeve.

After the duet, while Milman was tuning up his fiddle, Phillip asked about the petrol. Curling, lowering his eyes, and hoping that the other would not give so much as one glance at any member of the Broad family, whispered, "I was very pleased to be of use. Please forget it, Maddison."

"Well, thanks, old chap."

"Don't mention it."

While Milman was playing the dreamy, rather sad and beautiful *Alice, Where Art Thou*, that Uncle Hugh had played on his cigar-box fiddle with a brass horn so movingly, Phillip thought that Curling, despite his one pip, could not grumble. His father was very nearly a millionaire, and Curling was not likely to be sent out to France, when he was useful to the C.O. All the same, he was in half a mind to offer six shillings for the four gallons, but thinking of Curling's 'allowance from the guv'nor' of £600 a year, plus his pay, he thought better of it.

Sitting beside Curling, he noticed on the brown leather of his boots the black marks of spurs and chains, but no signs of rubbing on leggings or breeches strappings. Evidently Curling had glorified himself to equestrian status when he was home on leave, and out of sight of Colonel Broad. How funny that a baronet's son should want to swank. After the music, the piano was moved back for dancing. Phillip got away, before anyone could suggest that he dance with any of the girls sitting with their mothers. By the door he met Wigg, who said, "I met a friend of yours the other night in town. Her name is Frances. She says you know her cousin."

Frances, Frances, thought Phillip, who could she be? Fearing Wigg's cynical tongue, he asked no questions.

Chapter 5

TO THE BRIGHT LIGHTS

After lunch two days later Wigg came up to Phillip in the ante-room and said, "Would you care to come with me to Town this evening? I am meeting Frances, who said she knew you, and she has a friend."

"I have been wondering who 'Frances' can be, Wigg."

"All I know is that she is called Frances and that she is a mannequin."

"Then it must be another Maddison. A mannequin? I knew *of* one once, long ago, who wore a hobble-skirt."

"This one is too young for that. Are you on?"

"Thanks, I'd like to come. Shall we go in the Swift? I've just had some lamps fitted."

They went after tea through Romford and Ilford to the Bow Road and broad sett-stoned Whitechapel High Street; onwards to the City; down Fenchurch Street in the darkness—past Wine Vaults Lane, and the round face of the Moon hanging above the little office of many memories; Cheapside, with Benetfink's toy shop, belonging to an age now gone. How unsophisticated he was then!

"Straight on," said Wigg.

They turned off a crowded street of shops and hurrying figures into a side alley where a row of Post Office vans was parked.

"Stop here," said Wigg.

Walls arose on either side. At the corner was a building with open warehouse doors beyond which small gas-jets flickered upon elderly men in white aprons loading cardboard boxes into a horse van. He recognised the name of a fashionable West End shop which sold frocks and gowns to Society women; and a slight fear came to him as he thought again that the girls they were to meet were mannequins. Could "Frances" possibly be another name of Marie Cox, who had dared to walk down the High Street in that hobble skirt, to be jeered at by common boys? She had lived in Charlotte Road, and had bleached her hair—a very fast thing to do, Mother had said. She would be quite old now, quite twenty-four.

Wigg's pronunciation of the word *mannequin* in French made him the more uneasy as he waited in the dim alley. At one moment he had to suppress an impulse to touch Wigg on the arm and say he didn't want to go through with it. He would much rather go to a theatre or electric palace. What could he say to a mannequin? Worse, what was he expected to do? All he had heard about the West End at night was alarming. Also, he had only thirty shillings on him: mannequins would be used to dining at places like the Ritz or Carlton, where only champagne was drunk. The more he thought of it, the more he wished he had not come, and especially with an obvious *blasé roué* like Wigg. As minutes passed, the deeper his alarm.

"Give them a little grace. It's only five minutes after six."

The elderly loaders finished; the van doors were closed. There was, around the base of a lamp-post standing in a tiny pool of light, a suggestion of fog. The damp air hung tenuous; the horse whinnied as it tossed its empty nose-bag.

"I loathe women who keep a man hanging about," said Wigg, as a clock struck the quarter hour. "I was to see my brother at the Goat at twenty-past six." He looked at his wristlet watch. "My girl is called Frances, so don't try and get off with her. I know nothing about her so-called friend. That's your risk."

"I wish I could think how your friend Frances knows me. You say you don't know her surname?"

"I've told you, NO! half a dozen times! It can be Buggins, for all I care."

This harsh remark depressed Phillip further. He strolled down the street, and taking the three ten shilling notes from his fold-over case, hid them in different pockets. He was returning, hoping that Wigg would decide to leave, when two girls wearing large black straw hats, wider in the brim behind than in front, on which was a flounced bow of black velvet completing a band around the crown, and dressed in loose jackets with military cuffs to the sleeves and open roll collars, with wide flounced skirts of the same material, and each carrying a slim rolled umbrella with a floppy black velvet hand-bag came out of a door, hesitated by the lamp-post; then the taller one went forward to Wigg standing on the kerb with hands in pea-jacket pockets. Phillip heard a pleasant voice say, "Hullo! Are we very late? So sorry! How nice of you to have come," then a gloved hand, level with her shoulder, was held out towards Wigg.

Rather fascinated by the charm of her voice, Phillip walked towards them. Then to his alarm he saw Wigg take the girl in his arms, bend back her head, and give her a cave-man kiss, as on the films. "Well!" said the girl, when he released her. A scent of flowers hung in the air, and he saw that her face was fresh and young. She looked used to High Society. The other girl's face was shaded by her large hat.

"What a jolly runabout you've got!" said the girl who had been kissed, turning to Phillip.

After introductions, they all squeezed into the Swift, and he drove out of the alley with Wigg's girl sitting on Wigg's lap, and his girl wedged in between them and himself.

"Do you mind my arm behind you?" said his girl. He congratulated himself on having hidden the ten shilling notes.

"I'm afraid it must be frightfully uncomfortable for you." His thigh was rather frighteningly warm against her. "Which way, Wigg?"

"Turn left. Down Oxford Street, and straight on."

At the junction with Regent Street, Wigg said to the girl on his lap, "I thought we'd have a drink in the Goat. My brother is coming up from Pompey, and will be there."

"Oh."

"Don't worry, he won't be gooseberry, he's leaving soon."

"What is the Goat? Is it a restaurant?"

"It's a pub frequented by sailors."

"Well, thank you very much, but I don't think we ought to come, Mr. Wigg. We don't drink, you see. I'm so sorry if it looks like false pretences."

"Stop by the kerb," said Wigg.

Phillip could feel him turning cold and angry. From her voice she was much too good for Wigg. Fingertips lightly touched his cheek. Was the girl beside him trying to vamp him?

"Very well," said Wigg. "We'll go to the Nicosa."

"Where shall I drive?"

"Oh, down to Piccadilly Circus."

That was, for Phillip, a name holding further alarm. Were these girls high-class *demi-mondaines*? It was not reassuring that Wigg was fondling the breasts of the girl on his lap, as his voice grated, "At the Nicosa one can get broiled kid, and the wine has the tang of the pines of Greece, from the barrels in which it is shipped. The wine of Circe's Isle, and the pipes of Pan." Wigg gave a short, cynical laugh. Phillip wondered how he could get away. With relief he heard the girl on Wigg's lap saying,

"Well, thank you again, but would you mind if we all went somewhere more ordinary? We are both working girls, you see, and not used to such places. I'm sorry if it sounds horribly suburban——"

"What sort of place would you suggest, since you do not care for my idea of hospitality? The Apex House?"

"Well, the cooking is quite good there."

"Good God!" said Wigg. He appeared to be struggling. "Stop! Stop!" he cried.

Phillip drew into the kerb. Pushing the girl from his lap, who got out, Wigg sprang to the pavement. "I am going to the Goat! I promised to see my brother there! He's coming up from Pompey to see me, and so to the Goat I am going!" He said to Phillip, "if I don't see you later I'll find my own way back." Hunching his shoulders, Wigg walked away.

"I'm most awfully sorry Mr. Maddison," said the girl on the kerb. "I'm afraid it is all my fault. Have a good time, you two. Goodbye, thank you ever so much for the ride."

"No, don't go!" said Phillip, not wanting to be left alone with a vamp. "Wigg's a bit temperamental, that's all. Let's find somewhere to dine. Only, I don't know London very well."

"But two's company, three's none," she said, looking at him with serious eyes. "You and Alice go and enjoy yourselves."

Phillip had a wild idea to be seen in Freddy's with two such splendid girls: but they were used to the West End; and they weren't the kind to go into pubs. "I won't hear of you going off alone."

"Well then, I shall insist that you allow me to pay for myself."

"Of course not!"

"Let's talk about that later. Meanwhile may I recommend the Apex House? Or there's Snow's Chop House, on the corner, if you are enormously hungry. Both are inexpensive. I'm afraid I don't know any grand places, Mr. Maddison."

"I vote we go to the Apex House," said Alice, "and watch Piggy Wiggy playing the violin!"

"Oh, do you like music, too? How ripping!" said Phillip, as he made room for Frances.

"One can get a good dinner for half-a-crown at the Apex, Mr. Maddison."

"Good lord! I thought it would cost a pound each, and I've only got thirty shillings! Which way now?"

This was an adventure, he felt, driving into the wonders of the West End. He was actually in Piccadilly Circus! Scared of the rushing traffic, he went on in bottom gear and drew into the kerb at a place suggested by Frances.

There, having turned low the wicks of the oil-lamps, he left the Swift, with a backward glance of pride and gratitude, to walk between his two companions down the street. The pavement was crowded. Daring to hold an arm of each girl, he piloted them through a drifting mass of soldiers and women glimpsed in the lights of opened shop-door, oyster bar and jewellery store. There was the dark blue of Russian uniform, pale blue of French, Belgians in khaki wearing tall forage caps with tassels, grey Italian, greenish-grey Servian; while against the walls of theatres, upon sand-canisters, and by lamp-posts lounged homeless Australians and New Zealanders. He felt romance in every person and object that he passed: this was Piccadilly, here was the hub of the world.

Outside a theatre, revealed in the sheen of a lighted foyer, stood an old bare-headed man with long white locks and beard, and a face rather flat, but with an expression of remote idealism as he held up a tract.

"He looks like Tolstoi, doesn't he?" said Frances, smiling with eyes large and shining like cherries. Tolstoi? Tolstoi? Oh yes, there was a copy of the *Kreutzer Sonata* locked up in Father's desk at home.

"Do you think he *is* Tolstoi?" Could he have been looking at a real author?

"Didn't Tolstoi die four years ago?"

He felt a little ashamed of his ignorance; but her friendly squeeze of his arm was reassuring. He led them closer to the theatre, to examine the photographs of actors and actresses; and daring to look more fully at the other girl's face, saw with delight that she too was pretty. They were, in spite of being mannequins, only ordinary girls after all!

"Here we are," said Frances.

Proud to be seen with such beauties, he led them into a palace of marble and gilt, and chandeliers glittering with electric light: a hall of many vistas seen through doors of bronze and glass, of rooms seemingly endless with tables and electric lights.

Passing up a wide stairway they came to other rooms similarly large and lofty, and entered one with pale green carpets: a room full of Italian waiters gliding as they bore silver trays to tables, over which they bowed deftly. Could such a splendid place be as inexpensive as Frances had said?

He had thought that all the West End was aristocratic and fearfully expensive; now, with wonder and delight rising through his entire being, he heard his first string orchestra in a restaurant; and recognised Brahm's *Hungarian Dances*, hitherto heard only on the gramophone.

"Will you excuse us while we go and powder our noses? We left the shop in rather a rush, you see. Won't be long!"

He watched them going to the door, and for a moment wondered if they were leaving him, for they went down the stairs. Then he saw their rolled umbrellas, smaller and more slender than a man's, leaning across their chairs.

Looking around the room, he saw other officers like himself, and here and there a ranker; all quietly sitting, with wives and sweethearts, pink faces in the shaded lights upon the tables. So ordinary people like himself came here.

He watched the door; and with relief saw the girls returning. It gave him pleasure to see, as they walked across the room, several heads turning to look at them. Then Frances, the taller of the two, went off at a tangent to the orchestra upon a daïs. She spoke to the conductor.

Alice, sitting down, said, "Frances is asking for a special request. It's a surprise for you."

The orchestra began to play music from *Tonight's the Night*, and instantly the scene around him changed, so that he was drawn out of himself, and with a strange joy, re-entered a world that haunted him—and looking at Frances across the table he saw an expectancy in her eyes that he avoided. He felt thwarted; her look had spoiled his dream of the battlefield. He felt weary.

"I think you want some food," she said. "Or a drink—perhaps? I'll call the waiter—oh, here he is! Phillip—may I call you that? —will you think me horribly rude if I invite you, at your own table, to have a drink with me? For a very special occasion?"

His doubt returned. What was the 'very special occasion'? Were the drinks to be doped—or his glass? The waiter brought some sherry.

When the waiter had gone away with the food order—herb omelettes for the girls and roast saddle of mutton for Phillip—Alice said, as they raised their glasses, "Go on Frances, don't keep Phillip in suspense! He looks quite bewildered, poor boy."

The endearing tone of the *poor boy*, drew him in imagination to the silken bosom below the charming face of Alice; he drained his glass of sherry.

"Does the song they are playing now mean anything special to you?" asked Frances, leaning with an expectant smile over the table. She began to sing the words in a whisper, her eyes upon Phillip's.

And when I tell them, how wonderful you are
They'll never believe me, they'll never believe me——

then she broke off, and said, "A Decca trench gramophone? A dugout? Harold West?"

"'Spectre' West! How do *you* know about him?"

"He's my cousin."

It was unbelievable, it was marvellous. "Spectre" West in the trenches in front of Vermelles, badly wounded and ordering him to get round the flank of the Lone Tree position.

"Waiter, waiter, bring some more sherry! Bring a bottle!"

"A half-bottle," suggested Frances.

"A barrel!"

A half-bottle arrived.

"We must drink his health! How is the dear old boy? When last I heard of him he was at the Duchess of Westminster's hospital at Le Touquet."

"He's at Netley hospital now, near Southampton. I'm afraid he's lost an eye, and his left hand, poor dear, but his leg will be all right, he says. He was sorry you left the Gaultshires. He is very fond of you, you know."

The food arrived. The wine waiter gave him a list. "We must drink to Westy! How about a hock?" There was one for 2/6d. "Right, a bottle. It's probably made by the Jesuits on the banks of the Rhine. Wine and food should be in balance. One moment."

He ordered half a bottle of claret and filled the glasses three-quarters full. When they had eaten, he invited them to have some Christmas pudding, with brandy poured over it. Frances hesitated, looked at Alice.

"Very well, as it's a special occasion. But Phillip, remember that I am going to pay my share!"

"But this *is* a special occasion, not only because of the news of Westy getting better, but because you have both honoured me with your company."

"I believe he means it," said Alice.

"Of course I do," he said, looking from face to face, and thinking that he had never been so happy in his life before. Why wasn't Desmond with him? How pretty Alice was, the light brown hair clustering round her pink ears, her *retroussé* nose, and lips of coral. She was like Polly, but more delicate in feature. Her wrists, encased in white silk, were slender. What a pity Wigg wasn't more decent.

"I wonder what Mr. Wigg is doing," said Frances.

"I was thinking of him just at that moment!"

"It must be telepathy," said Alice. "Two soul mates!"

Elbows on table, hands holding glass, she saucily tasted her wine with repeated tongue dipping. Wigg had kissed Frances with his tongue. Did girls really like that sort of thing?

"Is Mr. Wigg a very great friend of yours, Phillip?" asked Frances.

"I hardly know him, as a matter of fact."

"Good for you," said Alice. "I don't like him. In fact, I thought him——"

"Now Alice——" warned Frances.

"Well, you thought so too, you told me so. Go on, be honest!"

Frances seemed to want to say something; then to decide not to say it.

"Men who look at a girl as though they are undressing her with their eyes bore me," continued Alice.

"Now you've shocked Phillip!"

"Oh, nothing shocks me, dear lady. All the world is my oyster! Who said that? Tolstoi, or Shakespeare?"

"Charlie Chaplin," said Alice.

"Let's go and see him after dinner, how about it?"

The Christmas pudding arrived. The waiter poured the brandy with a deft movement, then struck a match. While the flames were flickering away Phillip saw Alice turning to wave at someone. He looked and saw a naval officer lift his hand as he passed down the tables across the room.

"There's Timmy!" said Alice, excitedly. "I didn't know he was on leave!"

Phillip saw the animation on her face with dismay, and felt rueful when she cried, "I must go and speak to dear old Timmy!" and pushing back her chair, she almost ran to the newcomer.

"Don't be long," said Frances. "The pudding is nicest when hot."

"You eat my bit! I don't want any," Alice called back.

She returned when they had finished their coffee, about twenty minutes later.

"Timmy says would you two like to have a drink with us in the Café Royal? We'll meet you there."

Having paid the bill, Phillip and Frances went down to the street. Crossing Shaftesbury Avenue under the statue of Eros, they walked up a broad curved way of yellow painted buildings, and went through a door, to find themselves in a room of plush and crystal, of red walls with mirrors and sofas on which sat the Bohemians he had read about, behind glasses and cups on marble-topped tables. They looked to be an odd lot, not so much from their long hair as from the general ugliness of their clothes and the curious shapes of their pallid faces. Not all looked to be expressionless: one face was alive, with the bright-eyed glance of a fox: a red-bearded man wearing small gold ear-rings. He was talking in a low voice to a young girl in a simple, tight-fitting frock. Her face seemed to shine. Looking cautiously around the room, Phillip saw, sitting against another wall, a man with a putty-coloured face, and a brow over which hung small ringlets of hair. He looked to be un-washed, with a bulbous nose and expressionless dark eyes. He, too, wore large gold ear-rings, but under a shapeless black felt hat. When he spoke it was with a strange accent. Could he be an anarchist? Many of the other men looked queer customers, too, in their wide black hats, and coloured scarves round necks. He was greatly relieved to learn that coffee by itself could be bought, in glasses held in nickel silver containers.

"Good luck," said Frances, raising her glass, a little finger held out like a tendril. "You will write to Harold, won't you? You know his address? 'The Grapes, Lime Street, E.C.'. You knew his parents lived there, didn't you?"

"I had an idea that his mother did."

"Both his parents do. They will forward any letters. Or you can write direct to Harold at Netley Military Hospital, South-ampton."

"Does Alice know that naval commander well?"

"Fairly well, I think."

"I see."

"I'm sorry, Phillip. You like her, don't you?"

"Well, in a way. She rather reminds me of a girl I know." He meant cousin Polly.

"Ah, I thought you had a secret!"

This remark indicated the image of Helena Rolls. "Not really. I haven't a hope in that direction."

"How do you know? Have you asked her?"

"I did once, when I was rather young and foolish."

"Hark to the voice of hoary old age! But while there's life, there's hope, you know."

"But not much hope when there's death."

"Phillip, how very morbid! Why, you are only at the threshold of life."

"I mean that Helena Rolls"—he spoke calmly, to hide his alarm at his daring to speak openly of her—"loved my cousin, who was killed in front of the Hohenzollern Redoubt."

"Oh, how insensitive you must think me! Do forgive me."

"There's nothing to forgive. I just don't belong anywhere, that's all."

"No, I won't let you think like that! Time heals all wounds, you know—all wounds of the heart, anyway. And you are rather a nice person, Phillip. Don't you know it?"

She saw him shut himself away from her, and felt rebuffed. Shame rose in her; but she put it aside.

"Phillip, I am genuinely sorry that I upset you."

"Oh no, you didn't, really. It's just that I—well, I'm really no good, as I said. I've always been like it, long before I ever saw her. I just can't believe I shall ever be good enough, that's all."

"Did you feel like that when you were very small?"

"I think I must have done, for one of my aunts once told me that at nine months old, my 'baby eyes were filled with fear'. She said she knew why, but I would not like to be told the reason. I suppose I was born with something vital missing. I could never be really self-forgetful, as a child, except when I heard beautiful music. A freak, I suppose."

"I don't want to criticise your aunt, but she does not seem to be altogether an understanding person. Nine months of age! My dear Phillip, what next? I can tell you that Harold West, whose judgments I value, says that you are a person who inspires friendship. Those are his very words."

"I just can't understand why," he said, avoiding her eyes.

"Attraction of like minds is mutual, you know. You and Harold, for example. Didn't you like him at once?"

"Yes, as soon as I saw him. Others seemed a bit afraid of him, of his tongue, I mean, but I saw through him to his sense of humour. Even when he showed a side of cold fury, deadly serious and intent, it didn't really upset me. I suppose that was the effect of the drugs he had to take, because of his headaches?"

"I didn't know Harold took drugs, Phillip! How awful!"

He dissembled; and to hide his indiscretion, said innocently, "Oh, only when he was wounded, I mean! Not ordinarily. We all get morphia, you know, when badly hit. No, Westy was really awfully kind. Please don't think any more about what I said."

"Of course not! Cross my heart. Poor Harold, how he hates

war. His ambition is to be a country parson, you know, somewhere in Gaultshire. Yet he is a Cockney."

"How extraordinary! No, I didn't mean that. I know a parson who in his young days sailed before the mast all round the world. He's a very good sport. I say, how about Charlie Chaplin? Or don't you like him?"

"I adore the little man! But we'll wait for Alice, shall we? She'll be disappointed to miss you, I'm sure. Will you have some more coffee? It's on me this time! Good!"

While they waited, the red-bearded man got up, tall and lithe, and left with his fair companion, who looked enchanted, Phillip thought. As the door closed behind them, the broad-faced squat man with black ringlets bestrewing his bumpy forehead called out loudly, "Dere he goes, de 'Lion of Chelsea!' 'Vould you like a baby by me, my dear'?" he mimicked. "Pah! De ''coon of Chelsea'! Pah!" He spat vehemently upon the floor.

"Do you know," said Frances softly, "I rather fancy that there speaks the voice of envy!"

Alice arrived breathlessly twenty minutes later, saying that Timmy had met some friends, and they simply had to have a drink with them in the Cri. Well, here she was, what were they waiting for? How about going to a flick? There was a nice picture on just over the road.

"Hurray," said Phillip. "Let's get a taxi."

Outside on the kerb he hailed a passing hansom.

"But it's only just across the street, my dear man!"

"Come on, it's rather a joke to take a hansom to cross Piccadilly!"

"This is Regent Street, Phil. That curve of buildings was built by Nash. Isn't it beautiful?"

"Who cares?" said Alice, happily. "I want to see Gerald Ames, oh, I love him."

Horse and cab drew in, jingle and clatter. Alice put her foot on the step, but Frances said, "I simply will not allow you to waste your money like this!"

"Well, it's only a bob, anyway!"

Frances took his arm, and an arm of Alice, to lead them across the street; but he pulled back long enough to give the cabby a shilling. Then to the small and dark entrance to the cinema, with no posters outside. The girl in the wooden hut said all seats were full, but there was a box at half a guinea. Before Frances could object, Phillip put down the money, and triumphantly leading each girl by the arm, he followed an attendant upstairs, until they came to a row of doors like hotel rooms along a corridor, but closer together. The attendant opened one door, switched on a small light shaded in pink, and withdrew. There were four chairs, on a dark red carpet. The walls were red, too, with a spangle of tiny gold stars.

He hung up cap and belt, the girls removed hats. Then he was sitting between two curves of cheek below tendrils of hair, feeling romance as music from an unseen piano in the darkness increased the pathos of Gerald Ames, hatless on a horse, beside a dark girl in riding habit, after he had rescued her from her runaway mount, in a park, with fallow deer grazing quietly by. It was a story of love, misunderstanding, and of final renunciation, despite a brutal husband who drank, and beat his dogs with a hunting crop. As the hero rode away alone under the darkening sky, Phillip had to blow his nose. He saw Alice smiling at him in the dimness, and then turned to look at Frances, lest she feel out of it.

The next picture was a riot of fun and laughter, the one and only Charlie in flapping boots and trousers, bowler hat and whangee cane, being bullied, humiliated, and pursued, but always getting his own back in the most extraordinary ways, always polite, ready to smile, defend the weak, crawl through the big fat bully's legs, and give him unexpected kicks on his broad behind. Charlie was a scream.

A wonderful, wonderful evening; how sad that it had to end. If only Desmond could have been with them!

"I do hope your motor will still be there," said Frances, as they walked down to Piccadilly Circus.

"Oh, I never let little things like that worry me."

The Swift stood obediently by the kerb.

"Well," said Frances, "thank you for a most delightful evening, Phil."

"Yes, thank you," said Alice.

"Where can I drop you ladies?"

"We can go by underground."

"I won't hear of it. Jump in." He swung the handle. Passers by looked on admiringly, he felt, as he put on his British warm.

Frances said she lived in Bryanston Square. "If you're sure I'm not taking you out of your way."

Bryanston Square was in darkness. Frances asked him to stop at a corner. "The house is over there," she whispered. "My parents live in the basement. Mother's the housekeeper, so I'll say goodbye here, if you don't mind. Well, thank you very much, Phil, for the lift, and everything. Shall we meet again? Perhaps you can bring a friend? Write to D. and F's will you? And *do* write to Harold! Promise? Cross your heart?"

"Rather! Goodbye."

When the graceful figure, stepping softly in little black boots with fawn box-cloth tops buttoning six inches above the ankle had dissolved in shadow, he drove away round the corner, silent beside Alice.

"If you can take me to Vauxhall station, I can get a train there for Surbiton. The best way is to Hyde Park corner, along Park Lane to Victoria, then down Vauxhall Bridge road and over the river to the station. Are you sure you don't mind?"

"I'd simply love to, Alice, with you as guide and guardian angel," he said, wondering at his boldness.

She snuggled beside him.

They got out of the car by the Embankment, and looked down into the river. A smoky half-moon hung above the leafless plane trees.

"I love London," she said. "Don't you think it's fun?"

"Yes," he said, wanting to kiss her, but would she think him a bounder if he did?

They drove on across the bridge. On the dark platform, while the train approached under a ruddy haze of steam, they waited side by side. He wanted to ask her when they could meet again, but could not make the words come, until she kissed him. How sweet and soft were her lips. He kissed her, gently as before. Her lips fondled his. "You have such soft lips," she whispered.

"Alice, will you write to me, at Grey Towers, Hornchurch?"

"I may. But you'll come up soon, won't you? Can't you bring a friend for Frances?"

"I may not be able to come up often, owing to Zepp. raids. The moon's growing, you see. But I'll write."

The train came in, he put her in a carriage, he kissed her again as she leaned out of the window, then the darkened train was gone.

It was after midnight when he got back to Hornchurch. The house was in darkness, the fellows in his room asleep in their camp beds, including Wigg. He undressed without a light, and got into his sleeping sack, to lie still and live again scenes of the evening, and think of the mouth of Alice gently fondling his own.

He wondered whom he could invite to meet Frances. Milman, the piano player and violinist, would do, a very gentlemanly fellow, but he went always with his chum Thompson; besides, Milman was friendly with Miss Broad, the Colonel's daughter, a nice girl. Then there was a pink-faced amiable captain called Bason, who was second-in-command of the company, under Kingsman. But was Bason too old, being twenty-six? A fellow called Ray, also in the company, had tried to cadge a lift to Town; but Phillip did not want Ray. Ray was abrupt and cheeky, and simply awful with girls, picking up anyone in the streets of Hornchurch and asking one question, as he wore his sloppy trench-cap on the side of his head, pulled down like a pre-war nut's cap; he wore yellow breeches and puttees, and his nails were as dirty as his stories, which Phillip avoided. So he decided to ask Bason, who on the next expedition "up West" sat in the Swift beside him.

Phillip followed the routine of the previous visit almost exactly: meeting behind the shop, down Regent Street, Frances on Bason's lap, Alice's fingers gentling his neck, the bus parked outside the Criterion restaurant, dinner at the same table in the Green Room of the Apex House. After the meal, for which Phillip insisted on paying, they went to the Café Royal, and then to the picture house across the street. Phillip insisted that they were his guests, but Bason quickly put down what he called a bradbury, with a shilling, for two boxes.

"It's against King's Regulations to stand treat to a senior officer, old sport!"

Having already kissed Alice on Vauxhall station platform, Phillip was not shy of her for long; and during the picture, with Mary Pickford and her cluster of curls, he put his lips against her lips at intervals with remote feelings of pleasurable friendship. The time passed happily, and when they had seen the second picture, he tapped on the door of the box next door, and going in, found Bason and Frances sitting sedately side by side. They, too, were ready to leave; and Phillip led the way back to the Café Royal, where, feeling to be quite an old *habitué*, he ordered coffee in the Russian style, in long glasses. There on the plush settees sat the Bohemians in large dark felt anarchist hats, a guarded look in every eye.

The Lion of Chelsea was there, in the same place, with another, older model. This time he was smoking a large meerschaum pipe. He and his companion were drinking hot whiskies with lemon, which they stirred with glass rods. They seldom spoke.

The putty-faced man with the greasy curls and the large gold ear-rings was there, too, looking more unwashed than before, with the same dark woman looking like a gipsy. They left before the Lion this time; and Phillip heard the Lion say, as they went out, "Dirty little East Side Yidd!" to his companion.

Shortly after this Frances said, "I really think we should be leaving. I hate to say it, but Alice has some way to go. It's been such a lovely evening, thank you both so much."

At this, Bason said he would see Frances home in a taxi, and meet Philip in half an hour inside the Café. So Phillip drove Alice to Vauxhall, waited with her for the train to Surbiton, kissed her as she leaned out of the window, saluted, and watched, with his usual feelings of life coming to an end as the red tail-lamp grew smaller and smaller in the darkness.

Phillip and Bason saw the two girls twice more during the next week. Each time the same routine was followed; the gas-lit lane, the Apex House, Cinema, Café Royal, Vauxhall station, Grey Towers in darkness after midnight. Then, lighting the gas in the ante-room, a glance at Orders on the green baize board.

"I say, Bason, look at this! A new battalion is to be formed!"

Bason leaned on his shoulder as he read that officers whose names were posted below would proceed by train from Hornchurch to Northampton on the morrow to form the nucleus of the new battalion under (temp.) Major J. T. Gleeson, with Captain J. d'A. Kingsman as second-in-command.

"Good old Jasper," said Bason. "Now I'll get the company. I can do with some more dough, too. Blime, little old Milman's Adjutant! Bad luck, Phil, you haven't got a company. You should have got here last August. Tommy Thompson has, so has 'Brassy' Cusack. I bet both Wigg and Cox are fed up, neither's got a company!"

In the morning when Phillip came down to breakfast Milman was being congratulated on his engagement to Miss Gladys Broad, the C.O.'s daughter. Remarks at the lower end of the table were various: Wigg's was really dreadful, thought Phillip; while Ray said, with a laugh, "Fancy believing in love! Christ, they've got something coming to them!"

Later Bason said to Phillip, "Ray's old man deserted his mother when Ray was a kid, so of course he doesn't believe in any Ideal."

It seemed a strange remark from Bason, with his unimaginative face, thought Phillip; he felt closer to him, all the same, as he went to congratulate Milman, with others.

"Look at them," he heard Wigg say. "All sucking up to the little shop-walker!"

Chapter 6

CLICKETTING

In the early afternoon the cadre of the new battalion detrained at Northampton, and proceeded to billets in a residential part of the town. Bason suggested that he and Phillip should mess together in one house; they had a bedroom each, and a sitting-room where their meals were served to them by their servants. He said that Major Gleeson didn't know where they were going to eventually; meanwhile the company of less than forty men, all of them fairly young, was to carry on normal infantry routine training.

Company headquarters was in an empty Mission Hall. The men slept on the floor on straw palliasses. Routine inspections of feet and kit were soon over, when both officers and men were free for the rest of the day.

Two new officers had joined Captain Bason's company that morning. One was a tall, powerfully-built man who told Phillip that he had been a buyer of carpets for an Oxford Street store before joining up. The other, a short sturdy man, came from Grimsby, where he had been in the fish trade.

On the afternoon of the day following their arrival—a Saturday —the High Street of the town was thronged almost entirely with women and girls. Phillip, walking alone up the street to explore, passed hundreds of them. They seemed to scurry past, to be in unobtrusive hurry, as though they were fearful of missing something. He glanced surreptitiously at the faces coming his way hoping for one upon which he might fill his sense of vacancy. Reaching the end of the High Street, he felt himself to be on the verge of acute loneliness. Desmond would be back after his course at Waltham Abbey; and here he was, in a strange desolate place, where all the faces of the hundreds of girls walking up and down had the same white, subdued expressions. They seemed somehow to be furtive, mouselike.

With relief he saw the figures of the two new company officers in the crowd on the pavement. He went to them, and suggested that they have tea together.

"What a hot-stuff place," said the other, from Grimsby, appreciatively in his deep voice, as the eyes in his healthy face surveyed the hordes of girls. "Bags of it thrown at you."

"We're the first of Kitchener's Army, apparently, to be billeted in the town," said Paul, the carpet buyer before the war. "Most of these girls work in the boot factories. They get plenty of money now, on Army contracts."

"Aiy, they'll pay for your drinks, an' all," said the Grimsby man, named Flagg. "Last night I clicked with a bird——" With a frankness that slightly repelled Phillip he described his luck. As he turned away a young girl passed, and gave him a soft guilty look.

"Go on, Maddison, you've clicked," said Paul, turning politely to Phillip. His eyes were a bit stony, thought Phillip.

"Oh, I'm quite happy walking about by myself."

"G' a'ht!" said the Grimsby man. "It's here, why not 'ave it? You ought to come with me," he added, generously. "There's bags of it waiting, wherever you look. What did I tell you? I've clicked!"

He set off after a fair-haired pale girl, who had turned to give him a lingering look.

"I can see you are a fastidious man," said Paul. "I don't believe in indiscriminate picking up," he went on reflectively, "I prefer to wait until I see the kind of girl I like, quiet and respectable, with good face and figure, of course. On the other hand, as you've seen, Flagg goes after the first flapper who gives him the glad eye. I found a very nice piece last night," he went on, as though he were describing a Wilton carpet. "She had an excellent appearance, a wonderful soft skin, auburn hair, rich and thick, and took me home to introduce me to her parents. Her boy was killed in the gas attack on Ypres, and she said I reminded her of him. Her people gave me supper, and went to bed, leaving us alone. She got me a drink out of her father's whisky bottle, and sat at my feet on the hearth rug before the fire. She clung to me, and was very passionate. Very nice too." He smiled slightly, but his eyes were still stony. "But perhaps you don't care for taking what the gods provide?"

"Yes, of course I do."

"Well, take an older man's advice, and look for a girl who will take you home. If she comes from a respectable family, you can bet on her being quite safe."

"I know what you mean, Paul."

"One has to use judgment, as in everything else in life." Wigg, complete in pea-jacket and cap set slightly down on one side, sauntered up to them.

"Taking a look at the market?" asked Paul.

With a barren glance at him, Wigg strolled on, cane under arm, hands in flapped pockets.

"Bit stuck up, isn't he? A bit dissipated, too, I should judge. What was he before the war?"

"Tobacco at Smyrna, he told me."

"That explains his contempt for women, and also for me. His type is recognisable among the customers who used to come into my department, on leave from the East. Not quite pukka sahibs. I know the type well. Some of them brought home carpets to sell, and treated us rather as though they were still among dagos."

"Talking about tobacco, how about some tea?"

After tea Paul said he was going to call on his girl of the night before, and take her to the pictures; and alone once more, Phillip wandered up the High Street, wondering if he should go by himself to the flicks; but in the glow under a lamp-post he saw a girl walking alone. She gave him a half-look, and strolled on. Her white hungry face lured him to follow. He kept to a distance of about a dozen yards. At the top of the street she walked slower. He adjusted his pace, reluctant to meet her. She walked beyond the thinning throng of Saturday night shoppers, and stopped under a lamp post, as though waiting for a bus. She seemed nervous, and glanced about her.

At last he said, "Are you going for a walk?"

"If you like."

An iodine-brown moon rose over the roof-tops as they walked on up the street. He tried to see her face; and wondered what to say to her. Her compliant manner made him feel that he might be able to be like the Grimsby fish-salesman Flagg, with his muscular calves and thick thighs, full lower lip and resonant decided voice.

"I don't know my way about this town. Where are we?"

"We're in Gold Street now."

They walked on. "Where does this way go to, d'you know?"

"Gas Street. Down there is the Horsemarket."

They came to another cross. "That's Scarletwell, and down there is Silver Street."

"Silver sounds nice. I'd like to see it." At the end she said, "This is Sheep Street."

"That just about describes it!" He thought of the flock of girls from the factories, baa-baa'ing—and Wigg the wolf and Flagg the ram among them. "This way leads to the public park," she said, a little breathlessly. He took her arm and felt she was trembling.

They walked round an open space. The ground was damp and cold. He walked on, feeling more and more shadowy. They came to the gate, and were back where they started.

"Where else is there to go in this wilderness?"

"There's the churchyard near Green Street."

Side by side they returned down the Horsemarket, and came into Gold Street, where was the churchyard. In the yellow moonlight they threaded in and out of the graves, stopping at last beside a vault with a flat top, against which he leaned, while she stood a yard away, facing him.

"Is this a popular place for couples?"

"I don't know."

"Have you been here before?"

"No, never."

"Have you ever got off with anyone before?"

"I used to walk out with a boy," she replied, shivering.

"You're cold."

"Oh, I'm not really."

"Are you a native of this town?"

"No, my people come from Rugby."

"Have you heard of Rupert Brooke, by any chance?"

"No. Does he live in Northampton?"

"He was at Rugby. The school, I mean. His father was Head Master. Rupert Brooke wrote those famous poems, and died of pneumonia at Gallipoli last April."

"Go on."

Silence followed this remark. He wondered how he could get away without hurting the feelings of the pale face waiting—for what everyone wanted. Or did they? Was love no more than—clicketting? Yet, if only he dared—

"What happened to your boy, if it isn't a rude question?"

"He cast me off."

"I'm sorry," he said, "you *are* cold, I can hear you shivering. Let's walk, shall we. I fancy there's frost in the air."

They walked down to the main street. There he bought her an

overcoat, and while she was still struggling with words of gratitude he said that he had to go, and with a good night and a salute, returned to his billet.

Northampton
4 December, 1915.

Dear Westy

I was delighted to hear from your cousin Frances that you were back in England and getting along well. I have often thought of you and of the old days opposite the Lone Tree ridge, on that morning of 25 September when you copped a few packets. If only your plan to get round the flank had been carried out earlier, I think we should have got through to the Haute Deule canal. Even so, from what I saw of the reserves, we might have been surrounded in a counter-attack, for all their supplies had been lost. The staff work—well, *non est*, or should it be *non fut*? But they had their difficulties, and were hampered higher up, I fancy. Anyway my part was absolutely nothing. I was a mere spectator of something that was already decided.

When I got back on the evening of the 25th, to my billet, I was put on light duty for four days by an M.O. who wanted me, I fancy, as a fourth for bridge in the mess at night. So I was able to go here and there and see parts of the show as a mere spectator. Among other things I came across the Cantuvellaunians, with whom I had "trained" before I came out. I got involved and went over the top with them at noon on 26th. They had no idea of anything; they had also lost their transport, as had all the other 24 battalions of the two reserve Kitchener divisions which came up 12 hours late, unfed, without water, and exhausted by forced marches. As they crossed over the Lens—La Bassée road most of them went down in rows under m.g. fire from Hill 60, Bois Hugo, and Hulluch.

The attack fizzled out and the German Red Cross men let the walking wounded go back, me among them. About that time the entire front gave way; I saw thousands of our troops going back, for miles on either side. Poor devils, they couldn't stick it any longer, first time in, and no water or food. Anyway, they were up against uncut barbed wire, as usual.

Well, Westy, that is all my news. I'm now scrimshanking with what I suppose are pioneer troops, most of them old navvies with dry clay faces rutted by the tracks of cart-wheels, any age up to 70. They get six bob a day, as much as A.S.C. lorry drivers. They booze most of it away on Saturday nights. At least, that was so until now; we are an off-shoot of that lot, and forming anew.

We've only just got shifted here, and nothing doing at the moment; but I am looking forward to seeing Frances again shortly; and also to seeing you, so make haste and get better. I remember you whenever I hear *They Never Believe Me*; I shall never forget that dugout, and the clock that wouldn't stop ticking before Zero hour!

Walking about in this town tonight, I saw the moon rising over the roof-tops exactly the colour of iodine. Then it turned terra-cotta red, the hue of a neck-wound contused by internal bleeding, after death. I expect this is morbid, but I often amuse myself trying to connect one aspect of life with another, by means of similies.

Later, when the moon was higher, brighter, clear of factory smoke, I thought of it shining down upon Le Rutoire Farm and Mazingarbe, throwing long shadows from the crassiers and pyramidical slag-heaps around Loos, and dimming the electric sparkles of musketry around the Hohenzollern Redoubt, as seen from the high ground of Maroc. Isn't it strange what a fascination the front has for one, when one is away from it? Something seems to be drawing one back again; despite all the hell of it when one was there. I feel the romance of war, even in the dead lying on the chalk, to be absorbed again whence, originally, human life came. Our bones are calcium, and were not our original ancestors fishes? So we are cousins to the minute sea-shells that are the chalk-beds of the world.

I must stop before I utter any more bilge! Well, Westy, make haste and get well, and all the best, mon capitaine,

Yours till the last bottle,
PHILLIP.

P.S. Brickhill House, Beau Brickhill, Gaultshire, will always find me. It is my cousin's place.

Captain Bason came back on Sunday night and Phillip asked if he might have forty-eight hours off to go and fetch the Swift. On the way back, he thought he would go to Brickhill, and sleep the night with Polly. Beau Brickhill was, according to the map, only about twenty-five miles from Northampton.

"Sorry, old sport. You've got to attend a course on the Lewis gun, beginning tomorrow. By the way, I've invited Frances down for next week-end, and how about Alice coming, too? The land-lady says they can get a double room next door. I'll pay their fares, of course."

"Well, I'll pay my whack."

Frances and Alice arrived on the Saturday afternoon. They carried longer umbrellas, and wore what they called freedom skirts, with jackets of Crow Blue, a black material which had dark blue sheens on it at certain angles. They wore shin-high boots, a-swing with tassels. After tidying up, as they called it, in the bedroom which Bason had arranged for them to occupy in the house next door, the girls returned to the sitting-room, for what Bason called high tea.

Afterwards they played whist and rummy. Phillip played his trench gramophone. When he put on *The Eternal Waltz*, with its haunting lilt of faraway splendours and romantic loves, Frances and Bason rolled back the carpet, and began to dance. Phillip sat by the gramophone, his ear close to the tinned concave reflector. Alice raised eyebrows at Bason.

"Come on, you slacker," said Bason, kicking him as he passed, "don't leave Alice out in the cold!"

"I can't dance."

"Come, I'll show you," said Alice, holding out her arms.

"But I'm no good, really."

"It's quite easy. Just let yourself glide to the lilt of the music."

"I feel glued to the floor," he said, with a laugh to hide his fear of being clumsy and foolish.

"Come on," said Alice, smiling steadily into his eye, "you're not going to get out of it."

"My shoes have rubber studs on them, and won't glide."

To his relief the motor ran down at this point. He wound the handle, while Alice looked through the case of records, picking out one after another, swiftly to reject disc after disc and half-drop them on the growing pile. He wanted to ask her to be careful, but kept silent. Obviously she thought little of them.

"Haven't you got any foxtrots more up-to-date than Hitchy Koo?"

"Afraid not."

"Got any Winner records?"

"Sorry. Only His Master's Voice, and some cheap Zonophones."

"Do you like only serious music?"

"Well, yes."

She went to the gramophone. "Put on that waltz again. I'll show you the steps. It's simple—one, one two, one, one two. Take off your shoes, you can do it in your socks."

There was a hole in one toe; but he overcame his dread, took off the shoes, and stood trepidant before her.

"This arm goes round my waist, like this." She hid his hand behind her, pressed it firmly. "Now give me your other hand." A whiff of La Rola scent, as in the advertisements of the girl with wind-blown hair, further discomposed him. "Now, follow my steps, one, one two, one, one two. That's right. Only don't hold yourself so stiffly, let yourself go loosely, as though you were balancing a pile of books on your head. Don't laugh!" She shook him, and said, "You're not trying! Now be serious," with a little shake. He felt easier, and thought it rather a joke when he bumped backwards into Bason.

Thereafter the joke was repeated at intervals, the two manœuvring to give one another bumps.

"How about a drink?" suggested Bason, when they were resting. "I've got some gin, and a bottle of crême de menthe. You ladies no doubt will plump for mother's ruin? No? Well, how about some of the green eye of the little yellow god?" as he held up the bottle.

"Only a little, please, Bruce," said Frances. "Not more than a thimbleful, really."

Bason gave them each half a small glass. "What about you, Phil? Mother's ruin?"

"Beer, thanks, Bruce."

They sat round the fire, and sudden complete easiness came over Phillip. He lay stretched out in an armchair, on the small of his back, feet stretched to the blaze, feeling that he had known them all his life. Outside the December afternoon died as it had begun, in dullness; within the room all was contentment. He marvelled anew at the wonderful turn his life had taken; he was living a man's life, every day brought its different adventures.

Seeing that Bason's glass was empty, he arose with Indian smoothness and unscrewed the top of a beer bottle, gently controlling the sneeze of gas, and then with extreme care three-quarter filled the glass which Bason held on his knee, as he lay back on the sofa beside Frances, one arm amiably around her shoulders. His company commander's face, with its expression of happy relaxation as he stared into the flames of the fire, conveyed perfectly his thanks.

Continuing his silent unspeaking glide Phillip went to Alice with the liqueur bottle. One raised eyebrow and a gap between finger and thumb of half an inch beside the small narrow glass held in her hand, a meticulous pouring of the thick green liquid, a little jerk to contain the drip; then in the same flow of silence, save for the flap of flames, he half-filled Frances' glass, and afterwards his own glass, from the beer bottle. Holding them in the spell of his movement, he glided to the gramophone, wound it slowly, put on a record, set it flowing in circular motion as the centre of a dark deep whirlpool, and gliding away, stood beside the aspidistra fern in its brass cup on the stand and held down his eyes as the two voices, one delicate and ethereal, the other deep and tender, brought back memories of "Spectre" West and Y Z night before the battle of Loos.

And when I tell them, and I'm certainly going to tell them
That you're the girl whose boy one day I'll be,
They'll never believe me, they'll never believe me
That from this great big world you've chosen me!

Pretending not to see that Frances' eyes were on him, as he lifted the sound-box from the last groove, and that Alice was patting as though secretly the sofa for him to come beside her, and that her lips were parted, and her eyes, smaller than those of Frances, had the dreamy look he had noticed when he kissed her in the cinema box, Phillip put on the *Liebestod* from *Tristan und Isolde*, and went back beside the fern, to feel the sad beauty of darkness, and the dying music of the sun.

"Play some more, Phil," said Bason.

There seemed to be a feeling of unity, of friendliness and ease in the room beyond ordinary hankering desires, by which usually he had wanted to escape from the dull and terrifying nihilism of being alone. It was dark outside, the flame-light jerked about on the ceiling. He lit a candle beside the gramophone, and played record after record.

"Oh, not that old thing! They play it in every electric palace!"

He felt foolish, and took off Sinding's *Rustle of Spring*.

"How about Tchaikowski? The *Sugar Plum Fairy* isn't bad."

"All right, if it's the best you've got."

"Don't be so beastly, Alice!" said Frances, sitting up.

"Oh, I don't mind," said Phillip.

"Have another crême de menthe?" suggested Bason, lazily, re-crossing his strapped leggings, and jingling his spurs. He yawned without putting hand to mouth.

"Can't we do something? How about going to a dance?" said Alice. "I like light and gaiety." She got up and danced by herself, round the table. Coming to Phillip, she put her arm on his shoulder. He felt proud and grateful, and crossed his arm with hers, on her silky shoulder. He was happy again.

"You want taking out of yourself," said Alice, nuzzling his cheek with her nose.

Bason lit the gas. Then he opened a box and produced three balls and a magic wand. He did things with the balls, holding them between the fingers of one hand, waving the wand, and with a twist of fingers, the balls vanished. There were several variations of this, then he did other tricks, remarking, "The quickness of the hand deceives the eye."

"I saw Chung Ling Soo once saw a woman in half on the stage, wonder how it was done," said Phillip, thinking of Desmond beside him in the sixpennies of the Hippo.

"Like this?" said Alice, doing the splits on the rug before the fire, showing a length of silk stocking. Bason pretended to hide his eyes with a hand. "Ooh," he said, grinning at Phillip.

"Really!" said Frances, as Alice began a *pas seul*, snapping her fingers as though they were castanets. Soon they were dancing again, to the Eternal Waltz. The table was shoved against the wall, and the fun went on, until the landlady appeared with a tray, to lay the table.

"My," she said, "you young people are enjoying yourselves."

Chapter 7

CHRISTMAS 1915

A move to a camp was made the following week. The huts were of asbestos, and cold, for although each cubicle, for two officers, had a cast-iron stove, there was no coal.

"We're in a K3 division now, old sport," said Bason. "What's more, we've got a good chance of going to France next year, perhaps in time for the Big Push! What luck, eh?"

Phillip's room-mate was an amiable, goggle-eyed, half-bald man of about thirty called Lord, who had been selected with him for the Lewis Gun Course. The camp was a big one; huts were going up for miles around. Every morning the two subalterns set off for a large hut where instruction in the new automatic weapon was given.

The mechanism was explained by a staff sergeant, whose sentences never varied. Having seen how it worked, by the pressure of gas behind a bullet coming through a port in the barrel and ramming a piston down a tube to work the feeding and extractor mechanism, while turning the black circular metal drum of ammunition holding 47 rounds which clapped on above the lock, Phillip had no interest in the technical terms. The gun was cooled by rayed fins inside a cylinder taking away the heat of the barrel. Cold air was drawn through the fins by the pumping action of a buffet ring on the muzzle; the gun could jam at various positions of the cocking handle, and these places, and the direct action to be taken to clear stoppages, had to be learnt by heart. Anyone could see that in five minutes; the rest of the jargon, to be repeated until one was a parrot, was a waste of time.

"Come, sir, what comes after 'The action of the cocking handle being drawn back on the rack——'."

"I can make the gun work, sergeant, but not those words."

"Come, sir, have another try. 'The action of the cocking handle——'"

Patiently the staff sergeant repeated the mechanical sentences for the various mechanical details, and in turn the assembled N.C.O.s and officers had to repeat them. The idea was to learn everything by heart, before going on the range to fire the damned thing. Morning after morning was spent in the hut with the verbiage attached to the Lewis gun. Regularly Captain Milman the new adjutant came in, to ask cheerfully how they were getting on. Every afternoon, following tea in the mess, Bason and Phillip set out to walk to the station, three miles away, to catch the train for Baker Street, and an evening with Alice and Frances. Night after night they returned to camp between one and two in the morning.

Christmas was only two days off when it was announced that one half of the officers were to have four days leave including the 25th and 26th; while the other half would go away, on the return of the first half, until New Year's Eve.

Phillip was not among the lucky first batch; he would have to take his after Christmas, as Bason was going to his home in Brondesbury for what he called the festive occasion.

On the morning of Christmas Eve there was a junior officers' test for promotion. Ah, at last, thought Phillip. After a little drill, forming platoons on the left, fixing bayonets, and marching a skeleton company about, their fitness was to be tested by a forced march. They had to cover ten miles in three hours across country, which meant a circular route round several lanes. A captain, a Scotsman from Glasgow, who had been prominent in the Trades Union movement with Colonel Broad before the war, was detailed to take a score of subalterns on the march. They got as far as a small public house down a lane, and then with a grin, the big ruddy faced Captain 'Brassy' Cusack, who was a father of a growing family, said in broad Scots, "Here's a guid wee bothy where I can test your various capacities, gentlemen," as he halted them and knocked on the door.

The landlord opened it, they went inside, and soon the captain was seated at the piano, his pint pot on the lid, playing while Cox, Lord, Flagg, and others roared out popular songs. There they stayed drinking beer and eating bread and cheese for two and a half hours, leaving to get back to camp with ten minutes to spare. Captain Cusack reported to the adjutant, who came out with Major Gleeson, pipe in mouth. After an amused stare around Major Gleeson told the adjutant to carry on, and relighting his pipe, went back to the warm stove in his office.

"Carry on, will you, Captain Cusack," said Captain Milman, and followed the C.O. into the Orderly Room.

"Fall out, you wretched lot of tipplers," said 'Brassy', "ye'll all be pleased to hear ye're fit for promotion."

"Hurray!" cried Phillip. "Up the Jocks, and down with the pints!" as he walked to the mess for tea, lots of tea to take away the saltpetre thickness of the beer on his tongue.

Bason had a bag to take on leave, and he and several others took a taxi to the station. "Room for a little one," he said to Phillip, who had written to Alice to say that he would expect her at the usual time on Christmas Eve at the Apex House for dinner, and would she like to go with him to the Coliseum afterwards. He wrote at the same time to the Coliseum, for two tickets in the front row of the stalls for the second house, enclosing a cheque for £1 as deposit.

In the train to Baker Street Bason said "Frances told me that Alice wouldn't mind being engaged to you, Phil."

This was so unexpected, and complimentary, that Phillip could think of nothing to say in reply.

Engaged to Alice! Every week there were pages of twin photographs, like two pigeon's eggs side by side in rows of nests, of officers and their fiancées, in *The Tatler* and *Bystander*. He sat in the train looking at his polished brown shoes, with slight feelings of pleasurable satisfaction, that he, Phillip Maddison, would have a girl of his own. But what could he say to ask her? He shied away from the thought, and by the time they got to Baker Street, it had passed from his mind.

Saying goodbye to Bason, he went on the Underground to Piccadilly Circus, where the outlet near the Criterion Restaurant was lined with what Bason called hoo-ers.

"Hullo, dearie? Want a sweetheart?"

He walked past several requests, saying cheerfully to each, "No thanks," but at the entrance into the street, by the dim blue lights, a dark girl took his arm, and said in a Scots voice, "Be a guid laddie and take my arm, a bluebottle is watching me, to arr-rest me." She held him with a strong bony arm, and they walked as far as the corner of Lower Regent Street, where she stopped.

"Gi'e me a wee drappie, and then I know a bonny place yonder, in Coventry Street. You can gi'e me what you like. I've seen you fre-e-equently, who are you, Broken Billy? Have ye no cash? I don't mind, for once, Billy."

"Well, thank you very much, but I'm meeting a friend," he explained; whereupon the croodling tone evaporated and in a voice hard and sharp and deadly as a hatpin she swore at him for half a minute, while binding to him with the bone of her upper arm, before becoming a shadow in the night. Perhaps she had dreamed herself almost to death, he thought. Her heart must be broken, beyond tears. Did she still long for true love? Could a *prostitute* love anyone?

Somewhat shaken, he crossed the road, and went into the gilt and marble Apex House, and upstairs to the Green Room, with pleasurable feelings that he would soon be seeing Alice.

When after ten minutes she did not come, he went downstairs to look for her, and after waiting there another five minutes, he returned to the Green Room, and at once saw that Alice was already sitting at a far table with Timmy, her naval commander. The commander was leaning over the table, his face close to hers. She was smiling, as she looked into his eyes. Pretending not to have seen them, he went on without pause to his table, and keeping his eyes down, sat there mournful and perplexed until his waiter came. Hardly knowing what he said, he ordered a bottle of claret and a herb omelette. This he ate, with draughts of wine, followed by toasted cheese, and angels on horseback.

Brandy and black coffee to follow; then, having got the bill, he tipped the waiter five shillings, and forcing himself to appear easy and nonchalant, like a misjudged hero in a magazine story, he walked across the room and out into the street and so to the Café Royal, hoping against hope that she would follow him, and a touching scene of wet-eyed remorse follow.

He swirled in black depression; and after sitting still for some time, turned suddenly to the red-bearded painter at the next table and said, "Please may I speak to you, sir?"

"By all means. Have a drink."

After an interval Phillip said, "I've got two tickets for the Coliseum. Would you—please forgive me asking—but would you care to come with me?"

"Unfortunately I have an appointment," replied the painter,

taking out a gold watch. "Some other time, perhaps. I won't have a drink, thank you. Good luck to you."

Phillip walked to the Coliseum, his hands clenched as he said to himself that this was the end of a friendship.

He hardly knew what went on on the stage before him. There was a long sketch called Potash and Perlmutter, which seemed to amuse the audience; it was all about men with voices like lizards selling ladies underwear, but how it was funny, he could not see. There were songs, the chief being one he knew, from a record of his father's, *The Bride of Lammermuir*, by Donnizetti. There were acrobats, some dancers, and two rather sweet sisters with dark hair, dressed in yellow, who were stars, called Beattie and Babs.

Christmas Eve! Eleven o'clock in London, midnight in Berlin. Now the lighted fir-trees would be on the parapets, voices singing *Heilige Nacht*. Why was he not there, how could it be the same without him, he thought, as he stood to attention for *God Save the King*.

And so to Baker Street station, through darkness without meaning, and the long walk to camp, while he lived in memory upon the frozen battlefield, where the morning star shone white and lustrous in the east.

It was one o'clock when he got to his cubicle, to see Lord lying on his camp bed fully dressed and snoring, an empty bottle of grocer's port and an untasted cup of cold tea on the floor beside him.

Christmas Day at the camp was given over to ghosts, though few knew it: the ghosts of lost childhoods, of lovelessness, of spiritual self denials and self-suppressions so normal that almost automatically most of the herded young men got drunk.

It began with a church parade which was for most a mere marking time, until they should get back to, or away from, camp, and so start the day. Rounds of drinks in the mess, joviality, rivalry, one bad quarrel—Ray calling Wigg a hoary old swankpot and Wigg calling Ray a little squit from the gutter—while others sought to get the insulted to shake hands: which both refused to do with mutual scorn. Christmas dinner, presided over by Major Gleeson, was of roast beef and baked potatoes dripping with fat inside and out; and the fat on the baron of beef was yellow. Lord, who had worked for a butcher in private life, said it was cow-beef, which was the cause of the toughness and the frill-like yellow fat. Lumps of it were left on the sides of plates.

"Goo on," said Major Gleeson from the top table, "eat it up, you fellers. Do you good. Provides 'eat, lines yer guts with plenty o' reserve energy." He put a wodge of the stuff on his fork and flipped it into his mouth, then steadily chewed, while an amiable grin spread over his face. The Christmas pudding tasted of gritty currants and water, its flavour all boiled away. The rich tawny port then began to circulate.

Lord, who shared Phillip's cubicle, was away, so Phillip had the brittle grey hollow—to which came most noises in the other eleven cubicles in the hut—to himself. The window was too high for an emergency, but he found his way out of the door and down the passage and away into the darkness where beef, pudding, and port left their temporary receptacle on the way back to earth.

When Lord returned soon after midnight he found Phillip lying in his bed surrounded by empty cups of tea, and an empty bottle of milk of magnesia.

"Blime," he said, "looks as though you've been enjoyin' yerself, old cock."

"For God's sake put out that horrible cigar," groaned Phillip.

During his four days leave he did not see Desmond, who had been home for Christmas. Mrs. Neville had been away on Boxing Day, she said, and on her return, had found plates and glasses "all over the place", with half-drunk cups of tea and a bottle of whiskey on her drawing-room table *with the cork out*, beside a pile of records and Phillip's trench-gramophone. Her son and Gene, she declared, with laughter, must have had an *orgy*. Well, how was Phillip?

He told her all about the visit to Tollemere, Father Aloysius ("Yes, everyone speaks well of him, Phillip"), the girls of North-ampton and the new fellows at the camp.

"We are no longer navvies, Mrs. Neville, but part of Kitchener's Army, and as such I suppose, will go out when trained to take part in the Big Push everyone is talking about for next summer. Ah well, I shan't mind going back there again, we're all in it together." Then he asked about what was pressing on his mind: had she any news of Helena Rolls.

"I see her coming up on her bicycle, Phillip, from the Hospital, and she always looks up at my window and waves to me. She is a brave girl, she has *pride* you know, but one can see from her face, how it has been refined by grief, that she still feels Bertie Cake-bread's death. Why don't you go in and see her one night? When the old man's away, of course, as he is from Monday till Friday. There can be no harm in it. Take your gramophone with you, why not, and let her mother and Helena hear some of your beautiful music."

"Oh, I daren't! They would think I am imposing on them!"

Instead, Phillip played his favourite *Liebestod* at the open window of the front room at home, as Helena walked by, pushing her bicycle, on two afternoons in succession; but on neither occasion did her footfalls pause behind the privet hedge; she was gone, remaining what she had always been to Phillip, a vision: but now intensified in his mind as Colour and Warmth and Light, great rest, and fullness after dearth.

Freddy's was not the same without Desmond; he knew no-one in the Gild Hall, and dreaded to go there, lest he hear laughter; so he spent the rest of his leave with Mrs. Neville, visiting his grandfather, doing nothing in the sitting-room at home, and going for long walks in the darkness.

On his last evening there arrived a letter from his cousin Willie, now in France after the evacuation of Gallipoli.

Christmas Day this year was somewhat different from the one we shared last year, outside Ploegsteert Wood. This time an order came round that there was to be no fraternisation. To see that this was carried out the Corps commander ordered the guns, both heavies and field, to start shelling at 7 p.m. on Christmas Eve. The old Ger. sent over very little by way of retaliation. It turned out that a deserter coming into our lines some days before had spoken of their pro-gramme of festivities, and exactly at half past ten at night, or half an hour before Berlin midnight, the batteries concentrated on a particular spot where a dinner was to be held, with Christmas trees and candles, and blew it all to hell. The comment of our C.O. was that "the honours of Christmas Eve belong to the British".

When he had read this to his mother in the kitchen, Hetty said, "Perhaps it would be better if you did not show it to your father, Phillip. He is so proud of Willie, you know, and so fond of him. Of course it is very sad that such a thing should have happened on Christmas Eve, but then the Germans have done terrible things to our men, haven't they?"

Without a word Phillip got ready to leave. Then saying goodbye to parents and sisters, he left for London, to catch a late train back to camp.

When he returned he learned that he and Lord had been posted to the Machine-Gun Training Centre at Grantham, and were to "proceed there forthwith, after reporting to the Orderly Room for railway vouchers".

Chapter 8

TRAINING CENTRE

"Gentlemen," said the captain of Grenadiers, who had been hit by eleven German machine-gun bullets during the first battle of Ypres, "you may stand at ease."

Six hundred officers, of all regiments of horse and foot—glengarries, trews, breeches, knickerbockers; puttees, ankle and field-boots, both black and brown, Norwegian-pattern trench-knee-boots, leggings; every kind of tunic button of brass, black composition, and leather—badges of every county in England, Ireland, Wales, and Scotland—yeomanry, infantry, cavalry, bicycle—stood before him in the new large hall built upon agricultural land.

The captain of Grenadiers continued to stand in a position which was the opposite to that of any suggestion of ease. Stiff, upright, withered arm held in a black silk sling, chin resting on a burnished steel cup, above which moustaches were horizontally brushed out, he spoke in a curiously muffled voice.

"You have come here to learn about the Vickers Mark Ten machine-gun, its virtues and limitations, its possibilities as a tactical weapon, used singly and in battery. First you will learn about the mechanism of the weapon, then you will fire it on the range. Later you will learn how to site your guns, always with a view to protecting your infantry against enemy attack, and supporting them in advance, by both direct and indirect fire. It has been decided that the officers of the new formations are to be mounted, so those of you who pass into the new Corps will go through Riding School, before being posted to your companies.

"The armament of each company, to be attached eventually to an infantry brigade, or in the case of cavalry, each squadron to a cavalry brigade, has been laid down as sixteen guns, divided into four sections of four guns, each commanded by a section officer. Four companies, one in reserve, will form a battalion, under a lieutenant-colonel at divisional headquarters. That, in brief outline, is the organisation into which those of you who pass out here will be absorbed.

"Officers will now be detailed into squads, each under its instructor. Will you take the parade, Mr. Bostock."

The stiff figure, converted into an enlarged marionette after being brought back from the dead, returned the salute of the promoted warrant officer from the Hythe Musketry School, and retired to the Orderly Room.

The officers of the new Corps settled into squads of a dozen grouped on wooden chairs around sergeant-instructors, each sergeant sitting at his squad's centre like a nurse with its charge, or a priest with its godling—Machine-Gun, one, Vickers, Mark Ten—guarded between khaki knees above puttees covering ankles and calves in herring-bone pattern. Not for them the common loops, which might, or might not, cling tightly to the outline of the lower leg. These wore, by order of the Corps Sergeant Major, their puttees in a pattern of the *élite*: these were the sergeant instructors of the weapon which could spit forth approximately six hundred rounds a minute, according to the tensioning of the recoil spring, a rate of fire to surpass that of the hitherto invincible German Spandau gun.

Mornings and afternoons wore away slowly, while dull verbal mechanical acquaintance was continued with the steel corrugated cylinder squatting low on three steel legs with spade lugs, concealing within its water-jacket all but the muzzle recoil cup of the barrel which could spit out ten nickel wasps with leaden cores every second at figures in *feld grau*, carrying rifle, stick-bomb and pocket Bible to the counter-attack.

> *This the Weapon*
> *This the Corps*
> *To foe and friend*
> *A crashing bore*

scribbled Phillip in his note-book, with a sketch of batteries of machine guns pouring forth streams of bullets.

"Now if I may turn aside for a moment to ask a question on another plane, gentlemen," said the instructor, as time for the fall-out for lunch was near, "What reference in Holy Writ could be applied today to describe the function of the Vickers Mark Ten machine-gun?"

> *The godling guns*
> *Of Vick and Span*
> *Will end the life*
> *Of everyman*

but the intended picture of corpses everywhere was not completed.

The instructor was young and gentle, belonging to the Artists' Rifles; he was patient and smiling, never varying his soft-voiced encouragement to the forgetful or the disinterested. He was said to be a volunteer lay-preacher on Sundays in a chapel in the industrial part of the town.

"No one knows the quotation, gentlemen?"

He smiled around the circle.

"The answer, which with the question is not part of the official curriculum of course, is, 'Saul hath slain his thousands, but David slew his tens of thousands.'"

The afternoon sessions were given over to lectures, including accounts of the parts played by the machine-gun in the battles of 1914 and 1915. The lecturers were all of them regular soldiers, and maimed: the leader of the veterans was now a major: he bore the name of Slaughter, this Guardee with one shoulder held high, crippled arm, steel-corsetted spine, broken neck, and indomitable moustaches bristling out of the steel cup. Phillip was glad that this officer would not be going back to the front, for, like "Spectre" West, he had really done his bit. It was rather wonderful that the Guards captain was always so pleasant in manner, as though unaffected by his wounds.

After nearly two months' instruction, including riding school and firing on the range, the squad passed out of the Training Centre. G.S. waggons took the kits to another camp, about two miles away. Here amidst trees, stood echelon after echelon of huts of creosoted wood, with roofs of tarred corrugated iron. They were built in what had been a deer park, in the centre of which stood one of the stately homes of England, its southern front covered with Virginian creeper from which nearly all the red pointed leaves had fallen in the fogs and frosts of the year's dead end. He wondered what the family thought of the way their beautiful park had been mucked up. At least the vista in front of the house had been left open, with its trees and sward; but immediately to either flank, and behind it, the concentration of dark huts, their stove-pipes issuing thick coal-smoke, was dense and extensive, each holding forty-eight men with a cubicle for corporal or sergeant; while the huts of the officers' quarters apart in a separate place were of equal size.

He walked round the house, taking care to keep his distance from it, for it was still occupied by the noble owner. Beyond the stables and outbuildings was a cookhouse; and farther on, among trees, and almost enough to fill an entire hut in quantity, was the usual dump of loaves, half carcases of sheep, quarters of bullocks and other food, beside another immense pile of large bully-beef tins. No doubt the lot awaited clearance in the carts of farmers, for their pigs. There had been waste of food at Hornchurch, but practically none at his last camp (Major Gleeson had seen to that); here the pile was ten feet high, and heaving in places with rats.

There were no duties after noon on Saturday until 9 a.m. on Monday morning, so he thought to go home by the one o'clock express to King's Cross. Officers of the new Corps being mounted, the dress regulations permitted field-boots and spurs. So he went to the Army and Navy Stores and bought himself a pair of long brown boots, breeches of fawn cavalry twill, with buttons, not laces; and short-necked spurs with leather straps under the instep, not chains. The straps were specially cut while he waited, for he wanted the spurs to be parallel to the sole of the boot, and high under the ankle bone, not flopping down anyhow as worn by some gunner officers.

Having admired his new appearance in a looking glass, he paid the bill, stuffed the hob-nailed boots in haversack, caught an omnibus to the Elephant and Castle, and changed there for one that would pass Wetherley's garage, while longing to feel the rush of wind past his face as, with *Helena's* throttle open and exhaust drumming harmoniously, the grey road rushed upon him in imagination and he flew upon wheels into the future. Surely the bike would not have been sold?

It was not sold. It stood beside the Swift, a FOR SALE notice on the handlebars. "I think," said Phillip, "I will keep both, after all. But thank you for trying. You must let me pay the garage fees, of course. Did you manage to get a new inner tube? Oh, good. I'll leave the Swift here, then. I'm rather fond of the old bus. I hope the bike will start after all this time."

The engine fired after the plug was heated in a blow-lamp, then he pushed off, and with the old half-roll vaulted into the saddle; and lying low over the tank, accelerated past the police station and over the bridge into Randiswell, the barks of the exhaust being answered by several protesting dogs in the gardens and by their gates in Charlotte Road. A glance up at the flat, to see Mrs. Neville waving from her armchair; and thinking that he would go down to have tea with her, swooped up Hillside Road, and braked hard outside No. 11.

Mrs. Bigge next door was standing, trowel in hand, by her rockery. "I thought it wouldn't be long before I saw you, you know! I said to myself, 'There's Phillip', when I heard the Chinese Crackers coming up Charlotte Road. That's what we call you among ourselves, 'Chinese Crackers'. How are you in yourself, dear?"

"Oh, still not properly outside myself, you know. I hope you and your family are flourishing? I'm just home for a few hours, to look round the old rat-runs."

"What say? I'm getting a bit deaf, Phillip, between you, me, and the gatepost! What was that you said?"

"I said I came just to see the dear old faces, Mrs. Bigge!"

"How very considerate of you, dear. Now if you had arrived five minutes earlier, you would have seen your father, Phillip. He just went down the road with his wheel-barrow and garden tools. He's taken an allotment on the field next to Joy Farm."

"I've got the very boots for him for that job, Mrs. Bigge." He took them out of the haversack.

"My, Father will be pleased," she said, nodding her head. "Now you go in and see Mother, like a good boy."

Hetty too said that Father would be pleased that he had come home.

"He'll be back for tea at five o'clock, why not run round to see him, Phillip, I'm sure he would like you to see his allotment. He's so keen on it. The vegetables will be welcome, too, prices have gone up so much all round. Well, my son, how are you?"

"Oh, all right, thanks. Is Desmond at home?"

"I'm afraid I don't know, Phillip." She tried not to show her hurt.

"Mrs. Neville will know, I'm going to have tea with her. I'll take the boots round to Mr. Pooter now, as you suggest, and admire his new allotment. Poor old Father, he used to tell us children such interesting stories, years ago, when he was always pretending to be a farmer, and saying what he would do with the crops in this field, or the tillage in that. Then the trams came, and the elms were cut down, and the fields grew bricks and mortar, he said, and then he didn't do any more farming in the fields beside the road to Cutler's Pond, on our Sunday morning walks there. And your little boy you tried to hush hush hush when he tried to say this and that grew into a string of Chinese Crackers."

Hetty was startled by the way he had spoken. He seemed to be almost a stranger; yet what he had said explained most, if not all, of Dickie's life. Was it by accident that Phillip spoke like that: or was he beginning to understand, to feel sympathy for others?

"Yes, Father was very keen on the land when he was a young man, but it was not possible, owing to family matters."

"Grandfather Maddison was a bit of waster, wasn't he? What in those days was called a ne'er do well? Something like me, only more so? Well, Lupin will buzz off now and visit Mr. Pooter, on his farm at last! Did Father ever say anything about that book, *The Diary of a Nobody*, by the way?"

"He said it was too much of a lampoon for his liking. Don't mention it, will you, or he may think that we are laughing at him, and feel hurt."

"But you think the book funny, don't you, Mum?"

The childhood address made her exclaim, "Sonny, it is the funniest book——!"

They laughed together; then he said he would go round to see Father, and come back to tea. She was happy once more; her son wanted to have tea in the place which, for the mother, was not truly home while her children were away from it. Indeed, she thought of them all the time; she had hardly any other life, except when, occasionally, she went to London during the day, with her father, and sometimes, Aunt Marian. "But don't call me Sonny, d'you mind, Mum?"

"Very well, Phillip."

The next afternoon, a Sunday, he left for London Bridge and the Great North Road by way of Islington and Barnet, where he arrived at four o'clock. Grantham was still one hundred miles north, and that meant the last part of the journey in darkness. The container of his carbide lamp held only ash, and all shops would be closed.

Why not spend the night at Polly's? At the fork of two roads he stopped, undecided whether to press on, or to turn left-handed for St. Albans, ten miles distant, and so to Beau Brickhill. He tried to thrust away Polly's challenging face, in order to think out a plan. At what time should he get up the next morning in order to arrive in camp for breakfast; and he must not miss Riding School, for those passing out well were sure to be chosen as transport officers for the new companies; and that meant a very good chance of seeing out the war in France. If he left Brickhill at dawn, he would be all right.

The motor-bike ran well, drumming between the hedges of the narrow, empty road of Sunday afternoon, coming to St. Albans in fifteen minutes. Then *Helena* was raising the dust of Watling Street lying towards distant downs; and passing through the small town of Dunstable, he continued for a few miles until the turning that led through the village of splendidly noble houses and cottages, and so to the Duke's park; and leaving behind the wall of dark-red brick, with massed trees behind its coping, with cock pheasants crowing to the drum-like beats of the open exhaust, sped down a sandy lane, over the well-loved bridge with the Satchville brook below, up the hill, and so to Beau Brickhill, to turn through the gate into the gravelled courtyard as evening was settling into night.

"Goodness gracious me, you gave me a shock, suddenly appearing round the corner, I was at that very moment thinking about you," exclaimed Aunt Liz. "Well, I am sure everyone will be very pleased to see you. Polly has gone for a walk with Percy, he's home on leave, you know, and goes back to barracks tomorrow, and then to a battalion at Catterick Camp in the North. Come in, my dear boy, and warm yourself by the fire. Mother is asleep, she often takes a nap, poor old lady, she wanders a bit now and then in her mind. I didn't light the lamp, as Grannie prefers the twilight."

"So do I, Aunt Liz."

"Yes, it is very restful. Now you go and make yourself at home, Phillip, while I lay the tea. I'm longing to hear all your news, and you must tell me all about Mother, and the girls, and Uncle Tom —all of you, in fact. Now sit by the fire, dear, and warm yourself."

He went softly into the little dim parlour leading off from the breakfast room. The thin figure of Grannie Thacker, in lace cap and black bodice and skirt, was upright and still on a horse-hair chair by the grate. He stood, leaning against the wall, watching her. After a few moments he realised that the figure was not asleep, for a craky voice said, as though in reply to a question, "You are quite right, Jim, Eliza is of course very worried, but we must keep cheerful for her sake, especially. We are all in the Lord's keeping. And to think that the Kaiser is a grandson of the Good Queen! Did he never learn from her that blood is thicker than water?"

Hands on elbows crossed on her thin bosom, she looked towards him with tiny points of flame in the eyes of her shrunken face, and said in a mourning tone, "I hear too, that a lot of men from the village have fallen down, the ones who joined up early, when the Duke first made his call. Why, is that Percy? How tall you look. Sit you down on the sofa, and warm yourself, do."

Phillip sat back in a corner of the sofa, his face part turned away.

The old lady, upright in the wooden stays which had belonged to her mother, and which were worn with filial love, gave a long sigh. "I can call to mind the time when the champion team of Clydesdales were taken from my father's farm, for the Russian war. The carter went with them, although he had a wife and children, and 'listed, specially to take care of them, but neither he nor his team ever came back. Now the Russians are with us. Ah well, our lives are in the hands of One Above. Do you say your prayers, Percy, every night?"

"I'm Phillip! I've just arrived! How are you?"

"My, my, it's the little fellow! How you have grown to be sure."

"I've come to pay you all a visit."

He had to speak loudly, for she was getting deaf.

"I have been wondering how many battles have been fought round about here! There was one at Barnet, another at St. Albans, but I suppose all the fields in England were once nothing but blood and acorns, you know, great forests and sabre-toothed tigers, mammoths, moose, and deer, before the clearings and the settlements, which were then fought for by people with different ideas of what life should be. Well, Grannie dear, I must not disturb you, I think I'll go and look for Percy," he said, meaning Polly. When she arrived with her father and brother he found he could not say anything to her.

"So you ride a horse now, Phillip?"

"Yes, we are mounted troops, Uncle Jim. When I pass out of the riding school, I hope to be posted as transport officer to a company. There are to be sixty-four animals—riding horses, light draught horses, and mules, in each company. When all of Kitchener's Army is out, the scale will be turned. Our artillery, too, is increasing greatly. By the way, I must leave here tomorrow at crack of dawn. I daren't risk being late for the riding course."

"Do you think the war will end this year, then, Phillip?"

"It's quite possible," he said, knowing tiny little Aunt Liz's anxiety about her son. "You're wearing a nice pair of breeches, Percy."

Percy Pickering looked down at the upper parts of his legs with approval.

"I got them for him from Murrages, from an advertisement in the *Chronicle*," said his father. "Then you consider they are a good cut, Phillip?"

"Very good," said Phillip, concealing his thoughts of the laces, the poor quality of Bedford cord, the sloppiness around the knees.

"I remembered what you told us when you came home last time," went on Uncle Jim, blowing smoke from his calabash, "about the transport being more or less out of the thick of the fighting, so I thought it advisable to get a pair of breeches for Percy. Then he will already be equipped if a vacancy occurs in the transport of the battalion he is joining."

"Good idea," said Phillip, brightly, seeing their trusting faces upon him. "The thing to do is to apply as soon as he gets there, and in his spare time help in the horse-lines, without making himself too much of a nuisance." He felt sad that they should be so helpless as to depend on him for advice to save Percy's life. "Percy is still a bit deaf from his childish illness, isn't he? It might also help if he pretends he can't hear the orders on parade. Then they might bring him into the transport."

"You mean he must practise deceit, Phillip?"

Aunt Liz did not seem happy, as she looked up at him from her small height. She was like a child, rather as Mother was. They had never really grown up: Father, Mother, Mavis, Aunt Dora—he saw them all in the shadows of their own pasts—disappointed, downcast. He saw them all in their different ways trying to straighten out the tangle of their thoughts. The soldier, shot and on his knees, had got beyond the tangle.

"Well, now you know what to do, Percy," said Uncle Jim, trying one last match to the ashes of his pipe, as a flash of optimism rose in him. He looked at Phillip.

"What time must you be off in the morning, did you say?"

"I'd like to be away by five o'clock."

It was arranged that Polly should have the alarm clock and set it for half-past four; then she would get him his breakfast, and he could leave without disturbing any of the others.

"And now," said Aunt Liz. "We must all have tea, for we want to go to evensong. You'll come, Phillip? That's right. I've got some of your favourite sausage rolls, you must be very hungry, so come and sit at table, your old place is waiting for you."

As they were walking back from church, behind the others, Phillip said, "Don't let's waste time arguing about the Duke, Polly. You think he's selfish and keeping people from building on his land, but I think it should be conserved. Anyway, I prefer what my friend 'Spectre' West says about the Duke, for he knows him personally, and not merely from village gossip."

"I say the Duke is thoroughly selfish, so there!"

"And I say he is not! He has been very good to everyone in the Gaultshire Regiment. The Duke, or his forbears—the Duke in fact, for the dukedom is a position, more than a mere man—built all the schools and churches in his villages, too, in the past. And the countryside is beautiful because the mob is kept out. You ought to see what the mob has done to the bluebell woods in Kent, now part of the County of London—tearing down fences and trees, and leaving the place squalid. No, you leave the Duke alone, for you don't understand him."

They turned in at the gate. "Let's play billiards."

"I'm going to help mother get the supper."

He caught her and put his arms round her. "You're going to stop with me."

"Who do you think you are?" She broke away. He let her go.

When he came level with her again she was standing outside the french-doors leading to the billiard room.

"Come on, let's have fifty up before supper."

"Why should I?" said Polly, with a toss of her curly head. "I dislike the Duke. He's made his eldest son an outcast, because of his radical opinions."

"Well, don't make me an outcast, I've got radical feelings, so how about coming into my bed tonight."

"That I will not!"

He lit the gas, chose a cue, set out the balls, spun a coin, and said, "Heads or tails?"

"How d'you know I want to play?"

"Because you are such a sport. That's what I like about you. I'll start. There you are, a nice leave, it's your stroke. No mercy! I've played a bit since I saw you last."

"I don't believe a word you say, so there!" said Polly, as she took aim. Her ball rebounded from one cushion to another, and returned diagonally down the table into the area of baulk with just sufficient momentum to kiss the red and the white. He put two on the board for the cannon. She got two more cannons; six in all.

Then she potted the red; and with following stroke, potted his white, leaving her ball in baulk.

"That will teach you!" she said. "Now kindly put the red on its spot for me. I haven't finished."

"Very sporting of you," he said sarcastically.

She went in off the red, leaving it in position to go in off again; and again; and again, until she had made eighteen. Then she left her ball and the red in baulk.

"Your turn."

He could not get the angles, so started to slosh the balls.

"You're not trying to win, are you?" she said, poking him in the ribs with her cue. He twisted the cue from her hands, and put it down to seize her. She twisted free, then started to box him, standing without flinch before his blows of pretence. Again and again she poked him in the ribs. He gave up.

"No man can fight a woman, slippery as an eel. By the way, did you know that female eels live seven or eight years in fresh water before going back to the sea, to breed?"

"Do they now!"

"The male eels spend their time skulking in the estuaries, afraid to go up into fresh water, in case they are gobbled up by the beastly omnivorous females."

"That's all you know! Eels don't lay eggs, so there! They come from horsehairs in the brook. Everyone knows that."

"So the eel's father is a horse?"

"You're just being a naughty little boy!" Polly could not help laughing. "You always were what Uncle Dick called a prevaricator."

"Eels never prevaricate, they glide away."

"You ought to know. You are slippery if anyone ever was."

"I can't help slipping on sea-weed."

"Really! What will you say next?"

He moved towards her. She moved away. "I don't want to have anything at all to do with you, until you cease being the silly little child you always were when you get into one of your moods, so there!"

"Good! Then how about another game? Only play properly this time. Take the game seriously!"

"I like that, from you!"

Polly was off her stroke, while he felt he had never played better. He won, just before the door opened and Percy and his parents came in, to say that supper was ready.

The door of his bedroom opened and Polly in her nightgown came silently on bare feet. He noticed how her toes were widely spread, and thought of sea-shells. She stood waiting, hugging herself lightly, standing on the carpet, until he opened the bedclothes beside him, and said, "Come on, get in."

She got in, and sat up beside him. He had no feeling for her now, although he had desired this moment ever since turning off the Great North Road that afternoon. He settled his pillow on the thick, long feather bolster, and lay back with hands behind his head.

She continued to sit up in bed, looking down at him as he lay on his back. At length she said, "Well, I think I'll go back now."

She pulled back the bedclothes, and put out a leg. The sight of her broad foot, with the big toe she could wiggle almost like a thumb, made him put his arm round her ribs, to prevent her going. Then sitting up, he examined the back of her neck in the light of the candle reflected from the walls, lifting up the black curls falling on the quilled shoulders of her nightgown.

"Let me shift the candle. I want to look at you properly."

Her eyes were smoke-grey, her nose looked to be slightly flattened on her face, due to the wide-spaced nostrils; her lips were full and red, the chin strong, the ears small and well-shaped.

He unbuttoned her nightgown, while she said, "What d'you think you're trying to do?" with the slight toss of her head, as when defying her father sometimes.

"I said I wanted to look at you. Keep still."

He opened the neck of her gown, and pulled her arms free, then worked the nightgown off her shoulders to her waist. It was strange to think of Polly as a woman. He put his lips to her breast, but drew back, feeling that he was being unmanly and weak to have the wish to be a small child. Yet the sight of her sitting there so calmly drew him back to her breasts, although they were not as he had imagined a hundred times, but ordinary flesh, and quite firm, although silky to the touch. They were pinky-brown at the tip, little rosettes in bud.

"I suppose you've got what is called a good figure?"

"I've never thought about it."

Her back looked broad and strong, tapered curiously to a small waist, and her belly was flat and hard when she filled her lungs.

"I've got good muscles, you know," she said, holding out a thin arm and drawing up her fist. "You feel."

"Quite a bicep," he said, amused at the idea of Polly wanting to be strong, like a boy. "Do you do much gym at school?"

"Yes, and also hockey and basket ball. And we play cricket, and have lots of swimming in the bath beside the river."

"Good for you, Polly." He felt warm towards her, her boyish ribs were slender, as she sat there, looking at him. He drew his hand over her shoulder and arm, and felt the bud of a rosette becoming hard. Then lying down, he put his head against her ribs and nipped a fold of her skin between his lips and held his face hidden, while his feet began to work, as though his thoughts were dissolving through his splaying toes. He breathed out a long sigh, and lay back, one arm round her ribs, while she leaned over and gave him a light kiss on his head.

"I wish I'd learned boxing, and played rugger at school. It makes you hard and daring. You're quite brave, really, aren't you? I always was a bit amazed at the way you stood up to Uncle Jim when he got angry with you. You never gave way, but faced him with your chin up. So did Doris, when Father attacked her for saying she would kill him if he made Mother cry. She was only about four, but she had the courage to defy him, saying she was going to kill him for making Mother cry. He gave her a beating, but Doris refused to cry."

"Doris said Uncle Dick could be very angry, but he was always very nice to me."

"I'll tell you something awful about myself when I was a boy. I planned one night to get you to come for a walk with me, and meet Jack Hart, who was later expelled from school for taking out girls from the High School into the Rec. at night. I wanted you to meet him in the sheep-fold on the Hill. I had a sneaking fascination for him at that time, I was very small and thrilled by the fact that he had developed into a man."

"I think lots of boys feel like that at times."

"I'll say one thing for you, Polly, you're a jolly good sport."

He turned and put his hands on her ribs. The small bones felt so delicate, she was only a little girl after all. He exulted as he leaned over her to blow at the candle, but he lost feeling in the darkness. He raised himself up to feel for the matches.

"I like looking at you."

As the flame rose guiltily on the wick, he looked down at her neck, with a beginning of lust; at her eyes grey as smoke; at the ridges of her collar bones rising out of white flesh, the suggestion of blue veins on her breasts. He put his hands on her shoulder bones and held her, thinking himself to be Jack Hart, and seeing her teeth, her lashes, the way her hair grew off her brow, the curve of her cheeks, he began to enjoy the feeling that she was his victim, and he would pay her out for being a girl.

"Don't forget the alarm, will you. I mustn't get back late to Grantham."

When she had gone he blew out the candle, pulled back the curtains and opened the window; and then, getting back into bed lay stretched out diagonally across it, and with a deep sigh of peace, as on the first night of coming out of flooded trenches for a rest, sank away into sleep.

Polly returned, dressed in her school gym-clothes, while it was still dark. He was awake at once, and alert. When he had got out to dress she went downstairs to fan the embers in the hearth until the dry sticks burst into flame; and soon she had slices of green sizzling bacon in the pan on the trivet. Then she went to find two eggs in the hen house.

Phillip washed under the pump in the scullery, and sat down at the table, to sip tea while the eggs were popping. He told her to take the heavy cast-iron pan off the fire, and let them sizzle in the heat of the iron.

It was half-past five when, trench coat buttoned to neck and flying helmet strapped under chin, he went out to the yard; and the first thing he saw was a flat back tyre.

"Damn Wetherley! I bet he didn't feel inside the canvas for the flint which punctured the old tube! Or else I've picked up a new one, or a nail. My God, I haven't any puncture outfit, either! I can't get back in time for parade at nine o'clock. What, you haven't got a puncture outfit either? Anyway, someone's pinched my pump. What a fool I was, not to have looked when I got the bike back! I'll have to wait and get it mended, and report sick when I get back, that's all."

They returned to the house. He felt tired. She suggested he should lie down on the sofa in the billiard room, while she made a fire. Afterwards there was a smudge on her cheek, and she looked such a neat little girl as she brushed up the fallen ashes of yesterday's fire, to leave the grate tidy, that he told her to come to him, and when she came he put his arms round her and drew her upon the sofa beside him. She was warm and passive, but when she closed her eyes he thought of his holiday in Devon just before the war, of himself watching anemones in rock pools left by the tide, as they waved their tentacles to catch small shrimps, little fish, and other underwater creatures. When he had touched an anemone, its tentacles had clung a moment, as though to draw in the tip of his finger; then they had closed, and he had stroked their softness.

According to Darwin, all life began in the sea; the ancestors of man were fish-like creatures. Was that why he was now thinking of Polly as an anemone, and of himself as a little silvery fish being drawn to its doom in a sea-pool?

Chapter 9

A SPOT OF LEAVE

When he got back to camp in the afternoon Phillip went to the Medical Officer's hut and said he did not feel very well.

"How are you sleeping?" he was asked, after his pulse had been counted.

"Not very much, doctor."

"I see that you were invalided for dysentery in 1915. Any trouble now?"

"None, doctor."

"Any cough?"

"Now and again, doctor."

"Do you sweat at night?"

"Occasionally doctor."

"Let's look at your chest." Knock-knock, knock-knock. "Turn round." Knock-knock. "H'm, sounds like a dull patch on this lung. Anyway, don't let it worry you. If it does not clear up, now the fine weather's coming, we'll send you to hospital for observation. You're run down." He plucked an eyelid. "I'm giving you seven days' leave, meanwhile." Phillip made his voice level as he said, "Shall I report to the Orderly Room, doctor?"

"No need for that. My returns for the day are just going in, I'll add your name to them. Now take things easy. Don't go gadding about too much."

"No doctor. And many thanks."

Jubilantly he returned to his quarters to pack a haversack with pyjamas, shaving kit, and gramophone records. He would miss the riding course, but there would be another. Would he miss going to France in time for the Big Push? No hurry; if it was to be anything like the last one, there would be another.

Gramophone tied on flapper bracket, he sped along the Great North Road, flying south in brightening spring weather to the steady beats of the exhaust, past fields of winter wheat whose plants were not yet tall enough to hide the clods left by November's harrowing, and other fields where teams of horses with cultivators, rolls, harrows, and drill were putting in the spring oats and barleys. Down a hill into Stamford, with its sharp turning upon narrow bridge over a river with a glimpse of rushes and swans, and ninety-two miles to London. A whole week's leave, on and on and on, no time for tea, onwards to Stilton and Buckden and Eaton Socon, a stop at Baldock for more petrol and oil, and London under forty miles away. He was beginning to remember names on the white-painted milestones, the names painted in black—Stevenage, Broadwater, Knebworth—past which the exhaust thudded sweetly and steadily. Green pastures and parks and great houses, southwards the road curving and stretching through villages and past coppices and woods where rooks were noisy at their ink-blot nests, onwards to Barnet, on the same road where had marched the Saxon army and later the barons with their men-at-arms, their bowmen and heavy Norman horses; down the cobbled hill from Barnet, with its drop on the other side to the vast level place where Barnet Horse Fair was held. Would he be home by nightfall, or should he stop and get a tin of carbide? He would risk it; his O.H.M.S. plate would get him past any copper.

Onwards to Finchley and the trams, and so into the City of London, with its drays and taxicabs and bowler-hatted civvies; across the sett-stoned bridge over the Thames; past the grim stations and on down to the Elephant and Castle and the Old Kent Road; over Nunhill and down into the Wakenham Road; and dullness taking the place of former hope and enthusiasm; trepidation, a flash of hope, as he banged up Hillside Road.

"Well, Phillip, this is a surprise! A week's leave, have you? Rather unexpected, isn't it?"

"You never know where you are, in the Army, Father."

"I'm afraid I've cleared away tea," said Hetty, "but I will soon boil you an egg."

"No thank you, Mother. I'm not really hungry. I'll see you later."

They heard the front door close quietly behind him.

"H'm," said Richard, as he picked up his newspaper.

Five minutes later the strains of *A Broken Doll*, followed by *O, that we Two were Maying*, came from Mrs. Neville's open window, while Phillip drank tea and ate buttered toast with bloater paste.

Afterwards, hearing that Desmond and Eugene were playing billiards in the Gild Hall, he went on down to the High Street, to surprise them; but the manager said they had left a few minutes before; so he returned through the foyer, with its goldfish pond and domino players, and crossed over to Freddy's.

Opening slightly the door of the saloon bar, to peep in, he saw Desmond and Gene standing one on either side of a girl who was perched on a stool by the bar. He saw her back only until she turned to smile at Desmond, when he noticed her white even teeth and large china-blue eyes. Freddy saw him standing there, but kept an impassive face when Phillip put finger to lips, before slipping through the door, to creep towards the stained glass partition of the billiard room. As he went softly across the floor he noticed that the peep-hole was open, revealing a section of face with buck teeth and sunken expressionless eyes. He pretended not to have seen that Detective-sergeant Keechey and his column-dodging bowler-hatted umbrella-carrying nark were spying there, as they sipped large hot Irish whiskey at Freddy's expense.

Turning his back to the unpleasant nearness of watching eyes, he saw the girl's face turning in his direction. She wore a little dark blue straw hat, with a veil hanging from its brim. Behind the spotted net two large blue glistening eyes and a loose smiling mouth regarded him. He returned the limpid look with pleasure. Then Gene, turning to see what she was looking at, recognised him. A light of welcome came upon his sallow face.

Freddy now tipped his straw boater, and said with extreme politeness, "I think you know both these gentlemen, sir?" as he played his part in the comedy of surprise. Then, lest the subtlety of his action be missed, he explained, "I perceived that you wished to be incognito pro tem, in a manner of speaking, so I refrained from my customary welcome to a customer of this 'ouse. May I introduce you to this young lady? Miss Lily Cornford, this is Mr. Maddison."

Desmond gave Phillip a sardonic, sharing look, as much as to say, Look what we've found! The girl, despite the sophistication of veil and rolled-gold chain with bangles on the white wrist of the hand she held out to Phillip, a little uncertainly, as though ready to withdraw it at a look of disapproval, seemed to be bash-ful—or a little timid. She was all blue eyes and lips loose with smile, and looked at him without speaking—could she be a little bit tiddly? The blue eyes behind the faint dark net were slightly alarming, so was the tall white neck and golden hair coiled under the straw hat with a spray of forget-me-nots circling its dark blue crown. Unspeaking, she let her hand remain in his; her gaze still a little unsteady, like her lips.

"How do you do," he said, then turning to Desmond and Gene, one on either side of the figure on the stool, "so I see you know these two pals of mine, who are covering your flanks. How are you Des? By Jove, I'm glad to see you and Gene! I've got a week's leave! Drinks all round, Freddy!"

Desmond, now shaking with ingroaning laughter, lifted his nose, to draw Phillip to one side, while Gene took advantage of this to lay an arm possessively upon the girl's shoulder.

"I nearly burst out laughing when you said that Gene and I'd been covering her flanks. In a way you're right! She's a damned fine girl!"

"I've had some sport with Polly, too. Now I've wangled a week's leave! How about you?"

"I've got four days. I'm in for a transfer. I've applied for a tunnelling company in France. I want to be in the Big Push before it's all over."

"In the Training Centre we reckon it will start in three months' time, when the first hundred machine-gun companies are formed."

"Our sappers are digging shafts for the mines now. I don't want to miss anything."

"I'm quite keen to get back, too, now I'm with mounted troops. Who is this bird?"

"Gene met her first, but now I've clicked with her. We're going to the second house at the Hippo."

"Oh, I see."

Phillip felt dismayed. Although in their friendship so far he had been frank, or natural, with Desmond in most things, both youths had avoided the subject of girls; indeed, with the exception of the phantasmal Helena Rolls, none had come between them.

"Well, so long," said Gene, raising his boater. "I've got two birds to see in the Gild Hall. Why don't you come and meet them, Phil?"

Phillip lingered, hoping that Desmond would suggest that he join them for the Hippodrome; but when nothing was said, he bade them goodbye and crossed the road to the Gild Hall, which was now three-quarter filled with skittering groups of territorials of the local battalion of the London Regiment, locally known as the Gild Hall Brigade, and more pairs of flappers seated at tables.

Gene was lolling back in his chair, obviously fancying himself, too, as he tilted his closely-woven straw-hat partly over one eye, holding his silver-topped ebony stick in yellow-gloved hands, while talking to two young girls, who said they had changed out of uniform of the High School, and this was their second visit to the Hall. They were expectant and excited, and exchanged glances whenever Gene or Phillip spoke.

Gene explained that he had been in the Army, but had been discharged because his feet had given way under prolonged marching. "In my country, we ride horses. For ten generations my people have been soldiers, always on horseback. Only peons walk; we ride. So here I am, since the Cavalry is full up."

Phillip began to feel embarrassed when Gene, fitting his eye-glass, began to talk of his flat in Town, and would the girls like to visit him and his friend there. Gene had an attic floor in West-bourne Terrace, a seedy row of houses drab with soot and flaking paint near Paddington Station, which he rented for fifteen shillings a week.

He wanted to get away from this man-about-town talk with two schoolgirls, one of whom had not yet started to develop.

"I'll be back in a moment, I've got to see someone," he said.

He crossed over the road and walked to Freddy's, but Desmond was not there. Loneliness came to him, so for old time's sake he had a large whiskey and stood Freddy a sixpenny drink from the land-lord's own special inverted bottle of water. Freddy, leaning over the bar, and moving his eyes only towards the stained-glass par-tition, said, "Your friend came back here after you left to ask me about what Keechey had on Lily, and then went out again. I thought you ought to know that Keechey has got his eye on her. She used to be one of his pieces, but she won't have anything to do with him now. He's got a down on her, and is trying to get evidence for a pinch for soliciting, also he says she's not eighteen. I'm cleared against serving liquor to her, as I don't know her age."

Freddy stood upright and was again the landlord. "Well, your very good health, sir!"

He went away to serve a customer, and when he came back Phillip said, "Tell me, Freddy, is Lily a tom?"

The landlord shook his head decisively. "Not within the mean-ing of the act. She works in Nett's Laundry, on the lower side of

Randiswell Bridge. Of course, I don't say she doesn't have a bit of fun at times, but that's her business."

"Quite. Does she often come in here?"

"Not often. Usually she goes into the Bull. It wants forty minutes to the second 'ouse at the Hippo, so you might catch them there."

"Well, see you later, Freddy."

"The pleasure will be mine, sir," said Freddy, tipping his hat an eighth of an inch from behind.

He felt unhappy at Desmond's apparent indifference, after he had come as fast as he dared all the way down the Great North Road. Desmond, his great friend, could forsake him almost at a moment's notice, for someone he had met in a pub. But he must think with his head, as Father Aloysius had said, and not with his feelings. Very well.

Until that evening, Desmond had not seen him for some time. During that period Desmond had been living his own life, as he had been living his. Why then was he worrying? Because Desmond had said nothing about meeting him again? Yes; Desmond was all his true life: Helena Rolls was an Ideal, far above life.

He went into the Bull, and saw the girl sitting on a long padded seat beside Desmond. Hoping that they would invite him to sit with them, he stood by the bar, and ordered whiskey, while keeping his back to the two on the long seat by the wall. Beyond the row of bottles on shelves in front was a looking glass, and while he was drinking, he saw the two get up and go out through the door.

I see, he said to himself, I see. I am not wanted any more. It is not true, of course; I am pretending to myself, pretending that my best friend does want me, except when he cannot get anyone better.

He saw Lily's eyes, blue as the water reflecting the summer sky in the Lake Woods; and remembered that Desmond had taken Gene there to fish the secret lakes, to which he had never taken anyone else except Desmond, although the permit was made out to Mr. Phillip Maddison *and friend*. Now my great friend has forsaken me because of a girl and when I go to find him to warn him that the unscrupulous and revengeful Keechey is waiting to find someone with whom to charge Lily with prostitution, he practically cuts me dead before I can even tell him why I came.

He left the Bull, and walked round the Recreation Ground, hoping to see there the familiar figure of his friend, hoping that

Desmond, seeing him, would respond with their old boyhood whistle.

He walked round again, and frenzy rose in him as he left the darkening, friendless place that was without a soul.

Phillip had had little food since breakfast, sixteen hours before; he did not know that his feelings of desolation came from physical exhaustion.

Trying in vain to control his feelings, he left the dark and silent grounds by the river and hurried to the place which was now more his home than the house of fear where his boyhood had been spent.

"Freddy, Freddy, you've no idea how glad I am to see you! Please have a real drink with me, Freddy!"

"Are you feeling all right?" asked Freddy. "You look as though you've seen a ghost."

"Give me a quartern of whiskey, Freddy, and have one for yourself."

"Never touch it, sir. But I'll have a gin and peppermint if I may—out of a real bottle this time! Are you sure you want a quartern? Well, you know best," tittered Freddy. "Only you'll have to have it in a large glass!"

Where could he go? To Beau Brickhill? He had no tin of carbide. And there was something about Polly he did not like. Back to Grantham? Blinding through the night up the Great North Road? They would think it strange if he did, and the M.O. might get hauled over the coals. He must find Gene—there might be time before the Gild Hall closed. Swallowing the nauseatingly strong liquid, he went out and to his immense relief saw the figure of Gene getting on a 'bus outside the Conservative Club. He ran after the 'bus, and holding to the brasrail, leapt upon the footboard.

"Thank God I've found you, Gene!"

"I waited for you more than an hour after those two birds had gone home. Where did you get to?"

Phillip told him, and Gene said, "You should have come back to me. I've tentatively fixed up with the girls to have tea next Saturday at my flat."

"But they are only kids," said Phillip, feeling unhappy and reluctant.

They got off at the Obelisk and Phillip walked with Gene to the junction station. Having seen him on his train to London, he returned by way of Mill Lane to the Hill, and down the gulley to his home, walking on tip-toe through the gate, letting himself in with his key, silently. On hands and knees he went up the stairs, out of habit, and along the passage to his room, feeling hopeless as he undressed and got into bed in the darkness. He heard Mavis in the next room turn on her mattress as though to raise herself on an elbow and listen. He lay still. Oh, why had he gone to Beau Brickhill? Now he had missed his chance of going out to France again; he would miss the Big Push, too; and a decent chance to be killed, and end it all.

"I'd rather not discuss it, if you don't mind," said Desmond the next day, in the yard of his headquarters in Horseferry Road.

"But Desmond, aren't we still great friends? Don't we tell each other everything? What has happened to change our friendship? Won't you please tell me?"

"What I said to Lily, or what she said to me, is not your business."

"But isn't it to do with me, when you pointedly get up and leave immediately after you know that I had come into the Bull specially to see you?"

"Do you remember when I asked you, on the way to Horn-church, if you were going to allow Helena Rolls to come between us?"

"Yes."

"Do you remember the off-hand way you treated my question?"

"I didn't mean to be offhand."

"Well, you were. In fact, you laughed at my concern for you. Well, the position is now reversed, except that I find no cause for laughter."

"But I have not asked you to give up that bird."

"Your remark is unfortunate, but quite apart from its bad taste, whatever my friend happens to be is no concern of yours." Desmond came to attention as a sergeant passed.

"Well," said Phillip lamely, "I just thought I'd call and see if you were all right, after your sudden departure last night. How about tonight? Will you be on duty?"

"No sir," said Desmond, stiffening to attention again as the sergeant returned. Phillip said, with assumed jocularity, "Stand easy, Sapper Neville. Look here, Des, don't let's fall out over nothing. Shall I come down to you after tea? How about going into the country, like the old days? The migrants will be singing now."

"I'm meeting Lily tonight, and we are going to the pictures."

Concealing this further shock, Phillip said, "I see. Well, I'll be in Freddy's about nine, if you call in."

"I shall be taking Lily home afterwards."

"Then we won't be seeing one another?"

"No."

"I see," said Phillip, bleakly. "Well, so long. Have a good time," and returning Desmond's salute, he went back to the street and his motor cycle. He felt shaken, and with the roar of London's iron-wheeled and shod traffic beating on his ears, stood upon the kerb and wondered where he could go to see a friendly face. Gene worked in Charles Mayer's corset factory, he remembered. Where could he find a directory? He thought of the thick red volume on the shelf in the office of Wine Vaults Lane. He could get there by crossing over Vauxhall Bridge and finding his way behind the wharves along the south bank, to London Bridge. The cobbles were slippery with horse-dung, but with legs splayed for a touch with a boot-sole he could now control skids from the smooth tread of the back tyre. He thudded around drays and lorries, past heavy pairs of horses, and farther on, bales and bales of pressed waste-paper, which someone told him was used for making high explosive. Father took his bundles of *Daily Tridents* for salvage, so an accumulation of splutterings from the armchair might very well turn into one big bang over the enemy's lines.

Mr. Hollis looked up as he came through the glass door of the office and exclaimed, "Good God, look what's blown in! Where's the pantomime taking place, eh?" as he stared over his desk at Phillip's riding boots and spurs. "Seriously, Maddison, I'm most awfully pleased to see you. Where have you sprung from? Machine guns, eh? I thought you fellows who come back from France usually got put on the Staff! Well, it's a good war for some people, full salary plus pay. Look at Downham, a blooming major, though he's never left England, second in command of a cyclist's battalion, wears boots and spurs like you, though what the deuce a bicyclist wants spurs for, beats me."

The door opened above the lead-sheathed stairs, and the familiar slow steps of the manager began to flap down.

"Howlett, guess who's here? Puss in boots, having mistaken the date of the Lord Mayor's Show. Yes, our one and only comic genius, Maddison!"

Phillip did not mind Mr. Hollis' banter, he was rather pleased to be thought worthy of his senior's regard; while the face of Mr. Howlett beamed as usual, as though very glad to see him.

Phillip found Gene's address, and saying goodbye to Mr. Hollis, walked with a feeling of happiness down Aldgate to Houndsditch, where he was directed to the factory.

There he was shown up some wooden stairs, and came upon Gene with stylograph and long ruled book writing down numbers called monotonously by a yellow-faced Jewish boy who was turning over and examining one large pink-paper packet after another in a huge pile on the floor, reading the labels, and then transferring the parcels to another pile on the floor.

"Hullo, old thing," said Gene, getting up. "All right, Morris, I shan't want you for a few minutes." The yellow-faced youth went away. "I'm stocktaking. I'm damned glad to see you; my stock will go up when the manager hears my friend, Lieutenant Maddison, has come to see me."

"Where will it go to?" laughed Phillip, thinking of a Bairnsfather cartoon, *Our stock has gone up since a visit of Herr Krupp & Co.*, —hundreds of tins of plum and apple jam flying up under a shell-burst. "Oh, it's only a joke. I say, how about some lunch? Can you manage it?"

"I'm off in fifteen minutes. D'you mind waiting? No smoking by the way, warehouse rules. Are you on for Saturday?"

"Well, let's talk about it later. I think I'll wait outside, crowds amuse me, Gene." The sight of so many piled pink corsets was depressing.

Phillip had been in the London Tavern once before; now he was surprised to see many dark faces, obviously Jews, among the business men of the Lanes, some of them still wearing top hats, their faces not quite so beefy, as before the war. But steaks were still being grilled over the chef's open charcoal fire. Gene, invited to say what he would have, after careful scrutiny of the menu, chose smoked salmon, to be followed by an underdone rump steak with fried potatoes, asparagus, watercress, and mushrooms. Asked if he would like some beer with it, he said that steak, underdone, should be eaten only with claret, and chose a bottle of 1904 Chateau Lafite. A little amused by his expensive tastes, but not put out, Phillip decided to economise by having boiled mutton with caper sauce, potatoes and mashed turnips, the cheapest dish on the card.

"I'm surprised at you, Phil," remarked Eugene. "You're not

taking advantage of the *cuisiniere* here, by having the equivalent of a cut off the joint and two veg., as in any small pub. By the way, before I forget, would you lend me a pound? I'm rather low at the moment."

"By all means, dear old boy," replied Phillip, taking out his wallet. "Anything to help a pal."

After treacle tart Gene ordered toasted cheese; this was followed by two glasses of port each, and black coffee with brandy, and long cigars; by which time Gene was saying that before he went back to Brazil after the war and opened up an import business, he intended to put a Patent Improved Corset on the market; and if Old Phil would swear to keep the secret he would tell him what the Eugene Goulart Improved Corset would consist of.

"Swear? Honour bright? Well, it is simple I use rubber instead of whalebone, to serve a three-fold purpose: one, to enable the skirt of the corset to sit higher up on the rump, two, to give a more svelte line for the figure, three, to enable the Nip of Admiration to be given without fear of fouling the hard marginal line of the ordinary common or garden corset."

"You're rotting!" cried Phillip, when he had finished laughing at Gene's solemn absurdity.

"On the contrary, I am entirely serious, my dear old Phil. In my country the girls are very proud of their figures, and it is considered a compliment to put your hand on the behind of a belle you admire, with a sliding caress, of course, and nip her flesh, gently but firmly. It must be done in the right spot, not too low down, but by the point of hip. C.M. corsets cover that vital spot, and I have a theory that most Englishwomen remain cold because they have not been worked up properly before they settle down to dull domesticity!"

Phillip thought this extremely funny.

"Why does it seem funny to you? One does it to a horse or a steer, and one gets an immediate response of gratitude. What are women but animals, or mammals if you like? Of course, I grant you that what is natural to women of the sun would seem only impertinence to the majority of those with frosty souls and complexions in this northern country."

"Well, don't let the manager of the Gild Hall see you pinching the behinds of flappers there!"

"One does not pinch green bananas to see if they are ripe, senhor! You may laugh, but I am perfectly serious! If I found

myself in a crowd coming out of, say, Piccadilly Circus Underground, and stood next to a beautiful Englishwoman in the lift,
and paid her a compliment due to the female form divine, what
would she do? Accept it as a tribute from a senhor whose grandfather was a general in the Brazilian Army? Not on your life!
She'd shriek with indignation, and give me in charge! The
average Englishwoman is frigid, a Puritan! It is the raw, foggy
climate over here, most of the year. In South America we have
the sun, we are alive, we haven't the love-taboos that you have!"

Gene stuck his cigar in his mouth, and frowning through his
eyeglass, sucked thoughtfully. Then he said, "Did I ever show
you the photograph of my mother's father, the general who saved
Brazil from revolution?"

"I don't think you did," replied Phillip. "But don't you have
rather a lot of revolutions in Brazil?"

"You are thinking of Mexico, maybe," said Gene, as he
fumbled in his pocket book, to bring out a dog-eared photograph
of a round-faced little fat man with terrific moustaches and staring
eyes, rows of medals and plumed hat and sword and spurs with
rowels like catherine wheels.

"That is my grandfather, Eugene Roberto Franco Carlo
Goulart Bolivar——"

"No wonder he looks bowed down by some weight," cried
Phillip, unable to control his laughter at Gene's big-cigar pride
in the ridiculous pot-bellied figure.

"If you spoke like that anywhere in Brazil," retorted Gene,
"You would have had a knife in your ribs by now. We Brazilians
are very proud of our national heroes."

"Have another brandy, old boy, then you can put a pistol to
my head as well as the knife in my ribs."

"No thanks. I must be getting back. I mustn't keep my staff
waiting."

"You sound like a general."

"I am the equivalent just now, being in charge while the
manager is away. My father is a great friend of Charley Mayer,
you know."

"Well, on with the corsets," said Phillip, rising. "I suppose
you don't make bullet proof vests as well? I've seen advertisements of them somewhere. Not that I want one. I just wondered."

"Good God no! We're C.M. Corsets, we're the leading house
in the trade!"

The bill having been settled by Phillip, Gene asked him to walk back with him, saying ingenuously, "I want my staff to see the friend I've told them about, Lieutenant Maddison."

"Well, I'm not much to talk about——"

"You're an officer, and you've been to the front, and I want them to see me with you."

Phillip walked with Gene to the factory, and prepared to say goodbye to him outside, where several tallow-faced girls and youths stared silently.

"Well old man," said Gene (who had hidden the eyeglass as they approached, Phillip noticed), "I'll be seeing you on Saturday at the flat, at half past three, if I don't see you again before then? If those birds don't turn up, it doesn't matter; you and I can easily find two more. Well, so long!"

Phillip saluted Gene, and turning away, took a taxicab to Liverpool Street Station, where he had left his motor cycle. There being nothing else to do, he went home, changed into plain clothes, and went for a walk on the Hill, longing to see Mrs. Neville, but not daring to call at the flat, in case she, too, had turned against him.

When he went down for early tea with his mother, she said, "I suppose you won't be here next Saturday, will you, Phillip? You have not forgotten what that day is, have you?"

"Oh no. Sometimes I wish I had not lived to see it."

"You are run down, dear, I can see that. Is anything the matter, anything serious? If you feel you cannot tell me, why not confide in your father? He complains that you never seem to want to tell him anything. And after all, he is your father."

"My parent would be a truer description of him. He said to me once, 'Why can't you be like other boys?' when the answer was, 'Why can't you be like other fathers', only of course the wretched, fearful, furtive little rat that I was then could not reply like that: only by tears from a hanged head. What sort of confidence did he ever inspire in anyone? You know that he's critical, prejudiced, and dictatorial. I can feel it, even when he says nothing to me."

"Well, you must see that you don't grow like that yourself, dear."

"Oh do stop dearing me, Mother! I am nearly twenty-one, and have my own life now."

"Yes Phillip, of course. By the way, what would you like for your birthday present? Your father and I——"

"Nothing, really, thank you."

"It's a special occasion, you know. If you think nothing of it now, you will later on in life, when you are the father of a family yourself, perhaps——"

"I shall never marry, Mother, so please don't talk like that. It's kind of you to suggest a present, and I don't want to hurt anyone's feelings, so would a signet ring be all right? A gold one. Not with a stone in it, but all gold. Some of the officers wear them. With a crest. There is a Maddison crest, isn't there?"

"I think that is a very good choice, Phillip. Grandpa also suggested giving you a ring, but thought that Father might like to suggest it first. So Grandpa and I thought of a silver cigarette case, with the date and your initials on it, if you would like that, of course."

"Yes, I would, thank you. I suppose I could not have the crest on that, too? It could be copied from the spoons and forks of the plate in Father's box."

Hetty said she would ask his father when he came home. Richard said promptly that he had no licence to display armorial bearings, so it would not be right to have the crest engraved on the cigarette case. "Moreover, I consider it to be a waste of money to take one out now, under the conditions in which we live, not to mention the economies we all should practice in war time. An annual licence used to be a guinea, it may have gone up since my young days. Anyway, what does Master Phillip want a crest for?"

"Some of the other officers have them, apparently, Dickie."

"Yes, and they are probably entitled to them. I am not. I consider now that I belong to the lower middle class, and crests and coat-armour have no part in the life we lead, in so far as I am concerned. To want to revive them now, would be pretentious."

Later Richard said to Phillip. "Oh, by the way, your mother and I have been talking about your coming-of-age. I don't know if you will be here for the occasion, but anyway, we thought of giving you, jointly, a signet ring, with a monogram of your initials on it. What do you think?"

When his son did not reply, he went on, "Well, if that does not meet with your approval, have you anything else in mind? You have a watch already, I think? How about a riding whip, to accompany you with your boots?" he said with a laugh.

"We are not allowed to carry hunting crops, thanks all the same, Father."

"Well, I'll leave you two to decide what present you want. I think I'll go down to my allotment, and dibble in a row of first early potatoes. With luck we'll be clear of late frosts by the time their little green ears come out of the ground, to listen to the skylarks."

Phillip thought this rather a strange remark for Father to make; he thought of it more than once that evening, as he walked up and down the High Street, from Clock Tower to Hippodrome, up and down, trying to exhaust himself, and hoping for the dreaded moment, which never came, when he would see Desmond and Lily coming towards him.

Chapter 10

TWENTY-FIRST BIRTHDAY

Hetty and her father went up to London to choose the cigarette case, and signet ring. Thomas Turney knew a commission agent, through whom he could get 17½ per cent discount. Richard had "washed his hands of everything to do with the affair", as he said, after his wife had asked again if it might not be possible to have the family crest engraved on it, without, on this special occasion, applying for a licence to display it. Honesty was honesty, said Richard, and if Master Phillip, after he was of age, felt that he could face life the easier with a relic of the past with which to adorn himself, then he could apply to the College of Heralds for a grant of arms.

"I feel it my duty to say that such grandiose ideas for anyone in his station of life should be discouraged, Hetty! There is the example of your brother Hugh, if you remember, and how he used to talk of the Turneys being descended from Norman knights, the Le Tournets."

"But this isn't a question of doubtful family origins, Dickie. Phillip is proud of being a Maddison, that is why he——"

"If he feels proud, as you say, why does he not take more pains to show it, then? You think I don't know that he calls me 'Mr. Pooter' behind my back, do you? At least, that is conjecture; but he has more than once signed himself, in a letter to you, 'Lupin', and the reason for that is plain to me. I am poor, I am a failure, I am something to be laughed at because I have tried always to do my duty. Very well: if Master Phillip does not like my proposed present of a ring with his initials in a monogram, then I can only repeat that I wash my hands of everything to do with the affair."

So Hetty and her father went to London by tram as far as Blackfriars Bridge, and walking thence to the wholesalers near St. Pauls, they selected a ring to Phillip's size, and a plain curved cigarette case, both to be engraved with mailed fist and dagger of the legendary Le Tournets, with date and initials inside the circle of gold and upon the silver panel. They were to be delivered by registered post on the Saturday morning, without fail.

Thomas Turney had suggested a supper party in his house for that evening, but since Dickie might be hurt if he knew about this in advance (he would be asked, of course, as on other occasions, and probably decline to come) it was agreed between father and daughter that the supper should be in the nature of a last-minute affair, anyone who liked to come being welcome. They must ask Dora, the boy's godmother, of course. She was still working in the East End, at her friend Sylvia's children's clinic.

After leaving the wholesalers, they walked to the Guildhall, where the City Tribunal for examining claims for exemption from the Armed Forces under the recently passed Military Service Act, was sitting. There was a place for the public, said a policeman at the door. Hetty had heard from Mavis that Tom Ching had decided to appeal against his call-up on grounds of conscientious objection to war; and his case was to come up on this day.

While they were waiting, Thomas Turney said, "I have been reading in the paper that Lord Derby, as Director of Recruiting, has been protesting against the numerous exemptions claimed by young men in the one hundred and sixty reserved occupations, and demands what the *Telegraph* calls a 'comb out'. Of course there are cases of hardship, some being indispensible to businesses. Hemming tells me that we have lost eleven youngsters in the lithographic room alone."

The members of the Tribunal took their places, and the first case was heard. He wore spectacles with thick lenses, and claimed that he had tried to enlist in the "terriers" three times, and each time had been turned down for bad eyes.

The Military Representative, a dark man with sidewhiskers and a hawk-like nose got up and said, "I am instructed to say that so-called defective eyesight is no longer a disqualification for the Army. It does not matter whether this man is short-sighted, so long as he is physically fit. If he is physically fit to wield a bayonet, he is fit for service abroad."

The members on the dais whispered together; then the Chairman announced, "Exemption granted for two months."

The next case was a young man with black hair hanging thickly over his shoulders, and a beard almost down to his waist. He said that he was a member of a sect which was against the taking of any life whatsoever, whether of man, bird or fish.

"I believe in the Divine Command, 'Thou shalt not kill'," he cried in a high, almost falsetto voice.

"Is that why you let your hair grow?"

"I allow my hair to grow long in accordance with the passage in Leviticus, 'They shall not make baldness upon their heads; neither shall they shave off the corner of their beard'."

"Do you then believe all that is in the Bible?"

"I do. By obeying Divine Command, I shall preserve my body from physical death."

The Military Representative then said, "At the same time, apparently, you object to exposing your body unnecessarily to danger?"

"I do."

"You have read the Bible assiduously?" said the Chairman.

"I have."

Another member looked at a printed card on the table before him.

"Then you will no doubt recall this passage, also to be found in Leviticus: 'And ye shall chase your enemies and they shall fall before you by the sword, for I am the Lord, your God.'"

He is trapped, thought Hetty, looking at the large dark eyes in the white face; agonised eyes, she thought, like those of Hall Caine the great novelist.

"I rely on the injunction, 'Thou shalt not kill'."

"What is the name of your sect?"

"The Israelites. We are descendants of the Chosen People."

At these words, Thomas Turney nudged his daughter. "D'you see how the Military Representative keeps his eyes on the table before him? What is that to an orthodox Jew, heresy? The hairy one has cooked his goose."

Unaware of the irony of the remark, Hetty was thinking, Poor man, he might be a saint; and tears came as she thought of Another, also bearded and sad of face, whose words had been dismissed. But there, everyone had their Cross to bear. She heard with anguish the verdict, 'Claim refused'.

There was a small stir in the well of the Court, then the next case was announced.

"Thomas Erasmus Ching!"

Looking very humble, rubbing his hands, licking his lips and glancing about him as though he were acting a part, Ching faced the row of hard faces.

"I claim exemption on the grounds that my conscience forbids me to take any man's life, friend or foe. When I passed for the Civil Service I prayed to God to have me sent to a department where I could carry out His will, and——"

"You are in the Admiralty?"

"Yes, sir. I took it that God's will was for me to be appointed to the Admiralty, after my prayer, sir."

"What do you do at the Admiralty?"

"Nothing to do with the actual war, sir. I am in the Stationery Department, sir."

"Are you prepared to resign your post in that department?"

"No sir. I am told I am still wanted in the Department."

"By whom?"

"By my superiors, sir."

"Then you obey the orders of your superiors?"

"In the Stationery Department, yes, sir."

They are trapping him, thought Hetty, with a feeling of suffocation; but the feeling was relieved by her next thought, Thank goodness Mavis cannot bear him at any price.

"Do you go to church? You do. Do you study the Book of Common Prayer? And you also believe in what it says? Very well, no doubt you are well aware of this passage—" the speaker read from the large printed card—"'Articles of the Church of England, Number thirty-seven, *It is lawful for Christian men, at the command of the Magistrate, to wear weapons, and serve in the wars*'. Claim refused."

"I shall appeal, sir," said Tom Ching, before he left.

Phillip went to the High Street, wearing his pre-war ready-made twelve and sixpenny Donegal tweed jacket, half-crown straw-hat, and five shilling grey flannel bags. After calling at Freddy's, where he heard that Desmond had not been in since Monday, he crossed over to the Gild Hall. There at a table sat the two flappers; they began to move about on their chairs when he appeared, as he could see in the retina of his eye. He sat down at another table, while avoiding looking at them. As time went on he felt foolish: either he should have acknowledged them at once, or gone to their table. Were people at the other tables aware of his stand-offishness? His dilemma was solved by the waitress, who said that two friends of his were at another table, and as though in surprise he turned round, and getting up, went to them.

"Do you mind if I join you?"

"We thought you didn't want to know us!"

He ordered coffee for three. "Well, how are you?"

"Very well, thank you!" they said in duet.

"Good. I saw my friend two days ago, in London. Did you really say you would go to his flat?"

"We really wanted to ask you, if you thought it was all right!"

"Will you promise to keep it a secret if I tell you something? Very well. You ought not to go to anyone's flat. Now don't forget your promise. I must go now. Have your friendships, but don't be too idealistic about anyone in uniform. And don't say a word, will you? Goodbye."

Feeling himself to be a complete hypocrite, he crossed over the road to Freddy's bar. There Mrs. Freddy said to him, "A friend of yours is lookin' for you, 'im with the ogglin' eyes, Ching. He said he would be in the next 'ouse, the Bull."

After a quick whiskey Phillip left and walked to the Bull, and saw Lily sitting on a stool, talking to the barmaid. Near her stood Tom Ching. Seeing Phillip, Ching almost rushed at him.

"I've wanted to see you, Phil, I want your advice about something urgent. Can we talk in private? It's very important—First, let me stand you a drink. What'll you have?"

"I don't want anything at the moment, thanks all the same," he replied, conscious of Lily waiting to swim towards him out of her large blue eyes.

"Hullo," she said, in her soft voice. He wanted to be with her, to be free of the cloudy-eyed Ching tugging his arm, saying, "Come on over here, I've been thinking of you for over two days." He followed reluctantly to a corner.

"Well what is it?"

"I may join the Army!"

"I see."

"But don't you realize what I'm telling you?"

"You said you may have to join up."

"The question is, if I volunteer quickly, I might be able to get into the best branch. I've always remembered what you told me about yourself when you came back the first time. Well then, what is the best thing to apply for?"

"The Army Pay Corps."

"I've tried them, but they've got no vacancies."

"Try the A.S.C. or the R.A.M.C."

"I had thought of the R.A.M.C."

"Rob All My Comrades, the tommies call it. That's at the base, of course, and on lines of communication. The stretcher bearers are decent blokes, they go right up into the strafe during a show."

Ching rolled his eyes in the direction of the bar. "I didn't know you knew that girl. Is she all right?"

Phillip laughed. Just what he himself had asked the A.S.C. officer about the barmaid, a year before, in the Belvoir Arms. No wonder he had been snubbed. At least he could not choke off Ching for what was the very same gaucherie.

"Yes, she looks a nice person, doesn't she? Well, don't let me keep you."

"I'm in no hurry to go."

"Well, I want to talk to that girl."

"You don't mind if I stay with you, do you? I've got no other friend, you see."

"All right, come and have a drink."

"Thanks, I will. A double rum."

"Will you have a drink too, Lily? This is Mr. Ching."

"Pleased to meet you, I'm sure." She turned round on her stool, revealing skirts well above her ankles, and held out a limp hand, allowing her fingers to be taken by Ching, who, to Phillip's annoyance, began to fondle them. He determined to get away as soon as he could, especially when Lily held out her other hand for him to take; and when reluctantly he took it, she held on to his hand, swimming into his aloofness from the lakes of her eyes. He took his hand away, and she gave him a sorrowing, reproachful look.

"You don't like me, do you?"

"I don't even know you, so I can't really say."

She swung round again on the stool, and taking her glass, held it up and drained it. He saw a crucifix on her bracelet, and a heart, and what looked like a dog, and a golliwog.

"If you could spare a minute or two, I'd like a word with you in private," he said.

The blue eyes shone upon him. She got off the stool, and said, "Shall we go now?"

"Good night," he said to Ching, and followed her through the mahogany swing doors. Outside in the street she said, "Do you mind taking my arm? I wouldn't ask you if you were in uniform."

So she knew all about officers.

"Where shall we go?"

"It's nice and quiet in the churchyard."

"Don't you usually go into the Rec.?"

"Oh no, not if I can help it. I don't care for the Rec."

Trying to show she is superior, he thought. Then with surprise he heard her say, "You don't remember me, do you? Well, do you remember when you used to play cricket on the Hillies, and some of the boys you played with used to call you Grandma, because you were very particular how they had to treat your bat when you let them have a lend of it?"

"Well, I didn't want them to break it, or hit stones with it. I know they laughed at me, for being a fusspot."

"You were ever so nice. We called you Grandma because you looked after the little ones. You don't remember me, but I was one of the kids from Nightingale Grove, who you allowed to join in. The other boys used to let us field the ball, but you let us have a go with the bat."

"Well, it was only fair."

"I called you Grandma first. Did you mind?"

"I hated it! I remember you now! You wore a boy's jersey and button boots too big for you. And you called me Grandma!"

They crossed over Randiswell Road, and passing the Fire Station, came to the shadowed wall of St. Mary's churchyard, with its trees behind. There she drew apart from him.

"Thanks for the arm. Keechey hangs about there sometimes, hoping for a chance to pinch me for soliciting."

"I see, I picked you up first!"

"Well, you asked me, didn't you? No, I didn't mean it sarcastic. You are very kind, just like you were when a boy."

"I was a cowardly little rotter."

"You a coward? I shall never forget one day when you stuck up for Jack o' Rags against four boys in the High Street. Later when they found you on the Hillies one Saturday morning they set about you, and you never ran away. Your friend Peter Wallace, what was killed with his two brothers early on in the war, he came to your rescue, and trimmed them up. But before that you squared up to them, and they got you down, they were the bullies, not you, Phillip. You don't mind me calling you Phillip, do you?"

"It's better than Grandma, anyway!"

They passed by the front of the church, with its broad stone steps, and came to the darker shadows of the yews which lined the flagstone path lying, between thin iron railings, through the old graveyard. Here, out of the diminished rays of a gas-light in its glass case, they stopped. Memories of the bulky dark figures waiting by the rustic bridges of the river and the hoarse wheedling words, *Want a sweetheart, dearie?* made him ready for what might be suggested next. From the vestry of St. Mary's Church came the sound of boys' voices. It was Choir Practice night.

"Oh, don't you love music? I love singing. I go to St. Saviour's to listen to the singing. I would like to be a Catholic, if they'd have me. Are you a Catholic? Your friend is, he told me."

In the darkness came the faint pure voice of a boy, through stone wall and oaken door, penetrating the blackness of the yews to where they stood just beyond the wan downcast circle of the small war-time gas-light.

> *O for the wings, for the wings of a Dove*
> *Far, far away would I rove*

"Oh, I love a boy's voice so!"

He thought of the last time he had heard the words and tune, sung by one of the survivors of the attack on 19th December, 1914, coming down on the corduroy paths through the wood. Part of him brooded desperately on the scene, longing to be back in the wood: a feeling no one would ever understand, who had not been out. Where life and death waited side by side, to be wed by bomb and bullet. If only he could write about it, as Julian Grenfell had done.

"Do you know Julian Grenfell's poem, *Into Battle*? In Flanders, just before he was killed, he wrote about the stars he remembered from his boyhood at Taplow, by the Thames,

> " '*All the bright company of Heaven*
> *Hold him in their high comradeship,*
> *The Dog-star and the Sisters Seven*
> *Orion's belt and sworded hip.*' "

"Oh, I never," she said, clinging to his arm.

> " ' *The woodland trees that stand together*
> *They stand to him each one a friend;*
> *They gently speak in the windy weather,*
> *They guide to valley and ridge's end.*

The kestrel, hovering by day,
  And the little owls that call by night,
Bid him be swift and keen as they,
  As keen of ear, as swift of sight.

The blackbird sings to him: "Brother, brother,
  If this be the last song you sing,
Sing well, for you may not sing another,
  Brother, sing.'"

When he had finished, the lamp-lit lakes of Alice's eyes were running over. "So he was killed, was he. D'you know, I think he knew he was going to die, and did not mind very much. I feel like that sometimes when I'm in St. Saviour's, listening to the chants. I feel all the hundreds of years ago and all the hundreds of years to come are the same thing, so what does death matter. I suppose you think I'm silly?"

He felt shaken. There was somebody else in the world who felt as he did. He said, "I feel that, too."

"You do? You really do? Then you don't think I'm silly?"

"No, of course not. It's like something coming into your life, from beyond yourself."

"Father Aloysius, him who has gone away now, said that that was the feeling of God."

"How very strange. I know Father Aloysius. I met him quite by chance in Essex, last winter. And now you, Lily. It does seem strange. Did you talk to Father Aloysius?"

"Oh yes. I wasn't a Catholic, but he never minded me talking to him."

"Why should he mind?"

"For what I once done."

To his alarm he saw she was crying. "I've been very wicked, you see."

"We've all been wicked, I know I have. And still am! Anyway, don't let's worry."

"I only told one other person what I done."

"Is it about Keechey?"

"Who told you?"

"Oh, I heard somewhere that you used to be rather thick with him—that at one time you walked out with him."

"Did they say anything more."

"No. Why should they?"

"If I tell you, promise you won't give me away?"

"Of course I won't," he replied, pleased to be trusted.

She sighed, blew her nose, and said almost inaudibly. "I was going to have a kid by Keechey, and done away with it."

Boyhood's horror about whores' babies being suffocated, tied up in brown paper parcels, and dropped into the Randisbourne, came to him. "Keechey told me to get rid of it. He said he'd get me five years if I told anyone who the father was."

"He looks like that."

"I was only fourteen, and a little skivvy, when he did it to me. He was a policeman then. He asked me to go for a walk with him on my afternoon off, and when it was dark he took me on the seat around the willow where they play football, d'you know it? He told me he'd cut my throat if I screamed."

"Do forgive my asking, but did you kill your baby?"

"I had to have an illegal operation. I wanted my baby, truly I did, only I couldn't, as I was in service."

"And you were only fourteen?"

She nodded.

"Well, do take care of yourself now, won't you? I promise to keep your secret."

He was still puzzled why she went in pubs to get off with men, apparently. He wanted to ask her, but shrunk from appearing inquisitive.

"I knew you were a real gentleman," she said admiringly. "You were always different from the other boys on the Hillies."

"Then you are the only one who has ever thought so!"

"Oh no, you've forgotten Horace Cranmer! You remember him, in your Boy Scout's Patrol? He used to go to work at Hern's the Grocer's. You were his hero, didn't you know that? He was killed too, wasn't he?"

The last of his reserved feelings about Lily dissolved.

"You know, I can't think why a girl like you, so pretty and kind, doesn't have a—well, someone who—likes you."

"Men only want one thing, usually. They know I am bad, so they try to interfere with me. Though someone I know likes me, but he is old and funny. He likes to kneel down before me and kiss my feet. But he never wants to interfere with me, only kiss my feet and my bosom. He looked after me when I'd had the illegal operation, for nothing. You know him. Promise you won't tell if I say who?"

"I promise."

"It was Doctor Dashwood. But he didn't do the illegal operation, he didn't know about it, until I told him. He's ever so nice.
He said he would have looked after me, despite what people would
say, and would have adopted my baby. He wishes I was his daughter, he said once. He never charged me anything for what he done
for me. If people say I go after his money, it isn't true."

"Don't you hate Keechey?"

"I'm sorry for him. He says he loves me, now I won't have any
more to do with him. Isn't it funny? But men are jealous like
little children, when you know them. All they want is to be
looked after."

With her eyes upon him shining in the dimness, he felt himself
beginning to be small, and resisted the feeling.

"Would you say that about my friend, also?" he asked, a little
timidly.

"All men are like that, when you know them. But Desmond
is more so, I think. That's because his father died when he was
young, I suppose."

"But his father is still alive, Lily!"

"Then he made it up, I wonder why. Perhaps he's ashamed
that he left his mother."

"Yes, you may be right. It never occurred to me."

"He admires you a lot. He says you are the only one who has
been kind to him."

"He's my great friend. Or was, until he met you. And that's
the truth!"

"You think I'm not good enough for him, don't you?"

"Well, you see, we've always been rather thick, until you came
along."

"Don't worry, I won't come between you."

"But do you love him, Lily? I don't want to come between you
and him, if you do. Also, I didn't know you, then, as I do now."

"You love a girl, don't you? I've seen her, she nurses at the
Hospital."

"She doesn't love me, anyway."

"How do you know? Have you tried her?"

"She loved my cousin, who was killed."

"Yes, I heard. She looked ever so sad. But any woman could
love you, I think. You are so kind."

The eyes of Desmond standing in the porch looked at Phillip
steadily when Phillip opened the door to his ring.

"Come in, Desmond. I'm very glad to see you. Gene and I are going to dine up West tomorrow, and we want you to come, too—as in the old days. It's my birthday, but I don't want any presents. Will you join us?"

"I want to speak to you privately, first."

They went into the front room. While Phillip closed the door, Desmond stood still. Then he looked across the table sternly, unhappily.

"What's the matter now, Des?"

"You know as well as I do."

"I don't know what you mean."

"You know very well that you saw Lily last Wednesday. I suspected that when I noticed her changed manner when I met her last night. You went behind my back, after I had told you she was my girl. And why did you tell her that my father was not dead?"

"I didn't realize you'd told her he was dead, before I spoke."

"But what right have you to take her for a walk?"

"I only wanted to find out what sort of a girl she was, that was all. How did you know I had seen her?"

"Ching told me first, then I went round to her home, and she told me herself."

"But it was all above board, Desmond."

"That isn't the point. The point is that you have deliberately betrayed me."

The face was set and pale; this was no joke, Phillip thought, suppressing a feeling to treat the matter lightly.

"How have I betrayed you? We hardly spoke about you."

"That in itself is an admission. I want your promise that you will not see her again. I want it before I leave this room."

"What do you think happened between us, then? We only talked."

"You've changed her towards me. You've wormed your way into her thoughts, that is obvious. If your friendship for me means anything, you will tell me what you said to her. And what she told you about me."

"We hardly discussed you. I wanted to find out what she was like, for your sake, if you want to know."

"Well, what did you find out?"

"I thought she was really a very good person."

"Then your object has been achieved, and you won't need to see her again?"

"Not unless she wants to see me. I can't cut her suddenly; be reasonable. I have told you there is nothing between us."

"Why should she want to see you again?"

"I don't know. But she might."

"What did you say to her, that she might want to see you again?"

"I spoke about music and poetry, and she told me about her experiences of some time ago, and reminded me that I was called Grandma when we used to play cricket on the Hill. That was before I knew you, Desmond."

"I shall ask her if that is true."

"You can ask her what you like! And I don't care for your manner of interrogating me like this! If you don't believe me, you can lump it! I tell you it was merely a friendly chat, and we both wanted to get away from that hanger-on, Ching, who was with her in the Bull when I went in there to find you, if you want to know."

"In that case, there can be no reason why you shouldn't give the promise I ask for."

"Just a moment, someone may be listening." He went to the Polyphone, and put on *Over the Waves*. The door opened and Mavis came into the room.

"How long are you two going to be in here, eh? Mother and I are waiting to come in."

"What for?"

"Mind your own biz!"

"Must you use that vulgar expression? I've asked you not to, before."

"Look who's talking! What about you in the Gild Hall, eh?"

"Anyway, you might at least say how d'you do when you come into a room. And this is a private talk, if you don't mind."

"Ha, ha, all your affairs are either private or secret! Except what goes on in Freddy's and the Bull!"

Mavis went out again, leaving the door a-jar. Phillip closed it violently, then faced Desmond, whose eyes were still fixed upon him.

"Will you give me your promise?"

"But why should I not see Lily again?"

"She is my friend, and I do not intend to lose her."

"Then may I suggest that you do not treat her as you do me, or you may find that what you fear may have come to pass."

"You are plausible, as always, and can twist anything round. I want your promise."

"Well, don't you twist anything too much, or you might find you've broken its neck. Shall we shake hands?"

"On your promise, yes."

"No! I have said what I have said about that. I ask you to shake hands because we are friends, and only on that. And friends don't let down friends."

"That's all I wanted to know."

As they shook hands, Phillip said, "I hope that Gene won't attack me now, because I said I wasn't going on Saturday to his flat with those flappers. Those kids are much too young. One of them even isn't developed."

"In other words, you do not approve?"

"If you put it that way, yes!"

"I see. I'm not allowed to do what I want to do, since you disapprove of Lily, and Gene mustn't invite two girls to his flat, because you don't think it's right?"

"Well, I'm older than you both——"

"Does it occur to you that sometimes you behave like your father, I wonder?"

"Look Des., let's stop all this rot, shall we? How about a song?" as Doris came into the room.

Desmond had a friend in the London Electrical Engineers, an older man who was a professional singer, who had invited him to his home in North London, and given him lessons. Desmond had a light tenor voice, and sometimes Doris played for him, and Phillip. In the past they had sung duets together, songs like *Shipmate o' Mine*, *Friend o' Mine*, etc., usually with three verses, the first two expressive of loving comradeship, the third and final verse dropping into a minor key, solemn with the impending shadow of the valley of death: late Victorian ballads in the spirit of London, with its fogs and dirt and fearful competition, its dread of "going to the wall", of loss through incurable disease, but with faith in a future life, the resounding of trumpets, and general freedom where before frustration had enclosed the spirit.

Doris sat at the piano, and opened the sheet music of *Elëanore*, by Coleridge-Taylor. This was a favourite song of Phillip's; a medium by which he communed with the spirit of Helena. He had not heard Desmond sing since he had been taking lessons; and he was surprised at the clear enunciation of the words, which now came with an almost piercingly pure ringing quality of each note, so carefully phrased. Before, Desmond had at times been nasal in his singing; while Phillip himself was, he knew, soft and throaty, quite hopeless. It was the same when they had sometimes boxed together: Desmond had stood and guarded his blows, which were never really serious; but when Desmond had hit, it was with determination and strength. Phillip could now feel a new power in Desmond, through his singing. There was deep sadness in it, too.

> The forest flowers are faded all
> The winds complain, the snowflakes fall,
> Elëanore, Elëanore——
>
> I turn to thee as to a bower
> Thou breathest beauty like a flower
> Thou smilest like a happy hour,
> Elëanore——
>
> I turn to thee, I bless afar
> Thy name, which is my guiding star,
> Elëanore, Elëanore——
> And yet, Ah God, when thou art here
> I faint, I hold my breath for fear
> Thou art some phantom wand'ring near
> Elëanore——

Desmond's eyes were on the ceiling as he sang, his hands clasped before him.

> O, take me to thy bosom fair
> And cover me with thy golden hair,
> Elëanore, Elëanore——
> There let me lie when I am dead
> Those morning beams around me spread
> The glory of thy face o'erhead
> Elëanore, Elëanore——

"That was very beautifully sung, Desmond," said Doris.

"Yes, thank you," said Phillip.

"Isn't it wonderful that Coleridge-Taylor is a black man?" said Doris. "*I* think all men are part of the same world, really, whatever the colour of their skins."

"The purpose of life is to create beauty, in spite of everything," said Phillip.

Desmond said nothing, as he stood there, head and eyes downheld.

"Would you two like to sing a duet now?"
Neither Phillip nor Desmond replied.

As they went out of the room, Hetty appeared, and said she wanted to say something to Phillip. Desmond said a laconic good-bye; and Phillip returned with his mother to the room.

"I was wondering, Phillip, about your birthday party. As you will be going back on Monday, Gran'pa says he would be pleased if you would have supper with him tomorrow night. Perhaps Desmond might like to come, too?"

"Well, I'm afraid I shan't be able to come tomorrow, Mum, as Gene and I have arranged to go out. In fact, I was just going to ask Desmond, too."

"Perhaps Sunday will be better, then? Would you care to ask Desmond to come then?"

"He said he was on searchlight duty on Sunday."

"Well then, shall we have just a family party, like old times?" with a gay little laugh.

"Oh, all right," he said, with the dullness of nearly a thousand Sundays at home in his voice.

"Very well, Phillip," replied Hetty, with forced cheer. "I'll tell Gran'pa that you will come on Sunday. It is a special occasion, you know. You will only be twenty-one once."

"Not being a woman, I suppose that's true, Mother dear."

He gave her an unexpected kiss, arising out of joy that he and Desmond were good friends once again, and he was going down to Freddy's bar, hoping to see him there.

When the front door closed behind Phillip his elder sister came downstairs. Mother and daughter went into the front room.

"Thank goodness they're gone out! Desmond with his senti-mental, lugubrious singing! Phew, the room smells like a pub with all this smoke hanging about! Why do men smoke, I can't see anything in it? Help me clear the table, Mummie darling, will you? The light won't last very much longer, and you know Father won't let me use the gas, because of this beastly economy. Why hasn't Nina come? She said she would be here at a quarter to six, and it's past that."

"Perhaps she has been delayed at the office, dear."

"Oh no, she gets off at five, and promised to come straight here."

Ornamental china bowl holding miniature orange tree was lifted off the table, tapestry cloth folded; now they were ready to cut out, from material which Mavis had bought at the Spring Sales, the gores of the new Freedom Skirt, a pattern of which had been given away with *Weldon's Home Journal*. Sewing machine, work-basket, scissors, were all ready; but where was Nina?

"We must start without her, that's all, Mother. Take my waist measurement, will you?"

Mavis had looked forward so keenly to this occasion, that her friend's non-appearance, together with her fear of her father coming into the room—scores of mental pictures of this had already turned the edge of the joys of anticipation—was almost a disaster. Hurry, hurry, there was so little time.

Twenty-three inches, said Hetty. This was awful news: for the tissue pattern of the gore, or long triangular piece, twelve of which were to be sewn together to make the Freedom Skirt, was for a waist of twenty-five inches. The problem, or disaster, pre-sented two alternatives: one, to cut the material to the pattern, and allow wider margins when sewing together; the other, to reduce the paper pattern by the difference, two inches, in pro-portion.

"Of course, after I've had my tea . . . but I don't always get blown out. . . . No! We must cut for what I am, twenty-three inches!"

"If only Nina were here! She is better at mathematics than I am. Two inches off all round, divided by twelve. That's one-sixth of an inch. Doris! Doris! Bring your ruler, please! Quick! No time to be lost!"

Doris came in from the kitchen, where she was doing her home-work. Her opinion was asked for; and immediately afterwards she was asked if Mavis' opinion was correct. Before Doris could adjust herself to this, Mavis said, "No! It would be fatal to take off one-sixth of an inch all down each gore! Don't you see, one-sixth of an inch at my waist would be the equivalent of ever so much more at the hem, for the hem is wide! The waist is narrow! So how can it be the same? Mother, stop laughing! Oh, you are silly! Now you've upset all my thoughts, and I'll have to start again!"

"I am so very sorry, Mavis," laughed Hetty. "I know it's ridiculous, but I saw a perfectly straight skirt, twenty-three inches all down, so that you had to hobble, like Marie Cox did when she wore her hobble skirt through Randiswell!"

"I know, and ragged boys followed her to the High Street, and jeered at poor old Marie! Little beasts! I was going to the High

School then, before I went to Thildonck. How *awful* she must have felt!"

Nina arrived at this point, flushed and out of breath, full of apologies that her train had been missed. All was well. Hetty went to make a pot of tea, the kettle already simmering on the gas—or wasting away, as Richard (and Phillip) would have said —but thank goodness both were out of the house. Raisin scones with butter, put on in thick pats, were nourishing, and would keep the girls happy until supper, which they were to have next door, with Papa and Aunt Marian. Ever optimistic in her clear moments, Hetty took the tray into what was originally her drawing-room, and still was; for Dickie, she reflected, seldom if ever went into it. To the children, of course, it was the front room, a place of withdrawal.

Three girls were working out sums on paper, with pencils: how to reduce the pattern by 2/25ths. Doris worked it out to three places of decimals, and on being scorned by her sister for this, promptly left the room, saying "Do it yourself," and returned to her interrupted Latin "construe", taking her ruler and two buttered scones with her.

Two minutes later Hetty joined her, laughing silently, all her suggestions and attempts to solve Mavis' problem having been scouted. Her laughter turned to tears as she set about washing up in the scullery: why, she told herself, she did not know. The sudden revelation had been smothered: an opening upon the evaded reality of her life: that nobody wanted her for *herself*, only for her usefulness.

Apparently Mavis and Nina solved the problem, for when her smiling, cheerful face looked round the door again, the Crow Blue material, with its dark sheens, was in strips, cut to a diminished pattern.

"I think," said Nina, in her sedate voice, which seemed at times to have been pushed back into her stocky Saxon figure, "we'll easily be able to finish it all by next Saturday. Mavis will look wonderful in it, her figure is just right for it, don't you think so, Mrs. Maddison?"

"Don't waste time," said Mavis. "We've got to make the jacket yet, don't forget!"

"Don't worry, Mavis, we'll get it finished all right."

Saturday was always a time of enjoyment for Hetty, for in the morning her dear friend and charwoman, Mrs. Feeney, came to work with brush, pan, polish, emery paper, hearth-stone, swab, and pail, practically all of her time on her knees, but for a break at eleven o'clock, when with bread-and-cheese, and bottle of porter, she sat at the kitchen table and talked to the mis'ess sipping a cup of tea. Doris was home, too, and the April sun was shining, the hawthorns in the gulley were a pale gentle green, and little children playing happily on the grass beyond the spiked railings of the park in front of the house; and her son, still her little son, was twenty-one! How the time had flown since they had come to the house, nineteen years ago, one Saturday afternoon, to find it all new and bare, the floors so clean, and the new bathroom, and the picnic tea which they had had together, and while she had nursed her brown-eyed baby by the fire, Dickie and his little boy, who so loved him that he imitated him in nearly everything he did, played hide-and-seek in the bare rooms upstairs, and Phillip was so happy because Dickie had saved a spider which had fallen into the lavatory pan, and put it on the window sill to dry, to her little boy's delight. "'at poor spider will find 'is mummy now, won't 'e, Dads?"

"Now ma'am," said Mrs. Feeney, cheerfully, "I must get on with my steps. Master Phillip must see them properly hearth-stoned for his birthday." She understood the tears in the mis'ess' eyes, God bless 'er.

Richard refrained from looking closely at the ring and the case when Phillip showed them to him on his arrival home in the afternoon. He could not help saying, "I am afraid I have no present for you; it was taken out of my hands, that is all I can say." Then he put on his allotment boots. Wheeling away barrow and tools, kept under a tarpaulin in the front garden (well into the privet hedge against theft) he felt grievous and unwanted; but walking in the sun along Charlotte Road his heart lightened at the vision of bringing fertility back to his few rods of soil which for so long had lain acid under the smoke of London, and now were in his tenancy, at a peppercorn rent of one shilling a year.

While Richard was trundling his one-wheeled wooden vehicle of gardening tools past the open gates of the cemetery, another manifestation of vernal hope was showing itself in the front room of the house in Hillside Road, where Mavis and the faithful Nina were busy completing the Freedom Skirt, in the sunlit air coming in through the open windows of the front room, and slightly stirring the leaves of the aspidistra on its tall stand.

Doubts, anguished and devastating, tightened within Mavis when first, in company with Hetty and Nina and Doris, she saw herself in the long looking glass in her mother's bedroom. The skirt was a complete failure. It hung on her like a punctured balloon. And the pleats! They looked shapeless, some thin and others puffy. The skirt did not swing when she turned round, it did not swish, the pleats followed sluggishly. It was the pattern which was wrong. She had known it all along. If only Mother had not laughed, just when Nina was calculating the amount to be cut off the pattern. Now there wasn't enough material round the hem to let the skirt down a couple of inches. It was a disaster!

"Nina, why didn't you tell me I was cutting the skirt too close to the pattern? O, now I look a *sight*!"

Mavis was near to tears. While Nina humbly said she was very sorry, Doris proclaimed stoutly that it looked very nice. Hetty agreed. Mavis sighed, and wondered. Doris said, "I vote it looks jolly fine, Mavis." Nina ceased to apologise and added her assurances.

"Are you sure? I wish I could see it from behind."

Mavis twisted and peered, while her woeful face in the glass stared back at her. Her mother made a suggestion which in reverse settled the matter.

"Why not keep it, dear, a little while, and see if others are wearing it first?"

"What? And let them say I am a copy-cat? Not likely!" exclaimed Mavis, the plaintive, almost helpless tones of her voice giving way to a rougher, slightly guttural note, as she summoned up resolution. "No, I shan't care what people say! What do I care what anyone says about me? I like it, and I'm the one to be considered!"

"Of course, dear, naturally."

"Why not let Gramps and Aunt Marian see it," suggested Doris, "if you can't believe all of us?"

"Pouff, what will they know about clothes?"

"At least, Mavis, Gran'pa is interested in his granddaughter. And if he approves, you will know it is all right to wear it."

The old man was sitting by the fire in his yew-wood chair, reviewing scenes of his living long past, in the kinema of his mind. Tibby, the household steer cat, lay stretched along the length of its master's right thigh. Its tail hung down by his groin; its paws, with claws half-sheathed, rested on the shiny, rounded blue serge trouser covering the cocked-up knee.

For more than a dozen years, ever since he had given up his country villa at Cross Auton in Surrey to be near his daughter in the Benighted Swamp, as he called the foggy environs of the south bank of London River, Thomas Turney had worn only one kind of suit during the day; a ready-made blue serge, one or another of a score hanging in the mahogany cupboard in his bedroom. He was a short man, with a round bullet-shaped head, now almost bald. His body was not fat—his weight was constant at what he called, in his older way of speech, "Ten stun twelve pun". Since his days of discretion, he was wont to say, he ate for nourishment only, he-he-he—the little wheezy laugh, emphasised by a chronic inflammation of the bronchial tube, was due to having smoked too many Havana cigars in the past.

His eyes closed; the kinema of his mind, its life, was dulling out; he was on the edge of sleep; only the ticking of the ormolu clock set in dark marble on the shelf above the fireplace was audible in the room. He had not yet begun to snore.

In a plush-covered armchair, with its back nearly upright, sat his eldest sister. Her eyes were open, her arms folded, her thoughts were composed; she believed implicitly in the Christian faith. At eighty-three years of age Miss Marian Turney was still active and alert. She had a mass of white hair, and a strong, resolute face, which was offset in conversation by the controlled quickness of her manner. She wore a striped flannel blouse with a stiff starched linen collar like a man's, a thin black bow hanging from it. Whenever she spoke, it was in a decisive, firm manner. She listened to whoever was speaking with marked attention, as though what was said was important to her. Now she was resting between tea and supper.

At the click of the gate she looked up, and light came into her eyes. She rose to open the door to her niece and the two girls.

"Do come in! Tom will be so pleased to see you! Mavis, how nice you do look, dear! What is it, *le dernier cri*? To be sure, it is! And Nina, too, what a pleasant surprise!"

She always made people who called feel welcome; so did her brother Tom. Their nerves were strong; centuries of work on the land had bred a generation which was uncomplicated by the constraints of urban living.

The *dernier cri* was examined, every exterior part of it: the material, the cut, the jacket with the roll collar, the new large hat, the parasol, the new Norvic glacé kid button boots, with patent leather toe-cap and cuban heel. O, the doubt and hope that had flowed away from Mavis, and Nina, in choosing those boots! First it had been a cloth-topped patent golosh; then a velvetta calf with mother-of-pearl buttons, until, with almost a fracture of the mind, Mavis realised that cockney pearly men and women wore such things when they drove out, with feather hats and great vulgar boas, from their awful homes on Bank Holidays, usually singing and the worse for liquor. So the unexceptionable first pair she had tried on were finally chosen . . . at the very stiff price of 19s. 6d. And she had promised to pay for them on the Monday, having spent two weeks' salary on the materials for the *ensemble*.

While she was showing herself off, Phillip arrived. He *would*, she thought. If he were sarcastic, she would die!

"Good afternoon, Aunt Marian! How are you, Mother? Hullo, Nina! How do you do, sir?" Facing his grandfather, he said, "I have come to thank you for the very handsome presents you have procured for me for my birthday. Also I must ask to be taken into consideration my lapse in not having replied to your letter of six months ago, but I still keep it in my pocket case. Now do introduce me to this charming young lady, won't you? Why, it's you, Mavis! And wearing a Crow Blue *ensemble*. My lady friends in Debenham and Freebody's would be envious if they saw you now. Oh yes, I know two lovely girls who are mannequins there. I was very nearly engaged to one, but that was some time ago."

Taking solemnly his grandfather by the hand, he said in voice of the dead Hugh Turney, "I shall carry the Le Tournet crest, sir, in the Field—and faithfully maintain its traditions in the face of the enemy." He displayed the 18-carat gold ring on a little finger. "Seriously, Gran'pa, thank you very much indeed! How's old Tibbles? Still torturing birds in the Field—I refer to the Backfield, of course, this time." He rubbed the cat's ear with his finger.

Thomas Turney, not quite knowing how to take the varying moods of his grandson, said, "Well, your mother tells me that you've changed your Corps, once more, Phillip."

"Yes sir, kicked out once again, this time arriving on the back of a horse. *Eheu fugaces, fugaces*—as Uncle Hugh used to say. I thought that it referred to the cigar smoke he used to puff out of his mouth. *Phew—fumes, fumes*, for the word fumes was connected in my mind with smoke, from hearing him speak of a chimney on fire, in Charlotte Road. Then of course he told me that it meant the old days gone forever. It's a habit they have, unfortunately."

Hetty feared that her son had been drinking: his mocking manner, too, was startlingly like that of her dead brother, Hughie. She glanced at her aunt, that tower of affection and strength.

"Let me make you a cup of tea, Phillip," said Marian, getting up from her chair.

"Thank you, Great-Aunt, but I would not dream of putting you to any bother on my behalf."

"No bother at all, Phillip!" said the old lady, on her way to the kitchen.

"Well, Phillip, we expected you for lunch, you know. Have you had anything to eat?"

"Yes thank you, Mother. As a matter of fact, I had lunch with some friends for whom I referee'd a hockey match this morning."

"I bet!" scoffed Mavis. "Who were they?" she challenged.

"Some girls at the High School, if you must ask questions."

"Ha ha, those flappers you and Desmond meet in the Gild Hall! Fancy running after flappers, at your age!"

"Mavis, how dare you," said Hetty.

"Well, the referee must run occasionally, you know," said Phillip.

"Will ye stay to supper?" asked Thomas Turney. "Escallops will do you good. You must not neglect the inner man, you know."

"Well, thank you, Grandfather, but I promised to dine with some friends in London tonight."

"Then come tomorrow night, why not?"

"Yes do, Phillip," said Hetty, "we are so looking forward to it."

"Thank you very much. Well, I must be off now."

"To Freddy's, I bet," said Mavis.

He looked at his wristlet watch. "I must rush! Desmond and I are meeting Gene at Charing Cross in less than half an hour. Goodbye, everybody."

Home again, Hetty said, "I think you are most unfair, Mavis, to say things like that, especially before other people. Why you do it, I can never understand."

"There you go, always defending Phillip, and never seeing what he really is! I have told you, I am ashamed of having a brother like him! Everyone says at Head Office that he is a coward, or words to that effect, and was sent home last time, because he was no good. And everyone there has to work extra hard, to pay the salaries of the men away at the war, and what is Phillip doing with the money? Spending it on drink, and then wasting it away down the drain! And worse than that, he goes with loose women down in the High Street, and was seen the other night standing with one for a long time, outside St. Mary's Church, a woman called Lily Cornford, who gets drunk in the Bull and Freddy's, and picks up with anyone in uniform that comes along."

"Mavis, what are you saying? How dare you?"

"Well, it's the truth, Mother! I'm not imagining it! Desmond knows her, too, he takes her to the Hippodrome. And she goes to see that awful boozy old Dashwood, too—quite shameless!"

"How do you know all this, Mavis?"

"I heard it from someone who knows Phillip very well, and has done for years."

"Who is it? Tell me, Mavis."

"Do you swear you'll never tell a soul, Mother?"

"Very well, if you insist."

"Well, it is Mr. Jenkins, who hears it from the detective-sergeant at Randiswell Police Station."

"I did not know that you have been seeing Mr. Jenkins, Mavis!"

"I often come across him, when I go to see Nina. He goes on duty near her home."

"Oh, I see. All the same, I wish you hadn't told me, I wish you hadn't," said Hetty, feeling one of her headaches coming on.

Mavis put her arms round her mother. "Don't you worry, darling Mummy, I love you very very much, you know. But how can I help feeling like I do, about Phillip I mean, when he upsets everybody in the house, including Father. He always did, from the very first. When he was quite tiny, he was always taking Father's things, and causing trouble. Then when he was bigger, look how he used to get Peter Wallace to fight for him, and pick on innocent, weaker boys! Such as Albert Hawkins, who was killed at Loos with the Blackheath battalion, and I liked him very much, do you know that? Yes, he was the only boy who has ever loved me! And I loved him, too, as much as he loved me! And I can't forget his face, all over blood, as he cried and hung for support to that little tree growing on the bank below the garden fence, where the marn pond used to be, when Peter Wallace had punched him!"

It was now the mother's turn to hold the daughter, shaking with sobs.

London, April 1916. A fine night over Piccadilly, hub of the machine-turning globe, its golden spokes covering one-fifth of the world, the British Empire, whose energy was now roused in unity for—its own destruction.

The hub was small, in the financial centre of an island; and like a device upon the hub the bronze statue of Eros, the Winged Archer, was ever about to shoot his arrow into the human beings circulating below, with their thoughts of food, fear, fornication, and death; and here and there an individual inspired by austere thoughts of love everlasting, of patriotism, of the hope of courage in the final test of duty.

Dim specks of oil-lamps on taxicabs, their bodies built high like hooded bath-chairs, and almost as slow; blue-painted street lamps above the kerbs of pavements; uniforms of the principal nations of the Entente, Britain, France, Russia, Italy; and of the Allied nations of Japan, Belgium, Montenegro, Servia, Portugal. Officers of Colonial troops from Africa, spahis and other coloured troops wearing the fez; Australians with bushranger hats, Canadians, New Zealanders, South Africans, and the Gold Coast Regiment, the King's African Rifles. Among the masses seeking escape and relaxation from their thoughts, three suburban friends in file pressed through the slow thronging uniforms making for a restaurant which one of them, who considered himself to be a Man about Town, had discovered. There, he declared, one could eat a very good dinner at a moderate price, and drink the finest wines in London—Tiger's Popular Restaurant, less than one hundred yards from Eros, on the northern side of Piccadilly. Doors of wrought iron filigree and glass; golden electric lamps on tables; a carpet soft as sand, a string orchestra playing.

German submarine warfare had not yet stripped the bottoms in which money through trade had come to Great Britain: food was plentiful for those with money: the Great Push of the New Armies would end in the splendours of Victory.

One of the things Phillip liked about Eugene was his love of music. Eugene had heard operas with his father, and could hum many of the airs of *Bohême*, *Tosca*, *Butterfly*, and others. He had told Phillip the stories of these operas, producing in his listener the emotions he himself felt. Therefore it was extra pleasure that Phillip saw Gene going to the conductor of the orchestra, to ask for selections from *Pagliacci*, with its wonderful *On with the Motley*, the broken-hearted clown's lament for his betrayal and ruined life. Phillip felt himself to be the clown and ordered for a start two bottles of claret with the porterhouse steak; which when it came was surrounded by mushrooms, fried potatoes, onions, with six poached eggs lying upon it —a South African dish Phillip had heard of from a Boer officer at Grantham. When the second bottle was empty, he proposed a toast of the Big Push, declaring that he was off to Grantham on Monday, to finish his transport course, and apply to be attached to an early company going overseas; after the third bottle, Desmond declared that he would desert to France if his transfer to a Tunnelling Company of the Royal Engineers did not soon come through; while with the fourth bottle Senhor Eugene Franco Carlo Goulart etc. was on his feet declaring that Brazil would soon be coming into the war to join the Allies and then the spirit of his famous grandfather the General would etc. At this point the manager requested him to be seated, as the other customers wanted to be quiet, he said. Not to be suppressed, Phillip ordered a fifth bottle, and when that lay under the table empty he began to see how funny the quiet people at the other tables were, and by God, the three of them ought to wake them up and begin painting the town red!

A wonderful dinner. The host, when he had paid the bill and tipped the waiter five shillings and pressed upon each of his friends a pound note, followed them into the warm darkness of Piccadilly, to be led by Gene to the Empire Palace Hotel, and sit in an immense room of cream and gilt, with walls like Gorgonzola cheese from which the blue had been transmuted into veins of gold, where a thousand odd people sat at tables drinking coffee and liqueurs, eating pastry of Oriental splendour, while thick-red-lipped they stared around with mental hunger in dark brilliant eyes for glimpses of beauty and distinction to uplift them from their levels of living; and finding nothing, sat back upon those levels, ruminating prospects of more and more business due to war. They sat, seldom moving, secure in their fat, transients from the east, from Whitechapel, Aldgate, and Houndsditch to the west and north-west, Maida Vale, Hampstead, and Golders Green, families rising on the tide of clothing, furniture, and armament contracts.

Eugene, looking round with superior feelings, began to say that Phillip had let him down, by not being in uniform. He would be dismissed as a slacker. That's right. Also, if he had worn his'h uniform, he wouldn't mind betting that those two birds in the Gild Hall would have come to his flat s' afternoon.

"Well, to tell you the truth, dear boy," said Phillip, "I was'h thinking of someone called—hush!—Lily—so—you see—I stopped 'em from comin'."

A taxicab took them to Westbourne Terrace, and the driver, deeming them to be seeing double, sympathetically adjusted the fare to this state; and was surprised to be paid treble the sum on the clock.

It took twenty merry minutes, while doors opened to emit angry human barks before abruptly closing to loud *cuck-oos* by Phillip, before the attic flat was reached, where they slept, fully dressed. All night trains whistled and shunted in the yards of Paddington station below the row of tall seedy houses, heard remotely by Phillip as he tottered to the lavatory with aching head, throat, and gut; murmuring never again.

The repentance of the sick devil, or weak saint, went the way of most good intentions, including the romantic determination under the tawny flag to return to Grantham early on the Monday morning; for after spending Sunday in bed at home, and missing the supper party next door, on the following morning, when he got up at his mother's earnest request, to say goodbye to his father, he felt so weak that he decided to see Dr. Dashwood again, and ask for an extension of leave.

When Richard had left for the office, Mavis ran downstairs, and after swallowing her breakfast, said, "Mother, I must have ten shillings, quickly! I promised to pay for my new boots today, and have only nine and ninepence, which will leave me threepence when I've paid for them. Quick, quick, you must help me!"

"You've had a pound this month already, Mavis, and it is only the second week. I really cannot afford any more out of the housekeeping."

"But I must pay for my new boots! I must! I must! I must! Don't waste any more time, or I shall miss my train!"

"I really cannot afford any more, Mavis. You must wait till pay day."

"Give me ten shillings! I saw a note in your bag. Let me have it!"

Hetty looked at the face of her child, which was contorted, and near to frenzy.

"Quick, I say!" cried Mavis, as she stamped her foot.

"You did promise it would be the very last time, only on Saturday, Mavis."

"Oh Mother, don't waste time!"

Hetty looked helplessly at her daughter. "Oh very well, but this is the very last time, remember."

Mavis snatched the note, and ran out of the room.

"Don't bang the door!" yelled Phillip.

"Mind your own biz!"

The door clashed behind the hurrying girl.

"That stained glass will get loose in the lead strips. Why do you give in to her, Mother?"

"What can I do, Phillip? She works herself up so——"

"Why does she always want to dress herself in all these ridiculous fashions? And why must Nina always go with her, 'to help her to choose' this and that? She doesn't. It is always Mavis who chooses, and Nina who must agree with her. Mavis only wants someone to fetch and carry for her. They're like two birds together, a parakeet mincing along beside a thrush, Mavis in her finery and Nina in her tweed overcoat, and plain little hat. And they're always having tiffs, Nina always humbly asking how she has offended Mavis, and it usually ends in her crying; while Mavis holds out, won't say what Nina has done, but seems to enjoy prolonging Nina's distress. You say that Father often accuses you of what you haven't done, then sulks and withdraws into himself, letting you suffer; well then, can't you see that Mavis and Nina are in the same relationship? Why do you pander to her? It only makes her worse."

"Phillip, my son," said Hetty, looking at him with a steadiness near to despair, "'Judge not, that ye be not judged.' Mavis has been very unhappy. The boy she loved long ago, Albert Hawkins, was killed last October, at Loos, the same day that Bertie was killed. Do you begin to understand, my son?"

Phillip sat still. Then he gave a long sigh and said, "Yes, I think I do. Mother, at least let me give you this money, it's only three pounds, only you must swear never to say that I gave it to you. Help Mavis. Help yourself, too. Before Desmond or Gene borrows it first!" he laughed. "No, I didn't mean that. I'm very glad to be able to share with my friends. Oh dear, I can't go back today, I'll have to get twenty-four hours' extension. Never again."

Dr. Dashwood, that most courteous and titubating practitioner, after insisting on what he called a couple of pick-me-ups and the

patient considered to be potential lay-me-downs, insisted on a
medical examination in the billiard room.

"Definitely a dull patch on this lung, Middleton. I can't let you
return to duty until you have consulted my colleague Toogood.
I will give you a chit to take to him, Middleton."

To the Military Hospital Phillip went, and without further
examination Lt.-Col. Toogood, R.A.M.C., gave him another chit
and told him to report forthwith to Millbank Military Hospital.

There Phillip—having left his motorcycle in the porch of his
father's house, where it dripped oil that stained the terra-cotta tiles,
hitherto kept scrupulously clean by Mrs. Feeney the charwoman—
was put in the Observation Ward, and told to get into bed, after the
usual preliminaries of written-down details; and await an examination.

Chapter 11

TWO MONTHS' LEAVE

A condition of anaemia was found. The left lung showed symptoms
of phthisis; a sputum test having proved negative, it was considered
possibly to be due to chlorine gas inhalation. The action of the
heart was intermittent.

"Of course," he heard the R.A.M.C. major say to the lieutenant,
"the absence of tubercle in the sputum is not conclusive. He needs
building up." Phillip heard this with impassive face, while thinking
what a fraud he was.

He was put on a diet of milky foods; this was succeeded by white
fish, and chicken, while he had to remain in bed.

The ward had twenty-four beds, twelve a side. Each bed was
occupied by an officer. He noticed, during the morning inspection by the R.A.M.C. lieutenant on duty, and more pro-
nouncedly when the major and the colonel came round during the
bi-weekly inspection, how some of the faces opposite took on expressions of dullness or weakness specially for the occasion.

Some of them talked among themselves of having had medical
boards, one after another, until an original three months' leave
had been extended to six, then nine, then twelve; and one officer, a
senior subaltern seconded to the R.F.C. from a regular battalion
of an infantry regiment, had been on sick leave, with brief periods
in hospital such as the present period, since November 1914.

He seemed to have had a wonderful time. His talk was of dancing at Grafton Galleries, actors and actresses like Teddie Gerrard, Phyllis Monkman, Matheson Lang, Gaby Deslys, Vi Lorraine, and other famous people.

His bedside companion was also in the R.F.C. He had P.U.O. on his temperature chart, and said it was trench fever, probably from lice. He spoke of the coming Great Push. It was to be in the chalk country known as the Garden of Eden, the quietest and most peaceful sector of the British front. This sector, he said, had been taken over from the French, since the German attack at Verdun. A new British Army, the Fourth, had been formed under General Rawlinson, especially for the Push.

"Does the R.F.C. have liaison officers in the trenches, as the gunners do?"

"No. My engine went dud and I crashed my undercart behind the front line near Hebuterne, in our new sector. The Old Hun strafed my bus, but I got away into the trenches, where I got crummy but thought no more about it after a lysol bath. Then I had ten days' leave and here I am."

He went on to say, "In that trench they were digging a large rectangular pit, with a notice board stuck in it, SITE FOR WATER TANK. They groused like hell having to hack out all that chalk, and the skipper who entertained me in his dugout said it was a blind, in case the Hun raided, to give the idea that our trenches there were a fixture. It was just like the staff, he said, to think out such a Boy Scout idea to deceive the Old Hun."

"Don't you believe it!" called out a man across the ward. "Those pits are for a new kind of armoured land-fort, on caterpillar tracks. They put up the notice about water tanks to bluff Jerry."

The man in the next bed to Phillip was quite old, and in the Indian Army. He cursed things violently, and grumbled most of the time: a yellow-faced swarthy officer who, when he got up, put on a light khaki drill uniform. He had served in Mesopotamia, and was one of the few who had got away from the siege of Kut-el-Amara, after the battle of Ctesiphon. He was in hospital because he had what he called the Tigris Jigger in his guts. This, he explained, was a swimming organism with a corkscrew on its head, with which it burrowed, causing pain and bleeding. He had permanent screens around his bed, because he could not hold his water. He was given sandalwood oil in capsules, and hexamine; and he was privately dosing himself with whiskey. "Fire drives out fire, and corkscrew corkscrew," he said. The whites of his eyes, Phillip noticed, were as yellow as his Indian drill uniform.

One night he came back very late, saying that he had been arrested for "indecent exposure of the person in Trafalgar Square". He swore and raged, saying it was the bilharzia in his bladder—the Tigris Jigger. He cursed the Government for letting down the Army in Mespot. "We defeated Adbul the Turk at Ctesiphon, eighteen miles from Kut—five thousand wounded, and only springless carts to bring some of the poor sods back, over rough tracks, while Arabs gnawed like bloody rats at the wounded left behind, cutting off their private parts and sticking them in their victims' mouths." He told about the hospital ship *Mejidieh* floating down the river in a cloud of flies and stink for seventeen days, the wounded helpless and unattended on the decks, lying in their own fæces, black with flies—the lads who had fought at Ctesiphon.

In went the corkscrew, up went the bottle of whiskey.

After two days in slacks and carpet slippers, Phillip was told, "Matron says you may go out today. Have you friends or relations to go to? London is a naughty place nowadays, for a lonely soldier," as she relished him with her eyes. He dissembled, looking innocent to keep his detachment. "Oh yes, thank you, I live not far away."

"Then see that you are back in the ward by nine o'clock," she said shortly, as she went away, with a glance of disdain at the yellow, leathery officer of Ghurkas, sitting on the next bed and manicuring his fingernails.

Phillip walked about on the Hill, talked to Gran'pa and Mr. Bolton in their shelter, and wondered what he could do until six o'clock, when Desmond would return.

At seven they were in Freddy's, at half-past eight he caught a 36 bus to Victoria, jumped off at the Embankment, and walked to Millbank Hospital. After a few days of this, he returned on his motor-cycle, wheeling it into the hall of the hospital, and leaning it against the wall near the foot of the stairs. In the morning he wheeled it out again, and in sunny weather went home. For a week he followed the same routine; until the D.M.S., the old boy whose velvet tabs and hat-band were the hue of claret, asked what this O.H.M.S. machine was, and what purpose did it serve, and to whom did it belong. On being told it was the transport of a young officer patient, he said, "A hospital is no place for transport, let him arrange accommodation for it with the D.Q.M.G. Horse Guards."

"I think it might be simpler not to leave it here any more," said Phillip to the Matron, who said, "We don't want to separate you from your beloved *Helena*, so the Senior Medical Officer has arranged a board for you both at Caxton Hall tomorrow."

He felt he would be sorry to leave; his stay had been quite pleasant. Ah well, back to Grantham after a wonderful mike. But to his surprise the kindly old R.A.M.C. colonel—one of many white-haired dug-outs sitting solitary at little tables in the large hall, each with a convalescent officer seated before him—said, "I am giving you two months' convalescent leave. I would like you to go into the country and take things easily. Do you fish? The very thing to relax those tautened nerves of yours. Have you a good appetite?"

"Fairly good, sir."

"Now have you friends or relatives who will take care of you? If not, Georgiana Lady Dudley will be able to fix you up at one of her places. Meanwhile two copies of the Leave of Absence Form D.3a will be sent to you, one for your retention, the other you should send to your regimental agents, if you draw your pay through that channel. Your own copy should be kept by you, in order to support any claim for allowances, should you be entitled to any. Now if you go to the sergeant's table over there, he will issue you with a railway voucher for the station you want to go to. Good morning!"

There were half a dozen officers waiting at the sergeant's table, where warrants were being issued. As more accumulated, the sergeant got another book of warrants from a drawer and said, "If you gentlemen will take turns to fill in the particulars of rank, name, and regiment in this book, I will fill in the counterfoils, and we shall halve the time of waiting that way. Block letters, gentlemen, please."

The book of warrants went from one to another, with an indelible pencil. At last Phillip's turn came, and he made out his warrant for Lynton. He would stay in Aunt Dora's cottage, where he had spent his holiday just before the war.

When he got home, he fixed the warrant in the looking-glass frame above the fireplace. Lynton! Had not Father and Mother gone there for a holiday, too, just after he was born? A wonderful, romantic place. He hoped Father would notice it.

There it remained for several days, seen by Richard every time he went into the sitting-room; until at last he said, looking up from his magazine, "What is the wild boy up to now, Hetty?

What is all the mystery?" He indicated the pale green paper, which until now he had refrained from examining or asking questions about.

"Phillip stuck it there for safety, Dickie."

"What is it, if I may enquire?"

"He is going to stay for a while with Dora. Apparently he is not very well, and the doctors have sent him into the country."

"Look here!" cried Richard. "What is the mystery about Master Phillip? Is he ill, or is he not ill? If he is ill, why have not I, as the boy's father, been told about it?"

"I think it is general debility, Dickie. He was never very strong in the chest as a child, you will remember, and we were anxious about his croup."

"Oh. I had no idea. Was that decided when he went into hospital recently?"

"I think so, but Phillip does not say much to me, you know." She said this to reassure her husband.

"Well, it beats me. I don't understand what is going on, not in the very least." Richard picked up *Nash's*, and read more of the latest adventures of Chota in *Billet Notes*.

"Phillip is ordered lots of fresh air and cream, apparently, Dickie, so he is going to stay in Dora's cottage. He says the doctor told him to fish, so he is waiting for a few days, he says, until the trout are fat, at the end of May."

"Good God!" cried Richard, now thoroughly aroused, "what sort of caper is this? Have the authorities gone mad? What are they doing, to allow a bit of a boy like Phillip to run wild—and then they send him fishing for trout! And he bides his time, mark you, he picks and chooses, he waits until they are fat, at the end of May! Then in Heaven's name how much leave has he got, pray? *Two months?* Then why isn't he in hospital, if he is not well, instead of gadding about as he does, turning night into day? What are the powers-that-be doing, I should like to know, to leave a young fellow, if there is something radically wrong with him, to his own devices, until the Lyn trout are in condition? No, I do not accept that explanation! There is something very fishy about the goings-on of Master Phillip, if you ask me! Some things that want looking into very closely indeed!"

"I expect the authorities know what they are doing; please don't upset yourself about it."

"Who's upsetting himself? Not me," said Richard, and taking up *The Daily Trident*, he read about massed German assaults on the forts of Verdun; after which, an attack on Asquith for mismanaging the war, signed *Castleton*, the name of the proprietor of the newspaper.

"Well, at any rate, Dickie, I notice a great improvement in Phillip lately. He was very poorly, you know, when he came back from France last winter, very much on edge. I promised not to tell you, but his superior officer wrote to him and said he deserved a military cross for what he did. I saw the letter myself. Phillip took charge, he said, when the other officers had been killed, and led the men to take the position."

"Why didn't I know of this before?" cried Richard. "Now I come to think of it, Phillip always was a bit of an adventurer. Well I'm blest!"

Hetty felt happy, as she looked out of the back bedroom window at Phillip, whistling to himself as he worked in the garden below. The beautiful weather seemed to have entered into him; his almost feverish manner had calmed; he was like his old self, when all that had mattered to him was the countryside.

Phillip was varnishing his three-piece hickory rod, which he had bought before the war at a pawnbroker's for fifteen pence. Strands of a plaited silk line, speckled black and white, called *magpie*, were stretched between elm and fence, for rubbing with boiled linseed oil, for stiffening and waterproofing. His grandfather Maddison's japanned box of flies was open, for the points of the barbed hooks to be sharpened on oil-stone.

It was a fine morning in the second week in May. The sumach tree in one corner of the garden was in gentle leaf; the blossom of its neighbour, a lilac, was beginning to turn brown. Leaning a branch over the garden fence, as though to touch sumach and lilac, an apple tree planted by Thomas Turney at the same time that Hetty had planted the two trees on her side of the fence, soon after she had come to the house in Hillside Road, bore little green pouts of apples, their throats as though tied with brown bows. To Phillip's fancy the apples were the little eyes of the tree, whose fruit had been snatched, immature and sour, by the old man's grandsons during all the sunlit, peaceful years before the war. Never, never again! Gerry and Bertie, Tommy and Peter, Alfred and Horace, and for the boy he was, never the same again, for tree or man or bird. Did trees feel, did they mourn when their fruit, cradling their seeds, was lost to them before the time of ripening at the fall? Birds and animals suffered for loss of their young; so did insects, such as earwigs and spiders which carried their eggs in a silken bundle; some fish did, like the stickleback, the little rufous-bellied father fish, with his spiny daggers, who built a nest among waterweeds and hovered on guard, dashing at beetles which dived down to snatch his young. Once he and Horace Cranmer had watched a stickleback dart at a big black water-beetle, called *dytiscus*, which Father had told him flew about at night, looking down for water (and sometimes flopping upon glass-houses in the moonlight). The beetle seized the little fish and chewed it up in its jaws. Cranmer had caught it, and put it in a matchbox, and it had started to tear the wood of the box. *Sticklebat*, Cranmer had called the fish. They had watched it in a pond in Whitefoot Lane woods, in the old Boy Scout days.

Up in the elm above him sounded petulant beseeching cries. Ten tomtits, with new yellow gapes at the hinges of their beaks, had left the nesting box and were awaiting, on various branches among the green leaves, their parents with caterpillars, spiders, and occasional bits of fat from mutton bones hanging from trees in some of the gardens down the road. In the Backfield a female cuckoo belled through the mist of morning air; from the distant cemetery came the urgent *wook-wook-oo* of a male bird. The morning seemed to dream in stillness before the coming of great heat, as on the moor above the shadowed valley of the Lyn, during that wonderful holiday just before the war broke out. Would it be the same now, when at the end of the week he and Desmond went together to the West Country?

Desmond seemed much more contented than he was; he still went out with Lily, or rather to her house in Nightingale Grove, just above the railway; but apart from that, Phillip knew nothing.

Soon Desmond was to have ten days' leave, before going over-seas to a Tunnelling Company of the Royal Engineers. Six of those days were to be spent in Devon. Only seven more days now, and they would be sitting in a carriage at Waterloo, for the long and thrilling journey to Barnstaple; then the change to the little narrow-gauge engine, with the brass funnel, of the Lynton railway, leading up to the heather and furze and red deer of Exmoor, the bright running streams, the far blue Bristol Channel, the distant coast-line of Wales—far, far away would I rove!

Rod, line, and flies having been attended to, Phillip went through the open french windows into the house, and played his father's gramophone, which had been locked, but one of the keys

on his mother's key-ring opened it. After a cup of tea at eleven
o'clock, brought by Mrs. Feeney the charwoman (his mother had
gone shopping) he went down to visit Mrs. Neville, and had another
cup of tea with her at the open window. They discussed Desmond's
transfer, and he reassured her that all Tunnelling Companies were
well out of the fighting, safe underground from shelling.

"I think Desmond applied because he was a little bit jealous
of you having been out twice to the front. Of course I could stop
it if I wanted to, but he would never forgive me if I did. He's so
big that sometimes I forget that my son will not be eighteen until
next September! And now he talks of being engaged to some girl!
You look surprised, Phillip; didn't you know? I hope I'm not
giving away secrets—perhaps Desmond wants to tell you himself.
Anyway, I expect you know Lily, one of the little girls in the Gild
Hall? I know nothing about her, beyond what I've told you. I
don't expect to share in a young man's life, like some mothers do.
But then, I'm not the possessive kind. I believe in letting the
younger generation find its own feet. What's she like, Phillip?
Some fluffy little thing, with goo-goo eyes?"

"Lily is fair, and rather pretty, Mrs. Neville. She's not exactly
a flapper, in fact she looks quite grown up. Actually, I think she's
the same age as Desmond."

"Thank God she isn't a canary!" Mrs. Neville cried, with a
little shriek of laughter. "Although, poor things," she added, as
suddenly reflective again, "they cannot help it. Haven't you
heard of the canaries at Woolwich, Phillip? That's what the soldiers call them. They're the girls working in the explosives department, whose faces turn yellow with the chemicals they handle.
They make a lot of money, and the soldiers know this, of course,
and go out with them only if the canaries stand treat! They're
doing well, you know, some of the working class, nowadays—
especially those on munitions. They're buying motor-cycles,
gramophones, and even grand pianos! That's respectability, you
see, Phillip—a grand piano. Nobody can play them, of course!"

When she spoke next, Phillip realised that she had known more
about Lily than she had pretended.

"Desmond says Lily is rather like Helena, Phillip, only quieter,
though what that means I don't know, for Helena is the last girl
to be called flighty! Still, it's only his first girl—all the boys in
khaki nowadays want a girl, don't they, someone whose photograph they can carry in their pocket-book, and show the other
fellows. You look rather sad, dear. Is anything the matter?"

"Desmond doesn't want me to talk to her, Mrs. Neville."

"A little jealousy, dear, that's all. Don't you take any notice of that! He's finding his own feet, you see. So far it has been you who has filled his life, for as you know, Desmond has not had a father's care, and a growing boy needs someone other than his mother to look up to. Why, he was jealous of your devotion to Helena at one time, and used to tell me that if you and she became, well—it's only a phase, Phillip! Have another cup of tea, won't you? Oh, it's the gramophone at the open front window again today, is it? 'If music be the food of love, play on,' as Shakespeare says. Which reminds me, I am so glad that your mother has found an interest outside her home, in the plays she sees with Grandpa! I see them trotting off down the road, to get the midday cheap tram! Then back again, before your father comes home. Why don't you go with her to the Old Vic one day, it would give her such a treat, and you'd enjoy Shakespeare too, with your fine perceptive feelings, dear."

"Oh, I had enough Shakespeare at school to last me a lifetime! Though I must admit bits Gran'pa used to read weren't bad. I remember the scene from *Henry the Fifth* he read, the camp-fires, and the armourers 'accomplishing the knights', knocking in the rivets to their armour. That was when Uncle Sidney and Uncle Hugh were going to the Boer War. Well, I must skedaddle now. Can you hear the gramophone down here?"

"Faintly, dear. But I shall be looking out when she comes past, wheeling her bike. She always looks up and waves to me, you know."

"You are my ally, Mrs. Neville! Well, I must rush now! I think I'll play the Nimrod movement from Elgar's *Enigma Variations* today, and not the *Liebestod*. Only four more days now, and Des and I will be on our way to Devon! It won't be the same, of course, for somehow in war-time the country does not seem to be as it used to be, but with Des, who likes fishing better than watching birds, I hope it will be like old times again."

Phillip's new mood of optimism, which might have been due to the slack time he had been enjoying, was not to last long. Detective-sergeant Keechey was to see to that.

Feeling happy with life, Phillip went down early to Freddy's bar; but going in out of the sun, which was slanting shadows across the street and half-way up the buildings opposite, he felt sudden longing to be in the country. The bar looked dull and ordinary;

he had never been in during a summer day before, only in the autumn by day, and gas-light during the darkness when the shadowy world was shut out. Now Freddy somehow looked older, and artificial, like his wearing a strawyard indoors, a man of straw and cash in the till, and with no other personality than that of a foreground figure to rows of bottles. He was reading *The Morning Advertiser* when Phillip went in, there being no customers in the three bars.

"I'll have a beer, Freddy. And one for yourself."

They were on terms almost of confidence now; at least in small things, such as Freddy having confided that the money he got for drinks stood to him went into a money-box for his little boy; but when a very special friend asked him to 'ave one, well, he took a little gin. To show his sincerity, Freddy poured himself a tot from a bottle from which he unpeeled the wrapper.

Having toasted one another, Freddy glanced around the empty bar, took a look into the snug next door, and into the four-ale bar at the end. Coming back, his eyes made a conspiratorial sweep before saying in lowered voice, "You know those two plain-clothes fellows from the station? I thought I'd warn you that they've bin making enquiries about you. I told them nothing, of course. Don't say I told you, you know they can make it awkward for the tenant of this 'ouse with the Council."

"The Council?"

"The Borough Council owns this house, you see, sir. It's not a tied 'ouse, like most houses, it's what they call a free house, leaving the tenant to buy where he likes. But we have to be careful, as the Council owns the place."

A feeling of being shadowed, in two senses, came upon Phillip. He thought that his happiness had been too good to last: something was bound to happen. He touched the mahogany slab of the counter.

"I think—only don't say I said anything, will you—but I fancy it may have to do with your being about here so long, and out of uniform. You remember that Australian what was here spending money like water a week or two back? You may recall you told me his medal ribands looked wrong, he wore one for Gallipoli, I think it was, and you said there was no such medal yet. Well, they questioned 'im in the billiard room, and later he was arrested in London, as a deserter, by the military."

"Good God, do they think I'm a deserter, then?"

"I can't answer for what a flatfoot thinks, but I know they are out to get all the pinches they can, for promotion. It's not for me to express an opinion, but I think you can guess what I think of them," tittered Freddy, his eyes closed to slits as he sipped his gin.

Phillip took a draught of his beer, and was putting down the glass when the swing doors opened. Giving a wink, Freddy took up cloth in one hand, glass in the other, and began to polish. Rubber footfalls came from behind Phillip, and he saw in the retinae of his eyes dark-clothed arms from which rolled umbrellas hung.

"I'd like a word with you," said Keechey, beside him.

Discomposed by the deliberate nearness of the two men in bowler hats, Phillip tried to show calmness as he raised his glass, to drink slightly, and, he hoped, with nonchalance.

When Phillip made no reply, Keechey went on, "Will you come with us into the billiard room? I want to ask you some questions."

Freddy went on polishing the glass as though he had heard nothing. Curious and a little upset, Phillip followed Keechey into the billiard room. The tall moustached detective came after him, and shut the door.

"You have been about here for some weeks now, off and on, and I have made some enquiries about you. I think I am right in saying that your name is Maddison? And it may interest you to know that we have made enquiries at the Motor Machine-Gun Section, Bisley, and they have no knowledge of you. What do you say to that?"

"Only that I am not in the Motor Machine-Gun Section at Bisley. I am in the Machine-Gun Training Centre at Grantham."

"Then what are you doing, sometimes in uniform, down here?"

"I was given two months' sick leave by a medical board at Caxton Hall, a little over five weeks ago."

"Two months. That's a long time, isn't it? Were you wounded?"

"No. As a matter of fact, I was given the leave to go away into the country; Devon, in fact. I'm going there on Friday. I've been given a railway warrant to Lynton."

"I'll take particulars of your unit. Grantham, you say, is your headquarters? What's become of your friend Devereux-Wilkins? Ever hear of him nowadays?"

"He's not a friend of mine. I've only seen him once."

"But you went down to see him the night you came back from France, the thirteenth of October last, didn't you? You went to the Roebuck for that one purpose only, I think. You spoke to him for less than two minutes, having called him away from a game of billiards. Then he left for London, and you came back here. You were accompanied by a Brazilian friend, I think. Shortly afterwards there was a Zeppelin raid. Then you met Dr. Dashwood on your way home and returned with him to the Conservative Club until shortly after eleven o'clock."

"You seem to have been shadowing me quite a lot. I suppose you've been talking to Mr. Jenkins?"

"Which Mr. Jenkins?"

"The special constable who lives in the same road. Anyway, what is all this leading up to? Some spy-scare business?"

"We have to take notice of everything, especially during a war, you know. How d'you think the war's going? When are we going to have a smack back at the Germans?"

This was so obvious a trap that Phillip laughed. He thought of saying that they might put on khaki themselves and go to France and find out, but he could never make the sort of reply to people that might make them feel awkward. It was because he was a weakling, he knew; quite unable to hit back at anybody.

"Oh, a big push is coming, all right. We've got a lot of water-tanks in position behind our lines in France, south of Arras, in order to make Jerry think we are there for life; but that's where the attack is coming, I hear."

"Where did you hear that?"

"In Millbank Hospital, about five weeks ago. From an officer there, who had just come back from the front."

"What are the tanks going to be used for? Poison gas?"

"No, for water, according to what I heard. It was obviously a blind, to puzzle Jerry, if he came over to raid."

"In a Zeppelin, you mean?"

Phillip laughed.

"So you think it funny, do you?" The buck-teeth were exposed, the upper lip slightly drawn back.

"Well, sort of Heath Robinson, you know."

"Who's Heath Robinson?"

"Haven't you heard of Heath Robinson?"

"I'm asking the questions," retorted the other, with a suggestion of snarl.

"He's a comic artist. He's as well known as Bairnsfather."

Looking at Phillip sideways, the plain-clothes policeman said, "Are you trying to be funny? Because if you are, two can be funny, see? Who d'you think you're talking to?"

"Who do *you* think you're talking to?"

"You'll soon find out!" And taking his umbrella, the buck-toothed man, the blood partly drained from veinous face, walked from the billiard room, and out of the saloon bar, followed by what Phillip, who had been reading a story by Harrison Ainsworth, thought of as his myrmidon. Then, peering through the open slot in the stained-glass partition, his glance met the sky-blue shine of the eyes of Lily smiling at him from the other side of the partition.

A glass of colourless chemical lemonade stood on the bar, with the penny bottle. Freddy stood opposite her, the Chinese expression on his face emphasised by the oval pebbles of his spectacles framed in thin gold wire.

"This young lady," said Freddy, "wishes to 'ave a word with you," and he went away to polish more glasses.

Phillip slid the cover over the spy-hole, and went out of the billiard room.

"Hullo," said Lily, softly, making as if to take his hand, but stopping herself. "I knew what Keechey and his assistant were after, when I saw them following you over the bridge as I came out of the laundry. So I came after them, just in case I could help."

"Well, that's very kind of you, but I'm quite all right, thanks."

"You don't know Keechey as I do. It was him what set about Dr. Dashwood last night. Haven't you heard? It was after he had come in to see Mother, after a late visit to a little girl with diphtheria a few doors up. The doctor came into ours afterwards, and Mother give him a cup of tea. When he left it was getting on for eleven, and he was on his way to the Conservative Club when someone set about him in the dark as he was walking down Courthill Road and crowned him, then kicked his face while he lay in the road. Of course it was Keechey; he's as jealous as a rat, as I told you."

"Did you know about Dr. Dashwood, Freddy?"

"A publican hears many things, sir," said the landlord, polishing away. "I did hear he had had some sort of an accident."

"Accident!" exclaimed Lily.

"Now, my girl!" retorted Freddy, sharply. "I know nothing, see? This is a respectable 'ouse, and what goes on outside is none of my concern, see?" Coming to be near Phillip, "A man can draw his own conclusions, so long as he keeps them to himself. You, sir, I think I am right in saying, can draw your own conclusions, too? Now will you have a drink with me? Lily, you take my advice and go back to work, and I don't mean that in any way unkindly. I'm old enough to be your father, see?"

"They're all old enough to be a father if you let them," said Lily, to no one in particular as she sipped her lemonade, "only the nice ones like to fancy themselves as babies first."

"That's what it's for, isn't it?" tittered Freddy.

"Go on, you're like all the rest of them!"

"Don't let the missus hear you say that," whispered Freddy, "or she might start creatin'! You're a very pretty girl, you know. You want to get a real sweetheart, and leave the boys alone. It's time you went steady."

"Like you did, you mean? Well, I may not be that sort of girl."

"You know the old proverb, don't you?"

"I know your old proverb," said Lily. "But you didn't run fast enough."

"She's a caution, isn't she?" tittered Freddy. "So'll my wife be, if she hears her say that."

"She knows it already," said Lily.

When Freddy had gone to the lower bar she said to Phillip, putting her hand on his, "I'm sorry you're going away, but glad for your sake, for I know Keechey will try and pin something on you else. If he does, I know a thing or two about him which would keep him quiet."

"Oh, it was nothing, a mere mistake on his part. It's cleared up now."

"Please," said Lily, swimming to him from the blue lakes of her eyes, "please take care of yourself. And don't think me too forward, will you?"

"I think you are rather nice, Lily."

"Do you—really?" The lakes of her eyes seemed about to overflow.

When she had gone, Freddy said, "I'll say this for Lily, she pays her own way, and don't come in here to pick up what she can, as some might think." He leaned over the bar, and whispered, "I have an idea that she fancies someone other than your friend, Desmond Neville."

Phillip felt a pang of disappointment; then he was relieved. "I'm rather glad to hear you say that, for quite apart from other things, she is much too old for Desmond."

Freddy looked at him peculiarly. "You don't get my meaning," he said. Then between his teeth, "Anyway, watch your step with plain-clothes coppers."

"Look here, Freddy, did *you* believe what Keechey thought, that I'd lost my commission, and was due to be called up under conscription? The mistake arose simply because he'd enquired about me at the wrong unit."

"I'm not doubting your word for a moment, sir, and it's not for the likes of me to inquire into your affairs, but you know what I told you about him and Lily, and he's not the sort to stop at anything to please himself. He's not got many friends round here, I can tell you! So if you don't mind me saying it to you again, watch your step. You know what 'appened to a certain party on a dark night, don't you?"

"So you think that Keechey may have a grudge against me, as he had against Dashwood, on account of his friendship with Lily? Well, I assure you, Freddy, that there's nothing like that between Lily and me! As for my great friend, he's a bit of a boxer, and if Keechey tries any hankypanky on him, he'll get a surprise! Anyway, Desmond's going to the front after his week's leave."

"Yes, he told me. Tunnelling, I think he said. He'll miss you, you've been like an older brother to 'im, almost a father, in fact! So you have to that Brazilian fellow."

"Is it Eugene that Lily is keen on, Freddy?"

Freddy looked amusedly at him, and said, "Don't you know better than that?"

"I don't know what you mean, Freddy."

"Well, they say the onlooker sees most of the game, sir, and at the same time, one can never be sure of anything where a woman is concerned, so it's really none of my business. Will you have a drink with me? It's a pleasure, I assure you!"

Freddy tipped his straw; the bar had come alive again.

The beautiful weather of late spring continued. Evening after evening Richard went down to his allotment, feeling the buoyant sunny air to be part of himself as he pushed his wheel-barrow, its tools wrapped in sacking against rattling, past the cemetery.

Having arrived at his rods of ground, he set about preparing for work. His Norfolk jacket, folded inside out with the cashmere lining exposed, was placed in line with his tools upon the flinty soil, all laid neatly parallel. Such alignment gave this lonely man pleasure, or rather a feeling of harmony: here he could live his own mental pattern, which almost chronically was broken for him in what he thought of as his own house. Fork, sieve, spade, hoe, line-and-winder, compost pail, two small bags holding hop manure and lime respectively, and a third smaller one containing soot— there they were in their places, keeping their distance from him.

Having rolled up his sleeves in the correct manner, two-thirds the way up the forearm from the wrist, he took up his hoe, and treading carefully, examined his small plants. He saw them suddenly as they had looked in boyhood: the lettuces so tenderly pale, the carrots like dwarf trees, while the onions and leeks were tiny twisted green poles with black seed-caps on their tips, cabbages a tottering line of tiny little fellows.

Now to let the air most carefully into their rootlets! The finer the tilth on top, the more moisture would be conserved.

As he worked, to Richard came a picture of himself hoeing as a boy, after the Home Farm had been taken in hand—the last effort of his father to stave off the inevitable collapse, before the mortgages were foreclosed and everything broke up. The picture dulled; he sighed, and rested. The sun shone; his forearms were brown; he rejoiced again. There was nothing to equal farming; he was hoeing, he was in the open air, the late spring evening was warm and glowing with the same mellow light of boyhood's evenings in field and lane and attic bedroom looking upon the Longpond at Rookhurst. In his mind he saw the steel chain of twenty-two yards dragging bright and jingling over flints upon a loamy downland field of arable, as the steward, broad-clothed and buskin'd, measured the men's plots. Here, too, were flints; but upon a gravelly soil made hard with clay, a field abandoned to building plots, reprieved by the war. It was still alive, flown over by the cuckoo; voles lived in the grassy lanchetts between the plots; the kestrel hung above, larks sang in the air.

In one corner of the allotment stood Richard's compost heap. It was rectangular, properly squared at the coigns, and level on top. Within, heating in the first process of rotting, lay grass cut with shears, hedge clippings, nettle tops, dock leaves, perishable weeds, and pailfuls of kitchen waste provided by his wife. Not all of the latest pailful had gone into the heap, for some of its contents had been what Richard had asked Hetty particularly not to include: greasy margarine wrapping-paper, which would not rot, but only make unsightly litter.

He looked up at the sound of a motor-cycle engine and saw a trail of dust behind the familiar figure of the wild boy riding, one negligent hand on throttle-controls, the other resting, theatrically, he thought, on his hip. Stopping a few yards away on the cart track, the rider propped up his machine and strolled over. Richard leaned upon his hoe.

"To what do I owe the pleasure of this visit?" he said affably.

"Oh, I thought I would come and see how you were getting on, Father. I'm off to Devon tomorrow."

"Well, give the Lyn and the sea my love. And of course Aunt Dora."

"Yes, Father."

Richard watched him casting his eyes around, until they rested on two small pieces of grease-proof paper, neatly folded into squares, and held down by a stone, near the compost heap.

"Yes, you may well look in that direction," he said, with a light laugh. "However, we must count our blessings. At least so far no broken glass or sardine tins have been included in my compost pail."

"You ought to see the heaps of rubbish in an army camp, Father. Tons of loaves piled high, with rotting carcases of meat."

Richard thought this an exaggeration, but he said, "Oh, the great mass of English people are the untidiest on earth, we all know that. Do you remember the litter covering the Hill after a band night? Well, how's the motor-cycle? Running well?"

"Yes thanks. I thought of going out to Reynard's Common to look at the Fish Ponds, and see if the carp and rudd are still basking on the top of the water."

"Desmond, I suppose, is coming home from Waltham Abbey tonight?"

"Yes, Father, if there isn't an air-raid warning."

"He told me, when you were in Millbank Hospital, and the Irish Rebellion broke out, that they had an invasion scare. I mention this because you always tended to scorn any idea of an invasion, I think."

"We've got a navy, Father."

"Well, yes, I give you that point," said Richard, reluctantly. Then in a lowered voice, "Strictly between you and me, I can now tell you that, on the night following the murder of British officers as they lay in bed in Dublin hotels, we knew down at the Station that the eight Zeppelins which came over, led by Mathy, were working with the German High Seas Fleet. We Specials were on duty until two o'clock in the morning. The invasion alarm fizzled out, thank the lord, and I was able to spend some of my evenings getting on with my cultivations here. Well, tell me what you think of my little holding?" Richard swung out the hoe to encompass his sixteen rods.

"It looks very good, Father."

"We want some rain badly, and I fancy some is on the way."
He looked up at the sky, where a pack of white cumulus cloud was
moving slowly towards the north-east. "They may be getting
rain in the West Country now. If so, it will bring the salmon up
the Lyn for you. They use worm there, you know, in the boiling
pools between those huge boulders. Are you off now? Well,
thanks for looking me up. Tell Mother I'll be home about nine
o'clock, will you? I want to put in my runner beans, they should
have been in long ago. I have to go on duty at ten tonight, so if
I don't see you before you go to Devon, I'll wish you a very
pleasant holiday, now."

"Thank you, Father. Would you like me to take the greasy
paper back for you?"

"Oh, no thanks, I shall burn it before I leave."

Now what did the wild boy mean by that, thought Richard, as
the motor-cycle thudded softly down the flinty cart-track.

Chapter 12

LILY AND THE NIGHTINGALE

Phillip, right hand on the single lever of the Binks 3-jet carburettor,
was driving by ear, listening to the soft slow beat of his engine,
as though, he said to himself, to the heart-beat of the beloved.
This was a familiar phrase from magazine stories; but the engine
beat was nearer to his love than any human heart had ever been.
He listened with concern: there was inclined to be a rough spot
between the pilot and second jet; and he did not want the engine
to choke as *Helena* made her easy, lackadaisical departure. The
flywheel was turning about two hundred times a minute: a heavy
flywheel, so the pulley did not snatch at the belt. Gently now,
open the throttle: his ear delighted in the very sensitive response
to the extra gas, and at little more than walking pace, and still
with almost silent heart-beats, *Helena* bumped over the pavement
and the kerb to the road, and continued along by the cemetery
railings until her rider was out of sight round the corner by the
iron gates . . . then, with nickel-plated lever pushed wide, she
gratefully drummed away down the road to the village of Randiswell, her rider now feeling that he was flying through sunshine in
pursuit of the angular shadow racing effortlessly before him, as he

rose up and down over the bridge, retarded the spark to make the loudest burst of machine-gun fire past the police station, and then slowing, turning into the High Street, driven by the idea of seeing Lily again, to find out, he told himself, the true position between her and Eugene, for Desmond's sake. Why, if she cared for Eugene, was she also pretending to be Desmond's genuine lover?

With this good intention he looked in at Freddy's, then at the Black Bull, to find her eventually in the Gild Hall, sitting alone before a thick glass cup from which the twopenny blob of vanilla ice had disappeared. She wore a new pale yellow straw hat, with a blue velvet riband fastened under her chin, the colour of her eyes.

She smiled when she saw him, and when he went to her table she said "Hullo!" almost inaudibly, as she lowered her eyes and began to play with the spoon on the plate in front of her.

"I've been looking for you," he said, avoiding the shiny blue of her eyes. "How about another ice?"

He gave an order for two, and when they were set down on the table he met her glance and asked if she were expecting anyone.

"Oh no!"

"Excuse my asking, but do you like Eugene very much?"

"He's all right," she said, dreamily drawing a smoothed spoonful of ice between her lips and sucking it slowly.

"But do you like him awfully?"

"He's a nice-looking boy, and knows it, but he thinks every girl can't resist him."

"Then it *is* Desmond you—care for most?"

"Don't you know?" said Lily, with an unsteady smile. He felt disturbed by the pulse beating in her throat.

"Well, as a matter of fact, Desmond and I really haven't talked much about it."

She stopped sucking her ice and was looking on the table, so that for the first time he saw what long lashes she had, and the curve of her cheeks. Perhaps she was disdainful of him asking questions like that. Awkwardly he rose to his feet, stammering, "Well, I think I'll go for a run on my bike. I'm sorry if I seemed inquisitive." When the azure limpidity of her eyes was upon him he said, "I want to see if there are still carp basking among the lily-pads of the Fish Ponds out by Reynard's Common. See those gold-fish down there? They're carp, but poor little tame things. The carp in the Fish Ponds, some of them, are nearly as long as my arm, and a sort of bronzy brown. Have you ever been out there?"

"Oh please, why are you so angry with me?"

"But I thought you were angry with me!"

"Angry with you," she said, as though he were far away. She gave a little laugh. "Is that where the bluebells come from?"

"Where they *used* to come from, before all the lou—— I mean the fellows on bicycles pulled them up. No, that's not quite fair. They lived in, well——" he checked himself in time from saying *poor streets*— "—away from the countryside, and wanted to take some of the beauty home, I suppose. Haven't you ever seen bluebells growing?"

She shook her head slowly, as though nursing him in her eyes.

"I'm afraid they're over now," he said, thinking that her eyes were the same misty blue. "What flowers are left will be ripening into little pods, rather like papery skulls, filled with shiny black seeds. I had an idea to collect some, and throw them out of the carriage window, on the way to London Bridge, just before the war came."

"Aren't you funny?" she said, her head on one side. "You've got the most beautiful eyes. Did you know it?"

He was embarrassed, thinking that she was trying to get off with him, when she was Desmond's girl.

"Do you mind me saying that? I didn't mean to say it. Dr. Dashwood told me it was bad manners to make remarks about anyone, or to ask personal questions. Do you believe that the eyes are the windows of the soul?"

Dr. Dashwood had obviously said that about Lily's eyes, thought Phillip.

"Dr. Dashwood likes you—Middleton. Do you mind if I call you Middleton?"

"I think it's rather a compliment to have a nickname."

"He calls me Bluebell."

"How is he getting on?"

"His housekeeper has left him."

"Why, because of what happened to him last night?"

"No, she left before that. He's been doing for himself for nearly a month now."

"He won't last long as a doctor, will he, with no one to see to his house."

"He has asked me to marry him."

Phililp felt a jolt. He was unable to ask if she had accepted, or not.

"He cried, and said nobody wanted him. You won't tell anyone, will you?"

"Of course not. Poor old chap. Are you—no, I mustn't ask that."

"He cried because I told him I could not marry him."

"Because of Desmond?"

She shook her head.

"Oh, Lily, let us be as we were in the churchyard. Please tell me something. Do you love Desmond?"

She went on shaking her head.

"Is there someone else?" Seeing her downheld eyes, he went on, "I don't understand. Can you like many—people—at once. then?"

The head was shaken once more.

"I suppose I ought to go," he said unhappily.

"Why?" she said, with such appeal in her eyes that, despite the hat she wore, he said, "It's such a lovely evening. I suppose you wouldn't care for a ride on the back of my bike to the Fish Ponds?"

"Oh, I would!" she said, her face lighting up.

In 1916 it was not easy to start on a motor-cycle driven by a rubber belt and a fixed pulley, when you were on level ground, unless you could run and spring on when the bike was in motion. But when you had a flapper on the bracket it was impossible. The way to start was to go to the top of a sloping street, wait for your passenger, let her seat herself on the bracket over the rear wheel, while you straddled from the saddle; then, all being balanced, you stood up and pushed off with your feet, the handlebars taking all the forward thrust. It was a precarious few moments while you wobbled forward, ready to drop the valve-lifter; and when you did so, and the engine fired, a quick adjustment of weight was necessary, for you who had pushed were now pulled. If your flapper was calm, you were all right; your strong forearms kept the bike straight, as you sat back on the saddle, trailing your feet a moment to show your easy mastery of the situation.

"Sit tight!" said Phillip, straddling the level cobblestones. "Here we go!" as he shoved off. "This three-jet Binks is marvellous!" as he dropped the valve-lifter. *Helena* fired with beats slower than those of his heart. He sat back, and opened the throttle. "Top hole!" he cried.

Safely past Freddy's, fire station, St. Mary's church, he told her to put an arm round his waist and hold to his jacket, relieved that she sat so steadily. Desmond of course used to sit astride; Lily sat at right angles to the frame, her back to the rubber belt, which otherwise might have caught her skirt. She saw the polished tram-lines rushing away behind her, she felt unsafe and fixed as it were upon nothing except bumps; she felt all was unreal, she glowed with pride. Gran'ma, she thought, again and again, Gran'ma, I am with you at last.

They passed Cutler's Pond, and got up Brumley Hill without falter, and through the town, along Shooting Common, and turned up the long gradual incline to the Fish Ponds, arriving without mishap.

"Were you very uncomfortable? I tried to avoid the pot-holes as much as I could."

"It was lovely! Thank you ever so, for asking me."

The pines around the upper and lower ponds were reflected in the water; and there, among the floating lily-leaves, were the brown dorsal fins of the great carp which were said to be a hundred years old.

"The carp is the fox of the water. No angler has ever been known to lose his bait of a small boiled potato, bean, or bread-paste, to these piscatorial wiseacres."

"They must be quite happy without what the fishermen want to give them," said Lily.

It was strange, he thought, how she seemed to fit into the countryside, accepting it as though she had known it all her life, while not knowing the names of anything—stonechat, linnet, and willow wren, wagtail flitting for water-flies around the verge of the pond, or running on the lily leaves, to take flies for its young some-where. They walked through the heather, while she stopped to touch the bells coming into colour, and the white bark of a birch tree, while he wondered about it, for in the past he had done the same thing, but always secretly, lest someone see, and know that he was, in Father's words from earliest memory, a sort of throw-back.

"Oh, isn't it lovely?" she said, as slowly, slowly she followed behind him, ribbon of hat in hand trailing the heather and bracken, her mouth loose and her eyes dreaming. He began to assess her: she was strongly built, her skin was very soft and white, her breasts were high and level, slightly moving up and down in her white silk blouse as she walked. Their movement kept him mentally apart from her, while the silk softness of the blouse was alluring, and sweet to see. He thought of her as a woman, older than himself; not that she was seventeen.

They came to the wooden steps through the oak paling fence of Knollyswood Park, and opened the swing gate into what he said used to be his preserves. It was the first time he had been there since the war, though he and Desmond had passed the fence on the way to Crowborough, more than a year ago, he remembered, when he was going to try to get a commission from the second battalion. How long ago it was, a world gone for ever.

They sat down on the grass in a glade bumpy with anthills. A green woodpecker dived out of the trees in the near distance and in sloping flight approached them, and knowing the gallypot's feeding habits he pressed her hand and whispered, "Don't move!"

After an abrupt flop down the bird lifted a crimson head to stare at them. Then with a wild cry it sloped off in wavy flight.

"Oh, what a funny bird. And what a funny noise it made!" said Lily, chewing the sugary knot of a grass stem.

"Did you see that sharp mad eye of the violent wood-hammerer? That's the woodpecker which haunts the family that owns this park, and foretells the death of a member of the house."

"Go on," said Lily, her eyes big.

"It came here as a rest from its eternal task of having to strike furiously at half-rotten trunks and branches of trees in the forest. The crest of the family coat of arms of the Earl of Mersea is a woodpecker, hence the legend. Its laugh, what is called a yaffle, sounds insane, doesn't it? Well, it comes here to rest, as I said, from slavery. It has a long tongue, which uncurls like a watch spring, and flips up ants. It saw us, and cried out of its broken heart. Back to hammering wood, striking furiously with its neck muscles, which must be terrifically strong; even so, it must get awful headaches."

"Are you joking?" asked Lily.

"Only if the whole world is a joke. For consider a moment: for thousands of years, hundreds of thousands of years, special forces have been caged in that frame of bone and flesh and sinew, and all inherited from tiny specks of life in a fluid inside a white shell of lime! Other birds, too, inherit special forces and actions; they can't escape their fates; the hawk must tear flesh, the owl must fly in darkness, the wren make its nest like a ball with a hole in the side, and persecute spiders. Spiders must give hell to flies, fish must eat nymphs. The chalk downs, farther on towards the Saltbox and

Biggin Hill, are but shells of trillions of little sea-animals, all gone, who have all yielded up their obscure little ghosts. Every dew drop which falls has been drunk by something, which has lost its life. Perhaps when death comes, that is freedom for a while, to get away from the destined will and task upon the earth."

He sat before her with bowed head, feeling alone and void. She put out a hand and stroked his head; he did not draw back, nor did he yield; but when he looked up and saw her eyes which had brimmed over he did yield, for a moment, and allowed her to take his head on her breast. Without thinking what he did, as he lay there, he nipped a part of the white silk blouse between his lips, gently, and closed his eyes.

"Oh you are sweet," said Lily, a deeper tone in her voice. "How your mother must have loved you when you were a baby."

He thought he could have her if he wanted to: he had impressed her. The moment was lost as he thought of Helena: that this was not Helena. She divined what he was thinking, and said gently, "You love that girl, don't you? I always knew you did. But don't mind me, Middleton! I always knew you were different from the other boys, as I said when we talked beside the cemetery. It is wonderful, I think, what education can do. I never got beyond standard four at Carlow Road School."

"Oh, one learns nothing at school, Lily."

"But you must have studied lots of books."

"I got most of them from the Free Library, years ago. Others were at home, they belonged to my father's father, such as Darwin's *Voyage of the Beagle*, and books like that. But out in a place like this, thoughts come to one, somehow. I think it is the spirit of the earth, which is hidden under pavements. I had a wonderful time out here when I was a boy, it was so wild and so quiet, the beautiful colours of the leaves and ferns, and if you sat still, you saw the life going on around you, all in beautiful shapes and forms. I saw a fox over there, once, suddenly looking at me beside some brambles. It seemed to shine with its fur, all russet, and its teeth so white, its tongue-tip pink, and its eyes, they were yellow gems. Then with a completely silent flick, it was gone. How or where it went, I didn't know. The bush was small; it just flicked out, like a camera shutter closing. Tell you what, let's creep down to the Lake Woods! They are very secret, and by the water we may hear a nightingale. They used to sing there when they had stopped elsewhere; perhaps it was the liquid echo they heard, coming back from the rhododendrons around the water, and they sang to it."

"How do you *know* so much about everything?" said Lily, as they came in sight of a tall barbed-wire fence among the trees in front. "Hush!" he whispered, as he went on slowly, crouching slightly, putting one foot before the other to press down the dead leaves and sticks of the ferny path, wary of cock pheasants whose pitter-pattering away on the woodland floor on all sides might at any moment break into raucous rising cuckettings of alarm, and so betray their presence at that very private and secluded place. Lily followed behind, thrilled with the mystery and beauty, with a feeling, as she looked up through the canopies of the great oaks, of being part of the pale blue sky.

By good luck the gate was not locked, only secured by a bolt; and sliding this back gradually, lest it squeak or clank, he pulled back the frame of iron and threaded barb, and closed it behind them.

"The Lake Woods!" he whispered, turning to her.

"Oh," she said, with a long sigh. "It's all just like a picture!"

The first lake was the deepest. It was surrounded by azaleas and rhododendrons, a boat-house with shingled roof among them, and waterlilies on its brownish-green surface. Old beech mast lay on the mossy path, crackling as they walked on, to the lower terraced ponds, where a heron flew up dishevelled and angular so that she clutched his arm, saying, "Is that a crane?" "Yes," he said, "that was the old name for it," as they sat down by the water, and watched a shoal of red-finned roach moving just under the surface.

"I can't believe it is true," said Lily.

"Yes, it seemed like that to me, when I came here first, about five years ago. It made all the difference to my life. I felt all the birds were mine. I watched them at their nests and saw what they did, and it seemed they were very much like human beings were, only truer, somehow. Oh, I wish we could hear a nightingale. I am sure it sings because it has a feeling for music. It's born with it. There must be a God, even if it is called evolution. Anyway, Spirit gave colours to some birds, speed to others, song to others, skill in architecture to others. There's the Bower Bird, but not in England, which adorns its nest and courtyard with shells, stones, and other things. They say it is only to attract a mate, but he brings in the things after the courtship, as well as before. Why shouldn't a man paint his house after he's married, if he loves his home, and is happy there? It's only the unhappy people who don't care what squalor they live in, don't you think?"

He now could look frankly at her, trusting himself to the blue pools of her eyes.

"'Bluebell', he calls you, does he? Poor old Dashwood. I think you are a lily, like your name.

> "'*Now folds the lily all her sweetness up*
> *And slips into the bosom of the lake.*
> *So fold thyself, my dearest thou, and slip*
> *Into my bosom, and be lost in me.*'

"Tennyson knew that at night the water-lily pulls its blossoms under the surface of the water. The lily closes her eyes, the lily withdraws her beauty. Your eyes are beautiful, too, human Lily! Eyes are made of water, so why should their colour not come from blue water, or from the sky, which after all makes all things? That poet I told you about wrote,

"'And Life is Colour and Light and Warmth'; well, they're all there in your eyes." Then alarmed at what he had said, "Shall we go on to the Saltbox, and have boiled eggs and bread and butter for tea? It's possible that there will be a nightingale singing in the steep lane below Biggin Hill there. It was another favourite place of mine, years ago."

They returned to the road, and on *Helena* pushed off on the slope beyond the turn of the road below the paling fence; and drummed along the road to Westerham until they came to the tiled and brick cottage built in the shape of an old-fashioned wooden salt box. After tea, served by the old woman in black bodice and lace cap, they went into the beechwood below.

"I'm afraid it's too late, Lily."

"Dr. Dashwood said there was one singing in the Infirmary gardens, what is now the Military Hospital, on the other side of the Randisbourne."

"Really? How lovely! I thought they'd all left the district, driven away by soot, moggies, and river rats. But I'd like to hear it. Do you mind going into the Rec.?"

"Not now," she said. "I don't mind anything now."

The young moon was showing brighter in the western sky. He looked at his watch.

"It's getting on for nine. If we go now, we'll be in time for a drink at Freddy's, and perhaps see Desmond. He's coming on leave tonight. We're catching the morning train from Waterloo tomorrow, so it will be the last chance to hear a nightingale this year."

Freddy said, as he poured two small whiskies, "No, your friend hasn't been in yet. What time are you expecting him?"

"He did say about half-past nine. If he comes, tell him we're going in the Rec. to try and hear a nightingale."

"Yes, Dr. Dashwood was saying only last night 'e 'eard one there. Though what colour it was, he didn't say," tittered Freddy.

"Oh, hell," said Phillip through closed lips to Lily, a minute later. "Here's Ching. Go out quick, I'll follow. Meet me in the churchyard." Ching passed through into the billiard room, apparently to the lavatory.

Phillip said to Freddy, "If Desmond comes, tell him we'll be between the two rustic bridges, for it's supposed to be singing in the Infirmary Gardens."

With a slight wink Freddy said, "I think I understand, sir," as Phillip swallowed his drink, then Lily's, afterwards leaving.

Ching had listened and watched from the sliding panel in the stained-glass screen. When, five minutes after Phillip had left, Det.-Sergt. Keechey came in with his plain-clothes man, Ching told them what he had overheard, while a thin wire of glee spread up from his middle, akin to that Phillip had felt when Peter Wallace had been punching Albert Hawkins' face held under his left arm.

"Come on," said Keechey. "Not you!" he shot at Ching. "You keep out of this!"

The night was quiet. Soft darkness brooded over the flats of the Recreation Ground. Clouds had come up, shutting out the after-glow of sunset. Rain seemed possible. Disliking the crunch of gravel underfoot, Phillip vaulted over the iron railings, and stood with his back turned while Lily climbed over. They walked across the grass of what once was a water-meadow beside a trout stream where salmon, coming up the Thames by the Isle of Dogs, had run to spawn, below banks flowery with meadowsweet and ragged robin. Now the Londonised soil was packed hard, sour with the soot of the age of factory and deflowerment, during darkness a place of hard-eyed fornication. But soldiers, like sailors, don't care for the warnings of the respectable, or knowledgeable; and here on that early summer night came Phillip and Lily, to sit on the circular rustic seat around a solitary aged willow that had somehow managed to live on. The tree was equidistant from a gravel path beside a pointed stockade fence, made of old railway sleepers, guarding the railway line on one side, and the gravel path beside the polluted brook, on the other.

"I feel this is a happy tree now, Lily."

"Oh, how did you know I wanted you to sit beside me here?"

"I think it's best, really, to face up to things that frighten one. I used to be terribly afraid of my Father; but suddenly, facing up to him on his allotment, I realized he was a poor old fellow, cooped up in an office all his days, working away to keep the home going."

"Oh, I love this tree over us," sighed Lily, as the leaves rustled in the breeze.

As they sat there two shadowy forms came towards the tree from opposite directions; and pouncing suddenly, confronted them with accusations obviously rehearsed.

"No need to ask what you two are doin' here! We both seen you. Did you see them, Jimmy?"

"I seed what they was doing, sergeant."

"Come along with me, you, to the station, before the Inspector! I've been watching you for some time."

"You can't arrest an officer of His Majesty's Armed Forces."

"You're not in uniform. If you resist arrest, I'll ring up the Horse Guards, an' inform the Provost Marshal's department. Your bluff is up! Better go quiet with my constable!"

"Don't say anything, Lily," said Phillip. "Not a word!" Then to the dim form of Keechey, "I refuse to leave my friend here with you. This is a conspiracy, and you know it!"

"You'll know something else if you don't come quiet," said the plain-clothes man with the black moustache, shining a torch in his eyes.

"Put that light out!" cried Phillip. "That is a military order!" Then he said in a quieter voice, "What is the charge, may I ask?"

"The Inspector wants to see you at the station. I am asking you to come along."

"That is better. Come along, Lily."

He thought that it was his word against that of the two plain-clothes men.

"Lily, I'll want you as a witness. We'll both ask for a medical inspection from Lt.-Col. Toogood. I'll demand that we both see the Inspector! Law-abiding citizens can't be charged for sitting quietly in a public recreation ground."

Lily walked quietly beside him. Outside the station Keechey said in an entirely different tone of voice, "The Inspector asked me to find you, because an urgent telegram came in duplicate to us, so I was asked to invite you here to read it."

"I'll see you later, Lily," said Phillip, as he went inside.

"I managed to locate this officer, sir. I told him you wanted to see him."

The Inspector said that a report had been called for from the Machine-Gun Training Centre, Grantham, as to why it had been necessary to make an enquiry about him.

"A report was returned from this Station based on what you told Detective-Sergeant Keechey a few days ago. A copy of a telegram sent to you was telephoned to us tonight, and on learning that you were in the neighbourhood, I gave orders that you were to be invited here to read it, in view of its urgency. Here is the copy."

SECOND LIEUTENANT P.S.T. MADDISON PRINCE REGENT'S REGIMENT ATTACHED MACHINE GUN CORPS LINDENHEIM HILLSIDE ROAD WAKENHAM LONDON REPORT IMMEDIATELY TO BLENHEIM BARRACKS WINDMILL HILL LONDON YOUR LEAVE IS CANCELLED

ADJUTANT M.G.C. TRAINING
CENTRE GRANTHAM

"There is another matter, concerning your motor vehicles. I think you are the owner of a Swift runabout, GT 18, and a motor-cycle, LP 1656? Have you taken out licences of £3 and £1 respectively for these vehicles? Well, if you use them on the highway in future, O.H.M.S. or not, licences should be taken out. You have a driving licence?" Phillip showed him his card. "Well, I won't go further in the matter of licences now, but you might remember for the future. Now will you sign here that you have read the copy of the telegram."

As Phillip went out through the doors his father came in under the blue lamp, peaked cap on head and special constable's armlet around sleeve.

"Well, Phillip, what is all this?"

"I've just been recalled to duty. It looks as though the Big Push is coming. I'll have to leave right away, I think, so if you don't mind I'll say goodbye now."

Shaking hands with his father he said, "Well, good luck to the allotment." Rain drops were beginning to fall. "This will help your plants. Au revoir."

He hurried after Lily, but could not see her. He must go back and pack. It was hardly worth while to light the acetylene lamp. The police would not be likely to report him for having no light now that they knew the urgency of his orders. Even if they did, to hell with the summons. Returning, after another cursory look around for Lily, to the fire station where he had left the machine, he thudded home in the rainy darkness. Leaving it under the porch, he walked down the road to say goodbye to Mrs. Neville.

Desmond came down to open the door. "I don't wish to see you," he said. "Come up, Phillip," called out Mrs. Neville. He followed Desmond up the stairs and went into the sitting room. A moment later Desmond looked round the door and said quietly, "I'm going to bed, Mother, good-night," and went down the short stairs to the kitchen.

"Well," said Mrs. Neville. "Can I believe my ears? Was that my son? What can be the matter with him? He was so looking forward to going away with you to Devon, too. You wait here, Phillip, I'll have a word with him."

She heaved herself out of her chair, and went down to the kitchen. Phillip heard her speaking; then the door closed. After some minutes, she came back.

"Well, I can only say that I don't understand what it is all about. Did you take that girl Lily for a ride on your carrier? Of course I believe you that you meant no harm by it, but it was just a little ill-advised, wasn't it, Phillip? Still, I see your point of view. A little country air would do her good, after all the steam in that laundry! Don't you worry, it will come all right in the morning. If I were you I shouldn't try to see Desmond tonight. He's in one of his moods, and tired. A good night's sleep will make all the difference. You look tired, too. Go home to bed, and you'll find that tomorrow it will all have blown over. What do you say, dear? You may be going to France? Your leave is cancelled?"

She read the telegram. "I must tell Desmond this! Desmond, come here, will you?" When he came she said, "I'll leave you two to talk, and make some coffee." She went out of the room and down the stairs; then with an agility surprising in one so heavy, she turned about on the third step, and crept silently into her bedroom, to stand behind the open door and listen. To her astonishment she heard her son's toneless voice saying,

"I am glad to hear that you are going back to France. I have come to the conclusion that you are too complicated a person to live. Perhaps this time your fate will catch you up."

At first Phillip was too shaken to reply; then he thought that Desmond did not mean what he said. He pretended to believe it, hoping that Desmond would relent. "My fate? What is that?"

"It will be best for everyone if you are killed."

"Well anyway, let's not part in bad blood."

"You have created the bad blood."

"Have it your own way.   Goodbye, and good luck to you wherever you are."

He saw Mrs. Neville as he passed.   "Goodbye, Mrs. Neville. May I write to you, or would you rather I didn't?"

"Why yes of course, dear! Don't take it to heart, Phillip, it's only a storm in a teacup!"

"Teacups sometimes get broken, Mrs. Neville. Goodbye, and thank you for all you've done for me."

Outside the flat Ching was waiting. "I thought I'd tell you that I heard what Keechey said to you in the Rec., and if you want a witness, I'll say what I heard."

"Oh, it's all over now, thanks."

"Lily went back to Freddy's, and met Desmond immediately afterwards. She didn't wait for you, I noticed. Women are rotten to the core, in my opinion. Phil——" He moved intimately close to Phillip.

"Get away from me!"

He took a taxi-cab from Charing Cross, and when he reported late that night, he found that his kit had already arrived, with a certificate of contents, from Grantham. The next morning he went before a medical board, was passed fit for active service, and given orders to leave with a draft of officers that evening from Victoria station. The barracks were almost empty, only the depot staff and those on light duty remained; for the coming offensive all available trained officers and men had been sent to France.

Part Two

THE SOMME

Chapter 13

QUERRIEU

Phillip tottered off the gangway at Boulogne having, as he said to his companion from Victoria, catted up his heart, despite the fact that the crossing from Folkestone had been made in sunshine on a blue and waveless Channel. Fear had taken the heart out of him: fear of being sick: fear of the idea of having to face machine-guns again. The apparition of death from the back of his mind had come forward to share his living thoughts, so the voyage had been a semi-conscious froth of nausea, of endurance despite abandon.

While the transport had been crossing, with its destroyer escort, there had been a constant heavy thudding of guns. Either the Big Push had started, along the coast towards Ostend, or there had been a naval battle. When the ship docked, they heard: the German fleet had come out, and there had been a tremendous battle in the North Sea. Rumour on shore said that a German invasion force was waiting upon the issue of the battle. Heavy distant blows were still burdening the air, far away to the north-east, across the sea.

Once upon cobbled streets, and after a brandy and soda in the British Officers' Club, followed by beef tea and soup, colour came back into Phillip's cheeks, and he began to feel that what others had to go through, he could go through; and even beyond, like Julian Grenfell.

> *And when the burning moment breaks*
> *And in the air death moans and sings,*

he would think of the sun, what astronomers called a dwarf-yellow star, slowly dying, as in the *Liebestod*; death came to all things upon the earth, and to the eventual sun: that must be the philosophy.

After lunch there were nearly two hours to wait for the train to Étaples. Ray, one of the original mess at Hornchurch, made a suggestion to pass the time, to visit a red-lamp house near the docks. They parted.

Phillip spent the time walking alone about the docks and the town, conscious of a new, alert feeling everywhere. If only he were going to the Gaultshires, and perhaps "Spectre" West, France would be quite bearable. Now—officers were liable to be sent to any regiment, it was said. Still, he might be able to wangle it.

The train for Étaples, the base for Infantry Reinforcements, left in the sunny afternoon—hundreds of officers, thousands of men, for its long, slow, clanking journey down the coast. It stopped finally in a siding surrounded by huts and tents to the horizon, and they had to jump down beside the track, and move up a loose sandy soil to level ground where acres of creosoted wood and dirty grey canvas seemed to enclose the spirit of herded nihilism. He followed other officers to the reporting centre; and when particulars had been given, Ray and he and two other officers were shown a tent by an orderly. Here their valises were dumped on wooden floor-boards. "What a ——ing hole," remarked Ray. The Officers' Mess, a marquee, had no food. Dinner was over. They managed to buy some bread and cheese, and ate this with pale French beer which Ray said ought never to have lost the horse. It was now half-past nine, by Phillip's watch. Was Desmond, at that very moment, talking to Lily in Freddy's? Or were they together in her house? What a strange person she was. What was she *really* like? But no man could ever understand a woman.

Ray was full of the details of his Boulogne adventure. When someone in the tent asked if he wasn't afraid of a dose, he replied, "I've got old man gonnock already, thank God."

"But oughtn't you to be in hospital?"

"No, it's only a gleet, but it will get me back to Blighty whenever I've had enough of out here."

Lying on the floorboards of his tent, Phillip passed a wretched night. Apart from sleeplessness, the feared body of Ray next to him would roll over against him, snoring and gurgling. So at first light he got out of his flea-bag, in which he had lain half-dressed, and went into the morning air, where gulls were crying and afar a cuckoo was calling. The town lay below. Between the estuary and the sea beyond was a wood. Returning to his tent, he dressed, and going to the empty mess, lay back in a wicker armchair, covered with newspapers for warmth; and feeling relief at being alone, slept.

The day was hot, the work tiring. Carrying rifles and the leather equipment of the ranks with water-bottles, bayonets, and entrenching tools, a company of subalterns set out for what was called the Bull Ring. It lay beyond a sandy road past hospitals and rows of bell tents, upon an open area of low sandhills where trenches were dug, bayonet-fighting courses laid out, with Lewis gun and bombing ranges. Scores of sergeant-instructors were waiting for them. Fall in on your markers! Carry on, sergeant instructors! Left right left right left right, about turn, left wheel, right wheel, halt! by the right, dress! Eyes front! Quick march!

After half an hour of barrack-square drill, they fell out for five minutes. Followed physical jerks; firing of rifle-grenades, throwing of Mills bombs; filing through a gas-chamber, wearing damp P.H. helmets; an obstacle race while the Canary—instructor with yellow band on his arm—yelled for greater speed from thudding hearts. Under coils and over knife-edge obstacles of barbed wire, down into the trench, to stab sacks of straw painted crudely grey and red.

"Stand on the Hun to get yer bayonet out! Tear out 'is guts. Round the traverse following the bomb! Smash 'is face before 'e can recover! Give 'im Kamerad with three inches of cold steel in 'is throat!"

On the way back to camp Phillip thought that the blue estuary, flecked with far-off tiny white wings of gulls seemed as remote as a half-forgotten holiday picture postcard. If only it were Devon.

The tens of thousands of other ranks in the camps were not allowed out. Their lines were enclosed by barbed wire like the German prisoner-of-war camp. Every day prisoner-squads were marched away, their *feld grau* uniforms patched with blue circles and squares, to work on fatigues. They marched with spirit. Individual Germans about the camps snatched off red-banded caps when officers passed, leaping to stiffness before saluting. There was no ragging or barracking during roll-call in the German officers' section of the camp, Phillip observed, as British officers were said to treat their camp-commandants in Germany. At night singing came from the prisoners' lines of tents, with the strains of harmonica and accordion.

One early evening Phillip and Ray, sharing a common loneliness, walked down to Paris Plage. He found it to be a deserted watering-place with a long and wide concrete promenade the colour of the surrounding sands. "I'd like to practise bayonet-fighting on some of the prisoners," said Ray.

"Why? How have they hurt you?"

"In retaliation for the way British prisoners are treated in Germany."

"You'll have plenty of opportunity for practising up the line," replied Phillip. "Especially if you meet the Prussian Guards."

"Not this baby," replied Ray. "I'm not out for the V.C. my boy. I'm looking out for No. 1. If I don't, who will? Sense, isn't it?"

"Can you really get back home at any time you want to?"

"A couple of bottles of Johnny Walker, and old man gonnock takes me back to Cherry Hinton."

Phillip had to put up with other details of his companion's philosophy of preserving life, against the blue and empty expanse of sea and sky. How could he get rid of him, without hurting his feelings? An excuse came when Ray proposed that they try and get off with two nurses who were laughing together as they strode along the promenade, having come down from the town on the steam tram. Phillip said he would go back on the tram and write letters, and left Ray to try his hand alone. Looking back, he saw him accost them, but the nurses walked on as before, leaving Ray looking about him on the otherwise deserted concrete emptiness of Paris Plage, with its little blue and white villas in the distance.

After three days at the Bull Ring, officers were posted to strange regimental units up the line. Many were dismayed, despite fore-knowledge of what had already happened to others. The posting system seemed to be senseless: officers in kilts were sent to southern regiments; Londoners to Scottish regiments; men of Kent to the Northumberland Fusiliers, Tyneside Scots to the Duke of Cornwall's Light Infantry; Rifle Brigade officers, with great indignation, to the Welch Regiment; all a complete muck-up, it was generally agreed. Some were less unfortunate; Phillip was marked for the battalion of his own regiment he had been with at Northampton. The wilderness did not seem so empty.

Among the others, there was much grumbling, but the base-staff would accept no complaints. It was laid down in orders from G.H.Q. One major said, "You are destroying *esprit-de-corps* by your damned stupidity! Three hundred men of my regiment, the Black Watch, have had to discard their kilts for an issue of khaki trousers, before going as a draft to the Somerset Light Infantry! While in the next camp an equal number of the Dorsets have been issued with kilts, to serve with the Black Watch! A Boy Scout could do better than this! Bloody base-wallah Huns! Eating your fat heads off one end of your bodies, and wearing out your trousers at the other end, blast you all!"

Steel-helmets weighing two pounds, painted khaki, were issued. With the strap fixed under his chin, Phillip felt new resolution, which induced optimism when they were told that the manganese steel was capable of resisting shrapnel balls coming down at 750 feet per second. He worked this out to be about 850 miles an hour, faster than the speed of sound: as if that mattered, for it was well-known that a man never heard the bullet that hit him.

The battalion was some miles from Querrieu, where he and Ray detrained, to find a G.S. wagon waiting for their valises. A guide led the way through the winding town and so to a country road in a valley beside a stream. Cuckoos were calling in the woods, mayflies rising in clouds over the meadows; but the scene for Phillip was empty, flat, without meaning; for this was not England.

Walking on, the two, now some yards apart, came to a track which bore much traffic, judging by the horse dung flattened by solid tyres of lorries, direction boards with arrows, canvas watering troughs, and dumps under tarpaulins; and topping a rise, Phillip saw before him hundreds, thousands of bell tents covering a wide and shallow valley filled with troops.

It was a division withdrawn from the line, to practise over ground chosen to represent the section of the enemy lines which it was to assault. Irregular chalky white worsted lines herring-boned the threadbare scene to the misty distance. The land-scape was downland, broken into arable and pasture, but now overlaid by the dusty squatting of an army, with its wheels and feet that had turned all the living garment of grass to a dust which arose with buzzing blowflies clustering upon open latrines and heaps of dung and garbage despite the scattering of chloride of lime. This was the reality of his life, now, thought Phillip, not the fancied coolth of clear water rushing past the boulders of the shadowy Lyn, or the high moor where the sun cracked the pods of the furze, and bees scrambled over the bells of the heather.

But Phillip's depression lifted when he saw in the orderly room a face he knew; and asking if Captain Milman was still the adjutant, learned that Major Kingsman was acting C.O.

"Welcome back," said Milman, rising from his chair. He was the only adjutant Phillip had known who did that, as though greeting a guest.

Companies were marching into the lines, singing *It's a long, long trail a-winding*, steel-helmeted, boots, puttees, and tunics grey with chalk dust, faces brown and cheerful. And there was dear old Bason on a horse.

Other familiar faces soon came to greet him—Bason, Tommy Thompson, Flagg, Paul—now a captain—Wigg, Cox, and finally, in the company mess with Bason, Jasper Kingsman himself. The extraordinary thing was that they all seemed pleased to see him! Why, Phillip could not imagine.

There was no officers' mess, for they had had no time, said Bason, to do anything about it, since coming out of the line. Bason now had a ropey moustache; Phillip thought he must grow one, too. Paul, the tall shop-walker who had come to them at Northampton, had a Charlie Chaplin. Phillip envied him his three stars: perhaps, if he had remained with them, he would by now have had a captaincy. Another new captain was "Brassy" Cusack, the Glasgow Trades Union official who had given them a beer party in the pub when on the exercise for promotion. Milman's friend, Thompson, was another—but Wigg, he saw with relief, still had only one pip, so had Cox, acting second-in-command of Bason's company. The establishment, he knew, was two captains per company; and since he was senior to Cox, he might stand a chance for promotion.

"So they turfed you out of the Emma Gees, did they, old sport?" enquired Bason genially, as they sat together in the tent that was "A" company office. "Give us the latest about London. Still pretty hectic, I suppose? Seen anything of Frances or Alice? I've lost touch with Frances. I was a bit gone on her y'know—still, it's all in the luck of the game," he said, playing with a pencil. Then looking at him sideways, "You took her out one night, didn't you? I rather fancy she was keen on you."

"Oh no, nothing like that," said Phillip, not wanting any more misunderstandings. He told Bason about the fiasco of Christmas Eve. "And that was the last I saw of Frances or Alice."

"Alice wanted to make you jealous, and bring you on, didn't you know?"

"Good lord, really? I thought she liked her 'sailor man', Timmy. Anyway, it's all over and done with now. What about this push? I heard in London it was to be south of Arras, in the new sector taken over from the French. When are we for it?"

"Couple of weeks, maybe three, perhaps four."

"Where do we go over, I mean, what are all the practice trenches copied from, what place?"

"North-east of Albert, astride the Bapaume Road."

"I've never heard of it."

"You will, old sport, or you'll see what remains of it when we go over the bags! To give you an idea, take a look at this bumff! It's going to be a cakewalk this time, for all opposition will be wiped out by our guns before we start, not like those dud attacks in the past." He tossed over a bunch of cyclostyled foolscap paper, headed

OPERATION ORDER NO. 1 (Part 1)

"It'll be altered, of course. More and more bumff keeps coming in from Brigade. We're doing another practice rehearsal tomorrow, that'll make five so far. When you've got the general idea, I'll show you your platoon, and your sergeant can give you the dope. By the way, who's senior between you two blokes?"

Cox, who was sitting in a canvas chair, reading a letter from home, eye-glass in eye, looked up promptly and said, "I am".

"I had an idea you were, Phil?" said Bason.

"No, it's the other way about, skipper," said Cox. "Catch!" He threw over a packet of cigarettes.

Phillip knew that he was senior to Cox by ten days, but did not like to say so. Bason took a cigarette, and flipped back the yellow packet.

Cox is a liar, thought Phillip; and went on reading.

The division will attack north of the Albert—Bapaume Road. The preliminary bombardment will be carried out during five days preceding Z day . . . during the hour before zero the bombardment will be intense . . . machine guns will fire heavy bursts ten minutes before zero . . . Code name for battalion is CLAY . . . battalion on the right, SHOV . . . on left flank, FORK . . .

TASK. CLAY will assault and take the trenches on accompanying map named Rudd, Pike, Chub, Roach, Bream, Eel. SHOV on right and FORK on left will pass through CLAY at Pike . . .

DRESS. Fighting order with two bandoliers S.A.A., full water bottles, mess tin, mackintosh sheet, iron ration, remainder of day's ration and two smoke helmets. Officers will carry rifles and conform to movements of their men.

I'll wear a tommy's tunic, thought Phillip, thank God. That will give me an even chance.

All N.C.O.s and privates (except battalion scouts, signallers, and stretcher bearers) will carry two Mills grenades, one in each side pocket, and three sand-bags. Officers commanding companies will be responsible for seeing that . . . no grenades are to be thrown by individuals except in grave emergency.

He read the next paragraph, and then sat very still, feeling that Bason must hear the thudding of his heart.

> *OFFICERS AND N.C.O.S TO BE LEFT BEHIND.* Fourth Army orders that not more than 23 officers are to go into action with the battalion. Seconds-in-command of companies will remain with the first line transport until ordered to rejoin by Brigade.

He looked across at Cox, sitting cross-legged in his canvas chair, swinging his whangee cane, and knew that Cox had read his thoughts when he said immediately, with an eye-glassy stare, "Go on, you one piecee bad boy, read the rest of it! Gasper?" He threw over the packet of Goldflakes.

> *OBJECTIVES.* "A" company will take Roach, point *Fin* of which is to be made into a strong point. Rudd will be defended by Lewis Gun posts while general consolidation is in progress . . . B company will . . . C company . . . D company will remain in reserve—
> *FORMATION.* First four waves as practised, platoons being in depth. Special duty of first wave is to clear any wire or obstacles which will hinder succeeding waves. *This is more important than making any immediate entry into the German front line.*

Like bloody hell it is, thought Phillip, recalling to mind "Spectre" West's company of Gaultshires hung up by wire in front of Lone Tree.

> *LADDERS.* These will be provided in, certainly, the front line, and perhaps in others at a scale of one ladder to two men. Just prior to the time at which men are to leave trenches these will be placed in position and the two men will stand by. The man on right going first.

Where will the ladders come from, and what about the jam-up they will cause in the jumping-off trench? And who will place them in position? The Angels of Mons? He saw again the chalk-filled bags of the parapet at Loos before Zero, torn by machine-guns to ragged ears of hessian.

> *BRIDGES OVER TRENCHES.* Local commanders will see that floor boards in the German trenches will be torn up and placed in position for following waves to pass over.

ADVANCE. At eight minutes before zero hour, the first wave will advance and lie down 250 yards in front of the front line. The second wave will advance and lie down 100 yards in front of front line.

At zero hour first, second, third waves will advance simultaneously.

At zero plus 2 minutes, the fourth wave will advance. At zero plus 4 minutes the fifth wave will advance.

At zero hour plus 6 minutes, the sixth wave will advance.

ON NO ACCOUNT WILL THESE TIMES BE EXCEEDED. *Strict silence will be maintained during the advance through the smoke and no whistles will be blown.*

"What sort of attack is it to be, I mean how wide is No-man's Land, d'you know, skipper?"

"Varies between six and eight hundred yards opposite our sector. Why?"

"That means nearly a quarter of a mile for the first two waves to go, after the first advance. What is the rate of advance, is it at the double?"

"What, with over sixty pounds per man of clobber we'll have to carry? Give us a chance, old sport! At present it's a hundred yards every two minutes."

"That's less than two miles an hour. Rather slow, isn't it, to go a quarter of a mile under fire."

"There won't be a Boche left alive after the bombardment, old sport."

Phillip picked up the pages, and glanced through half a dozen more. An item caught his eye.

BATTLE POLICE. Their duties will be to see that no one except linesmen use the new communication trenches across Noman's Land from the German side. They will prevent any N.C.O. or private leaving the German lines who is not wounded. They will direct men who have lost their way, and messengers or carrying parties.

CASUALTIES. All officers will send casualty estimates with all reports . . .

LOOTING. Most extreme disciplinary action will be taken in the case of any officer, N.C.O. or private found in possession of any article from the dead.

PRISONERS. These will be escorted on scale of 10 per cent of their numbers. Prisoners will be searched at once for concealed arms or documents, always in the presence of an officer. Guards are forbidden to talk to prisoners, or to give them food or tobacco. Identity discs will not be taken from them.

There were many other paragraphs, including RATIONS, WATER DUMP, REGIMENTAL AID POST; and then his gaze fastened on something which accentuated his thoughts.

> *TENDING OF WOUNDED.* All ranks are forbidden to divert attention from enemy in order to attend wounded officers or men.
>
> *WHITE FLAGS.* All ranks are to be reminded that these are not a sign of surrender, but an implication that the enemy has a communication to make. During action, firing will NOT be discontinued on any account. The showing of a white flag will be reported to Divisional Headquarters.
>
> *WARNING IF CAPTURED.* All ranks are warned to give only Name, Rank, Regiment.

He put this bunch of papers down, then took up OPERATION ORDER No. 2, which consisted of four cyclostyled pages. Then OPERATION ORDER No. 3, which was of three pages; followed by OPERATION ORDER, *Amendment No. 2*, and OPERATION ORDERS, *Additions and Amendments No. 3*.

"Cox, here's the Imprest Account for the company's pay to-morrow. You'll find the Field Cashier at Querrieu. Now don't go to Amiens with the cash and paint the place red, will you?"

"What, with my missus expecting a baby next month? No damned likelihood of that, skipper!"

When Cox had gone, Bason said, "Cox likes to think he is very much the family man these days. Now I'll take you to your platoon, and introduce you to their feet and kits. The usual inspection. Then you're free till tomorrow. I'm going down to Amiens this evening, to get a bath, and then a bite at the Godbert. How about coming? We can ride over, it's only ten kilometres. Are you on? Good. Remember when we used to go up together to Baker Street from camp, and our long walks back after midnight? Good old days. We had some sport, not half we didn't!"

They walked down to the company lines. Phillip was taken to his platoon sergeant, a small alert, wiry man.

"You'll find him a good chap," said Bason, aside. "Between you and me, he asked to be transferred away from the platoon last week, under Wigg. You remember the old lizard? Fortunately for us, Wigg's just got himself another job."

"What kind of job, skipper?"

"Acting Area Commandant—and I hope he stays there—we don't want him back. All the other chaps in the company are keen as mustard."

"For the attack, you mean?"

"What else? It will be a cakewalk, with one howitzer for every forty yards of Hun front, and one field gun to every twenty-five! That's in addition to gas, smoke, all the trench mortars—light, medium and heavy—Stokes, Christmas Puddings, Flying Pigs, all going the bundle! We'll all be home by Christmas, old sport, I'll take a bet on it. How about a bradbury, level betting?"

"Do you think the war will be over by then?"

"I'll make it five to one, that it's over by Christmas! Are you on?"

"All right. Only it will be like robbing an incubator."

Speed with the lightfoot winds to run

the words flashed in his head as he reversed his puttees preparatory to riding into Amiens for dinner with Bason. Followed by two grooms, they avoided the main road, with its heavy traffic, and went along a track which passed away from the practice area of facsimile German trenches. He had a 16 h.h. chestnut, with a white blaze down its face, and a hard mouth; temporary gentleman with temporary charger's manners. However, behind Captain Bason bumping up and down on a bay mare, like the Galloping Major of the song, he felt like a cavalry wallah. His mount kept shaking its head. He dismounted to loosen the curb-chain, which had been hooked too tight under the animal's jaw. The groom didn't know his job.

"Two fingers should slide easily between jaw and curb, like this!"

"Very good, sir."

The wind-waves were upon the corn. Larks sang in the sky. There was no other sound save the clop of hooves, the creak of leather, an occasional clink of the loose curb-chain, as the chestnut behaved, he thought, with gratitude.

Thus began one of the most pleasant periods of Phillip's military life, brief as it was. It was a time given not only to the practice assault, but to sport. There was cricket in the long evenings between the companies, and inter-platoon football matches. Running events, too, and boxing. The company boxing instructor was Phillip's platoon sergeant, an alert, cheery man with a brown face and pale blue eyes, part Welsh and part Devon, coming from a village inland from the Exmoor coast—so he and Phillip soon had plenty to talk about. Davy Jones gave him boxing lessons, using patience and kindness, and away from the men, because Phillip was shy of his inability, at first, to avoid blows, which wove around and under and through the almost static guard of his right arm. He used the posture taught him years before by his father, left arm straightly extended, right arm covering chin, with no idea of working the forearm to divert blows. But he persisted, and learned the elements of countering, the use of his toes and calves when striking—it could not be called punching.

The frame of Davy Jones was spare and hard as the ash handles of the shovels, paring hooks, mattocks, and picks he had used since boyhood with precision. Phillip persisted, and the exercise gave him confidence and some sort of belief in his body powers. He went for long runs, loping along, mile after mile with the athletes of his platoon, and practised deep breathing in the early morning and at night.

This was after Sergeant Jones had said, "I've been a-listening to your breathing, sir. It's in-out, in-out, like putting three inches of the bayonet in a sack. Lungs is like bellowses, sir, they work best with deep draughts, in and out at the same rate, slowly. Town people don't know how to use bellowses," he went on scornfully. "They puff and blast away, scattering the embers, instead of fanning them, sir, to give them new flame with the air in equal proportions, if you understand my meanin'. There's so much power in an ember, and no more is gained by blasting it to sparks, when its heat is wanted to bake a stick, then fire it. And 'tes the same wi' breathing, a lung is nothin' but a bellows. Take in slowly, like, and let out slowly. I breathe eight to a minute, and can expand my chest five inches. I'll show you."

And putting a piece of string round his chest, Davy Jones asked Phillip to tie it tight, with a double knot. When this was done he said, "Now watch me!" and with his eyes fixed on Phillip's he drew in breath slowly, more and more, until the string broke. Holding up a hand for silence, he completed his act, letting out air slowly as he had drawn it in.

"Twenty seconds you'll find that took, and I could run a mile without breathing any faster if I'd a mind to!"

After parades, in the calm summer evenings, there was the

bioscope, with one riotous night, a Charlie Chaplin film. In another barn in Querrieu was the Ah-Rays concert party, run by some gunners. This, like the mobile cinema, was also packed every evening. Some of the actors dressed up as girls, with various types of wigs. Each man in the audience dwelt upon the plaits, golden curls and rouged faces, upon the eyes made large, liquid, and luring with red specks of paint in the corners and crowsfeet of black extending the lids made shadowy with blue powder. Each herded man in the audience was fascinated, filled with longing, stirred by lust which made him shout or grin or hide his facial feelings according to the experiences, or lack, of his body.

Phillip sat motionless, for one of them looked like Polly, with short dark curls to the shoulder; he soon transferred to another with fair hair and eyes which reminded him of Lily, as he longed for her with regrets that he had not had her on Reynard's Common, since Desmond had cast him off, in the words of the girl in Northampton who had been chucked by her boy after he had had her. Why hadn't he had that girl, too? What was the point of being idealistic, when no one but yourself cared, really, for ideals? He stared at "Lily", with unutterable longing, until another "girl" with golden curls sang the duet *They'd Never Believe Me* with an actor who, Bason said, was a West End matinée idol, and the eyes and curls were those of Helena Rolls, remote and beautiful above the tragedy that was ordinary life.

"Cheer up," said Bason, behind his hand, "still thinking of that girl who's 'too good for you'?"

"I don't know what you mean."

"All right, old sport, don't get huffy. Frances told me all about it."

The introspective mood passed when other songs followed: the Cobbler's Song from *Chu Chin Chow*, and others from *Razzle Dazzle*; and by the time they were over, he had revisited many more scenes of his secret life, with their array of swiftly-passing faces, longings, and regrets. Then he forgot himself and lived in the present, thinking of dear old faithful Eugene when the star-turn came on towards the end. This was the West End actor, now in the Kite Balloon branch of the R.F.C., who was famous before the war for his song *Gilbert the Filbert*. He sang it now—glass in eye, walking to and fro, so debonair with silver-topped cane, silk hat, morning coat and striped trousers with white spats—and brought down the house.

I'm Gilbert the Filbert
The K-nut with the K!
The pride of Piccadilly
The Blasé Roué!
Oh Hades, the ladies
Who leave their wooden huts,
For Gilbert the Filbert,
The Colonel of the K-nuts!

After this someone at the back—it was Ray, it *would* be—started others to join in a parody, beginning

I'm Charlotte, the Harlot
The Queen of the Whores
The curse of Piccadilly
With——

at which the man at the piano promptly played *God Save the King*, for some padres and staff-officers were in the front row. Among them, unknown to Phillip, was Father Aloysius, now a chaplain to one of the Irish battalions in the division.

> 8th (Service) Bn. The Prince Regent's Own Regt.
> B.E.F., France
> 4 June, 1916

Dear Lily,

How are you getting on? I often think of our jaunt to Reynard's Common and the Fish Ponds, and the reflections in the water. You are I hope well, and things have not been too bad for you with our mutual friend K. As you can see, I am out here again, and the old life at Freddy's etc. seems already a far memory. I thought that my feelings for the countryside had gone for ever, but when you were with me, I felt them very much as in the old days. I mean the beauty and the wildness, the enchantment of so much colour and life and warmth of the sun. Most people are restless in the country, they feel a vacancy, and want to get back to the shops and pavements and traffic; what they call life. Sometimes the war seems to have come directly out of that restlessness. This is awkwardly expressed, and probably silly, but you may know what I am trying to say.

Write to me if you have time. But only if you want to. I mean, if you find or know friends you are happy with, please don't bother. I send in this letter a poppy and a marigold. They grow quite a lot out here, in this chalk country rather like the North Downs, but smoothed out, made larger, and so much more empty, if one forgets for the moment the vast swarming masses of troops, camps, convoys of lorries and guns and horse-transport for ever passing in a haze of dust.

The last of the nightingales still sing. Late at night the notes seem to travel from afar, bird answering bird under the pale glow of the midnight sun in the north-west, the glimmer of the stars upon the chalk of our practice trenches, and the ghostly lines of tents wherein, for the moment, hopes are at peace. Sometimes the thought of the hundreds of thousands of our men out here is momentarily overpowering, when I think of so many individual lives, and what they are really thinking, and hoping. Sometimes I feel that I must know everything that everyone is doing and thinking. I have an idea that a stream of English thought runs through all our days—not like the Randiswell which is no longer a living brook—but like a brook which is crystal clear and pure, with fish in it, and lilies, and dragon-flies.

Do you remember those lakes in the woods we saw together? The time I was there last, before we went together, was on the Saturday before August Bank Holiday. How far away it seems now, that time before the war! Yet it is always near me, sometimes seeming to pass right through the strange life one lives out here, an outward life, in a sense quite unreal. My cousin Willie's roach pole is still in the rhododendrons where we hid it, by one of the lower lakes—we were coming back for it on the following Saturday. Somehow you seem to be part of the spirit of the Lake Woods: the trees so quiet, the water so cool, the lilies resting among their leaves, whereunder pass the red fins of the roach.

I would like to go there with you again when and if I come back. *Please tell no-one this*, if you chance to meet any friends (or otherwise!) of mine. They might not understand. Well, I must get down to it now; I write by candlelight, and the three other subalterns sharing the tent are asleep. Write if you feel like it, but don't tell anyone if you do, or that I have written to you. The reason for this, as I have said, is that some people might misunderstand. *Méfiez-vous, les oreilles ennemies vous écoutent*, as they write up in French railway carriages: Keep your own counsel, enemy ears are listening.

Yours sincerely
PHILLIP MADDISON

Somewhere in France

5 June, 1916

Dear Polly

How are you? As you can see, I am out again, this time it is do or die. For great things portend. I thought of you last night, at the divisional concert party, where were to be seen some most beautiful actresses, who sang some of the current London hits, *Razzle Dazzle* etc.,

How is your Father? Enjoying good health, I hope? And Grannie Thacker? And of course Aunt Liz, whose sausage rolls I shall never forget. How is Percy? I am sorry I have not been to see you lately, duty calls, etc. etc., but when I get some leave I will make amends. Ye olde mo-bike is laid up at ye olde Wetherley's, he of ye olde long curling moustaches, in ye olde High Street of ye olde Borough. Do write if you have time and give me all your news. How is ye olde woodpecker in ye olde room with ye olde tester bedde, is he still glinting i'th' eye when ye candelle shineth on ye patchwork bedspread where of yore these my bones rested, so well cushioned on ye most soft and delightful dove-like sweetness of my dreams?

Until we meet again, book-boo-roo-roo, as the ring dove croodles to his mate in the tall holly hedges of the village I remember so well in Gaultshire.

With love to all,

PHIL.

British Expeditionary Force

6 June, 1916

Dear Mrs. Rolls

I write this in my tent, where all is grey, from the marching hosts sending up the chalk dust of Picardy. I trust that all is well at Turret House, and that no cockchafers under monstrous cocoons have been droning across your skies of late. We are now well behind the front, and what can be seen here makes one realise how mighty is the strength of Albion when once it is aroused. Thousands of shunting trains heard at night from the Hill, from the district beyond Shooter's Hill, have it would appear discharged their loads upon the rolling downlands where until recently all was pastoral peace and agricultural activity.

There is a stream here where we bathe, to the unhappiness of various French fishermen, who now that the mayfly is up would prefer the solitude of human herons. This is understandable, although not to hordes in khaki who consider that Piscator, as Isaak Walton calls him, would be better equipped for present-day activities with a rifle and bayonet than with a green-heart rod. It does seem strange to be fishing amidst all this activity, until one considers that one was oneself about to go to Lynmouth for the very same purpose, until the threat to Verdun called for a counter-stroke, as the military writers say. I don't think I would like to fish here, all the same; for it is not England, where my thoughts lie, as do those of most of us.

Tomorrow we are leaving here, and will be marching nearer the sun. We had divisional sports today, including judging horses, vehicles, etc., a wonderful spectacle. Bands played, and the chains of our transport glittered so brightly that the French interpreter asked if they were nickel-plated. It is all quite different now from what it was when

I was out before; leather straps and breechings are saddle-soaped and spotless, waggons and limbers painted and oiled, even the horny feet of the horses are polished with ox-blood shoe polish! Ready for the triumphal march into Berlin, in fact. At least, that is the feeling here. For myself, I think it will not be such a cake-walk as the others seem to think; but at any rate the spirit is that of your favourite character in a book, as you once told me, *Richard Coeur-de-Lion*.

I expect the green slopes of the Seven Fields will be echoing, during these long summer evenings, to the crack of Mr. Rolls' rifle. This country is in places not unlike the landscape there, although it is more continuous, like a prolonged swell of the open Atlantic compared with an inland sea. France is less populated than England, Major Kingsman (a friend of mine from Hornchurch days) tells me, in relation to the rural areas. The French farmer has heavy grey Percheron horses to work with, and they go with his wooden sabots and imperturbable mien. I expect they will not be sorry to see the troops off their crops, especially as the corn has come into ear, and the wind-waves rush over the wide fields, carrying the butterflies in the hot sun and the swallows skimming high after gnats and other of the ephemeridae from the water meadows of the stream, which flows, under its green mail of water-weed, on its way to join the Somme, and the sea which washes the chalk cliffs of old England.

It is past midnight, I must say, "Out brief candle!", and turn in upon the floor of my tent. This day we march towards the unknown. Please will you give my kind regards and my best wishes to all for a fine summer. Shall you be going to the Isle of Wight this year, or will war-time restrictions prove too much to overcome? Salaam!

Yours sincerely

PHILLIP

He felt suddenly tired after writing this letter, lost confidence, and tore it up.

Chapter 14

HAPPY BREED OF MEN

They left camp and marched away in the afternoon, for the sun was approaching the solstice, and the light was long. The sun rose in the north-east and set upon the north-west; the roll of the earth from darkness into light was brief, so that the hues of sunset were scarcely gone down when the sky was in glow again with the transfiguring pallors of dawn.

The soldiers sang as they marched in the shadows of the poplars enclosing the cobbled road.

> *A German officer crossed the Rhine,*
> > *Skiboo!   Skiboo!*
> *A German officer crossed the Rhine,*
> *Out for to get him some women and wine,*
> > *Ski-bumpity-bump skiboo!*
> *Oh landlord where is your daughter fair?*
> > *Skiboo!   Skiboo!*
> *Oh landlord where is your daughter fair,*
> *With lily-white breasts and golden hair!*
> > *Ski-bumpity-bump skiboo!*
> *Oh yes, I have a daughter fair,*
> > *Skiboo!   Skiboo!*
> *With lily-white breasts and golden hair,*
> > *Ski-bumpity-bump skiboo!*
> *But my daughter fair is much too young*
> > *Skiboo!   Skiboo!*
> *But my daughter fair is much too young*
> *To be pushed about by the son of a Hun*
> > *Ski-bumpity-bump-skiboo!*
> *O father, O father, I'm not too young,*
> > *Skiboo!   Skiboo!*
> *I've been pushed about by the parson's son,*
> > *Ski-bumpity-bump-skiboo!*
> *It's a hell of a song that we've just sung,*
> > *Skiboo!   Skiboo!*
> *It's a hell of a song that we've just sung*
> *And the pusher that wrote it ought to be hung,*
> > *Ski-bumpity-bump-skiboo!*

He thought of Lily, of her white throat and yellow hair, with a rasp of longing for her tenderness. What was she thinking, in the steamy rooms of Nett's laundry, with its soapy water gushing into the Randisbourne below the arched bridge, bubbles riding away below the backs of houses and the garden of the Conservative Club with its weeping willow. The water was dead now. He remembered his father saying to him, when he was little, that the brook had given up the ghost when the officials of London County Council crossed the Thames and asked for the fair daughter of Kent. He hoped his letter would reach Lily, c/o the laundry.

He must also write to Father; and to Mrs. Neville. And to dear old Eugene, and Mr. Howlett at Wine Vaults Lane, to show him he was in France again, in case Downham came in, and belittled him.

The wind waves of young summer were upon the barleys, the wheat was upright and rustling, the oats shook their green sprays. Old men with scythes were cutting hay to the tramp-tramp-tramp of nailed boots between the ever-widening rows of poplars shaking all their leaves like little heliographs or as though waving goodbye. They marched through villages of lime-washed *pisé* and thatch, where children stood and stared, but waved no more; for hundreds of thousands of *les Anglais* had already passed that way, singing, whistling, and shouting the same remarks. Old women scowled, their thoughts shut away like their hens, as they stood beside the drying stagnancy of dirty grey washing water they had poured from their thresholds into the gutters.

The column swung along past them, singing happily. What a difference in the spirit of these men, thought Phillip, and the old survivors of the battles before Loos.

> *Wash me in the water, that you washed your dirty daughter*
> *And I shall be whiter than the whitewash on the wall*
> *Whiter than the whitewash!*
> *Whiter than the whitewash!!*
> *Whiter than the whitewash on the wall!!!*

Unused to marching on the hard stone-setts, soon he got blisters; but he set himself not to think of them, thus to train himself to subdue his feelings. Do not think of the past, or of the future, when the burning moment breaks—or the burning blister. Think only of your men, never of yourself. Having thus told himself, Phillip tried not to limp; blisters must be squashed down.

In the heat they rested on the grasses along the verges of the road, under the poplars with their ceaseless flashing leaves. Or was it, he thought, as he lay on his back, with arms under head, that every leaf was saying no to the wind, no no no, leave us upon mother tree, O wind. No, he must not put his feelings into leaves, as though he were of leaves crying to the wind, Strew me not dead upon mother earth, nor these poor men with me, brown withered leaves upon the earth, lost to the sun.

"The C.O., sir," said a hoarse voice near him. He sat up, and saw Major Kingsman, coming down the road. He got up and saluted, and was gladdened to hear Major Kingsman say,

"Welcome back to the battalion, Phillip. By the way, you remember Lulu, Father Aloysius? He's come to the Liverpool Irish in the Division as padre. We must foregather one evening."

"Oh good. I hope Mrs. Kingsman is well, sir?"

"I heard from her this morning. One of her redpoll heifers made top price at Chelmsford, she's very bucked."

"Oh good."

Major Kingsman talked to him for some minutes, then returned up the road to the head of the column. Could he have come down specially to see him?

Seated upon the grass again, Phillip saw the glitter of light upon the shaking poplar leaves above as part of the joy of green summer upon the earth, and the morning air was blessing the membranes of the leaves.

Heavy with sweat and dust they marched on, turning into a road where dust lay thickly on the grassy verges with old petrol cans, rusty tins of bully beef, and other signs of an army's desolation, including bashed trunks of the poplars at wheel height, telling of the passage of lorries and caterpillar-drawn guns. Motor convoys passed them, both ways; the march became wearisome with halts. At last, when the sun was gilding the poplar leaves and casting long shadows, they turned off the main Amiens–Albert road and halted for the night beside an oak wood, where each man and his mate made bivouacs of their two groundsheets laced with string. Then companies were taken in turns to a river across a marsh, where ran clear water on a bed of chalk and flint. They undressed, and soon were splashing, crying out, and joking. Their brown arms and necks and faces contrasted oddly with the grey-white of their bodies and legs. Phillip among them felt reborn in a new world. Forgotten was the war and homelessness; here was cool clear water, here was the joy of life, which took one by the throat.

Sunshine floated upon the countryside, as though for ever. Twilight filtered clear light upon a blue distance. A solitary white owl flapped and skimmed slowly and silently over the swathes of hay. The last of the old men and women in sabots clattered down the road, unspeaking with their long pronged forks, thinking of calvados before coffee.

Fires speckled the margin of the wood. Mouth organs played.

The moon rose up across the hayfield. Umbered faces broke into song. *Umbered—Henry V.*

> *There's a long long trail a-winding*
> *Into the land of my dreams*
> *Where the nightingale is singing*
> *And a pale moon beams—*

Melancholy, romantic, a little sad, they sang together words by which they visited and were blessed by images of tenderness and longing, in the land of their birth, in the dream which was England.

"Care for a cupper char, sir? With the boys, sir?"

It was the hoarse voice again. He had been wondering about that face, dark and cleft with little scowl-ruts; the man wore the two ribands of the South African war. The face was now offering him a mug of tea. "It's quite clean, sir, I jus' washed it aht in the stream."

He remembered the prisoner in the guard room at Hornchurch —what was his name? To show that you remembered names bucked a man up—as Major Kingsman's *Phillip* to himself. It was the name of a City brewer, famous for stout.

"Thank you, Pimm. Where have you sprung from?"

"'Ospital, sir. Shrapnel in m' arm, sir, not enough for a Blighty one."

"Bad luck."

"It's all in the game, sir."

"May I sit by your fire?"

Half a dozen men eagerly moved to make room. He sat by the cheering flames, and sipped the strong sweet tea. He had been delegated by Bason to pay five francs to each of the men— there was a Y.M.C.A. marquee in the camp, and wheeled canteens from Division—the previous afternoon, and had made a point of speaking to each man by name, as he gave to each a green note. He must imitate the Duke's way, in the Gaultshires, according to "Spectre" West, of asking questions about their homes, encourage them to speak. He had learned that they had been out from England for six weeks, and had had several spells in the trenches; he acted as though they knew more than he did. They seemed to like him; had Pimm given them a picture of him as a proper toff—all because he had played the sahib in the guard-room and spoken amiably to a poor devil up against it?

He wanted to leave while the good impression of him remained. Should he say *Goodnight, men*, as was correct, or *Goodnight, you fellows*? Which?

"Goodnight, boys!"

"Goodnight, sir!" in instant chorus. He felt himself to expand in the darkness, the darkness now glowing alive with a spirit beyond death, as he walked back to the bell tent he shared with three other junior subalterns, all near-strangers, all recently joined, and ready to defer to one who had been out in '14, and '15. Bason must have told them; he had kept to his role of quiet veteran, determined to make no mistakes this time. Jubilant that, at last, he felt that he belonged to the men of his platoon, as they to him, he washed and cleaned his teeth, got into his camel-hair bag and said a prayer for himself and others before trying to sleep. Nightingales were singing in the wood, and through the open flap of the bell-tent shone the pale moonbeams.

The next afternoon, when the marching battalion approached the turn-over point of a long slope leading up to the sky, suddenly upon the air fell the intermittent rumble of guns; and during a 10-minute halt, the rumour came down the recumbent men that Lord Kitchener had been drowned in the North Sea, on his way to Russia, in H.M.S. *Hampshire*, which had struck a mine. This added to the stillness of thought within Phillip as, later, he waited for dusk on the northern slope of a hill overlooking the tributary river, with its marshes and watery cries of wildfowl; for now it was known that the battalion was going into the line, for a tour of duty, to relieve other troops. Phillip lay near his men, listening to the singing of larks through the thuds of howitzers, the remote cork-screwing of shells travelling east into the height of the sky. Poppies shook in the evening breeze, with marigolds and scabious. Below the hill, to the north-east, lay the ruinous town of Albert. To the left of its red-brick sprawl was a large building, which might have been a church, with shell-holes in its fabric; and towering above the walls was a campanile with something upon its summit glinting in the western sun. Focusing his field-glasses upon it, Phillip saw a figure, which once had been upright, but now was, upon its iron frame, inclining downwards at an angle, so that the object held in the figure's arms seemed about to drop into the void below. With a shock of recognition he saw that it was what he had seen photo-graphed in newspapers—the Mother of God with the Babe in her arms. The iron frame supporting the figure had been struck by a shell, and had remained half-broken in that position, to be seen by all going into the line, month after month, to inspire the legend that the war would end only when the Golden Virgin fell into the ruins below.

They spent the next week providing working parties for the Engineers, while occupying support trenches. One of the fatigues was the digging of ditches for the burying of water pipes. Phillip enjoyed the work of supervising his platoon, and learning about something he had never thought about before. Water, it appeared, was quite a problem when hundreds of thousands of men and animals had to be provided for. A friendly captain, entertaining him to lunch in the sappers' mess, explained the set-up.

On the staff of the Chief Engineer of the Fourth Army was a Water Supply Officer, with three assistants, and each Corps had a Water Officer. For many months they had worked to improve existing water-supplies, and build and bore for new points. The Engineer-in-Chief at G.H.Q. had bought a large quantity of water-supply machinery and equipment from England—pumping sets of every description, including powerful steam fire-engines from the London County Council. Two water-barges, fitted with purification plant and large rotary pumps for forcing filtered water through pipes, had been sent up the Somme from Amiens. Trenches had been dug for iron pipes of 4 in. and 6 in. bore, eventually to be laid up to the British front line and beyond into re-conquered territory. Water-points, led off the main pipes, filled canvas troughs for horses and mules, and provided other points with taps for refilling eighty extra water-carts or G.S. waggons fitted with 200-gallon tanks in each Corps area, in addition to the regimental water-carts.

"A pity the water has to taste so filthy," said Phillip.

"We can't run risks. One carrier of paratyphoid 'B' in a village, chucking the old slops into a stream, might bring down the corps."

"Even so, the chlorinated water, with the petrol taste, makes me feel sick."

"The remedy is to dry out the petrol cans thoroughly before filling them with drinking water, surely?"

"I'll speak to the Adjutant about it."

The engineer went on to say that a Fourth Army Water-tank Column had been formed, for when the advance moved forward. To give an idea of the amount of water required, he said the Column consisted of 192 three-ton and 111 one-ton lorries, each carrying 550- and 135-gallon tanks respectively. Each lorry carried chloride-of-lime purification apparatus, for dealing with surface water, and water in shallow village wells. Attached to the Water-tank Column was a Flying Repair Column, with special tools and steel bandages with which to repair pipes gushing water out of breaks made by gun-fire.

These lorries, together with tens of thousands of other wheeled vehicles, could move properly only on metalled roads; and the problem of keeping roads in repair, and of building new ones across what would be a devastated area, was one of some concern to the engineers. For the French railways behind the battle front, largely an agricultural area, were insufficient for the needs of the Fourth Army which required, every day—the engineer captain said—eleven trains to carry supplies, fourteen for ammunition weighing over 5,000 tons, and six trains for reinforcements, remounts and stores; while the Third Army up north, which was to fight part of the battle, required twenty-eight trains.

Once the Push had started, he said, it had been estimated that the daily total of trains needed would rise to one hundred and twenty-eight, including Red Cross trains for the wounded.

This number of engines and waggons was not available upon the broad gauge of the Chemin de Fer du Nord, unless the carrying of stone for the roads was cut out.

"So it will be rough going, at first, for the transport. We'll have to re-metal the roads across the area of annihilation, as we call it, as best we can. In the back areas of the Fourth Army there is only one solitary quarry, and that's nine miles back, at Corbie. The stone is inferior, too, with a lot of clay between the strata. In peace-time the metal for the Picardy roads came all the way from Belgium, you see."

Later, metalling for the destroyed roads had to be brought by ship from the granite quarries of Jersey and Cornwall.

Chapter 15

THE RAID

At the end of the week "A" Company went into trenches upon the gently rising downland nearly two miles north-east of Albert.

Phillip looked across a no-man's land of tall grasses, thistles, docks, and wild flowers and saw—nothing: no movement, no sign of life. Half a mile away was a village of skeleton roofs, and some trees in leaf, forsaken upon a fossilised chalky landscape, void of life and movement. Yet the pale summer sky of morning was suspended in a feeling of terror: within the delusion of forsakenness a thousand hidden eyes watched with the invisible sharpness of death. The sniper's bullet cracked as it passed faster than sound, sometimes sparkling at night upon the chalk-filled bags of the parapet—the bleached and grey hessian bags, some broken with rot, with fatigue, and not renewed; for their purpose was almost served.

The British front line lay upon a plateau one hundred metres above sea-level. It faced the German lines on the slope, rising imperceptibly past the two fortified villages of Ovillers and La Boisselle to the horizon of one hundred and forty metres, where lay, beyond periscope visibility, the third enemy line. Behind and hidden below that downland crest the towers of Bapaume arose in open country between the rivers Somme and Scarpe. There, he thought, was the open country awaited by the cavalry for more than a year now.

There were moments when Phillip's imagination overwhelmed him. He wanted to feel all the excitations, the hopes, the determinations, the fears of every soldier in khaki and *feld-grau*. With fascination, with glamour, with occasional tremulous thoughts of glory, he imagined the hundreds of thousands of hidden men, dusty with chalk, in khaki on the one side, mingled with an equal fascination of curiosity and romantic wonder about, and innocent pity for, the hundreds of thousands of men in coal-scuttle helmets and *feld-grau* on the opposite side—men lost to home upon that ancient bed of the sea raised by elemental cataclysm aeons since. Father Aloysius had said that there had always been war; that the surface of the earth would not be fertile without death and decay. Beyond such seeming destruction was the harmony of God, striving that men should see clearer, and live happier, according to their true natures. The eternal processes of decay and redemption had never ceased; they were eternal. He imagined the rain falling under the ocean winds from the south-west, and dripping through the chalk, to break out upon the hillsides as springs of water which, falling, falling, falling to the sea, widened the valleys in whose sides and upon whose plateaux, *at that very moment of time passing through his brain*, millions of men were digging and tunnelling, one race against another, reinforcing shelters above ground with concrete and steel, protecting them with barbed-wire strung on angle-iron and screw-picket, behind which machine-guns, mortars, gas cylinders and flame-throwers were hidden from view, in chalk-bagged bay and traverse, against blast; steep wooden steps leading down through timber-framed doorways to rooms and corridors panelled with wood, as in the flash of a torch he had seen during a static moment of raging hot coolness during a raid to get a prisoner for identification: a raid carried out in silence on both sides until Mills bombs had been lobbed down dark rectangular holes below the German parapet, ominous with wooden steps disappearing down into—what? *Back! Back!* he relived the moment with thin tense steel-wire fear, as a prisoner, gibbering and slavering, was kicked and prodded out of the deep trench, a young soldier with shaven head laced with blood after being hit by an entrenching-tool handle enwound and weighted at the end with barbed wire. What had happened? Where were the other Germans?

They had crept across no-man's land, guided by little posts, in the split tops of which hens' feathers had been stuck. They had known the way by feeling the quill-ends; they had got into the trench, without a shot being fired; they had scrambled back, ripping hands, sleeves, trousers, puttees on trip-strands of loose wire, swearing with fear and interior galvanic flashes of terror in illumination from the bursting of green and red rockets over no-man's land, rising above scores of calcium flares, soaring up from the German lines, a moment before sheet-lightning from the east told that the German protective barrage had started, to add coarse buzzing and swishing of howitzer and field-gun shells, with red-stabbings of rifle fire from ground-level and distant flashless enfilade of machine-guns firing north across Mash Valley from Y Sap just over the Bapaume road, also from higher ground in front of Ovillers. When he got back or rather fell into the British front trench he could not speak, his throat being dried up and partly closed, while the sweat from his armpits soaked the arms of his flannel shirt almost to the wrists; but the release from fear was exhilarating, the feeling of being alive most wonderful; for all of the raiding party had returned safely, bringing the prisoner, who had held up his hands in supplication, that his life be spared. He was very young, and soon calmed down, on being given a drink and a smoke, despite Divisional Routine Orders, while waiting to be sent down under guard to Brigade headquarters.

"The new C.O. is expected tonight," said Bason, "and the Adj. wants to hold the prisoner, who won't be seen by Army Intelligence anyway until tomorrow morning. I've sent your report down. By the way, Major Kingsman wants to see you at the Post."

"What about, skipper?"

"Search me. He's just telephoned. That's all I know."

Major Kingsman's headquarters were in the support trenches six hundred yards behind the firing line, at the cross-roads known as Ovillers Post. Behind the Post the road led on down to Aveluy village across the river marshes, a mile north of Albert.

Major Kingsman was standing behind a hurricane lamp at a table in a dugout four steps below the grassy surface outside. He said "Well done", and then he said towards the haze of the hurricane lamp, "This is the officer who was in charge of the raiding party, Colonel. Mr. Maddison."

"Thank you, Major Kingsman. Will you be ready to go round the lines with me in half an hour, please? Sit down, will you?" said a voice spoken through jaws nearly closed.

His sight still dazed behind smarting eyeballs, Phillip sat on a ration box. Across the table was a figure with a black patch over one eye, and a pink scar drawing together the flesh below it. The hand of the arm laid on the blanket-covered trestle-table was hidden under a black glove; and around the wrist of the black hand was a strap with swivel, which could be fastened to a ring on the tunic. He had a glimpse of a silver rosette upon the riband of the Military Cross, and looking up, saw a pale blue eye in a pallid face.

The black hand pushed over an enamel mug, a voice said "You need a drink; help yourself, Phillip," which was another shock on this night of shocks, so that he felt that his life floated unreal in waves of remote nothingness. He was unable to speak or to move. The reaction to intense stimulation was still upon him. He held up the mug of whiskey and chlorinated soda water with shaking hand, and then he felt tears running down his cheeks, why, he did not know, other than that he could not believe that he was in the presence of "Spectre" West. He drank, and the mug was taken from his hand.

"Have some more."

The Sparkler syphon hissed. The mug was put before him. He drank, and began to feel his glassy self thawing.

"I want to hear about your raid, Phillip."

"Very good, sir."

While he was trying to speak coherently there was a commotion outside. A sergeant's face leaned down and said, "Beg pardon, sir, but the prisoner's in a fit, sir."

The prisoner lay with bitten tongue, and snoring; he recovered for a moment some minutes later, and sat up, to glance wildly around and to cry "Mutter, Mutter" before dropping back and lying still. When the doctor arrived, he felt the prisoner's pulse; then with his stethoscope confirmed that the heart was not beating.

"Too bad he died on us before he could be interrogated," said the doctor, adding, "Otherwise the only good Hun is a dead one."

"Bloody fool!" muttered the Colonel, as the M.O. left. Then Phillip was asked questions, before a trench map spread upon the table. He was asked about the direction of machine-gun lines of fire, direct or indirect. He was told that observers in the trench and behind it had been trying to spot them, but no flashes had been seen. The Spandau guns were thought to have been firing down pipes, from fixed positions behind the front line, and from the strong point to the south called Y Sap. While the questions were being asked, Captain Milman came into the dug-out.

"I'll be ready to come round with you in ten minutes, Captain Milman. I want to talk to this officer alone, if you please."

Captain Milman looked surprised at the curt tone of voice, and went out again. Then "Spectre" West, his eyes fixed on Phillip's face, began again, somewhat curtly, to ask more questions. How long before he had gone over had he known of the raid? Had any details been discussed or imparted by telephone from battalion headquarters to his company commander's dug-out? Had any been telegraphed on the buzzer? Had he seen any Hun sentries in the trench? Had any stick-grenades been thrown? Any rifles fired?

"I didn't hear any, Colonel."

"It looks as though they knew of the raid. The question is, how?"

Captain Milman came back. He bowed to the Colonel as he saluted, and smiled at Phillip.

"I've sent in a report about the raid to the Brigade-major, sir."

"Spectre" West said evenly, "In future it will be my reports that will go to Brigade, Captain Milman."

"Certainly, sir."

"I think, too, that, except on parade, I would prefer to be addressed by all my officers as 'Colonel'."

"Certainly, Colonel."

"That, I need not say, will not appear in orders."

"Certainly not, Colonel."

"Now will you be good enough to ask the Brigade-major, from me, if someone from Army Intelligence can be sent here to identify the dead prisoner as soon as possible?"

"The Brigade-major has already asked me to get the kadaver down to Albert tonight, Colonel. Intelligence from Army is coming to examine details tomorrow."

"Tomorrow? God's teeth! Why not tonight?"

When Captain Milman had gone, "Spectre" West said, "I want to ask you a particular question, a personal question. I have a reason for asking it. It is this. Why did you tell 'Crasher' Orlebar that you were up at Cambridge University before the war?"

Phillip remained silent.

"It was untrue, wasn't it?"

"Yes, Colonel."

"You didn't feel good enough, did you? So you pretended?"

"Yes, Colonel."

"Well, you *are* damned well good enough!" shouted "Spectre" West in sudden rage. "You are an Englishman! You were in the Gaultshire Regiment! You fought at First Ypres! You *are* good enough, and do not need lies to bolster up your fancied feelings of not being good enough! Do you understand me?"

"Yes, Colonel."

"But I know how you felt," said West, reflectively. "You need not think you are the only one."

The air of night under the stars was being charged by a magnetic awareness that drew up the larks which lived upon the battlefield to rise above the calcium flares. It was not yet three o'clock. A thick mist lay upon the valley of the Ancre. The guns were for the moment silent. Only occasional rifle-fire sheared flatly in the distance; spinning shapeless richochets fell with chromatic piping sounds into the marshes.

Phillip was instantly awake when a hand touched his shoulder.

"The goddess Aurora," said "Spectre" West, in a whisper. They stood together outside the shelter, looking towards the east. "The pale brow of Aurora." He added, "Pale with sight at the bloody filth of Mars. All this has happened before. What a pity you were not at the 'varsity. You should have read Greats."

"Look!" said Phillip, "that lark up there has a red breast. I am sure they fly to see the sun, when they go up at dawn. 'Bird of the wilderness, blithesome and cumberless'."

"Yes, cumberless. That is what the infantry should be on Z morning, not line upon line of pedlars."

When the last lark was back in the wilderness grasses again, Phillip was drinking tea with "Spectre" West, whose face in daylight looked if anything more marmoreal than by candle. He wondered if "Spectre" had been cured of his dope-taking; and remembered Dr. Dashwood saying that topers and drug-takers who had been cured lost some of their old personality, their minds became slower, their thinking involved, together with their talking. Dashwood had made a joke about it. What they lose on the swigs, Middleton, they gain on round-about talk. It did not seem so funny now.

"Did you think of letting a Mills bomb, without its detonator, roll down the steps of one of those Hun dug-outs? You did not. You did not think to meet silence with silence, on the principle of softly, softly catchee monkey? Comparative silence, of course. Bompity-bompity-bompity! all the way home, otherwise to the bottom of the steps, while you counted the number of bompity-bomps? What, you weren't ordered to count the steps? Of course you weren't! Why should you be? Who knows anything but damn-all about anything in the line, except P.B.I.? You should have taken that priceless opportunity, as you went down, to find out the depth of the Hun's fortress shelters. In future raids in this battalion will be made in plimsolls, by thieves and cut-throats, not by officers imitating hearties smashing glass at a Bullingdon dinner. We'll have another dart at them, but I doubt if the old Hun will be so obliging a second time. I'll have to get the B'grdear's approval, but if he won't give it, we'll take out a strong patrol and get it lost the wrong side of the wire."

Phillip heard this with misgiving.

"How long have you known this battalion?"

"I've only rejoined less than a fortnight, Colonel."

"Is it the same battalion you wrote to me about, when you were at Northampton? When Frances came down?"

"Yes, Colonel."

"Drop the 'colonel' when we are alone. I speak to you as to an old comrade. You are a second-lieutenant: my substantive rank is lieutenant. Otherwise I am merely a temporary captain with the ephemeral rank of lieutenant-colonel. And apart from that, I know damn-all about what is behind the Hun wire. G.H.Q.

knows damn-all. Aeroplane photographs are deceptive. They give an illusion that much, if not all, can be reconstructed from them. But they don't tell what we want urgently to know. For example, the Hun's probably got listening apparatus that picks up our telephone talks. He must have, otherwise why the suddenly evacuated front trench, and that idiot left alone there? Of course he may have unexpectedly thrown a fit, and they left him there, after cutting off his shoulder numerals, and taking his identity disc and papers. I wouldn't put it past the Hun to have cleared out and left him there, from a misplaced sense of humour."

"He was crying when we got into the trench."

"Poor little sod."

"Spectre" West took up a dossier of operation orders. "You've seen the battalion orders for the attack?"

"Yes."

"What do you think of them?"

"I don't really know, except that they seem to be part of an ordered scheme."

"Oh, for God's sake——! Must you talk in clichés? I suppose you don't know what a cliché is? Well, it's a stereotyped phrase, which old compositors, in the days of picking out type in single letters, kept made up, to save time. 'A wedding was solemnised', 'the contracting parties were . . .'—that sort of thing. So no clichés of thought or phrase with me, if you please. Here's a book for you. It's the *Everyman* edition of Smith's *Smaller Classical Dictionary*."

"Thank you ever so much."

The colonel's servant brought in another pot of tea. He wore Gaultshire badges. "Good morning, sir. Permission to say, sir, very pleased to see you again, sir." It was Boon, last seen when "Spectre" had been hit at Loos. Phillip shook him by the hand. When Boon had gone, "Spectre" said,

"You must forgive my sharpness, Phillip. I have been an usher too long. Now I want to know what you *really* think. You saw what happened at Loos. Haig's orders were for every brigade to get out into the blue as fast as it could, and if Sir John French hadn't kept back the Guards Division and other reserves, the Hun might have had to pull back to the Scheldt, and the war been over by Christmas. Now, this time, it is the opposite principle; limited advances to be made at a slow but steady pace, wave behind wave; every man having a special job, like the caste system in India, and incidentally carrying over sixty pounds. The idea is to be ready to meet the counter-attack from the Pozières ridge, and smash it.

Then the cavalry passes through the gap, to hold the ground beyond Bapaume until the infantry can come up and break out, and roll up the Hun's flanks. Are you listening?"

"Yes, sir, of course!"

"To all objections by local commanders, Army replies, in effect, 'But me no buts'. The enemy positions will be rendered untenable and the Germans in them 'wiped out' by the preliminary bombardment. Those were the very words used by Rawlinson at the Corps Commanders' conference at Querrieu yesterday. You will of course keep what I have told you strictly between us two."

"Yes, I promise."

While he had been sleeping in headquarters dug-out the previous night, the kadaver in *feld-grau* was carried on a stretcher, amidst oaths and whizz-bangs, down to Albert. There, at 10 a.m. the next morning, after a breakfast of scrambled eggs with bacon and devilled kidneys, followed by toast, Oxford marmalade, farmhouse butter and coffee with fresh (not tinned) milk, three A.I.D. officers arrived in a Vauxhall motor-car, to try and identify from the kadaver's remains the German regiment holding the sector opposite Usna Hill. Since neither shoulder numerals, letters, nor identity disc were available, they held what they called a sartorial post-mortem; and decided that, according to the kadaver's tunic, he was a Bavarian; from his trousers he was a Saxon; his shirt made him a Prussian from Wurtemburg, his boots a Swabian from Pomerania; his socks gave no clue to identity, since he was not wearing any; he had a five-pfennig piece in one pocket and so (ran the joke in No. 2 mess later) he must have been a Scotsman.

Comic Cuts, the Corps Intelligence broadsheet, did not mention the raid. There was, however, an indirect reference to it.

> There are grounds for believing that the man-power shortage among the enemy has caused young recruits of a low category of physical health to be put in the foremost positions confronting our lines.

Phillip got back to Keats Redan by the communication trench, and reported to Captain Bason in the support line as a smell of frying bacon was coming from the servant's shelter next door. "Just in time, old sport," said Bason, cheerfully. "What happened last night? Did you have a binge? I hear the new C.O. can put it away. What's he like?"

"He's Frances West's cousin! My friend I told you about!"

Bason looked sideways and said, "See any green in my eye?" and maintained a sceptical attitude until Phillip overcame the nuisance of his manner and made him listen to his story, while keeping back 'Spectre's' confidences and saying nothing about the raid being repeated; but he wondered if he had said too much as soon as he had replied to Bason's question, "Was Brigade pleased about the raid?" with "It was a failure, like all the others on the Corps front, I heard"; for thereupon Bason became indignant about 'the bloody brass-hats moaning about failure, just because the prisoner was a ponkey and had kicked the bucket'.

"They ordered us to go Hun-pinching and you did it, didn't you? Anyway, I've put you in for the M.C."

Phillip was too astonished to say anything but, "Well, skipper, I think I'll go and have a look at my platoon, then if it's all right with you, I'll come back and get some breakfast."

"You're very keen all of a sudden, old sport. Come and tuck in now, it's all ready."

After enjoying a breakfast of bacon, fried bread and coffee, with tinned butter and marmalade to follow, Phillip went down the communication trench, passing painted signs on stakes driven into the chalk, and brass 18-pounder shell-cases used for gas-gongs, and came to the front line, where men were shaving, cooking breakfast bacon on tins of solidified spirit, cleaning rifles, writing letters, in an atmosphere of cheerfulness induced by the haze of the morning sun. One man in twelve was on look-out duty with a periscope above the parapet of chalk-filled bags.

He sat down on the fire-step, asking about their rations, particularly bread; the daily ration was 1¼ lb. per man, but they seldom got more than half a 1-lb. loaf each in the line; and if the water tasted of too much petrol; if letters were arriving all right from home, and separation allowances being paid to their families?

"When do us go over the plonk, sir?" asked the platoon sergeant, who came from the West Country.

"I don't know any more than you chaps."

"Any chance of home leaf after the push, sir?"

"I hope so."

"The gunners have a rumour we are going to Verdun, sir. Is it true?"

"More likely that Jerry's coming up here."

"Are we down-hearted?" cried someone.

"No!" they shouted.

"They say you knew the new C.O. before, sir."

"Yes, I did, at Loos. He's the finest officer I know."

"A fire-eater, sir?"

"No. A real soldier. I'd follow him anywhere, so will you."

"Why was Jerry silent last night, sir?"

"Perhaps we caught them all with their trousers down."

That made them laugh. He left them, and went to his shelter, *The Demi-Lune*, made of curved elephant iron covered by three layers of bags, and entering past the gas-blanket, found Pimm his servant sitting by a steaming kettle. Telling him that he had had breakfast, Phillip lay down on a mattress of sandbag bundles, and thinking of a purple-and-white riband on his tunic, settled contentedly to sleep . . . until he recalled 'Spectre's' words, and remained with his eyes open.

Getting up after an unrestful half hour, he asked Captain Bason's permission to go down the sappers' mine-gallery. For months the Royal Engineers had been driving a gallery under the German position opposite, where the northern shoulder of the salient made by the enemy's trenches around La Boisselle, known as Y sap, was a strongpoint of reinforced concrete forts with splayed slits at ground level holding machine-guns. Y sap was to be blown up just before the infantry assault on Z day.

"I've seen the sapper subaltern, and he says he'll take me down."

"You must want a job, old sport. You wouldn't get me going anywhere near the Glory Hole for a hundred quid!"

Phillip set off for the main shaft of the tunnel, with two ideas in his mind: to enquire if the sappers knew the depth of the German dugouts; and to find out if, by some extraordinary bit of luck, Desmond had been posted there. After all, he had never expected to see Westy; it was a small world.

South of Keats Redan the British front line ended in a barricade of sandbags laid header-and-stretcher, a dozen courses high and two courses thick. The barricade was usually riddled by day, and rebuilt at night. Here, across no-man's-land, the German front line turned back east along rising ground. The white scar of trench lay beside the Bapaume Road for a quarter of a mile, before returning north again across a shallow valley in the downland imperceptibly rising to a skyline of 110 metres. This slight hollow between two spurs was known as Mash Valley, up which the battalion was to advance on Z day.

Through a periscope Phillip looked out over no-man's-land, as he had many times before, with fascination and wonder for its human lifelessness. To leave the trench and advance over the open was something that thought broke down upon; yet one day it would have to happen.

Far away on the skyline, beyond two diminishing lines of trees marking the straight road to Bapaume, he could see a faint serration of roof-tops: Pozières, the final objective on Z day.

Pozières was two and a half miles distant. He could get there in three minutes on his motor cycle, if by some miracle every one of the hundreds of thousands living underground suddenly were to be lifted away, if the shell-holes and trenches were filled in, and the wire removed in the same instant, and all become as it was before 1914. Vain thought: the seasons of the world had changed: summer was harsh and bright and meaningless; winter cold and wet and pitiless; spring was a time for the greater activity of death; autumn for the dissolution of bodies into the soil, under the little hammers of the rain.

If only he could stop thinking like that: if only he could enjoy the moment, as Bason did, and most of the other fellows: if he could feel as Kingsman felt, serene because he believed in God, that what was to happen was inevitable, and so all things must be accepted *cum aequo animo*. Did prayer really help? But first you must believe. He did not know what he believed; first he believed one thing, then another.

To the right of the Bapaume road the salient in front of La Boisselle projected like a shattered reef of white coral upon a grim and empty prospect of grey. Here upon the white reef of the German lines had burst storm upon storm, until immense troughs and crests of waves, expended, lay as though fossilised in Time.

The Glory Hole was a litter of skulls on which tufts of hair remained, beside puttees coiled upon air and leather knee-boots empty save for each a bone; of charred fragments of cloth, once khaki or grey, sewn with buttons now black with sulphurous fumes, embossed with the Royal Coat-armour of Great Britain and Ireland, or the Imperial Crown of Prussia above the Gothic letter W. The Glory Hole was no charnel-house, for all flesh had long since leached into the chalk; it was a boneyard without graves, an uninhabited area making a gap of five hundred yards in the British line, an abandoned no-man's-land of choked shaft and subsided gallery held by a series of Lewis-gun posts. Nature was trying to return here, with thin, one-stalk weeds of poppy and charlock, and those other plants of the wilderness, ragwort and dock.

In the Glory Hole lay many British shells, of the largest calibres, which had failed to explode on impact. Observers upon the Fourth Army front had been reporting that one, sometimes two, and occasionally three of a salvo of four shells fired by the Corps siege artillery were duds.

KEEP LOW
SNIPER

said a notice board, for the German front line was less than a hundred yards' distant from the barricade beside the road. Suddenly the grey sea rushed, the wave broke; the shock was like an interior explosion; Phillip sat down while little triangles and splinters of looking-glass tinkled down. He threw down the shattered periscope and hurried away, remembering that this was Minnie Corner—the minenwerfer wobbling up into the air, the dreaded oil-drums filled with ammonal turning over and over, falling with smoking fuse visible as sparks at night, like a Chinese cracker: thump, on the chalk; silence; then in a vast flash everything blown flat and sideways. The Germans sent them up in home-made wooden mortars like long thin barrels bound with wire; he laughed as he imagined Heath Robinson figures running away solemnly as soon as they had lit the charge with a candle, for if the wooden barrel burst before the drum left, the present to Tommy would deliver itself backwards.

"I'll have to ask you to remove your boots when we're farther down the sap," said the lieutenant of Engineers, leading the way down the shaft with an Oerlix flashlamp. "And no talking, please. No smoking, either. We have to move slowly, especially at the face of the gallery, to conserve the oxygen in the air. We've had several cases of mine-gas poisoning."

There were three separate shafts leading to the gallery, for safety. Wooden steps went down into a series of tunnels, some of which appeared to be store caverns. The main gallery led away south. It was low and narrow; he had to bend down, feeling direction with his fingertips on the walls, elbows well in, the gallery being only thirty inches wide. He was glad to stop in a bay cut into one wall, where candles had made the chalk smoky. Here puttees, boots, and socks were taken off.

The floor of the gallery from here onwards was laid with sand-bags. He was sweating, and his back aching when they rested in another bay, where the sapper officer whispered that soon they would be crossing the line of a counter-mine the Germans had been digging until ten days before, when all sound of picking had stopped.

Phillip knew enough about mining and counter-mining to know that this might mean the blowing-in of the gallery any moment. "Camouflet or stifler no bon," he said, making a joke of it.

"We've got a listening set continuously manned, we'll be passing it soon."

Padding on the sand-bags, on which his big toes sometimes fluffed, and sweating in the close air, they came to a bay lit by a candle stuck in an alcove in the wall, where a man in shirt-sleeves was sitting, back to bag-upholstered wall, reading a book, head-phones over ears with wires leading into a box beside him.

"That's the C.R.E.'s new pet gadget—he calls it a 'geophone'," whispered the subaltern.

The listening man lifted his eyes from the book, made a washout movement with one hand, then went on reading. When Phillip bent to find out what the book was, the listener held it up, open at the title page for him to see; he nodded as though with anticipatory appreciation. It was *The Egoist*, by George Meredith, an author Phillip knew only from a poem in one of his younger sister Doris' school-books, *Love in the Valley*, which was pretty good, with true descriptions of a barn owl flying, and a nightjar reeling above the bracken on Reynard's Common, sitting along a branch of a silver birch. But he could not read such things, or think of them, out of England.

After a long time, it seemed, the tunnel became slightly wider, and they came upon men sitting on the floor, silently passing back a solitary sand-bag as carefully as if they were middle-aged devotees of some secret baby-cult. The sand-bag was laid, with extreme care, on another bag stacked with others beside one wall. The sapper officer put finger to lip before creeping forward, very slowly, to the end of the gallery.

Two men only were standing at the face of the chalk. One held a carpenter's wooden auger. He turned it with extreme caution several times, before pulling out the bit slowly, for the chalky droppings to be caught by his mate, in cupped hands, beside him. The droppings were put into a sand-bag held open by a third man sitting on the floor. A fourth man then gave the second man a bottle, which was tilted into the auger hole. When the liquid had been in about a minute—while everyone waited in complete silence—it was then scraped out in the form of chalky paste, with the aid of a long thin wooden scoop. Then the boring began again, as slowly and silently.

When they were up in the trench again, in dazzling light, the sapper subaltern explained that the gallery was one thousand and thirty feet in length, which brought it directly under the German fort at Y Sap. The extreme caution was necessary, he said, because of what had happened recently when the 183rd Tunnelling Company had been mining Russian saps, to provide covered communications across no-man's-land into the German front trench— "The idea of these is to blow the ends in by small charges, for the infantry to debouch through at Zero hour. This particular sap was considerably deeper than the others, and the chap pushing the auger at the chalk face suddenly staggered forward, the point of the bit having unexpectedly penetrated a Hun officer's dug-out."

"Good God!"

"Fortunately our men are Tynesiders, miners in peace-time, and were on their toes. They saw what had happened, and stood absolutely still. The bit had come through the last of the chalk, and was up against the upright deal planks lining the dug-out, with a couple of inches of air-space in between wood and chalk, to act as a buffer I suppose. The old Hun didn't suspect anything, and there's a hundred pounds of ammonal tamped in at the end of that particular Russian sap at this moment, ready for Zero hour."

"How deep was the dug-out?"

"Well, our sap was thirty feet down, deep enough to prevent it being blown in by all but the heaviest howitzer shells."

"Has that been reported? I mean, that the Hun dug-out roofs are thirty feet down?"

"I don't think a point was specially made about it in the report."

Thanking his host, and inviting him to call and have a mug of whiskey and a slice of plum cake in the company dug-out when he passed that way, Phillip hurried back to Captain Bason, who was seated at a table signing returns with the company clerk, a lance-corporal.

"I say, I think I ought to see the C.O. at once, skipper."

Captain Bason went on writing. Then, after some time he said, "What about, old sport?"

"I think I have something he will want to know, rather urgently. It's really a sort of private matter between us."

Ray, who was in the shelter, said, "Don't tell me you've got the job of private bum-boy already?"

Ignoring this remark, Phillip said, when Captain Bason continued to write upon the paper before him, "Well, I didn't mean exactly private, but I think I've found out something the C.O. wants to know."

"You don't say!" replied Bason, good-naturedly. "What do you know that only a colonel should know? By the way, he was round here while you were on your Cook's tour, with Kingsman and Milman, and asked where you were."

Before Ray could say anything further, Captain Bason went on, "Ray, go round to the C.S.M. and check up the trench stores that we'll have to hand over when we go back to Querrieu. Come along in, corporal. See that these returns go down to Ovillers Post with the ration party this evening."

When the corporal had followed Ray out of the shelter, Bason said, "Now then, what's the trouble, young Phil?"

"I think I may be on to something the C.O. wants to know rather urgently."

"Then it's personal? Nothing about the battalion?"

"In a way, it concerns the battalion. But he told me in confidence."

Looking at him sideways, with narrowed eyes, Bason said, "Can't I, as your company commander, know about something that concerns the battalion?"

"Well, skipper, I think Col. West ought to know it first."

"If that doesn't take the biscuit! Who the bloody hell d'you think you are?"

Phillip had not seen Bason looking before as he was looking now. The amiable, easy face, with the long thin brown moustache, untrained and untrimmed, had a look of a stubborn pink pig standing motionless, its eyes fixed sideways and upward. "If you can't tell me, as your company commander, then I'm b—d if I'll let you go sucking up to the Colonel, just because you knew him socially before you joined this regiment! Who the hell d'you think you are? What's the idea? Want to push out Milman as adjutant? Why, you're only a wart, and under my orders, and don't you forget it! You'll bloody well stop with your platoon until I bloody well tell you to go, and anything you have to report, you'll report to me! Now clear off back to your post, and let's have no more bloody nonsense from you!"

Standing to attention, Phillip said, "Sir! I request permission to see the Commanding Officer."

"I'll bloody well put you under arrest if you don't bloody well obey my orders!" shouted Captain Bason, rising from the table. "Push off!"

"Very good, sir!"

He went back to his platoon.

Two hours later a company runner came and said he was wanted at Coy. Headquarters. There Captain Bason told him he was to report at Battn. H.Q. The skipper eyed him keenly, saying, "Now look out what you're about! No talking out of school, mind!"

"Of course not, sir."

"G'r'rt yer!" said Bason, imitating George Robey's famous remark in *The Bing Boys* at the Alhambra. "G'r'rt yer! Come back later and tell us all about it."

Phillip was glad that the Bason was his old self again.

Boon brought in burnt corks and 'Spectre' West praised Phillip for his information, but said more definite evidence was required, and that the Brigadier had already approved his plan of trying to get into the Boche trench opposite. A box barrage was to be put round the sector at seven minutes past midnight for four minutes. Shrapnel and high-explosive from field guns would plaster the front line, leaving the section to be entered unshelled until the last two minutes. Then all batteries would put down a barrage from 12.9 a.m. until 12.11 a.m. That would get the Hun garrison down into the dug-outs. Meanwhile flanking parties would occupy shell-holes and sweep the rear lines while a party of picked men, cricketers all, would get into the front line. They would be armed with Mills bombs, daggers, and knobkerries. They would have blacked faces, and wear wash-leather bags over their boots.

Two parties, each under a sergeant, would get along the trench, from both sides of the centre of the chosen sector, and form bombing blocks. "Your centre party will carry these experimental grenades of yellow phosphorus. You will detail men to stand by three dug-out entrances. The grenades will be thrown down the two outside shafts, leaving the middle shaft un-bombed. The phosphorus will release dense white smoke, and choke any Hun below. They might still be able to fight, but there is no question of a fight. The sole purpose of your entry into the Boche line is to find out how deep the dug-outs are. You yourself will descend the middle shaft, wearing a P.H.G. helmet. This has special eye-pieces set in rubber sponge. It

will have been soaked in a concentrated solution of sodium bicarbonate, to counter the fumes of diphosphorus pentoxide."

"Very good, sir."

"I repeat:—The sole purpose of the raid is to enable a descent to
be made down the steps of one dug-out. *You are to count each step
going down, and again on coming up.* Visibility for your descent will
be provided by strontium flares. These flares on being tossed down
the central shaft will burn red and give the effect of the dug-out
being on fire. Any Boche below will, at first, keep clear of that
entrance. When you have come up, a sergeant will go down, to
check your count. Meanwhile the space between the top ledges
will be measured, to get an average measurement of the drop
between each ledge. Is that clear?"

"Yes, sir."

Phillip left a letter, to be posted to his mother, if he did not come
back. In it he put some pimpernels and speedwells picked from
around Ovillers Post.

It took two hours to get into position, crawling and resting, by the
gap through the German wire. Singing in chorus came from the
trenches in front. It was drowned when the barrage opened up
with its intensive summer lightning over the valley behind,
followed by the shriek and score of air. Red stars burst in the sky,
arcs of fire opened in the German lines, while Lt.-Col. West
crawled from one black face to another, pressing the hand of each
man.

Three streaks of fire arose from the German lines. Two broke
into red balls, the third became a silver pheasant's tail. Down fell
the German barrage on their own parapet.

Phillip pushed himself flat, next to "Spectre" West. His eye was
near a wan green dotted circle on the ground: the luminous wristlet
watch strapped to the black wrist of the wooden hand.

He felt a strange exaltation. The light and clangour took away
all feelings, so that he was a small centre of calmness.

They lay there for what seemed a very long time, until the British
barrage stopped. The German barrage was still dropping. When
it stopped, suddenly, they heard shouting coming from the dim
white German parapet.

With hot-bowelling suddenness machine-gun bullets were
cracking from groups of sparkles to left and right, all cutting across
the German parapet, sweeping just in front of it from the left and
from the right, so that some bullets seemed to be striking each other

with extra large flashes. Then stabs of red came from the trench itself. The front line was held in strength.

They lay there until the firing died down, and singing once more arose up from the dug-outs.

"The Brocken," said Lt.-Col. West at midnight, when they arrived at Battalion H.Q. "Or some other midsummer-eve festival. I don't know much about German mythology, but I fancy they celebrate in the Hartz mountains with song and dance about this time. Well, I've been able to get on the right side of the Brigadier, but Division is strafing him. Corps wants to know why they weren't told in advance. I suppose I'll be returned to the Commanding Officers' Pool."

He pushed over mug, bottle, and siphon of chlorinated water. Phillip saw that his hand was shaky.

"But surely, sir, with your record——"

"My dear Phil, colonels are as common as peas in a bushel measure. One or another is *degommé* every day. One third of us get bad reports from our brigadiers."

"Good lord!"

"Oh, stop being jejeune, for Christ's sake! Everyone wants a scapegoat, and Corps is in very hot water already. Haig, I hear from the Brigadier, has complained that not one of the trench raids on its front has come off. Why? Because they're held in strength. Why? Because the Boche knows our plans and realises they are based on illusion. If that illusion persists, the greatest slaughter in the history of the British Empire will occur on Z day!"

"Spectre" West emptied his mug of whiskey, and cried, "Were you bloody well telling lies again? Did you pick up that prisoner in no-man's-land? Was he in their front line, as you said at the time? By all the angels of God, if you let me down, Phillip, I'll have you shot!"

"I am sure the dug-out was very deep. It took me quite a time to go down, and then up again."

"Then why didn't you report its depth to Milman?"

"It didn't seem important, then. I thought it must already be known. It was only when you made a special point of it, sir, that it occurred to me."

A salvo of 5.9's swooped over, making for the valley beyond.

"Spectre" West called to his servant to bring another bottle of whiskey. He poured himself a terrible lot, thought Phillip.

"You know, the entire future of Britain and the Empire depends on the success or failure of the coming battle. The flower of the British nation, all the ardour, guts, and intelligence of a generation which has volunteered to do its damndest for what it believes in— Great Britain, and all that the *Pax Brittanica* stands for throughout the world—under the proud words *Ich Dien*—is gathered here in Picardy. I must empty my bladder. Don't go away."

When he came back to the shelter he said, "How old are you, Phillip? Twenty-one? God, to be twenty-one again! The world in 1906, when I was up at Wadham, was from everlasting to everlasting, as Traherne wrote in his 'Immortal Wheat' passage. Now at twenty-nine I am a wreck, mental and physical. Do you know why? Shall I tell you?" He poured himself more whiskey.

"Steady on," said Phillip, putting out a hand to take the bottle. "Please don't have too much. I give you my word that I know that dug-out was very deep, if that's any help."

"Oh, I'm not thinking of that. Why didn't you go and see my people at their pub in Lime Street, as you promised me when I was hit in front of Le Rutoire Farm last September? Does not your word mean anything to you? Or haven't you got a word?"

"I saw your letter from the Duchess of Westminster's hospital on the ante-room board, in which you wrote that you were hoping soon to rejoin the battalion, so I thought it wasn't necessary."

"You didn't forget?"

"No, of course not!"

"Well, well, well," muttered "Spectre", staring at nothing. Phillip thought that he looked dreadfully ill. "I suppose Frances told you? No need to pretend, my lad. You don't know? Well, here it is. I've been in love with her, my cousin once removed, since I came down from Oxford in '09. Nothing doing."

He looked at his mug of whiskey. On impulse Phillip took it, and put it at the other end of the table.

"You know," went on the other, apparently not noticing, "I had a hell of a job to get back here again. I wouldn't have had the hope of a snowflake in hell if 'Nosey' Orlebar hadn't been at the War House. He got me posted to the seventh battalion, as second-in-command. Then I was offered a battalion."

"May I be excused, Colonel? I must empty my bladder."

He took the mug with him and swished the whiskey away. When he returned, "Spectre" West with elbows on table was saying to himself, "Bompity-bompity-bompity-bompity! A cricket ball would have done the trick. How many steps leading down? Bompity-bompity-bompity! How many bompity-bomps?"

"I can only repeat that the Mills' reports were muffled and soft, but then I was standing six or seven yards away from the shaft. I could feel them, remote and dull, to be far under my feet, allowing for the fact that they were only Mills bombs."

"That's the kind of objectivity I want! Chalk is soft stuff, of course, and absorbs an explosion. If those dug-outs are more than seven to eight yards below the surface, then only a 12-inch or 15-inch howitzer shell can blow them in. And in confidence, mind!—as is everything I'm saying to you—there are only sixteen really heavy guns on the Corps front. One 15-inch and three 12-inch on railway mountings, and twelve 9.2's. Sixteen heavies to poop off at dug-outs possibly eight metres deep underground, in soft, shock-absorbent chalk, honey-combing half a dozen lines of trenches along three thousand five hundred yards of Corps front. Divide three thousand five hundred by sixteen, and you have one dug-out-busting howitzer or gun to every two hundred and twenty yards of front. Multiply that a mile for depth, for raking back, that's one heavy shell for one-eighth of a square mile. In that area will be scores of machine-gun teams down in those deep dug-outs, each team of which has practised bringing up its guns and mountings in pieces, to fit together as soon as the bombardment has lifted. Where will their targets be then? Six hundred yards distant from the muzzles of their Spandau guns! I tell you Fourth Army is MAD!" he shouted, banging the table with his fist. Then he uttered a long sigh and lay down on his bunk, face to the wall.

Phillip took the bottle from the table, and going outside, hurled it into the air. Then climbing out of the communication trench he walked beside it on its way to the line. Hearing the voice of the Brigadier coming down the trench, and since it was against orders to walk over the top, he cleared off before questions could be asked. Thank God he'd chucked away the bottle in time.

Chapter 16

THE YELLOWHAMMER

There were four sections of eight men under a corporal in his platoon. Each section had rehearsed its particular and detailed function, for almost every moment of the assault, during the many practice advances, before he had joined Captain Bason's company.

Every man knew what to do, how to do it, and the precise time it should be done; but now, for the final exercise before the Generals, the time-table had been changed.

At Zero minus 8 minutes the first of six waves was to advance upon the fluttering line of flags held by distant figures representing the final barrage, in order to cross three hundred yards of ground by Zero. There was sixty yards between each wave, and the pace had to be set so that the last wave rose out of the earth at the moment that the flags stopped fluttering: when a more distant fluttering indicated that the guns had raked back upon the second objective at the moment when the leading infantry wave was five hundred yards away from the German front line.

Lt.-Col. West was addressing the assembled officers of the battalion.

"On our right," he said, indicating two straight lines of pegged white tape, "lies the Bapaume road. Across the Bapaume road to the north-west, lies La Boisselle. It will be attacked by the North Country division, but not directly. Mine craters lie between our lines and the fortress of La Boisselle, and the area of these craters, as many of you are aware, is known as the Glory Hole. The Glory Hole won't be attacked directly. Columns of troops will pass on either side of it, and bomb their way into La Boisselle, which is a maze of trenches and dug-outs. Lewis-gun teams and batteries of Stokes guns will support them. So much for our right flank.

"Now I come to our own problem.

"As you know there is a salient around La Boisselle, pushed out like a great fist, half a mile wide, forming a re-entrant into our lines. Machine-guns on the end knuckles of this fist can sweep across all the lower ground of Mash Valley over which we have to advance. Their fire, as things stand now, can take us in enfilade, at precisely one hundred and eighty degrees. From Y Sap, which is at our end of the German fist, machine-gun batteries can fire right across our line of advance."

All eyes were fixed on the speaker's face.

"Likewise the southern knuckle of the fist, at the far end of the Glory Hole, is able to enfilade the advance there. That is what you all know."

Lt.-Col. West paused.

"Well, gentlemen, I have some news for you! Both knuckles of this fist are to be sent sky-high, from two mines packed with about fifty thousand pounds of ammonal apiece, at Zero hour. The mines will not only destroy the Boche's flanking m.g. fire, but will throw up many hundreds of tons of chalk. This chalk will drop around each crater. The dropped tons of chalk will be in the way of all enfilade fire. The crater lips will be about fifteen feet high, enough to do the trick. Thus our flanks, in the coming assault, will be secured."

The commanding figure looked at his watch, took their salutes, fastened his wrist by the swivel on his belt, then rode away with his adjutant.

Deployed upon the rolling downland three brigades of four battalions each, with subsidiary companies of engineers and pioneers, waited for a rocket to splash its yellow plumes against the blue summer sky, signal that the imaginary barrage had started. Distant flags began to waggle.

A second rocket burst on high, to fall in red rain, denoting that 45 minutes had passed and it was now Zero minus 15 minutes.

The brigade-major cantered up to Lt.-Col. West and said, "The Brigadier wishes to emphasize that on no account will the times of advance be exceeded, sir," then he cantered four hundred yards away to the next battalion of his brigade. Far away other mounted staff officers were to be seen, cantering.

The troops waited.

At Zero minus 8 minutes, the first wave got up, and moved in line towards the faraway flags. Although it was early morning, the heat of the sun was great. Soon dust was arising above the extended lines of men moving forward. They were followed by groups of companies in diamond or artillery formation. Six hundred yards farther back the supporting battalions, in lines of columns, moved forward meticulously in time with the plan of advance, thirty-three yards to the minute. Aeroplanes on contact patrol flew overhead.

Upon the field, junior staff-officers with printed tables and stop-watches beside them checked the rate of advance.

"God's teeth," muttered "Spectre" West, "they knew better than this at Waterloo."

The sight of the waves and the masses of waves following was exhilarating to the young inexperienced officers and their men who, although ordered to be silent, gave to one another small greetings with hand and lift of chin. They had been told to imagine that they were carrying, beside their rifles, water-bottles, entrenching tools, and haversacks, an assortment of spades, bandoliers of ammunition, picks, rolls of barbed wire, pigeon baskets, electrical-buzzer gear, drums of telephone wire, water-cans, sandbags filled with bombs, and other gear; and such was their ardour and enthusiasm that they imagined what they had been told. Metallic discs were stitched between their shoulder blades; coloured ribbons tied to their shoulder straps.

Each man of Captain Bason's company, plodding astride a mock Bapaume Road made of white tape, had a red ribbon tied on his left shoulder. The three other companies of the battalion wore blue, yellow, and green ribbons; while every rifleman with wire-cutters had a white bow tied upon his right shoulder—the bridegrooms, Bason called them.

Bridegrooms of death, thought Phillip.

Unimpeded, irresistible, the division went forward in six waves, up slowly rising ground to the final objective, a large white notice board on which was painted in black letters

SITE OF POZIERES

While strict silence had been observed and no whistles had been blown, occasional cigarette-smoking had been observed by the brass hats; so the attack must be made again. More dust arose with a greater heat; sweat, flies, boredom, and thirst. The gilded staff lost its pristine glamour in the eyes of the once-ardent. Then the whisper went round that the Field-Marshal himself was coming to watch the rehearsal.

There was the C.-in-C.'s pennant, carried upright by a first-class warrant-officer of Dragoon Guards, an object of mahogany, bristle, and brass with the appearance of one who had never been boy or man but always a figure of impersonal military power. The spit-and-polish of this equestrian figure was such that Phillip thought of him as altogether inhuman. He wore brown riding boots so straight in the leg and so polished that they looked as though before coming on the field they had been kept in a show-case: as in fact they had been—breathed upon, boned, saddle-soaped, boned and waxed and boned and polished, boned again and waxed again and polished until they resembled brown lustre glass. Behind rode an awe-ful figure, grey-moustached, keen of eye—Sir Douglas Haig. With the group of generals, a little in rear, rode a svelte, sallow young man with imperturbable manner more Eastern than European, with eyes both cervine and calculating, a two-legged deer of the oases who had somehow come to stand beside the British lion, immaculate in uniform with gorget patches and brassard of G.H.Q.

Peasant *cultivateurs*, whose roots and tillered corn had been crossed again and again, ceased to pause in their work of hoeing down the rows of beet-sugar and mangolds, as they struck at thistle and spurrey with feelings of violation, of outrage, for the destruction of their crops. The soldiers from office, factory, and machine shop considered these morose individuals to be hardly more animate or intelligent than the roots they tended.

There was one exception. While "A" company was resting near the notice board for the third time, a short fat Frenchman in peaked cap, dark coat, and trousers clumsily tucked into black leather leggings, showing laced ankle boots of *glacé* kid below, appeared out of nowhere with a gun under his arm and an angry expression on his face nearly covered by thick black beard and whiskers. Judging by the string bag stuffed with red-legged partridges and other smaller birds slung on his shoulder, he had been having a successful day. He was, moreover, equipped for comfort. He was complete with rolled cape, leather wine-bottle, cartridge belt, and *La Vie Parisienne*. A thin unhappy-looking setter with over-worked dugs quivered behind his heels.

"Hullo, cock, how's yourself?" cried a wag.

"Pah!" With indignation the French sportsman surveyed the soldiers lying down on his land. "Les autres Boches," he announced to himself.

At that moment a yellowhammer flew over the grass. The *tireur* followed it with eager eyes. It lit on the board, and sang in a small, flint-chip voice. The *tireur* raised his gun—*crack!* The brown-and-yellow bird dropped as to a puff. Breast feathers floated in the air. There were ironical cheers from the men as the small body was picked up and the sportsman strode away, towards a wood, followed by his bitch and a cry of, "Next time, Pah, 'ave a go at Fritz!"

Phillip picked up two of the breast feathers and put them in his pocket book, beside a poppy and a marigold picked in Tara Valley. He was keeping them to send home in the next letter to his mother.

Back at camp, rumour spread like a chill. The Colonel had been removed from his command.

"Have you heard anything, Captain Bason?"

"Straight from the horse's mouth, otherwise our one and only Wigg. He has honoured us by visiting the mess—complete with red tabs, crown, and spurs. Blimey, some people know their way about, all right! But why the 'captain' all of a sudden? Cheer up, old sport!"

Phillip left the letter he was writing and went with Bason to the mess marquee.

"Your pal has mucked himself up good and proper this time," said Ray, with some glee.

"What happened, skipper?" asked Phillip, feeling weak.

"You ought to know, he confided in you, didn't he?" Bason could not help saying.

While they were discussing it, Major Kingsman came to see Bason. Captain Paul was with him. The three walked up and down side by side, a hundred yards from the lines, talking together for several minutes.

The battalion officers had not dined together in mess since leaving England, until the previous night. For this second and final occasion before returning up the line for the Show, as it was now called, a special dinner had been arranged in a marquee, with champagne, provided by the C.O. The occasion had been much looked forward to, a grand send-off in the spirit of Eat, Drink, for tomorrow—the Break-through! And then the news about Colonel West leaving, and Major Kingsman commanding the battalion. Would the old C.O. be present? And would he now pay for the fizz? asked Ray. Beaucoup fizz was what he wanted; lashings and lashings of the stuff. And all buckshee.

The dinner took place. Major Kingsman, after His Majesty's health had been drunk, proposed the toast of the Regiment. Then he read an apology for absence from Lt.-Col. West, who said that to his very great regret he would not be leading the battalion into action. He knew, however, that they would give whole-hearted support to their new Commanding Officer, and do their damndest to get the Hun out of France, and so play their part in bringing Victory to the Allied Arms. He himself would be taking part in the offensive with his own regiment, to which he would be on his way, to serve in any capacity that he was ordered, when his Farewell Message was being read by his good friend and comrade-in-arms, Major Kingsman.

He wished them God Speed, and Good Luck.

There was prolonged cheering as Major Kingsman sat down. Beside him was Captain Paul. Toasts were drunk to "Spectre", by which name he was by now generally known, in the wine he had provided. But it was not the old colonel they cheered, so much as their thoughts of the Great Push that was imminent.

Major Wigg, sitting on the other side of the C.O., drinking his seventh glass of gin and lighting his second cigar, was a more refined sardonic self, as befitted the gilded frame of his self-portrait as a G.S.O. 3. He never drank champagne, he explained, it was bad for his liver. He was a man of gin. To those beside him—Captains Milman, Paul, Thompson, Cusack, and Bason—he gave the inside information.

A man of manners on occasion, Major Wigg, now a guest, withheld his personal views and spoke objectively, although in a dry tone of voice as befitted one on the staff of Army, with a comprehensive point of view.

The rate of advance, "Spectre" had complained, was too slow, and it began too far off. The German front line should be rushed, he had most considerately explained to a mere G.O.C. Army, from close up behind the barrage. Army's plan, he maintained, was based on a fallacy, that "the opposition would be wiped out by the preliminary bombardment". Even if this "wiping out" were feasible, and he had reason to doubt it, Field Service Regulations made the principle of the assault after bombardment perfectly clear: the phrase used was "rush the position". The Regulations also laid down that troops, even under the orders of junior commanders, seeing an opportunity to get in quickly, should start off under their commander's own initiative, and "others were to co-operate as soon as possible". That was the principle of successful attack in all wars, and this war was no exception, the "mushroom colonel" had argued.

Putting down his damp cigar, and choosing as though carefully a cigarette from his gold case, Major Wigg continued, in a voice of gravel, "Our would-be military genius went on to say that he had heard that the Field-Marshal himself had suggested that the advance should be made in small rushes. This view of the Field-Marshal—our late schoolmaster was kind enough to lecture his seniors, who by this time were wondering why Old Man Rawly had put up with such damned insolence for so long—was based on the 'historic principle' of overcoming the enemy's unformed resistance speedily at close quarters, before it could cohere into resistance. With the usual sweat bedewing his brow, 'Spectre' went on to say, 'The Field-Marshal's suggestion, I understand— and I say it with the very greatest respect, and in humble duty'— for all the world as though he were the P.M. before H.M., and about to kiss hands—'has been rejected by the Fourth Army Commander.' His very words. So," concluded Major Wigg, with satisfaction, "Mr. Bloody West's goose is cooked."

At this point Phillip, wishing he had not had any champagne, made his way back to his quarters.

The post corporal had left parcels in the tent. Among them was one for him addressed in a strange, unformed handwriting. In the parcel were two tins, one of sardines, and another of café-au-lait, a packet of cigarettes, some chocolate, a cake, a packet of ginger snaps, a tin of Zam-buk, and a glossy picture postcard of Gaby Deslys dancing with Harry Pilcer. There was also a letter written on cheap lined paper.

The sender thanked him for his ever-welcome letter, and hoped he was well. She asked him to take care of himself, and prayed for his return every morning on waking up, and every night before going to sleep, and hoped he would not mind. The Zam-buk was in case he was wounded, and had nothing handy to kill germs with. She had seen none of the old faces, as she was now doing hospital work in the evenings, after the laundry. *Yours truly, Lily.*

He was ending a reply to the letter, and about to take one of the yellowhammer's feathers from between the pages of the book Westy had given him, to put it in the folded writing paper, when Bason came into the tent and said, "Hullo, where did you get to?"

"I didn't feel too well, skipper."

"What's that you've got, a canary's feather?"

"No, it's one of the yellowhammer's, shot by the Frenchman this afternoon."

"Well, old sport, I just looked in to suggest that perhaps in future you'll remember the old saying, 'Easy come, easy go'. And I'd like you also to know, for what it's worth, that you have a company commander who is also your pal."

Bason put his hand for a moment on the younger man's shoulder, and went out of the tent.

Chapter 17

WAITING

8th Bn. P.R.O. Regt.
B.E.F.
27 June, 1916

Dear Mother.

I am sorry I have not replied to your letters before this, or written to thank you for your two excellent parcels; my only excuse is the work out here, and the hectic time accompanying great preparations.

There is now an interval: I am lying on a little hill above a river valley and the sun is going down upon the long straight road we have marched up to our destination. The company is billeted in bunks put up in outhouses and barns, for this area is almost as crowded as the Hill on a Thursday band-night before the war, when people waited to see the fireworks from the Crystal Palace. We, the officers, have a room in the farmhouse, on the floor.

We started our march up yesterday morning. The road was much congested, for it is the main route to the Picnic, as we call it. Often we had to leave the road and walk in file the other side of the poplars, in and out of the ditch. At times it was a bit trying, as after the bright weather the sky became dull with heat. Then rocky grey clouds moved over, sullen and hard; the air became more oppressive; lightning struck, and the heavens began their bombardment. We were soon soaked to the skin, but afterwards regained cheerfulness, for after the rains, which fell upon an almost silent countryside, the sky came clear, the sun flashing. At night an Aurora Borealis greater than the one Father used to tell us about, when in the hard winter before I was born you were living in the canal-keeper's house at the end of Comfort Road (I have sudden vivid pictures of a life that is gone, it seems forever, out here), filled the night sky. From where we were last night we heard nothing, for by some freak of the strata underground or the atmosphere above all the thunders of man were inaudible. The eastern sky was a wonder; the winter-god was conquered by Proserpine; a thousand butterflies fluttered there, soundlessly fluttering on wings of light, tremulous at times, suddenly flushing gold as though with some discovered nectar in the flowers of the night. It was wonderful, it was terrible, it was music and poetry and all the power of life come to play upon our little world—or should I write worlds, for each one of us is a little world, which in course of time will dissolve like the animals that once inhabited the shells, now chalk, upon which soon we are to move, as in a new creation by fire, and, for some of us, darkness evermore. For the wondrous light is not of Proserpine; the nether world of Pluto has opened upon the earth, with the fires of hell.

When a man dies, does a wraith issue forth from the poor shell, to find its way across the sea, perhaps as suspended thought, to visit the world it has abdicated, by right of being of the European generation which has been called to account for itself? I write European generation for I know that our feelings are shared by those who are opposed to us. It is not easy to write this, in fact I feel damnably nervous, not so much about what is to be, but because what I think is, I feel, not acceptable to others.

If it happens that my fate is already resolved, I ask you not to grieve. As I wrote to you before I went out in 1914, I have had a happy life, when I have not been selfish and contrary; and so what happiness I have had has been owed to you and Father, to my sisters, my Grandfather, too, and Aunt Marian, and my neighbours. If I have been in conflict with some of the latter, it was, I am sure, due to my fault, or error.

Do you, Mother, remember our picnic on Reynard's Common, before I left for the front last September? I remember all you told me about prayer helping to overcome fearful thoughts, by thinking of others before oneself, that is, of one's men. They are very simple and trusting, these men, and so cheerful. For myself, to whom they look, I have accepted the idea of death, if it is to come, as pre-destined, "when the burning moment breaks".

Reynard's Common, when we were little! It was wonderful to go by train to the end of the line, where Father in his bicycling suit was waiting to meet us. He used to wait patiently to allow us to watch the engine being disconnected, and then put on the wooden turn-table, which was wound round by hand, until the engine pointed back to London, to puff away until it came back to the guard's van, ready for the return journey.

I can see it all so vividly now, Reynard's Common and the heated air over the pebble beds, where the gorse grew and the linnets nested, their breasts coloured as though with flame from so many fires in those dry summers long ago. Do you remember the chiffchaff's nest near where we once picnic'd? Father made us bury our orange peel, but I left a little piece of yellow showing, because I wanted to go and watch the nest.

I have met Father Aloÿsius, of St. Saviour's, again. He is attached to the Liverpool Irish in our division. He came to dinner in the Colonel's billet last night; I was invited, too—just the three of us. I told you about our C.O., he was a captain at Hornchurch, and lives at Tollemere Park, and is now in command. Both he and Fr. A. were Balliol men. It is very interesting to hear them talk; I now see what Aunt Dora was driving at, with her talk of ancient Greece, etc. Fr. A. told me that in France the symbol of religion is the mother and child, not the father as in Protestant countries.

Below me, and to the north as I sit here on the hillside, I can see a cathedral half-broken, and the Golden Virgin on the campanile, leaning down—struck by a shell—but still holding the Babe in her arms. After dinner I went to Fr. A's billet, and we had a frank talk. I told him how Desmond and I had quarrelled, and how the misunderstanding had come about; and how I knew that a bitter remark made by D. just before I left for the depot after the telegram, was only the measure of his affection turned to bitterness. So if it happens that my turn has come, please assure Desmond that his friend understands, and sympathises with all that he has suffered through me.

The padre and I talked quite frankly about death. I told him that I had heard dying soldiers, both English and German, calling out for their mothers; he said the spiritual feeling between a mortally wounded boy and the image of his mother was of the same relation between the Son and Mary, the Mother of God, but lifted beyond the struggling human spirit into the realm of the soul, what the ancient Greeks called Eirene, which was everlastingly as a light over the Abyss.

This Abyss, said the padre, is in every man until impersonal love for his fellow men comes into his life, as a motive force for living. In a war like this, he said, which is a manifestation of the Abyss, of the eternal war between love and hate, the individual is able to escape his own terrors of the mind only by encouraging, through prayer, the good within him to dominate his life; the greater love.

He said that the Church was by no means perfect and admitted that dreadful things had been done in the past; for men were only human, and being human, could be one thing or the other. This is a bit muddled, I fear, but I think I know what he meant. Father Aloysius is very popular with the troops.

I hope that Father's allotment flourishes, and all goes well in Hill-side Road, and that your jaunts to the Old Vic with Grandpa continue. Major Kingsman, who is keen on history, told me that Henry the Fifth crossed the Somme somewhere near here, on his way to fight one of his battles. Do you remember Grandpa reading the prologue of *Henry the Fifth* to us the night before Uncle Hugh and Uncle Sidney went off to the Boer War? Major Kingsman lent me his Shakespeare, and told me to read the passage where the King visited his troops round their camp-fires. I must say it was a revelation to me, after the impression of complete nothingness I got from having to do this play at school. The Prince of Wales, from what I've heard, is rather like that. When he was dining at the Officers' Club at Boulogne one night he invited an officer I know to have a glass of port with him at his table. He (the officer) was badly hit at Loos, and came to this battalion recently, from the regiment to which I was originally gazetted, but now for various reasons he has returned to his battalion. I wonder if by any chance

Percy Pickering will come across him, if and when Percy gets out here.

No more now. By the time you get this, perhaps Father will be reading rather special news in *The Daily Trident*, which, by the way, seems to be the only paper to be bought out here, in the back areas. We never know what is happening out here until we read of it in the papers; though not everything we read is what we know has happened.

I bought some excellent *patisserie* in the town below us this afternoon; almost as good as that we bought in Brussels five years ago. Do you remember?

I watched a thrilling sight today—three of the German sausage balloons behind their lines brought down in flames, leaving black smoke in the sky—coal-gas, I suppose. I have seen other wonderful sights, but cannot tell you what they are!

Your affectionate son,

PHILLIP.

Sursam corda! That's what Father A. said to me. It means, broadly translated, Keep Smiling!

After hesitation he added two words to the beginning; but seeing that the addition was obviously an after-thought he rewrote the first page, beginning *My dear Father and Mother*. Then doubts of what Father, who scorned the Roman Catholics, might think arose in him. The letter began to look fanciful; then the word *throw-back*, so often heard about himself in boyhood, rose before his mind like an apparition in black. He regarded the rapidly-written pages with indecision; then tore the letter up and buried the fragments.

If one of the least of temporary junior officers of what was called the Citizen Army suffered from frustration, so did the greatest soldier of the British Expeditionary Force. Neither the place nor the time of the offensive were of F.-M. Sir Douglas Haig's choosing. He had wanted to make the attack farther north, in Artois and Flanders, later in the year; for while the New Armies were in good heart, they lacked both experience and sufficient training. His own ideas and wishes had been set aside when he responded to the French call for help; Maréchal Joffre had demanded an attack in Picardy, the country of the Somme, to relieve the sufferings and annihilations of French divisions upon "the anvil of Verdun".

Having subordinated his strategy to that of the French Maréchal, he had next to give way on tactical points. Sir Douglas Haig had wanted the infantry assault to start at first light, before the German machine-gunners could sight their targets properly; both Maréchal Joffre and his subordinate commander General Foch had declared that the battle must begin at 10 a.m., for their artillery observers to have a clear view of the infantry in *horizon bleu* advancing on the sector of the Sixth French Army south of the steep cliff-like right bank of the Somme.

The British Field-Marshal had chosen one of his senior generals, Rawlinson, to command the new Fourth British Army, which was to fight the battle, and had suggested to him the need for a quick preliminary assault, immediately the final intensive bombardment lifted, to rake back upon the successive German lines. Sir Henry Rawlinson had not agreed with this suggestion; the Field-Marshal had not pressed it since, having delegated responsibility, he was loyal to his subordinate's wishes. To have forced his views upon Rawly would have been, in the English idiom, "not cricket": a term often derided because misunderstood by those who did not play that game wherein only the better feelings of man, by the very nature of the game, can be exercised.

An obscure lieutenant of militia, holding the acting rank of lieutenant-colonel, had left his command during manoeuvres to address himself to Sir Henry Rawlinson, a guest of the Divisional Commander, without permission, without introduction. He had persisted in stating his uncalled-for views beyond the limit of what was considered good form. He had insisted on saying that a strong line of skirmishers should be sent to enter the enemy lines before the German machine-gunners had time to climb up and out of their dugouts: that this preliminary penetration must be made in the first light, the *prima luce* of the great commanders of the ancient world. Holding himself rigid against his discomposure in the presence of soldiers of high rank belonging to an assured caste of which, owing to his humble birth, he was ever conscious, with beads of sweat upon his forehead, "Spectre" West had quoted, in the original Greek, from Euripides, following it by a translation— "Danger shines like sunlight to a brave man's eyes"—but, he said, with unseen machine-guns firing into those eyes from under the blaze of the risen sun in the east, it would be a fearful price to pay for courage thrown away.

"With due respect, sir, and in humble duty to his Majesty the King-Emperor, I submit that, whatever the hour or state of light when the main assault takes place, that assault, or ordered advance of what are practically porters, must be preceded by a line of mobile skirmishers, thrusting forward immediately behind the barrage in order to contain, or to destroy, the enemy garrisons underground, until the impedimenta-laden waves of infantry arrive."

He was listened to in silence; and when he had seen that his remarks were apparently to be ignored, he asked formally to be permitted to see the Commander-in-Chief.

Afterwards, at Querrieu, in the garden of the château which was General Rawlinson's headquarters, he was courteously taken by the General's A.D.C., together with his Brigadier, to the office of a Major-General in one of the many wooden huts of Army Administration. There the matter of the existence of deep German dugouts, "some possibly between thirty and forty feet underground," which he had spoken about previously, was discussed.

"You know, Colonel, one is inclined to be puzzled as to the reason why no subsequent report about the alleged existence of such deep shelters was sent in by you, after you took command of your battalion. A pity you did not think of it at the time. In war, and indeed in all aspects of life, everything depends on the question of timing. To cast doubt at this late hour, and without substantiation of what you say about the depth of the shelters, is only to cause uncertainty, even alarm, as by now you probably realise," said the Major-General.

Later, over a peg of whiskey-and-soda in his living quarters, he said, "How was 'Nosey' Orlebar when last you saw him at the War House? I was runner-up in the middle-weight boxing tournament at Aldershot in '06, and had the distinction of helping to get 'im 'is nickname, you know. He put me down well and truly in the next round by way of retaliation! Now about this question of tactics that worries you. I think in the circumstances you may wish to consider yourself free of all responsibility in the matter. So if you will be so good as to come with me, I will take you to the D.A.G., and you can have a word with him about it."

In the Deputy Adjutant General's office Col. West asked to be allowed to see the Field-Marshal. The response was curt. He was told that no useful purpose would be served by an interview, since he had already been relieved of his command. Any remarks he wished to make should be put in writing, and forwarded through the usual channels.

"Meanwhile would you prefer to go home to England on long leave, or to rejoin a line battalion of your Regiment?"

Captain West asked to be allowed to rejoin his Regiment.

Having written his farewell message to the battalion through

Major Kingsman, he went back to the 7th Gaultshires in the Eastern Division at Carnoy, which with another division of the XIII Corps was to attack opposite Mametz and Montauban, adjoining the French Sixth Army.

During the darkness of the next night four raids were carried out by units within the area of the Fourth Army. In one, near Carnoy, enemy trenches were found empty and damaged by shell-fire. In the second, north of Maricourt, the trenches were lightly held, and a prisoner was captured. The third raid took place south of La Boisselle, near the Schwarben Hohe. Here the trenches were strongly held, and the raiders were shot on the wire. The fourth raid was opposite Ovillers, upon the sector where, a fortnight before, Phillip's party had scrambled into trenches ten feet deep, with a firing step seven feet below a loop-holed parapet built up by coloured dazzle sandbags, and revetted by stakes and withies. The trenches on this raid were full of Germans, one of whom was hauled back. To all questions, except those demanding name, number, and regiment, he replied *Bitte! Nicht sprechen!*

No question about the depth of dug-outs was asked either prisoner of these raids; no requests for this particular information had come from Division, none from Corps, none from Fourth Army.

When was Z-day?

It was still unknown to the troops in the valley of the Ancre. The company waited in barn and billet. Sentries with whistles stood outside to give warning of aeroplanes, revealed by irregular dots of white, the bursting shells of Archibald, the anti-aircraft gun. Well in front of drifting cotton-wool was a tiny white speck, as diaphanous as one of the pale watery ephemeral flies dancing in clouds among the poplars in the water-meadows. The whistle blew; no faces looked up, to where almost imperceptibly high in the blue was moving the frail wraith with black crosses.

"Anyone got any rumours about Z-day, skipper?"

"Nothing from the Adj yet, old sport."

Excitement among the herded men was intense. Bets were made, in plinketty plonk (*vin blanc*), *rhum*, and *vin rouge*—to be paid in Brussels; or Berlin.

"A gunner officer told me the attack had been put off!"

"Did you hear, the Hun has asked for an armistice, after mutiny down at Verdun!"

"Well, you see, Asquith has shares in Krupps, and so he's

delaying the attack as long as possible, for the Germans to increase their armaments!"

"That's bloody rot, Cox! Like his wife visiting German officers at Donnington Hall!"

"Well, don't lose your wool, One-piecee!"

Clouds moved in drifts across the summery blue, wind poured into the valley of the Ancre, tributary of the Somme, from the south-west. The shadow of Nimbus raced the golden glow of Phoebus across the undulating country that was to be the battle-field. Again the concentrated bombardment of destruction broke upon the air, while the ground seemed to be shaking in one continuous rumbling, as of the boiling of an immense cauldron. When it had boiled itself over individual salvoes of batteries could be heard, but seldom a moment in the day or the night passed without detonation.

"Jerry's copping it," said Pimm to Phillip, with dark satisfaction. The bombardment continued all the next morning, but at 3.30 p.m. it ceased abruptly. The silence was blank and irritating.

What had happened?

Why were so many scout aeroplanes going over?

Flight after flight of D.H.2's, Nieuports, Sopwith two-seaters and F.E.2b's passed in formation above slower reconnaissance B.E.s.

A rumour went around that the Kaiser had offered to surrender, that the R.F.C. were sending planes to escort a delegation of staff officers to deliver terms.

"From the latrine, like all the others," said Captain Bason. "Hell, I'm a platoon commander short, now Ray has gone sick, with a dose of clapp."

"So he's got away with it?"

"You've said it, old sport. He's just been taken down to the field ambulance. You'll take command of the company while we're in, if anything happens to me."

"What about Cox?"

"The order remains that all seconds-in-command of companies are to remain behind, with two sergeants per company, to form a cadre on which to reform the company in case of heavy losses. Cox is to be promoted to Captain."

"Does second-in-command go by seniority, skipper?"

"Sure thing. Cox is senior, isn't he, to you? Anyway, he's going to the Chinese Labour Corps being formed now, as he speaks the lingo. He put his name in for it a week or two back, when we were at Querrieu. That rumour about the Kaiser asking for peace is bilge, by the way. Those aeroplanes went out to photograph the shelled sectors, protected by scouts. I saw Quarters just now. He's just come from railhead, and says Duggie Haig has moved his advanced headquarters to Beauquesne, only a dozen miles back, so it won't be long now."

Phillip walked down the muddy street to Cox's billet. It had rained during the night and early morning. Cox was lying down on his flea-bag, a bundle of old letters and a bottle of whiskey beside him on the floor.

"Hullo, One-piecee. What brings you here?"

"Cox, why did you tell Bason you were senior to me? You know you're not. I was gazetted ten days before you."

"So you've got the wind-up, have you, One-piecee? Have a choc."

"No thanks. I hear you're going to the Chinese Labour Corps, anyway."

"Ha!" exclaimed Cox, letting his eye-glass fall as he sat up. "Has it come through?"

"I don't know. Bason said your name had gone in. The point is that I was gazetted on March the fourteenth last year, and you on March the twenty-fourth. It's in the Army List."

"My dear One-piecee, you appear to forget that I was appointed second-in-command before you rejoined. So I am senior in service with the company. Help yourself to some whiskey, if you don't mind drinking out of the bottle."

"I think you ought to tell Bason the truth."

"My dear One-piecee, do you want Bason and everyone else to know that you're showing the white feather? They will think that, you know. After all, I'm a man of thirty-five, and my wife is going to have a baby. And I'm going any moment to the Chinese Labour Corps, as an interpreter, so if you kick up a shindy, it will be obvious that you are trying to save your own skin."

"You told me you were twenty-five, when we were at Sevenoaks."

"Everyone lies about his age in the army. I did, to get in quickly. Well, go and tell Bason, if you feel like that. Only don't be surprised if everyone thinks you're yellow, will you? How are the pigeons? Why not go and see? I'm rather busy. Tootle-oo, One-piecee!"

Phillip had been appointed Pigeon Officer for the battalion. When Captain Bason had asked casually what he knew about birds, "of the feathered sort, of course, old sport", and then said that the

Adjutant had suggested him for the job of Pigeon Officer, he felt relief mingled with regret that he would not be with the men of his platoon any longer. They seemed to like him, and he did not want them to feel deserted.

However, the job was only part-time, to last only until the attack. The birds arrived from the Corps Mobile Loft (which was built on to a London omnibus) in a large wicker basket strapped on the back of a despatch rider riding a Triumph motorcycle. The corporal showed Phillip how to take a bird out, by holding the legs placed backwards in the hand, together with the wing-pinions, and departed. Later, a bag of split peas, tares, limestone grit, and grain arrived from the Quartermaster. The birds were fed and watered from zinc trays attached to their baskets. They were to be taken into action housed in smaller baskets, one for each company. Having showed four chosen runners, one for each company, how to hold the birds, and to remove the aluminium leg-capsule for the message, the job of Battalion Pigeon Officer was practically ended.

Now he went to look at the birds, which were kept in a pannier in a barn. One bird in the top compartment of the basket had laid an egg, while another in the lower section was trying to get at it, udging by the way it was croodling and looking up at the shiny white shell through the wickerwork. Did pigeons suck eggs? He decided to find out, and having taken the egg, put it in the lower section. At once the pigeon bowed to it, dropping its wings before straddling the egg and settling upon it, in one corner. While he was watching, Pimm, who was looking after the birds, joined him. Pimm had kept pigeons in civvy street, he said, and so had been given the job of carrying the advance basket, which was to accompany Phillip who, as the senior subaltern in the company, was to lead the attack.

"That's an old bird, a cock, sir," he told Phillip. "Jimmy, I call 'im. I've been watching Jimmy. He wants only one more egg, and he'll be happy. An old cock will always brood eggs; he love a squab, you see, and cares for it all right. Some people think pigeons too free with one another's mates, in a manner of speaking, sir, but I've proved the contrary. Like a gander, sir, a cock pigeon will always look after a pair of young birds, what we call squabs, or some calls 'em squeakers. I love to see 'em, sir, with young 'uns. I used 'av an old cock what we called Romper, what used to caggle a hen away from another cock, not exclusive for the tread, like any old barn-yard cockerel, sir, if you understand my meaning, but to get her to lay him a couple of eggs, in a nest he'd already prepared for them. Once laid, Romper never so much as looked at her, but cuddled them eggs between his 'ams until they was 'atched. What a daddy he was, too! Nothin' was too good for them squeakers, and he kep' by them until long after they was grown up, a feeding of them with 'is milk, sir."

"This old bird won't have much chance to hatch that egg, I fancy."

"By rights Jimmy ought to be took out of the kit, sir. He won't fly back to the Corps Mobile Loft, sir, but come back here, with any message. It's home to a bird, sir, cock or hen, where their eggs is, what they've fixed on in the eye. Jimmy'll be 'overing about back here, come to look for 'is egg."

"Poor old bird. What ought we to do with him?"

"I'll keep 'im back, sir, in the basket. He can come for a walk acrost Jerry's lines with us, sir, like he was a mascot. Then Jimmy can come back with us when it's all over, can't you, Jimmy boy?"

Phillip tried to ease his fears by telling himself that it was Cox's wife and her unborn baby that mattered, and for this reason he would say nothing to Bason about seniority. With Pimm beside him, he would be all right. He would stick with his boys, and damn the captaincy. He went to see how they were, and sat with them and smoked his pipe in the barn, while the rain fell and the guns made a continuous rumbling; bringing the rain, everyone said.

That night the battalion went into the line for the attack. There they spent the rainy darkness, each man laden with 66 lbs. of equipment, while the squalls lashed down, making white or rather grey their uniforms and rifles. Soon after midnight they filed out of the trench, and were brought back, to make what shelter they could in the wretched hour before dawn upon the streaming ground. Phillip made a fire and sat by it, waiting for daylight.

In the morning everyone in the Ancre valley knew that the attack had been put off. Drivers astride mules drawing limbers shouted the news to G.S. waggon drivers; lorry drivers flogging ration cigarettes in estaminets near Amiens talked about it as they downed café-rhums made from coffee that was more than half chicory.

"I believe," said Bason, in the continuing silence of the German guns, "that Jerry knows all about this attack, and is waiting for us. They're damned clever, you know, the Germans. Anyway, we've got two days now before Zero, but keep it under your hat."

During the preceding month of May General von Bulow, commanding the Second German Army, had proposed from his headquarters at Bapaume "a preventive attack astride the Somme". On 6th June he sent a report to O.H.L., the German Headquarters in the West, at Mezieres, containing the following:

"It is said that the preparations of the British indicate an attack north of the Ancre on the projecting angle of the *feste* (super-fortress) of Gommecourt, and south of the Ancre upon the *feste* of Fricourt. In view of the ground and run of the trenches it is quite imaginable that he will only try to hold fast the front between these two points by artillery fire, but will not make a serious attack. This possibility is however provided for."

On 15 June, when the Kaiser visited Crown Prince Rupprecht of Bavaria's Sixth Army Headquarters at Douai, Lieutenant-General von Falkenhayn, the All Highest's Chief of Main General Headquarters Staff, said that he could not understand why the British should attack on the Somme. In the event of success, he said, the further fighting would take place in Belgium, which would be devastated, a thing the Allies would not want; nor would they want Northern France, with its rich coal mines and iron industries, laid waste.

Crown Prince Rupprecht stated that increased railway traffic had been noticed behind the British front on the Somme, together with many new artillery emplacements and assembly trenches; while camps had been built near Albert and on both sides of the Roye-Montidier railway, well to the south of Field-Marshal Haig's back-areas.

General von Below proposed that, should the attack on the Somme materialise, the British forces should be let through into a large salient or pocket, and there be encircled by attacks driven into the flanks.

The Crown Prince Rupprecht then informed the Kaiser that agents' reports had spoken of a British attack about Whitsuntide (11 June) but it had not materialised. This had puzzled his Intelligence Staff until they had received a report of a speech by Lloyd George, the British Minister for Munitions, to owners and workmen of munition factories on 2 June, where Lloyd George stated,

"I am asked why the Whitsuntide holidays are to be postponed until the end of July. How inquisitive we all are! It should suffice that we ask for a postponement of the Holidays until the end of July. This fact should speak volumes!"

The Crown Prince Rupprecht commented, "It certainly does so speak; it contains the surest proof that there will be a great British offensive in a few weeks."

The speech of the Minister of Munitions had been reported in London morning newspapers of the 2 June; copies of which in due course had gone to Holland, and thence to Germany.

The Crown Prince Rupprecht went on to say that, according to a report of an agent at The Hague, the British attaché there said that the offensive in the West would begin at the end of the month.

On 24 June, he wrote in his journal,

A prisoner of the British 46th Division captured at Gommecourt stated that a 5-day bombardment will begin on 26th, and an attack on a 30-mile front will follow on the first of July.

Some of the French newspapers, notably *La Victoire*, write a good deal about the impending British offensive, in which at last the great British Army, the work of Kitchener, will make a decisive attack and show what it can do.

On 26 June,

Reports of the German military attaché at Madrid and an agent agree that the enemy offensive will begin on 1st July.

On 27 June,

North of the Somme 14 captive balloons have been counted, corresponding to the 14 British divisions in line there. In the morning the British guns ceased. Will the British, recognising their lack of skill, yield precedence to the French?

On the night of Thursday, 29 June, the weather cleared, and for miles up and down the Valley of the Ancre thousands of little fires burned in the darkness, below the sight of the Germans on the high ground above. From far and near came the sound of singing under the stars. Before one of the fires Phillip sat beside Sergeant Jones, dreamy with flames, his spirit happy with these men who looked to him for almost everything. He thought—as was true—that they were proud of their "Old Sticks", because he was the only officer in the battalion who had been in an attack before: he would know what to do, and they would follow him anywhere, Sergeant Jones had told him.

The fires died down, the stars moved westwards, water-birds and frogs called and croaked in the marshes; and under a shimmer of gunfire the men crept into their bivvies and slept their last sleep before the battle.

In the morning the sun shone into the valley. Flying was again possible, though at times low cloud dragged across the wide and gently swelling downland. The bombardment continued, though not so intensely, as supplies of shell, owing to the postponement by two extra days, were limited. Early that morning the Germans stood to in their trenches, and fired their machine-guns, while their artillery put down a barrage in no-man's-land. This was soon known among the waiting troops: faces at times were serious.

Phillip wrote two letters to his parents; one to be sent off—"good luck to Father's allotment, tell him not to trench too deep, or he may find himself in Australia, after all"—the other to be posted if he were killed, thanking them both for a very happy life, and concluding that they must not worry when they heard that he had come to the deep, deep sleep.

"Company to parade in battle order at ten o'clock, sir!"

Now the period of suspense was over. For Captain Bason and his company officers it had meant much work, in detailing and instructing ration- and water-parties (all water in 2-gallon petrol tins); in checking equipment, examining maps, instructing N.C.O.'s, signallers and runners, for each man had his detailed instructions for the assault. The times of the artillery lifts had, together with the signals by Very light and rocket for the gunners, the code words of companies and neighbouring units to be transmitted by visual signalling lamps, by flags, discs, shutters, fans, pigeons, ground-sheet-patterns for the R.F.C. contact patrol aeroplanes—all these had been learned by heart, for nothing must be written down, in case of capture.

Months of training, lecture, rehearsal; of working parties under the Engineers for the digging, sand-bagging and roofing over of pits for guns, scores of guns, hundreds of guns, in orchards, woods, and on the open hillside; fatigue parties unloading shells and mortar bombs at hidden dumps; carrying parties humping up barbed wire, trench ladders, wire-netting to be laid over assembly trenches and covered with grass—all was done with now, as in the last night of June the company paraded silently, while the croaking of frogs in the wide marshes of the Ancre became insistent.

Chapter 18

THE CAKE-WALK

In the courtyard of the farm he shook hands with Cox left in reserve, called his platoon to attention, and marched off along the road leading to Albert, followed, at 100-yard intervals, by the three other platoons of Captain Bason's company. Each platoon pulled two ropes hooked to a little two-wheeled hand-cart in which were the Lewis guns and drum buckets.

He carried a rifle, and wore the same makeshift leather equipment, in lieu of khaki webbing, as the men. Like them, he was in fighting order: bayonet in scabbard, entrenching tool, water bottle, steel helmet, rolled groundsheet and haversack in place of pack on back.

In his haversack were towel, soap, shaving kit, message book, spare socks. In the mess-tin, covered by khaki cloth, was the "unconsumed portion of the day's ration", with two cheese rations, hard wheaten biscuits, tin of bully beef, and a selection of small pieces of cake, chocolate, lozenges of meat extract, and a tin of café-au-lait. The rest of his mother's parcels he had had to leave behind—feeling that he was abandoning her with them.

In his left breast pocket was a small khaki Bible, covering the heart, gift of the Church Army hut at Querrieu. Round his neck hung, on a leather boot-lace, a small *papier-maché* identity disc, with his name, rank, and regiment, and religion, C. of E., for burial purposes. On the bootlace hung the ebony and silver crucifix his mother had given him in 1914.

The regimental device was stencilled in white on the front of his helmet, while on the left side the divisional colours were painted. These were repeated in a small rectangle of two-coloured cloth, sewn on the back of his tunic, centrally below the collar. A white riband on his left shoulder strap indicated his company. Thus docketed and tagged, he was, as Bason said, all ready for the Summer Sales.

Like the men, he carried two gas helmets and a pair of tear-gas

goggles, field dressing, and iodine capsule. In addition, together
with other company officers, and N.C.O.'s, he carried four flares.

The flares were to be burned in answer to long blasts on the
klaxon horns of R.F.C. contact patrols, which meant, *Where are you?*

The night of 30 June 1916 was fine in the valley of the
Ancre, and fairly quiet. Cries of water-fowl came through the
darkness as the column frequently halted in the traffic congestion.

The last hues of sunset were congealed upon the north-west
rim of the earth above which arose a steely haze of light. Phillip
wondered, as he leaned on his rifle, if this was the glow of the
midnight sun, the distant rays in space rising millions of miles
beyond the horizon of the battlefield. How small it must all
seem to the sun, which had looked upon so much life and death
on the planet. Everything was vast to one human brain, but to
the sun, how small. A few miles farther on—across the slag-heaps
of Loos—onwards to Flanders—over the Channel—beyond the
South Downs and the North Downs—even upon London Bridge
—thousands of human eyes were seeing a different sunset, each
pair of eyes with different sets of thoughts. So there was seldom
ever complete agreement. It was a terrifying thought, a revelation of man's puny helplessness behind the great machines he made
to ward off his fate, or to preserve it for awhile, with howitzers
and high explosive. Where was God in the actual scheme of
things? His Son had failed to alter the scheme; He had died on
the Cross, condemned to death by the makers of iron; and all
God's Mother could do was to stand below the Cross and grieve;
and later, to be erected as a Virgin with the Babe in her arms, to
ward off the Abyss—into which, originally, both had fallen.
It was all right for Father Aloysius to talk; but it was a fairy
story.

He quivered with terror of death, waiting to enter the dead
town of Albert, with its ruins blanched repeatedly by white stabs
of field guns and bulging yellow fans of howitzers.

They moved on slowly. They halted and shuffled on. At last
they were over the old double-track railway-crossing and into the
outskirts of the town. Many of the walls of the buildings were
standing, but roofs gaped and window spaces showed blackly, in
the ear-ringing white stabs of 18-pounders among the ruins.

Other streams of traffic were converging upon the town, which
was filling up everywhere with the rolling grind of wheels and
the tramp of boots, shadowy with infantry columns side by side

with files of led pack mules and horses pale-marked on their flanks. Each paleness was an oblong wooden box slung in a stirrup leather, holding two field-gun shells. Movement of foot, wheel, and hoof was continuous, and most strange without the sound of one human voice, a descent of the hosts of the dead into the Underworld.

No palm of hand glowed with concealed fag, no jokes were made during the halts: all was earnest, and curiously unreal.

The main roll of traffic went away to the right through the town, following the Rue de Bapaume. The platoon marched straight on, passing under the red-brick mass of high walls and shattered roofs above which the Golden Virgin leaned down from the campanile, high over the street, gleaming in every gun-flash.

From the cellar of the last rubbled house came a glint of light. Above it was the dump, where the platoon had to take up three picks, twelve shovels, and six pairs of wire-cutters, to be given to those men already chosen to carry them; while others were given two sandbags and two Mills bombs each, with additional tools, bundles of sandbags, and barbed wire twisted on two-handled stakes. Two men were given a dixie of hot soup to carry, on a pole.

Looking in the cellar through a grating level with the street, Phillip saw four officers within, seated at a table, playing cards by candlelight. A whiskey bottle and glasses were on the table. Coloured pictures of adorable girls from English magazines were on the walls. The inmates of another world were leaning back in their chairs smoking and throwing down cards. O fortunate inmates! Probably they were field-gunners off duty; their battery was among the ruins, their guns under roofs of timber baulks and sandbags. If only he were one of them! Then he thought of his men; pray God he did not let them down.

Beyond the church was a wooden bridge over the river, then a track across low ground marked by a line of hurricane lamps painted black with small green spots stretching away up the gentle slope of Usna Valley to the horizon of flares.

Along the front to be assaulted, of more than twenty miles, from the river Somme in the south, to Fonquevillers in the north—opposite the most powerful German fortress of Gommecourt Park and village—fourteen British infantry divisions were moving into the line. Hundreds of columns were a-foot, on routes marked by tapes, posts, and lanterns.

There was little enemy shelling in retaliation to the usual British night bombardment; but on the northern wing of the attack, from behind the fortress of Gommecourt Park, its wood and village, two divisions, the London and the North Midland, suffered many casualties as their assembly trenches were blown in. Elsewhere only slight enemy shelling "confirmed the belief that the seven-day preliminary British bombardment had done its work": that trenches and dug-outs were levelled, wire shot to pieces or buried; the garrisons, cut off from relief and supply, demoralised.

At Ovillers Post, where two tracks crossed, the Brigade-major was standing near the entrance leading down into the ground.

"Who are you?"

He acknowledged Phillip's reply with relief, and asked what had caused the delay.

"Held up on the road into Albert, sir, and again up the track. The men found the weights somewhat heavy, sir. Shall I lead on?"

"Yes, yes, of course. You know your assembly trench, and your duties. Good luck," he added, as an afterthought, as he waited tensely to check the next platoon.

"All the best," added another voice. It came from Paul, now second-in-command of the battalion.

The flares from the German lines in front cast pale shadows of laden men. Overhead the copper driving-bands of heavy howitzer shells, spinning up into the height of the sky, made bass dronings, while under them 18-pounder shrapnel, shedding sparks of burning fuses, tore screaming away east, to burst as red stars pricking the horizon, while yet the 9.2-inch howitzer shells were below wallowing-point at the tops of their curves, eight miles up.

"With so much stuff going over, it will be a cake-walk," said the Adjutant to Phillip, as he followed Lt.-Col. Kingsman round the line of the battalion front. To each platoon commander the C.O. read a message from the Fourth Army Commander; after which Captain Milman, cheerful and dapper as ever—"Little Marmaduke" to the men—told Phillip that Zero hour was at 7.30 a.m., the intensive bombardment to begin an hour earlier.

Watches were synchronised. They were already advanced by one hour on Greenwich Mean Time, as the new Summer Time had begun in the B.E.F. at 11 p.m. on 14 June.

"Soup will be up shortly," said Captain Bason. It would keep hot for some hours, he added, in the new containers.

"There's one container for each platoon. The C.O. thinks that hot pea soup will be more staying than rum. See that it's dished out to your blokes about ten minutes before the guns let rip at half-past six, will you, old sport?" He went on to say that the rum was to be kept for later on in the day, when they were at their final objective. "What do you think of Rawly's message? He's changed his tune somewhat, hasn't he?"

Phillip did not say what he thought: that "Spectre" had been right.

When Bason had gone he put the rum jar beside his rifle, and telling his men to get some shut-eye, seated himself on two petrol tins containing the platoon's water for the next forty-eight hours, closed his eyes and tried to sleep—one of nearly three and a half thousand temporary British infantry officers, of the rank of captain and below, in the assembly trenches cut in chalk.

Phillip sat on the petrol tin, repeating one of the verses of *Into Battle*, in order to fortify himself against the fears that hovered on the borders of his mind.

> *Nor lead nor steel shall reach him, so*
> *That it be not the Destined Will.*

Try as he might to hold himself firm in this belief, a persistent picture arose before him, crying as it were upon him with angry edges, of the poet bursting with a stock-whip into the room of another undergraduate, furnished with oriental silks and cushions: a man who did not play games, but was an "aesthete", whose father was a Bombay merchant-banker named Sassoon, and a friend of King Edward the Seventh.

Then there was the case of another *nouveau riche* Jew who had been ragged in the Cavalry Barracks at York during May 1915, and who had committed suicide, about the time that he himself was being ragged at Heathmarket by Baldersby, senior subaltern in the first officers' mess he had joined. Baldersby had led on the pack of subalterns while blowing a hunting horn, before they had stripped him naked and beaten him. Had Baldersby suspected himself of having Jewish blood?

For Father said that Grandfather Turney was a Jew, who had taken the Gaultshire name of Turney, and then made friends with some of the real Turney family and so bluffed people that he was English. That was rot, anyway, for Cousin Polly's Grannie was

Gran'pa's cousin, and she had said that Gran'pa's forebears had farmed in Gaultshire for centuries. In spite of this, Aunt Victoria Maddison had persisted in declaring that the reason why Father did not get on with Mother was because she had Jewish blood, and therefore belonged to a world entirely different from that of the English Maddisons.

At the same time, Father hated the Germans, although his own mother had been German. As for Aunt Victoria, she was very religious, and a Protestant, and yet she disliked, even feared, all Catholics; she even thought that they were barred from Heaven. Yet Jesus had been a Jew! And He had, moreover, certainly ragged some people, and with a whip—the local bankers sitting in the Temple!

Phillip looked at his wristlet watch; it was getting on for half-past one: in five hours the guns would open up. Quick! Quick! He must settle his mind now: if he did not, Fear would tear him apart: if the worst happened, and he broke down, he would have to shoot himself. If only he had dared to tell his fears to Father Aloysius, when he had had the chance!

But what were his fears? He must know them, if he was to master them.

Julian Grenfell hunting Philip Sassoon; the cavalry subalterns in York hunting Otto Beit's son; Baldersby hunting himself; himself hunting Albert Hawkins. Ah, the missing link! Albert Hawkins! Now the chain was complete! Albert Hawkins waiting behind the garden fence to see Mavis, long ago! "Go on, Peter, give him a good lesson!" Albert Hawkins had stood still and let himself be hit by Peter Wallace until his face was woeful with tears and his new butterfly tie spoiled by his own blood.

That was far worse than what Baldersby had done; anyway, he had deserved the ragging he had got at Heathmarket, for his conceit and bad manners. Why then was he worried because a high-spirited poet had merely cracked a stock-whip at someone he did not like? He had been only nineteen at the time; it was some years before *Into Battle* had been written: had he, too, perhaps grieved in retrospect when he thought of how he had bullied the man who 'was not English', and who now, by the irony of fate was, as Kingsman had told him, Aide-de-Camp to Sir Douglas Haig; while Julian, and young Beit, and Albert Hawkins, and Peter Wallace, lay in their graves?

Phillip prayed for forgiveness; then he got up and went to see how he might help his men, each in a separate loneliness.

Summer stars shone over the battlefield, owls called in the woods above the marshes of the Ancre; while away in the west, trains loaded from the pit-heads around Béthune were rolling southwards to Paris, hauling trucks of coal for the hotels, factories, power-stations and living rooms of the Gay City, at the rate of one train every half hour of the day and the night.

At 2.45 a.m., Berlin time, the German Reserve Regiment in its battle headquarters underground at Contalmaison, three thousand yards behind La Boissele, reported a portion of the British Fourth Army Commander's message, which had been sent out by field-telephone to the troops under his command. The message had been picked up by the Moritz overhearing post in the German lines immediately south of La Boissele.

"In wishing all ranks good luck the Army Commander desires to impress on all infantry units the supreme importance of helping one another and holding on tight to every yard of ground gained. The accurate and sustained fire of the artillery during the bombardment should greatly assist the task of the infantry."

This message told the German commander that the general offensive was to begin that morning.

Orders were given for the machine-gun garrison to evacuate the *festung*, or strong point known to the British as Y Sap. Under the *festung*, as the Germans knew, was the mine driven by the 179th Tunnelling Company, to be touched off just before Zero hour, to pile up around its crater lips loamy earth high enough to obstruct the otherwise perfect field of fire of machine-gunners across the bare, open ground of Mash Valley.

The German machine-gunners were now waiting well away from Y Sap, in deep dug-outs behind the trench running east and parallel to the Bapaume Road, thus facing Mash Valley at right-angles, well beyond the mine area.

The steely light above the north-west horizon, beyond the valley of the Ancre and Athuille wood, had scarcely begun to fade when a new light, as of an electrified and glowing energy, began to rise in the north-east, over the Bapaume Road and the fortress of La Boiselle. Soon larks were rising above no-man's-land, eager to see the sun.

With the lark-song came the hot soup containers, each slung

on a pole borne on the shoulders of two men. Phillip saw his sergeant, and told him to dish it out at 6 a.m.

The larks, small of impulse, had long since dropped to feed and rest among the poppies and marigolds of the open land (where still the grey stubble of the 1914 corn harvest was to be seen in places) when the sun rose above the serrated rim of the east. One whole hour and a quarter had to pass before the concentrated bombardment started. Never did time knot so tightly within the human diaphragm. Phillip tried to take interest in the outward scene, but his thoughts were of home. Would the morning be fine on the Hill, so clear and sunny and green in the early mornings of summer? At home they would still be sleeping. In the Valley of the Lyn the amber waters would be running cold and clear. Summer in England! It was as though he saw through thick plate glass soon to shatter into splinters that would pierce all his body.

At a quarter to six Pimm brought a mug of hot tea, with the remark,

"Proper day for a race, sir."

Heathmarket, Godolphin House, *The Belvoir Arms*, trainers on the Severals, strings of bloodstock walking back to stables. Soon the July races, Rolls-Royce and Daimler, old gentlemen and young officers, society girls in summery hats—just the same in England, goodbye, goodbye.

He must talk about horses, to keep his mind from fastening upon death's bitter dark in the spoke-burning sunshine. High up in the blue, a flight of scout aeroplanes was flying towards the east. For a moment he felt heavy as stone.

"Yes sir, as I was saying, when the baskets are opened——"

Baskets? Why must he talk? For God's sake leave me alone.

"——up they all flies, sir——"

"What, horses? Oh, you mean pigeons. I see. How many have we got, did you say?" At all costs, keep the fox gnawing his guts under his cloak hidden.

"Four birds, two blue chequers, a red chequer, and a mealie. Nice lookin' birds, sir, all fed. Now as I was saying—up they all flies, and 'eads for 'ome after a few circles, to get direction. Some knows it at once. I can, myself, tell a good bird by the eye it has. Would you credit that I can tell a bird's powers by its eyes, sir? Or its many eyes, for a pigeon has three in one, sir. Just you take a look at Jimmy here's eye, see the orb and circles, sir, two circles there be, one for range and t'other for intelligence, and locked up in the apple, sir. But it's in the 'ollow bones of the wings where their lungs extend to, that there's the sense of homing, sir, though some say it is inside the skull, or the little bones in the ears, filled with spirit and a hair bubble, sir."

"Spirit? What sort of spirit?"

"There's no telling, sir, but Sergeant Jones thinks it's like the hair bubble in a joiner's level, keeps the bird on a level keel, and magnetically on the course for 'ome."

What rot it was, a bird flying magnetically.

"How very interesting. Now I think I ought to go and see Sergeant Jones. Keep an eye on the water cans, *and* the rum, and see that no one touches it, or the rum jar."

The platoon sergeant had spent part of the night straightening up part of the trench wall, digging at great and continuous speed. He had removed, he claimed, seven cubic yards, from ground level down, in the four hours of darkness, picking and shovelling without help, and leaving the wall as plumb as any mason would want to see it. At the end of the self-imposed task Sergeant Jones was as fresh and cheerful as at the start.

"Gives a bit more room for the boys to stretch out in like, you see, sir!"

Thereupon Sergeant Jones' manner changed; he became confidential, almost intimate, as with a slight knock of the back of his hand on Phillip's ribs, as though he were still a Devon small-holder striking a bargain, he said, "Yurr!" while lifting his nose to suggest a withdrawal out of hearing by the others. His speech, too, changed in places, back to the Devon brogue.

"It be one of the bombers, sir, Howells. His pluck's left 'im, sir. 'Owells never had much, but what there was has gone and left 'im."

Phillip had particularly noticed Howells because he had a look of cousin Willie about him. He was a young soldier with delicate face and features, and large brown eyes which usually were reflective, even sad.

"He be down yurr, sir."

Howells was lying back against the bottom wall of the meticulously plumb trench, looking as though he had been hit. His face under the sun-burn was a greenish-white. His eyes stared fixedly. Other men were standing and sitting on the floor of the trench, smoking, talking, or with arms folded, resting.

"What's the matter?" said Phillip, stooping down beside Howells. Had his face looked like that, before advancing up through L'Enfer wood to the crest of Messines in October 1914? What would have been the best way, then, to help him over his terror? "I think we all feel pretty bad, Howells. So don't feel that you're all alone."

The large eyes showed blue-white as they looked at him. Phillip bent down to hear what was said. Howells had to swallow several times before he could speak. "I can't go on, sir. I feel bad."

"How old are you?"

"Seventeen, sir. I gave a wrong age, please sir!"

"Are you thinking of your mother, Howells?"

"Sort of, sir. I feel all giddy and sick when I stand up, and my legs give way, sir."

"You're not the only one, Howells. Try not to think about anything, that's the best thing, I find. I've been just like you, the first time over. Anyway, if you feel too awful, stay here in the trench when we go over the plonk. I know how you feel; I am scared stiff myself, and look to all you chaps to help me. Can't you think of how you will be able to help them with your grenades? They may make all the difference. We need your help, Howells."

The boy seemed not to be hearing. He stared sickly in front of him. Sergeant Jones again beckoned Phillip with his nose. "He's got on a bullet-proof vest, sir, that's part of the trouble.   He bain't got the frame vor carry that and his clobber, as well as his sand-bag of thirty-two Mills bombs, sir. He was crying, coming up the Green Track last night."

"I've told him to stay behind, if he can't face it, sergeant."

"Yes sir," said the sergeant, absently. Then, "The others don't like him, sir. They say he won't muck in with them, as us says, sir. He's greedy with his parcels, and won't share and share alike."

"That's because his mother sent them, sergeant. It's fatal to imagine your mother in everything from home."

"Us be all in this together, sir."

"But Howells doesn't feel in it yet. He's still very young. What he needs is friendship, not scorn."

"Yes, sir?"

"How are the others?"

"They'll do, sir. They don't believe all they've been told about a walk-over, you know. Some talk about the old Colonel being right on Jerry's deep dug-outs, sir. Others say us be starting too far back. But you know what talk is. They say 'a leary cart maketh the most noise,' dont'm? But they won't let 'ee down, sir."

"I only hope I don't let you chaps down!"

"No fear of that, sir. The men know a proper officer when they see one." How easily taken in they are, thought Phillip, while Sergeant Jones went on, "Only they say it's a long way to go, sir."

So they know it, too, thought Phillip. As though he had read his thought, small-holder Jones came near, and lifting his nose up in beckoning, struck him with the back of his hand on the ribs and said, "Yurr! The men'd rather get close up to Jerry while 'e's keeping 'is 'ead down, like. Then again, with all the clobber they have to carry, sir, they feel they can't get down quickly to give covering fire, if it's needed, and then get up again. It be worryin' of them, like."

Phillip wished that Jones would keep his distance. He came as it were under his guard. He must pretend not to be affected, lest he hurt Jones' feelings.

"What is a leary cart, Farmer?"

"That's what us calls a butt, sir, wi' nothing in it."

"I see. I feel a bit leary myself, so how about dishing out the soup?"

"Very good sir."

Sergeant Jones turned away and said, "Corporal Nolan, tell off two men from each section to fetch along the canteens for themselves and their butties, we don't want no bunching. And keep some soup for me, and the officer. Get a move on!"

Then turning to Phillip, Jones struck him again—a purely involuntary action observed and adopted since childhood in the West Country—and said, "Yurr! I was going to say, the men don't like there being no rum issue before we go over the plonk, sir."

"The C.O. thinks it best kept for later, when we've got to our objectives."

"That's a long way for a jar of S.R.D. to walk, all the way to Possyairs. 'Twill be a pity if it don't arrive, and a miracle if it do, sir," said Sergeant Jones; while Farmer Jones looked up and pointed. "See all they starlings, zur, flyin' as though nought was happening out of the usual! Tes early for they birds to be gathering, don't 'ee reckon?"

A long loose flock of small dark birds, flying strongly, passed about six hundred feet over no-man's-land, going north.

"I wonder what can have disturbed them?"

"I've a-got it!" cried Sergeant Jones, "it be the petrol shells what have driven they birds out of Fricourt Wood! See the black smoke a-goin' up? They'll burn any Jerries up they trees, won't 'm tho! My Gor, it must be gettin' on for the time for the guns to

start!" He jerked about in his excitement, balancing his weight
on his feet.

"Any moment now," said Phillip, looking at his watch, and
feeling himself unstable.

Why was Jones grinning at him fixedly? He could not look at
the watch any more, but only stare back at the small, lean, brown
face. He wanted to say that he needed rest, but his tongue felt
as though it would only clack dry if he spoke. Jones was more
successful in trying to say something. Hoarsely, with his involuntary back-handed nudge, "Yurr! What about they soup containers? I mean to say, do us leave them yurr? Or do us have
to take 'em with us?"

At that moment, from behind, an enormous furrow seemed to be
opening in the sky, a vast unmusical wind-sound, followed by a
small flat concise *pop*, from the 12-inch naval gun firing on its
multiple-bogie railway mounting thirteen miles behind Albert.
The report had travelled through the morning air slower than the
velocity of the shell.

On the shell was marked, in chalk, the words A PRESENT FOR
VON STEIN XIV HUN CORPS BAPAUME.

It was followed by many other shells, of all calibres, which
passed over the British trenches in a ceaseless screaming, tearing,
screeching roar, a broad torrent of multi-curving steel, shattering
the air and rocking the ground. The men stood up in the trenches,
exhilarated by the immense rush of shells; some shook hands,
others danced a little jig. Jokes were made, but heard by none;
only miming was understandable. Phillip went down the trench,
borne on the spirit of exuberance. Surely, surely this was going
to be different from Loos. The German lines were hidden in smoke
and dust and rising chalk, as though a stormy sea was breaking
in great waves there.

Not all of the shells fired during the preliminary bombardment
reached the German lines. Some burst either just beyond the
muzzles of gun and howitzer, or in the barrels themselves. These
prematures were due to defective workmanship. In peace-time
about one-third of a steel-ingot in a British foundry was rejected—
the outer metal, nearest the air—but since early 1915 this had
been reduced to one-fifth. Thus some of the steel had lost its
temper, and crystallised after cooling in the foundry. Invisible
hair-cracks had opened in it; and when such steel formed a

shell-casing the terrific pressure of the flames of detonated cordite striving to expand penetrated the cracks and burst the casing prematurely, either while still in the bore or on leaving the muzzle.

In some of the 60-pounder guns, for counter-battery work, prematures occurred owing to the shrapnel heads, called fuses by the troops, coming off in the bore. Worse were the 4.5-inch howitzers, which so frequently burst their shells two barrel-lengths from the muzzle that the crews of such batteries told one another that they belonged to the Suicide Club. Not only were the fuses dangerous, but owing to the cordite in the cartridges not always being burned out, but remaining in the bore, flashes occurred during re-loading.

Faulty annealing of copper driving bands on shells—so that the copper was hard, and not pliable—caused the rifling of bores to be torn, and worn erratically. H.E. shell fired in the 18-pounders sometimes burst or bulged the barrels. Weak buffer springs, which did not hold and contain what recoil was not absorbed by the piston of the oil buffer, sometimes broke, and the gun had to be run up to fire again by hand.

Again, hot summer weather caused the high explosive in a heavy shell sometimes to exude and form a film which was tricky to scrape off.

All these, and many other defects, were due to haste in an improvised and expanding munitions industry, where often amateur workmanship was employed upon second-rate material; but when after the beginning of the Battle of the Somme, the wholesale and terrible defects of guns, ammunition and fuses were reported, Mr. Lloyd George, Minister of Munitions, said, "The Garrison Artillery in France is entirely untrained, it cannot shoot, and is quite unfitted to work the perfect weapons which I have provided'.

Meanwhile in the front assembly trenches before Ovillers on that summer morning which was to become a day of great heat the first wild hopes of the one-way bombardment had subsided: trundling quarry-heavy noises filled the brain as with stone. Men sat or lay down, apathetic, apart, each one with his thoughts.

Sitting on the came, Phillip could feel the water vibrating under him, as he strove to overcome the knotted feeling in his stomach, to prevent the saliva in his mouth from making him sick. He clung to himself in the rushing weight of noise, which made his head ache without his realising it. He tried to fix his mind on the starling on Grandpa's red chimney-pot. Now it would be singing into the freshness of the morning air, just as he had seen it a hundred times on awakening. There it was, turning its head first one way, then the other, like a speaker by the Socialist Oak on the Hill; and as it turned it squeezed out a sort of one-bird-band music—concertina, mouth organ, jew's harp, and penny whistle—head thrown one way, then another. From its quivering throat, surrounded by its own feather boa, the starling uttered every kind of noise and call to be heard in the streets and gardens; errand-boy's whistle; *milko* of milkman with clank of milk-cans; cat's wail, dog's bark, blackbird, thrush, tomtit, even Grandpa clearing his throat in the bathroom, and gargling. Think of the starling, of the sky above the red chimney pot, which was red because Grandpa used a gas-fire in his bedroom, think of the silky blue sky of early summer morning at home. Would they be getting up yet? Father sometimes went on the Hill, to walk alone in the fresh air of morning, Think! Think! But his mind seemed to break like glass, his being to leap out of his body, as he saw the chalk lip of the trench jumping in spits and splatters. There was a machine-gun playing on it, and thirty more minutes to go to Zero hour!

He felt himself to be all water from mouth to stomach. With a fearful start he felt someone touch him. Jones was mouthing something but all sound was ground away by the glacier of shells. Jones cupped his hands and bawled so that the extra noise was hurtful, unendurable, and he pushed at the shoulder below the face, crying soundlessly, "I know! I know!" as Jones pointed to the edge of the chalk, where the long grasses fringing the shine of the unseen sun were being flicked off like little pieces of straw.

It was five minutes past seven. Phillip hurried to get the rum jar, pushing past faces looking at the breaking parapet. When he returned, followed by Pimm with pigeon basket and water-can, Sergeant Jones took the earthenware gallon jar, and held it while Phillip ripped his mess-tin out of its cover. Out went cake, chocolate, cheese, tomatoes; in slopped rum, dark brown and oily, while the tin rattled. Thrusting the cork back in the jar, and stamping it in with his heel, he left it in the charge of Pimm crouching beside the pigeon basket, and went with Sergeant Jones down the trench, squeezing past men waiting there, some pale and shaking, others composed, all quiet. To each a double spoonful, fed baby-fashion by the sergeant. They were for it: bompity—bompity, all the way down to a soldier's grave.

He looked at his watch. It was 7.10 a.m. Howells was lying still and void of face on the floor of the trench. His head was bent on his neck as though it were broken. In five minutes' time the Stokes mortars out in front in their pits would open up, and the first waves would climb up into the deadly vacancy above. The Spandaus were being aimed low. If he could get clear of the parapet, there was an even chance of a leg wound. Yet, lying upon the ground, his head might be hit. The enemy gunners' sights would not be lowered while wave after wave passed through the same area. But he must think of the men.

"Come on, drink!" he yelled, inaudibly. Howells' mouth opened and worked, as though he were drowning. Sergeant Jones knelt and put his arm behind his shoulders. He dipped the spoon, and pushed it between chattering teeth. It ran down Howells' chin.

"Come on, pour it into him!"

Sergeant Jones tried again. Howells choked. "Stand up! Get up! Or I'll shoot you for cowardice!"

Phillip hardly knew what he was saying. In his own deadly fear, holding him in a vice, that "Spectre" West was right, that the plan was wrong, that the most terrible disaster for them all was imminent, his attitude towards the younger, weaker Howells was that of his father to himself in the past. He saw the nervous lovelessness of a past self confronting him in the deadly white-faced fear of the broken Howells. He knelt and levered open the jaws with finger and thumb, thrusting in the spoon, holding the nose while Jones held the feebly fluttering hands. Another, another. Then he pointed at Jones' mouth; down went the rum; now me! me! pouring red-searing liquid past his own teeth. Howells was raising himself on an elbow, life returning to his eyes; Phillip, inflamed, thinking of Albert Hawkins as Howells got on his feet, put an arm round his shoulders and pressed him to him. "I'm with you! I'll look after you!"

When the canteen was empty he went back for the jar, and spoonfuls were given to all and every open mouth, including Pimm, the Oliver Twist of the trenches, as the men called him.

Oliver Twist had a pigeon in his hands. "Kiss the tippler for luck," he said, offering the bird to Phillip, who touched its feathers with his cheek. Pimm went on to other men. "Kiss Jimmy for luck, cully!" Laughing, they kissed the pigeon. Phillip passed down the trench, shaking hands with his men, under the glissade of shells swooshing through smoke and air-buffets crushing ear-drums to talking voiceless shaking-hands-mouthing-nothingness thrust out from sleeves white with chalk. Howells, seen to be lifting up the bag of Mills bombs, was given the bag of lighter special phosphorus grenades instead, Phillip slinging the bag of Mills bombs over his own shoulder. He shouted unheard orders—"Jones, we go right through! Bring the Lewis gun! We'll go right on! Forward! Forward! Chuck off your equipment all of you, come on, chuck it off!" He undid his leather belt, threw off the shoulder straps, unbuckled haversack and water bottle.

"Rifles, pouches, bombs and bandoliers only! Fix bayonets! We're going over now! They can't see us in the dust and smoke, we'll get right up to their wire, all the way! Pimm, bring the pigeons and one water can, leave the rum jar. We'll show them!" he shouted unheard even by himself, obsessed by the idea of getting across no-man's-land before the bombardment lifted. The wild boy had taken over.

But now not so wild externally. At 7.20 a.m., two minutes before the practised time of advance of the first waves, he got up a ladder and immediately found himself alone with the unhelping indifference of wild flowers and grass in a glassy-gold world of dust and chemical air. He ran forward until he was breathless, then stopped, curiously observing little tufts of grass being spat out of the ground all around him. Life was automatic movement beyond reality. He beckoned with his free arm to bring on the running figures faster in the noiseless bone-thundering air, figures in the sun-smoke seen to be throwing up arms and sinking slowly on their knees, to lie still as though tired or to twist about with open mouths and hair untidy without helmet covering in front of more upright figures advancing at the double. Men caught up with him as he ran on. His legs moved without conscious motion except their dragging heaviness. To left and right the line, bunched here and gapped there, was going forward with him. He felt an incoherence of joy that he was not afraid and that Westy would approve. He was detached from what was going on, he felt that nothing really mattered, barely aware of Time that raced yet was fixed. Now Sergeant Jones was running towards him with the black Lewis gun, and on the other side of him was Pimm, running with eyes staring and mouth open. The pigeon basket on his back was jumping up and down and the sandbag holding the water-can was swinging in one hand, his rifle at the trail in the other. A line of OPERATION ORDER NO. 1 ran zigzagging through Phillip's head. *Strict silence will be maintained during the advance through the smoke and no whistles will be blown.* He began to laugh.

"Two-fifty paces, sir!" the sergeant yelled in his ear, as he pointed to the ground, meaning that they were to lie down, as practised.

"Forward! Forward!"

They must get over the bare and open ground. They must get as far as the German trenches, where at least would be cover in shell-holes. There they would have a chance to find where the Spandaus were firing from and to put a burst into at least one of them; but even as he flailed his arm to bring the first and second waves on, he saw that the whole line was staggering and falling, four and five men together at a time. Then he was tilting up against the sky in a moment of suspended amazement before the rim of his helmet wrenched his neck against grass. His legs had given way under him, how queer. In the same moment he saw a great ugly grey bulb arising out of the earth, with a cracked dome. It became a huge cauliflower turning into black smoke. It was some time—about two seconds in reality—before he realised that the mine under Y Sap had gone up, without the other mine farther south, the Lochnager. The shock had flung them all to the ground.

He began to think coolly. Now the lip of the mine crater would be in the way of the machine guns firing at them. They were lying down, according to orders. The mines were to be fired two minutes before Zero hour. The barrage had two minutes to go. The first German line was still out of sight, about a quarter of a mile away. They were wasting valuable time. Westy was right; a line of skirmishers, lightly equipped, but all with bombs, to stop the Germans getting up from the deep dug-outs.

Forward! Forward!

A thousand wires hummed high and shrill in his ears as he hurried on. He saw Sergeant Jones shouting; helmets were rising up, falling, rifles dropping. A steam-harsh noise filled the air. He knew what that was: machine-gun bullets, each faster than sound, with its hiss and its air-crack arriving almost simultaneously, many scores of thousands of bullets in the air together at the same time and coming from all directions.

Brilliant spots of light broke above the rolling smoke, far away. Each coloured spot hung there, burning, before dropping down into the dusty storm below. Rockets calling for help: the German barrage fell on no-man's-land.

The guns that morning were heard in south-east England, through, some said, reflection of sound-rays from the layer of heated ozone far above the earth's atmosphere, to the ground below. Others declared that the vibrations travelled through the continental chalk ridge of north-west Europe, the base of which extended under the Channel. Whatever the means of travel, the bourdon of gunfire was not heard on the south coast of England; but it was heard most clearly by Richard Maddison, who had gone up early, drawn by the beauty of the morning, upon the pleasaunce of the Hill.

He wore his old striped flannel trousers and white shoes with brown leather borders, pleased that the clothes he had first worn for tennis in the 'eighties were still comfortable. He felt the warmth of the sun upon his face and bare head; his old tennis "togs" gave him a feeling of youth. He was now in his fifty-third year, and was good, he told himself, for another twenty years. Nothing like digging to keep a man fit!

He had the Hill to himself, except for the rooks busy in the grass where the sheep had been grazed until a fortnight before, when the fly, of both the green and the blue bottle variety, had begun to be active, from so many dust-bins in the streets which had arisen out of the burnt subsoil of clay like continuous reefs or cliffs around the Hill. There was danger of spotted fever, the dreaded cerebro-spino-meningitis from such flies. He must get some chloride of lime for Hetty's dustbin.

However, London River was to be seen as of yore, the woods on Shooter's Hill, and the North Downs; while the Crystal Palace, glittering grey, was a mark that he saw, in such free moments, with romance, for the old days a-wheel into Surrey and Kent.

He had a new romantic feeling that morning; for as he walked upon the crest of the Hill, before going down the gully, he heard all about him, in the air of the splendid summer day arising, a continuous heavy undertone, almost from the ground under his feet; or was it from the air above?—a heavy undertone, with dull faraway boomings, which remotely seemed to thud upon the ear. The guns in France! The Great Offensive, of which so much had been spoken and speculated upon in the City, had started that morning!

He kept the news to himself when he arrived home; and having had his cold tub, and put on his City clothes, he went down to breakfast with a feeling almost of freedom.

"Well, Hetty old girl, I've some news for you. The guns in France were going well, great guns, as I came down from the Hill just now! Something is in the wind, you mark my words!"

"Oh dear, I do hope—yes I expect it will be all right," answered Hetty, not wanting to upset his happy mood. "Your bacon is almost ready, Dickie. It won't be a moment."

"The mid-day editions of the evening papers will have it, I've no doubt."

He ate his bacon happily, and helped himself from his especial pot of Cooper's Oxford marmalade.

"I shall be home early today, by the way, about half-past two. It was my Saturday off, but I agreed to forego it until the Mid-summer rush of renewals is over." He looked at his half-hunter gold watch, thinking that he might have a turn or two upon the Hill before descending for his train. At that moment he heard Mavis walking along the passage to the bathroom.

"Now I want to clean my teeth, Mavis must of course choose this very moment to lock herself in the bathroom! All this prink-ing and prettying of herself is ridiculous! Why cannot she come down to breakfast at the proper time, like any normal, decent person?"

"Well Dickie, she waited until you had had your cold tub. She didn't want to be there when you came back."

"That is no reason for lying in bed, and on such a beautiful morning, too! Why, bless my soul, in my young days, my sisters and I——"

Richard went into the front room, and sat down, tense with resentment that he should have to wait to get into his own bath-room; and his wife's attempt to make things easier, by saying that he had plenty of spare time before leaving for the station, only added to his irritation. His routine was put out; the habits formed during thirty-five years in the City, when never once had he defaulted, as he put it, by being late at the office. If only he had been twenty years younger, or even ten, then he might by now be in France, living a comparatively free and spacious life, instead of slaving to keep going a family that had no understanding of responsibilities and duties.

The brushing of teeth, preceded by work with a rubber band to clear spaces of food, made him feel less burdened by himself, but when he walked up the gully again, into quiet air, romance was gone from the Hill.

Phillip was then lying down in no-man's-land, with the fragments of his platoon. He had been going forward, carrying the Lewis gun which Sergeant Jones had dropped on being hit, when an apparition in coils of white smoke had run to him, screaming to be saved. It collapsed and hung to his legs. The sandbag of phosphorus grenades carried by Howells had caught fire, to enclose him in crackling loops and spurtings of white thick smoke. His tunic smouldered; fuming ulcers ate into his flesh; he ran to his officer for help. Phillip tried to knock away phosphorous fragments like broken nuts, which were dividing and sub-dividing on Howell's uniform and equipment. His efforts were vain. Shrieking, Howells began to roll and squirm upon the ground. Phillip was about to turn the Lewis on him when he felt himself to be scalded all down his left leg. He saw Pimm sitting up, the water can torn open a few yards away, and thought that a shell had burst near and heated the water to steam, which had scalded him. He was now behind the front wave, and seeing this he hurried on. Shouldering the Lewis he tried to catch up, raging and cursing incoherently, beyond the fury of fear, followed by hoarsely yelling men. He turned to tell them, with gestures of his free arm, not to bunch—to spread out—they would draw more fire—when he felt a terrific blow on his behind, and fell over. He thought that he had been struck by a piece of shell coming from afar; the weight of iron had knocked him over, and numbed his leg. Obsessed with the idea of getting on with the Lewis gun, to give covering fire for his platoon, he started to get up, but his leg gave way, as though it were not there. The lump of iron had obviously numbed a nerve. He lay a few moments, waiting for strength to come back. When it did not, he crawled into the crater of a shell which had blackened the cracked chalk.

His left hand was smarting and looking at it he saw the flesh blistered in spots and the centre of the blisters stuck with bits of smoking phosphorous. Dare he pour water on the biting, throbbing sores, or was it only oil that would stop them burning? There was oil in a brass cylinder in his rifle-stock—where was his rifle, the thought passed in his mind as he tried to push the Lewis gun over the torn lip of the crater. Had phosphorus been kept in the laboratory at school in oil, or water? If only he could remember. Phosphorus burned on contact with oxygen in the air, but had it, like metallic sodium and potassium, power to break up water into hydrogen and oxygen, and release the choking white fumes of Diphosphorus Pentoxide?

The knowledge-pictures from the past occupied his mind for an instant only. They were succeeded by a raging, tearful complaint that he must catch up with the few figures advancing through the smoke in front. The nerves of his leg were still numbed, so he tried to raise the Lewis gun upon its steel prong in order to give covering fire from the lip of the crater, but he could not lift it so far, and this made him cry. Lying back, he realised that his trouser leg was soaked not with water, but with blood.

Opening the front of his trousers, he saw a small blue puncture near the top of the thigh. Experience told him that the main wound would be at the back; feeling down his trousers he touched with his finger tips what seemed to be an enormous hole, as ragged as it was sticky. This made him feel weak and sick, so he lay back until he felt better, when he tried to break his glass iodine capsule while lifting up his leg to pour the iodine into the hole. While he was doing this a shower of earth fell over him from a machine-gun burst traversing to catch what he imagined to be the other waves coming up. He heard shouting, screams, and hoarse cries under the harsh bands of metal tearing the air. He gave up.

When he recovered he pulled up his trousers upon the wound, after picking earth from it. The iodine capsule was lost. Figures charged past the sky-line. He heard a yell of *Erin go bragh!* and thought that the Liverpool Irish had come up. They were in the reserve brigade. He crawled to the lip and looked over. They were all running together, in bunches, and falling fast. He shouted and cried, pulled at the Lewis gun, and fell back helplessly, sobbing.

He was next aware of someone beside him. The face was far away, then it came clearer. The face was reading a breviary, the lips praying. "Where are you hit?" The little book was put in a pocket.

He saw that it was Father Aloysius, and said, "In my leg. It's not much, but I can't walk, Father. What's happened to the others, do you know?"

"We seem to be held up. Are you sure you are all right? Let me look." After looking he said, "I must leave you. Lie quiet, won't you. Don't drink any water until the stretcher bearers have got you down to the Aid Post. Promise me?"

"My bottle is gone anyway, Father, but I promise you. Is my intestine showing?"

"No. But there's a remote chance that it may be punctured. You'll be all right if you don't drink. Now I must go."

Earth spat into the crater. "Please don't leave just yet, Father."

"There are others, my son."

"I didn't mean it that way, Father. I meant the sniper might get you. He is lying out in front somewhere, not far, judging by the crack."

"Why, you are Phillip Maddison! I did not recognise you. Bless you for your concern." He smiled and said, "Do you remember the Rough Man's poem, Phillip

> '*Nor lead nor steel shall reach him, so*
> *That it be not the Destined Will.*'

"Let me go instead, Father, I can crawl. Look, I am all right now! I can get to them. Anyway, let me come with you. I must see what happened to my chaps, honestly, Father. I can't bear lying here, when they need me." He began to cry with weakness.

"No, you lie here, dear boy, and take your rest, for the journey you will have to make when the darkness comes. Now I must go on. May I say one thing to you? The Virgin and Child is not a symbol of what should be, but of what *is*, Phillip. That Love is in the world always, waiting for all men. It is the love of God. Now I must go. Good luck!"

The glacis between the fortresses of Ovillers and La Boisselle was strewn with men of all misshapes and sizes, lying amidst blind shells of many calibres.

Later, the Corps assessment of casualties in the division which had attacked immediately north of the Bapaume road were: 99 officers and 1,828 other ranks killed, with 92 officers and 3,003 other ranks wounded.

The corresponding casualties in the two German front-line battalions of the 180th German Regiment which had opposed the division were: 4 officers and 79 other ranks killed, with 3 officers and 181 other ranks wounded. Most of these losses occurred among the two front battalions of the 180th Regiment, for only one part of one company in reserve had been called upon to help during the British assault.

Chapter 19

REST AFTER STRIFE

The Germans immediately north and south of the Bapaume road ceased firing when the local attack was over. The commander of the 180th Regiment not only allowed stretcher-bearers to take away the British wounded, but sent some of his own medical men to help them. By the morning of July 3 the last of the wounded were got away.

Phillip, between periods of semi-consciousness following bouts of pain from the burns of phosphorus, and a greater drag of thirst, managed to crawl back on the afternoon of the first day, obsessed by one idea: he must get back for the sake of his mother. He could not walk, because another bullet had gone through his left boot, penetrating the metatarsal arch. On his way back through no-man's-land he passed Pimm, lying dead among others whose lips and eyelids and wounds were already yellow-edged with blowfly eggs. He saw many rats, too. After a rest, brow on earth, he released the pigeons fluttering in the basket. Whether or no they flew back to their loft, he never knew.

At one period on the crawl back he seemed to be hearing the bell-like colours of wildflowers with startling clearness—field scabious, poppies, marigolds, small pansies, and others he did not remember having seen before; and about these flowers were wild bees and grasshoppers, scarlet soldier flies, and bronze beetles among the grasses. They glowed and shimmered with varying sounds and colours. This period of hopeful beauty did not last long. The sunlight became harsh, frazzling all things with the return of pain. He tried to pick out bits of embedded phosphorus with his nails, and found that he was gibbering a sort of plea to himself, a beholder. Thereafter at times it seemed that he was three people; one feeble and struggling, the other a critic of his feeble self, the third a beholder watching in the air, above the back of his mind on a sort of invisible gossamer.

The critical self knew that the feeble self had gibbered for effect. He *could* bear the pain if he did not pretend to himself that he could not bear it. Very well, he would show himself that he could. The beholder, without feeling, watched the body crawling on: while he mocked at the feeble self humming a fragment of tune in a minor key, the sort of song he had made up, when alone, in childhood, to show himself how sorry he was.

Why did he have to think like that? *Why in the name of Christ should he bloody well have to*? His head was heavy and the untidiness of everything made him feel like screaming all of his bickering little two selves away. That feeling, too, passed, leaving his mind fixed with desire to take his shadow from the battlefield, while he had a shadow. He would lose his life if his shadow sank into the ground. It will not wait for ever, his mind told his champing jaws.

When the top of the leaning gilt figure on the church in the valley came into view, another feeling, of shame for his abject condition, came upon him as he saw hundreds of curious faces of soldiers waiting on their way up the line. Why did they have to stare like that? Why must they look at him, had they no manners?

Progress now became extremely painful. He resented the many curious faces. Their staring made him press back against the groans that alone could help him escape part of the pain. Every time he rested, his thigh felt heavier, as though his leg were nearly dragged off. When, when, when could he reach the small red-cross flag of the First Aid Post.

The sunlight was vibrating in corrugated waves when he got there, to rest on an elbow, to sink into himself, one of hundreds of waiting figures. Some were smoking, and talking. Their words jarred about the wavy bars of sunlight. Orderlies were kneeling among them. At last a face looked at him, and told him to lie back on his elbows. Then with a knife that had a point of terror lest it touch the purple hole in his buttock, the bloody-handed orderly started to rip his trousers. The awful noise ground through his nerves.

"I put Zam-buk in my wound, orderly."

"You've got several other blighty ones, sir," said the orderly, as he painted iodine on the blue puncture in front of the thigh. "Now over on your right side, sir. It may sting a bit—that's right. We'll soon have you away." As he was tying a bandage, Phillip said, "Not too tight! I don't want to get gas-gangrene."

"I'll watch it. Now will you be able to walk, sir, if I get someone for you to hold on to? Stretchers are somewhat at a premium."

Phillip pointed to his ankle.

He felt as the puttee was being ripped that the woollen cloth was in his mouth and he was chewing it with his back teeth. He tried not to be sick. "Steady, steady!" he quavered, as his boot seemed to be wrenched off. To keep hold of himself he tried to think of "Spectre" West not complaining after he had been hit in front of Le Rutoire Farm during the battle of Loos ten months ago; but Westy had been doped with morphine.

"Went clean through, this one," said the orderly, holding the heel in one hand and working the toes with the other. "No bones gone."

Phillip showed his burned hand.

"I'll put some iodine on them."

Phillip shook his head. "No good," he said through rigid jaws. The pain had throbbed back.

"I think in that case you'd better wait till you get to the Dressing Station in Albert, sir."

As he lay there, covered by a blanket, a chaplain came and gave him a cigarette. "Are you badly hit?"

"No, padre."

"Good man! Keep smiling. You'll be pleased to hear that things are going well down south. The news has just come through that Mametz is taken, and also Montauban, with thousands of prisoners. The French, too, have got all their objectives."

"Water, padre."

"You must wait, I'm afraid," said the chaplain, seeing the bandage, "until the doctor has seen you."

Later in the afternoon he was taken down a track on a wheeled stretcher which passed under the campanile of the church. With a sort of mild wonder he saw a bearded man in uniform sitting at an easel beside the road. He was painting a tree growing near a broken wall. It was so strange a sight that Phillip asked the orderly to stop. Then he saw that it was the same man he had seen in the Café Royal. He wanted to let the painter know he was there, but could not make himself speak. The painter went on with the picture, as though nothing else in the world was happening.

While the wheeled stretcher remained there, six feet away from the easel, two red-cross orderlies came down the road, holding between them a man who could not walk properly. He was being held under each arm, his head hung down, he was blowing and slavering, froth on his lips. Deep, rasping shudders came from his throat. His spirit had obviously been broken into pieces within him. Somehow this was more terrible a sight than that of a wounded man, or rather one whose body had been blown to tangles and mangles, for this one's body was apparently unhurt. All the nerves seemed to have come unhooked from the sinews. Would he be an idiot for life? Better to be that than to lie in the sun, waxen before swelling black, and turning into green and pink pudge.

The painter glanced at the man, and went on painting; and as he was wheeled away, Phillip thought it strange that anyone could sit calmly painting while over the brow of the hill hell was going on.

The Advanced Dressing Station was a red-bricked house of gables and little turrets, as he saw when the stretcher stopped before an archway leading into a courtyard. The lower walls and entrance were protected by solid-looking sandbags. He had a glimpse of wounded men inside the courtyard, sitting about. Many more were coming down the road, among the wheeled stretchers. A padre in the road was in charge of traffic.

"Wounded officer? Buttocks and foot? Wheel him through the archway and take the stretcher carefully off the carrier. Then pick up a spare stretcher and return to the Aid Post you came from, there's a good fellow."

Another padre in the courtyard came forward, with an orderly, to supervise the lifting of the stretcher from the carrier. Phillip recognised, with a flush of happiness, Father Aloysius. Somehow he had felt he would not be killed. He was recognised as the priest came forward to examine his bandage; and felt resolute when he heard him draw in his breath before saying, "Is the pain very bad, Phillip?"

"No, Father," he heard his voice croak. His tongue felt like a wooden clapper.

"Is there anything you want, Phillip? Shall I send off a field postcard for you?" The padre knelt beside the stretcher.

"Water—please, Father, if there's any to spare."

"You know, I think you'd better wait, until the doctor has seen you. I'll come back—I must see to the poor fellow over there."

A German with a large black beard lay upon a stretcher, groaning. His brow and cheeks were grey-green. When Father Aloysius lifted the blanket, Phillip saw that both legs were blown off at the knee. Father Aloysius pointed to a room, beyond a sand-bagged door, hung with white sheets.

"German prisoners go down the road, sir," said the orderly.

"Never mind that, take this poor fellow in next, will you?" said the priest. Then he knelt by the Bavarian, and finding a crucifix on a chain round his neck, gave him absolution. Later the stretcher went into the operation room.

When Father Aloysius came back, he said, "Are you sure your wound is clear of your intestines?"

"I don't know, Father."

"You must be patient, Phillip."

"Yes, Father."

He became aware of the moans and groans all around him in the courtyard, of the stretchers that were continually being brought in through the archway. He watched for awhile, trying to make himself not think of his own pain, but of those worse-off than himself. Heads in bandages like turbans of white and red cloth held in bloody hands. Slit-trouser'd legs big with white cotton and soaked through and through with crimson splotches. Boots and puttees and tunics all mud; had they come from the valley below Thiepval wood? They were Inniskillings. He listened to them talking to other lightly wounded men of the Ulster division, who had gone over before the Schwaben redoubt on the high ground above the valley. They had climbed out of their trenches before the guns lifted and got up close to Jerry's front line. At Zero bugles had sounded the advance. They got into the German front line just in time to catch Jerry coming up from the dugouts, and having scuppered them, went on to the Hansa Line, where they sent back hundreds of prisoners. Carrying on, they reached the final objective, beyond all the shell holes and barbed wire, where the grass was tall and green, giving plenty of cover. They were so far in advance of the others that their own shells were dropping behind them. They had looked down into the valley and seen the steam of the train bringing up Jerry reserves into Grandcourt station.

So 'Spectre' West had been right. He felt suddenly very cold, and cried silently. The tears loosened dust in the eye-sockets.

Working among the British orderlies was a German in a green tunic with a red-cross band on his sleeve. He went from stretcher to stretcher, bandaging quickly. There were occasional screams. He heard a cry of "O my God" made in a voice twisted with despair. He noticed a young, clean-shaven clay-yellow face beside him. The lips were quivering, the face began to contort. With an anguished cry of "Mother" the young soldier rolled off his stretcher. When he saw Phillip looking at him he said in an imploring, weak voice, "I think I'm going to die. Please ask them to send for my mother."

He elbowed himself off his side, meaning to give the frightened youth his right hand. Before he could do so, his left hand was seized, and he fell back. As the nails of the youth dug into the ulcerous burns, he had to press his lips and eyelids tight to stop himself from crying out. An orderly came, and opened the grip of the fingers; then looking at the staring eyes and open mouth, said to Phillip, "A stomach wound. I'll get the M.O. to give an anti-tetanic serum injection." He went away, but no doctor came. Flies settled upon the open mouth, drinking the bloody froth on the lips. Later, Father Aloysius came, and knelt by the stretcher, and prayed. Later still two bearers carried the stretcher to the cemetery.

When Phillip's turn came for treatment he was carried into a room opposite to that hung with white sheets. It had electric light. After an anti-tetanic injection, his dressing, caked with blood and dust, was pulled off, the wounds examined. "Flavine," said the doctor. While an orderly sprayed the wound the doctor looked down at his face.

"Is the pain bad?"

Phillip shook his head: he would hold out against himself.

"You were in luck. Another inch higher, and the colon would have been perforated by that bullet. You've got shell splinters in your leg, too. Now we'll put on a fresh dressing, and give you an air-ring for your backside. That will make you more comfortable. Let me look at your burns." He sniffed them. "H'm, still oxidising. We'll soak your hand in a solution of sodium bicarbonate, then put it on as a powder until the burns cease to fizz. Finally, a pack of the same stuff, and down you go to Field Ambulance."

The doctor gave him a cigarette, and said, "Now it will hurt a bit. I've got to dig out those bits of phosphorus."

He thought steadily of Joan of Arc burning at the stake: his pain was nothing to what others had to go through. When the doctor had finished bandaging he apologised for having taken up so much of his time. The doctor laughed, and said, "I suppose I could say the same thing to you. Anyway, you've got plenty of guts."

He was carried back into the courtyard. There, while his hand lay in soak, Father Aloysius brought him an enamel mug of tea. There were bloodstains on it, but he took it gratefully. The sweet taste of condensed milk brought instantly to mind an afternoon on Reynard's Common in the early days of the Bloodhound patrol. The vision was so clear that afterwards he felt distress that he could not find himself back there. Another picture floated before him, of himself during a summer in the Backfield, cooking bacon and tomatoes over a fire in a deep crevice of the clay. He saw the grass-fringed sky above, and felt a blissful happiness that he was in his hiding place, away from all the world, as he ate his "biltong" and read a green-covered *Gem Library*.

This contentment, like the period when the flowers and butter-flies in the grass had suddenly seemed so beautiful, was brief. The nagging dullness of pain returned, with unhappy mind-pictures of his home. The orderly brought more tea, which he drank so eagerly that some of it ran down his neck and chest. The thought of his clumsiness worried him; and the further thought that he had messed himself added to his own disgrace. He began to think of his platoon, and cried silently.

The injection made his head throb, throb, throb. The corrugated rays of the sun solidified into hot brass. Time was suspended; he floated; he slept, and saw with delightful clearness when he awoke; and was almost crying-dull when his turn came to leave. Never again, he thought, would he see the doctor or the priest or the orderly, whose care had taken away the burning pains. But life was like that. Nothing ever was the same again. Friends were lost by misunderstanding and death. Goodbye courtyard, goodbye you blokes. Thank you, Mother of Jesus, for helping my spirit.

The stretcher was lifted and taken through the archway, and slidden into a Ford ambulance.

The ambulance held only one other stretcher, the space opposite being occupied by four sitting cases. One of them was swathed in many bandages, crossing and recrossing his shoulder and chest. He sat in the care of a sergeant with a bullet through his jaw. The other two sitting men were lively, and talked a lot together at first. Seeing Phillip looking at the listless, swathed man, the sergeant explained with painful slowness, pointing to the mass of bandages.

"Hickinglung, hir, ussenk igh gown," he said. Then the two slightly wounded men explained together, what the sergeant with the bullet in his jaw had tried to say. "Hit in the lungs, sir, mustn't lie down," while the other said, "'E may drown in 'is own blood if 'e lies down, see?"

The ambulance buzzed along the straight road under the poplars, climbing and running easy as the contours rose and fell. The Amiens road was empty of troops, as he could see by looking out of the back. But soon the fast pace slowed down; for they had come to the head of a new division marching up. There were halts. Helmeted faces peered in the back.

"What's it like up there, chums?"

"Not so bad, mate," replied the two lightly wounded cases with shrapnel-balls in calf of leg and arm—not good enough to be Blighty ones, they had agreed.

The sun-burned faces looked cheerful. "Good luck, boys! Have a pint for us in Blighty!"

The lung-case groaned wearily. The sergeant with the swelled iodine-brown jaw said something which was meant for encouragement. Phillip felt sorry for the fresh brown faces. Still, everyone was in it now.

The ambulance left the long straight road and bumped and swayed over a dusty track to some hutments. Red crosses in white squares were painted on black felt roofs. Here it was easier than in the courtyard at Albert. Bandaged men talked cheerily to one another, smoking and laughing. Their spirits were already on the way home. He watched the sergeant with the smashed lower jaw helping the lung case, now spewing a froth of blood, to walk to a hut. They went inside; he saw them no more. The two lightly wounded men talked hilariously with some pals they had met. Then he recognised Captain Bason's servant, and learned that he was there. He had been hit in the arm, not badly. The servant went away, to return with Bason.

"How goes it, old sport?"

"Oh, not so bad, Skipper."

"Where did you get it?"

"In the thigh."

"Jasper Kingsman and Milman both copped it. So did Tommy Thompson, and 'Brassy' Cusack. And Paul."

"Killed? All of them?"

"All gone west, so has the Brigadier, and his brigade-major. In fact, the whole brigade's copped it."

There was nothing to say about that.

"How far did you get before you were hit?"

"About halfway across no-man's-land."

"How did your chaps get on?"

"It was so difficult to see, skipper, in the smoke. I think all of them must have been hit."

"Tommy Thompson got into their first trench, along a hundred yards of it, just north of the Bapaume road, and held on for about two hours. He was killed on the way back. You know, I reckon your pal 'Spectre' was right after all. But one man can't fight a system, old sport."

"Who's in command of the battalion now?"

"Cox!" laughed Bason. "I expect what remains of the brigade will be withdrawn tonight. Anyway, write out a report as soon as you can, and send it to the C.O., for the battalion diary, will you? They'll want to know what happened."

His wounds were inspected, a label tied to the second button-hole of his tunic with the letters *G.S.W. back*, *left foot. Phosphorus burns hand and arm*. Thus, after more tea, he was sent down to the Casualty Clearing Station at Heilly.

There he was carried into a hut for officers, with beds, into one of which he was put, on a rubber sheet, and covered with a blanket. Flowers in a jar on the table and wide open windows: how strange to think of the battle raging not many miles away, and here nobody seeming to care.

More tea, with bread and butter and jam, brought round on a tray by a nurse, changed his mournful feeling. He began to feel happy; his left hand no longer throbbed. After tea, face and right hand washed; nurse bringing him the latest number of *The Bystander*; time began to flow almost sweetly, as he thought of going back to England—of the months of rest before him, with accumulations of pay at eight and six a day—for his promotion was to be ante-dated to June—and also his salary from the office.

Voices were talking happily outside the windows. They were discussing the attack, seeming to regard it as a bit of sport. Had it been sport at the time for them? It was so easy to forget, in the relief of afterwards.

A padre came up the hut, holding by the arm an officer who dragged his feet and clung to him, while darting dark eyes about in a sallow face, and talking wildly, as though he were still in the attack, and expecting enemies. He was put into a bed opposite, and constantly beat his hands on the blanket. He had a moustache, not clipped like most regimental officers wore, but long; and seemingly in imitation of the Kaiser's. He was constantly smoothing out the ends, and pushing them upwards, with his fingers. Once Phillip caught his eye; immediately a hand went over the eyes, the cries broke out. Phillip had an idea that he was putting it on.

Soon afterwards the padre was back again, holding the arm of a very young officer, who was weeping, and had to be restrained from beating his own head with his fists. He looked really shattered. He cried, "Don't let me go back, I can't go back! Why did it happen? I can't bear any more!"

The padre spoke to him, soothing him. The man with the darting eyes and rat-whisker moustaches was watching. Phillip saw his face contort before he sprang out of bed and rushed across the hut, screaming, "Shoot! Shoot! They're coming! Where's my rifle?" Whirling his arms, he smashed himself into the wall, punching with his fists. Then he sank down, moaning.

"Don't worry, old fellow, you'll soon be better after some rest and sleep, probably in England. You're quite safe here."

The officer stared and gave a mad laugh, then started to do P.T. exercises. The padre led him back to his bed. The officer held out his hands, with fingers spread, showing his broken knuckles.

Later on an R.A.M.C. sergeant asked his name.

"I don't give information to Huns!"

"This man is your friend," said the padre. "He is in the R.A.M.C. He wants to know your name."

"I don't talk to Huns! I claim the Berne Convention!"

The sergeant moved to look at his identity disc. The officer clung to it.

"Oh no, you don't! I need give you only my name and regiment! I'll give you no information about code names!"

"Very well then, give me your name."

"I refuse!"

"What does it say on your identity disc? Come on, sir, let me see."

"I put you under arrest!"

"Very good, sir. Meanwhile the senior medical officer wants to know all the names here in this ward. Won't you let me see your identity disc?"

"What's wrong with my name?"

"I only want to write it down here. Come along, I've got other officers to see."

The man now appeared to be dazed. Phillip felt sure that he was pretending to be mad. As the sergeant looked at the disc a terrific flash-report shook the hut. Whimpering cries broke out from the very young officer; the man in the bed opposite gave a scream, threw off his blanket, and crawled under his bed, to curl up and lie still.

"What is it, the twelve-inch railway gun?" Phillip asked the man next to him.

"Fifteen-inch, I believe," he replied, in a voice that appeared to be in shreds. Phillip wondered if he had been gassed, for his face was the colour of rotten eggs, which was also what phosgene tasted like if one smoked when it hung about.

"Were you gassed?"

"Hit in the stomach," the voice said, with extreme weariness. Then he began to groan, and twist under his blanket.

"You'll be all right," said Phillip. "Try and keep still, old chap. Sergeant! Please come!" for the officer had fallen out of bed. An R.A.M.C. lieutenant came to join the sergeant. They kneeled beside the man on the floor. He was so near that Phillip could see a small brown hole in his stomach beside the navel. "Bring him to the operating table," said the doctor, getting up. The man, his eyes staring, was carried away to the end of the hut on a stretcher, to some screens. A nurse with flurried ginger hair ran past.

More and more stretchers were being carried in. When the spaces between the beds were filled up they were placed at right angles to the beds, leaving only a narrow foot-way. An R.A.M.C. colonel appeared, with a major, who looked worried. "We can't take any more," the colonel said.

"There's a queue outside, two hundred yards long, and three Dressing Stations have telephoned urgently for ambulances," replied the major.

The R.A.M.C. lieutenant came down the hut from the screens with the nurse and said to the sergeant, "Get two orderlies to remove the case on the table to the mortuary line."

"What happened?" Phillip asked the ginger-haired nurse, later on.

"Must you ask questions? Can't you see we're more than busy?"

"I'm sorry, nurse."

"That's all right. I didn't mean to be sharp with you. Was he your friend? I'm afraid he died under the mask. Now before you ask me what the mask is, I'll tell you that it holds the A-C-E mixture which is sprinkled on it before we put it on a patient's face, to give him a whiff. Don't look so alarmed, you're not to be operated on! You're far too well!"

"Thank you for telling me, nurse."

"Now lie still, like a good boy, and don't ask any more questions. We all realise what you have to put up with in the line, but you aren't the only one carrying a burden, you know."

That morning, of the first day of the battle of the Somme which was to continue during one hundred and forty-one days and a hundred and forty nights, the total of the British Forces in France was 1,489,215. Of this number, 1,206,704 were in the battle areas of Flanders, Artois, and Picardy, and by the afternoon many were coming sick and wounded into the aid posts of battalion areas, thence to dressing stations of brigade, field ambulances of division, and casualty clearing stations of corps areas.

When the battles of the year were over, 643,921 men had been admitted to hospital sick, together with 500,576 wounded, a total of 1,144,497: a number nearly equal to that of all the British combatant soldiers in the B.E.F. on July the First.

Such was the metal of the British pastures, and slums.

Many of the wounded returned, like Phillip, to fight again in due course; while the dead lay unburied, or in shallow graves upon or just behind the battlefield, the falling or resting places marked by rusting helmet, cross of ration-box wood, or bayoneted rifle stuck in the ground; while never for a moment during the night or the day, in rain, frost, snow, or sunshine, did the artillery cease to thunder, machine-gun and rifle bullets cease to shear the air, or bombs to burst with their sharp, gruff noises in dug-out and along broken trenches in ruinous fields, woods, and villages upon nearly two hundred thousand acres of upheaved subsoil that was the battlefield of the Somme.

Meanwhile, on the late afternoon of the first day, with its 57,470 British casualties among the assault troops, Phillip was lying between rough brown blankets in the C.C.S. at Heilly.

The ginger-haired nurse came back, looking more composed; her hair was brushed, she felt renewed desire to be of service as she carried round a tray of bread and jam and mugs of tea. Phillip found that he was both hungry and thirsty; the unchlorinated tea tasted wonderful. He began to enjoy the adventure of being wounded, with months of ease in the sunlit sweetness of England before him. He was one of the lucky ones, he told himself: he was alive. For the moment, pain was gone. He lay back happily; but pain returned, so throbbingly and twistingly heavy that he was given an injection of morphine sulphate. Some time hazily later his stretcher was slidden, with eight others, in the open body of a lorry, and driven to the station. The jolting made the stretchers jump, causing cries from those badly wounded, whose bone-fractures grated together; but he was able to hang on in silence against crying-out until they came to the siding beside a long hospital train.

There, he felt better, and interest in the scene about him came back. Where were they going? Rouen, said the train orderly, his appearance nearly as strange a sight as that of the bearded man painting in Albert, for the orderly was not only shaved, washed, and hair brushed flat with oil, but his khaki trousers actually had a crease.

No. 9 General Hospital at Rouen, used by the Germans during the Franco-Prussian war, was so quiet at night that he could not sleep until he was given an injection of morphia, when the rough waves of excreta zigzagging awfully became smooth waves drowning him with spike-haired-Streuelpeter-terror until he rose slowly above their smooth and awful horridness and floated smilingly in silk-hanky pink-petal breast bliss, on the edge of sleep, but not over it because it was all so silent.

In the next bed lay a mass of bandages which moaned and whimpered through the darkness, heedless of cries of *Shut up, for Christ's sake pipe down*, and more violent curses from the length of the ward. The bandaged man had belonged to a party which had tried to storm the redoubt on the Bapaume Road and been burned to death by flamethrowers as it reached the parapet, with the one exception. When Phillip looked in the morning, the bed was empty; the man had died, and been wheeled away.

Later, Phillip was lifted upon a rubber-tyred trolly and wheeled along a passage, to stop outside the operating theatre door. Before he could ask what was to happen a mask was put over his face, with pipes attached to cylinders. So he was to have a whiff. His hands were held when the cocks were turned on. He wanted to say to the nurse that he would not struggle, he would lie perfectly still, so would she please trust him and not hold his hands; but she held his hands, and as he lay immobile he felt distress that he could not say with the mask on what he wanted to say. Down down down he sank into a deep dug-out shaft, seeing the sky above turn green with sparkles and spangling flashes, the pollen of the lilies of the dead, far far far above him—

Then a face in a tilting room was very large, speaking foggy words, while waves washed in sounds somewhere and the angles of the rocm were acute, then right-angles, then obtuse, always trying to steady themselves while his hands were held and the voice of the face spoke his name and tried to draw him out of a wide open ragged space like a shell-hole under the sky which was whitewashed like the ceiling of the room. He was sea-sick with the waves, and with a roar vomited froth into a basin which was part of the white shell-hole. He was sick again and again, and was only half

of himself, the other half burning and held down by the grey-
starched bosom of the nurse whose voice boomed as she spoke his
name and said, "Come on! Come on! Wake up!" as she pulled
him to her in a horrid froth-making way. He tried to push her
away, uselessly, and saw her face clearly, as it shrunk; she said,
"Lie still, I'll fetch you a drink", and the thought made him feel
swelled and sick, and why did she have to bang the door with a
fearful noise that hurt like thunder when she left the room. Why
was he alone in the room, why was he not in the long rather dark
ward, why was he isolated, what had happened. He sank away
under nausea.

Two days later he was gliding in a hospital ship down the
Seine. All base hospitals were being cleared to take the wounded
coming down from the battlefield, many of them by barges on the
canals.

He read a newspaper, *The Daily Trident*, which spoke of the
continued British advance along the road to Bapaume, of the fall
of La Boisselle and the imminent capture of Contalmaison, two
miles beyond the old British front line. He wondered if "Spectre"
West, who had gone back to the Gaultshires in that sector, had
had anything to do with the success there.

Trees on the tall wooded river banks glided past the port-
holes, green and pleasant as he lay canted on his side, easy with
milk and sugar in his belly.

He took up an old copy of *Nash's and Pall Mall Magazine*, one
of a bundle left on his cot by an orderly. He told himself that he
must read carefully, so that when pain began again he might be
able to hold his mind above matter. He began with the advertisements.

On the first page there was a picture of an officer in the trenches
stropping a safety razor. The loop of the strap was held by a
tommy with rifle slung, while another looked on, grinning.

IN FRANCE, FLANDERS, GALLIPOLI—or wherever he is—
send 'him' an AutoStrop Safety Razor Set, the gift he most needs.

Comforts are few at the Front; therefore give 'him' the very real
comfort of an AutoStrop Shave. Send him the only razor that strops
itself whether in Field, Camp, Dug-out, or on Ship-board.

Opening his fountain pen, he gave the officer a beard; then the
written comment, *If it strops itself, then what is the officer doing in the
picture?*

The next advertisement was of a tommy holding an immense tin of Fry's Pure Breakfast Cocoa, while a shell burst behind him, and underneath the words, WHAT I HAVE I'LL HOLD.

Then one of a small boy, finger to mouth, saying *I'se found out where Mummy keeps Ficolax.*

There is no need to cheat your children with nasty powders secreted in jam, or to give them horrid doses of castor oil . . .

Ugh, castor oil and licorice powder, given while Father stood by; for Mother alone could not get him to swallow such filthy stuff.

ONOTO the Pen. IT CANNOT LEAK. Do not make the mistake of sending the wrong pen to the front. The Military size exactly fits the Soldier's pocket, 10/6 in Black Vulcanite, £5/5/- in Gold.

Phillip took his pen and shook blots all over the advertisement, then smeared the blots, and wrote across the advertisement, *PROOF!*

FREE! from Asthma. Specially suitable for Children. Potters Asthma Cure, Artillery Lane, London E. Recommended by many doctors, it has proved its efficiency for Asthma, and also for Bronchitis, Croup, Whooping Cough, and other Lung Troubles.

Including Phosgene, Chlorine, and all Hot Air from Behind the Lines, he added.

LOVE & KISSES from Wright's Coal Tar Shaving soap, the Ideal Antiseptic. No slimy lather.

There was the picture of a man holding the waist of a girl in a nightdress who was lathering his chin.

Two jobs in one, as Freddy would say.

Then came the familiar picture of a man enclosed in a wooden box, his head sticking out.

TURKISH BATHS AT HOME. All the delights and benefits, etc.

Now that Gallipoli is no longer available, he wrote, as he gave the man dundreary whiskers.

A man in morning coat, with sahib-glance, stiff upper lip, jutting chin, stared out of the next photograph.

£2 to £10 WEEKLY, FOR ONE HOUR OF YOUR TIME DAILY! No matter what you are doing; no matter how low your salary, or how poor your prospects; no matter how discontented or discouraged you are; no matter how incapable of achievement your family or friends think you are—you can at once become the partner of the world's greatest mail order enterprises. You can begin, for the first time in your life, perhaps, to see the money roll into you at every visit of the postman, without grinding out your heart, soul and body for every shilling of it. Right now I offer you the money-making chance of your life, without asking you to mortgage your life to me, without driving a grim, cold-blooded, Shylock's bargain with you. I started with £2 and made a profit of £5,000 in two years in the mail-order business. I will teach you how to look the whole world in the face and never ask your shillings where they came from.

If, wrote Phillip, beside the photograph, *you don't ask your shillings where they come from, what sort of a business man are you? Better get into khaki, and be really sure where your bob a day comes from.*

Superfluous Hair Permanent Cure Guaranteed by my ELECTRO-LYSIS HOME TREATMENT by Madame TENSFELDT, 122N, Princes Street, Edinburgh.

PROTECT YOUR SKIN against Cold Winds by Glycola. Neither greasy nor sticky, cannot be detected.

A USEFUL BOOK, which should be in the hands of every adult—Married or Unmarried. Skilfully the author guides his readers past the treacherous snares and unwary pitfalls that lie about the path or the unwary wedded . . . he shows how to guard against those body-blighting sins which married people know so much. . . . There is no shuffling or beating about the bush here, but a straightforward explanation of matters usually kept secret.

The heavy down-dragging weight was coming back, the nausea of pain, turning the mind from clear glass to frosty glass, to sooted frosty glass above London Bridge station, all the engine safety-valves blowing off in one great screeching tearing from which away he could not drag his feet. It was too much, it was happening all the time, it was going on night and day, never-ceasing, flesh splattering and bone splintering, shell splottering, bullet bizz-buzzing, bombwompering mortar crackrending. Rough awful

waves of corrugating glass embedding him silent-screaming into
smooth thick thickening thickest stifling excreta of licorice powder
bubbled with castor oil breaking into smoke and flame and white
flossy caterpillars of silent-screaming fire-terror Mavis.

"You must try not to cry out."

"It was Mavis. She——"

"Drink this."

"But my sister——"

"Now try and go to sleep again."

"Was I asleep?"

"You have been, for the past hour."

"Thank God, O, thank God!"

"Be a good boy, and I'll bring you some tea."

He took up the magazine, rejoicing secretly with it, as with an
old and trusted friend.

"LIFEGUARD" Patent Collapsible Pocket Periscope. Used by
over 8,000 Officers. To be without it is taking needless risks. Costs 20/-.
It's cheaper than life. From all Opticians or direct by return from the
Sole Manufacturers.

There was a man with revolver in hand gazing calmly into a
looking-glass on an expanding stick, while beside him stood another
man with rifle, fear on his face as he had not got a Lifeguard
Patent Collapsible Pocket Periscope. Perhaps he was also thinking
that his wife could not afford 20/-.

IN A BAYONET CHARGE one of these watches had the bezel,
glass, and hands torn off and the dial cracked but the watch NEVER
STOPPED. Isn't that PROOF POSITIVE that it's just the watch
for Active Service? Price £1 15/-. Every one Guaranteed.

Every one Guaranteed: what, never to stop—running? He
began to laugh. Hero-proof watches, wear one and never stop
running.

TOILET REQUISITES.

Handsome men are slightly sunburnt. "Sunbronze" gives this tint,
detection impossible; genuine, harmless. 5,000 Testimonials. 1/3, 2/0,
10/6. Sunbronze Laboratories, Stoke Newington, London.

"Don't cry, ducks," said the nurse, bringing the tea, "you're
going to get well very soon. Now drink your tea, it's nice and

sugary, good for little boys." Little London Cockney boys, he thought, no longer slightly sunburnt.

When sending a present to your Soldier friend include a set of the famous coloured Harrison Fisher Beauty Pictures—"Betty", "A Fair Breeze", "Good Morning", "Dad's Girl", "He won't Bite"—the five pictures will be forwarded post paid on receipt of a postal order for 2/6. All orders to *Nash's Magazine* Print Dept., 69 Fleet Street, London, E.C.

O love, my love, did you but love me. There she was, his golden girl, in five poses by Harrison Fisher. He ached with longing.

LITERARY. If you can write an interesting letter you can learn to be a free-lance journalist, and increase your income by spare time writing and earn while learning at home. Send (with stamp for return) specimen letter, article, or story for Scholarship competition. No Entrance Fee. Freelance Correspondence College, 6 York Buildings, Adelphi, Strand, W.C.

He would write to them when he got home, and send an account of the attack of July the First.

WHY "NASH'S" WINS

In the year that has passed, the sales of Greater Britain's Greatest Magazine have greatly increased since the war. There is of course a reason for this. No such group of famous writers and great artists has ever before contributed to one magazine.

During the last twelve months, when so many magazines have been compelled to cut down expenses, the following writers and artists have contributed to *Nash's*: Rudyard Kipling, W. J. Locke, Gouverneur Morris, Ella Wheeler Wilcox, Hilaire Belloc, Booth Tarkington, Israel Zangwill, Cynthia Stockley, André Castaigne, Frank Craig, Frances Hodgson Burnett, Maurice Maeterlinck, Robert W. Chambers, Princess Troubetskoy, John Galsworthy, Perceval Gibbon, F. Peter Dunne (the creator of the inimitable "Mr. Dooley"), Fortunino Matania, Harrison Fisher.

During the present year the following eminent writers will join the large family of *Nash's* contributors.

Marie Corelli, Elinor Glyn, A. E. W. Mason, E. Phillips Oppenheim, and Jack London. Mr. Rudyard Kipling will also contribute, and Mr. Hall Caine's next serial will appear exclusively in our pages.

He looked through the pages. There was a story called *The Fear*, by Charles G. D. Roberts, about prehistoric cave-men and women (one woman was naked, leaping forward, big toes spread, wild hair flying, with smoothed-out breasts) and mammoths; *The Wonderful Year*, a serial by W. J. Locke, to which he would return, as the woman looked luscious and sunny, with golden hair; "Mr. Dooley," a fat Irishman with a funny face apparently cheating at cards; an essay by Dr. Frank Crane, called *Bunglers*, with a buxom angel visiting a girl in Greek robes, sewing beside a basket of pears, in a Mediterranean setting.

We educate everything except our souls. Is it not worth while to master the technique of failure, to turn disappointment into amusement, to handle crabbed natures so they show their sweetness, to make soured souls conscious of their bit of nobleness, to be an expert in hearts and a virtuoso in human nature, is it not the art of all arts? Why bungle?

Phillip thought of Grandpa, of Father, of Desmond, of Mavis: in future he would be to them like Col. Kingsman, putting himself out to understand others.

He turned over the pages, and settled to read *Billet Notes, being Casual pencillings from a Fighting Man to his Mother.*

Dearest,—I have just emerged from a dug-out that would make you stare. Now there are dug-outs and dug-outs. They all aim at being a home from home, but this one was fairly It. It hadn't a carpet, but it was fashioned with old oak (loot from a German trench whose previous occupants had obviously looted it from somewhere else). In it we ate our dinner off delicate Sèvres plates and drank out of rare old cut glasses. A dug-out de luxe! But even the common or garden dug-out shows some attempt at cosiness.

We always have a desire to make the best of circumstances. We collect (or steal) planks, bricks, doors, and windows to help give a semblance of civilisation to our funk-holes. The men keep the trenches neat and make gardens behind the parados. A sense of humour gives spice to the task. It shows in the names bestowed upon our residences—"The Keep", "Minnewerfer Villa", "The Gasworks". "Myholme" is also very popular. But there's something beside humour that incites Tommy to put up a board marked "Trespassers will be prosecuted" over his kitchen garden. He means it. His impotent rage when a German shell ignores the prohibition is comic to a degree.

After one of these annoyances some of the men of my company in desperation stalked a German sentry, brought him in alive, and made him write in huge German characters the words KARTOFFELN GARTEN—VERBOTEN, which they hoisted on a board facing the enemies lines. I believe that sentry is secretly being kept as a hostage against further damage!

Your loving

CHOTA.

The notes continued with a long description of Chota's dog, Little Kim, being sniped by the Germans, for daring to bark at them from the parapet. The "Boches" had thrown over written messages, "more than once informing us that they meant to get him if they could. We hoped, unconvincingly, that Little Kim had gone rabbiting."

Little Kim eventually was traced by "a thin blood-stained trail to the bunk in my dug-out". He had "a nasty hole in his chest".

Our trench first-aid outfit doesn't include any quick means of deliverance for a mortally wounded dog, and we hadn't an R.A.M.C. man handy. Somebody volunteered to fetch one. Waiting, it was evident to me that if the medico couldn't do anything, I should have to do so.

Phillip felt fretful. How could troops, apparently in the front line, since snipers were watching it, make and tend an allotment just behind the parados? Seeds took weeks and weeks to grow; and a battalion was not likely to remain in the line for months. Well, perhaps some had. But this battalion seemed rather strange; why was no stretcher bearer, or first-aid man, in the trench? And who ever heard of a "medico" in the line?

He read on, feeling twisted.

Kim was only a puppy, and as guileless a one as ever I'd known, yet he was made to suffer for something without purpose and for something beyond his comprehension. Is it fair? Tommy and I know we play with chance if we show our heads over the parapet and jeer at the Germans; but Kim had no knowledge of the risks he ran when he barked at them out of sheer *joie de vivre*. Poor little chap! Best of four-footed pals! I wished the Little Mother had been at hand. She would have made him understand that I was not angry with him. He got colder and colder, and I drew the blanket over him, but it moved tremulously with his shivers. And all the while his sad eyes were on mine.

At last, when the medico was brought in—one of the Vet.-corps—I saw there was no hope. "His number's up, I'm afraid," he said, and offered to shoot him for me. I told him I would rather do it myself.

I think Kim knew and understood my reason. At least, I hope so.
He lay still, very patient . . .

I had no idea the men would take it so badly. One or two fairly
blubbered. They asked, as a favour, to be allowed to bury the little
body . . . It went hard with them that they were not able to do it with
full military honours . . .

Thank goodness we've been told to hold ourselves in readiness to
move off first thing in the morning. There's a rumour that we're in for
the Big Push at last. If it's true this time, it's enough to key the men
up to concert pitch; but there's something more in it to them than
crumpling up the Germans (if we can do it): they mean to avenge
Kim's murder. They're getting ready grimly, tidying themselves.

If Tommy has sufficient notice, he likes to fight trim, dressed for
the part. He shaves, brushes his hair, mends his kit. Also he sees
carefully to the action of his rifle, and he finds something wherewith
to put a fierce edge on his bayonet.

They'll be difficult to hold back this time. I don't feel like holding
them back, either. Goodbye, dearest; I must tidy up too. I want
to get a bit of my own back as well.

                                                        CHOTA.

He lay back, exhausted. The whole account was a fraud. How
could they have fetched a Veterinary Officer, from Division, miles
behind the front line, so quickly? And anyway a wounded dog
would feel like a wounded man, and cling to life, in a world of its
own terror, the more terribly the worse it was hit, at least while it
remained conscious. Howells had screamed when he had pointed
the Lewis gun at him; he had known his intention, and had been
almost out of his head with fright. Perhaps his so-called bullet-
proof vest had saved him; more likely it would have roasted him.
He felt distress as he thought of it; his body was hot, his leg aching,
and a new pain grew in it, like the gnaw of phosphorus. He
pushed *Nash's* through the bars of his cot. The author of that piece
had not been anywhere near the line. It was all of it untrue. Why
were such pieces printed? Father took *Nash's*. He would hate the
Germans more than ever when he read about the dog's death, and
so help to make the war last longer.

The war began to ache in his wounds, as he thought of going
home to hear again the same old talk. Then the ache spread to his
head, and the glazed-glassy world came back, which was before
the rough-and-smooth nightmare feeling. His temperature was
taken. The nurse went away, and returned with the doctor. He
was given something to drink, then an injection in his leg, and his
pillow turned over, so that it was cool. Soon he was sinking down

into calmness and bliss, while the sun shone with a mellow light which bore him along a lane across a heath, with shadowy forms around him. He could hear voices, but not what they were saying. He could see the whirr of wheels, and heat was shimmering from gravel spread upon tar which had come up in black bubbles. The tar clung to the bicycle tyres. They dragged and made pedalling hard. Phew, the day was a scorcher! The last day of July, 1914.

They were sitting outside the little brick Greyhound Inn on the left of the road. His bike and the three others' bikes were leaning against the dingy yellow brick wall. There was a wooden trestle table outside the inn, and two wooden forms, unpainted and grey with exposure to rain and sun.

Pink china pots of cider were on the table. They were sitting on a bench by the wooden table, while gorse-seeds popped on the common. Willie, Desmond, Eugene, himself—all viewless.

They were all at the beginning of a great new friendship. He was taking them to the secret Lake Woods, and their rods were tied on their bicycles. Then with running leaps they got on their bikes and were racing up the slope towards the windmill, and he followed, but his heart was thumping black, his eyes were sparky, as he tried to catch up with them; then they were gone, and he saw the oak paling fence of Knollyswood Park, and turning north, was swooping downhill past the Fish Ponds, gleam of water under pine-trees, ratchet-click of free-wheel past the lodge, he was at the end of the cleft-oak fencing. At the boundary the footpath led under trees into the unknown. On the upper side was a tall taut barbed-wire fence, on steel angle-iron posts seven feet high. How could he get over it, and where were the others? He could not see them, although he could hear them talking but without any sound. He saw them, far below him, scraping a hole in the leaf-mould under the lowest strand. Then he was floating under pigeon-clattering tall hollies and oaks. He came to the Lake Woods, one terraced above the other. They were surrounded by rhododendrons and towering firs. He heard dry patterings, sudden startling wing-drumming *kock-karrs!* of upbursting cock pheasants, flying away with tails rippling.

There was a peacock in full blue-and-green display on the grassy dam between two ponds. Its maniac cry rang through the woods. Then from an upper lake flapped a grey heron, its legs trailing. It dropped a thin white thread, which fell across the leaf-reflecting surface. He watched it dissolve palely in the water.

The bailiff, in grey whip-cord, was walking to the higher iron gate. They all hid. They watched him go away up the woodland ride. Cole-tits in the fir-tree tops talked to one another as they flitted in and out of the sun. The ring-doves cooed serenely. A figure was now quite near him. It was fitting together a long bamboo roach-pole. He tried to speak, but was unable even to move. There were four lengths, fitted together without brass ferrules. It was a Thames roach-fisher's pole. It was being taken apart and the figure was pushing the sections, now tied together with string, into a rhododendron bush, where it would be hidden until they came again.

When they had all gone away and left him he felt desperately ill because he could not recall their faces. Then he saw Mavis. She wanted to follow him, but he tried to escape from her. She was very small, she had left Mother's arms, she was trying to walk after him, round the sitting-room table, and the guard was not up before the fire. He said go away and she still followed him, and because he wanted to be alone to stand still and grieve by himself he pushed her backwards and she fell into the fire, and she was screaming until Mrs. Feeney ran in and pulled her out, her clothes burning. O Master Phil whatever made you do such a thing he heard Mrs. Feeney's voice saying, but he could not see her, or find the room again. He was alone, suspended in a void. He searched but could not move, called but could not see, looked but could not hear. Everything became rough, and then sickeningly smooth.

When he woke out of this torture he was wet with sweat, and tried to steady the swaying ship by holding his eyes upon a trolley with tea being wheeled round the ward. He told the orderly he was feeling sea-sick, but the orderly said they had docked at Southampton. The orderly did not bring him a bowl, so to his shame and degradation he was sick on his pillow.

On the hospital train, gleaming white in the long ward-like coach, a lady came round with telegraph forms and pencils. Would he like her to send a telegram to his next of kin? No thank you, he said, unable to bear the thought of what Father or Mother or Mavis or anyone belonging to the old life might say, their shame and their criticism, and now probably saying how proud they were of him, when he had failed utterly.

Part Three

THE QUIET BOY

Chapter 20

LILY'S RESOLUTION

Phillip had written a letter to his mother from Rouen, saying that he was wounded, but not badly, and would she please not be worried (he meant fuss) about him, as he was really lucky to be where he was, considering all things. He added that he might not be at Rouen very long, so no letter should be written to him. He would write when and if he got to England. He also sent a field postcard to Freddie, hoping that Mr. Jenkins, when he went there, would see it.

Considering all things was his way of under-stating what, in fact, he could not bring himself to write; he could not even think it to himself. It was too much: the mind flinched from thought of the grinding advance up the slightest of grassy slopes to the chalk thread of the German trench seen only occasionally in hazy gaps of wafting smoke and spouting earth. Indeed, on that day, until he was taken down to Albert he had not seen a German, nor during the advance had he known where the firing was coming from. Punctured khaki figures had fallen, to writhe, cry out, crawl, twist, or lie still. That was all he had seen of the battle; half-realised scenes of which recurred again and again, in flashes and shards within his mind, as he lay in bed, fixed by an iron ache of pain which the feeble dribble of the glass tube in his buttock wound, sucking at the pus, failed to relieve, while the smell of iodoform in his nostrils mingled with the nauseating scent of roses in the bowl on the table.

He endured long moments of self-exasperation before he could assemble himself to overcome the shame of asking for the bed-pan; while to ask for the screens at the same time was a thought of horror because it would reveal his feeble weakness. Black and bitter laxative was another dread, lest the inevitable pain occur when sister was engaged elsewhere, and he disgrace himself in her eyes. Thank heaven she was not a lady. "Haven't you got anyone coming to see you?" she said on the third day. "My, you're a real lonely soldier, aren't you. No letters for you this morning. Were you expecting any?"

"Oh, we don't write much in our family, sister."

The morning probing, after the doctor's inspection, was an agony, while he lay on his face, and got the cotton of the pillow slip between his lips, to hold hard against crying out. Caked and stinking swabs were lifted out by tweezers, then the tatters of muscle, otherwise flesh, which had rotted in the night, must be picked away. All the damaged flesh had to loosen and go before new growth could begin. He sweated violently. Drain tubes, which had been removed, were then replaced to rasp away elsewhere in the foetid yellowing crater.

"Tell me if I hurt you."

"Oh, it's nothing, sister, really," came the muffled voice from the pillow. It was nothing, he thought, compared with the chap in the next bed, who had had his private parts shot away, and his thigh-bone broken by a shell splinter. He groaned a lot, his monstrous plaster leg under a wooden cage. He had pince-nez spectacles, and his wife came to see him every afternoon, bringing black grapes.

Then the merciful cool spray of malachite green; it was all over for another twelve hours, except the putting on of fresh swabs and bandages.

"I suppose the bandages have to be very tight, don't they, sister?"

"The binders, you mean?" she said, taking a safety-pin from her mouth with one hand, while holding the end of the roll tightly with her other hand. He wondered if it was healthy to hold it in her mouth; but no doubt it was sterilised. "Yes, as tight as possible, so don't you start complaining."

Why did she say that? He had never complained. For a while he had wanted to die, since nothing was left to live for; but that had passed, and with it his mood of not writing to his mother.

"What day is it, sister?"

"Saturday. Have you lost count? You must pull yourself to-gether!"

"You've done that for me, sister!"

"That's better! The shock is wearing off, I see."

"What shock? I've had no shock!"

"That's what you think! Now be a good boy, and write to your people, and they'll get the letter in time to visit you tomorrow, and take tea with you in the ward. Sunday afternoon is Visiting Day, from two o'clock until half-past four. I'll post the letter when I go off duty at nine o'clock, if you hurry up."

He wrote to his mother, asking her to come with Doris, as only two visitors were allowed in, he said, for each patient. He felt ill at the thought of his father, or Mavis, coming to see him; and tore up the letter. He wrote another, and screwed it up half way through. Then he wrote a third, and while he was writing it the sister returned and stood by while he addressed an envelope; so that one was posted.

On the Saturday afternoon of July 8, Richard Maddison was working in his allotment, with a satisfaction based on two thoughts that gave him a calm feeling: one, that his son was at least out of the battle, with wounds that were not so severe as to lead the authorities, in whom he had implicit trust, to send for his mother and himself; two, that the benefit of sub-soiling he had done upon his rods of land was to be seen in the healthy appearance of the growing crops. It was helped, of course, by the half-rotted compost he had trenched-in a spit deep, and the hop-manure raked into the seed-beds.

Bran, mixed with powdered napthalene, had accounted for the slugs. A maze of black thread, thought of as barbed wire defending his main-crop position, had kept sparrows from the peas. Thin lines of lime around the lettuce plants in their straight rows were his outposts against skirmishing snails.

On his way to the allotment, pushing wheel-barrow and tools, he had noticed a young woman looking at him as though expectantly; she had made as if to smile, and he had been quickened by the wide-spaced blue eyes in a pleasant, open face which reminded him of his young sisters, Effie and Viccy, when they had been in their early 'teens. Effie had died young, of phthisis; she had been the beauty of the family.

He was thinking of past days as he mixed sand with lettuce seed for economy of sowing, when he noticed that the young woman, who had apparently been on her way to Joy Farm, was gazing in his direction as she stood, with an open sunshade over her shoulder, on the gravelley cart-track which led to the farmhouse, or what was left of it now that it was almost entirely surrounded by rows of houses in yellow brick.

He knelt to release the seeds and sand carefully between finger and thumb, looking through his gold-wire reading spectacles, to make sure that the line was absolutely straight. It was most important that his sowing be along a precise line, in order to hoe within half-an-inch of the "drill" (as he called it) and so catch the weeds before they grew to the two-leaf stage. If it rained, the weeds would grow fast; the guns in France were said to be causing precipitation of cumulus into nimbus by percussion, according to an article in *The Daily Trident*.

When he had drilled the seed to the end of the row, he stood up to straighten his back, and saw that the young woman with the sunshade was still dawdling upon the cart-track. She was looking his way, and appeared to be hesitating. Then she smiled.

The good news in the paper from France that morning, the friable state of his soil, the colour of his plants, and now a smile from the lady-like young woman on a summer afternoon, freed the automatic reticence of a Victorian upbringing, based on what was correct behaviour towards all women, and he called out,

"Are you waiting to see me, by any chance?"

The Vision—as he thought of her later—of pink cheeks and smiling blue eyes came forward, and said in a soft voice, "Please excuse me intruding, sir, but I heard from a friend that Lieutenant Maddison had been wounded, and as I happened to be passing, I thought I would ask you if he is all right."

"We have not heard particulars yet, but no doubt no news is good news."

"Oh I am so glad."

It was then, with disappointment which showed itself in a masking of his affability, that he recognised her as the young woman he had seen leaving Randiswell police station on the night of his son's recall to France. She looked quite a nice girl, too; but one could never tell by appearances.

"I hope you don't mind me speaking to you, sir."

"Well, as I expect you know, there has been a lot of fighting in France, and no doubt the authorities are hard put to it to communicate with the next of kin of all the casualties."

"Yes, Mr. Maddison, these last two days the Borough Military Hospital has had no beds vacant."

"Oh, you work there, do you?"

"Yes, sir. I do volunteer work there nights."

Richard felt easier. She had a frank, open face. Her next remark pleased him, for the consideration it showed.

"Well, sir, I must not keep you from your work. I hope you will excuse the intrusion."

"Oh, no intrusion, I assure you. On the contrary, I am most obliged to you for your kind inquiry."

She blushed prettily, he thought, while a feeling of pleasure spread up from his knees. Thereafter she was the Vision.

"Thank you ever so, Mr. Maddison."

"I will let Phillip know that you asked after him, when we get in touch with him. May I inquire your name?"

"Lily Cornford, sir," she said, and then, after slight hesitation, "I hope your son has a speedy recovery."

"Thank you, Miss Cornford, I will tell him when I see him," he said, giving her a little salute. He restrained himself from looking after her as she went away; and was surprised that he felt a pang that his visitor was gone. The allotment seemed stony and flat for a few moments. And when he glanced at the plot adjoining his own, he felt its tangle and untidiness acutely. He sighed, and went on with his task.

The allotment next to Richard's was in the occupation (as he phrased it to himself) of his neighbour and fellow special-constable, Mr. Jenkins. Or, more correctly, non-occupation, for Mr. Jenkins was, he thought, in the nature of an absentee tenant. Only a fifth of his ground had been dug over, and so long ago that it had re-covered itself with couch grass, for Mr. Jenkins—despite the trouble he had taken on his behalf to tell him what the rubbishy condition of the land needed—had made no attempt to trench or deep-dig his plot.

When the young woman was at a safe distance, Richard looked in her direction, and saw that his dilatory neighbour was approaching. He watched him stop when he came to the young woman. How came that fellow to know her?

When he arrived at his allotment, Mr. Jenkins immediately made the matter clear.

"Hullo, Sergeant! Busy as usual, I see."

"Yes, Mr. Jenkins. The time of year is passing."

"You don't say, Sergeant!"

Richard's neighbour of No. 8 Hillside Road used the Randiswell's Specials mode of address to Richard when off-duty as a kind of criticism of his senior's aloofness, and of the older man's disapproval of the habits of the majority of Specials, e.g. slipping into a saloon bar to "have a quick one" while on duty during Zepp-less nights.

"Well, it will soon be too late to put out any seeds, I fancy."

"What do you think of the news that Phillip and Desmond have both been wounded in the advance, Sergeant?"

"Oh!" said Richard. "I had not heard about my son's friend being a casualty, Mr. Jenkins."

"Then you are almost the only one of our squad, Sergeant, who hasn't."

"Oh!"

"Both Phillip and Desmond sent a field-postcard to Freddy, the landlord of their favourite house of call, Sergeant, and Freddy has the cards pinned up side by side, for all to see. Both will be home shortly, the cards say."

"Well, that is news to me, Mr. Jenkins."

He thought that Phillip might at least have sent a field-postcard to him at the office, rather than to a publican who, in the nature of things, was little more than a stranger. Before he could check himself, he said, "But there, Phillip has always shown more interest outside his home than in it."

He regretted this admission the more when the other man said, "Well, I mean to say, Sergeant, to understand the younger generation, it is only necessary to remember our own young days, in regard to our fathers' heavy attitude towards us, isn't it?"

This remark affected Richard strongly. What did Mr. Jenkins know about his Father? Whence had he got his information? From Master Phillip, who apparently could not keep a still tongue in his head—where outsiders were concerned, at any rate? Had his own son told Mr. Jenkins, and others in that pot-house haunt of his, that his grandfather had been killed in an accident when under the influence of liquor?

"I cannot discuss such topics, Mr. Jenkins; but I will say this! If you are hoping to get any crops from your allotment this season, may I suggest that you are leaving your cultivations a little late? After all, rationing of food may come yet, you know. We have been warned."

"There you go again, Sergeant! Your attitude is, well—always so disapproving. Why can't you be human sometimes? I know you have your troubles at home; so do lots of other men. But does that give you sympathy for others in the same boat? Not likely! 'Judge not that ye be not judged!' We're told that, aren't we? But how many of us practise it, eh?"

"Mr. Jenkins," said Richard, straightening his back, and feeling that his lumbago might be coming back, "I do not know why you are condemning me like his. And if you have any complaints about me as your sergeant on duty, I suggest that you lay them before the proper authorities. In the meantime I should be obliged if you would observe a common civility."

"There you go, you see! I can't make an ordinary remark to you, but you immediately take umbrage, Sergeant! It is the same with all the specials at the station! You put everyone's back up, but don't seem to know how or why. As Burns said, 'If ye canna' be aisy, be as aisy as ye can.' Well, it is still a beautiful afternoon, and I came down here, I don't mind telling you, very much looking forward to a neighbourly chat and to tell you the good news about Phillip, and what do I get? Not bread, but a stone!"

"Sailor" Jenkins then put on his yachting cap, gave Richard a salute, and taking his tools, walked back the way he had come, thinking with longing of Lily, who had refused his invitation to go with him to the New Cross Empire that evening, saying she would be working at the military hospital. He imagined himself kneeling before her, while she took his head tenderly upon her breast, and his weariness left him. For a moment he felt weak at the knees.

On her way back, as she walked up the asphalt path between the spiked iron railings of St. Cyprian's churchyard—uncultivated, a genuine prairie of long wild grasses on the yellow clay of a prehistoric river-bed—Lily stopped to listen to organ music coming from behind stained-glass windows. The *vox humana* spoke to her like a heavenly voice, a voice of eternal love. So moving was the music, that she determined to do what hitherto even the idea of had made her quail: she would call on Mrs. Neville, in the hope that it would lead to the two friends, who had fallen out over her, making it up.

Mrs. Neville had heard about Lily from Desmond after Phillip had gone off into the night six weeks previously to report back to his regimental depôt. Coming out of the bedroom doorway where she had been listening, she had asked her son what he had meant by saying such dreadful things to his best friend: to learn that Phillip had not only broken his promise not to see Lily again, but had taken her into the country on the back of his motorcycle.

Seeing how upset her son was, she had tried to reassure him, by saying that it was probably a harmless whim of Phillip's: that he was a generous person, and might have wished to cut a figure with a pretty girl on the carrier of his motorcycle, as well as give her a view of his beloved countryside. If, as Desmond had inferred, it was for another reason, then it was the girl's fault.

"What is this Lily, anyway? A girl who goes into public houses to find men is hardly the sort of girl that any son of mine, surely, would want to bring home to meet his mother?"

Even as she said that, Mrs. Neville knew herself to be a hypocrite: for had she not met Desmond's father in the same way, in the promenade of the Alhambra in Leicester Square? He was then living in chambers, and on the point of qualifying as a solicitor. His university degree had been the equivalent of the preliminary exam; he had passed his intermediate while articled to a firm in Lincoln's Inn; and when she had met him, he had told her that he was about to spend the next six months with Gibson and Weldon, the coaches.

A girl of strong will and daring vitality, Hilda Carey had left her home in Brixton, and gone to live with him, feeling herself to be the New Woman.

What a disaster the marriage, precipitated by parental opposition on both sides, had been! Their ideas had kept them apart, as she knew now. He had left her six months after her baby had been born, and now he had another family in the county town of Essex, by a woman who had changed her name by deed-poll to Neville. He had wanted a divorce, of course, but as a good Catholic she had refused.

So tolerant and understanding of most other people, Mrs. Neville was adamant about the wrongs she had suffered from Desmond's father. Her opinion of him, as Desmond had once overheard her to say to someone when he was little, was "the greatest cad I have ever known".

The hours, the days, the months alone with her baby, on a mere pittance, living in a single room in a shut-away London square: yet in her clear moments she saw that it had been wrong from the start. What had she, a young girl from the suburbs of London, daughter of a warehouse clerk, known about life? His undergraduate friends had come to see them in their chambers after the marriage; he had complained afterwards that her laughter was too loud, that she was lacking in reserve, with no knowledge of how to carry on a conversation obliquely, so that one's personal feelings were not obtruded upon others. Tears, remorse, reconciliations; he had ceased to invite his friends of Clifton and Trinity.

They moved to the flat in Red Lion Court, for economy. O,

the loneliness! The only friend she had kept among all his friends had been Maude Hudson, of Highgate, who had a *salon* where writers, journalists, musicians, and actors used to congregate. And Maude had remained her only friend to this day; for she had grown away from those she had known before her marriage. She lived between two worlds.

How true it was that a woman might marry beneath her, and adjust herself to her husband's life and environment; but not when she married above her.

And now this girl Lily setting her cap at her son, barely seventeen years old! And meeting Phillip, promptly attaching herself to him! In all probability she had got herself into trouble, and was fancying herself as a war-bride! If she met the precious hussy, she would soon settle her hash! She had half a mind to go down to Freddy's bar and give her a piece of her mind; but she must not do that, of course, for it would add to Desmond's embarrassment, when he came back.

When Desmond had gone overseas, Mrs. Neville had known what it was to lead a life in suspense; but she also lived steadily in her faith that life was a spiritual thing; and on the Saturday afternoon she was about to go out (having watched "Father", otherwise Mr. Maddison, out of the way with his wheel-barrow) to call on Mrs. Maddison, when she saw a strange young woman looking up at windows, and thought to herself that she must be Lily.

"I feel ever so nervous, Mrs. Neville, please excuse me daring to call on you like this."

"What can I do for you?" replied Mrs. Neville, in a voice of polite condescension. Relenting as soon as she saw the pulse beating in the girl's neck, the widening of the most amazing blue eyes she had ever seen, and their long childish lashes when her glance dropped in nervousness, Mrs. Neville went on, "You are Lily, aren't you? Then come along upstairs, my dear, where we can be more comfortable than on a door-step! You go first, will you? I'm rather slow nowadays, with my weight." She looked at the girl's legs and clothes as she followed behind her. Neat ankles, black stockings, well-brushed boots, no spots on her blue serge skirt, small waist (thank heaven, nothing unusual under it), neat jacket pressed under a clean damp cloth with no threads of cotton left anywhere, worn lining carefully darned under the hem of her jacket.

"Round to the left and up the three steps into the drawing—well, it's really a sitting room! Here we are! Now sit down and make yourself comfortable. You know, I expect, that both Phillip and Desmond have been in the fighting, and got themselves wounded?"

"Oh yes, Mrs. Neville! I have just come from seeing Mr. Maddison on his allotment, and he told me, too."

"Really? Do you know Phillip's father, then?"

"Yes, Mrs. Neville. He is ever so nice and kind."

"Do forgive my curiosity, Lily, but was there any special reason for going to see Phillip's father?"

She saw faint colour come in the girl's cheeks, as she lowered her eyes. Mrs. Neville waited, and when Lily said nothing further, she said, "Well, I expect you would like a cup of tea? I'll go and put on the kettle. Don't get up, I'll be back in a moment."

This needed some thought. What was coming next? How long had the girl known Phillip? Under two months: absurd! Hilda, my dear, she said to herself, do not force the pace! Leaving the kettle on the small burner, she went back to her drawing room. "It won't be long, Lily! Now tell me, how was Phillip when you last heard from him? He does write such an interesting letter, doesn't he? Did you hear from Desmond also? No? Well, I expect he was underground most of the time, tunnelling, you know, and he had time only to write to his mother."

"Mrs. Neville!"

"Yes, Lily?"

"I came to say that I am very sorry I came between them, but I did not mean any harm. I hope that Desmond, if you don't mind me calling him that——"

"Why of course not! I hope you don't mind my calling you Lily? Anyway, you know how young they both are, in their ways, I mean, and I am sure when they meet again they will be as if nothing had happened. And, after all, what has happened? Nothing but a little jealousy over a pretty girl! What else, indeed?"

What a beautiful expression she has, her eyes seem to glow, they have a look of Phillip in them, so gentle and—young. She is a good girl. So she had a crucifix among the charms on her bracelet!

"Lily, dear, look at me. I want to be your friend," she heard herself saying, against the catch in her voice. What was the matter with her? The girl's eyes were tender and, yes, they too were brimming with tears.

"Here, give us a kiss, ducks!" cried Mrs. Neville. "I'm as soppy as you!" she shrieked, wiping her eyes. "And not a drop of drink have either of us had! Wait a moment, I'll shift the kettle to the big ring, then we'll have a proper talk, dear! Are you a Catholic? Not yet; well, I can only say I have found comfort and direction in the Faith. I've got a gooseberry tart, I'll bring it in. Play the gramophone if you like, it's Phillip's, he would like to know we are enjoying ourselves. Here! Come on in the kitchen and help me get the things on a tray, there's a good girl!"

So Lily confided in Mrs. Neville, that she had decided to go away and find work elsewhere before the two friends came home again. She told about the jaunt to Reynard's Common, the search for the nightingale in the evening. Before this, she said she had gone out with Desmond, and—eye-lashes on cheeks—she had felt sorry for him.

"Are you trying to tell me that you love Phillip, dear?"

"I don't matter, Mrs. Neville. I know he loves someone already, somebody good——"

She told Mrs. Neville what she had told Phillip, about her trouble when she was a servant girl.

"Yes, of course, of course! I see the reason for everything now, Lily. You've never forgotten your baby, have you?"

Richard walking up Hillside Road, pushing his barrow of tools, all carefully cleaned, as befitted a countryman, met Mrs. Rolls coming down. She was her usual gay and friendly self, and when she said, "What big boots you are wearing, to be sure, Mr. Maddison!" and he replied, "Yes, Mrs. Rolls, these are the boots my son wore in France!" the pride she saw in his face made her exclaim, "Yes, we are all proud of Phillip! He was so charming when we saw him last, when he came to tell us about his cousin Bertie. So modest and considerate! I hope we shall see something of him when he is well again. Are you going to the Seven Fields Rifle Range now? Gerard is going, I left him oiling his precious three-o-three, as he calls it, whatever that may mean. Do give Phillip all our very best wishes for a speedy recovery when you write to him next, won't you? The success upon the Somme is wonderful news, isn't it, wonderful! Helena now has some of the men back from July the first, in the Military Hospital. We are proud of them all. Goodbye, goodbye!" and with a wave of her hand, Flora Rolls tripped on down the road, just as Lily was saying goodbye to Mrs. Neville.

Chapter 21

THE HOME FRONT

One day towards the end of the month Richard was visited in his office by his younger brother, Hilary, who wore the uniform of a captain of the Royal Naval Reserve. Captain Hilary Maddison, R.N.R., had returned from the Far East, in a convoy through the Red Sea and Suez Canal to the Mediterranean, where his ship, the *Phasiana*, carrying troops, had been torpedoed. Hilary, a fine swimmer and well-covered, had remained twenty-four hours in the sea before being picked up. He was far from well, but made nothing of his heaviness of spirit. He was staying a few days in London to attend a Board of Trade enquiry, and other affairs at the Ministry of Shipping.

His old chief, the Earl of Capewroth, had arranged for Hilary Maddison to be placed in the Ministry, in order to watch over his interests in the MacKarness line; so Hilary had two jobs at the same time, an official position under the Admiralty, and an unofficial one for the rugged ex-Glaswegian who had started his career at twelve years of age as an office boy in a house of East Indiamen which later was amalgamated with others to fly the MacKarness house flag.

Hilary had his own side-line, as well. German submarines were sending tonnage to the bottom at an increasing rate; and in sympathy, as the term went, freight rates were rising fast. Speculators in all the great ports—clerks in shipping offices and agencies, with a sprinkling of ship's-chandlers and petty lawyers—were beginning to form into groups to charter rusty old tubs, obsolescent piston-engined tramps, most of them held together by paint, for the Atlantic run, carrying munitions. Hilary had some of his money in two Maritime Investment Companies that bought up such sea-coffins (as the crews called them); one registered at Bristol, the other at Cardiff. The Treasury indemnified the owners against loss. Hilary's investments were immensely profitable.

The freight rate of grain from Argentina, for example, had been 12s. 6d. per ton in July 1914, to the Port of London; now it was 183s. 6d. Excess profit taxation at sixty per cent, imposed by the Government, had stimulated the rise; even so, the profit was more than seven-fold. Coal from Cardiff and Swansea to Genoa in Italy had been carried for 7s. 6d. a ton; now it was 100s.

At the moment Hilary felt that his life was a failure. On arrival at his club, he had found a letter awaiting him, from his wife in Hampshire. It told him that she could not live with him any longer; that she wanted her freedom. She asked if he would be a gentleman, and let her divorce him. Just that; no other details; written on one side of a piece of writing paper. She had waited, she added in a postscript on the other side, until the children were grown up.

Hilary at once went to see his solicitor, who called in a private enquiry agent. He knew his wife Beatrice did not know when he would be home again, now he was part of what was called the Silent Service.

The upshot was that he secured immediate evidence of his wife's misconduct. Now, at fifty, he would have to rearrange his life. There was his sister Victoria; she was a lonely woman; he might buy a smaller house somewhere, and start again. With this in mind, he went to see his brother Richard in Threadneedle Street one morning, walking up from MacKarness House in Cockspur Street.

Hilary reckoned that since the war his capital had increased to six figures. His regret that he had no children of his own was increased proportionately. There was, of course, his step-son from the previous marriage of his wife Beatrice, and a step-daughter, but he did not care much for either. He had done his duty, provided the means for their education; but neither had shown any real interest in the home he had given them. The boy had left Winchester and was now at Sandhurst; the girl at a finishing school in the Isle of Wight.

"I don't know what it is, it must be the stock," said Hilary. "Bee, as you know, is a Lemon, and you don't need me to tell you what happened to George, our late lamented brother-in-law. Well, now she's gone and kicked over the traces with some young whippersnapper half her age, in the Navy. She turned the house into a convalescent home for officers, you know."

"Well, I can only say that I am extremely sorry, Hilary, that it should have happened, particularly so in war-time, to add to your other worries."

"I shall divorce her, Dick. Look at this!" He showed his brother an envelope, containing a single sheet of writing paper with one word written on it, *Forgive*.

"It arrived at my club this morning. She knows I have got evidence that she's been carrying on behind my back for a long time, while I was away at sea. She's turned of forty, and won't find it easy to begin a new life. But she should have thought of that before. Well, how are things with you, Dick?"

Richard told Hilary about Phillip, adding, "I have not seen him yet, he has not asked for me."

"But why don't you go and see him, Dick."

"Oh no, I know when I am not wanted, Hilary."

That evening Hilary went to Wakenham, to sup with his brother and Hetty, and have a talk about the future. He was going to sell the Hampshire place, he said, and would have a fair amount of money, which he wanted to regard as eventual capital for the family.

"I'm going down to see John next week, and sound him about an idea I have, of buying back some of the Rookhurst land sold off by our father, Dick. You know, I've an idea that things will never be the same again after the war. Land won't sink back as it did in the 'eighties and 'nineties. Now that both Willie and Phillip have shown what they're made of, on the Somme——"

News had come to Richard that his nephew had been wounded in the attack on July 14; and Willie was now in St. George's Hospital, Lancaster Gate.

"I must go and see them both, Dick."

Hilary wrote down the address in his pocket book. "Where's Phillip lying?"

"At the Royal Free Hospital, Hilary. As I told you, I have not visited him yet, but his mother has, with Dora. I thought I would go along when he is more recovered. Poor chap, he has had a rough time, so I gather, though he has said very little of what he has been through, to his mother. These soldiers won't talk about their experiences, you know. They are all the same. From what I can hear, Phillip received two bullet wounds, apparently in the one leg. No bones broken, fortunately, but he has some way to go to mend." Richard laughed. "You remember Nipper, our terrier, when we were boys at Rookhurst? How he had to be bitten on the nose before he would tackle the rats we let loose in the brew-house? Well, I can't help wondering if his recent experiences will help to cure Phillip of his illusions about the Prussian militarists."

He went on to tell his brother about "the boy's curious beliefs", and Hilary said he would soon clear that up with Phillip when he saw him.

"Taken on the whole, it appears that our mother's people are a highly hysterical lot. As you know, the Bavarians hate the Prussians, and yet admire them for their strength. This hysteria explains the contradiction in their make-up. Take an instance from the German White Book, published last year. A Major Bauer testified that after the massacre of seven hundred civilians at Dinant, coffee was given to the survivors, 'with every kindness', he said, and also 'chocolate was given to the small children found alive under the bodies'. That is the German record, mark you, so it cannot be dismissed even by pro-Germans as propaganda."

"Exactly!" said Richard.

"Well, this Major Bauer apparently made his testimony in order to show how humane his people are. All in one breath—the massacre for military frightfulness followed by extreme sentimentality, and chocolate! And that is their vaunted Kultur, and inability to see themselves as others see them, Dick!"

"We have our sentimentalists here, Hilary. In Lord Bryce's Report, the statements are never definite; every incident is 'alleged'. I blame Asquith for that. It's time he went."

"These armchair humanitarians and pacifists should serve at sea, Dick! Their eyes would be opened, and their playing-for-safety soon changed if they'd seen crews of merchantmen picked up after weeks in an open boat, half mad and croaking, unable to speak from thirst! The submarine commanders treated them with punctilio when they set them adrift, giving them cigars and brandy, but at the same time they took away all charts and compasses!"

They spoke of their sister Theodora.

"We saw her last Sunday, before she and Hetty went to see the boy. Dora is well, and is still carrying on her work among soldiers' dependents in the East End."

"Well, that's better than agitating for votes for women! You look to be in good shape, Dick. Have you had any holiday this year?"

"Oh, one can't have holidays in war-time, old man! We gave up Whit Monday Bank Holiday, you know, and now we shall all have to work throughout the August Bank Holiday. After all, the soldiers and sailors cannot rest in their duties, and the least we civilians can do is to hold the Home Front. However, I manage to get an evening or two on my allotment; that tones one up wonderfully, you know."

"How are the crops coming along?"

"Fairly well, Hilary. I fancy the deep trenching, and breaking the hard pan underneath, with the pick, has made all the difference. I don't suppose that you will have time to walk round to look at my work?"

"I would very much like to, but I have to get back to town, Dick. Another time, perhaps. Well, I must say goodbye to Hetty. It has been ever so nice to see you again, old fellow!" Looking almost happy, Hilary tore up the letter, with the single word *Forgive*, from his wife.

Now that the Somme casualties were appearing in the Roll of Honour, Phillip was able to learn something of what had happened to the faces he thought about. Letters, too, had been sent back from France, and others to his bankers, for forwarding. One was from "Spectre" West, written from the Duke's hospital in Gaultshire. He had been wounded in front of Caterpillar Wood, beyond the third and final objective of the White trench near Pommiers Redoubt ("the Hun's *Jamin Werk*, and pretty jammy it was too, the men said, when we finally got into it"). He had gone with a patrol as far as the Willow Stream which rose in Caterpillar Wood, he said, and if they had had the reserves which were thrown away up north at Gommecourt, Beaumont Hamel, and Ovillers, they could have got through the Hun's second line to the Bazentins and High Wood, past the Purple Line and on to the Hun's third and last positions along the Pys-Sars-Eaucourt l'Abbaye-Flers line, and to open country for the cavalry beyond Bapaume, not only turning the flanks of the German Northern Army Group, but rolling them up to the North Sea. It could have been done; our lines from Arras to the coast were strongly held, and the Germans would not have been in a position to launch a counter-offensive, after their losses and disorganisation at Verdun.

Phillip thought this a wonderful letter. He studied maps in *The Times*, *The Daily Trident*, *The Illustrated London News* and other papers, until he was confused.

Westy was all right, that was the main thing, he told his mother when she came on the following Sunday, once again with Aunt Dora and his sister Doris.

When they rose to go, Hetty stayed behind to say, "Both Father and Mavis would like to see you, dear; perhaps now that you are a little stronger——?" She stopped, seeing his face. "Of course, they would not both come at the same time—— What is it, dear, won't you tell me?"

"Well you know I can't get on with either, don't you?"

"But they are both so very proud of you now, Phillip—— So is your Uncle Hilary. Well, anyway, there's no immediate hurry. Goodbye, and don't forget your prayers, will you? I am sure the dear little crucifix from Thildonck has brought you safely through. You will never never lose it, will you?"

"I'll try not to, Mother. Don't turn round, someone is coming —— O, why must you?" for Hetty had turned her head. Down the ward, dignified and smiling, came Mrs. Neville, accompanied by a thin woman with a patient sweet face, who turned out to be Mrs. Hudson, the friend she had often spoken about, from Highgate. Phillip's heart felt lighter; though he sighed when his mother said, after talking to them for a brief time, that she must go. He felt he had turned her away. Mrs. Neville saw this, and did not stay more than five minutes: a quiet, pleasant time for Phillip. He liked Mrs. Hudson at once, she was so sympathetic and understanding, in manner rather than words, for she said very little. Mrs. Neville, too, was quite different from the rather boisterous person he had known hitherto. She seemed to feel the ward was a sad place, with all the frames and "boxes" keeping broken bones and legs away from the bed-clothes, for he felt a tear fall on his cheek when she bent over to kiss his forehead, before leaving.

When Uncle Hilary came he began by saying that although they both had German blood in their veins, it was not anything that one could be proud of, particularly at the present time. Then he went on to say something about cigars and cognac to torpedoed sailors, and coffee and chocolate to survivors and children of the massacre at Dinant.

"Well, Uncle Hilary, I do know that they gave some of our chaps cognac after our attack on Hulluch and Hill 70 had failed at Loos, last year, and——"

"That's just the point, Phillip! They shoot you down first, then treat you like that!"

"But it was sporting of them, all the same, Uncle! If they had attacked us, we wouldn't have gone out to help them afterwards. Look what happened last Christmas Eve in France!"

"What did happen?"

"According to Willie, who was there, they thought it was going to be a truce as in 1914, and were singing carols and lighting

Christmas trees when our artillery opened up and blew them all to hell. I don't call that sporting."

"Well, there's another side to that, Phillip. They're deeply engaged in Russia, and it pays them to keep their army fighting to a minimum in the west. But wait until Russia collapses—then you see if they'll be wanting truces and Christmas trees in the trenches!"

"But who is 'they'? You're talking of the German High Command. I'm talking of the ordinary regimental soldiers."

"I'm talking of the two sides of the German character, or nature, Phillip," said Hilary, leaning over the bed in persuasive earnestness. "The side that ruthlessly massacres innocent civilians *en masse*, and then immediately afterwards hands coffee to the survivors—stolen from the estaminets, no doubt—and chocolate to the unhappy little children. Chocolate, in compensation for the death of their parents! Think of it, Phillip! They stop firing, and then play the host."

"Well, they also stopped firing when our stretcher bearers came out to help bring in the wounded before La Boisselle, Uncle. I was there, I saw them!" said Phillip, in a tremulous voice. He felt he could not breathe.

"I am glad for your sake, Phillip," said Hilary, trying to speak amiably. "Still, one isolated example does not alter the fact that they are a brutal people by nature, despite superficial kindness. One swallow does not make a summer, you know."

Swallows usually come in April, in the spring, thought Phillip, faintly. He felt himself to be feeble as frayed blotting-paper.

"Well, I told your Father I'd have a word with you in the matter. He is bothered by your attitude to the Germans, but I told him that it was nothing to worry about, especially as you'd done your duty so splendidly against them. It's our life as a nation or theirs, you must never forget!"

Phillip lay back limply, fighting remotely against the wire in himself becoming a thin, thin scream.

"Now, before we leave the subject, just let me tell you one more thing, nothing to do with bloodshed this time, Phillip. It concerns the way they have treated, and still are treating, Belgium, which is a small country, and can hardly be regarded as having been a threat to Germany in any way—of course the Germans want the mouth of the Scheldt, which is also the mouth of the Rhine, and all it entails, with the port of Antwerp, and other facilities. Well, the economic stifling process was put into operation as soon as war broke out, when the Federation of German Manufacturers, *die Grossindustrielle*, urged that they should pay no taxes for the continuance of the war, but that the Belgians and French of the occupied areas should pay instead, by fines imposed by the Military Governor. This was pure extortion, Phillip. It was continued until March this year, when the idea of 'speedy victory' was modified, by the non-success of their land and sea strategy, and they had to float war-loans. You know what they are, I expect?"

The head on the pillow nodded.

"I won't go on, but I must say this, Phillip. The war is by no means only the fighting, you know. Well, about money, which is the sinews of war. These loans the Germans have floated in Berlin, carry interest to be paid out of reparations to be imposed *when* they have won the war! If that isn't a swindle, what is? The bonds will be worthless in a defeated country, of course. Meanwhile another kind of swindle is taking place. Big firms are now clearing off their debentures, using the inflation of the mark. Krupps have done this, and have made a profit of ten million pounds, in our currency, by the manoeuvre."

Phillip saw Gran'pa Turney in his mind, and felt reassurance coming into him.

"But aren't debentures usually held by the family that owns the firm, Uncle? Grandpa's debentures are, anyway; that's why he wants them to remain in the family. And isn't Krupps a family concern?"

"Well, if they held all the debentures, they wouldn't want to sell them, would they, Phillip? No, take it from me, it's a swindle, and shows up the entire character of the financial-military combine, the pan-Germans, who want to rule the world, to aggrandise the Prussians!"

Phillip felt like the small boy Uncle Hilary had trapped between his legs, chuckling as he had tried desperately to escape.

"Well, there you are! That's what we are up against, and what you fellows are helping to destroy, in a war to end war, to destroy militarism for ever. Well, Phillip, my advice is, don't bother your head further about sympathy for Germans. You do your job and let others take care of the rights and wrongs of how the war is being run. You've done well, you're a credit to the family, and just to show my appreciation, I propose to buy in your name one hundred pounds of war loan, to be left in trust for you until you are twenty-five."

When he was alone again Phillip lay back with closed eyes, wondering why Uncle Hilary always made him feel as though he were nothing.

"You've been talking too much," said sister, coming to stand by his bed. "Now try and get some sleep." She put her hand on his forehead. "As I thought, you've got a bit of a temperature, naughty boy! That comes of talking too much!" Flicking a thermometer, she put the bulb under his tongue. "There, it's up to a hundred and one! Any pain?"

"No, sister, thank you."

Reading again, later that evening, a letter from cousin Willie, who had been in the attack when La Boisselle and Ovillers had been taken at dawn from the southern flank at Contalmaison, and the high ground before the outskirts of Pozières had been reached by the end of the day—the final objective of July the First—he felt a wild regret that he had not been there. He saw the battlefield as in a dream, something that could never be properly realized, which made his breast ache with all longing when he tried to enter in upon it, silent and without physical movement, the red-hanging brick dust over the villages, the sun shining down on the still, still bodies of the dead: the same sun, but O so different, whose light was reflecting from the polished wooden floor of the ward and making a haze about its flowers, coming in under the blinds half-drawn against the August sun staring down upon the hot baked brick wall and white-painted sill of the open window beside his bed, with the murmur of traffic in the London street below. In his mind he was a spirit, feeling the radiant heat of the chalk of the trenches; cooling himself in the flicker-rippling Ancre. O, to be able to see it all again, a ghost world of gun-flashes at night. O to see it all, to grasp all of it, without violence, without pain; to share the marching and the singing of the living that were part of the great dream of life and death.

It was a strange feeling to be out of bed, his foot still itching inside its plaster cast, with a pair of crutches, and sister beside him, to explore a new world. The figures in bed, the beds, tables, doors —all looked so different. It was quite a surprise to realize that there was a passage outside the door, leading in two directions, instead of it being a sudden-appearance place of doctors, nurses, wheeled stretchers, and food trolleys. It was sad that the world seen from the safety of bed had already vanished.

He visited other officers still prone, and sat beside them, and they talked about anything but the war. It was fun to play draughts with them, and have little championships. They were not the dangerous or bad cases, which were in another ward.

The morning came when his foot was taken, pallid and warped, out of its plaster cast. Exercises began in another room between parallel bars, the crutches put away—a perilous feeling, to be all alone in a polished, swaying room. Then the crutches were exchanged for a walking-stick with a rubber ferrule, although his leg still felt to be hooked to him, rather than part of his body. Further exercises brought the aching flaccid muscles back into tension.

The London Gazette had his promotion in its close-printed columns one morning. He was a senior subaltern! He cut two cloth stars off his spare tunic and asked for a needle and khaki thread. The sister asked him what for, and when he told her, took away stars and tunic, and returned it with the new rank upon the cuffs, leaving the mark of the old star unfaded in the middle of the twin stars. It was a wonderful sight, at which he glanced again and again during the day.

Sooner than he imagined he was one of a party of officers taken to the theatre. They saw *Chu Chin Chow*; two days later, they went to see *Romance*. They were taken to a tennis party in Regent's Park, where he met delightful people, who sent their motors to fetch parties of officers from the hospital, and take them back again.

"I think we can let you out for an hour or so this afternoon," said the doctor one morning. "Only no drinking of spirits, mind!"

Joyfully he took a taxicab to Charing Cross Station and in the train smelt, by the open window, the familiar smells of fish-glue, vinegar, sulphur, hops, tan-yards, and a new one of iodoform. Then the junction, and the line parallel to the brook running polluted and dead behind tattered drab fences of flowerless back-gardens, and so to the old dark station with its old dark dog-chasing cat, the walk through the village and up Charlotte Road, under the same old peaceful chestnuts, past summer-dulled privet hedges, rain-worn oaken gate-posts, up the asphalt of Hillside Road with its cracks where, thank God, pink convolvulus flowers were growing; and at last to the so-narrow gateway and the porch beyond.

Mrs. Bigge, Mrs. Feeney, Gran'pa and Aunt Marian, Mrs. Pye fatter than ever, and—a dared visit to Turret House. Mrs. Rolls said how thin he was, and so much more grown up. Helena arrived from the hospital, and he was asked to stay and take pot luck. He sat on his hands when he was not eating, trying to say acceptable

things, feeling strained into a state half-dream, half-shyness, feeling
he was talking jerkily, flippantly, about his fellow patients, doctors,
nurses—and at ten to two when she had gone down the road again
—rather a relief that she was gone—he felt he had said and done
everything to put himself in the worst light.

The day came when he could walk almost normally except for a
tight feeling when he sat down. He thought to go and see his father
and sister at Head Office in Haybundle Street, but when he saw the
building, and the smiling moon in silver hanging over the door, he
felt he could not face Martin the messenger there, after all Mavis
had said about everyone at H.O. knowing what had happened on
Messines Hill; so he crossed over and walked through the streets
and Leadenhall Market, meaning to call in at The Grapes, and see
Westy's parents. It was after closing time, so he went on into
Fenchurch Street and to Wine Vaults Lane, where Mr. Howlett
said,

"You could not have come at a more opportune moment,
Maddison! Downham's up in town. He and Hollis and I are
going to have tea at four o'clock at the Crutched Friars' Mecca
café. It's my birthday. We always meet there once a year, you
remember? You'll come? Splendid! How's the leg, better? Oh,
good. Be here about ten to four, will you? You must tell me all
that's happened."

Phillip went on to see Eugene in his warehouse in Houndsditch,
where he learned that he was on holiday; and so he sat in the
churchyard in Gracechurch Street where often in the past he had
eaten his sandwiches, among others who had always seemed to be
poor, in that dark place splashed by pigeons.

He found Mr. Howlett and the others at the bottom of coffee-
smelling stairs, in a large room with tables topped by brown
glazed tiles, some scattered with dominoes. Downham was in
field boots and spurs; and noticing Phillip's limp, he made a joke
about his wound.

"Shot in the arse, were you? What were you doing, running
away again?"

"Come, come," said Mr. Hollis, sharply. "That's not fair!
Anyway, you've damned well taken care not to present your precious
carcase anywhere near the Germans!"

"Well, how do you get on with your father now?" asked Mr.
Howlett.

"I haven't seen him yet, Mr. Howlett."

The next day the doctor said, "You're better. I'm sending you for a Medical Board at Caxton Hall tomorrow."

He was given six weeks leave, to be spent in a convalescent home.

"Go and see Georgiana Lady Dudley," said Matron, on his return. "She'll fix you up at a place in the country. Tell her where you want to go. She's got lots of places on her list. Don't be put off by her painted face, she's a dear old thing."

Almost from the beginning of the war private fortunes had been expended to equip hospitals, in both England and France, by many of the great and famous hostesses of Society for the sons and brothers and cousins of their own and their friends' families, whose names were beginning to fill the casualty lists . . . until now all were spilled away, and the names in the Roll of Honour were of strangers.

But England had need of them, and soon after the Battle of the Somme began there were few country houses which had not answered the appeal of Georgiana Lady Dudley and her friends, to open their doors to men of the New Armies recovering from wounds and sickness. By the month of August over a hundred officers a day were being sent to houses great and small, from Sutherlandshire and Caithness in North Britain, to Kent and Sussex and Hampshire in the South, Lincolnshire, Norfolk, and Essex in the East, to Devon and Cornwall in the West Country.

At first, it had been possible to discriminate: to send only men of one's own class—those who had been at the only three possible schools, and who therefore knew good form—to one's friends' places as guests; while the other kind, the vast majority of half-and-half people, could be disposed of to the smaller places—dower houses, manor houses, and even Highland lodges—where they would be able to amuse themselves in their own ways. For the deluge had arrived.

With a pile of papers, telegraph forms, and card indices before her on the desk, Georgiana Lady Dudley disposed of one temporary officer after another, as he came with respectful affability, as though assured in his new status, before her. For Georgiana Lady Dudley induced no feelings of awe as she sat, her luxuriant white hair crowned by a circular floral hat, and her complexion all cream and roses, on a hard wooden office chair giving forth, but not radiating, an impersonal, all-enveloping geniality: this hostess of Edwardian luncheon and dinner parties of from a mere dozen or score of faces to hundreds of guests, many of them enveloped with the spirit of the cream and roses of the earth, upon whom had fallen the bloom of gold of hundreds of thousands of sovereigns every year from carbonised vegetation lying in seams below their estates and properties.

What magic, what splendour, what heights above the congested areas of surburban living did the presence of Georgiana Lady Dudley suggest to many of the temporary officers of the New Armies! The very name was a necklace of precious sparkling jewels to some who sat before her.

What did Georgiana Lady Dudley think of them? They were the half-and-half people, so very polite, poor dears, so formal, trying hard to appear above themselves; but all was forgiven them for being what they were. Had they not come out of their unknown places and answered the call, from their obscure streets and small houses, to replace, with their plain names in the casualty lists, those of the splendid young men who had fallen in 1914 and 1915?

This lady with the face of youth and the bright friendliness of age sat behind a desk, her floral hat nodding and moving but never jerking as she arranged the immediate future of captains of eighteen and subalterns of forty-five, in slacks and trews, kilts and breeches, pale cotton of Indian Army and double-breasted "maternity jacket" of Flying Corps; dear boys all—a tick against a long list, a name written down with a gold pencil set with diamonds, and one more was sped to Yorkshire or Cumberland, to Dorset or Flint, to a house by the sea or a lodge on the side of a strath, to have the time of his life.

From the watershed of the Somme, from charred wood and desolated valley, amidst the fragmentation of steel and flesh and the dust of detonated village hanging in the sun, was coming the thought that would bring not only the end of the old order, but the end of ideas that had endured a thousand years.

"Devon, or is it Devonshire, it's so muddling," said Georgiana Lady Dudley brightly, as she flipped a card index. "It's Devonshire cream and cider, one supposes, and also the Devonshire Regiment, but no doubt you will know. Now let me see," she went on briskly, as her eye ran down a list. "All the places in Devon appear to be filled. What have we here—Dorset? No? Derbyshire? No? Durham? No. I agree. Much too cold and smoky, and those everlasting east winds! Denbigh? Very rainy, and the south-west blows all the time. Flint? No? How about Gloucestershire?"

Discomposed by her bright, bird-like speed, Phillip tried to force himself to ask if he might be allowed to go to his aunt's cottage at Lynmouth, and have treatment from a local doctor. Willie, whom he had visited in St. George's, had suggested this for both of them. He felt more uncomfortable when the amazingly alert Georgiana Lady Dudley looked at a gold watch hanging on a diamond and platinum brooch inside her jacket pocket. It was almost one o'clock, and he was the last to be seen.

"I would rather go to Devon, ma'm, if it isn't giving you too much trouble. Perhaps I could come again, later on, when it is not so inconvenient?"

"Miss Catesby, have we any places in Devon, in this morning's post? We have? How splendid!" Papers were put before her. "Here is the very thing, perhaps. Sir George Newnes' Hollerday House, Lynton. Two beds will be vacant in a week's time. I'll mark you down for one of them. We drove through Lynton once, when I was a gal, from Lee Abbey. I expect you know it, high above the cliffs, with Wales just across the water? The hills were terrifying, and we all had to get down from the coach and walk. The wheels caught fire! What was the name of the spot! Watersmeet, was it? Of course. Very well, your Matron will be notified."

Georgiana Lady Dudley gave him a brilliantly enamelled smile of dismissal.

"Thank you very much, ma'm. I am afraid I am rather a nuisance, but I have a great friend, a cousin, due to be b-boarded at Caxton Hall any day now. I wonder if it would be possible for him to have the other bed? He asked me to put in a word, I m-mean, to enquire for him."

"What a close family yours must be, Mr. Maddison. How nice that you all want to be together. Where is your cousin? At St. George's Hospital, Lancaster Gate. Very well, if you will give my secretary particulars, she will arrange it. Good morning!"

Georgiana Lady Dudley, a new light upon her face, cleared as it were for action—she was having luncheon with some friends who were planning a counter-attack on Mr. George, "the Little Welsh lawyer", who was preparing one more of his low-down tricks against dear Henry Asquith—left without further thought of the young man whose face she no longer saw. Nor did she realise that he had sprung up to open the door for her: accustomed to footmen all her life, she no more thought about doors than Phillip had about those in his ward until he had learned to walk again, on crutches.

Chapter 22

THREE TEAS

"I've got a week before I go," Phillip told Mrs. Neville. "Nothing to do, really."

"Have you been down to Freddy's, dear?"

"Once, but it seemed so different. I don't want to go again."

"Ah, I expect you have outgrown your old haunts, Phillip. One does, you know, as one grows up. Must you go now? Well, come to tea tomorrow, will you?"

She was determined not to tell him that Lily had been to see her. The sooner the whole thing was forgotten the better, for the girl's sake. The boys could look after themselves. It was Lily who had her sympathy now. That brute Keechey! If she ever came face to face with him, she would give him a piece of her mind—and her umbrella, too, and let him sue her for assault and battery, if he dared! Anyway, Lily was safe from that beast now, for she had become a Roman Catholic, and was (Mrs. Neville thought) a changed woman. So Mrs. Neville was resolved not to mention Lily in any way at all.

This good resolution having been made, and what she thought of as her higher self having been satisfied, Mrs. Neville's lower self began to feel curious. What *had* happened between her son and Lily? Was it as she had suspected, that Lily had been anybody's— including Eugene's—for the asking, before she met Phillip and fell in love with him? Such devotion as Lily had revealed, though the girl had tried to hide it, might have come from either of two things: from an attachment of the animal that was in every woman to her mate after he had satisfied all her feelings, or from a spiritual love that was based on the highest aspirations of the soul. Mrs. Neville liked to think that it was the soul of Lily that had been touched by the sweetness and gentleness in Phillip—oh yes, of course it was! What was she thinking of? Just because Lily worked in a laundry, did that mean that she was not capable of the highest aspirations of the soul? How was she herself any better than Lily? Hilda, my girl, watch your step, or you'll be growing into what Maude Hudson's husband used to call an intellectual snob!

Having come to the conclusion that she was no better or worse than anyone else, Mrs. Neville felt life to be serene. If only people could know themselves properly, how much easier and simpler living would be!

She went into the kitchen to prepare her tray for tea: best teapot, early Georgian, the ivory knob to its lid yellow with age, the pawnbrokers' scratches on its bottom adding to its history.

While she polished it, Mrs. Neville had the wild idea of asking Phillip, when he arrived, to take a note down to Lily's house in Nightingale Grove, inviting her to call that evening. The idea so overpowered her that she had to sit down.

My God, she said to her image in the looking-glass, a few minutes later, as she powdered her nose and cheeks, whatever will you be thinking next? What part was she intending to play, that of a scheming *duenna* out of *The Decameron*? Yes, Hilda my girl, you may well look like that! All you really want is to find out what happened, not by questioning, which is the refuge of the banal, as Mr. Hudson used to say, but by watching the two young things together. Hilda, you are a monster!

Ah well, aren't we all? she said to herself as, having cut a plateful of thin cucumber sandwiches, and then another of Phillip's favourite Old Sea Dog Bloater Paste ("Refuse all imitations"——how they had laughed over that on the label!—Phillip declaring that they were special bloaters because caught by the Old Sea Dog diving overboard and bringing them up in his mouth, like a seal) Mrs. Neville carried her tray to her sitting room, and put it on the table. Beside the Georgian teapot was the tortoiseshell tea-caddy that had been given to her husband for a wedding present by one of the Nottingham uncles. Then came milk jug, sugar bowl, and kettle pivoted above a spirit lamp.

Thus fortified by her *lares et penates*—the phrase, picked up at Highgate in the Hudson *salon*, gave her a pleasant feeling of culture—Mrs. Neville awaited the arrival of her guest.

The familiar exhaust beats of *Helena* came up the road. With a series of whistling hisses, as the valve was held up, it stopped. The tall figure in white flannels and Donegal tweed jacket got off and leaned the footrest on the kerb.

"Hullo, Mrs. Neville!"

"Let yourself in, will you, dear?" the creamy voice said from the open window, as the key fell on the lawn.

She listened as he climbed up the stairs: yes, as she had thought the day before, one foot did thump more than the other.

"Ah, just like old days, Mrs. Neville!" he said, seeing the tea tray.

"Help yourself if you're hungry, Phillip. I'll go and get the hot water."

He got up at once, saying, "I'll fetch it, Mrs. Neville."

"But your leg, Phillip——"

"Oh, the stiffness is almost gone. In fact, I thought about playing tennis again, only——"

She waited until he returned, when he filled the silver kettle with steaming water, afterwards lighting the spirit lamp for her. Then he sat back in the armchair.

He looked tired and dejected, she thought.

"Only——? You must not try and do too much all at once, you know."

"Oh, my leg's all right. But I made such a fool of myself just now. I'd go back to France tomorrow if I could. Thank God I'll be in Devon soon."

"I expect it will take some while for you to re-adjust yourself, you know, Phillip."

"Oh, it's not that, Mrs. Neville. It's my idiocy in trying to join St. Simon's Tennis Club. It's Mother's fault, in a way, though I must blame myself."

"Why shouldn't you join the Tennis Club? I don't understand, Phillip."

In a satirical voice directed against himself he told her that he had gone round to see if Helena was playing; and not liking to be seen hanging about outside, had walked through the gate and watched through a gap in the trees. A set was in progress on the court, Helena and Milton, whom he had known at school, playing against two others. She had waved her racquet at him, and smiled. When the set was over, she had introduced him to the secretary, also the churchwarden, who had just come in, with his wife, carrying a basket of tea things, and kettle and teapot, from the parish hall.

"Then like a fool I asked if I might join, Mrs. Neville. The secretary said that membership was limited to parishioners of St. Simon's church, and I must get someone in the club to propose me, and then someone to second me. Helena and Milton were standing by, and I think they were going to offer, when the secretary said, 'I wonder if it is tennis that is entirely the attraction, Mr. Maddison? I notice a certain name painted on the tank of your machine.' And Helena heard, Mrs. Neville, and turned away her head. I think she was laughing, as she went away with Milton. Damn! Damn! Damn! Why did I come home at all? What a bounder they must think me, with that name ostentatiously in gold paint on the tank!"

Mrs. Neville had never seen him so upset. His eyes stared, the nose seemed thinner, the cheek-bones more prominent. He had a look of Uncle Hugh on his face. What she had regarded as a rather prolonged case of love's young dream now seemed to be something much more serious. But *did* he love Helena? How could he *love* her, when he did not know her?

"'A bounder,' Phillip? My dear, you are anything but that. And surely you have proved yourself to the world now? Don't you know it?"

"Oh, that business on July the First was nothing! I *mean* nothing! It *was* nothing! We had to go over, and that was all; hundreds of thousands like me. No proof of anything there, Mrs. Neville. The others, who had never been in action, were optimistic; those who had been, were pessimistic. That's all. No, what I mean is that I seem to be two people, almost; one fairly serious and reliable, and the other a stupid sort of jack-in-the-box, doing things suddenly, thinking they might be a great joke, and then finding what a silly stupid fool I've been all the time! I've often wondered what made me set fire to Colonel Heycock's newspaper on my first guest night with the Cantuvellaunians at Heathmarket. It was a bounderish thing to do. I may have had something to drink, but I wasn't drunk; I just thought it would be damned funny. Whereas it was merely damned impertinent. And now this utter stupidity of mine, painting that name on the motorbike, and not realising how it would embarrass her!"

"I don't suppose she thought of it at all, Phillip, in that way. Why, most girls would be proud of having their names on——"

She stopped. It occurred to her that Phillip was right: it was *not* quite the thing. She pretended to think of something else, knowing how perceptive he was. "Of course, in the old days, a man tilting at the jousts would wear his lady's favour, wouldn't he? It was usually a glove, if I remember rightly. Not that I was ever there!"

"Yes, Mrs. Neville, but even the strangers who came to the tournaments were knights. I mean, they belonged—they had status. They weren't outsiders, like me."

He must be low, after the loss of blood, and the shock, she thought. What he wanted was feeding up, and to get away from himself. Desmond had been just the same; there had been that strange scene, when he had shown her Phillip's letter urging that bygones be bygones, and Desmond had become so bitter about his father. He had even asked her if he had been born illegitimate! Where did these boys get all their ideas from? It was the war: it had upset everything in life.

"You'll feel better after a week or two in Devon, Phillip. Mr. Hudson used to say that our physical condition had a lot to do with our thoughts, and that when a man had influenza was not the time to look at the Stock Exchange prices in the paper. That may sound banal, but there's something in it. Anyway, dear, don't you worry any more about the affair. What else did the secretary of the tennis club say?"

"I didn't wait to hear, Mrs. Neville. I damn well left straight away! I must have looked a frightful fool, from first to last."

"I am sure no one thought anything of it, beyond the fact that you had called to ask about joining, to make an enquiry. Oh dear, what the young have to go through. The more sensitive, particularly. You remember Lily, of course? Well, she came to see me, after suffering agonies, Phillip. What a sweet girl she is! I don't think I'm breaking any confidences by saying that she told me what she told you, about her past life, I mean. That is all over, I am glad to say. Yes, Lily is now a Catholic, and making a fresh start. No more Freddy's bar. No; Lily has a fine future, I think, if she can meet the right man. The trouble is, of course, that so many rogues look like the right man at first! Anyway, I hope that she won't allow herself to be imposed upon, for she has a very sympathetic nature."

Phillip was silent.

"Phillip, do you mind if I am very frank?"

"No, Mrs. Neville. I like it best when you are."

"Very well, dear. You know Lily loves you, don't you?"

"I didn't really know, Mrs. Neville."

"But can't you tell, Phillip?"

"Well, you see, in a way I was frightened of her."

"But why? Because she was in a public house?"

"Yes, I suppose so."

"You think that makes a difference, then? Oh, of course I know what you mean! A loose woman?"

"Well——"

"Did you feel attracted to her?"

"In a way, yes."

"But not as my son and Eugene felt—'what the gods provided'?"

"No, not in that way."

"What way then, dear?" said Mrs. Neville, very sympathetically.

"I was just very happy when I was with her. And knowing what had happened with Keechey, it didn't seem fair to—well—to impose myself on her."

"I see. Did the thought of Helena have anything to do with your attitude, Phillip?"

"No, I don't think so. Once or twice I felt that I would like—well—to give way to Lily, only I expect that seems weak and silly."

"Weak and silly? Oh, Phillip! Why, my dear, to be kind, to show tenderness, and to receive tenderness, is part of the love of God."

"Well, anyway, Mrs. Neville, I'm always thinking, my brain never stops. And if I see the other person's point of view, it kind of stops mine. If I have one. I just don't know."

"Do you want to see Lily again, Phillip?"

"I thought I would when I was in France, and again when I was in hospital; but now I'm home I don't think I shall."

"For her sake?"

"Not particularly."

"Then is it Desmond that's worrying you?"

"Oh no. If he wants to believe what he says he believes, he must continue to believe it, that's all I can say."

Mrs. Neville sighed. She was no nearer to understanding him; in fact the new personality he seemed to have developed baffled her thoughts. The silver tea kettle was steaming away. "Oh dear, while I've been talking, I've quite forgotten to give you your tea! It just shows how interesting a personality you are to me. Now do eat up everything you can see. You like China tea still, don't you? I got some specially for your homecoming."

After tea he asked her if she would like to hear his new gramophone records. "I've got some of Kreisler, and also some yellow and plum labels—Caruso, Galli-Curci, Scotti, some of Cortot playing Chopin, and Harry Tate's *Motoring*. Which shall we have first?"

"Harry Tate!" She uttered the little shriek she gave when changing gear from the sublime to the comic. "It's time we came back to earth!"

"You know, Mrs. Neville, I've been thinking that I ought to sell the motor-bike, before petrol becomes unobtainable. I must paint out that name on the tank first. I've sold the Swift already.

Private motoring will soon be a thing of the past. I see the laundry
van has already got a big gas-bag on its roof, and I hear others are
fitting vaporisers, to run on paraffin. I had a talk with a sergeant
of the A.S.C., in the Tillings Omnibus Depôt near Cutler's Pond.
His name is Martin; he was a crack racing driver before the war."

"And what did he say?"

"He told me that he held records for a Singer motor car on
Brooklands; also hill-climbs at Aston in Buckinghamshire. He's
got a huge bike with a twin-cylinder J.A.P. engine, with stub
exhausts. It makes a noise like four machine-guns. My hat, it was
fast—he told me it could do just under a hundred miles an hour."

"You're not going to buy that one, I hope!"

"Oh no. I just happened to see him with that bike, Mrs.
Neville. I asked him what he thought about fitting a vaporiser
for paraffin. 'Not on your life,' he said. 'It will cause unequal
over-heating, distortion will result, with consequent cracking of
the cast-iron pistons, and everything will be peppered inside that
isn't smashed.'"

He went on to tell Mrs. Neville that Martin, a small dark
man with a pale face and black moustache with waxed ends, had
said he might find him a customer for *Helena*. Being in the
A.S.C., they had no need to worry about juice.

"Well, see that you aren't swindled, Phillip. And if you see
Lily, you won't do anything to make her really fond of you, will
you? You know what I mean. She's too good to play about with."

"Ah, but you've aroused my interest, Mrs. Neville!"

"Oh, Phillip! Don't joke, for God's sake!"

What had she done? What a fool she was! She must say no
more, never mention the name of Lily again.

"Hullo," she said, looking out of the window, "Father's home
early from the allotment, isn't he? He only went down to it a few
minutes before you came. There he is, wheeling his barrow back,
Mother beside him. I wonder what can have happened?"

Hetty had gone with Richard to look at his allotment, carrying
a new wicker trug, a present from Hilary. For both of them it was a
very special occasion; for Richard had grown the first peas since
those planted in his very own garden plot which he had tended
nearly fifty years before, when a little bony thing in a tartan kilt;
and those peas were now to be picked in Phillip's honour for a
dinner with lamb chops that night, with a bottle of claret.

Reaching the allotment, Richard saw that most of his carrots had been dug up and taken away, together with the new potatoes, and all the peas and most of the lettuces; while the brassica plants looked to have been trodden down deliberately. The only signs of footprints were those of a large dog across a soft patch that Richard had left fallow.

He stared unhappily. "Never mind," said Hetty, trying to show sympathy, while hoping that she would not laugh, for the idea of a large dog helping itself to peas and carrots and potatoes arose ridiculously before her. Alas, she could not help the look in her eyes; and seeing it, Richard turned and walked back the way he had come. She caught up with him by the cemetery gates. He stood still while a funeral procession was going in.

"Well, that is the end of it. I shall not try again."

"I am sorry I laughed, Dickie, but *could* it have been a dog?" Then she caught a glimpse of an old man in the solitary cab following the hearse, and realised that it was the funeral of Mrs. 'Lower' Low. After some hesitation, she asked Richard if he would mind going on alone; and then she went through the iron gates of the cemetery, to stand near the thin figure in black bowed by the grave: the only other mourner.

Within the flat in Charlotte Road, Phillip was listening to Mrs. Neville, while the tolling of the cemetery bell came regularly through the open window.

"You know, dear, everything in this life comes full circle. The mills of God grind slowly, but they grind exceedingly small, as Mr. Hudson used to say. How time flies! It seems only the other day that Purley-Prout, that cunning rogue—what a scout-master! —was sitting in the very chair you are sitting in now, with brazen effrontery suggesting to me—to *me*, mark you!—that Lenny Low had invented the whole story, in order to get a new bicycle out of him! *That* poor little mite, as Lenny was then, with his legs not quite straight from early rickets, blackmailing that great big swanking bully! Can you imagine it! Purley-Prout was in a deadly funk, of course. He thought he would be sent to prison, I could see that. But the effrontery of it! I soon sent him packing!"

At this point all trace of sardonic merriment left Mrs. Neville's big pale face. In a subdued voice she continued, "Ah, we can laugh now, but the sequel was heart-breaking, Phillip, after Mr. Low had made Lenny return that half-sovereign Purley-Prout had given him. Lenny's poor, poor Mother! She was in debt to the money-lender, you know. She still owed the ten shillings

she had borrowed, years and years before, to buy Lenny a winter
suit, as you may remember; but the years of trying to get disen-
tangled had left their mark on her. She came here, you know, just
before her mind gave way and they took her away to the Infirmary. Her husband, she said, had refused to speak to her for
years. Her heart was broken. As long as I live, I shall never forget
the story that poor creature told me.''

Phillip saw tears dropping from her grey eyes. She dabbed them
with her handkerchief, sighed deeply, and after a few moments
continued, ''Poor thing, she was worn out, trying all those years
to make ends meet; for that old devil, her husband, kept her so
short that she had to make artificial flowers half the night, with
her failing eyes, too, by the light of a candle, for he would not let
her use the gas. Do you know the rate those flowers were paid for,
Phillip? Violets and buttercups, and other small flowers? Sevenpence a gross! Think of it! One hundred and forty-four to be cut
out, to be tied on wire which she had already wrapped with green
material; and in the end, only sevenpence to show for it all!
Roses, which took her a long time, were never more than three-
and-six a gross, she told me; but more often it was two shillings,
or half-a-crown. She used to work all day, while Mr. Low was at
his office, and seldom got more than four shillings for a week's
work. Then she had to take her flowers up by tram, paying her
own fare, to Clerkenwell.''

Mrs. Neville wiped her eyes. ''And all the time, Phillip, that
money-lender down in Limes Grove was charging her a shilling
a week interest on the ten shillings she had borrowed more than
six years before. She slaved away at her flowers, so that Lenny
should have enough food to eat, and proper clothes to wear.
Then she was told no more flowers were required—they went out
when feathers became all the rage—and so she used to make up
black tulips, and ragged roses, as they were called, with scraps of
black silk, for poor people to wear for mourning. She used to sell
them to one of the old women outside the cemetery gates, for
threepence the spray complete. It would take her, she told me,
the best part of a morning to make one spray, with her failing
eyesight.''

Mrs. Neville sighed. ''But there, she's at rest now, and thank
God for it, I say! Her eyes had a growth on them, and it affected
her brain; so they took her away. When your mother went round
to see if she could help in any way—what a *kind* woman she is,
Phillip!—there was old Low with his head on the table, crying.

Yes, and talking to his wife, too! Now that she was dead and it was too late! He was old when he married her, you know, and always believed that someone else was Lenny's father. So he didn't speak to her for years, eaten away with jealousy. Well, that is life, Phillip! My, what a morbid creature I am, crying like this, and upsetting you, and after all you have been through."

"I understand, Mrs. Neville. Life is tragic. One has to accept it. I wonder what happened to Lenny Low."

"Didn't you hear? He was killed on July the First, with many others of the Blackheath battalion of the London Regiment."

"Oh well," said Phillip. "He's out of it. That makes four of the old Bloodhounds gone west, Peter and David Wallace, then Horace Cranmer, now Lenny Low. I think I'll go and cheer old Low up. D'you think he'd mind? Hullo, there's Mother coming back. I'll go and see Mr. Low after tea. At home, I mean. Don't tell Mother I had another tea here first, will you? She said Father hoped I would be in to tea, though why, I can't understand. Well, it's been lovely seeing you again—au revoir—and many thanks!"

It was Phillip who helped Richard to forget the calamity of the stolen vegetables, which he heard about at the tea-table. He had seen some bundles of plants on the market stalls in the High Street as he had motored past; and leaving the table, went away on his motor cycle and was back again within five minutes, with two bundles, each of fifty. He put them into a bulb bowl he found under the kitchen sink, and having washed both bowl and plants, took them into the sitting-room.

Richard hardly knew what to say, the gift was as sudden as it was unexpected. The way it had happened made him feel resentment that the matter had been taken out of his hands: he did not want cabbages; it was not too late to sow swede turnips; he had been imagining them, pale green in beautiful rows, during his tea. It was, of course, very kind of Phillip: but why hadn't the boy asked him first? The pale green rows wilted away; he supposed he would have to plant the cabbages instead. Then he saw the scars on his son's hand and wrist, and his slight limp as he went round the table to his chair; and he imagined his baby son, smiling at him, liking him—and the cabbages in the bowl began to look much fresher.

"Well, that was kind of you, Phillip, I must say."

Phillip looked at his father's face for a moment without dropping his eyes: it was the first time he had looked without flinching, did he but know it, since he had been beaten at three years of age for opening his father's cases of butterflies without permission, and .breaking some of the frail coloured wings in an attempt to make them like fairies.

Now Phillip looked into pale eyes, faded almost to the colour of washing ammonia, and saw friendliness, timidity, hesitation; and was amazed, and discomforted, when Father's glance dropped first.

With determination he went round to see Mr. Low, finding him about to fry a kipper; and there he had his third tea, Mr. Low insisting on sharing the kipper with him.

Chapter 23

IONIAN COTTAGE

Phillip, sitting in a corner of a first-class carriage, *The Morning Post* on lap, remembered his journey to the West Country before the war as something in a world gone for ever. Khaki now took the place of corduroy and fustian; camp after camp of tents and wooden huts, convoys of lorries on the roads, and soldiers on every station. Brooklands was an aerodrome, with several triplanes of a new type flinging themselves about in the air over the track. He hurried to the next carriage, a third, to point out the exciting news to Polly and Doris. Might he not transfer to the R.F.C.? Pilots got 20s. a day, plus 5s. a day flying pay.

Doris had the picnic basket. After Salisbury he invited the girls into his carriage, which he called the mess, to eat with him; but no crumbs on the seats, please, or paper thrown under them; if the ticket inspector came round, they must pretend not to know him, but say they had made a mistake. Nobody disturbed them; Afterwards, to prove how fit he was, he turned inside out, holding to the luggage racks, and did various exercises, until the loose change dropped out of his pockets. It was time now for them to go back into their steerage cabin, and leave him alone to smoke the cigar he had bought at the kiosk on Waterloo Station.

Life was good. He had £110 in his account at Cox's, his convalescence at Hollerday House would cost him nothing, he had sold *Helena* for twenty-five pounds to an officer of the A.S.C. at the Omnibus Depot, and given Sergeant Martin a fiver for his part in the deal. They had exchanged addresses; after the war he would try his hand at motor-bike racing on Brooklands. Meanwhile life was more of an adventure than ever. Willie was coming to the convalescent home later on, and they would have a wonderful time together, fishing, swimming, and exploring the countryside. His other cousin, Percy Pickering, was also coming for part of his overseas leave. Poor old Percy, soon to be going out, a footslogger, into that hell.

Looking at his newspaper, he ran his eye down the column of *Awards*, and thus saw a familiar name, under the heading *Distinguished Service Order*.

> Lieutenant (temporary Major) H. J. West, M.C. (and bar) 3rd Battalion attd. 7th Battalion The Gaultshire Regiment. This officer has consistently shown high qualities of leadership and resource, combined with devotion to duty and complete disregard of his personal safety. In the attack on July 1 Major West led his companies close to the preliminary bombardment. When the guns lifted he showed exemplary dash, entering the first position before opposition could be effectively organised by the enemy. Leading his men on, he overcame the enemy's resistance in successive lines of trenches, and continued until the final objective was reached. The initiative displayed by this officer was the admiration of all ranks, and though wounded in the shoulder, he remained in command of the position won until ordered to the rear.

He hurried into the girls' third-class compartment, waving the newspaper, crying, "There you are! Westy was right! My God, why did I ever leave the Gaultshires? The attack of July the First failed practically everywhere else, but not where dear old 'Spectre' was allowed to use his napper! You won't understand what I am talking about, so goodbye!"

The train rushed on under the sun shining down upon the green fields and stubbles of Dorset, Somerset, and at last Devon. Here was the River Taw again, the thunder of carriages over iron bridges, with the brown shrunken waters of the river winding through the meadows, and then the marshes before Barnstaple. There they changed into the little light-gauge railway. Phillip started off in the first-class coach, as befitted his status; the girls in the yellow wooden third-class coach. Then, after Snapper Halt, he joined the girls. At Chelfham they all went into the glass coach. At Blackmoor Gate he rode beside the driver, and worked the throttle to Wooda Bay station. Then back into the glass coach, with its blue upholstery, for the arrival at Lynton. For an hour and a half the squat, tank-square engine with the brass funnel had puffed on and up, rising above oakwoods and steep coombe sides to the moor; now it was running down to its destination, the little wooden platform at the very end of the line, whereon a thin, tall Aunt Dora was waiting, smiling with her teeth protruding, her eyes pale and her hair grey but her voice soft and musical as ever.

"How good to see you all! And how kind of you to come all this way to see an old woman. You must be tired, Phillip, after all your adventures. And you are little Polly, how you have grown! And Doris, you have grown too! We will go down the cliff railway, it is only a step or two away. And we shall be seeing you, Boy, when you are rested, no doubt. You know the cottage, don't you? Was it only two years since you were here? Well, here is Buzzacott with the jingle to take you up the steep hill to Hollerday."

Phillip wondered which was Buzzacott and which was the Jingle. Was the pony, between the shafts of a small tub-like cart, called Buzzacott? Probably, by its appearance. Then the groom, or driver, must be Jingle. Beside the pony stood a foal. Amid exclamations by the girls, who tried to stroke the leggy young animal, small enough to be carried under a man's arm, Phillip got into the tub on wheels, to be taken forward at little more than a snail's pace, while the driver, a man as shaggy about the head as the pony, talked a language less comprehensible than that of the animal; for at least a whinney was a whinney. Dressed in corded coat and trousers, and old bowler hat, he sported mutton-chop whiskers, shaggy brows, and teeth that were but brown stumps; even so, Jingle was evidently a privileged person, for as they crept out of the station yard he put a clay pipe, with a horrible dark brown stain half way up the bowl, between his blue lips. The bowl, gurgling and faintly screeching, gave forth an acrid smell so strong that, when the procession, in silence save for the repeated breaking of wind by Buzzacott, left the high street of the town and turned up a steep slope to a lodge beside iron gates, Phillip decided to get out and walk.

He saw before him a stony lane leading up into a gloom of trees, so steeply set that the pony could hardly pull the tub, let alone Jingle. Very slow, clack by clack, the pony went on and up, past a row of monkey-puzzle trees, coming to a gorge, where the way had apparently been blasted through rocks. Slower and slower stepped the pony, issuing forth more and more salvoes of wind, shaking the whiskers of the driver, who sat and sucked his pipe for comfort and occasionally flipped the reins and squeaked something, in odd contrast to other expressions of a peaty, brackeny voice. After the next bend the way got so steep that the pony, with a final detonation, stopped altogether.

"What does it work on, compressed air?" enquired Phillip. "Seriously though, don't you think it's too much for such a small mare? And she's in milk, too."

"Ooh, 'er's used to'n maydeer. Sot yew doon in yurr beesade me," as he opened the small door at the back.

"God's teeth, Buzzacott can't pull us both!"

The groom rattled and squeaked with laughter. "A'y, tes a lazy 'oss what zweats vor zee th'zaddle!" he cackled. "Yesmye! Come yew in maydeer, sot yew beesade me, yew'm zo thenza dashel."

"I'm afraid I can't understand what you say, Jingle. Anyway, I'll help poor old Buzzacott by giving a shove behind."

This offer produced a throaty cackle, a hand like a root slapping a knee, a head held back and brown teeth stumps visible. When the pony stopped again a tangle of vocal chords issued past the gurgling pipe.

"Blarm'd if I c'n unnerstan' a bliddy word on what you'm telling maydeer! G'wan, g'wan!" The last two noises were directed towards the pony, who pecked slowly onwards, while Phillip pushed, and the driver sat still, except for an occasional shake of the reins.

The way became steeper. Phillip felt his heart thudding. As soon as he stopped pushing, the pony stopped.

"Yurr! Why don't ee ride upalong me, maydeer? There be plenty room voor two in this yurr jingle. Come yew in and sot yew down."

"I thought your name was Jingle!"

More laughter, and "Noomye! My name be Buzzacott."

"Really? I thought it was a case of the pony being buzzacott by name and buzzacott by nature."

Again the cackle, slap, and hawhawhaw of stringy laughter. Phillip went on, followed slowly by the little cart. He saw a stone house with a red-tiled roof through the thin pines. Breathing deep to steady his heart, he went to the oak door and pulled the bell. He thought it must be the matron who came, for she said, looking at his face, "Have you walked all the way up?

And you only just out of hospital with a leg wound? Where is Buzzacott? Didn't you see him at the station?"

"Yes, but I walked up for exercise."

"Well, I like that! We take the trouble to send the jingle down, and you walk up! Now straight to bed you go! And there you'll remain until Dr. Minstrel comes tomorrow and gives you permission to get up!"

"But I am up already, Matron," protested Phillip. "I've been up for weeks!"

"Not here, you haven't! Come now, orders were made to be obeyed."

"I quite agree, Matron, but might I be allowed to go down to Lynmouth and see a relation there, for a minute or two? I know the way down by the water lift, so I shan't strain my leg by too much walking."

"You can go tomorrow. You've had a tiring journey. Now I want you to take a hot bath. Dinner is at seven. You can have it on a tray in bed."

"I am used to having cold tubs in the morning, Matron, and a hot bath might open my pores too wide, and allow influenza germs in, perhaps?"

"Aren't you awkward! You're the second devil we've had back from France. The first one who came last week is enough of a handful, what with his fire-pail filled with flotsam, and his plans to attack the Germans every night. Now be a good boy, and try and help us, will you, and do what you are told without argument. It's my evening out tonight, and I've got a lot to do before then."

"What time does Dr. Minstrel show up? Before or after dinner?"

"Dr. Minstrel will be here at eleven o'clock tomorrow. Your room is number eight, at the end of the passage on the first floor."

He went upstairs and sat on his bed. Through the window could be seen vast levels of the Severn Sea turning purple in the westering sun. Tidal races ripped white around the feet of the Foreland precipice. The scene was one of lonely emptiness, in tune with the desolation of his life. What was life for, anyway? A mild terror of the great rocks and the sea and the sky possessed him. He must get out of the new prison as soon as he could, change into mufti, and have a few drinks. The girls and the cottage were dimmed in the feeling of universal desolation.

He looked at some books. They were by Ethel M. Dell,

Elinor Glyn, Charles Garvice, and Marie Corelli; nothing he wanted to read. Matron's footfalls came along the passage. He was relieved to see her face again.

"You look properly tired out! And wanting to exhaust yourself further! Now be a good boy and have a bath. You'll find a dressing-gown in the cupboard, and also a bath-robe, for if you want to go sea bathing. Dr. Minstrel's permission must first be sought, of course."

"Thank you, Matron. By the way, do you know when another officer of the same name as myself is coming?"

"William Beare Maddison? He's our third wounded case, and is due next week."

"What's the other chap from France like?"

"Piston? Oh, he's a mad devil."

"I see. Are there any more patients here?"

"Certainly! But they're all home service, thank goodness. What you need is a nice quiet time, and you'll get it here at Hollerday."

He felt more depressed than ever.

"Now I'll run your bath. The smell you'll smell will be Sanitas. It's bracing, as well as antiseptic."

When he had bathed he felt better. A nurse brought with his dinner tray a Late Extra copy of *The Globe* evening newspaper, which had come all the way from London by the same train as himself. It contained a violent attack on Asquith, blaming him for the "virtual failure of the Battle of the Somme".

At eleven o'clock next morning the doctor, who arrived on a pony, gave Phillip leave to get up, with orders to take things easily for the first week or two. As soon as he could he got out of the gloomy house and went down the cliff railway to the village below, to stroll around with the two girls until it was time to return up the watery cliff, green with ferns, for luncheon. Down again afterwards, and back in time for dinner; one more visit, up again by nine o'clock, and bed; a few pages of *Only a Girl* until, feeling sleepy, he turned the ivory button of the shaded lamp by his bed, and snuggled down to sleep. One more day, and Willie would be coming, and then Percy Pickering. Life could not be better.

Theodora Maddison had been using her cottage during the spring and summer months as a rest home in connexion with the "Mothers' Arms", the old public house turned into a *crèche* in the East End, where babies could be looked after while the mothers were out to work. During the early summer she had invited some of the mothers down for a change of scenery; but this had been a mistake. They missed the familiar streets and faces which helped them to bear grief, the suspense of their men being at the front. One of her visitors had heard that her husband had been killed on the Somme; for her the green glooms of the valley had been the very loneliness of death, the sea was grief itself, with no children to give consoling warmth. So back trooped the resting mothers, to find relief in known factory smells, dolman capes, black bonnets and lined faces, by which hope flowed back again.

So let Ionian Cottage be for the young people; and here they were, five young faces around her table, Percy and Willie having arrived the evening before, Percy for but three days. As soon as he arrived Dora saw by the bright eyes of Doris, and the bloom upon her cheeks, that the two young people were in love. She felt warm liking for Percy: an honest, rosy-faced country boy, a little slow perhaps, and with an ordinary mind, but that was all to the good; there was enough nervous tautness already in the family. How little Doris, stout defender of her mother against the paternal irascibilities, had come on! How glad she was that she had invited them all, these young people with their fresh young faces, in the very springtime of life. The continuity of a family was so important: all members of a family should come together at least once a year. Let them differ, by all means; but let them hold together, let them know the feeling of belonging to a family. Could she not persuade Dicky and John and Hetty to visit her also, as they had twenty-one years ago? Twenty-one years—it seemed little more than yesterday, that summer of 1895, when Phillip had been a baby, and Willie still in the aetherial world. They should, of course, meet in the old home at Rookhurst: but brother John was hopeless, with no feeling of responsibility as head of the family.

It had rained almost without break for a week; the mouth of the valley was overhung darkly, the river in spate, salmon running. Then the clouds lifted; but rain fell again, and in the dark of the valley Dora lost some of her feeling of hopefulness, and relapsed into her reflective mind, which had given up the struggle for a fairer world, and accepted the literature of the Ancients as a revelation of the inevitable fate of European civilisation. In this mood the happiness of the young people was poignant, so gay and care-free were they, regarding the war as something entirely apart from their lives. They appeared to accept it without question.

In Dora's mind the war had entered upon its most terrible phase; she realised now that it would be a long and bitter struggle. Once single-minded in opposing the war, her mind was now cleft: the run of her thoughts went in two directions; that no military tyranny must be allowed to dominate the world of Christendom; that the cousin nations of Europe were likely to bleed themselves to death. What new world could come, as many were saying, out of the chaos that so titanic a struggle must leave behind it? This lonely woman reflected upon the rivalries of the Hellenic City states, which had destroyed one another until the fairest and clearest light of the ancient world was extinguished. No, not wholly extinguished: Pallas Athene had survived, flying in the twilight from the sad ruins of Athens, to settle for awhile with the white bird of the Khristos, uneasily in the kingdoms of the West.

If only she could feel sure about the sole responsibility of Germany for bringing about the war! Surely in both cousin countries *hubris* had been long growing; materialism, based on coal and iron, had dulled and despoiled the plumage of owl and dove. Was Christendom, surely arising from the spirit of Hellenism, to sink forever under the machines of Armageddon, above the valley of Desolation, which history might well decide to have been the valley of the Somme? Where, even in one year's time, would be the faces around the cottage table, laughing now over games of rummy and nap, snakes-and-ladders, ludo, tiddlywinks and halma— bought at the village shop which was also the post-office—while it rained and rained outside. Would they be lost in the flames— that innocent, guileless country boy Percy, with his rosy cheeks, his slow speech? Phillip with his ready smile, his wit, his startling resemblance to the bust of Alcibiades in the Vatican at Rome, his look of trying to resolve some problem which he did not fully understand—his mind still clouded, an effect, perhaps, of having been the unhappiest small boy she had ever known? Willie with his warm, brown-eyed eagerness, his quick, intelligent movements? Were these faces fated to vanish in their generation, with the singers, the poets, the splendid young men who had already fallen, voices of a generation doomed before it could come fully to flower—Rupert Brooke, Julian Grenfell, and unknown others whose deathless verses would, in Time, be all that remained of a generation lost in the holocaust?

"Have you still got the copy of Rupert Brooke's poems I sent you, Boy?"

"Oh yes, Aunt Dora."

"What do you think of the 1914 sonnets?"

"I think they are very fine, but—— Well—it's only my opinion, of course—probably quite wrong——" He looked uncertainly at her. "Yes, I think they are very fine."

"What are?" asked Willie. Dora told him and he said promptly, "Yes, but they could only have been written before Gallipoli and the Somme."

"I think he's right," said Phillip. "Also Julian Grenfell's *Into Battle*."

"I am glad you are not afraid to speak your minds," said Dora, coming between them, and taking an arm of each. "I am most interested to hear what your generation has to say. So far I know you only by what your poets have said. Won't you tell me more? What do you think about it all, Phillip?"

His mind winced; imagination fluttered hopeless into the void. Dora sensed this. "I expect the thought of the war is too overwhelming—it will take years to see it in perspective. And why should you have to think about what you have passed through, to satisfy an old woman's curiosity? Now I do declare," she said, going to the window, "I see the sun coming out! That is one of the virtues of our West Country weather; one moment a sky black as your hat, as they say in the village, and then the clouds lift, their tails drag, and lo! suddenly it might be the Aegean!"

"Well, with all due respect the Aegean is one place I don't want to see again," said Willie.

When he had gone away Dora, who felt herself rebuffed by her younger nephew's manner, said to Phillip, "I wonder if you can spare a moment to glance at a book I have here, before you go for your walk."

She put a large book on the table, containing photographs of sculptures ranging from the ancient to the modern world, beginning in Greece, continuing past the Dark Ages to the Renaissance, and ending in a Paris garden. She hoped he would be interested; he was more composed than Willie, who was too restless, too taut. She was happy to see Phillip settle down to the book, apparently finding it interesting. When he had come to the end she asked him which period he liked best. He said that he preferred the last statues, then the ones in the middle, and the early ones last of all—Rodin, Donatello, Phidias.

"Now that is most interesting! You are for the romantic, rather than the classic. Do you know what I mean?"

"Yes, I think so. It was explained to me by my colonel, Jasper Kingsman. He said that the classic is the hard, objective line, the romantic the tender, subjective line."

"Well, can you see the difference between Rodin and Phidias?"

"One is beautiful; the other is beyond the beautiful. But both dream, you know."

"How well you express yourself! In saying that you reveal the classic basis of your mind! You understand both subjective and objective attitudes."

"I like both Rodin and Phidias."

"Phidias, to me, is perfection. He was responsible for the temple of Athena in the Acropolis—you have heard of the Parthenon?"

"Only just."

"Such genius of course caused jealousy, and Phidias eventually was accused of impiety, in having put both his own likeness, and that of his patron Pericles, on the shield of Athena the goddess— what in a later age would be called blasphemy. So he was cast into prison, where he died of disease—the greatest sculptor of the ancient world. But that is the idiom of history, of all the poets and the great men, in any age. We have to accept it. It is the spirit of man at its highest expression, confronted by ordinary men. But you will be wanting to join the others in their bathe. I must not ride my hobby horse."

"It is the winged horse, Aunt Dora!"

She was charmed by his grace and courtesy, and felt herself no longer to be the odd one out of the family. For the rest of the morning, while the young people were away enjoying themselves in the sun, she felt no longer to be a woman lost to life in her own aloneness, which had become loneliness. Soon, soon, she had been thinking, soon the young faces would be gone, and the cottage would reveal itself, in appalling moments, to be a home without atmosphere; it was an empty cottage, spiritually speaking; it was bare, without a soul. Now, it had a living soul; the world was eternally young, despite its shadows.

Why had she allowed herself to be downcast before? Was her mood taken from the running noises of the stream below, the water everlastingly hurrying, blindly, despite its clearness when no rain had fallen, to the sea, its blind parent? The sea, "the unnumbered smile of ocean" of her youth, now blind, for ever set upon its task of reducing rock to sand, and sand to dust? Water in the end wore away the hardest stone.

Deeply within her, Dora was afraid of her cottage; she feared something intangible about it; an indefinable remote dread haunted her, as though the Erinyes, avenging spirits of twilight, dwelt in the dark glen above the village.

"Your colonel sounds a nice man, Boy," she said, when they returned.

"He's dead now, of course. Our other colonel was a great character—'Spectre' West. He was a classical scholar, too."

It was the first time he had spoken to her of the war.

"Do tell me more about them, if you feel like it."

"Jasper Kingsman was a classical scholar at Balliol. So was his friend Father Aloysius, a Catholic padre—the troops all called him 'Father'. He went over the top with his battalion, reading his breviary. His real name is Llewellyn Vaughan-Herbert. He was also at Balliol, but later, and knew Julian Grenfell. It was wonderful to hear Father Aloysius and Jasper Kingsman talking; they were very great friends, but always so polite, in an easy sort of way, all the time."

"What did they say, can you remember?"

"Well, vaguely. Jasper Kingsman saw the Christian religion as something grafted on to pagan rites, and bits of older religions, as described in Frazer's *Golden Bough*. I think it was called that. He said that it was all part of man's spiritual life; but Father Aloysius said that Christ's coming was a complete revelation, the first, the only, the final truth revealed by God. He said the fact that other superstitions and beliefs existed, and had existed until they passed with the civilisations which had engendered them, made not the least difference: they were limited, temporary truths, while Jesus had brought the whole, or permanent truth. But they didn't argue about that."

" 'Vaguely', you say! I think you have understood the whole of what was said. And what lucidity you have, to be sure. It's amazing to me how your outlook has developed during the past year or so. Both your Colonel and Father Aloysius seem to have been splendid men. They are both dead?"

"Jasper Kingsman is. Another friend was 'Spectre' West. He gave me this book."

"What a splendid gift! The *Everyman Library* is a most excellent series."

"Would you like to borrow it?"

"May I? How kind of you."

Dora knew it well; but she looked into it as though she had seen it for the first time.

"I think I'll go and find the others now, Aunt Dora. We're going to bathe this afternoon, when the tide is right in."

"You will be most careful, won't you? The currents are dangerous."

The tides in the Bristol Channel ran so fast that they gave a permanent cant to the paddle steamers plying between Cardiff, Swansea, Ilfracombe and Lynmouth before the war. The summer sky was blue, reflecting its colour upon the waters flowing into the harbour. Walking on the quay, with its crab-pots and nets, they put up a greater black-backed gull, which flew with weighty slowness of wings to a post marking the channel, where sat another black-back, presumably its mate, for the newcomer soared up, and with wings held gracefully aloft to hold the air, dropped lightly down to sit upon the other bird's back. For a few moments the under-gull put up with this, then giving way under the weight, dropped down and flew to the next post, leaving the usurper upon the pole.

"You see!" said Willie. "The soldier's philosophy also applies to the gull world."

"I bet she was his wife," said Doris. "How like a man!"

"Here, I say," said Percy, looking at her with simple eyes.

"Ah, Percy, don't forget that probably he's been feeding her all the while she was sitting on the eggs, so why should she take his armchair? Down with votes for women!"

"I don't think he was very nice," said Polly. "He thought only of himself." She tossed her head at Phillip.

"Apart from all rotting, Polly, it was probably the bird's post, and the second gull was using it as a vantage point, to rob the first gull of anything it found in between the boulders at low tide. I saw a gull the other day snatch a sea-trout of over a pound, working its way up the stream."

"Well, what can the gull have been looking for now it's high tide."

"Fish heads and guts the cottagers chuck into the river, or other things."

"Do they really? Then I certainly don't want to bathe here," said Polly.

"Why not, Polly? What's wrong with a fresh fish head?"

"Anyway, if I had been the bird on that post, I would have stood up for myself," said Doris. "I hate all bullies!"

At this moment the bird which had been turned off its post flew back and pitched upon the back of the usurper. They all laughed at the ridiculous sight, which was interrupted by a salmon leaping straight up out of the water, a few feet from the quay. As it fell back with a smack the two black-backs, uttering gruff bass cries, flew across the harbour to the far bouldered shore, to stand together at the water's edge.

Phillip and Willie watched them from the quay, with Percy. The girls had gone on, to get undressed behind some boats drawn up, with a pile of crab-pots, under the cliff.

"I wonder what made it jump like that."

"They say to knock off the sea-lice, Phil. The lice suck blood around the vent, and it must itch like hell. After a day up the river the lice die. They can't live in fresh water."

"What a lot you know. I wish we'd lived in the country."

"But you know a great deal about the country."

"All picked up from books at the Free Library, my dear Coz!"

"You're jolly lucky to have one to go to!"

This led to talk about their fathers. Both agreed that they lived extremely narrow lives. Both were in ruts. A pity that they never visited one another.

"I believe they did once, actually, Willie, a tremendously long time ago, long before the Boer War, even. Aunt Dora had that cottage over there then—that one behind the pub," said Phillip, pointing at the sett-stoned narrow lane leading up from the quay, to a cottage red with rambler roses. "Does Uncle John ever go to see Uncle Hilary?"

"Father's always saying he'll go, but seldom leaves the library where he practically lives nowadays. He likes fishing, too, and says that Uncle Hilary's beat on the Avon is a jolly good one, but he doesn't care for Aunty Bee. Anyway, she's gone. Uncle Hilary is selling his place there, and is going to buy land at Rookhurst."

"I wonder what for, Willie."

"Get it back in the family, I suppose."

"Oh, good. Father will be jolly glad to hear that!"

Chapter 24

PISTON

The girls had bathed before, but this was Phillip's first swim since bathing in the Ancre. He was apprehensive of the deep water, lest he got cramp in his leg. They strolled on to the boats drawn up beyond the lift. The girls, walking on ahead, were opposite the entrance when three young officers from Hollerday House appeared. Two wore bath-robes, with towels round necks; the third was in plain clothes. He had been on leave when Phillip had arrived at Hollerday House; but as soon as he saw him, Phillip had recognised him as the man at the Casualty Clearing Station at Heilly who had come into the hut on the padre's arm, and pretended to be fighting the Germans.

His name was Piston. It was the first time he had seen the girls, but he treated them immediately as though they were old friends.

"Hullo, dear ladies!" with a double flip of his rat's-whisker moustaches. "Welcome to Lynmouth! Delightful spot down here, don't you know! I'm from the same jolly old place as Phil and Bill, you know, Georgie Newnes' shack built on *Tit-Bits*, and looking like it, too. These Cheap Press Wallahs get my goat. I don't care who they are—Billy Castleton, Alf Harmsworth, Arty Pearson, Georgie Newnes—the whole bang lot of them ought to be shot in my opinion, for feeding the muck they do to the hoi polloi. They're all yellow bellies," he went on, with a high-class drawl. "I know quite a lot about Fleet Street. The Hidden Hand, and all that. *Wang!* I'd shoot the whole dam' lot!"

The dark eyes darted from face to face as he went on, "I was with dear old Phil in the Somme show, you know. Ac-tually, I got lifted sky-high by one of the mines in front of La Boisselle. Lost my memory, or parts of it, ever since! And the trouble is, strictly between ourselves, which parts! God knows who I am. Sometimes I don't even know myself. Ever had the feeling of being reincarnated? If so, take my advice—don't!"

The speaker's face had gone pale. He looked exhausted. With a glance at Polly, half-shy, half-furtive, he went on, "I expect you think my name sounds a bit odd. Ac-tually," with a flip of moustaches, "one of my great-great-uncles invented something that made little old James Watt's steam-kettle idea practicable.

Few people realise that, as they equally fail to realise that Major Shrapnel invented the shell, Sir Hiram Maxim the machine-gun, and old Uncle Tom Cobley Gatling that barrel-organ thing they used on the Fuzziwuzzies in the Sudan."

Phillip wondered if his manner was due to his trying all the time to get away from something he could not bear to think about, so he was always talking and imagining things in order to forget what had hurt him. Perhaps he had suffered from "the battle of the brain", when he was a boy? Had the war frightened him, literally, out of his wits? So much so, that he was pretending to be mad, in order to get out of the army? Poor devil.

"Let me introduce you to my sister and to my cousin Miss Pickering—Mr. Piston."

"Somewhat belated!" said Piston, saluting. "Well, I can see that you are all straining at the leash to get on with the old trudgeon stroke, invented by a bloke called Trudgeon, by the way, a pal of mine, so I'll leave you to it. Cheeroh! I'm unfortunately not swimming just now. Concussion!" He coughed hollowly, wheezed, and thumped his chest.

Phillip was glad that the blue cloth of his bathing dress covered the ugly purple-red crater on his left buttock, and that the bullet hole in his foot just above the instep was hardly noticeable. Willie's wound was through the shoulder, and had healed cleanly. They were both being worked upon twice a day by a Swedish masseuse, who pulled and pushed, to ease away any stiffness in the new muscles. He was glad, too, that both Polly and Doris looked all right: Doris in her bathing dress with its frills round neck, knees, and elbows: Polly in an overcoat. However, she should have worn a bathing cap, like Doris, her hair tucked up into it. As it was, with her white skin and black curls all over her shoulders, Polly looked rather fast, he thought. He hoped she would not attract attention from the others.

With some uneasiness he saw, when she took off her overcoat, that Polly was wearing a boy's bathing dress, which showed her legs above the knees, as well as an arc of her white neck; while her bosom pushed out the loose worn blue stockingette of her costume and showed the swelling of her breasts. What would people think of her?

He was not left long in doubt. Piston, who had taken a quick, almost guilty look, which had in it some satisfaction, offered to hold Polly's coat. Phillip began to regret that he had been so friendly towards Piston; he was going to be beastly familiar, he

considered, already calling her by her christian name. The other
two from the house were waiting by the little lighthouse on the
quay. They ran their eyes over Polly's figure, too. He wasn't
going to introduce them, and run the risk of having them hanging
round the cottage.

Dared he go in? The water was deep; the surface was two feet below
the quay, and he might do a belly-flopper. While he waited, Polly
prepared to dive. He felt anxious about currents, although at the
moment there were none; the tide was still flowing in, but he knew
that it began to go out strongly at the turn, and also there was much
fresh water coming down from the moor. How well could she
swim? He watched her getting a grip with her toes on the edge
of the stone. She placed her feet together, threw back her arms,
bent her knees, she sprang, he saw the pink palms of her feet,
instep to instep, as she curved in, leaving only a round white ring
in the water, much neater than the salmon's. He saw her pale
shadow down in the green before she bobbed up a dozen yards
away, shook water out of her eyes and hair, and with swift over-
arm strokes made for the quay, leaving behind a wake of white
water. Ignoring Piston's hand, she drew herself up, sleek and
dripping, to stand, arms by her side, one knee slightly bent, while
about her feet formed a pool of water. She was as self-possessed as a
statue; she was transformed, like his thoughts of her. He felt
proud that she was with him; her white arms and shoulders were
like the sculptures of Rodin. Could this be Polly?

"Top hole!" said Piston, holding her coat. "I mean that,
Polly!"

The others plunged in, leaving Piston, Phillip, and Polly on the
quay.

"Don't you swim?" said Phillip, moving between Piston and
Polly.

"No costume, old boy, there's been a war," said Piston,
darkly. "Pity we can't all go in starko. Why should we be ashamed
of nature? It's only the blasted beaks, all puff and paunch, that
made the dam-silly laws. Your Cousin Polly is a peach. Beats
Annette Kellerman, in my not so humble opinion."

"Are you sure you will be all right, with your leg?" said Polly,
turning to Phillip.

He wished he had gone straight in; the more he hesitated, the
feebler he would look. So arms over head, and pray that it would
not be a belly-flopper. It was, and it stung. Exuberance rose in
him. He could still swim! He saw Doris sitting on the edge of the

quay, beside Percy. "Come on in!" Then Polly dived in and rose up beside him.

"I'm going in off the tower."

"No, it's too dangerous! You might hurt yourself!"

"Pouff!"

"Polly, come back!"

Polly walked on. He watched her open the door of the lighthouse, and go inside. She reappeared on the balcony, climbed upon the parapet, and stood there awhile, looking around with assumed unconcern. Was she brazen about her figure? Treading water, he saw that people up the street were looking at her. Among them was Aunt Dora, with a sunshade. Others were staring up, too. He wanted to call out that it was too risky. Supposing she hit the edge of the quay? He felt distress.

But Polly, unknown to Phillip, was the champion swimmer of her school beside the river in Gaultshire. She crouched and swung and came down in a swallow dive into the water, leaving a small shell-splash behind her.

"Hi-ee-o!" yelled Piston, as he jumped into the water. He swam about, singing, "My old man's a fireman; He puts out fires!" His head was dark and sleek. Reaching for his tweed cap which was floating in the water, he flung it on to the quay. Phillip thought, after Piston had tried to duck Polly, that he was a bit too much of a good thing.

The water in the harbour was from the Atlantic, pressing up between Cornwall and the south-east coast of Ireland. It had the chill of the ocean main; soon Phillip felt the cold strike him.

"You stayed in too long, you know," said Dora, seeing his face. "Now go and dress quickly, and then come back to the cottage and let me give you some hot milk. What was that odd-looking creature doing, swimming about in his clothes?"

"He hadn't got anything else to swim in."

"Of course not, poor man, he has come straight from the battlefield. I must look him out something."

When Piston swam again he wore a heavy worsted combination suit of blue and white rings, which buttoned up from the middle of the chest. It covered all his body except his neck, head, forearms, and legs below his kneecaps. It had been left behind by Richard after the visit to Lynmouth in 1895.

As Phillip had imagined, Piston became almost a fixture in Ionian Cottage. Still, he wasn't such a bad chap after all. He offered to do odd jobs to help Aunt Dora, being handy with saw, nail, hammer, and mason's trowel. He also must have peeped into the pages of *A Smaller Classical Dictionary*, for one afternoon after all of them had returned from fishing in a hired motor-boat, he said to Dora, "One of my ancestors was called Pistor, I've just remembered. I lost my memory after that show, you know. Ancestral memory goes back a long way, under stress. Funny, it all came back to me as I pulled in that pollock that it's been a tradition in the family for God knows how long that the old boy invented a stunt of chucking out bags of quartern loaves to the old Gauls when they were besieging Rome, to make the old Gauls think the blokes inside the fortress had lashings of grub to eat. Whether old Pistor got away with it I don't know, anyway later on one of the family came to England with the Romans, and founded the English branch of our family. That's the rumour, anyway. Probably all bilge, like most pedigrees, you know, bars sinister and all that hoodoo."

Dora, who had never met anyone like him, thought that he had the innocent make-believe imagination of the child. This was shown also in the way he had made friends with various children, whose company he seemed to prefer. Then there was his strange devotion to his fire-pail, as though to some *penates* of his mind, a bucket he had found somewhere, perforated with a number of holes. He claimed that it was a fire-pail he had brought back with him from the trenches in Plugstreet Wood.

"Actually, Aunt Dora, it is the original bucket that suggested to Bruce Bairnsfather the idea for his cartoons."

"How very interesting," she said, not realising at first that this statement was in the same category of fancy as the "Pistor" story. Had she done so, she would not have continued, "Willie will be most interested to hear that—he was in Ploegsteert Wood during that first winter, too."

She saw his eyes dart about before he replied hastily, "I got blown up there, too, and can't remember anything about it, except the jolly old fire-bucket and Bruce's face when the idea came to him to do the first picture for *The Bystander*."

Was he inventing this too, she wondered. Could the source of his fantasy be disturbance to the brain when he had been blown up with the mine before La Boisselle, a graphic account of which he had given her, of himself rising high in the air, and being saved on returning to earth by the cushioning effect of powdered chalk? Might not the shock in some way have brought to the fore a primitive part of the mind? Who knew the mysteries of the brain?

"Piston by name and Piston by nature, that's me, temperamental you know, up one moment and down the next." He was, she told Dr. Minstrel, a kind young man. Not only did he play with some of the village boys at being a pirate, collecting "pieces of eight" in his fire-bucket—circular corks off fishing nets—but he entered into the spirit of the children, making camp fires on the boulders by the shore, and roasting potatoes in the embers. "He is one of them," she said, and thought of him as The Innocent.

"I'm bung-full of Devonshire Cream and ozone, Aunt Dora. I say, old thing, do you mind frightfully if I call you Aunt Dora? I haven't any aunts of my own left, you see. The last two, God bless 'em, were killed in Mathy's raid on Hull on the fifth-sixth June last year. So may I have the honour to call you Aunty, please?"

She thought he was most pathetic, a pleading in his eyes like that of a spaniel, and replied impulsively, "Of course, dear boy, I am most touched by your request! Now do please stop lime washing the scullery wall, and go out and enjoy yourself with the others while this fine weather lasts. Mrs. Sloly and I can manage these walls, can't we, Mrs. Sloly?"

"Aye aye!" roared the semi-bearded fat cottage woman who came in every day. "Us can manage thaccy, midear, yesmye!"

"Ah midear!" he shouted back. "Leave it to Piston! Piston always pays! Piston will do it more quickly than slowly, no-yesmye?" to the woman's bellows of laughter and "You'm a praper pup, midear, you be!"

Then seeing Dora's face he said with little-boy brightness, "That's all right, Aunty, I'm quite happy doing this until the little tackers come along, honestly Aunty! Cross my heart!" The tackers were the small fry which formed his band upon the bouldered beach.

The easy days passed in a bright flow of summer weather. Phillip and Willie went about together; Doris and Polly, too, were the firmest friends. The officers at the convalescent home came down to bathe, or fish, or sail offshore in the charge of fishermen. There was a boat-house belonging to Hollerday, and among the boats there was a dinghy, and also a small outboard motor. Phillip managed to make this work, after removing and drying out the coil, and adjusting the contact-breaker; but Matron said it belonged to the house, and should not be touched. So the two cousins hired a boat, and went fishing for pollock and mackerel and other fish offshore. Phillip learned how to sail. They hired ponies in Lynton, and taking lunch with them, rode up the valley to the high moor. Westward lay the Atlantic; and Dartmoor to the south rose dimly in the hazy harvest air murmurous with bees at the heath bells. Once the air seemed to quiver with distant and continuous reverberations: the guns in France, the Somme battle still raging.

They walked, too, up Beggar's Roost, a steep track of red rock under a tunnel of over-growing blackthorn and ash, and Phillip showed Willie where he had been caught in a cloud-burst two years before. August drew out its golden days of halcyon blue seas and moorland of yellow furze and purple heath, beyond rumours of war, where two-day-old newspapers arrived, never to be looked at; a timeless age while it lasted.

The day came when Doris had to leave for London. Polly and Dora went with her to the station, and saw her off. Mavis was coming down for a week the next day, a Saturday. Dora did some shopping, before going down the cliff railway, having said that she would see Polly at luncheon. Polly did not turn up; but Willie and Phillip did, declaring that she and Piston had taken the dinghy from the boathouse and with buzzing outboard laying a trail of blue smoke on the calm water, had disappeared round the Ruddy Ball, swiftly on the ebb side. They would come back all right, said Phillip.

Dora tried not to show her anxiety as she served sea-trout with cucumber slices and new potatoes. She knew that the cliffs went sheer down to the water, and also the force of the tide. Supposing the engine broke down? Or ran out of petrol-and-oil, for it was a two-stroke, and would not run on petrol alone. She was *in loco parentis*, and what would Lizzie Pickering say if her only daughter were to be drowned, the body perhaps never seen again, as the tides swept away between Land's End and Ireland?

"Piston is naughty to do such a thing! He should have known better. I am quite cross with him!"

"He has only gone round the Ball, and may be back by now, Aunt Dora."

"But there are no landing places before Wooda Bay!"

"And the tide will be against him," said Phillip.

Immediately after luncheon Dora left for the quay. No, the little boat had not returned. She asked about hiring a motor boat to look for them. The tide was out, the river low, a few inches deep, between the boulder ridges. She wondered if she should telephone the coastguard. What an idiotic thing to do, really, Piston was completely irresponsible, and Polly should have known better. The girl lacked imagination. There was the incident of her bathing in a childish bathing dress when she was already a woman: it showed that she lacked a sense of the feelings of others. But then she was only a child of sixteen!

The tide began to flow up the Severn Sea again; but no dinghy, no Polly. Dora telephoned the Matron of Hollerday House. Was Mr. Piston there? No, he had not been in to lunch, nor had he signed the book that he would be out for lunch. Was anything the matter? Dora then learned that a letter had come from London ordering Lieutenant Piston to proceed to a special hospital in the North, where cases of shell-shock were to be treated. This information led Dora to speak of the missing boat.

Later, a message came from the post-office asking her to go to the telephone. There she was asked to ring up an Ilfracombe number.

"Hullo, Aunt Dora? I just thought you might be worried, old thing. Oh, everything's quite all right, in fact it's better than that. The jolly old engine conked out and we took turns to row here. I'm bringing Polly home by hired car, fairly soon. Yes, everything is top-hole. The sea calm as a mill-pond. I'm getting the old engine fixed up and shall come in another day and bring the dinghy back. Where am I telephoning from? Oh, the jolly old police-station. Yes, of course Polly is all right. Damned good scout, Polly! See you later! Cheero! Keep smiling!"

When Piston came back with Polly he was apologetic, saying that he had meant only to go out to spin for mackerel for half-an-hour, but the outboard had conked and the tide took them down the coast before they could say Jack Robinson, and the only thing to do, honestly Aunt Dora, was to make for the nearest harbour.

"Well," said Dora, "if you want to take Polly out again, I must ask you to let me know first!"

"Trust me, cross my heart, Aunt Dora!"

Phillip told Piston when they were alone, "Orders came through while you were away. You're being sent up to Scotland, to a new hospital."

Piston's eyes became wild. His face looked haggard.

"Why, old boy? What's the game? What have I done? Is this a punishment? Who told you?"

"Oh, I think it was the major. It's just an ordinary move, I suppose. I expect the medical authorities can't quite make out your case. By the way, I saw you at the C.C.S. at Heilly on July the First."

"Was I there? I can't remember, old boy. When have I got to leave, d'you know?"

"Tomorrow, I fancy."

"Let's go to the pub and have a drink, for Christ's sake. I want to think. Also I am overdue in celebrating Leefe Robinson's V.C. I was at school with him. Spotty-faced little scug, he was, too. My fag, at Harrow, actually," drawled Piston.

Phillip had read that Leefe Robinson, the lucky pilot who had got the wooden-framed Schütte-Lanz, had been at St. Bee's School, Cumberland; but he said nothing as they walked down to the quay, and turned up a steep path to the Rising Sun. There Piston began to drink brandy, drawn from an earthenware barrel on the shelf. Phillip drank beer. He missed Willie, who had gone home. After one more week he was leaving, too; a further week at home, and he would be boarded. He hoped to go back to Grantham, if he could wangle it at the War Office, and become a transport officer to one of the new companies, which, he had heard, were going out to France in increasing numbers. That was the only life, really.

Piston seemed to be greatly afraid. His dark eyes stared; he kept brushing up his moustache. Perhaps he really had been blown up, and was shell-shocked, like the man he had watched being led down past the painter at his easel in the ruins of Albert.

"Masson old man"—Piston imitated the small boys who called Aunt Dora "Miss Masson"—"Masson, what sort of a place are they sending me to, did Matron say? What will they do to me? Cook me up and bung me back to France? Or is it a bloody mad-house?"

"They'll build you up, I expect. You know, they've got all sorts of ways now of finding out things about shell-shock cases I was reading about it in *The Times* the other day."

"Christ, I don't want to go back again. I couldn't stand it. Could you?"

"Oh, it's not so bad, when it happens, as you think it's going to be before you start." He left Piston in the pub, and went on the cliff railway, and the long slow pull up to Hollerday House, for dinner.

When he went down to the village afterwards he saw an object in front of him, apparently having come up from the beach, carrying a fire-pail full of driftwood. It had a cork-blackened face and wore a wig of sea-weed. It was followed by a score or so of children, shrilly crying out and jeering. Piston appeared to be in a panic, as he turned round to curse the children. They stopped at the cottage gate, when he disappeared round the wall leading to the scullery.

As Phillip arrived, Dora came to the gate, and telling the children they must not abuse the friendliness of Mr. Piston, asked them to go back quietly to their homes.

"Mr. Piston is not very well, you know; he was hurt in France, at the war."

Shrieks of laughter from Mrs. Sloly were coming from the scullery.

Dora went there with Phillip.

"Oh my dear zoul, 'a be a proper mazed man, 'a be! 'A saith 'a be Feyther Neptoon, and 'a's eyes be dartin' about in 'a's 'ade, I be proper scared, m'm! 'A looketh at me like an old rat peepin' through a broom!"

"Hush, Mrs. Sloly, he may hear you. It is only his fun."

They went into the scullery, and saw smoke rising from the fire-pail. Piston sat on the lime-ash floor, warming his hands. Oddly enough, his eyes did remind Phillip of a rat's, except that they were bloodshot.

"What are you doing? You will have the place on fire! Have you lost your senses? This is carrying a joke to excess, surely, Piston," said Dora.

As he did not move, Phillip seized the handle of the pail and held it under the pump.

"Stop acting!" he said, when Piston jumped up, crying, "They're all around me! They've broken through! Where is Sergeant Oldfield? Tell him he's under arrest! Stand to! Stand to!" Then he leaned his head against the wall, and uttering a long sigh, turned to Dora with round and simple eyes. "What's happened? How did I get here? What's all this camouflage?" He ran a finger down his face. "Who did this? Have I been in a raid?" Then he began to cry. "I can't stand any more. My head is splitting, Aunty."

Phillip felt that he could not stand any more either, and walked out.

"Cannot you remember? You were playing with the children, and came up from the beach like that."

"Did I?" he said vaguely. "I can't remember a thing about it, Aunty."

"Now wash your face and hands. Here's a bowl, and soap and towel. Mrs. Sloly, please do not say anything about this in the village. Mr. Piston is still suffering from shock. Fortunately Dr. Minstrel will be here shortly, and I will ask him to see you."

"No, please don't say anything about it, Aunt Dora! I'm quite all right now, honestly I am! You see, midear," he went on, in a different voice, as he pulled out the ends of his moustache with finger and thumb, "if you tell the jolly old doc. he may get me sent away among the genuine dippies, and I'm not really that, you know. You see, what happens is this. I can't control my thoughts of what happened when that mine went up, taking me for a joy-ride. I break into a cold sweat—sorry, perspiration—and then everything goes blank. I can see myself all right, I know what I'm doing, but someone else seems to have taken over. I saw myself putting a match to the old fire-pail, but at the same time knew that it was quite safe, on the stone floor. I felt terribly cold, and then I was back in the trenches. When you spoke to me, it was like being woken up out of a sleep-walk. The old cranium seems to swell up and burst. Sometimes I wonder if I am all of me, or should it be I? Anyway I'm not me, after that jolly old joy-ride."

"Our leading psychologists are only now beginning to realise the nature of the most subtle injuries to the mind. Indeed, there is a special hospital, for what they call shell-shock cases, in Scotland now. I was reading about it in *The Times* recently. The doctors are very clever people, I am sure."

"Shall I have to go to Scotland, Aunty? It will be very cold there, won't it?"

"They will help you to get well again, dear Piston."

Piston left, with his fire-pail, which he had now christened Old Contemptible. He collected more drift-wood before going up the cliff railway.

"So Piston thinks you are a darned good scout, does he? I wonder how far his scouting got with you?"

"You better ask him, if you're so interested."

"I'm asking *you*, Polly."

"I don't see what it has got to do with you."

"Only that you're my cousin, and he's obviously a——" He stopped; the thought of what he was going to say came back like a boomerang.

"What is he obviously, pray?"

"Ssh, don't talk so loudly. Aunt Dora might hear us."

"I've nothing to hide."

"God's teeth, I'm in your bedroom! Don't you realise what she will think?"

"You used to come in and talk when Doris was here."

"Well, you fool, she isn't here now!"

"Then what is the difference, may I ask, if I am such a fool?" said Polly, very politely.

"This," he replied, opening the front of her night-gown. She closed it, holding her hand there. "No! You do not really care for me. You want me only as a plaything."

"That's right! 'A Broken Doll'. Poor old Polly! Quite a shame, isn't it?"

Polly could not help laughing at his comic face. This was the Phillip she had liked ever since she could remember.

"I think it was a compliment, when Piston called you a good scout, Polly. But tell me honestly, did you and he, well, you know——"

"I do *not* know," said Polly, loftily.

"I mean, what you and I——"

"Oh, I see what you mean. Certainly not! Piston is a perfect gentleman. He treats me as a chum, and a good sort. Not like somebody else I could mention, who has hardly bothered to speak to me all the time I've been down here."

"Rot! I thought you were jolly good when you dived off the tower, and said so."

"Yes, when others had said so first."

"Come on, let's stop this rot!" he said, as he got into bed beside her.

Later, he said, "We're supposed to be back at Hollerday by ten, but I can get in through the window of the library, and then creep upstairs. That's the way we all get in, after lights out."

He fell asleep, and Polly did not wake him, for she liked to hear him breathing gently beside her, as he lay with cheek against her bosom and his long dark hair, so soft and silky, against her throat. She dozed, and lay thinking of scenes in her past life, scenes which were always happy, so that every tree in the garden and the plantation behind the boxwood hedge, in which was the little summer-house where a wren always nested, every field footpath and lane, the Satchville brook where she had paddled, and later the river by her school where she swam, the playing fields, the tennis courts, the gym, Daddy and Mummy and Granny and Percy and everyone she had known were of that happiness. And now Phillip was friendly once more, and not snubbing her, and some of that happiness had helped him, she dimly thought; for to Polly he was still "a bit funny".

She may have slept, lulled by the Lyn water running beneath the window, feeling peaceful that the soft hair and gentle breathing was beside her; for when she thought of things next it was to wonder why the ceiling was moving with just perceptible hues of pink, or was it her imagination? No, it was a fire somewhere; and getting out of bed, she went to the window and looking up saw flames high up in the sky.

Polly was not the only one to see the fire on Hollerday Hill. Ships passing up the Severn Sea saw what looked like a beacon burning on the moor. The convalescent home was well alight. Piston had lit the fire-pail, which he kept beside his bed, to warm his hands in the trenches, he said afterwards.

Three months later, when Phillip was back in France, Piston was invalided from the Army with a sixty per cent disability pension. Bowler-hatted, carrying an umbrella, wearing the Old Boys tie of his adopted *alma mater*, Captain (sometimes Major) Piston had a job in the London Area Inspectorate of the Ministry of Munitions. He visited suburban factories in garages by motor-car, being driven by a uniformed chauffeuse of the Women's Legion, who fetched him daily from his parents' home in Finchley, and took him back there at night. He was quite a character, she thought, and always so chivalrous that after awhile she did not think of him as a real person at all.

Chapter 25

A MAN OF SOCIETY

As soon as he arrived home, Phillip went to see Mrs. Neville, to give her a detailed account of all he had done, except with Polly. He told her how he had gone up the path beside the cliff railway, which was not working at night; and then up through the fir and monkey trees to the blaze above.

"I must be pretty fit, I got up in about ten minutes, and it's nearly a thousand feet up, well, eight hundred anyway, and was only slightly puffed. The Lynton fire brigade arrived about the same time, with a beam pumping outfit, but their hose wasn't long enough to reach down through the wood. I gave them a hand with the hose, and having established an alibi, appeared among the others, who seemed to think I had been burned up. Oh no, I said, I'd been helping. They found rooms for us in an hotel, but I went back to Aunt Dora's eventually, when the fun was over. All my kit was burnt up, of course, so I'll get a new outfit. Fortunately my old tunic was at the cottage, so I've got that. I like it, it's had many adventures with me, Hornchurch, Tollemere, Northampton, Grantham, Boulogne, Etaples, Paris Plage, Amiens, Querrieu, Albert—dear old tunic, what memories it has.''

"What goings on, to be sure," said Mrs. Neville. "Of one thing, you know Phillip, I am certain: this world will never be the same place again when the war is over. What will become of all you boys then, I often wonder. What experiences you have lived through, to my knowledge! Well, so far Desmond has not set fire to Bognor Military Hospital! Of course, there's no telling, he may do so yet! My son may turn out to be another Piston!" she shrieked. When she was calmer, "Well, your mother was pleased to see you, I expect. Are you going to another convalescent home?"

"No. We were transferred to Watermouth Castle, but I asked for a Medical Board at Exeter, and was passed fit for Garrison Duty, with three weeks' leave; and here I am."

"But you won't be going out again, of course?"

"I hope so. I want to see 'Nosey' Orlebar at the War Office, and ask to be posted back to the Training Centre as a transport officer. I'd rather be out there than on home duty, or Gibraltar, or Malta, or somewhere like that."

"Quite the soldier, aren't you, dear?"

Phillip went up to London, and saw Colonel Orlebar, finding him quiet, friendly, and helpful. He apologised for his lie about having been at Cambridge before the war.

"My dear fellow, say no more about it. Westy told me the circumstances; one lives and learns, at least the good'ns do, I suppose. War finds out all our weak spots. We all get it in different ways, you know. Well, I'll see what can be done. But you're still B2, you know. Take it easy meanwhile. Have you seen Westy? They peppered him a bit more this time; he'll soon be as full of holes as a colander if he goes on at this rate. Earned his gong, if ever a fellow did. I heard from him yesterday; he's at the Duke's place in Gaultshire. He'll be up in town shortly, for H.M.'s Investiture at Buck House; he'd like to see you, I know. The best of luck to you, Maddison."

Phillip went out of the room, feeling keen and happy. He walked down the Strand to the City, to see his father. Richard was pleased to see him. Phillip invited him out to lunch, but his father said he "would rather not, thanks all the same". The habit of frugality in the middle of the day was now set in Richard's life. So Phillip went on to Wine Vaults Lane, and saw Mr. Howlett, who insisted on taking him to the London Tavern, where Phillip picked his own steak and saw it put on the grill above the charcoal fire before sitting down at a table with his old manager, who asked him to "tell him all about it". Phillip found that there was nothing to tell.

Afterwards he went on to Houndsditch, and called at the C.M. Corset factory. Eugene was delighted to see him, and they dined together at the Popular restaurant that evening, afterwards going to see *The Lilac Domino* at the Empire Theatre. He got home at midnight, just as Richard returned from his patrol. Phillip told him about his plans to return to Grantham, and Richard heard them with some misgiving. Was his son strong enough? He looked too fine drawn; but Richard said nothing. He was relieved to see no sign of drinking.

"Your cabbages, Phillip, you'll be interested to hear, are doing well, and are already hearting up. The only trouble is the white caterpillar, but I hope to settle that problem by the aid of soapy water."

"Oh, good."

Hetty, hearing amiable voices, came down in a dressing-gown to share the new feeling. Her hair looked grey and wispy, Phillip thought: she was only a small girl who had lived longer, that was all.

"Well old man, you are ready for bed, I expect?"

"Yes, there's a lot to do tomorrow," said Hetty.

There was nothing to do, he thought with dullness, almost dread: nothing. And once more the dream of Helena Rolls held him.

"Good night, Mother."

"Kiss her, Phillip! Go on, she's your mother," said Richard. "You're not really too big yet, you know!"

"Yes, you're still our little boy," said Hetty, with a smile that was not far from tears.

Phillip kissed his mother hastily on the cheek, and saying good night, left the room, to wash quickly in the bathroom before Father came up.

"Well, old girl," said Richard, when they were alone. "What do you think of your best boy now?"

"He seems so different," she replied, with a half-resigned smile of loneliness. She meant that her son, the little son she always thought of, seemed to have grown away from her almost entirely. Richard smiled too; the tears were in his heart. He felt the barrier between himself and the rest of the family sometimes with despair; for unlike Hetty, he had no hope of his life changing now. The gift of cabbage plants had moved him deeply: every time he saw them, he felt tender towards the tiny boy who had climbed his knee, and once had seemed to love him.

"Ah well," said Richard. "The wild boy seems to have settled down. I suppose," he added, "that we can give a certain young lady credit for the improvement?"

This remark renewed an anxiety that Hetty had been feeling since the previous evening, when Doris had told her something as they walked home across the hill after Evensong at the church of St. Simon.

"Mother, Phillip has no right to think of Helena Rolls any more."

"What is the reason, Doris? You must have some reason."

Phillip had gone to church with his mother and sister solely in the hope of seeing, from the gallery where they usually sat, the figure of Helena Rolls in the light of incandescent gas-mantles shining down upon her rented family pew. The pew was still empty when the organ began to play. He hoped until the last moment; but when Mr. Mundy came in from the vestry with the choir, he knew they were not coming; and there was nothing to live for, once again. The years' depressions were upon him.

On the way home he strode ahead of his mother and sister, trying to outwalk his thoughts, to hurry on towards—what? Why had he not gone up to town, to be with Gene? At least Gene could feel the real things of life: he was alive, he loved music, he *understood*: a feeling that did not exist in Wakenham, except in Mrs. Neville. No, no, he must not think unkindly of the place: these people did not know what he knew. They had been stuck there all their lives.

Striding on alone, missing the joining lines of the paving squares lest, treading across one, it bring him bad luck, he reached the gates of the Hill, and felt some relief that the houses were left behind. Before him in the mellow light of evening he saw the grass, the railings, the seats, the row of elms—all things which once he had known better than he had known himself, for they had been intensely visible, standing out sharply in the life that was out-ward, every blade of grass, flake of bark, grain of wood on almost every seat. He knew them all. But the life that had been on the Hill then, had passed away. All was gone. Dully his shoes crunched the gravel of the path, as he strode in the wind which was clearing the sky of the greyness of Sunday-afternoon smoke from all the rows of houses suffocating the Hill.

A group of young boys chivvying a group of young girls sported on the grass; challenges and laughing cries came on the wind. He thought of Uncle Hugh, thin and shambling, and his remark once to them when they were playing Robber Bands. *Keep it going, boys; your race is nearly run.* Had he seen the war coming? Striding on, he passed another group; the boys were trying to tear up a seat, to show off their prowess to the girls. Or were they tearing up hurtful authority? All the canings and the silences before authority? They were silent as he strode past them. Was he "an old man" to them? Just as in his boyhood, the seats of the L.C.C. were stronger: the oak bars were bolted to galvanised iron frames, which were likewise bolted to iron under concrete slabs, as in, it was said, the German concrete shelters under which their machine-guns fired. These seats had been designed to withstand the little "Erkles" of the Hill, as Shakespeare might have called them. Keep it going, boys; the war is not yet nearly run.

On other seats, spaced along the crest, quiet couples sat, close together, wrapped in one another's arms, unspeaking, unmoving, unseeing. He passed them without a glance, leaving them to their thoughts. Were they dreaming of happiness everlasting, so different from their parents' lives, perhaps? Up and down to the office, twice a day over London Bridge, nearly six hundred times a year: could Love endure such sameness? Love endureth long, and is kind: Father Aloysius among the wounded: perhaps he was dead by now. Mrs. Kingsman, why had he not written to her? What could he say? That Jasper was with God? It was too late to write now, nearly ten weeks afterwards.

Lily on the seat, by the weeping willow tree, weeping for the baby they took away, her baby wrapped in brown paper and dropped over the rustic bridge into the Randisbourne, leaving Lily with blue-glass eyes, Lily weeping diamond tears, Lily a large wax doll, and the river ran black with death. Poor Piston, promoting himself to Harrow. What fears had riddled his soul?

Lily was gone, to make a new life for herself, to train to be an army nurse, Mrs. Neville said. Nothing was left of his old life, nothing, nothing, nothing. Damn his B2 category. He would ask for another board, and apply to be sent back to the war, to the life, to the death, of the battlefields.

Hurrying to keep the tall figure of her son in sight, Hetty said, "What is the reason, Doris? You must have some reason."

"I just think that Phillip ought not to go running after her anymore."

"I'm afraid I don't understand, Doris."

"I don't think it's right."

"But why?"

"Very well, if you promise you won't tell a soul. Polly is going to have a baby, and Phillip is the father."

"Oh dear."

It was a shock. Hetty had hoped the *liaison*, as she called it to herself, between the two had long ago been ended, a single episode in fact, now forgotten. At that time she had blamed Polly as much as Phillip, for after all she had gone into his bedroom.

"Are you quite sure it's true, Doris? There are often irregularities when the period begins, you know."

"Polly's first came on when she was thirteen, and she says she's always been regular so far."

"Was it before Phillip went out to France the last time, Doris?" If so, it would be over three months.

"Oh no, Mother. It happened at Lynmouth."

"We can be thankful for that small mercy, anyway. After all, Polly is still at school. I must talk to her when she comes next week."

"Mother, you promised!"

"We'll have to see what happens, dear. Now, whatever you do, don't mention it to Mavis, will you? She is so easily upset, and is the last person to know about this. So is your father. Has Phillip spoken to you about it?"

"I don't think he knows. I only heard about it from Polly in her letter yesterday."

Happy voices of three figures were coming nearer upon the gravel path of the Hill at its highest point. With a feeling almost of

sickness Phillip heard a merry laugh, a throat-laugh possessed by
only one person in the world, a laugh that had power to lift him
momentarily out of the dullness of ordinary life. He assembled
himself for the longed-for, dreaded meeting.

"Good evening, Phillip. So you are back again. Did you have
a good time in Devonshire?"

"Oh yes, very, thank you, Mrs. Rolls."

"How long are you home for this time?"

"I've got three weeks' leave, then I report back for duty, sir.
Then with luck I'll be back in France again."

"So soon?" said Mrs. Rolls. "My dear boy! Well, you will
let us see something of you before you leave, won't you? Are
you sure you're well enough?" The voice seemed to brood over
him.

"Oh yes thank you, Mrs. Rolls."

Helena was looking at his face, too, he could see, as he stared
at the ground. He felt lame before them, as though his leg were
crippled. Then looking for a moment at her face, he saw its full
beauty.

"The secretary of the tennis club says you're an honorary
member, being in the Forces," she said. "So do come and play,
before the season ends."

"Oh, thank you."

"We must be getting along, Phillip. We're going to sup with
Mamma and Papa. Come in some evening and tell Helena and
me all your adventures, will you, and bring your gramophone."

"Thank you, Mrs. Rolls."

The Hill was transformed. There was no hurry onwards now.
With assumed calm he waited for his mother and sister.

From just before the turn of the century until the outbreak of
the war, the Hill had burned with thousands of invisible flames
of shrill sound. Poor children from the slums south of the river,
freed from asphalt playgrounds and narrow streets, freed from fear
—of fathers, policemen, the whooshing flop of cane and underlying
dread of Cat-o'-nine tails—had swarmed in summer upon what
they called the 'Illies, to hear the wonder of bands playing, and to
see the magic of fireworks from the Crystal Palace. Under Lord
Rosebery, Chairman of the London County Council, the invisible
flames of fear had been, for the moment, released upon the green
and pleasant spaces of what once had been forty acres of church
land.

Few men and women of the class and generation of Flora and
Gerard Rolls living in the district saw through the shrill screams
and shouts, the litter of paper and orange peel, the incoherent
rushing about and the not infrequent bullying and, above all, the
appalling raggedness and malnutrition, to the radical causes
underlying the unpleasantness. There had always been the poor,
and there always would be the poor. Did not Holy Scripture
declare it? Such children were not as their children; their feelings
were different; they belonged to an entirely different stratum
of life, which was bridgeless, except as between employer and
employed.

Flora Rolls had always been attracted by a certain look in
Phillip's face, though she had disliked many of his ways: the little
ruffian who set fire to the dry grasses in the Backfield, scattered
orange peel and paper thoughtlessly on the Hill (not, of course,
during a paper-chase, which was permissible) and filled the bushes
of the gully with broomstick rushing about and howling of his
Boy Scout patrol, some of whose members were most emphatically
not of the class she would have allowed him to mix with, had he
been a son of hers.

In addition to his wild behaviour as a boy, it was the swearing,
the use of unmentionable words which had decided her never to
invite him to the children's Christmas parties: a thing which had
darkened Phillip's life, convincing him that he was not good
enough for them, the most beautiful people he had ever known.

Dear Helena,

Life was a dream before it appeared on this earth; and the look on
your face is the most beautiful thing I have dreamed. Your laugh
is as the music of the Lyn under the green beech leaves. Your blue-
grey eyes are the Greek sea, *thalassa*, the sea that is the mother of man.
Your straight nose and calm brow would have inspired Phidias, so
serene and classic is your profile. No-one sees himself or herself as others
see them. Therefore I am your poet, though I do but limp in prose.
I see upon your brow, which is even as that of Aurora, the thick gold
hair arising in two waves, diverging from the peak in the centre of your
forehead: twin summer waves rearing upon some remote Aegean
shore of white sand, the light making them green-glass-clear before
the fall of *thalassa*, *thalassa*, which imitates the sound of the golden
tresses of the sea.

In ancient times the Greeks would have declared you to be the
re-incarnation of the daughter of Zeus and Leda. In the Greek legends,
Helena is all beauty, calm and serene as the tall summer wave falling

upon a mere mortal, breaking without hurt upon the neck and shoulders, while drops glitter in the sun as they fall past his eyes; then the crash, *thalassa*, upon the immortal shore of the world.

This evening of corn-coloured light you looked straightly at me, smilingly, as did your father, so tall and upright, and as Zeus himself. Now I must make a confession of ignorance: for if your Mother is Leda, I do not think your father could be Zeus, for did not Leda fall in love with a swan? So I am not sure of my similes. However, your mother is very beautiful, with perfect features, and violet-coloured eyes; she, too, has the soft throat-laughter inherited by you——

At this point Phillip's afflatus left him; and he scrumpled the letter, then burned it in his bedroom grate, thinking that it must be the first time that anything had been burnt in it; which was just as well, as in the old days he had hidden his tin of forbidden gunpowder up the chimney, and it was still there, forgotten.

When he rang the front-door bell of Turret House the next evening he heard the footfalls of Helena as she strode out of the front room, to pull the door wide and, stepping back, smile in greeting. He saw that she wore upon her white blouse the gold brooch, the Star of the Garter, that Hubert had given her. He flinched; but must go through with it.

"Come in, Phillip," called the voice of Mrs. Rolls from the sitting-room. He heard a rumbling growl from Rastus the bloodhound as it got out of its master's armchair. Entering, he saw the dog lifting off its square of carpet, to lay it beside the copper coal-scuttle.

"Rastus is now trained," the caressing voice explained, as Mrs. Rolls bit a thread from the nightshirt she was sewing for the Red Cross. "Put the gramophone on the table, and come and let me look at you, Phillip." His hand was taken affectionately. "How thin you are! You always were thin, of course, but now you are much, *much* too thin. How are you feeling in yourself?" Violet eyes looked tenderly up at him. "Draw up a chair, and sit beside me, and tell me all you have been doing. That's right, make yourself comfortable."

Try as he might, he could not feel at ease within himself. What could he say? He must say something to break the mask constricting him.

"What do you think of the Ancient Greeks, Mrs. Rolls?"

"Which ones, exactly, do you mean, Phillip? Have you any particular one in mind?"

Phillip mentally raced through the small print of *A Smaller Classical Dictionary*. He began to dread that he might mention Zeus or Leda, for then he would surely give away his thoughts. Also, Ancient Greece now seemed to get fainter and fainter in his mind.

"Tell me about them, won't you?" Stitch, stitch.

"Well, they fought among themselves, you know, and so destroyed what was the fairest light in the world. Phidias, you know, and all those other sculptors."

"Yes, Lord Elgin's marbles," said Mrs. Rolls, knowingly. "In the British Museum. Most interesting! You should talk to our Vicar about that, Phillip. Ancient Greece is his pet hobby horse. The Archæological Society has had to give up, you know, for lack of members. Such a pity. Wasn't your father once a member? I seem to remember him telling me something about it, oh, a long time ago now, before Gerard and I were married."

"Oh, I didn't know that, Mrs. Rolls."

"A hobby is so essential for a man, to take his mind off his work, don't you think?"

"Yes, I do."

"You sound much more determined than you used to be. I like a man to be determined, to know what he wants, and to go straight to his goal. Don't you?"

"Yes." He thought of "Spectre" West getting to the third and last objective beyond Contalmaison on the first day.

"What else have you been doing? Don't get up. You are so polite!"

Helena had come into the room. Drawing up a chair, she took her sewing.

"Well, I helped to put out a fire." He told them about Piston, making him out to be a comic character, instead of someone riddled by fear from some early hell. Laughter removed part of the constraint.

"Phillip believes that the Ancient Greeks had a wisdom which we don't find in the world today. What do you think, Helena?"

"I don't think anyone would dispute that," said Helena, stitching away.

"I was in Rome with Gerard many years ago, indeed we went there for our honeymoon, and the ruined buildings were most awe-inspiring," remarked her mother, as she wound cotton round a button energetically, secured it with two loops, and snapped the thread. "Most impressive."

"That was the Romans, mother!" laughed Helena.

"Well, the same sort of thing that Phillip is telling us about, surely?" said Mrs. Rolls, as she threaded another button.

"I rather fancy," said Phillip, smoothing his hair several times, "that the Romans adopted the culture of the Greeks. Eos became Aurora, and things like that." What a fool they must think him.

"Did they now? I know they came to Britain, and made all those wonderful straight roads. They went to Bath, too. I remember seeing the ruins there, with my parents."

"The Barbarians came after the Romans, or rather they poured in, didn't they?" said Helena.

"Yes, and Nero fiddled while Rome was burning, of course. Fiddling reminds me of your gramophone. What are we going to hear, now? Helena, will you fetch the coffee, darling?"

When Helena was in the kitchen, Mrs. Rolls said, "I am so glad that she has got over the worst of the shock of Hubert's death, Phillip. She is still very young, you see, only nineteen. When the war is over, Gerard will be going to the Far East again, on business—he's in bristles, you know—and will probably take Helena with him, to see the world. Everyone should travel when young, don't you think?"

"Yes," he said. Helena all in white, brilliant sunshine, gay laughter on deck, fashionable people, handsome, well-bred young men, evening dress, waltzing.

"It helps to broaden the outlook. No young person can really know his or her own mind until they have left home, and seen how wide the world is. Don't you agree?"

"Yes," he said again, sinking into darkness. She was letting him down gently, giving him a diplomatic hint. Thank God he had not put that letter in the box last night.

Flora Rolls saw the droop of his mouth, the corners turned down, the look on his face that she had so often seen when he was a boy. "You look tired, Phillip. I think I shall give you some Benger's Food instead of coffee."

"No, really, thanks, I am quite all right."

What a mess he was making of the conversation, which he had fervently anticipated to be about music and sculpture.

"You are still depressed by your wound, I can see that. Helena! Heat some more milk, darling, will you. Phillip must have some Benger's. You can have the coffee afterwards, if you are good!"

His spirits rose, that she was concerned that he should be well.

"May I play the gramophone?"

"Do. I adore all music, or nearly all."

"Do you like Wagner, Mrs. Rolls?"

"No, I can't say I do. It's all so heavy and ponderous, don't you think, even morbid. Gerard calls it a filthy Hun din, but then he likes Gilbert and Sullivan. Play something jolly. I'm sure you've got something jolly?"

"I've got a Harry Lauder, Mrs. Rolls."

"Oh, *Roamin' in the Gloamin*? Or *Annie Laurie*, perhaps?"

"No, I'm afraid it's rather silly."

"As long as it's not vulgar, I don't mind what it is."

He was transfixed. The record was *Stop Your Tickling, Jock*. It was absolutely vulgar. Hastily he put on Tosti's *Goodbye*.

Falling leaf, and fading flower,

the sad words, so clear and elegiac, came out of the tin concave of the open black cube.

Shadows falling on you and me—
Goodbye summer, goodbye, goodbye.

Helena came in with a tray, on which were cups and plates and jugs, and a plum cake, at the wonderful, tempestuous climax.

What are we waiting for, ah my heart
Kiss me once on the brow, and part
Again—again
Goodbye for ever! Goodbye for ever!
Goodbye—goodbye—goodbye.

"Very beautiful!" murmured Flora Rolls. "But too sad. Almost morbid, in fact. He was Count Tosti, wasn't he? An Italian, of course."

"I think so. The singer is John McCormack."

"I know it well, of course. Gerard used to sing it."

"Did Daddy actually sing *that*, Mummie? I can't imagine it!"

"It was before we were married, dear," said Flora Rolls, lightly. "He was terribly jealous, you see, and had morbid thoughts."

"What, Daddy? It doesn't sound at all like him!"

"Ah, he was in diggings then, you see. He did not need to sing for his supper, after we were married," she laughed, turning to Phillip. "Feed the brute, that's what I did!"

"Bravo!" he said, thinking, Food, when there is so much beauty in the world! He tried again.

"This is *The Dance of the Flowers*, by a Russian, Tchaikowsky. No, I think I'll put on *Souvenir de Moscow* first. Or how about Van Biene's *Broken Melody*?"

"I hope they're jolly ones," said Helena. "What's that I heard about Harry Lauder? Daddy likes him. So do I."

"All right." In for a penny, in for a pound, as he selected the record, and whizzed round the winding handle.

> *Stop your tickeling, tickel-ickle-ickeling,*
> *Stop your tickeling, Jock!*

It was a great success, especially when Rastus lifted up his snout and joined in.

After that things went better. At half-past nine, seeing a gold tooth revealed by the tremble of a yawn starting on Mrs. Rolls' face, promptly to be concealed in the white folds of a hospital nightshirt, Phillip thought it time to get up, and say goodnight. He must not outstay his welcome.

"Must you go so early? Well, thank you for the delightful music, and your company, too, of course, sir! Now, Helena, did I hear something about tennis tomorrow afternoon with Joe and Cherry Milton?"

"Yes. Would you like to make up a fourth at the Club, tomorrow afternoon at half-past two, Phillip?"

"Oh, thank you!"

"I suppose you'll be going on that noisy bike of yours?"

"Oh no, Mrs. Rolls, I've sold it."

"Then can you walk so far, *and* play as well?"

"Easily! Or I can borrow Father's Sunbeam."

"Well, do take care of it, won't you. I know how proud he is of his 'machine', as he calls it."

"Oh rather. Well, thank you for a ripping evening. Half-past two at the club, then? I'm a bit out of practice, you know, so you must excuse my bad play. Well, goodbye once again. Cheerho, Rastus, now you can have your chair."

Rastus growled, as much as to say, *I know that*, as he got up, assembled his loose bones and skin, and laying the square sample of carpet on the seat, slowly, like half of a big-skulled spider, lifted his body into place; then turning round to encircle himself, collapsed with a sigh.

Decca trench gramophone box under one arm, case of records in hand, Phillip almost skipped into his grandfather's house, to tell him about the beauties of Ancient Greece.

To his surprise, Gran'pa had been there, years ago, making a tour with Mr. Newman, who had died of the heat in the hot summer of 1911.

"Everything comes from the energy of the sun," said Thomas Turney, to his grandson. "The sun of the Mediterranean is bright, the sea is deep blue, the land is bare and rocky. The Greeks were great sailors when Britain was a wooded island, almost entirely covered by oak scrub, the indigenous tree of this island, that was sacred to the Druids, because of its great usefulness. It is the conditions of a land and its surrounding sea that produce religions, you know, or rather the thought from which religious systems are made. I've been reading a remarkable book, Frazer's *Golden Bough*. You must read it one day. The atmosphere of the eastern Mediterranean produced the hard bright poetry of the Greeks, and also gave them their tragic background, of exploration and war, for the two go together. This present war is a maritime war, y'know. A century ago it was Napoleon; his war was a war for the sea-lanes of commerce."

"I didn't know that you knew all about the Greeks, Gran'pa. Where did you pick it up?"

"Well, where did you pick up what you know, my boy?"

"Oh, here and there, but chiefly from two friends I made in the army—classical scholars of Oxford University."

"Travel is the best university. It broadens the mind, prepares it to assimilate classical knowledge later in life. Look at my poor boy Hughie, he learned nothing at Cambridge, except to drink, and keep up with bad companions. Now if ye'll take my advice, after this war you will learn Spanish. America is the coming continent, and especially South America. Learn Spanish."

"Well, I'll see, Gran'pa. Good-night, sir, good-night, Aunt Marian."

When he had gone, the old woman said, "What a nice boy Phillip has become, Tom. How well he looks, too, after his visit to the West Country!"

Richard was delighted to lend his Sunbeam bicycle, which after a dozen years of the most careful use was still without a chip on its many coats of stove-enamellings, and its thick nickle platings. The chain, running inside the patented "Little Oil Bath", the sprockets, the Sturmey-Archer 3-speed gear, were all as new, after more than four thousand miles on the cyclometer. Indeed, Richard was proud that his son should want to ride his "machine", which he never rode himself nowadays.

"You're becoming quite a man of society, aren't you?" he said.

In whites, with pipe-clayed shoes, wearing Donegal tweed jacket and silk scarf round neck, Phillip free-wheeled down the road, waved to Mrs. Neville (who had been told, the previous night, all about the visit to Turret House), nearly fell off, his racquet being held across the handlebars, and in second gear pedalled up the slight incline of Charlotte Road, watched by his mother from her bedroom window, hidden behind lace curtains, since she knew his dislike of being observed.

"Mr. Phillip's his old self again, ma'm," said Mrs. Feeney, who had watched from the front-room window. "And fancy, on the master's machine! Merry and bright, and holding himself upright like a real gentleman. Ah, but you can't beat a uniform for smartness, ma'm! Now you can leave the house quite safe with me, and go up with Miss Doris to meet Miss Polly at Euston. I'll wait until you come back, and get the master's and Miss Mavis' tea if anything happens to hold you up. So don't you worry, ma'am," said this poor woman of impeccable Victorian manners.

Chapter 26

LAWN TENNIS

When Phillip arrived, the grass court behind the cleft-oak fence and privet hedge was empty. His first feeling was to leave: then he went through the gate and lay down on the edge of the lawn in the shadow of a linden tree, and held his face to the sun. Five minutes or so later he heard a scurr of tyres on the dusty road and the soft double pad of Helena's alighting plimsolls. He lay still, pretending to be asleep; but his heart thudded so hard that he decided to get up, lest he be giddy when he did so in her presence. Also make-believe belonged to the past; he must act the man.

The gate clicked, she passed through, and was walking in shadow, smiling, her eyes steadily on his, and a faint blush on her cheeks that he had seen when she had looked at Bertie on the Hill that Sunday of May, 1915. No longer did the blue-grey eyes seem proud and confident; and at the sight of them he felt himself quiver, as though stricken.

They began to play a sort of pat-ball. He thought she was the nurse taking care that the patient did not do too much, so he began to serve as his father had taught him years before, pitching the ball high and striking it with the racquet so that a left spin or a right spin could be put on the ball as it was struck, with arm extended to full height, against the gutted frame. Thus the ball, descending fast over the top of the net, had swerve on it, to break away left or right of the line.

A puff of whiting on the grass, the ball was gone past Helena. Three more puffs; and game to the server.

"I say, you're quite hot stuff, aren't you?"

"Sorry. I'll serve slower next time."

"Rather not! No favours!"

Helena's back-hand drives and volleys were as good as her forehand drives and volleys; Phillip's were erratic. Game to Helena. One all.

She was two games ahead when Milton arrived, hatless, wearing white flannels and khaki tunic ... a staff-captain! And never been to the front! How did they wangle it? *Major* Wigg, *Captain* Cox, *Captain* Milton, all with red tabs, or were Cox's yellow, for the Chinese Labour Corps?

"Hullo, Milton, you one-piecee bad boy! Long time since I saw you."

"Let me introduce you to my sister, Cherry. This is Mr. Maddison."

She was as tall as her brother, but with hair, eyebrows and lashes almost the colour of silver sand. Rather delicate, he thought, as they spun for partners, and he and she paired off. He played badly, his thoughts not on the game, but on Milton and Helena opposite, as he watched for signs of something more than friendship between them. Was that an endearing glance from Helena to Milton? He began to pay attention to his partner. Why was she called Cherry? A cherry should be dark, with black shiny eyes and ringlet hair. This Cherry was not delicate, she was strong, she could hit hard, her breasts moved up and down together, quickly. Assiduously he collected the balls for her, darting after them between the services, handing her two promptly each time, noting that Helena's glance was often his way. This was encouraging. He played with spirit; and when it was his turn to serve, won a love game. Cherry's "Well done, partner", with upward glance of sea-green eyes, her rather fascinating silver-sand eyelashes and brows kindled him. Then at one particular moment he felt the clearness of himself in freedom. The shadow was no more. Could he believe it? Yes, it had actually gone! It was startling; he wanted to give an enormous shout. It was a wonderful feeling.

He swirled; and leaned upon his racquet handle.

"Are you all right? Phillip, would you like to rest?"

Cherry spoke through half-closed lips, demurely; she glanced slyly out of the corners of her eyes. "I hope you don't mind my calling you Phillip, Mr. Maddison?"

She was a white-fleshed cherry, a white eating-Morello. There was a little down on her upper lip, the faintest little moustache, soft, downy. Gentle, soft white cherry; breasts of half cherry.

"I'll be all right in a moment."

"Are you sure? You can't be very strong yet, after your leg——"

"Oh, that was nothing."

"Nothing? The Vicar mentioned you in prayers, for three Sundays running."

"Hi, what are you two doing?"

"Do you mind if we stop for a few moments, Helena?"

"No, I'm all right, really."

"I want a rest anyway," said Cherry, striking her racquet on her starched and laundered white skirt; while her brother lit a cigarette. He had a gold case, Phillip noticed, like that of Mr. Bloody Wigg.

After two sets they went into a room behind the parish hall, where was a trestle table and plates and cups and saucers, a gas-ring and a kettle. He felt himself to be floating in the warm friendly sunshine of the mellow September day: a most extraordinary feeling of contentment that he was no longer apart from life. He was living in the present, careless. How had it happened? Was it the presence of Milton, who showed consideration and obvious liking for him, almost a deference? Did Milton remember how he had cribbed from him in the Arithmetic paper, when their desks had adjoined in Hall during the Oxford Local examinations; and how he had not told the truth, but allowed another to be flogged instead, and so saved himself from possible expulsion?

Had Milton told his sister what a little hero he had been, and was that the reason why she was so friendly? Or was it all his fancy, and had Milton forgotten it long ago: or even believed now, if he ever thought of it, that he had told him the correct answers, as Milton had inferred to the Magister? Anyway, what did it matter, that insignificant episode of long ago? Funny how he should remember it now, after all that had happened since August, 1914.

As a fact, the injustice of the flogging in the Magister's study in 1913 had come to the forefront of Phillip's mind on one other occasion: when he had shouted against the Magister during the bayonet charge with the Guards Brigade against the Prussians in the wood near the Menin Road on 11 November 1914; but he had not known that he had shouted his most harming thoughts, in the midst of frenzied men shouting theirs.

After tea more players appeared. The Vicar came, with his wife, whom he called Miranda. Phillip remembered that Mrs. Mundy's hair used to be red; now it was almost the colour of lead peroxide, much darker. Her eyes were still green, though the lashes were thicker, as though black cotton had been gummed on to them. Surely she did not paint, or use rouge? Mr. Mundy was quite bald, very red in the face, and rather bouncy in front, fatter in fact. He hoped he had forgotten the copy of Gould's *British Birds* he had taken out of the Free Library immediately after it had been returned by his wretched, schoolboy self, with the awful remarks he had scrawled on some of the plates, particularly that of the Shag.

"Coming to the dance tonight, Phillip?"

"I didn't know there was one, sir."

"Oh yes. It's Leap Year, and so the gels are bringing the boys. We must see about finding you a partner."

"Really, sir, thank you all the same, but I'm not much of a dancer."

"I can only dance the hornpipe, but I'm coming! What about you, Cherry dear? Coming? Good, that's settled. You'll bring our wounded soldier boy."

"Are you sure you don't mind?" she said, when the Vicar had gone away. "I wasn't going to come, but I will if you'd like to." Silver-sand lashes fluttered.

"I haven't got any dancing pumps!"

"There are some in the shops!"

"All right, I'll get some. But I'm a cave-man dancer, I warn you!"

"How exciting!"

"What time is the hop?"

"Eight o'clock. It's a flannel dance, by the way. Or hop, as you say. I'll meet you here in the hall, shall I?"

"Rather. Shall I bring my trench gramophone?"

"That would be lovely. We can play it when the pianist is having a rest."

"It's mostly classical stuff, I'm afraid. Greig, Elgar, Brahms, and Chaminade's *Autumn*."

"I simply adore that French woman's stuff!"

They looked at each other delightedly.

St. Simon's Parish Hall was *en fête*. Strings of flags of the Allies crossed diagonally from the wall-plates. Bowls of chrysanthemums stood on little tables around the walls, at intervals in the rows of chairs. On each table was a candle standing on a white plate, illumining the flowers. The curtain'd windows, the rafters and beams above, the pitch-pine panelling below, gave the place a cavernous appearance, wherein white forms with happy faces and gleaming eyes passed, to the haunting lilt of Leo Fall's *Eternal Waltz* on the gramophone, while feet susurrated on the parquet floor made smooth, and in places almost slippery, by scatterings of french chalk.

At one end of the hall was a daïs, and on the wall at the back hung a lithographic portrait of Edward the Seventh in a red cloak trimmed in ermine, and white satin breeches, wearing the crown and holding ball and sceptre—a Coronation portrait. Beside this picture was another, of Queen Alexandra; each had its candle, for the Vicar once had been presented to both, as Prince and Princess of Wales, when he had served as a naval chaplain in a dreadnought.

Phillip was going round the floor with Cherry. He had not asked Helena to dance; he was hoping to make her keen thereby: while at the same time feeling that by continuing to ignore her, he was, as he put it, throwing away his chances. This made him feel the keen wire, on which his feelings seemed to be twisting, tighten into faint self-torture. With this was a desire to make Cherry bend to his will, as he felt her nature coming warm upon him as they pressed together.

There was an interval for coffee and cake; it was half-past ten; the hop ended at midnight, and there was, when dancing began again, only an hour and twenty minutes to go. He danced on, with Cherry, feeling after each sitting-out period that he was destroying himself in Helena's eyes.

At half-past eleven Mr. Mundy the vicar beckoned him into the room behind a hanging curtain, where tea had been made; and there he took a bottle of whiskey out of a cupboard, and they had a secret drink together, clinking glasses.

"Your health!"

"Cheerho!"

The bottle was hidden, and as Phillip passed under the curtain he saw Helena coming down the passage beside the platform, where sometimes amateur plays were performed. The passage was hardly wide enough for two to pass abreast, but something in Helena's smiling face drew him on, politeness forgotten, and as they passed he realised that he was leaning forward and sideways to her at the same moment that she inclined her head towards him, and as they passed they kissed one another, hardly stopping. He went on into the hall, feeling to be gliding on air, with no desire to look back, as though a gleam of sunlight had fallen on both their heads at the same moment. With the sense of gliding on air he went to Cherry and sat beside her, feeling that he did not exist, that it was a dream, and Cherry's face was glowing, too. Then Milton came over to them with a look of subdued contentment, and sat on the other side of him. Milton leaned forward, resting elbows on knees, and stared smilingly at the floor.

Then he turned to Phillip and said, "Congratulate me! I see you have already done so to Helena."

Phillip's heart seemed to explode; then it dropped away deeply beneath the floor. He controlled his breathing, and glanced at Milton, realising that he had a look of cousin Bertie on his face. He was the same build, the same broad face, relaxed and easy.

"I do congratulate you, Milton."

Helena came back and sat beside Milton. Her face was shining. Phillip looked at her, smiling, but with tremulous lips. Then to his alarm he felt he was going to cry, and saying, "I'll be back in a moment," returned to the room behind the curtain. There the Vicar was helping himself to a quick one from the bottle.

"Ah, you've caught me, Phillip! Well, join me, dear boy."

As they clinked glasses, Phillip said, "Did you know before, about Milton?"

"What do you think?" said the Vicar, looking over his spectacles, and smiling. "Don't take it too hard, will you? There are others, you know."

"I was so surprised, sir. I hardly knew what was happening just now. It was a sort of butterfly kiss, a light touch on the flower of her lips, and she was gone."

"Helena told me, dear boy. Your health!"

"Cheerho!"

The Vicar looked at Phillip's face, and said, "These things are made on earth, but they begin in heaven. I have known both Joe and Helena since they were kids, and they are as alike as two peas from a pod. Or should I say two finches of the same sub-species. You know, a chaffinch is a finch, but it knows better than to mate with a sparrow, or a bullfinch. Their patterns are different. Think of the confusion in nest-building! You know what I mean?"

"Yes, I think so, Vicar."

"Of course we must not tell anyone, Phillip. Joe will have to ask her father's permission first."

Phillip broke into tears. Mr. Mundy put his hand on his shoulder. Phillip looked up. Soon he was smiling.

"There!" said Mr. Mundy. "The emotional constraint is gone! You are free, dear boy. Now go back and dance with Cherry. And shall you ask Helena to dance? Perhaps too much of a gesture? It's rather strange, isn't it, suddenly to feel an old self slipped away, like casting a slough? But that is how we develop. Suddenly our lives are changed. Go back and dance with Cherry, dear boy."

The Vicar squeezed his arm, and in a daze where before it had been a dream, Phillip went back to the piano music, the candles, and the revolving figures in white.

When Mrs. Neville threw down the front-door key next morning she could see Phillip had some startling news. He came so slowly up the stairs. He was so grave and calm.

"Well, Phillip, how did the dance go?"

"Oh, quite pleasant, Mrs. Neville. The light touch, you know. I kissed a girl or two, and they kissed me, including Helena."

"Oh no, Phillip! Oh no! It can't be true. Don't you dare to play any tricks on me! I couldn't stand it!"

The round eyes stared at him.

She was not pretending; at least, not wholly. The *feuilleton*, the serial story of Phillip's vain dream of Helena, had been going on in monthly, and sometimes weekly and even daily instalments, for nearly ten years. And now, unexpectedly, the climax! The habits of mind of many years are not easily relaxed. Mrs. Neville's round eyes stared at Phillip, as she sighed deeply, and resigned her bulk to the back of her chair.

"I've lived in your life, so long now, you see——"

"It's no joke, Mrs. Neville. I just kissed her, and she just kissed me."

"What else, Phillip? What happened next? Don't keep me in suspense like this!" She flipped a hand at him.

"Nothing. Or everything!"

Mrs. Neville stared at him. "Were you drunk, Phillip?"

"No, but I had just had one with the Vicar, in the room behind the stage."

"What was it? Napoleon brandy?" she cried.

"Just ordinary whiskey."

He told her what had happened, and having sworn her to secrecy, announced the news of Helena's engagement to Joe Milton.

"And that's why she kissed you, Phillip! How sweet of Helena! And what a compliment to you! She must be fond of you, dear. Well, I don't wonder! You're attractive, you know, and have the lightest touch, a gracefulness, at times. Now what about Cherry?"

"Well, as Milton took Helena home, I took Cherry to her house, kissed her at the gate, and then we kissed again, and she ran up the path blowing kisses to me, a dim ghost. It was all like Tennyson, in those songs in *The Princess*. So I set out for a long walk, as the night was too beautiful to go to bed. In fact, I walked about most of the night, and had an early breakfast at a carter's pull-up in Brumley at 4 a.m. After that I walked home."

"What did Father say?"

"I didn't see him before he left for the office."

"Did Polly arrive last night? Have you seen her?"

"No, she and Doris went out before I got up. You know, I don't think I've ever felt so free in my life before. I can't realise it all yet. The way her lips parted, her eyes shone! The way her neck turned, and the chin came up, you know how rounded it is, and then the lips, slightly parted—it was so spontaneous! It should have happened in the bright sunlight of ancient Greece, where the atmosphere of eternal summer on the bare and rocky ground produces that hard bright classical poetry. Ah, if only I could write poetry, Mrs. Neville!"

When next Mrs. Neville tossed the key upon the terra-cotta tiled approach to the flat, the face looking up at her was as dejected as it had been exalted.

"I must see you!"

He came up the stairs so fast that she feared for his leg.

"I shall have to get married!"

"Oh, Phillip, what are you saying now? Don't tell me Helena's jilted Joe, and wants you!"

He collapsed into his chair, and rested his face in his hands. Mrs. Neville could see that something serious had happened. She waited. At last she said,

"Well, Phillip, what is it, dear?"

"Polly."

"Polly? What do you mean?"

"She says she's going to have a baby." He looked into her face, as though expecting her to cry out; but two could play at being extremely calm.

"How very interesting life's becoming for you, Phillip, isn't it, when one comes to think of it? But do tell me how you know that you are going to be a father? Did Polly say so?"

"Yes."

"Did she give any particular reason?"

"Well, yes. She said that her, you know, has stopped."

Mrs. Neville laughed lightly. "Well, I doubt it is the first time a woman has thought she was going to have a baby, when she wasn't. Did she give any dates?"

"No, Mrs. Neville."

"When was the last one, did she say? About six weeks ago? A fortnight late is nothing. I was afraid at first that she was going to say from last June, just before you went out to France. Now tell me, does she know what happened at the tennis dance?"

"Only what she heard from Mavis, that I didn't come back until half-past five the next morning. 'Where did you go?' she asked me. 'In the sheep-fold?'"

Mrs. Neville shook with laughter. Now she knew where Polly had been with Phillip in the past; and the idea of Helena being there for five and a half hours during a dewy September night with Phillip, his head filled with lyrical notions, was extremely comical.

"I must say, however, that this, coming right on top of the other thing, would depress anyone. But don't worry. Polly will be here staying with your sister how long, five or six days? Until Sunday? I see. School begins next Monday, of course. Well, before she goes, bring her to tea, and then leave her with me, and I'll find out about Miss Polly, and how far she is gone, if any way at all! You get on with your tennis, and think no more about marriage."

"I wouldn't like Polly to have an illegal operation, Mrs. Neville."

"Of course not! The very idea! But I wouldn't mind betting it's just an ordinary lateness; don't you worry your head about it. Desmond will be on convalescent leave any day now, and I'm sure he'll be only too ready to make friends again. Oh, the boys and their girls! Go and play some more tennis with that Cherry, she sounds rather nice. Kiss Cherry, by all means. What harm is there in a kiss? If there was more genuine kissing in this world, I don't mean the Keechey sort of kissing, which is done with razors, thinking only of one thing, the rat—no, Phillip, a genuine kiss, a token of warm affection, which is what the world so sadly misses today—— Oh fouff! What am I talking like this for—let's go the whole hog and have a little drop out of the air-raid brandy bottle!"

"Yes," she went on, "don't take life so seriously, not girls, anyway, though what else there is in life, when you come to think of it, but men and women—— Anyway, keep to your new-found light touch. And don't, as I said, think too much of one girl, not yet, anyway. Man is a polygamous animal, at least most men are, until they find the one woman who satisfies them. Look at Byron, what he went through, trying to find happiness! Why, at one time he even had to have an affair with his half-sister, Augusta, to find out where he stood! It can't be proved, of course, but one day something may come to light, to confirm what biographers have only surmised so far. Anyway, this Cherry sounds interesting; but don't go and make her fond of you unless you really want her, will you? As for Helena, although she is a very nice girl, I never really thought she was your spiritual sort, dear. What has happened is that you've dreamed about her so long, that she became a beacon in your life. You see, Phillip, you have an imagination beyond the normal, and so you are bound to suffer when life does not appear to come up to your expectations of it. You are an idealist, you know. Try not to anticipate, take life as easily as you can. You've always worried far too much about things, you know; and as for being selfish, don't you believe it! Why, you've been like an elder brother to Desmond and Gene, and Desmond will see it one day. When my son was young it was Phillip says this and Phillip does that, all the time. That little misunderstanding about Lily will blow over, you mark my words. She is a very nice girl; she's been here to see me, you know. Oh yes, Lily and I are very good friends!"

"Where is she, Mrs. Neville?"

"Oh no, you don't! You know very well that Lily is fond of you, and you don't want her, so let her alone, Phillip."

"I wouldn't hurt her."

"No, not deliberately, Phillip; but Lily has been very badly hurt, as you know, and if it were to happen again—— No, it must not happen again. Lily has found her vocation, and soon will be leaving the district."

"Mayn't I see her before she goes?"

"Well, you know how attractive she is, don't you? She's such a sweet girl, too. No; I am sure that it would be for the best if you did not see her again. Besides, she's not really your sort, quite apart from her station in life."

"How do you know she isn't my sort, Mrs. Neville?"

"Well, Phillip, to be frank, I doubt if you know yourself yet. One has to find oneself, you know, by losing self-centredness. I can say this, now that you have begun to see Helena without rose-tinted spectacles. You will need someone with what the French call *sensibilité*, someone instinctively in tune with all the things you love, which are your real life. You remember Mrs. Hudson? Of course you do. You two got on well immediately, I could see that. Did you notice the way she held her hands? And her head?"

"Yes. She looked so graceful, and young somehow, in spite of her grey hair. I liked her from the first look at her."

"She said the same thing of you, Phillip. You both have an inward grace of the spirit, you see, which informs your movements."

"What, me, Mrs. Neville?"

"Yes, you always did have that grace, Phillip, but only lately has it begun to show itself steadily. You are so much calmer since you came back this time. I suppose it is due to many things, all of them helping to form character. That's the other word I wanted, to describe Maude Hudson—she has character, as well as sensibility. Sensibility without character is rather like water running to waste in sand, Mr. Hudson used to say. Sensibility is kept in focus by a formed character—the most valuable thing in the world. All the great artists had it, otherwise how would they have done all the work they had to do? Genius is fairly common, Mr. Hudson used to say; but what is rare was to find one that had been sober, industrious, and in his last situation for a number of years. He got it from Bernard Shaw, of course, who often came to Maud's *salon* in Highgate, with others of the Fabians, you know," concluded Mrs. Neville, in her most elegant voice.

"Now don't worry about Polly, will you? Just have a good time, and begone dull care! Oh what the devil am I talking to you like

this for? Of course you know what to do! But I will say one thing.
I have a feeling that everything is going to come right for you now.
You know, I was quite taken with that girl Frances, the *mannequin*
you told me about. Now she seemed to be a really nice person!
Have you seen her since you came back?"

"No, Mrs. Neville, but I might when Westy goes to Buck House
to get his gong from H.M."

"My, aren't we getting up in the world, Phillip! Well, you will
find your proper level one day. But you must leave Lily alone.
What that girl needs is a husband, so that she can have the babies
that every woman wants, Phillip."

Chapter 27

COMPLICATION

Phillip went down to Freddy's bar. It would not be deceitful, he
told himself, if while he was there Lily happened to come in. In
his fatigue, the heaviness upon him, he longed to rest in the image
of her tenderness. He could be himself with her; safe with her;
he understood her, through and through. He saw that Helena,
throughout the years, had been like a light at sea to a drifting
hulk; a light that was the bright star in the poem by Keats; an
ideal. While Mrs. Neville had been speaking of Lily, the image
of her large shining eyes had seemed to hold warmth, rest, peace,
tenderness. He could be himself with her, as with no other person
he knew. Just by thinking of her, he felt himself to be gold-dust,
like a humblebee in a yellow flower. His inner self cried to be
with her, to lose itself in her tenderness, to be absorbed, his face
to be covered with her hair, his spectral self to be lost in the
silver-gold glow of Aurora, the dawn of new life. *Leave Lily alone*,
said Mrs. Neville. As though he would hurt her! Physical love
was nothing; it should be for children, not for triumph and con-
quest. Love was not love that had strain in it.

"Well, I'm very pleased to see you again, sir!"

The eyes of Freddy almost disappeared in his smile as he looked
into Phillip's face. After some time, Phillip casually mentioned
the name of Lily.

"Now, isn't that funny? The wife and I were only saying just
now that we haven't seen her all the summer. She went to be a

nurse, you know. She was down here at the Infirmary for a while, and then got moved to the London Hospital in Whitechapel. I fancy Dr. Dashwood will know if she is still there, he got her into it. Or if you don't want to see him, her mother lives close by, in Nightingale Grove."

He walked up and down past her house, on the opposite side of the road, unable to make up his mind; then turned away, meaning to walk to Cutler's Pond, and so tire himself out, and be able to sleep. But the prospect was now flat and damp, not as when he had walked there, after the dance, inspired by Helena's kiss; so he went back to Freddy's, there to see, to his immense relief, his old school-friend Cundall. They fell upon one another, while Freddy looked on and said,

"I can't tell you how seeing you two back again 'as cheered me up. It only wants your friend, Desmond Neville, to come in, for it to appear like old times." Then seeing Phillip looking at the stained-glass partition of the billiard room—"You won't see our friend there for a year or two, if ever again. Keechey got pinched by a special Investigation squad trying to induce an old woman what lived alone to make a will in 'is favour, by threats and intimidation. It was just after you went out to France the last time. The case comes up at the Sessions at the end of the month. So you won't have any more worry from that direction."

"And no more, I hope, from them bleedin' gas-bags o' yourn!" remarked Mrs. Freddy, looking at Cundall's R.F.C. maternity jacket. "But don't try and kid me it was you what got that one down at Cuffley, for I seen the curly-haired feller's face in the papers, 'im to 'oom they gived the V.C."

"But what is more," said Cundall, "Leefe Robinson's been given the freedom of the Piccadilly Grill. God knows what he'd have got the freedom of if it had been the redoubtable Mathy in L 31 he had sent to Valhalla. All the duchesses in London, I expect. And look at the cash he's picked up! Cheques pouring in by every post, two thousand quid from someone called Joseph Cowen, one thousand from Lord Michelham, five hundred from a bloke called Bow, a shipbuilder of Paisley. What it is to be a national hero. He's doomed."

Cundall went on to tell Phillip that Robinson was in the same squadron as himself, No. 39, but in No. 2 flight stationed at Sutton's Farm, between Hornchurch and Dagenham.

"Good lord, I know that country!"

"Robinson had all the luck, to run into that Schutte Lanz where he did. He spotted and lost another first, over Woolwich. I was up with the second patrol, from Hainault Farm, at one o'clock. I'd got to five thousand in my B.E. 2c and saw Randy Rupert scissored between two searchlights over Woolwich. That was the one Robinson saw about the same time from thirteen thousand feet. I saw it turn north and then lost sight of it, so I went on climbing, and went for a joy-ride back over London. At twelve thousand feet I was over the north-west suburbs, and then I saw another, held between three searchlights, and Archie bursting well under it, but it was too far away. Robinson had got there first. He put a drum of alternate New Brock and Pomeroy along one side of Randy Rupert, then another drum along the other side. Nothing doing, so he gave it a third drum up its arse. I didn't know this at the time, of course, but I knew there was something doing when archie stopped and the searchlights. Then a glow like a Chinese lantern, only red, grew into an inferno of fire with shreds of flame dropping away from it. Then all of a sudden, it was brighter than noon up there! It had a wooden frame, and burned incandescent as it rushed down. In fact, it was a comet. White, blinding. Almost screaming, the thing was. A great white comet with a tail, heading for the earth. We heard afterward that people could see to read by the light at Tunbridge Wells in Kent, at Guildford in Surrey, and at Baldock in Hertfordshire."

"Good God!"

"I prayed, I can tell you! Also, on the principle of Cromwell, who believed in himself as well as in God, I switched off my engine, and watched Leefe Robinson diving away and pooping off red Very lights, then a parachute flare. Then I stalled, and had a most unholy feeling that I was a flamer as the thing began to break up, and turn slowly into a yellow skeleton. Then I realised I was for it, if I couldn't start the engine, but have to force-land somewhere in the dark. When she spluttered and gave her revs. I said another prayer, promising I'd be a good boy in future. When I got back to the drome at Hainault I was a mass of sweat, and half an hour later I was up to the back teeth in whiskey. That's the birdman's life on the Home Front. You've been in the real war, I hear, so has your pal Neville. How is he?"

"He's back, too. Got blown up. Haven't seen him yet."

"You heard about our conchy school chum Ching, of course? No? Well, he and lots of other Cuthberts have been combed out of Whitehall. Ching's now in the Artist's Rifles. When I saw him last he asked me if I could advise him how to get a commission as a kiwi."

"What's that?"

"Equipment officer in the R.F.C. A mere groundling who has all the fun with none of the fury."

"I wonder if Ching really does believe all that stuff in the Bible."

"The literature of cranks and cowards? As Bernard Shaw said, 'The last Christian died on the Cross'. Basically, conscientious objectors want to save their own skins. Why not? If you're a professional soldier, it's different. He's a man of honour. Honour is a professional bargain. You stand by me and I'll stand by you."

"You always were a brainy bird, Cundall. But surely Bernard Shaw is an ass? Everyone knows it."

"You've been reading newspapers. Bernard Shaw is the modern Voltaire."

"Who's he, when he's at home?"

"Only the greatest thinker of the eighteenth century."

"Well, to come back to Ching. Why don't people like him? He tries to be kind and considerate to me, yet I simply can't stick him."

"Ching doesn't belong to himself. He's grown up skew-wiff to life. No real base. He's Jerry-built. Don't ask me why."

"Just like me."

"Not on your life! Your trouble is that you always think everyone is like you. Ching's not like you. He's a nasty piece of work."

"Do you think it's born in a person, Cundall?"

"Partly. Western man is rotting, that's the trouble. The war is the epitome of the sexual rot, the sadism, the bunk in Western man. Christian bishops quote Jesus Christ in support of it, the corrupt ones, anyway. The German bishops who have come out for the war, with the French and English bishops, are equally corrupt. They're killing Christendom between them."

"Where did you get all your ideas from?"

"Gibbon's *Decline and Fall of the Roman Empire*, Carlyle, Havelock Ellis, Bertrand Russell, Bernard Shaw, Tolstoi, Keats, Shelley, Shakespeare, Voltaire, among others. Read them, and you'll get a glimmer of what civilisation is heading for."

"What is it heading for?"

"We're all on a voyage of death. The prophets have seen through civilisation to the reality behind it—the sickness in our souls, the obscenity of present day living, because love has been lost, and fouled, in the grime of industrial fog."

Phillip saw that Cundall's face, always pale, was set and strained.

"Civilisation has got the death urge of self-destruction. 'Kill Huns' we say, to escape our own torments. We really want to escape our own death-feelings like that. We get this death-wish in our very early years. We really want to kill our fathers then, because they take away our mothers, when we are very small. We don't realise it of course. That's why fathers and sons are usually antagonistic. It was known by Sophocles, for his play *Oedipus Rex* illustrates it."

"Do you mind if we sit down? It's rather airless in here."

They sat on the horse-hair settee.

"I thought about all this as I watched S.L.11 going down over Cuffley the other night, when my engine was dud. Both engines, in fact: my own, and the B.E.s."

"I think I know what you mean," said Phillip. "Let's have another drink. Desmond will be home next week, we must have a night out together."

"Doubt if I'll be able to manage it. Meddlesome Mathy and his myrmidons will be about in the dark of the hunter's moon, with little presents from Krupps."

After closing time he went round to Nightingale Grove and knocked at Mrs. Cornford's door. She opened it and invited him in. He told her about France and she told him about Lily, saying that her girl was getting on well in her training, and would be pleased to hear that he had called to ask after her. She was ironing clothes. After asking if he minded her continuing she put on a kettle for a cup of tea. Then she made him a cheese sandwich, which he ate, hoping it would stop the old swirling feeling that he dreaded from many past experiences of swallowing too much whiskey.

"I'll open the window, Mr. Maddison," she said, in an even, quiet voice as she worked at the ironing board. "We have to be careful about showing a light, with the Zeppelins about, as I expect you know. Yes, Lily is getting on nicely, and will be coming home just for the Saturday night next week-end, if all goes well. That will be, let me see—" she looked at a calendar on the wall, "the 23rd of September. She has to be back at five o'clock on the Sunday afternoon. Shall I tell her you will be coming on the Saturday? Or would you rather leave it open?"

"I would like to see her, but perhaps she will have other plans—"

"None that I know of," said the quiet, soothing voice. "I am sure she would be sorry to miss you. I usually go up to see her on

Wednesday afternoons, so I'll tell her, if you like. How do you like your tea? Weak? Perhaps you won't mind putting in the milk yourself? I'm sorry there isn't a lemon, they are getting scarce, owing to the shipping losses. They say rationing will be coming in soon, have you heard anything about it? No, I don't suppose you would want to bother your head with such things. Does my bumping with the iron disturb you?"

"Oh no, Mrs. Cornford."

After swallowing the tea he felt the swirl, and got on his feet. "I think I ought to go, Mrs. Cornford. Father goes to bed at eleven o'clock, and he's a bit overworked. He can't go to sleep happily until everyone is in bed."

"Parents seldom cease thinking of their children, Mr. Maddison. We know the Sergeant round here, of course. We can put our clocks right by his rounds, so reliable is he. No danger of lights showing while he is on duty. A greatly respected gentleman, if I may say so, is Sergeant Maddison. Lily told me he has a beautifully kept allotment."

"Yes, Mrs. Cornford. Well, thank you for your hospitality. I will look forward to seeing Lily next Saturday."

"I'll give her your message. She often talks of the country ride you gave her on your motorcycle, and the woodpecker you saw. Have you still got your motor?"

"I sold it before I went out, Mrs. Cornford. I loved that expedition to the Fish Ponds."

"You'll be able to talk over it when you see Lily, won't you?" said the grey haired woman in the white apron, serenely. "She comes off duty at five, and will be here, by Tube from Whitechapel to New Cross, and then tram, by about a quarter to six. It will be coming to the moonless nights then, won't it? So if there are Zepps about she might be delayed, or even kept back to look after her patients. You'll understand then, won't you? I'll give her your message when I go up to see her on Wednesday. Thank you for coming, I am so glad you could spare the time. Good night. I'll close the door quickly, if you don't mind, just in case there's something about——"

The next day was Polly's last but one before going back home, so Hetty proposed a picnic on Reynard's Common. Would Phillip care to join them?

"Do, Phil, it will be like old days," said Doris.

"Oh, all right."

So far he had avoided Polly, after her announcement to him;

but meeting her unexpectedly on the landing, he said "I suppose you blame me entirely?"

"It never occurred to me to blame anyone."

"I wish I had let sleeping dogs lie, anyway."

"I don't know what you're trying to talk about."

"Well, if you had not worn that faded, cast-off bathing dress, and shown yourself off in the way you did— As it was, metaphorically speaking, the dogs woke up and gave tongue. After all, you did ask me to dry your back with the towel in your bedroom, after we returned from the swim."

"I called you in only because I knew you were interested in birds, and there was that little bird hopping about by the river, below my window——"

"Anyway, you had no clothes on."

"Dear dear. Were you shocked? I never thought about it."

"Sandpipers hopping! They're waders!"

"Have it your own way."

"It's not my way, it's the sandpiper's way."

"I think you are funny. You always were funny. You always made me laugh."

"Give me a straight answer. Do you, or do you not, think it's all my fault? Anyway, I don't think there's anything funny about it."

"Well then, we need not discuss it further, need we? I am going to help Aunty Hetty and Doris with the picnic basket." And lifting her chin Polly said, "Let me pass, please," and walked downstairs.

It was a mellow day, air calm, the sky blue, as though vacant, but with the last quiet warmth of summer. Phillip hired a Humberette runabout from Wetherley's garage, and drove them to the Fish Ponds. They sat upon the exposed roots of the pines, at the verge of the larger pond, placid with water-lily leaves beginning to decay. The two girls had brought their bathing dresses, but Polly, who had been silent during the drive to Brumley—where she and Doris had done some shopping—did not bathe. She said the water was too cold. So Doris swam alone, while Phillip wandered about, mourning for the care-free days that were gone for ever.

When they returned home he went to see Mrs. Neville. He showed her a prayer-book, with ivory covers, that he had bought on the return through Brumley. "I thought Mother would like it, to remember me by, Mrs. Neville. I saw it as we were going to

Reynard's Common, in the shop next door to the haberdasher's Polly went in with Doris."

"What did she want to buy there?"

"I didn't ask."

"And then she didn't bathe? And she a fine swimmer? And you buy a prayer-book for your mother—all in one morning. Oh dear, I must look into this, Phillip! You bring Polly down here, and leave us alone for awhile, will you. Only don't say it is my suggestion! Ask her down will you, to hear the gramophone."

The Decca had been at the flat since June, except for the evening at the Rolls'.

Having taken Polly down, Phillip returned to his house. Ten minutes later, as he was sitting in the front room—where Father seldom went, so one could be apart there, and feel apart, too, from life, since life as it was known to the family was all about them in the sitting room—he saw Polly come in the gate. He opened the front door. She came in without a word; but as she started to go up the stairs she whispered. "I didn't think that you were a sneak!" and went on before he could think of anything to reply.

Down he went to find out what had happened. Once again Mrs. Neville dropped the key from her window, then went on with her crochet work while he sat before her, waiting for her to begin.

"Well, what did Mother say to the prayer-book?"

"She seemed a little surprised."

"I don't wonder!" cried Mrs. Neville. "The devil was sick—!" Then seeing his rueful face, "It's only my fun, Phillip."

The crochet needle worked up and down. "I'm a little behind-hand with Maude Hudson's birthday present. I want to give her a set of six doilys for her tea-table, so you won't mind my working away while we talk, will you."

"How many have you done so far?" He felt he was splendidly restrained.

"This is the third, only the borders of course, then they're sewn on to the centres. I do think a dainty doily looks well under a silver cake-stand, don't you?"

"Yes, Mrs. Neville. What did Polly say?"

Needle and thread promptly went down. Eyes in the large pastry face became round as pale green grapes.

"Oh, what a brazen hussy! She defied me! 'That is my affair entirely!' she said, holding up her chin. I began by saying, 'Now Polly, let's have no nonsense. Who else did you know in Lynmouth? What about that fellow Piston? Phillip tells me you went out in a motor boat with him one day, as far as Ilfracombe.' 'So I did,' she said, 'but there was a boatman there all the time.' 'Even when you landed to have tea? Come now, don't let's have any nonsense about it,' I said. 'You're talking the nonsense,' she says looking at me, as bold as brass! 'And I'll go further,' she says, 'and tell you that you don't know what you're talking about. So there!' she says.

"'Oh ho, my girl, it's like that, is it? Well let me tell you that your whole attitude is causing Phillip a very great deal of worry, and while I don't for a moment say that Phillip is blameless—boys will be boys and girls will be girls, we all know that, I've been young myself you know—but there's a feeling about this affair I can't quite feel happy about. And you know what I mean, don't you, Polly?'

"'I haven't the least idea what you're trying to say,' she says.

"'Very well, let's get down to brass tacks, since that's something you'll understand, my girl,' says I. Oh, I could see it was going to be a contest of wills, Phillip! And I admire her for it! Well, as I was saying, 'There's nothing the matter with you, Polly, and you know it. Now tell me this! Where did you spend that ten shilling note Phillip gave you, for that medicine? You didn't buy anything with it, did you? Until, that is, you found that you suddenly had to go into a haberdasher's shop this morning? Was it anything to do with the fact that you, a fine swimmer, didn't swim afterwards in the Fish Ponds? Answer those questions, my girl, if you can!'

"'Why should I?' she says, oh, bolder than ever she was, the minx!—'I shall not, if I don't want to, so there! It is entirely my business,' she says, 'and none of yours, not in the very least!' she says."

Mrs. Neville exploded, "I expected her next to ask if I had been given power of attorney!"

"Well, she admitted that she was sometimes irregular in her ways. You know the business women have to put up with I expect. Anyway, she could not bathe today for a very good reason, and so you have nothing more to worry over."

"Then she's not going to——"

"No, dear, she's not, so you've no need to worry," said Mrs. Neville gently. Then the comic side of her rushed in. "But don't go and do what a fellow I knew once did—he worried so much over a girl he'd got into trouble that in his relief after getting her clear of it he promptly put her back in the family way again!"

"No fear. I've learned my lesson, Mrs. Neville. Well, thank you ever so much." Then thinking of Lily, he got up.

"What are you going to do now!"

"I'm going to have a word with Polly. I think I ought to say I'm sorry for having worried her."

Mrs. Neville, a look of wisdom on her face, slowly shook her head. "No, dear, women are not like men. After all, Polly is a woman, and a woman's dearest wish is to hold her baby—" out came the little square of lawn—"in her arms." Having recovered from her momentary melting mood, she went on. "So say nothing, Phillip. And don't be too kind, or she may begin to hope——" More eye attention. "I feel a brute, you know. After all, isn't it natural—even if it was all pretence—to want to be a mother? Instinct, you know, is after all an agent of Creation, and in war-time, with all its death and destruction, the spirit of life works on—faster than before, judging by all I hear!" the voice ended on the familiar ribald note. Mrs. Neville sighed.

"Don't think me cynical will you, Phillip? But as I get older, you know, I see the comic side of life more and more. No, don't go and tell her you're sorry. Polly is evidently fond of you. You can be attractive at times, you know!"

Another line of thought opened up. "I wonder what Helena is thinking. She always looks up at this window, you know, and waves to me. Still, no harm has been done there. She probably feels as you do—glad that you're free of your *idée fixe*, as Mr. Hudson used to call it. And after all, you know, you are Bertie Cakebread's cousin, and Bertie liked you, and so there you are. Ever hear from that mannequin, and her friend Alice."

"No, but that reminds me, I mustn't forget to try and see 'Spectre' West on Wednesday, when he goes to Buckingham Palace."

"Will you be able to get in, do you think?"

"Oh no, I shouldn't want to, even if I had the chance."

"Why not, dear?"

To her surprise he broke into tears; but almost immediately recovered. He did not tell her what had suddenly caused him to break—a vision of thousands of still figures lying in Mash Valley as he crawled away from his dead platoon on that afternoon of intolerable sunshine.

Later in the evening Phillip hurried down to tell Mrs. Neville the latest news: a telegram had come from Polly's mother saying that

Percy had been killed during the battle of Flers, on the 15th September.

"Oh no! Not that young country boy! Oh no, Phillip, it isn't fair! That little thing, his mother! She doted on him! We all went to Greenwich Park for that picnic, in the hot summer of 1911, do you remember? And now that red-cheeked country boy is dead, you say? Killed? Oh, it isn't fair, Phillip, it isn't fair!"

He sat before her, while her face fell into ruin. "Don't worry too much, Phillip," she said when she had composed herself. "I know just how you feel. What a pity you and Polly aren't suited to one another, isn't it, so that you could comfort her. Oh, I can't get that little mother out of my mind! She was just like a pawn on a chess-board, the resemblance struck me immediately I saw her. And as good and simple. She must feel herself broken, poor little soul."

"Doris is very cut up, Mrs. Neville, too. She and Percy were very thick. I only wish I could be simple and ordinary, like Polly or Doris, or Percy."

"Go back and be very very kind to them all, dear. Go and comfort them, your mother and sister, and Polly too. At such a time a woman wants someone near her to be strong and stable, to give her extra strength. After all man was made for woman, and woman for man, whatever Darwin may say about it . . . and I'm not sure that his species idea isn't already in the Bible, in Genesis, you know. He merely dug up some old bones and fossils and if he'd read Chapter One of the Bible he would have saved himself a lot of trouble, anyway, that's what Mr. Hudson used to say. 'What's all the fuss about this feller Darwin?' I can hear his very tone of voice now. Still, death is death, and however clever a man fancies himself, we've all got to come down to fundamental realities in the end, so you run along home, dear, and do your best to cheer up your mother and the girls."

What could he say? Percy had copped it; he hadn't been one of the lucky ones. Still, he must try and say something.

Polly, her bag packed, was in her tweed coat and skirt, topped with small fur toque. She looked calm and self-possessed.

"I'm awfully sorry, Polly, really. It was very bad luck. Are you going home now?"

"Yes," said Polly. "I've explained to Aunt Hetty why I must go home tonight, and I'll tell Mother what you say, Phillip."

"Yes, please give her my love, and also Uncle Jim. I'm terribly sorry, Polly. Let me run you up to London in the bus. I was just going to return it down to Wetherley's but I'd like to take you to Euston."

"I do not want to keep you from your friends, thank you all the same."

"Let Phillip take you, dear," said Hetty. "And perhaps Doris could go with you as well, Phillip?"

"Yes, of course I'll come," said Doris, with quiet determination. He could see no signs of weeping on his sister's face. Perhaps women were like men in action; grief came afterwards.

So Polly said goodbye to Aunt Hetty and Uncle Dick, Gran'pa and Aunt Marian, Mrs. Bigge, and Mavis; and if she felt anything she did not show it, not even at Euston station, where just before the train left Doris clung to her and let tears fall.

Phillip stopped at three pubs on the way back, to stoke up, as he put it, while Doris waited in the Humberette outside. He was callous, he told himself: the truth was that the news of Percy being killed had not really affected him, except as a surprise. Why was it, that he could not feel like other people: but only for certain things, like poetry and music and the *idea* of things, and not for the things themselves?

Returning the runabout to Wetherley's, having taken his sister home, he went into Freddy's, and soon felt merry and bright. Tomorrow he would be seeing "Spectre" West. But why was he thinking of Polly, and Percy, and the grief that must now be felt even by the walls of Brickhill House?

He went up early the next morning to Charing Cross, and walked down the Mall to Buckingham Palace. A crowd was outside the tall black and gilt railings, before which sentries of the Welsh Guards in khaki service uniforms with fixed bayonets marched up and down, stamping at the turns. He hung back from the entrance through which motors and taxis with soldiers, sailors, and airmen of all ages and ranks, showing cards of invitation, were allowed in. He did not see his friend.

They began to come out soon after noon: admirals and generals, captains and commanders and colonels, field officers and junior commissioned ranks with their ladies; then the warrant ranks of the Navy and Army, the chief petty officers and the sergeants, with their wives; the lower deck and other ranks with their women, as the official description of the period ran. Hundreds of them; gold

braid upon blue and scarlet; pins on tunic breasts whereon Victoria
Crosses of the bronze of captured guns of the Crimean War, gold
and enamel Knight's Crosses and Companionships and Orders,
smaller crosses and medals of silver had been hung by the gruff-
voiced, bearded King-Emperor.

There were Indian troops as well, some of high rank in turbans
and general's gorget patches, with subahdars and jemadars,
all of whom he saluted, saying to himself that if they had fought
for England then they deserved to be saluted by an Englishman,
whatever the latitude line of the sun shining upon their heads.
Besides, since 'all handsome men were slightly sunburnt', according to the advertisement, ergo, these wallahs being more than
slightly sunburnt were the more entitled to be treated handsomely,
especially as so many of them had the fine, slightly aloof bearing
of aristocrats. Let them therefore be saluted by one who bore upon
his tunic only two slender gold stripes on the left sleeve, since
wounds were all he had gained in battle. If only he had a ribbon
on his left breast; but that was never likely to be.

When he saw "Spectre" he went forward eagerly, but remembering the last occasion when he had shown enthusiasm for his old
friend and been put in his place for it, he walked slowly to where
his group was standing. He recognised Frances, and thought how
top-hole she looked; the two old people were probably his parents.
With a manner of slight self-withdrawal, he hesitated before going
up to them, as they stood, apparently waiting for a taxi. While he
stood there Frances turned her head, under a large picture hat,
and recognised him. With a smile she came to him, showing
delight in her face, as she laid the fingertips of one gloved hand
gently on his forearm.

"Phillip! We wondered if you would be here—— Come and
congratulate Harold. Don't take any notice of his gruff manner,
he's really tremendously pleased to see you, but hates showing it.
Come and meet his parents, my respected uncle and aunt."

Phillip's eye was drawn, with wonder, to the new blue and
cerise riband of the decoration added to the purple and white of
the Military Cross, with its central silver rosette; to the seven
wound stripes on the sleeve, above the wooden hand encased in its
black glove. He saw in a glance that Westy had a torn ear, and
one side of his face had a hollow between cheek and jaw, where a
bullet had ploughed through, leaving the jaw slightly lop-sided. He
hid his thoughts, and kept his gaze on his hero's eye when he
greeted him, after saluting Mrs. West, and bowing.

"Congratulations, Westy. I am so glad."

"You know very well that such things come up with the rations. Are you doing anything for lunch?"

When Phillip said no, Westy told him to hop in when the taxi drew up. He did so last but one, waiting for the old people and Frances to get in first.

Mr. and Mrs. West were modest and self-effacing, concealing all pride in their son. They hardly spoke in the taxi, which turned out of the Mall and went past a dark brown building by iron gates which Frances said was where the Prince of Wales lived when in London. They turned down Pall Mall, which Phillip recognised as the street where Uncle Hilary's club, the Voyagers, stood. If only Uncle could see him riding past, he might realise that he was not the washout that he obviously considered him to be.

The taxi went up the Haymarket to Piccadilly, and stopped outside the Café Royal.

"Well, my dear mother and father, I'll see you later."

"Very well, Harold. We'll expect you when we see you."

"I'll tell the driver to take you home. Thank you for giving me your moral support."

"We can just as well get a bus going east, Harold——"

"Now, Father," said Mrs. West. "No fuss. Goodbye Mr. Maddison, it's been so nice seeing you!" and the taxi drove away.

"'Nosey' is coming up from the War House," said Westy, as they went into the room of red plush, mirrors, and white marble tables. "Let's have a drink, for God's sake." Frances was carrying the case with the decoration. "Do you mind if we look," she was saying, when the expression on her cousin's face stopped her, and she looked whimsically at Phillip.

Gazing around the room, he saw the painter with the beard, sitting alone. Their eyes met. The painter beckoned a waiter, and said something to him. The waiter came over to Phillip. "The major's compliments, and will you and your friends take wine with him at his table."

"Yes indeed," said "Spectre". "He's a very great painter."

Champagne was brought in a bucket of ice. When they were seated at his table the painter said to Phillip, "You've changed since I saw you last, on Christmas Eve. You were most doleful, having lost an illusion."

"Well, sir, that was not the last time I saw you. It was on July the First, and you were painting a broken wall at Albert, as I went past on a stretcher."

"I remember you. You were on a wheeled stretcher. I remember your eyes. I wanted to paint you, but you had to go down the road." Turning to Frances he said, "I remember you, too. You came in here with this boy about a year ago. I remember the line of those shoulders under your coat. I wanted to paint you. You walked like a ballet dancer, in pure horizontal motion, from feet to crown. Most women merely hold up their heads; your mind carries yours, and your entire body. Oh, don't think that you are entirely responsible! Art can do much—sometimes—but Nature can do more. The moment you came in just now, I saw the correlation between you and your brother, or cousin at least— the same genetic traits rule both your lives," he said, turning to "Spectre".

"I am called Harold West. This is my cousin Frances. The boy who ruined a masterpiece with two bullets through his leg is Phillip Maddison."

"A Celt, as you are Norse. The moment of fusion of sight and feeling comes and goes in the Celt; the Norseman is less fluid, like his icebergs and rocky soil. I am a Celt. We have always respected Vikings, and that offshoot tribe the Normans. We may not have defeated them, but we have eluded them, and to some extent tamed them. Perhaps you—", the gay and expressive face of fox into gentleman inclined towards Frances—"will allow me to paint you?"

"I feel highly honoured," said Frances. Her lips suddenly seemed to be pinker, or was it the colour in her cheeks, thought Phillip. Poor "Spectre's" jaw muscle was working, he saw. Was he still in love with her?

"Oh, that crafty fox, how I can see him, the fascinating creature, Phillip! Of course I heard a lot about him when Mr. Hudson was alive. He's a genius, there's no doubt about that; and as a lover I'd rank him far above Byron, for he's a real, full-blooded man whereas poor Byron never really could forget himself, or his club-foot, could he? Well, as I was saying, if that Frances is not very careful, she'll find that she's carrying more than a head filled with compliments!" laughed Mrs. Neville. "Why, you look quite shocked, Phillip! You have a lot to learn about women. We're materialistic creatures, you know. And every woman is at heart a rake, you know. Now tell me more of your luncheon party. It's years since I used to lunch and dine in the West End. Tell me everything."

"Colonel Orlebar came, with his wife. She had smoothed out lines on her face and neck, and was quite old, over thirty I should think, and yet she was gayer than a very young person. I felt a little out of it, for another colonel of the regiment came too, Colonel Mowbray, now a brigadier-general. He came with his daughter. Aren't they terribly polite, Society girls? Are they always on their best behaviour, I wonder?"

"Oh yes, Phillip, they're trained from the cradle—good manners are second-nature to them. Mrs. Hudson has the most exquisite manners. The three rules of manners, she used to say, were, Keep your distance; never repeat the gossip of the servants' hall; never ask personal questions. She is very well-connected. Oh, very! All her brothers went to Clifton, with Desmond's father. Hudson's 'Bristol Ship Shape' tobacco, and wine, you know—one of the old Merchant Venturer families. Some of them are Quakers, of course."

Phillip began to laugh. He saw a family party of Hudsons, all quaking as they tottered away, each seeking a lonely corner in Bristol, after smoking 'Ship Shape' thick twist. Rather as he had felt, half way through his cigar after the luncheon, on top of six glasses of champagne with smoked salmon, lobster, various *gateaux*, a *pêche Melba*, and two Napoleon brandies (at seven-and-six a little glass like a finger, too) all floating about inside him.

Awful! He had locked himself in one of the lavatories, and two hours later, when he had recovered, everyone had gone from the restaurant.

"What a fool I was to drink all that wine! Still, I'll never see any of them again. Even so, I feel awfully ashamed. But the waiter kept filling my glass, and everything was so happy. Still, the real test of a gentleman, which I'm not, is if he can hold his liquor, isn't it?"

"I should think it's much more likely the sign of a healthy stomach if it gets rid of all that poison as soon as it can, Phillip! Mr. Hudson always said that the average healthy human liver can stand no more than two fluid ounces of alcohol. He used to tell us how the French specially lace some of their champagnes with brandy, for the English market; but that they'd rather be found dead in a field—or dead drunk more likely!—than drink it themselves. The English have little regard for the niceties of the palate, you see, Phillip, they drink, Mr. Hudson said, to forget their eternal winter of climate and thought. Anyway, don't you worry yourself unduly. Just write a little note to 'Spectre' West and thank him for his hospitality, and explain that you were not feeling well, and were overcome. He'll understand."

"Yes I will. Thanks for the tip. All the same, I wish I'd pretended when I saw him outside Buck House, as they call it, that I'd promised to go to lunch with someone else. Apart from drinking too much, I didn't really know what to say to them. They talked of India, pig-sticking, polo, friends in the Regiment, while Tenby Jones told the most amusing stories about famous people. He kept them roaring with merriment, but as I didn't know any of the people, I had to pretend to be in the know."

"I expect they understood, dear. A young man in the company of elder men does not have to try and compete, you know. Indeed, if he sits quiet, and is a good listener, they like him for his diffident manner. Youth," pronounced Mrs. Neville, "has one trump card that older people never get dealt to them as they journey on through life."

"What is that, Mrs. Neville."

"Why, youth, dear. '*Ehue fugacious, fugacious*', as Mr. Hudson used to say."

"I know the feeling, Mrs. Neville," he sighed.

Life was not only fugacious, it was stagnant and dull. What could he do, to kill time until Saturday? Play tennis in the evenings? Somehow, he did not feel like going to see Cherry. Nor did he really want to meet Helena, after the really wonderful tennis dance. What was the matter with him? Why, after all the years of intense longing, was Helena now ordinary to him? It was the same about the war, which was fascinating but only when he was not in it: but the moment he was apart from what it really *was*, it seemed romantic and enthralling. Was his brain injured perhaps, by what had happened before he was born, when Gran'pa Turney had knocked Mother down, and she had lain unconscious for several hours, as Uncle Sidney had told him? Perhaps the brain had slipped, and so could never think properly except afterwards, when it changed things from what they really were to something quite different. A misfit of a brain! It missed gear, as it were, and the 'bus didn't go forward properly. Perhaps he was fated to become insane, and these were the symptoms.

He tried to outwalk the thought. He really was a bad person. For example, he had felt an utterly selfish, mean desire to hurt Polly, to put her in the family way, to pay her out—for what? She had never harmed him. Yet others as well felt like that

towards girls, wanting to "teach them"—why? Girls never wanted
to harm boys. "Put it acrost them"—that's what common soldiers
wanted to do. Harm them. Grind them down, in more ways
than one. Why? What did it all mean? Why had Keechey behaved towards Lily as a ferret to a rabbit? Lily—when he saw
her, what would he *really* feel? How much would he pretend?
Was pity unnatural, a weakness? There was no pity in Nature,
really; was that why wild birds and animals were so beautiful?

From a seat on the Hill below the school he saw Desmond
arrive at the flat below, and felt that he could not face him. He
walked up to the crest ready to clear off if he saw Helena walking
rapidly in her white tennis things, swinging racquet and string
bag of balls. He did not see her, and was disappointed. Probably
she had gone round by road on her bike. Should he walk to the
club, and peer through the privet hedge? As soon as he thought
of it, he started off; but veered away when he got to the dog-
marked paving stones of Foxfield Road, and went down to Pit
Vale, and so to the Obelisk, meaning to call on Mrs. Cornford;
but veering in his mind again, he crossed the bridge over the
Quaggy, dead in its oval concrete bed, and went to the Bijou
Electric Palace, to see the new Charlie Chaplin film. Veering
once more at the box office, he followed boyhood's way up the
steep hill, to his old school, and so to the upland levels of the
Heath, which Cundall had told him was a reserve landing
ground for anti-Zeppelin aeroplanes at night. Football was
being played everywhere. He walked across grass and gravel
patches to Greenwich Park. The place looked colourless. The
fallow deer were gone. Huts stood on the grass under the trees
where they had driven, as children, in a wagonette, for their
picnic. He stood still, trying to re-enter the past, to drag it
out of memory, to make live again in his mind the dappled
sunlight under the trees and see himself, his sisters and friends and
all who were there on that hot summer day of 1911, when in the
shade the temperature was a hundred degrees, according to
Negretti and Zambra, the instrument makers who were always
mentioned in the newspapers before the war. Come back, he
cried wildly in his mind, come back, O summer day of my childhood, let me re-enter just one crystal moment; but he could see
nothing, all was beyond invisibility, far away in ancient sunlight,
life lost for evermore. For the moment he felt stricken into stone;
then turning away, walked out of the park between the avenue of

chestnuts planted, Gran'pa had said, in Charles the Second's reign. Layer on layer of ghosts, perhaps helping to suspend sunlight in the air, atoms pressed tightly together like invisible golddust, by which the electricity of creation was brought to the living. After all, if matter was indestructible, why not spiritual force? Everything was built up of atoms, held together by the spirit of life. Feeling suddenly happy, he looked at his watch, and thought that Lily would now be in a tram, on her way down Pit Vale and the High Street, and so home. Was she thinking of him, with her shining nature, and had he caught her thoughts through the *aether*?

He set off across the Heath, walking all the way, to delay his arrival, becoming more and more nervous as he descended the hill into the High Street and drew near the railway bridge just beyond which was the Conservative Club on one side of the arch, and the Gild Hall on the other. Then a turn to the left, and he was walking up towards Nightingale Grove. He walked past her house, telling himself that he ought to give her time to be with her mother and at last, almost with a feeling of going over the top, he swung back the tiny iron gate and knocked at the door.

Chapter 28

NIGHT AND MORNING

Lily came to the door. For a few moments she looked at him without speaking. She did not swim from her eyes towards him; she was a different Lily.

"I am so glad that you could come."

"Oh, thank you."

"Won't you come in?"

Mrs. Cornford came from the scullery to welcome him. She was impersonal, as before; contained within herself, keeping her distance with amiable reserve. He thought how very nice she was; much calmer than Mrs. Neville at her creamy best. Lily's mother kept back her personal feelings, she was a natural lady, he thought. Lily had changed, she was like her mother now.

"Have you had tea?"

"Yes thank you."

Lily looked at him with a smile. "Sure?"

"Well, actually I seldom have any tea."

"We're just going to have ours," said Mrs. Cornford, serenely. "Perhaps you would like to join us. I must watch my toast."

She went into the kitchen, leaving them in the sitting-room.

"I must draw the blinds. Mother is frightened of raids."

"She doesn't show it, she looks always so calm."

"She was well trained as a servant, in her young days, you see."

"Weren't they rather hard days? I mean, it was rather a severe life, wasn't it? below—er—I mean, in the servant's hall?" This sounded a bit better than below stairs.

"Oh no, we all enjoyed ourselves. It wasn't a very grand house, of course, like the county-and-town gentry live in," said Mrs. Cornford, coming into the room, with a tea tray. "My master and mistress were quite comfortably off, as they would have said. We lived in one of the houses in the Paragon on the Heath, I expect you know it. My master was a City gentleman, with a carriage and pair. It was some time ago now, of course. He used to drive to the City wearing a deerstalker, and just before he got to Lower Thames Street he would take it off and put on his topper. They were fine old days," she said, as she went out of the room. "I'll bring the toast shortly."

"Mother was trained under the housekeeper, and when the butler left she became head parlourmaid," said Lily. "When she left service to get married, she and her mistress cried together like sisters, she always says."

"I see," he said, thinking of his own sisters.

"Won't you sit down? You look tired."

She sat at the other end of the sofa, and looked at him. "Was it very bad, out there, I mean?"

"It was for some, but not so bad for me."

"You won't go back for some time, I expect?"

"I want to get back as soon as I can."

"You're still not very happy, are you?"

"Oh, I'm quite happy, thanks."

"Oh, Phillip," said Lily, moving to him. "I have thought about you all the time you were away."

"I thought about you, too," he said, formally, feeling himself to be melting.

She took his hand, and opened the fingers, one by one. "You've been sitting here all the time with both hands clasped tight, as though waiting to fight something. You were like that when I first saw you. I look after little children in the ward, you see, and all the unloved ones hold themselves in at first, and hands clasped tight are one of the signs. Please don't hold yourself away from me. I'll never do anything to hurt you."

"I know that."

"It probably looks as though I'm vamping you, but I promise I'm not, and never will. For one thing, I've taken a vow."

"A vow?" He was startled, and disappointed.

"Here's mother. I'll tell you after tea."

He munched toast, and sipped hot tea, wishing that he could speak without feeling stilted.

Mrs. Cornford said she had to do some shopping after tea, and left the house. Sitting again on the sofa, with sudden ease he took her hand. "Were yours ever clenched tight?"

"Yes, once or twice. But I was lucky to have Mother."

"Do you confide in her?"

"Some things, yes. But not everything. She wouldn't like me to."

"How do you mean?"

"She says it's best to have a little reserve in all friendships. Don't look at my fingers, they are very rough."

"It's a nice shape, your hands. I like rough hands best. They look honest. A bird's pads are very rough."

"Oh, I've often remembered our walk in the country!"

"Yes, it has often been in my mind."

"Has it? Oh, I am so happy." She lifted his hand to her cheek, then kissed it lightly. He put his cheek against hers, and felt its kindness like an invisible light. He thought of Keechey, and felt himself harden against the fat, buck-tooth face; and knew she had felt his thought when she said,

"I am sorry for Keechey's wife and little children. If he goes to prison they won't have anything to live on."

"I hadn't thought of that. Did you know I was thinking of him?"

"I thought so, when your hand closed up."

"What am I thinking about now?"

"I don't know. But is it Desmond?"

"Yes! How extraordinary! He arrived home this afternoon, but I haven't seen him yet."

"Are you friends again?"

"I'm afraid he's rather adamant."

"He'll want to make it up again, you'll see if I'm not right. Then I shall be ever so happy."

"What is your vow, Lily."

"It was when I turned Roman Catholic."

He felt fear, and loneliness. She took his hand.

"No," he said, taking it away. Always the misfit; he did not belong anywhere.

"I made a vow to Our Lady, that I would serve Her."

"You're going to become a nun?"

"No, it is a private vow I made. I was selfish before, seeking happiness in the wrong way. Now I want only to serve."

"I see," he said bleakly.

"Don't you see, I've got to make something of my life, not just drift along as I was before. So I became a nurse, and when I'm trained I hope to be sent out to France."

"No more Freddy's?"

She shook her head, looking at him.

"I met you too late," he said as he got up, his hands clenched tight. "I suppose you think that I should have taken what the gods provided, like Desmond and Eugene did, and your other men friends?"

"Do you really believe that, Phillip?"

"What does it matter what anyone believes?"

"Oh, it does matter. You don't really believe that, do you? I hope I haven't upset you. Please don't go. I didn't mean anything, truly. I'll do anything for you. You know that, don't you?"

She looked at him humbly. "I thought you didn't want me, because I'd been with other men. I couldn't bear you not to like me."

He sat down, hands still clenched.

"I'd give anything to see you happy, honest I would. Only I know I'm not good enough for you."

"I'm not good enough for you. May I tell you something just to prove it?"

He told her about Polly.

"You didn't love her, that's why you acted like that. But if she really loved you, you would have felt safe with her, I think. I think she was in love with you, only."

"Do you feel safe with me, Lily?"

"Oh, it is so lovely to hear you call me Lily! Of course I feel safe with you. Didn't you know it?"

Touched by his unhappy look she said, "Can't you tell when anyone is fond of you, Phillip?" Then the desperation in his face made her exclaim, "Oh, you're so tired! Lie down awhile, why

not. I'll get you a cushion for your head. Now lie down, and rest
your poor head. Dear head," she murmured, sitting by him and
stroking his brow with her finger-tips.

He held her hand and with a distraught expression in his eyes
bowed his head and hid his face in the crêpe-de-chine of her blouse,
feeling her warmth and softness; while as though to a child who
had yielded to her, given up to her the ghost of itself, beyond the
fatigue of its wilfulness, she murmured as her lips touched his hair
and brow. "O, I love you, I have always loved you, my only dear,
and now you have come to me. Do not be afraid, I will not harm
you."

All purposelessness fell from him with repeated sighing, and
then he sat up and stroked her forehead, and her hair, touching
with finger-tips her eyelids and smoothing her eyebrows, before
clasping her head and feeling its ordinariness, its smallness, its
skull-shape, with its curving bump at the back, so tender. It
seemed that his eyes were filled with her thoughts, the sky-blue
thoughts of Lily, no longer to be afraid of, for she was only a little
girl, of bone and flesh and hope like himself. She was a spirit, he
could feel her clear feelings, as simple as his own.

"And I was so afraid of you, little head, poor little head that
worried so much, in the darkness of the Rec. Can you be the Lily
I saw on that stool in the Bull? The Lily in the lamplight by the
yews in the churchyard, longing for the Wings of a Dove? You are
a dove, I think. You are gentle, and kind, like a dove."

"Oh, you are sweet! You look just like you did on the Hillies,
when we played cricket, and you showed me how to hold your
bat," she said, with glistening eyes turned upon him.

"Yes, I suppose we are all the same inside, really, under all
the wrong things we do." He stroked her forehead. "I love the
way your eyebrows grow in straight little hairs, like silky gentle
porcupines." He put his arms round her, and kissed her cheekbone.

"I can't believe you are here with me, at last," she said.

He saw tears in her eyes, and touched them with his lips, tenderly.

"Did you really like me years ago?"

"I liked you very much. Then when you walked into the Bull
that night I knew I could love only you."

"I was frightened of you when I saw you on that stool between
Desmond and Eugene. I was afraid of the look in your eyes. You
know, I had a feeling that only beautiful courtesans, the terribly
alluring kind, had eyes this colour."

He kissed one, then the other, of her closed lids, while the corners of her lips quivered with smiles.

"Women are rather alarming, you know, very beautiful girls like you, I mean. I think I know why some men make jokes about love. It's the same reason that Bairnsfather is popular, he jokes about what everyone really is afraid of. Tom Cundall would have a theory about that, I expect, he's a brainy bird. Do you know him?" he asked, with a twinge of jealousy.

"I've only seen him with you. He looks a nice boy."

"How about Ching?"

"I've only seen him in the Bull, or Freddy's."

"What do you think of him?"

"He's terribly hurt in himself, isn't he?"

"That never occurred to me. Yes, I suppose it's true! Who else do you know?"

"Nobody else, now."

"Were you ever sorry for Keechey?"

"At first."

"Why?"

"He was unhappy."

"He told you the tale, in fact!"

"But he *was* unhappy. Else he would not have told the tale."

"Only the loveless tell lies, in other words. I suppose you're right. Who else have you known beside Desmond and Eugene?"

"I've forgotten."

"Come on, tell me."

"You need not be jealous of anybody," she said, touching his cheek with her lips.

"But did you love them?"

"I was sorry for them. Also——"

"Also what?"

"Well, the one I wanted I couldn't find, so who I went with didn't seem to matter."

"Oh," he said.

"I wanted to be liked for myself alone, but it did not seem it would ever happen. But after I saw you in the Bull I never went with any other fellow, old or new. What big eyes you have, Grandmother!"

"Grandmother! What a name!"

"Oh, I loved it, and always shall."

"Isn't it strange, we two being so ordinary together? Let's wash up the things for your mother, shall we? I think it's fun to work together."

"Ah, but you might not feel the same when you're gone away from me."

"I shall always feel like this."

He took off his signet ring. "Wear it on your little finger—but keep it a secret, won't you?"

She stared at the ring, gave it a series of small kisses, and held it to her heart.

When he had dried the tea things and spread the cloth on the clothes horse before the fire he said, "I think I ought to go now, Lily. I promised to meet Desmond and Gene. I shall have to tell Desmond. Shall I see you tomorrow?"

"I go to mass in the morning, at St. Saviours."

"May I come, too? I'll meet you outside the church. What time? All right, till then. Thank your mother for me, won't you? Au revoir. Till tomorrow!"

They kissed lightly, tremulously. Her last whispered words to him were, "You are my child."

Phillip and Desmond went up to Charing Cross, then by tube to Paddington to call on Eugene in his garret flat in Westbourne Terrace. Eugene was delighted to see them; his sallow face lit up. He had just opened a tin of sardines for his supper, thinking they were not coming, he said. There it was, on the kitchen table. He eyed it thoughtfully, and said, "It will do for me tomorrow," then he put the tin back in a box on the window-sill where he kept his grub. Having washed, he stood before a long looking-glass, adjusted his bowler hat at the correct angle for a man about town, took his yellow gloves and silver-mounted second-best ebony stick, returned to the glass to erect his blue, white-dot bow tie, and said, "I am ready. Where is it to be this time?"

"How about the usual place, Gene?"

"Well, the Popular has become too well known, since you've been to France. It's crowded with all sorts of people from the suburbs nowadays."

"Where do you suggest then? You're the expert."

"How about the Piccadilly Grill?"

"I've only got five quid."

"That ought to do, if we don't have vintage wines. It's *infra dig* to ask them to take a cheque, of course."

"I see. Let's get a taxi."

Outside the Piccadilly Hotel stood two enormous grey Mércèdes motorcars, with great brass flexible pipes snaking through the bonnets.

"The Royal Flying Corps always comes here when there's nothing doing," explained Gene.

The hotel foyer was full of what Phillip thought were the most beautiful girls he had ever seen. Gene took off hat and coat and gave them to the cloak attendant with what he considered to be the air of a Brazilian aristocrat, and led the way down to the grill room, where amidst masses of yellow and bronze chrysanthemums on a dais an orchestra was playing. The restaurant manager bowed him to a table; lifted a hand to a waiter, who hurried forward to draw back a gilt chair for Eugene, bowed to the other two, and withdrew; to come forward again, after an interval, with three enormous *cartes de menu*.

"Let me see," said Eugene, fitting his eyeglass.

A second waiter attended. "Cocktail, m'sieu? Sherry?" Eugene shook his head, the waiter bowed and departed.

Phillip thought the prices were very high. Still, he had five pounds and a few shillings.

"Do you mind ordering, Gene? I've rather lost touch since coming home."

"How about our usual porterhouse steak, with onions and fried potatoes? And a Burgundy? I'm going to lunch with Charlie Mayer at his house in Sydenham tomorrow, so I fancy something simple tonight."

The leader of the band came forward, violin under chin, bow in hand. People clapped.

"That's de Groot, the famous violinist," explained Gene. "He's made dozens of gramophone records."

"Good lord! Of course! I've got his Selections from *Razzle Dazzle*!"

The band played selections from *Chu Chin Chow*. The lights, the gaiety, the food, the wine, the laughing faces were all around; yet something was absent. It was not like the old days. Since meeting again at the door of the flat, he and Desmond had not spoken much. Desmond seemed subdued; he was still, he said, passing a hand across his forehead, liable to headaches, from being blown up.

"What happened?" asked Phillip. If only Lily were with them, and they were four friends together. Polly—Percy—Jasper—Bason—no, the old days were gone.

"Oh, we were in a Russian sap, in front of the infantry, and when we blew in the end of the tunnel the blast came back and the roof fell on us," Desmond's low voice was saying.

"What was the idea of blowing in the end while you were still there?"

"For the infantry to debouch. It was a shallow tunnel, you see, and the end was under the German front line. The blast was supposed to lift the lid off the end, but it didn't, so we were all trapped."

"How long were you there?"

"I don't remember, but it must have been a long time, for when I recovered consciousness, I was lying on a stretcher, and it was night."

"You were lucky."

"I know. It got me out of that hell."

"Where were you?"

"In front of La Boisselle."

"I was in Mash Valley. On the left of the Bapaume Road."

"A very unhealthy place. It's no good asking me about it, I can't remember anything since the explosion." Again the hand across the brow. Was Desmond doing a Piston?

"Ought you to drink wine, if your nerves are bad?" He winked at Eugene.

"Oh, that doesn't affect me. I drank the best part of a bottle of rum last night, and was the same afterwards as before."

"Seems rather a waste to drink wine then, doesn't it."

"That's the sort of remark you would make."

"Well, I didn't mean it that way."

"But you said it."

Phillip looked at Gene, whose faint eyebrows on the edge of a slightly receding brow were lifted.

"Now then, Des, Phil didn't mean it the way you took it. Can't you take a joke?"

"Drink up," said Phillip, filling the glasses. "Waiter, bring another bottle."

At this point the R.F.C. pilots dining somewhat noisily at one of the large tables in the middle of the room got up and left, after the manager had spoken to them.

"First warning," said Desmond.

The band went on playing, while many heads were turned to the departing officers in their riding boots and double-breasted jackets. The waiter whispered: the famous Leefe Robinson, V.C., had been among them. The life of the restaurant seemed to have departed, too. When the music stopped it was quiet, even subdued. Desmond seldom spoke. Phillip felt the secret satisfaction of his thoughts of Lily going from him. How much was Desmond putting on his having-been-blown-up mood?

After their dinner they left for the cheaper Monkey House for coffee. The vast carpeted room with its marble pillars and mirrors and chocolate-gilt decorations seemed to be filled more than before with full-lipped dark-haired people in family parties with eyes like black grapes gazing at ease among figures in khaki, a few wearing the new gold-braid wound-stripes on their left-arm sleeves, sitting with patient faces and shut-away thoughts.

Phillip was drinking coffee with his cigar and looking upon the scene into which, it seemed, music like golden-shred marmalade was being poured with the din of voices, when a fat young man wearing homburg hat on his head, a smart new overcoat with astrachan collar, and pointed yellow boots pushed past to a family party near them, and beckoning with a fat hand on which many rings showed, said something which made them all get up and walk away together. Other dark-eyed groups followed the general exodus, until khaki uniformed figures here and there with their womenfolk became prominent.

"See how they run," said Gene. "There's absolute panic in the Whitechapel Road when a Zepp is anywhere near. Here in Piccadilly the wealthier ones are the first to get down into the Underground. They all ride round the Inner Circle on a penny ticket until the raid is over. How about going to Hampstead by tube, and looking over London from the high ground? It will be safe up there."

Outside in Piccadilly the crowds were thick as before, taxi-cabs with their little yellow oil-lamps, newsboys in the faint glow of the Prince of Wales theatre foyer crying the names of evening papers—*Star*, *Globe*, *Pall Mall Gazette*, *Evening News*—All the latest! Advance on the Somme continues!—Italian Victory on the Isonzo!—German Food Shortage!—All the Latest!—Hullo Dearie, looking for a Nice Girl? No thank you. Well then, push off! That's just what I'm doing, good night. Obviously Ray, dug-in at Cherry Hinton, had graduated in Piccadilly Circus.

"It's too bloody far to Hampstead. Let's go and see Freddy."

"That means I'll have to come back to Town by myself," said Gene.

"You can go all the way by tube to Paddington."

Piccadilly Underground was crowded with people, so they walked to Charing Cross. Lily, would she be in Freddy's? Had she changed her mind? He felt heavy with longing.

"I've heard nothing down this way," said Freddy.

It was not the same place any more. He did not want to drink whiskey, and led the way to the Gild Hall. New flappers, new faces, innocent eyes and fresh complexions, young soldiers seeming smaller, shy-bold, callow. Had he once been like that?

> *Now folds the lily all her sweetness up*
> *And sinks into the bosom of the lake—*

He wanted to be alone, to dream of Lily, to nurse the ache within him. Was he lost again, as he had been with Helena? When Desmond suggested a game of three-handed snooker, all against all, he made his excuses.

"If you don't mind, I think I'll go home. I'm still a bit under the weather with my leg at times, so I'll leave you two, if you don't mind."

"Just a minute," said Gene, drawing Phillip aside, "I wonder if you could lend me a pound? I'm rather hard up at the moment. My quarterly allowance is due next week, at the Brazilian Bank, so I'll be able to settle up all the other money I owe you then."

"I've only got fifteen bob left, but you can have ten, if that's any good. Righty-ho, see you soon. Thanks for coming with me tonight."

"Don't mention it, it's a pleasure. You know very well how I feel about you, Phil." Eugene pressed his hand.

He walked home, hesitating at the chinks of light around Mrs. Neville's window; then went up Hillside Road, where the two lamp-post lights were out.

His house was dark.

"Is that you, Phillip?" How anxious the voice seemed.

"Yes, Mother."

"Don't make a noise, dear. I'll come down."

How small she was, in her bare feet and dressing-gown, her hair so thin, a grey wispy rat-tail.

"Father was called out. Don't say a word to Mavis or Doris, will you, but Zeppelins have been reported on the way here. Doris is all right, but Mavis is terribly nervous, and she's not well, either."

Mavis' voice called with wild fear from her bedroom door at the end of the house. "Who is it, Mother?"

"Only Phillip, dear."

"I thought I heard one just now! There was a flash right across my window!"

The window looked east, towards Woolwich and Shooter's Hill.

"It was only a tram," said Phillip. "Don't get the wind up."

"You'll wake Doris, and she's got to take her College of Preceptors exam this term."

"I'm awake," said the voice of Doris. Her dim face looked over the banisters of the landing above.

"If you all go on talking I shall never get to sleep," came the complaining voice of Mavis from down the passage. "Phillip turns night into day, just as Father says."

"That's better than turning night into fright, anyhow."

"Night into getting tight, you mean!" came the satirical laughter. "Where have you come from now, eh? Freddy's, I bet! How's the washerwoman's daughter?"

"I'm going for a walk on the Hill, Mother."

"Down to Freddy's, you mean," Mavis called out.

"Mavis, will you stop taunting your brother!"

"Well, he began it."

"Yes, I made the mistake of being born before you," said Phillip, closing the door behind him.

It opened again. "You won't be late, will you, dear?" whispered Hetty.

Outside the gate the shadowy figure of Desmond awaited him.

Across the North Sea from Germany nine airships were flying. Six of them, of an older type, were making for the east coast of England north of the Thames estuary. They were loaded with two-hundred-kilogram bombs and thermite canisters. Their objectives were factories, foundries, and industrial plant in the Midlands.

Three others had been ordered to bombard London, now declared to be both fortress and arsenal by the German Supreme Command. Driven at fifty miles an hour by Maybach water-cooled engines housed in gondolas suspended under rigid frames of aluminium, each of the silken envelopes contained a million and a half cubic feet of hydrogen gas. They were the new and improved type of Zeppelin, capable of a maximum air-speed of sixty miles an hour.

Shortly after six o'clock, *L 31* and *L 32*, based on Ahlhorn, had crossed the industrial areas of the Rhineland. Far to the south the crews could see Cologne Cathedral. Then in the dusk, at six hundred feet, they continued side by side above the glimmering Belgian roads, lined with trees, which guided them as they flew by map and compass.

Darkness settled upon the earth as they rose above the gathering mists, heading for Ghent, on course for Ostend. With the coming of night, direction by wireless came to each airship from ships of the German fleet, which gave bearings from List, Nordholz, and Borkum.

The cold which had come into the air with the setting of the sun increased the buoyancy of the gas in the envelopes. A difference of three degrees in temperature meant one per cent in weight-carrying capacity, or three hundred feet in altitude.

Shortly after ten o'clock that night *L 31*, *L 32*, and *L 33* were passing down the coast of Northern France. The crews saw on their port beams, like a great livid wound lying upon Europe in the darkness, the lights of the raging battlefield of the Somme. For nearly an hour the pallor in the night accompanied each man in his loneliness, remote from the turmoil upon land and sea, but not from the fear and resolution of each mind, as slowly the wan ghost receded astern, while they hung under the stars, to the throbbing of exhausts.

One of the commanders was Mathy. He had planned to make his landfall upon the coast of Kent—a dim wandering line of chalk awash with the fret of shallow waves—and then turning nor'-nor'-west through wingless darkness to follow the lines of the London, Brighton, and South Coast Railway into the City. Thus he hoped to avoid the formidable defences of the guns, lights, and patrolling aircraft concentrated upon the north-east approaches to London.

Desmond sat upright at one end of a seat on the Hill. At the other end Phillip was lying back, feeling smoothed and selfless, neck resting on hands behind head, feet stretched upon the gravel before him. It was a warm night, with a gentle wind. Remotely above them the Milky Way lay across the depth of the sky. It was the beginning of the season of meteors and shooting stars.

Now slides the silent meteor on and leaves
A shining furrow, as thy thoughts in me.

He could never write poetry like that. It was as unattainable as the pale star-dust of the galaxies, which had been burning aeons before man had come upon the earth, in his earliest amoebic form. Yet Love was before the stars were flames, and Love would remain when they were burned out. Love was the spirit of the universe, shining in the Abyss.

"This situation between us has got to be settled now, one way or the other."

"I agree."

"I've hardly had your betrayal of our friendship out of my mind for more than a few minutes during the past three months. I've been in hell. I've thought about it at night. It begins the moment I wake up. Now it must be settled one way or the other."

When there was no reply, Desmond said, "I thought you would not answer. I told you before that it was in my mind to kill you, and you laughed cynically. Well, before I decide whether to kill you or not," the low voice went on, "I'll give you one more chance to tell me the truth. Did you see Lily tonight, before you came to see me? I want just a plain yes or no."

Phillip wondered if the fact that Desmond had been blown up had worn down his nerves to what engineers called the flash-point of gaseous liquids such as when paraffin and petrol turned to flame. He told himself that he must be careful. Had Desmond got a revolver in his pocket?

"Yes, I did see Lily tonight. I went to say goodbye, as she is going away soon. I called to see Mrs. Cornford some days ago, and she told me her daughter was coming home, and invited me to tea. Now may I ask you a question. Why do you ask?"

"Because I also have seen Lily tonight."

"Then why didn't you tell me before?"

"Why should I? What has it to do with you?"

"I might have asked the same question, Desmond. But I didn't. I don't mind if you see her or not. Both of us have been friendly with her, you know; though not in the same way. I told you that before I went back to France, when you were kind enough to wish for my death. Incidentally, it might be argued that your remark was hardly that of a friend. Whether it was a betrayal of friendship, or not, you can decide for yourself."

"As usual, you are very plausible, and can twist anything round your own way."

"Well, everyone has his or her own point of view, you know."

"Did you promise me on one occasion, and did you promise my mother again the other day, that you would not see Lily again? And have you broken both promises?"

"I don't remember making definite promises."

"Well, let me jog your memory. Do you agree that my mother asked you not to see Lily again, for her own sake, because you had made her fond of you, but did not care for her? In other words, she asked you to play the game with Lily. Do you admit that?"

"She did ask me. But the reason, as you put it, to play the game, wasn't mentioned, so far as I recall."

"But it was inferred?"

"Yes, in a way."

"Would it be true to say that as soon as you got from Polly what you wanted, you had no further use for her?"

"Yes, I think that is true."

"Furthermore, having achieved your desire at last with Helena Rolls, you promptly lost interest in her?"

"That's probably true, too. But no harm has been done to her."

"How do you know? You had your triumph, and that's all that matters to you. You don't really want love from anyone, you want to be able to gloat over them. It is what is known as diabolical possession. So if you do not leave Lily alone I shall consider it my duty to kill you. Then I shall shoot myself."

"Well, that would not exactly be an act of friendship, would it? Also, wouldn't Lily tend to blame herself all her life? She does now, you know; or did. She told me so. She felt she had come between us."

"On the contrary, it is you who have come between Lily and me. Your shadow lies upon her—what the Germans call a doppelganger. She's fascinated by you, as a dove is by a snake."

"Do you really believe that?"

"Yes, I do. I remember your power over Peter Wallace, and how you got him to fight your battles for you. He believed everything you said—until he found you out! You got him to thrash Albert Hawkins, merely because he dared to talk to Mavis behind your garden fence. What harm could that do—childhood sweethearts? By your act Albert Hawkins' heart was broken, as well as his face. That never occurred to you, did it?"

"I don't know why you're talking like this. It happened a long time ago, anyway, and I admit I was a bit of a coward then."

"Are you any different now? You may think so, perhaps. Let me remind you. Didn't you clear off and leave your pal Martin in the lurch on Messines Ridge, in 1914?"

"How do you know that?"

"You told me yourself."

"It's only partly true, anyway. The Bavarians had broken through. Martin wouldn't get up when I tried to get him up, so I retreated, with many of the others. No one knew what was happening."

"Except Peter Wallace and his brothers, who had the guts to stay, and were killed."

"Why are you using all that I told you against me?"

"To prove to you that you always twist everything in your own favour, regardless of the truth. You make up all the rules to suit yourself, don't you?"

"Isn't that what you're doing now?"

"You'd wriggle out of anything. But you won't wriggle out of your treachery to me over Lily so easily. You've seduced her spiritually—that is your power over people. I tell you now, and I swear it before God, that if you see her again, I'll put a bullet through you, Phillip Maddison!"

Did Desmond really believe that Lily would be able to love him if the so-called diabolical influence of himself were removed? And thinking thus, he was jagged by the thought that Lily might have said that to Desmond. Lily had turned Catholic; Catholics believed what their priests told them about such things. Could Lily, after he had left her that evening, have confessed to a priest that she was being pulled back from the Love of God by himself? Well, if that was the Love of God, the sooner he was dead and in hell the better.

"Do the Catholics go to confession on Saturday night, Desmond?"

"Yes. Especially round here, because many are working all the week. Why do you ask?"

"I wondered if the idea of my diabolical nature had come from the priest's confessional box. You are a Catholic, aren't you?"

"Yes, but you can't bluff me. What you really want to know is what Lily said to me."

"Tell me if it was Lily who first talked of demoniacal possession."

"Would it surprise you if I told you that she did?"

Phillip made no reply.

"I saw Lily tonight," said Desmond, quietly. "I called round after I'd said goodbye to Gene."

"Is it true that Lily said that? About me? On your honour?" It was now Desmond's turn to be silent.

"Answer me, Desmond! You *must* tell me!"

"Why should I? You don't tell me the truth, so why should I answer your questions?"

"Then you are a wriggler, and no better than I am, are you, according to your ideas?"

"Except that I love Lily with all my heart and soul," said Desmond. "Tonight I asked her to marry me," he said, hardly above a whisper.

"What did she say?" Phillip said, putting away his feelings.

"I've told you in so many words. Your influence, or shadow, stands between us."

The night wind moved slightly in the hawthorn standing by Phillip's end of the seat. He heard a brown leaf dropping through the spined twigs, making the slightest of sounds, like broken sighs, as it left the parent tree for ever, its brief summer over and done with.

"Desmond."

"Yes."

"If it could do any good, I would go away for ever. If it would do any good between you and Lily, I mean."

"How do I know that you will keep your word this time?"

"I said I would go away if it would do any good between you and Lily."

"Well, I have told you it would."

"Did Lily tell you that? Please tell me the truth."

"You ought to know the answer."

"Did she kiss you, Desmond? I mean, tonight?"

"Yes," said Desmond, and at this Phillip felt black depression gripping him. But he managed to say, "If she kissed you as though she loved you, why are you worrying about me?"

"She kissed me on my forehead, she kissed me goodbye, because she's possessed by you!" cried Desmond, as he got up and walked away in the darkness.

Some time later Phillip arose and walked round the Hill, filled with thoughts of Lily streaming in the night sky like meteors from the constellation Berenice's Hair, her eyes the light of the morning, her brow the dawn, Eos of the Greeks, driving her chariot up to heaven from the River Oceanus, to announce the coming of the sun.

He had picked up these crumbs of learning from the *Smaller Classical Dictionary*; how Eos had carried off youths distinguished for their beauty, such as Orion, Cephalus, and Tithonus, whence she was called by Ovid *Tithonia Conjux*. "By the prayers of Eos (Dawn) who loved him, he obtained from the gods immortality, but not eternal youth, in consequence of which he completely shrank in his old age; whence a decrepit old man was proverbially called Tithonus."

The fate of Orion seemed to be linked with his own conduct: for Orion the hunter had treated the maiden Merope badly, after falling in love with her. Her father in revenge had his eyes put out. But Orion recovered sight by exposing his eye-balls to the rising sun; and after death he lived among the stars, with lion's skin, girdle, club, sword, and Sirius the hound trailing him as he bestrode the universe.

There it was, the constellation of Orion: low over the horizon: far beyond the Weald of Kent, beyond the battle raging from North Sea to Alps, beyond the sands of Africa and the coral strands of the south. Lily, Lily, be thou mine, save me from the terrors of the world. No, no; stand alone, Phillip. Even as "Spectre" West.

When he returned to the seat, he saw Desmond sitting there. Something in his humped-up attitude made Phillip say,

"Desmond, I'm awfully glad to see you back! I've been thinking. There's a lot of truth in what you said to me."

"Phillip," said a low, quiet voice. "I've been talking to Mother."

"I see."

Desmond sighed deeply. "She says I am wrong. So I've come to say one thing to you, before I volunteer to go back to the front."

After a long silence Desmond began in a voice almost inaudible.

"First, I must tell you about my mother. But before I do that, I want your word of honour never to tell anyone what I am going to say."

"I promise."

"My mother, when she met my father, used to haunt the promenade of the Alhambra. She was very much the same as Lily was when I first met her in Freddy's. Lily, you know, used to go in to pubs in order to get off with men——" the deep voice quavered to a stop.

"We all seek for the one true love, Desmond."

"My mother walked the Alhambra Promenade because she was a prostitute."

"How do you know? Did she tell you?"

"No, I heard it from my uncle in Nottingham. He is my father's brother. He and his sister—they are both unmarried—pay my mother a monthly allowance."

"Forgive my asking, Desmond, but did they say that your mother took money from men?"

"No, but they inferred it."

"Nottingham is quite close to Grantham. When I get back there, I think I'll go and see them—not about what we're talking about, of course."

"I shouldn't do that. You see, they don't approve of you."

"How do you know?"

"They told me so."

Phillip felt subdued: a familiar feeling: otherwise he might have wondered how it had come about that people who had never met him could disapprove of him.

"My father," went on Desmond, "has another family."

"I see."

"I know what you're thinking. But you're wrong. My father and mother were married. They still are, in fact."

"I see."

A large white brilliance opened in the darkness of the sky, low in the south-west. It hung steady, shedding its beams softly.

"Hullo!" said Desmond. "What is it?"

The light floated, swimming in its own solitary brilliance. Then a red shearing flashed upwards to the light. A few seconds later came the deep crump of a bomb. There came a shout from the silhouetted mass of the school.

"It's a parachute flare dropped by a Zeppelin!" said Desmond.

Searchlights were now weaving about the sky, trying to pierce the ball of brightness hanging over the distant streets and houses. Shouts and cries came from the roof of the school, as a pale blade arose towards the stars. It seemed to burst, with the throbbing of the engine driving the dynamo in the sheep-fold, into a lilac blaze, reaching up until it dissolved wanly in space.

"What the hell are our guns doing? There's a three-inch on One Tree Hill," said Desmond. "Look! The blasted thing's coming our way!"

A second flare scalded the sky with brightness dazzling the eyes; followed by another ruddy flash.

"Come on, under cover!" cried Desmond. "We can get over the railings into the lavatory."

"What's the odds? I vote we stay and watch what happens."

"She's making for Woolwich Arsenal," said Desmond, listening to the growl of engines. "I bet it's Mathy! What an idea, to blanket our lights with flares! The guns can't spot her, either."

Searchlights were fumbling nervously. Then one swung around in a complete arc, before making a steady point.

"They've spotted her!"

All the lights rushed together and clustered upon a tiny yellow length, tilting steeply, yellow-brown as its nose bored a way out of sight into a cloud.

"It was over twelve thousand feet," said Desmond. "And rising fast. One of the new thirties. I'll swear that's Mathy."

One after another the searchlights died away. The beam lancing up from the roof of the school glowed a pale pink before leaving an eye-daze upon the darkness.

"There must be an aeroplane about," said Desmond. "Listen!"

They heard the throb of engines.

"The note is too heavy for a 90-horse Raf engine in a BE2c. Those are Maybach engines. Hark!"

The scoring hiss of a bomb travelling aslant scalded the sky. There was a leaping flash, and three to four seconds later a rending reverberation. The sword lights leapt up and pointed about the sky again.

"Swine!" cried Desmond. Phillip, too, felt hot and angry. "That one must have fallen right into the High Street."

"Come on, man! Let's go down and see!"

"No, I want to watch what happens. We can see best from up here. There must be a reason why the guns haven't opened up. An aeroplane above the Zeppelin would see it against those flares you know. What's the time?"

"A quarter to one."

"Look, there it is! I knew there was a reason for the guns not firing!"

The rod-like yellow length was now seen in the massed beams to be as though dragging a money-spider on a gossamer, which glistened now and then.

"He's firing tracer and incendiary!" yelled Desmond. "He's into her! Look! In Christ's name, look! He's into her!"

The glistening money-spider was beside the Zeppelin. Then the searchlights flicked out once more.

"Have they lost her? Have they lost her?"

"Wait! Wait!"

Desmond gripped Phillip's arm. "They've got a platform on the top, and a machine-gun mounted there. The aeroplane was visible to them, in our lights, you see!"

They waited, tense and anguished. A scarcely audible rattle, like a woodpecker drumming, came from the stars; again, and yet again. Then a wriggle of red showed in the northern sky. It moved slowly, it extended and broadened, flames were seen, growing wider until the whole of the Hill, every tree and seat, pebbles on the path, Desmond's face, the hard bony lines of his brow and cheeks and jaw, glowed with fire. Then from all around the Hill, sounding far away, came thin flame-like cries, recalling to Phillip children screaming on Band Night, but these cries were deeper, harsher, from all the streets of London.

One of those streets had been opened out, and thither policemen and special constables, nurses, and ambulance men who had been waiting at police stations came hurrying; while in Randiswell fire station firemen were sliding down the polished steel pole through the holes in the floors of their quarters leading direct to their engine on the ground below. Brass helmets on heads, bell dashing its chimes into the flaming night, the engine roared down the High Street, to where men and women in nightshirts and nightgowns covered by coats, wearing slippers or bare-foot, were hurrying out of houses.

Special-Sergeant Richard Maddison was sitting in the gutter of Nightingale Grove, dazed. He had been walking down the road, looking for light-glints in one house after another, when he heard a high-pitched scream coming down aslant the High Street. The aerial torpedo struck a house and passed through it and continued on through the party wall of the next house and burst in a third house, blowing out the walls and causing the collapse of five houses altogether. Richard was caught in the blast which blew out windows and turned glass to dust, so that when he was helped to his feet he was white as with frost. When some people tried to help him away to hospital, he said, "Thank you, but it is my duty to attend to the injured," for screams and cries for help were coming from the chaos of rubble and rafters and other things shattered and heaped together. But he fell over, and was unable to get up for some minutes; his sight was dazed, the stench of powdered brick and mortar sickened him, he felt weak and thin. Then the fire-engine clanged up the road, and the firemen, together with others, began to pull and lift away the masses of broken masonry. Richard got upon his feet and helped.

From the first house was withdrawn a bed, doubled up by the explosion. In it lay a woman also doubled up, with a grey face; she appeared to be sleeping. She had been killed, it was said, instantly by shock. They they found the body of a young girl. Seeing her face in the light of a torch, Dr. Dashwood, who had hurried up the road from the Conservative Club, immediately knelt beside her, to listen through his stethoscope. When the onlookers saw him take off his bowler hat, they knew that Lily Cornford was dead. At least, they said, she had gone with her mother. It was then that Richard was seen to stumble and fall. He was taken, with the other cases of shock, to the Military Hospital.

When Phillip and Desmond arrived at Nightingale Grove they saw Dr. Dashwood standing alone, tears streaming down his face, as he looked at the ruin that had been the home of Lily. They set to work with others, to help get clear those whose voices were crying for help under the bricks.

The ambulance returned. Stretcher cases were taken away.

Soon afterwards a squad of elderly civilians, with G.R. armbands —known locally as the Gorgeous Wrecks, a punning reference to Georgius Rex—arrived, and a cordon was put round the damaged buildings. Phillip and Desmond went home.

They did not speak until Phillip called out good-night to Desmond as he put his key in the door. Then, hearing Mrs. Neville's voice in the downstairs flat, he went in. Mrs. Neville was sitting with old Mrs. Tinkey and her daughter, by a table on which stood a candle and the bottle of brandy kept for an emergency. The bottle was open, and seeing his condition, dishevelled and covered with dust, Mrs. Neville said very quietly, "Thank God you are both all right. You've been doing rescue work, I can see that. Help yourself to some brandy. Even if Gran'pa does write you another letter, Phillip!"

When he had finished his tot she said, "Now, dear, I won't ask you any questions, because your mother is expecting you. Doris came to ask if you were here, saying that Mavis has fallen unconscious, so I think you ought to go home at once."

Mrs. Neville's big face was calm, she felt herself to be all queenly dignity, as befitted the tragic circumstances of the night.

"You'll let Desmond and me know if we can be of any help, won't you, Phillip? I suppose you haven't seen Father?"

"No, Mrs. Neville. Good night, Desmond."

Doris came to the door. She said that when the sky had turned red, lighting up everything so terribly, Mavis had screamed "Mother! Mother!" and then given a kind of wail. Doris had leapt out of bed and run to her sister's help. As she was hurrying down the passage she heard bumping sounds in the end bedroom. Then, said Doris, Mother came.

"In the light coming through the window we saw Mavis jerking about on the floor. Her eyes were glazed, and there was blood on her lips. She had bitten her tongue." They had lifted Mavis on to her bed; she had awakened a moment, said, "Don't leave me, Phillip," then fallen into a deep sleep.

"She asked *me* not to leave her?"

"Yes. I heard it distinctly. She said, 'Don't leave me, Phillip'. Ask mother if you don't believe me."

Phillip was sitting in the kitchen when there was a ring of the front door bell. Mr. Jenkins had come to say the sergeant had been taken to hospital, suffering from concussion.

Phillip took charge. "Thank you for coming, Mr. Jenkins. Now don't worry, Mother, I will look after Father. The raid is over. Have some hot milk ready to heat the moment I return, for Father. And water for a bottle, for his feet. And keep calm. No fuss, please."

He ran most of the way to the hospital, and arrived as Father was about to leave. Father seemed surprised to see him, and said it was very good of him to have come down. He was all right, except for being deaf in one ear, and his head was still ringing with the explosion. His spectacles had saved him from flying glass; he had only just put them on, he explained, to look the more carefully for any light escaping past a blind, which might very well betray to the raiders that there was a target for their campaign of frightfulness.

"It was *awful*, Phillip!"

"Yes, Father, I quite understand. Don't worry any more."

"No, oh no. Of course this is all new to me. I suppose," he said, "you have many times experienced the effects of bursting shells? Well, this one was an eye-opener to me, I can assure you! They tell me that a splinter no bigger than an acorn went right through a pillar box, and out the other side. However, retribution has come, as no doubt you know, to one of the raiders, at least. Let us hope it is Mathy. You look very pale, Phillip. Are you sure you are all right?"

"Yes thank you, Father."

Richard went to thank the matron. They walked through the yews of St. Mary's churchyard.

"Well, this is a night we shall remember for the rest of our lives, Phillip!"

"Yes, Father."

Mavis was in a deep sleep when they returned.

"She had some tripe for supper, at Nina's, and it did not agree with her, Dickie. She was ill once before, after eating tripe. It was very foolish of her, but she won't do it again."

Richard remembered the time, nearly twenty-two years before, when his wife had had a similar collapse, after being knocked down by her father, when she was *enceinte* with Phillip, and the old man had found out about the secret marriage. That old tyrant next door had much to answer for, in his opinion.

"Well, I suppose she had better see Dr. Cave-Browne tomorrow. But why does she eat tripe, if it disagrees with her? It is beastly stuff, anyway."

The doctor, in frock coat and silk hat, drove up Hillside Road in the morning, and advised rest, and a tonic. "It is purely functional," he said. "She is highly strung, and should eat plenty of fresh vegetables. Cabbage is the stuff, but don't throw away the so-called greens-water. And no more excitement, young woman. Learn to take life calmly. You're always hurrying somewhere whenever I see you." His hands were stained dark brown. He had been called out the night before, to help the bomb victims, and had used many handfuls of potassium permanganate on shattered flesh, to stop bleeding and infection. "Rough and ready treatment," he said.

When the doctor had driven away, Hetty said to her son, in the privacy of the front room: "Try and be kind to Mavis, won't you. She is your sister, after all. I wonder why you never liked her, from the earliest days you would not be reconciled. I remember when she was a tiny baby, in my arms, you tried to get her away from me. Then you once pushed her in the fire."

"Did I? I don't remember it, Mum. What a little swine I must have been." He went up to his sister's bedroom. "I'm sorry I have been so beastly to you, Mavis," he said, and kissed her.

Afterwards he walked down to the High Street, to the Roman

Catholic Church. When the service was over he bought a candle to place on the iron ring before the image of the Virgin. On the way back he called at Wetherley's, to hire the Humberette, thinking to go that afternoon to see the fallen airship; then he went into Freddy's bar.

The landlord leaned over the counter and said quietly, "The wrong ones were took last night over there," as he jerked his head in the direction of Nightingale Grove. "It would have saved a lot of trouble if it'd been our friend who we all admire so much. But Keechey's got a stretch in Wormwood Scrubs coming to him all right."

Phillip could not help thinking about his wife and small children. As he was drinking a glass of beer Dr. Dashwood came in, and taking him aside, gave him the signet ring which, he said, he had seen on the finger of someone in the mortuary.

"I recognised it, Middleton. God bless you, God bless you," he whispered, and then he went away without having a drink.

"I must go too," said Phillip. "God bless you, Freddy."

L' ENVOI

Again Desmond and Phillip were driving through the Blackwall Tunnel, out past riverside docks of the East End to fields of stubble and roots, along narrow lanes through the villages with names like Little Warley, Childerditch Street, and Herongate, passing hundreds, thousands of men and women on foot, clad in their Sunday best, farmers in dog-carts and traps, bicyclists and bands of boys, all hurrying east as they made their way to Snail's Hall Farm, where the Zeppelin's empty frame lay glittering like part of the Crystal Palace in the bright sunlight of the hot day as it straddled two burnt fields across a scorched hedge, broken in the middle where it had sunk down upon an oak tree. It was seven hundred feet long.

Outside the cordon of sentries with fixed bayonets stalls had been set up. The vendors offered cakes and mineral waters, cockles and oysters, even picture postcards and Sunday newspapers. Many people were moving towards the webbed broken frame rising above the fields.

Phillip led the way direct to the line of bayonets.

"Sapper Neville, I think Intelligence demands that we both make a closer inspection."

"Certainly, sir."

"Walk just behind me, with a confident air."

"Very good, sir."

Phillip, booted and spurred, his badges of rank hidden by a British Warm, walked towards the wreckage. A sergeant came forward, but before he could speak, Phillip said, "Have you seen the General Commanding the London District, Sir Francis Lloyd, sergeant?"

"No, sir," replied the sergeant.

"In the circumstances the General will not expect a General Salute when he does come."

"Very good, sir."

Approaching the buckled frame, they saw the white corrosion of fire on the aluminium girders and cross members, and the oak tree, forty feet high, with all its branches crushed around the trunk. Many R.F.C. officers were peering at equipment from one of the gondolas laid out by mechanics. A smell of burning hung in the air.

Phillip overheard a major talking about the crew in the barn, and soon found his way there, without asking questions.

At the door of the barn he said to the sergeant of the guard, "Have you seen Colonel West of the Gaultshires?"

"I don't know the officer, sir!"

"You can't mistake him, sergeant. He's got a black patch over his left eye, and a hand missing. If you do, tell him that I've arrived, will you? He'll know who I am."

"Very good, sir," replied the sergeant, as he sprang aside.

Two rows of bodies lay on straw. Their faces looked to have been tarred, and the tar to have cracked, revealing old red paint beneath. Their thick greatcoats were frizzled, their long felt boots grew black lichen. The arms and legs were those of dummies, ready to dangle loose about skulled faces with stubbed ears and noses, and flat eyes. He counted twenty-one. The twenty-second corpse, lying apart, was not burned. Grass stuck to the Iron Cross in the button-hole of the reefer jacket.

"He's the commander, sir," said the sergeant. "He was picked up in the field, some way off of the airship. There's the impression, six inches deep in the ground, where he plonked down. He was lying on his back, with his hands still clasped behind his head, as though to protect his skull. Pity it wasn't Mathy, sir."

"His turn next, sergeant."

Prophetic words: within a week Mathy was to perish with his

crew in the flames of *L 31*, shot down by Tom Cundall, whom Phillip met again on this Sunday afternoon.

"When are these chaps to be buried, d'you know?"

"I did hear in Great Burstead churchyard, on yonder hill, next Wednesday, my beamish boy. Not even lead-lined coffins. War-time economy."

"They'll need some chloride of lime before Wednesday."

As they walked to the runabout, Phillip said to Desmond, "How about coming to see the funeral?"

"Not me. I've had enough. Besides, I'm going on Wednesday to be interviewed for a commission in the gunners, at Woolwich. I've got a lift back in a tender to London, so I won't be returning with you."

"Well, goodbye, Desmond. And the very best of luck."

But Desmond was already walking away.

"Lily?" said Cundall.

Phillip nodded. Cundal squeezed his hand.

Great Burstead church stood on high ground beyond the town of Billericay. It had a square tower, from which arose a pointed shingled spire. Phillip arrived at Snail's Hall Farm three days later just as the procession was starting along the narrow lane winding up to the graveyard.

On a lorry, covered by a black pall, lay twenty-one coffins.

Behind them was a trailer pulled by a second lorry, bearing the coffin of the commander. It had a brass plate on it. *Commander Brodruck, killed on Service Sept. 24, 1916.*

This was a mistake. Later, it was known to be Petersen.

Following the coffin was an open Crossley in which sat officers of the R.F.C. No Cundall's face. At the tail of the procession was a squad of airmen, and then a few sightseers.

Last of all walked Phillip, feeling lost, wondering if the spirits of the dead men were lingering in the autumn air, looking down, faintly curious, at the poor little bodies below. Was Lily there, too? He felt that the dead would not be angry, nor would they know any more fear. If only he could write poetry in which his feelings, and the scenes he had known, would live forever, like Julian Grenfell's poem.

The leaves of the elms were turning yellow. Gossamers glinted across the stubbles, the drift-lines of hundreds of thousands of unseen little spiders come to earth, each a thread of hope. The threads made vast tunnels to the sun, like fragile formless airship frames. What happened to the myriads of tiny travellers, floating in the warm air, all going—whither? For what purpose? To flee the frosts, to reach the haven of the golden sun, each to return its gift of life, like the hundreds of thousands marching into the sunrise of July the First? Male spiders, thin and nervous, died for love: did each one have a speck of soul, of love, within its frame?

The mass grave was in one corner of the churchyard, beside a small pit for the commander. He hoped no one had taken his Iron Cross, for a souvenir. It should be kept, and returned after the war to his wife, for his son; but perhaps he had not been married. Then for his mother.

The blue sky was as gentle as the eyes of Lily. She and her mother were being buried that afternoon. She would understand why he had come to this funeral of the unloved. Surely thoughts had their own existence, like gossamers.

The six R.F.C. officers carried the coffin of the commander to the pit beside the other coffins around the mass grave. Was God, during the service, looking down sadly upon the scene? Now the Vicar was saying, 'I am the Resurrection and the Life', but when he came to the 'our dear departed brothers' he changed it to 'these men here departed'. Dear departed brothers, thought Phillip, while it seemed that the eyes of Lily were regarding him steadfastly.

Soon, too soon, it was over, and bugles were sounding the Last Post. Goodbye, brothers: your mortal envelopes lie here in Mother Earth, your spirits drift as gossamers across the sea, to where thoughts of love will help you on your journey to the sun.

He went to Tollemere Park, but Mrs. Kingsman was away. Dust sheets covered the furniture. He learned from the butler that Father Aloysius had died of wounds. The butler asked him if he might offer him luncheon, but Phillip declined, and after a drink said goodbye, returning by way of Horndon-on-the-Hill, to see the church where, a year before, Kingsman, Cox, Wigg, and he had stopped on their way to Southend. Goodbye, Jasper Kingsman: will there be a wall-memorial for you, in due course, with your son? In quiet autumn sunshine he drove on down to the marshes of the Thames, and boarded the ferry for Gravesend, to cross the estuary with its smoking steamships and brown-sailed barges borne upon the tarnished waters rushing to the sea. Standing by the rail, he was beset by anguish so piercing that he felt he must go to the other passengers, and beg to be allowed to speak to them. But he stood still. The anguish passed, with his tears.

When he got home, what would there be to do?

For it seemed that the old life was now gone for evermore. The next day he would be going back to Grantham, to rejoin the Training Centre. This time he would work hard, and do his job properly. What "Spectre" West could do, he could do. When the time came to take over a section he would live for the horses and mules and grooms and drivers which would be in his care. He would be part of one of the many new Companies which were going out every week, to the Battle of the Somme.

Devon—Suffolk.
January 1956—January 1957.